SACRIFICE FOR A KINGDOM

Patricia D'Arcy Laughlin

ISBN: 1484036107
ISBN-13: 978-1484036105

Library of Congress Control Number: 2013907136
CreateSpace Independent Publishing Platform
North Charleston, South Carolina

ABOUT THE AUTHOR

Patricia D'Arcy Laughlin was born in Trinidad of British and French ancestry, educated there, the U.K. and the U.S.A. A world traveler and award-winning artist, famous for developing her 'Unique Stainings On Wood,' although having composed poetry and songs, '*SACRIFICE FOR A KINGDOM*' is her first novel. Married in her teens, she lives in Florida with her husband, has three children, and is "blessed" with five grandchildren.

Watch for her novel's sequel - '*KINGDOMS AND SACRIFICES.*'

DEDICATION

To my husband, Peter, who has sustained me through this daunting journey with whatever I needed, love, nourishment, encouragement, and, at the most frightening time of our financial lives, courage, I gratefully give you my heart, *"till death and even beyond."*

To my precious children, Natalie, Duane, and Tonya, and my grandchildren (who will not be allowed to read this book until they have reached the age of maturity!), I thank you for your love, understanding, and support. You are eternally cherished.

ACKNOWLEDGEMENTS

I am overflowing with gratitude for the assistance given to me during the writing of this first effort of a novel by many special people, just a few of whom I have space to mention.

My husband Peter, and my family, who have supported me in every way possible, and to whom I also owe apologies for my distractedness at inappropriate times and events because I was consumed with thoughts of compositions and formulations for *SACRIFICE FOR A KINGDOM*. More apologies in advance as I embark on its sequel, *KINGDOMS AND SACRIFICES*.

My son-in-law, Andrew Tanner, for much and varied, patient, computer assistance. My cousin Christine Caruzzo for some Internet research. Dr. James Marsh, and Dr. Brad Lerner and staff, for medical authentication. My cousin Giancarlo Caruzzo who served in Afghanistan and South Korea, for military and weaponry advice. Rev. David Owen Ritz, and Rev. Don Fern, and the many other clerics, and scholars, who wish to remain anonymous, for their information, insight, and inspiration.

Stella Yumani, for her intelligence, intuitiveness, and education.

James Gladstone, computer consultant, who organized me with a computer and educated me in the rudimentaries of using it, I having never even sat in front of one before, and, was devoid of typing skills! (I wrote the first ten chapters in longhand, often while being driven somewhere, or in various waiting rooms.)

I am especially honored by, and appreciative of, two extremely busy, esteemed persons: Myrna Welch, English educator and philanthropist, who read and complimentarily critiqued my first draft (730 pages) and the final manuscript (636 pages); and, Dr. Larry Thompson, President, Ringling College, who, despite lugging the final manuscript file through North Carolina, and a field trip with students to Venice, Italy, gave rave reviews for *SACRIFICE FOR A KINGDOM*.

My many dear friends (you know who you are) who, though sometimes feeling neglected by me, still stuck with our friendship, and after I divulged that I had been writing, which added to some social hibernation the last few years, forgave me, and elated me with their admiration, encouragement, and unstinting support.

To all intrepid authors, poets, composers, and singers of songs, I lovingly, admiringly, respectfully, express my gratitude to you for your courage, inspiration, and talent, and for always enriching my life, and that of all humanity.

CHAPTER
1

*T*he hotel's luxury penthouse suite was bustling with adrenalized activity. Elizabeth was examining her Paris original and accessories for the third time. Olga, the Portuguese housekeeper whom Elizabeth's Aunt Ruth brought with her from New York was needlessly ironing Ruth's dress for the second time.

The irritated hairdresser was rearranging Ruth's hair yet again, while the frustrated manicurist had to keep getting out of his way and at the same time try to do her own job properly.

She still had to do the pedicure as Ruth insisted on soaking her feet in a mineral solution for one hour. She complained her feet have always been the weakest part of her, and she was ensuring they won't be an impediment to her enjoyment of such a rare event.

The make-up artist stood by impatiently waiting to apply her final touches, while a maid served refreshments to everyone.

Ruth's husband Robert, still undecided about a suitable tie, called Elizabeth over to select one. She looked carefully at the unnecessarily large array of expensive ties and chose one that was elegant yet subtly festive in design.

"The young lady has excellent taste," the man from The Gentleman's Store remarked while repacking the rest of the ties.

"Bu…but," stuttered Robert, "i…it's too simple, doesn't make any statement."

"Yes it does," said Elizabeth, "it states that you're a gentleman of quality and distinction."

She pecked her uncle affectionately on his cheek and walked back to her room leaving him staring at the tie in his hand. The last thing Robert needed was another tie but unfortunately, out of the scores he had back in the States, Olga unthinkingly packed the few that were unsuitable for this event, for which the hapless woman had been thoroughly lambasted.

Elizabeth decided to leave all the excitement for a while and have a leisurely warm bubble bath, she felt a disturbing need to soak her troubles away.

Compounding a preexisting dilemma was a new worry about her safety because of her upcoming controversial speech. She had been warned that fanatics will find it inflammatory and therefore could very likely put her life in danger.

Stripping off her clothes, she caught a glimpse of her nakedness in the mirror. A brief remembrance of the multifarious pleasures she once enjoyed caused stirring in her genitalia. But she quickly, determinedly, renewed an old anger which assisted in casting away any salacious thoughts, and just as quickly, she cast aside the anger to indulge in a different pleasure. Sinking her tanned curvaceous body in the bubbly water, she luxuriated in the feeling of its tenderness that mixed compatibly with the tranquilizing scents of lavender oil and rose water.

Luxury was not new to Elizabeth. Her life had always been privileged to the extent that afforded her almost immunity from discontent, until the catastrophe struck that shattered her idyllic world. Her perfect life was now forever blemished by, *"The tragedy."* As intelligent and sophisticated as she was, having copiously searched the labyrinth of her mind these past sorrowful debilitating months, it was still beyond her imagination that she, of all people, could ever be in this predicament.

She knew she faced making extremely difficult decisions that would forever affect her life, and those of her loved ones, in the tomorrows that would inevitably come, but today, she was putting the past away that caused the problems for the future, and was going to enjoy and live only in the present.

Not trusting others to not be extreme, she did her own hair and makeup, she wanted to look perfect but natural for this very special occasion.

She and Ruth had gone to a lot of trouble, and expense, to ensure they would be the best dressed threesome at this event. The cost of this extravagance was not her concern, Robert had his accountants pay all bills with merely perfunctory glances at them. They had brought several fabulous spring outfits from top designers in America, the weather forecast being for an unusually cool June. However, these clothes were no longer suitable; the unpredictable European weather had turned to summer heat.

The fallible weather forecasters were now declaring "*due to global warming this June promises to be the hottest in decades*."

When Ruth and she had realized there were only three days left and the temperature kept steadily rising, they flew to Paris in Ruth and Robert's private jet and went directly to the business house of that most famous couturier who designed only for nobility, the very aristocratic, and the very rich.

After much discussion with a person of uncertain gender, they were shown to an inner salon where they were haughtily told, "Be seated, and wait."

Ruth became furious, "Doesn't *it* know who *I* am? Imagine my having to wait on a mere dressmaker!"

Elizabeth calmed her down with a reminder, "Right now, we need him more than he needs us." At that moment, the couturier himself waltzed in and bluntly informed them he knew of their request and was sorry, but they had given him too little time and it was impossible to accommodate them.

As he turned to leave, Ruth said sweetly, and somewhat desperately, "But cheri, we'll pay *anything*."

The couturier stood still, his ear cocked, "Anything?"

"Anything! We want the best, and you're the best."

He strutted ahead of them loftily, "Tres bien, follow me to design salon, we start immediatement." Unknown to them he had an assistant Google the Robert Charles Grangers and therefore was well aware they could indeed afford his idea of "*anything*."

They followed closely on his heels as he snapped orders to everyone he passed. It was astonishing to see how they dropped whatever they were industriously undertaking to follow their master. Within an hour the outfits were designed, measurements taken, fabrics chosen, materials on the cutting board.

While being measured the couturier told Elizabeth she was "*a true beauty*," and if she lost four pounds he would have her model in his upcoming fashion show. She politely thanked him for the compliment but declined his offer claiming pressing work commitments. She modestly didn't tell him how trite his offer was, she having heard it numerous times before. Additionally, she dared not tell him she had model friends in New York who were constantly stressed over having to maintain their stick-thin figures, some even taking dangerous drugs to achieve the practically anorexic look most designers seem to prefer. Furthermore, still fresh in her mind was how difficult it had been to regain the twelve pounds she lost after the depressing calamity that turned her life upside down. Moreover, every man she ever dated, and many others she had not, complimented her on her "*perfect figure*."

The couturier's interest in her gave her the courage to charm him into allowing her to be involved in the designs of her own outfits, but Ruth gave him carte blanche with hers.

For the special event Elizabeth chose a rich lilac Shantung silk fabric, the color setting off her golden tan beautifully. The dress was sleeveless, form fitting, with a slim skirt ending above the knees and a high slit in the back. She designed an open weave crisscross bodice just above the bustline in front but low to the waist in the back, and requested a matching long-sleeved jacket the same length as the dress.

The couturier insisted on throwing in a broad-brimmed sunhat in the same fabric with the remark, "Leettle tan on body's fine but you moost protect zat exquisite face."

Despite Elizabeth's protests, Ruth insisted on having extra outfits made for her, saying, "It's been too long since I've had the enjoyment of giving you special treats."

They were told to come for fittings at ten in the morning and collect their outfits at six in the evening. Elizabeth marveled at the entire occurrence. It reconfirmed for her the outrageous power one wields when one is extremely wealthy.

Clasping her amethyst and platinum necklace that matched her earrings, bracelet and ring, she checked herself in the mirror for the last time feeling pleased. She knew the entire ensemble exemplified sophisticated chic. *This, is what Uncle Robert would call "making a statement!"*

The three partygoers looked each other over appraisingly while Olga fussed with Ruth's pillbox hat which kept tilting unattractively sideways. Elizabeth took over from Olga and fixed it with an antique diamond clip Ruth had been given by her now deceased mother-in-law who had adored her.

Ruth was relieved, "Perfect. Thank you, darling. It's the fussy hairstyle he gave me, nothing sits on it easily. You don't know how lucky you are having such lovely hair, not having to go through what I do to get mine looking thicker with some style."

Ruth was incorrect in that statement, Elizabeth knew very well how fortunate she was to have inherited her father's genes for lush auburn hair. It was easy maintenance and she kept it long, past the middle of her back. The reddish-brown tresses had natural golden highlights and would obediently go wavy or straight, depending on however she chose to style it. Her friends often complimented her on her "*crowning glory*."

She was grateful to Mother Nature she was given what she was frequently told was "*natural beauty*" as she had neither the patience or desire to spend much time titivating to achieve attractiveness. The one thing she didn't much care for and considered it a flaw, was the upward tilt at the tip of her nose, although her parents, loved ones, and actually everyone who saw her, thought it adorable. Even as an adult she was often given affectionate pecks on the tip.

She felt it made her look too juvenile, as, especially when in America, she was usually carded and had to show identification to prove she was of legal drinking age.

However, she was now grateful for her height of five-feet-nine-inches as it frequently saved her from having to rummage in her bag for identification when a wait-person saw her standing.

She hardly thought about having to maintain her slim curvaceous figure because she loved to exercise; it was a rewarding part of her hectic life. She usually exercised five days a week, alternating swimming, speed-walking, dance classes, light weight training, Pilates, and yoga.

As a little girl her first love was ballet, for which she had an inherent talent and gracefulness that was admired and encouraged by her parents, teachers, and everyone who saw her dance. Unfortunately, on becoming a 'young lady' at age eleven, not only did her breasts substantially sprout out, but her legs substantially sprouted up, and she became the tallest in her class. She felt she could eat meals off her partner's heads, began to feel gawky and uncomfortable in her own skin and tutu, gave up her dreams of becoming a famous ballerina, and turned her attention to her other love, music.

One Christmas when she was seven years old she was given a guitar, and a quatro, by two older cousins who had not consulted each other on their gifts. All her family knew she had a lovely voice and loved to hear her sing. She had an innate aptitude for those instruments, learning to play them well in no time, accompanying her singing. She loved every kind of music, from country to rock'n'roll, classical to calypso.

At age eight her parents gave their upright piano to a less fortunate but talented cousin, and bought a Steinway baby-grand. They increased Elizabeth's lessons from once to twice weekly and she became an even more proficient pianist.

Although she loved the classical pieces her teacher usually chose, the moment he left she would put away those music books in the piano stool and start pounding out the latest popular songs or calypsos, singing to her heart's delight, thrilling the domestic staff, and amusing her parents.

When she was fourteen, the crime in her country increased rapidly with the incoming flood of illegal immigrants from smaller poorer islands, along with oil revenues. With barely enough jobs for the better educated locals, and the introduction of the drug trade from the South American mainland, kidnappings of the wealthy or their offspring for ransom became prevalent. Her terrified parents quickly took her, and her childhood best friend, Judith, to attend boarding schools in Europe. From then on her love for travel and learning about other cultures was fed, not only by her doting parents, she being an only child, but also by her equally doting, childless, American Aunt Ruth and Uncle Robert.

Now in her adulthood, with the many responsibilities she had taken on, traveling had been recently curtailed to places closer to home due to the demands of work, family, school, and philanthropy. So, with now exhumed excitement and renewed enthusiasm, encouraged by those few of her family and friends who knew of her heartbreaking suffering, and bolstered by a philanthropic endeavor, she seized the opportunity given to her to come back to Europe, and once again indulge in her taste for faraway places and different cultures.

Accompanied by complimentary "Ooo"s and "Ahh"s through the lobby from the staff who knew where they were going, along with admiring guests, they arrived at the Bentley waiting at the hotel's entrance. Settling themselves in the car they chatted animatedly like excited children on their way to Disney World.

Elizabeth sat back thinking that although, except for the "*Shocking tragedy*," she had been blessed with an abundantly rich fulfilling life, this would probably be one of the more unusual enjoyable events. After all, it could only be once in a lifetime that an ordinary commoner, with as yet no international claim to fame, could be invited to a very exclusive, very rare, 'Royal Palace Summer Garden Party.'

The chauffeur eased the car into the queue of expensive automobiles unloading their assorted and honored passengers and Elizabeth observed the scene looked like a meeting of The United Nations. There were people of every race, conceivable color, size, and attire, with some in national costumes. It felt uplifting to see everyone smiling and chatting gaily together, as if they had no differences, there were no conflicts anywhere on the planet, and the world was, at last, at peace.

Along with scores of other important guests the Robert Charles Grangers and their niece Elizabeth were presented to His Majesty, King Alexander IV, his sisters, and several senior royal cousins. Elizabeth surprised herself by accepting His Majesty's compliment, "It's always a pleasure to meet a beautiful young lady," with graciousness and calm.

Her aunt and uncle beamed with pride. Feeling embarrassed, she said on moving into the crowd towards a refreshment bar, "I see some people I know under the trees, shall we go over or do you want to stay here?"

Ruth, thinking she probably needed the companionship of contemporaries because they had monopolized her since they arrived in the country, said quickly, "Darling, you go, have fun. We'll stay near the refreshments."

She walked towards the young people and had almost reached them when she realized she was mistaken and didn't know anyone in the group. She turned away embarrassed, because they were all watching her intently, when a young but self-assured male voice called out, "Hey, don't go, we're dying to meet you."

She turned back to the now smiling group who introduced themselves. They were tastefully, expensively, attired in the latest designer fashion trends, but with that relaxed carefree look of teenage youth. She found it curious the boy and girl who were twins, unlike the others, gave only their first names, Megan and Mark. She soon forgot about it as they were extremely friendly, taking her into their confidence about amusing and embarrassing incidents involving older members of the nobility present, at similar events of the past.

They showed great interest in Elizabeth, asking numerous questions about her schooling in Europe and America.

Their interest became further aroused when she revealed she was not only born there but was presently living in Trinidad, in the West Indies. This topic of conversation took up an additional hour. Beginning to feel guilty about leaving Ruth and Robert for such a long time, she politely explained this to the group who apologized for keeping her away. She assured them she enjoyed their conversation immensely, and they made her promise to come chat some more before leaving.

She strolled towards the area where she had left the Grangers but they were nowhere to be seen.

Walking briskly up to the group whose eyes were following Elizabeth, with an inquisitive grin on his strikingly handsome face, he asked, "Alright, who's the beautiful young lady? She's obviously smitten you lot."

"Isn't she gorgeous, Michael? She's like a model." Megan gushed to her older brother.

"She's more like a goddess, really. A goddess with style," effused Mark, "she has a strange mysterious air about her." The others all agreed.

Showing his perfect white teeth the twin's elder brother laughed, "That's the craziest remark you've made yet, Marcus. The last time you sounded so enthusiastic about anything was when you begged to borrow my T.V.R. sports car to impress a hot date. Well, seeing the young lady's made such a deep impression on you, I'll have to go meet her myself, find out what this "*air*" is all about."

Chuckling at them, he started after Elizabeth. He deliberately omitted telling them he had been watching her for some time before he approached, and he too was intrigued, but could not say why. He wanted to go over to meet her the moment he first saw her talking to the twins, but he was frustratingly, albeit politely, trapped in a lengthy, and to him, trifling, discourse about fashion, with four dowager members of visiting aristocracy. He eventually, with some degree of difficulty, managed to extricate himself from the loquacious ladies before the conversation turned to what he humorously titled, 'The Usual.' It never failed to amuse him to see how all the older women maneuvered, jockeyed, and practically fought, to gain his attention, each extolling the virtues of a marriageable daughter, or granddaughter, or niece. Over time he had met or seen photographs of every one of the propounded young, and not so young, ladies, and was not in the slightest attracted to any.

Elizabeth's back had been turned to him and he found it an exceptionally shapely one indeed. He could see only her profile when she moved which he thought very pretty. He could not see her eyes because of the fashionable broad-brimmed hat she wore but enchantedly took in her high cheekbone and refined chin line that led to her long stately neck. Definitely attracted to her lips which were full, he thought them extremely sexy.

Then looking at her tilted up nose, although he thought it rather sweet, he decided she was probably too young to waste his precious time on. After all, she enjoyed the company of his teenage siblings so obviously they were her peers. She was taller than everyone in the group except for his brother who matched her height, but that was not the reason he was drawn to her. It was something about the way she moved, her mannerisms, her poise, or in Mark's words, her "*style*" and her "*air*."

Elizabeth had a distinctive feeling of being watched but dismissed it thinking it was probably some of the grand old dames, who all seemed to have such poor fashion sense, enviously admiring her outfit. She could not see the Grangers anywhere, and the aroma of food reminded her she had not eaten since breakfast. She bent over an elaborately decorated buffet table which was lavishly covered with a variety of unusual delicacies.

She placed a tasty looking canapé on a napkin and turned, straightening up quickly, to continue her quest for the Grangers. She bumped into a man who must have just walked up because he certainly was not there a moment ago.

Both said simultaneously, "I'm so sorry," and she looked to see if any of the crushed canapé had soiled his jacket, which it had not, then she looked up at his face.

Startled, she blurted, "Oh, Your Royal Highness! I…I'm so sorry. I…I didn't know you were there and-"

"Please don't apologize," he interrupted softly, "it's my fault, I was too close behind you. I'm terribly sorry, did your beautiful dress get soiled?"

She looked down at her dress but could not see anything, she could barely think. Her heart was racing, her usually strong legs felt gelatinous, and long banished stirrings in the pit of her abdomen surprised her. His face was mere inches away from hers and he made no attempt to move away.

She stuttered, "N…no, i…it's alright, thank you. Please forgive me, Your Highness, I must go. My aunt and uncle must be looking for me, I've not seen them since we arrived. Excuse me."

Despite her weakened legs she wanted to run, not walk away, *He wasn't supposed to be here.* She didn't understand why she became so filled with consternation when she didn't even get the proverbial '*butterflies in the stomach*' on meeting the King and other members of the royal family earlier. Was it because of the way this hot Prince's blue-gray eyes with sparks of silver gazed at her intensely, or because his luscious lips parted to a seductive smile, or the nearness of his perfect physique that she knew existed under his exquisitely tailored gray suit, or the masculine smell of him that mixed provocatively with his cologne? Or, just the fact of being in the presence of *this* particular prince, now so alarmingly close to her?

He held her arm firmly, "But we haven't even met. You can't run away from me in this manner. How would it look to all these people, seeing the most beautiful young lady at the party running away from who the media refers to as 'the world's most eligible bachelor,' not to mention the heir to the throne?" His voice was stern, making Elizabeth feel doubly embarrassed at her ostensibly improper etiquette with royalty.

Trying to think of a suitable apology she slowly lifted her head and looked up at his face. He was grinning impishly, obviously taking great delight in her discomfort.

She drew in a breath, attempting to contain her growing annoyance. Discerning it, he softened his smile, stuck out his right hand, and straightened himself with overstated formality, "Allow me to introduce myself. I am Michael Alexander Stephen, and a string of other more impressive names I won't bore you with. May I have the honor of knowing who you are?"

In spite of herself she was soothed by the easy yet somewhat shy charm of this charismatic man of royal blood, who seemed so unpretentious he did not deem it necessary to use his full formal title in his introduction to her. She took his hand with a firm handshake, "I am Elizabeth Angelique Richardson. I'm here with my aunt and uncle, the Robert Charles Grangers."

"The American oil tycoon?"

"Oh, you know him?"

"No, I know of him, there aren't too many oil billionaires left. I'd like to meet them," he gave her his left arm where she reservedly placed her right hand in the crook, "shall we go look for them or do you know where they are?"

Looking around, she shook her head gently, "No, I don't, but I simply must find them now, we should be leaving soon, we have an important dinner engagement-"

"More important than a royal party?" he interrupted, arching an eyebrow but smiling teasingly at her.

This time she smiled back, "Don't think you'll have me trying to stammer out another apology, Sir, I've caught on to you now, I realize you're a terrible tease, so I won't let you upset me anymore." He laughed appreciatively. "Oh, there they are!" she exclaimed on seeing the Grangers chatting amiably with a distinguished looking gentleman.

They walked quickly towards them, Prince Michael nodding and smiling at everyone who greeted him as they passed by.

The gentleman smiled and said as they approached, "Michael, my boy. And who is this little beauty?"

"This little beauty happens to be the niece of the people with whom you are speaking, Uncle Patrick. May I present Elizabeth Angelique Richardson. Elizabeth, my uncle, His Royal Highness, Prince Patrick Barrington."

Shaking Prince Patrick's hand, Elizabeth noticed his eyes had his nephew's teasing gleam, accompanied by unabashed admiration, "Ah, I see you two have known each other for some time. Where've you been hiding her, Michael?"

"Well…ah…actually, we've only just met."

He grinned at Michael, "Oh? This is surprising for you, calling a lady by her first name when you've only just met," he turned to Elizabeth, the teasing gleam increased, "usually takes a few dates before he gets to know a girl well enough to call her by her first name. You must have something *extra* special."

Elizabeth felt herself blushing and turned her head to look away but her glance caught Prince Michael's face. She gazed at his eyes and smiled teasingly at him, for he too was blushing. She introduced the younger prince to the Grangers and after the usual polite pleasantries and compliments were exchanged, Michael diplomatically swayed the conversation to oil and alternative energy, he and Robert becoming engrossed in the latter subject. It was well publicized that the very astute, very wealthy, American oil magnate was investing heavily in alternative means for sustainability of continuing a civilized and eventually more economical lifestyle, for the people of a future ecologically healthier planet Earth.

Michael kept asking questions and listened attentively, Robert answering everything with calm authority.

Ruth, tiring from standing the entire duration of the party with her already weak feet said softly to Elizabeth, "I'm afraid we'll have to leave soon. My feet are giving out on me, and, we've got that Alternative Energy Dinner tonight-"

Overhearing her, Michael interrupted, "I realize you must leave shortly, Mr. and Mrs. Granger, I'd like to ask your permission to take your niece to dinner tonight. May I?"

Elizabeth was flabbergasted. Not only was this totally unlike the *'reserved, conservative, very proper'* heir to the throne the media was always writing and talking about, but his assumption that she would spontaneously go out with him when he had not even asked *her,* was the height of conceit.

Seeing Elizabeth's astonished look he added quickly and somewhat apologetically, "That is, of course, if the lady wishes to honor me with her company?"

Elizabeth didn't respond, she had not yet regained her composure. Robert cleared his throat and said courteously, "You certainly have our permission, Your Highness, I'm sure she wouldn't be in better hands. But," he looked at Elizabeth with concern, "Elizabeth will have to give you her own decision. Ruth and I will be waiting at the entrance for word from you. An honor to meet you both, goodbye." The Grangers shook hands with the two princes, smiled faintly at Elizabeth, though she caught a half-wink from Ruth, and left.

Prince Patrick, observing the way his nephew was admiring Elizabeth, also took his leave on the pretext that he must, "Be courteous and circulate."

Elizabeth was livid. *How could they! Leaving me to handle this alone. They know my position! And Uncle Robert not even trying to get me out of a spot like this! Granted he had to be diplomatic, but sacrificing* my *dignity in that manner! Then this presumptuous, cocky prince, putting me through more embarrassing moments in one day than I've had in years! It's all too much!* "How dare you," her tone was soft but harsh, "embarrassing me in front of everyone. What type of person do you think I am? Someone you could pick up at a party, order to do your bidding-"

He stopped her before she could go on, a decidedly deflated expression on his handsome face, "I'm terribly sorry, I realize now how it must've sounded, but I really felt, in all sincerity, you wouldn't mind going out with me. I apologize for having made such a bold-faced assumption. Please forgive me. I...I...would really be honored if you would have dinner with me?"

She calmed down on seeing he actually looked distressed, "You didn't ask *me* first, and it was more of a command."

Looking into her eyes he smiled shyly, "Elizabeth Angelique Richardson, would you like to dine with me tonight?"

She was trapped. How could she say no now, besides, looking at that face, hearing that voice, feeling that presence, she didn't want to. She responded with exaggerated formality, "Yes, Your Royal Highness, I shall be delighted."

"Terrific," he grinned, giving her his arm, "let's go."

He took her by surprise again, "Now?"

His eyes twinkled but his voice was firm, "Right now."

Realizing he wanted to be alone with her she argued, "But it's early, you can't leave now, with everyone here."

Determination dominated his tone, "Why not? I can slip out just as easily as I slipped in, I do it all the time."

"Bu...but...I have to tell my aunt and uncle goodbye."

"We'll send a messenger, it would take too long for us to get through this crowd." He motioned to a wiry fiftyish gentleman in a navy-blue suit whom Elizabeth had noticed earlier walking a few paces behind, "Jenkins, this is Miss Elizabeth Angelique Richardson. Elizabeth, Jenkins is my right hand, sometimes my left as well." Jenkins half-bowed to Elizabeth. Cautiously shaking the hand she held out his piercing black eyes gave her a calculating look, causing her to feel a faint sense of uneasiness, his physiognomy confusing. The look did not escape Michael's observation but he ignored it, "Send Brian with a message to the American couple I was speaking to, please."

"The Grangers?"

"Yes." Michael showed no surprise at Jenkins' knowledge of who the Grangers were, that was part of his job which he handled with great efficiency and pride. Michael wrote a note on a card embossed with the Royal Coat of Arms Jenkins handed him and gave it back to Jenkins, "They'll be waiting at the entrance."

Jenkins bowed his head politely, walked towards a red-headed young man who stepped out of the crowd, and handed the card to him. They exchanged some words and Brian left for the entrance, Jenkins remaining unobtrusively in the background.

"Wait," she touched the prince's arm, "I'd like to get my jacket please, the nights can get chilly. It's in our car."

He motioned to Jenkins, who overheard her request and signaled to another man named Eric, who seemingly materialized out of nowhere, and dispatched that burly figure to fetch it.

"He'll put it in my car," Michael said offering her his arm again, "may we go now, Your Highness?" he enquired facetiously.

She eyed him with caution, "You're teasing again."

He became concerned, "Does it annoy you? Should I stop?"

A smile twitched at her lips, "No, because I really don't think you can. It's part of your personality, and why should you change just to please a passing acquaintance."

Taking her hand away from his arm, he held it in both his hands and looked at her in earnest, "You are not a passing acquaintance, Elizabeth."

CHAPTER
2

They were about to slip away from the crowd when Elizabeth caught a glimpse of the group who had befriended her earlier, "I forgot to say goodbye to those lovely young people."

The prince looked in the direction in which she was looking, "Ah, the twins, and their friends. I'll tell them you had to leave in a hurry, later."

"You know them?"

He grinned, "I should hope so. I've spent eighteen long years helping them grow up. They're my sister and brother."

Elizabeth could not hide the surprised look on her face. She had not recognized them, all grown up now. She smiled at him, "This day has certainly been full of surprises."

The biggest surprise of all was at herself. She was amazed she was not irked by the way he took control the moment she agreed to go with him. It had been a long time since she allowed a man to take control of her. Somehow it seemed natural, comfortable, with him, and after all, she *was* in his territory.

He warned they had a long walk through the Palace pathways and hallways to get to his car, much of it paved in cobblestones, rough terrain for her heels, so he must hold her hand to keep her steady and prevent her from tripping.

At first she thought, *Yeah, right,* and gave him a cynical look to suit as she felt this must be some sort of 'royal come-on.' Because of the intimation of where a 'Garden Party' would be, she had deliberately worn just two-inch-high thick-heeled shoes, instead of the three-plus-inches stilettos that she normally preferred when dressed up. He caught the look but simply smiled and said nothing.

Within minutes she was grateful for his hand and clung to it tightly as she almost stumbled when she came upon the "*rough terrain*" he warned about, aged and rounded cobblestones with wide grooves in-between. It was his turn to give her a look, it said teasingly, 'I-told-you-so.'

They passed through several interior hallways and rooms with smooth marble or wood floors, guards standing at attention at each end, but he did not release her hand.

Pointing out historical rooms that existed behind closed carved wood and iron doors, he told her interesting anecdotes about them. He began asking her questions about herself, starting with where did her "lovely unusual Britishy-American accent come from," expressing surprise when she told him she was educated in various European countries and the United States but was born and presently living in Trinidad in the Caribbean. Intrigued, he remarked, "I haven't been there but a bunch of my cousins have. They sneak in for your famous Carnival every year," he smiled and winked, "I'll obviously have to join them next year, I hear it's a blast."

She feigned nonchalance, "Oh, it's alright, if you like that sort of thing."

He gave her a look of disbelief, "Don't you play mas'? I thought all the young people would be involved. From what I've heard, and the pictures, magazines and films I've seen, everyone was having enormous fun."

She was not surprised at his using the Trinidad Carnival terminology 'play mas" which meant dance in masquerade in the streets, while following calypso-soca playing bands or disc jockeys in trucks, the Monday and Tuesday before Ash Wednesday. She knew his cousins would have told him the terminology, but she wanted to discourage any further conversation about Carnival, and Trinidad. Under no circumstances did she want him coming there for any reason whatsoever, especially to do with her, which she surmised was why he gave her that smiling wink.

"It would be too dangerous for you," she lied.

Despite the crime increase in Trinidad after the oil-money started flowing in as the oil flowed out, Trinidadians did not allow crooks to spoil their Carnival. It was their annual much awaited heavy dose of contradictorily stimulating yet tranquilizing therapy, for a normally hectic past year.

Unlike the comparably dangerous Carnival in Brazil, except for a rare jealous lover's *crime passionnel*, the worst crimes committed were pick-pocketing, or a drunken fight, which more sober masqueraders, band security, or police, would soon put to a stop before any real harm could be done.

She also didn't want him to realize not only did she know that, along with hundreds of other celebrities, his cousins sneaked in for Carnival, but she herself often danced, or in Trinidadian lingo, 'jumped-up' with them. They played mas' with the same band she had been a member of since she was seventeen, when her parents first allowed her to play mas' in costume on the streets with her own older cousins.

Moreover, not only was she involved in every aspect of Carnival, socializing and helping with costume-decorating at Band Headquarters, going to steelband rehearsals at panyards all around the city, attending all the fetes and shows that started taking place around Christmas; but she so loved it all, her most disturbingly haunting nightmare was that she would fall asleep on a Carnival Sunday night after partying all weekend, and not wake up until Ash Wednesday morning, to depressingly discover she had slept through the whole of Carnival!

Michael sensed she was uncomfortable with this subject and decided to let it drop, although he wondered if her discomfort had anything to do with her being white in what he thought was a predominantly black country.

He pointed to a wing of the palace, "That's where my family's private quarters are. I have my own apartments on the far side overlooking the gardens. I'll show it to you sometime…if you would like, that is."

The stirring in the neglected area of her otherwise well looked after body returned, but she simply smiled demurely, not knowing how to respond verbally. Then she got concerned that he might think her silence meant consent so she asked, "Does every member of your family have their own apartment?"

"No. The twins sill live with my father, he keeps a strict eye on them. So does his two older sisters who live in their own apartment next door. But me being the eldest, and the heir, I get to have my own space, and…privacy." He gave her a look again, this time there was no smile, no wink, it was serious though not solemn, and she was unsure of how to read it. What she was sure of was that it sent sensations in her to the place she had been deliberately ignoring for quite some time.

They walked slowly through The Great Hall, taking in its regal grandeur. Heavy crimson embossed velvet draperies trimmed with gold fringe and tassels, adorning the tall arched mullion windows, complimented the ornate gold-gilt framed museum quality paintings, tapestries, and life-size marble and bronze sculptures. Everything was strategically placed around the enormous room for viewing enjoyment, the wall hangings enhanced by giltwood scrolled carvings surrounding them and attached to ivory colored walls.

Standing under them like inanimate antique sentinels were mahogany and gilt sideboards, commodes, and glass gilt and rosewood cases, all displaying untouchable priceless treasures of splendiferous bygone eras. On the perimeters of the ceiling and down its center in six equally distanced sections were detailed relief scenes, in plaster and alabaster, of flying cherubs playing various musical instruments, trailing vines with fruit and flowers in abundance. Hanging from the six center sections amidst the playful gesso cherub musicians were enormous but exquisitely delicate Austrian crystal and gold chandeliers.

Elizabeth took it all in with quiet dignity which did not reveal her feelings. Haunting memories evoked nostalgia for majestic elegant places and times she had so much enjoyed in the past. With it came a strengthened reminder to never again take anything for granted.

Prince Michael acted like an enthusiastic docent as he gave brief histories and symbolic meanings of many objects they paused in front of, so proud was he of his family dynasty, despite the reduced power of the monarchy at this point in time.

As the attending guards opened the last door for them, he stopped and held her back regarding her speculatively, "You're not very impressed, are you?"

"Oh? Oh but I am, it's all very impressive. And your extensive knowledge of the history is most admirable."

"I get the impression you've been around palaces before, which ones have you seen?"

"Um…actually, all the major ones…including yours."

"I see. As a tourist?"

"Yes…of course, as a tourist." She lied again. It bothered her how easily this new mendacity came to her, she had always prided herself on being scrupulously honest. However, she felt it necessary to keep everything simple and restrained between them, as of right now, she could not handle another complication invading her once perfect life. So, the less he knew about her, the better for all concerned.

On entering a large courtyard with a wide driveway that circled around a three-tiered marble fountain, Jenkins, who had suddenly disappeared during their walk, sheepishly rushed forward to escort them to a large silvery-charcoal colored Rolls-Royce that was parked between two less prestigious cars. After settling into the luxurious comfort of the softest suede upholstery, and two large matching down-filled silk cushions, Michael resumed asking Elizabeth questions about herself.

She answered as congenially as she could hoping he would not pick up on her reluctance to divulge too much information. Now that they were alone and seated close to each other, she was finding it extremely difficult to relax.

Jenkins, who was driving, and a bodyguard named Tommy seated next to him, were separated from them by a thick upholstered and black glass panel and could not be seen or heard. It felt like the prince and she were totally isolated from the world outside.

In response to more questions, she told him briefly about her early childhood in Trinidad, her schooling in Europe and America, and that she was being groomed by her father to take over the running of his companies when he retired.

Struggling to not be mendacious, she began to feel discombobulated as the intrusive inquirer relentlessly persisted in digging into her private life. She strived to steer clear of details, attempting to make it all sound as humdrum as possible.

After concisely answering more probing questions about what it was like to have lived in New York with the Grangers, she said quickly, "Well, that's it. You have my life's history in a nutshell, and quite frankly the subject is tiresome to me, therefore must be to you too. So why don't you liven things up, tell me about your life. The real one, not the publicized, it must be really exciting."

He remained silent and motionless. She looked at him tentatively. Scrutinizing her face his expression was skeptical, "What are you hiding from me? Your life could not possibly have been so dull. You're not only strikingly beautiful but you have a charming stimulating personality. You're trying to subdue it, but it seeps out. The twins remarked that you had a certain "*air*" about you. Now I understand what they mean, although I can't explain it. So someone like you doesn't lead a practically boring life such as you've described."

Elizabeth swallowed, "Wha…what else do you want me to say. I can't give details. That'll take a lifetime. After all, I spent a lifetime living it."

"What about romances?"

"I've had my share, like everyone else."

"Were any serious?"

"They were all serious."

"You know what I mean."

"You mean were they lovers? Really Prince Michael, I don't mean to be rude, but that's no business of yours."

Suddenly humbled, he sounded contrite, "You're quite right, I stand corrected. That's twice you've put me in my place today, a new experience for me."

Elizabeth again thought she must have overstepped the boundaries of proper protocol with this royal personage and hastened to apologize, "Prince Michael, I'm sorry, I didn't mean to offend you, but please try to understand-"

He pressed a finger gently to her lips stopping her. The touch felt like an electric shock speeding through both their bodies, the sparks not visible but inwardly contained, "When are you going to stop calling me 'Prince Michael,' must you be so formal, don't you think you know me well enough yet?"

"What would you like me to call you?"

"By my name of course, Michael."

With jest in her eyes, a small pout of her lips, and a dramatic haughtiness to her voice, she responded, "I don't know that I should. I hardly know you, and actually, I'm not sure my parents would approve."

They both laughed merrily at her playful raillery but then Michael became silent. After a few awkward moments, looking nervous, he spoke cautiously, "Elizabeth, I need to know something…how old are you?"

The surprised look on her face made him immediately regret the question. She responded with pretended indignation, "Why, Your Royal Highness, didn't your mother teach you it's impolite to ask a lady her age?"

He was visibly embarrassed, "Well, yes, but I think it's necessary, under the circumstances, that I know. Surely you understand that?"

Thinking, *Here comes the whole age 'thing' again,* she worked hard at keeping a straight face, "Circumstances? What circumstances?"

Twitching, he stammered, "Wel…well…you know…oh lord! Don't tell me you're not even of age?"

She enjoyed his squirming, "Of age? Of age for what?"

He looked uncomfortably at her, "For…um…things legal."

She feigned puzzlement, "Things legal? What things?"

A sigh of exasperation escaped from his lips, but then he broke into his famous boyish smile, "I'd like to know you could at least have a glass of wine with me."

She laughed, "Michael, how old do you think I am?"

"I daren't hazard a guess," he said coyly.

"Oh go on, I dare you," she egged, then added in a more serious tone, "I promise not to get upset with your answer."

Looking even more embarrassed, he spoke slowly, "Well, you confuse me. You're a bit of an enigma, actually. You *look* like you could be anything from seventeen to…say, twenty-two, but you have the poise and comportment of a woman in her thirties, even forties." He sighed again, this time conveying utter frustration, "I give up."

Although at first she was highly amused at seeing this esteemed, powerful, self-assured, stud-handsome prince, discomposedly struggle through these last moments of their dialogue, she was now beginning to feel sorry about it.

She never intended to belittle him, just simply to have some fun, so she took pity on him, "Okay, I'll put you out of your misery, I'll be twenty-eight next month."

He raised an eyebrow in surprise, "Really? I would never have guessed. Your looks belie your age. Except for your stature you look so young, you could pass for a teenager."

She pursed her lips, "Oh, so is *that* what Your Highness is into, underage girls?"

Although amused at her teasing accusation he responded seriously, "Good God, *no!* I need a real woman, such as your manner and intelligence suggests you are…it's just that you remind me of someone…

from a very long time ago." She observed that he developed a far-away expression in his eyes as he took her hand. After a moment he squeezed it and asked, "Where would you like to go for dinner?"

Her own faraway thoughts having entered her psyche, she hid her sudden discomposure, "Wherever you can go."

"That's anywhere, so the choice is yours."

"You go anywhere? Is that safe? I thought-"

"It's perfectly safe. We've five Secret Service bodyguards, two in the front car, two in the rear, and Tommy in our front seat with Jenkins. The car in front checks the route, and a couple men check the place before giving the okay to go in." He gave her a reassuring smile on observing she became concerned.

Sympathy mixed with her dismay, "My lord, how terrible! You mean you can never sneak out, do something privately, all on your own? Can't you wear a disguise?"

He chuckled, "Oh yes, I have my private moments. On such occasions I do often wear a disguise. Promise you won't tell anyone?" She nodded conspiratorially. He reached forward and pressed a tiny button across from where he sat. The suede upholstery slid out of sight exposing a surprisingly large compartment filled with assorted spectacles, sunglasses, caps, hats, scarves, wigs, beards, and moustaches. Picking up a blond wig, a sandy colored moustache, and a pair of large horn-rimmed tinted glasses, he quickly put them on and turned to face her, "How does this look, shall I wear these tonight?"

The wig was askew, allowing his shiny brown hair to hang out on one side, the moustache was lopsided, and the glasses too low on his nose. He looked comical, absolutely ridiculous. Elizabeth burst into laughter.

Glancing at a small mirror obliquely across from him, he saw his clownish reflection, whipped off his disguises, threw them on the seat, and he too collapsed into laughter. They could not stop laughing for several minutes. The ice was now broken and there was a feeling of warm familiarity between them, the kind of feeling one develops only after one has known someone for a long time, or with whom one has shared a private joke.

They stopped laughing, their heads resting against the back of the seat, almost touching, and turned to face one another. Michael tilted her chin and softly kissed her lips.

She turned her head away slowly, "Michael, we mustn't." Unable to stop himself, sensing the chemistry between them, he ignored what he assumed to be a false protest and took her in his arms. She tried to resist without pushing him away, "Michael, please, we...don't have the right-"

He kissed her again. She tried to move away, but he held her tight and kissed her harder, his tongue pressing between her lips, trying to get her mouth open.

Elizabeth's heart began to hammer in her chest. Sensations were racing through her to just one place. She had not had these feelings in a long time and didn't know how to cope with what was happening. She knew it was wrong for her, and for him. Being here with him was wrong. Everything she was doing was wrong. Then why did it feel so right, so natural, so perfect. Why did she have this compelling attraction to him? Her commonsense told her she was simply flattered by his attentions, that it is a great thrill for even the most blasé of women to be dated and kissed by a prince, particularly *this* hottie.

However, the fact was, he had aroused in her something once so familiar, but had been too long dormant, and she felt herself wanting to succumb and revel in it. She desired this as much as he did, opened her mouth, and let his tongue reach for hers.

After a slow sensuously satisfying kiss he released her a little saying softly, "I couldn't help it. You're so irresistible. I wanted to kiss you the moment we were alone although I knew it wouldn't be right, that you should get to know me better before I dared, but I couldn't wait. It seemed so right for us. I could tell you felt it too. Why did you resist me at first, didn't you want to kiss me?"

Quickly containing her emotions she sighed, "Yes, Michael, more than anything. But, please don't do it again." She pushed at him gently, "Please, let me go."

Taking offense, he released her quickly, "Why are *you* so proper? Are you trying to give *me* an inferiority complex? I'm the one who's supposed to be "*hard to get*" and "*untouchable.*" Is this some kind of game you're playing with me, Elizabeth?"

Seeing the hurt look that clouded her face he felt some guilt about what he said so hastily, but became unsympathetic as she said nothing and looked away, and that deeply hurt his proud ego. This was the first time in his thirty-two years a woman told him to release her. Never in his life had a female resisted him, even when he traveled incognito and she had no clue as to who her handsome charming suitor might be. When she did know, as is the case right now, every woman was always too eager to hold on to him, and acquiesce to his most intimate desires.

The experience of being rebuffed by the 'goddess' creature was shockingly foreign to him, he was unsure of what to make of it. *Perhaps I came on too strong, too soon for her. But I feel the chemistry connection between us. She wanted to kiss me as much as I wanted to kiss her. The moment she relaxed she totally surrendered to the enjoyment of it. I know she's attracted to me so what's this rejection all about? She doesn't seem to be the type to play games, at least I hope not. I've neither time nor patience for childish nonsense. She's somewhat reserved and proper on the surface, but I can tell there are embers smoldering the interior of her sometimes icy exterior. My challenge is to figure out what it'll take to get her inflamed.*

They rode on in silence. Elizabeth kept trying to think of the most diplomatic way to get out of her present situation, but she was distracted by his nearness, and the coolness that had developed between them strangely saddened her.

Michael was trying to compose in his head words that would sound like an apology but without him actually apologizing, when the sound of a buzzer disturbed the uncomfortable silence.

He flicked on a switch near his head, "Yes, Jenkins?"

"Begging your pardon, Sir, but you haven't said where we're going. Shall I drive around The Park while you decide?"

"Sounds good." He flicked the switch off and turning to Elizabeth asked in a markedly formal manner, "Well my dear, have you made up your mind about where you'd like to have dinner?"

She responded unhesitatingly, "Under the circumstances, I, should go to my hotel."

Turning to face her he fixed startled eyes on hers, "Oh no, you don't. We're not going to end the evening on a bad note. It started out very well, until I made the faux pas of kissing you. Which I shall not apologize for because I'm not sorry, and I don't think you are either." Determining that to cast his macho ego aside and swallow his pride to be the most effective way to achieve his desired outcome, he broke into that irresistible, famous boyish smile he knew how to use only too well, and pleaded tenderly, "But can we please forget about it, and my reaction to your rejection, and start afresh? Alright? Pleease?"

With a melting heart, she sighed acceding, "Alright."

"Good. Now, where would you like to dine?"

"I honestly don't know. What kinds of food do you like?"

"All kinds. With my type of upbringing, traipsing all over the globe with my parents, I've had to develop a rock hard palate and stomach, so I've learned to enjoy the foods of all nations. What kinds do you like?"

"I too have been raised to enjoy a sophisticated palate, but quite frankly, I'm not terribly hungry."

He wished he could say straight out the kind of repast he really wanted to enjoy with her was of an entirely different nature to that which would fill their stomachs, but managed to say politely instead, "Actually, neither am I. Would you settle for sandwiches and salad in The Park, we could have a picnic?"

"Great idea. But…you know what…I just thought of something… I'd like you to try a special curry sandwich that we have in Trinidad, it's called Roti."

"Oh, what's it like?"

"It's curried meat of any kind, chicken, beef, goat, shrimp, or beans, with potato. It's wrapped in an Indian bread, soft dough like a large flour tortilla, with crushed peas inside. It's absolutely delicious."

"It sounds delicious. Actually, I think I've had that bread in India or Pakistan."

"You would've had the bread only, I believe the sandwich is a creation of our East Indians in Trinidad. The bread you had is what encases the meats."

He stuck his tongue in his cheek, "I see. Well, shall I order the jet to be readied for the flight to Trinidad so we can go pick up our Rotis?"

She laughed, "No, silly. There're Roti shops dotted around the city, I could phone a friend, find out where's the nearest one. Couldn't you send a car to pick them up?"

Even her laugh is beautiful. He flicked the switch on the intercom, "Jenkins, we'd like to eat Roti."

Jenkins responded hesitantly. "Roti…Sir?"

"Yes, ever heard of it?"

"I believe it's some sort of West Indian peasant food."

"Trinidadian-East Indian actually. Know where we'll get some?"

"No, Sir, but I'll find out soon enough."

Elizabeth expressed surprise at Jenkins, he seemed to be a storehouse of information. Michael explained that Jenkins had one of the most retentive minds he had ever come across, and a keen sense of observation, and he relied on him heavily. In fact, Jenkins had become his almost constant escort, so indispensable was he.

Jenkins was neither valet nor butler but held the more prestigious title, 'Prince Michael's Personal Assistant.' His wife and closest relatives died many years ago. He lived entirely in the palace since he was thirty-five, in quarters next to Michael's apartments. Not controlled by frivolity, his worldly important belongings consisted of twelve suits, an equal number of shoes, five dozen shirts, and a nice collection of ties, belts, and cufflinks, which Michael generously added to through the years. His prized possessions were two engraved watches given to him on different occasions, an Audemars Piguet by the Queen, a Bacheron Constantine by the King. Apart from these his material needs seemed to be few, and those were met satisfactorily by the royal household. He appeared to be content just protecting, grooming, and guiding his charge, whom he had care of since Michael was fifteen.

The buzzer interrupted a humorous anecdote Michael was giving about an incident in his adolescent years when Jenkins first came to the palace, and he flipped on the intercom switch, "Yes, Jenkins?"

"Sir, I've got the location of the nearest Roti restaurant, but begging your pardon, it's not the type of neighborhood you should be in at night. May I suggest we send a car to pick up the food, you could stay in The Park and eat here?"

"That was exactly our intention. Look for a private spot."

"Of course, Sir. How many of the Rotis would you like?"

Michael looked at Elizabeth enquiringly.

"You could probably eat two," she said, "maybe three, it depends on the size, they vary. I can just manage one. Better get four to be safe. What about Jenkins and the guards?"

"Oh, don't worry about them, they'll look after themselves. Look, I want you to relax, forget they're here. Just think you're alone with me, alright?"

She gestured toward the front seat, "Alright, I'll try, but you must realize this is a new experience for me."

His face softened, "This seems to be a day of new experiences all round. A day to remember."

Elizabeth wanted to touch his handsome face and tell him it was a day she could never forget, but she controlled her feelings and simply flashed him a demure smile, "Oh, we'll need to tell Jenkins what kinds to get. Do you have any preference?"

"Beef, you?"

"Beef too, but let's also get a chicken and a shrimp for you to try, alright?"

"Great." He gave Jenkins the order then said to her, "The car's stopped, would you like to get out for a bit?"

"Yes. Let's go for a walk, the air is so fresh and clean here," she replied, removing her hat so as not to look too conspicuous to passers-by.

They strolled hand in hand along the more private pathways, admiring the swans and ducks floating gracefully and lazily across the large pond, and came to a grouping of lush rose bushes, abloom with almost every color of rose in existence. He pointed out two hybrids that were named for his parents, a white for his mother, a yellow for his father, and asked what was her favorite color rose.

"I don't have just one." she replied, "I love them all."

"So do I, but everybody has at least one special color that appeals to them the strongest. Surely you must prefer one, or even two, that stand out from the rest."

Amused that Michael was so insistent on fishing out of her a special color rose, she decided to humor him, and pointed to the two he had just shown her. "Alright, if it makes you happy that I choose, I choose those two, the white and the yellow."

He smiled, pleased, and looking deep into her eyes, touched a lock of her hair and rhymed, "Yellow for golden streaked hair and eyes with flecks of gold. White to illuminate the purity of your beautiful everlasting soul."

Her cheeks blushed and she felt a tingling sensation all over her body but managed to say teasingly, "Oh, I dare say, we have a Royal Poet in our midst."

His smile fading, the look in his eyes held something more than sincerity, "You have the most beautiful and unusual eyes."

She felt her blush spreading to her breasts and said modestly, "They're just light brown."

Cupping her chin in his hand, with a riveting gaze, he continued his poetry, "The golden flecks signify illuminating rays of sunshine for the day's light. The black rings encircling them signify mystery and romance for the dark of night."

She had previously heard her amber eyes described in a variety of complimentary ways but never before had someone composed poetry about them. She hoped he wouldn't notice the goose bumps rising all over her naked arms. Too late. He caressed both arms slowly downwards with his palms, then held her fingers with his own. Striving for words to distract him she said with a hint of sarcasm combined with humor, "You're quite the romantic poet aren't you, Sir? Who knew the always cool and collected Prince Michael Alexander Stephen had it in him?"

He smiled flirtatiously, "You bring it out in me." Michael was not teasing this time, and was actually quite surprised at his new found talent that suddenly manifested itself. In all his years of wooing and romancing women he had never been inspired to compose poetry.

Their verbal intercourse was disturbed by the bustling of Jenkins's and Brian's arrival with two baskets, "Excuse us, Sir," Jenkins said somewhat apologetically, "do you wish to eat out here, under that tree, or in the car?"

Michael didn't take his alluring eyes off Elizabeth's, "Under the tree, thank you."

CHAPTER
3

*A*way from curious eyes, Jenkins and Brian smoothed out a blanket on the lawn at the back of the tree and bushes that faced a small pond, placing the two silk cushions from the car on top of it. Michael seated Elizabeth on a cushion, then sat on the other next to her. The two men proceeded to unpack the baskets in almost reverent silence.

They spread an embroidered linen table cloth on the blanket, placing two settings of matching napkins, Limoges china plates, and sterling silver cutlery engraved with the Royal Family Coat Of Arms, directly in front of the couple.

Holding them cautiously as they were steaming hot and wrapped in tinfoil marked with the first letter of each flavor to distinguish them, they removed the rotis from paper bags. Placing them in a silver chaffing-dish, covering it with a matching domed cover, the handle of which was embellished with a small jeweled crown, the men withdrew quietly and walked back to the car to keep an eye on their charge from a discreet distance. Elizabeth sat still throughout this entire performance trying to decide if she was shocked or amused, wondering what a Trinidadian would say if he were to pass by and see a common Roti, usually eaten with just hands and paper napkins, often while standing on a sidewalk or in a crowded shop, being eaten in such regal elegant formality.

Jenkins returned and sheepishly proffered a small notebook to Michael, "I'm terribly sorry, Sir, but they're not allowed to sell alcohol there. Unfortunately we didn't know and the Rotis would've cooled if the men went back to the palace again for wine. This is a list of the drinks they purchased. Brian recommends the fresh pineapple juice."

Elizabeth could no longer contain herself, she began to giggle, *Imagine, Palace wine! With Roti! What next!*

Michael looked at her in surprise and she turned her head away because, try as she might, she could not stop giggling. He took a while to read the "*list*" and eventually handed it back to Jenkins, "We'll have pineapple juice please."

Jenkins walked away with a puzzled expression, as Michael, his own expression even more baffled, turned to Elizabeth, "What on earth's the matter with you?"

She suppressed her giggles, explained to him the usual manner in which Roti was eaten and went on to say she doubted any Trinidadian would believe Roti could reach to such heights, being eaten by royalty with Limoges plates and sterling silver on antique hand embroidered linen. He appreciated the humor and asked her to show him the "proper" manner in which it should be eaten. She placed the napkin on her lap, unfolded the tinfoil from around the Roti on one end, and bit into it with relish.

Copying her perfectly, he smiled happily after swallowing his first bite, "Hmm, this *is* good."

She laughed, "I do hope Jenkins won't be disappointed in me. He may think I'm lacking in finesse, and, corrupting his precious prince."

Ignoring stirrings in his loins he laughed at what he thought to be her incongruous remark, seeing he had a different idea as to who would corrupt who, "He won't think that, he comes across as puritanical but is actually very broadminded. Anyway he knows you're a lady of good breeding."

Suspicion overtook her, "Oh, how does he know that?"

"Well…by your manner…and your dress, you know-"

Her chariness showed, "Oh come now, Michael, anybody can cultivate good manners and fashion sense. Jenkins doesn't strike me as the type who can be fooled by those things."

Michael's integrity prevailed over caution, "Well…I feel I should tell you anyway, he ran a check on you."

Elizabeth almost dropped her Roti, "What! When? How?"

"After we met at the garden party. Don't get upset. It's part of his job, does it automatically with anyone I show an interest in. He's simply protecting me."

She paled, "Wha…what did he find out about me?"

"Not much really, there wasn't enough time. Of course he knew about your aunt and uncle, then he checked with your schools and confirmed what you told me. Except you neglected to tell me you had a Bachelor's Degree in Business from New York University, and studied languages and music. If I know him, he'll probably check with your embassy in the morning to see what more information they'll give him."

Her mouth already open in disbelief, she spoke slowly, "When did he tell you all this?"

He smiled guardedly, "He slipped me a note with the drinks list."

Fear combined with anger building inside her, she sucked in a breath, "Michael, I'm shocked, horrified! You make me feel suspect, cheapened. Like an alien spy or something sinister! I don't think I've ever felt so disgusted, demeaned, and denigrated in my entire life! To think that complete strangers have been checking up on me, digging into my past, probably hoping to find something sordid and degrading so they can put me, 'the common little upstart,' back in my 'place.' Well, *I* happen to know where my place is, and it certainly isn't here with *you!*" She stood up in a huff and stalked past the car.

Michael jumped up, and catching up with her, grabbed an arm swinging her around, "Elizabeth, wait! You don't understand, it isn't like that at all! Every new acquaintance I make has to be checked out.

It's for security reasons only. Surely you can understand that, with the way the world is today?"

She turned her head away, unable to look at him. She was extremely shaken and afraid it would show on her face. Misconstruing her angry demeanor to be solely a feeling of denigration, he determined that he had better do some fast-talking to convince her to stay, "Elizabeth, please don't take this personally. Investigations are done on all new friends of royals just to protect us from scandals. I can't begin to tell you how many innocent situations have been turned into something destructive, despicable, resulting in blackmail attempts, reputations almost irreparably damaged. The investigations are called 'Standard Procedure' and are automatic now. They're simply done to avoid future embarrassments, that's all, not to downgrade anyone." He let go of her arm, turned her face to look at him and said softly, "Do you understand now, Elizabeth, it's not just you personally, but everyone?"

She nodded slightly, but not convincingly. Seeing the dubious expression in her golden eyes, a foreboding overtook him as he perplexedly felt he was about to lose the most precious gift that had ever been given to him, this goddess who had already entrenched her spirit in his heart.

He knew her allure was undeniable, felt compelled to concede to what he assumed she was thinking, and lightened his voice, "I'm sorry this has upset you. That's the last thing I want to do. I'll tell Jenkins to drop Standard Procedure immediately. I promise. If there's anything in your past I should know about, I want to hear it only from you."

She remained silent, wondering why she didn't feel any sense of relief on hearing his concession. Perhaps she wanted him to discover all the secrets of her past, get it over and done with before she got in any deeper, while she could still walk away without too much pain being added to the one she was already enduring.

Her conscience had become schizophrenic. A part of her mind felt obliged to tell him the truth about her, but the other felt no guilt at all about hiding it from him. *Surely there could be no harm in this brief encounter with this special prince? We'll go our separate ways at the end of the evening and we'll both soon forget the whole thing ever happened. Why doesn't this thought console me? Why does it fill me with such dread?*

"Elizabeth?" His concerned voice interrupted her thoughts, "Are you alright?"

Repressing her emotional abnormalities she looked in those incredibly unusual blue-gray-silver eyes and made her voice sound light, "Yes, I'm fine, now. Thank you for understanding…and…for your trust. Shall we go finish our Rotis?"

His own emotions of fear and regret drowned by relief, Michael's confidence returned as he looked into those bewitching golden eyes, held her hand and thought to himself, *I'm looking forward to taming this one.*

They walked back to their old spot under the tree, sat down, and with her eyes avoiding his, silently resumed eating.

Elizabeth sensed from his fidgeting that Michael was having some difficulty in keeping his Roti bread from unfolding and spilling the curry out from it, and looked over at him.

He grinned embarrassedly. His face was a curried mess. He had a mass of thick curry barely hanging on above his top lip about to be inhaled into his nostrils. Two large blobs on each side of his mouth were sinking into his dimples, and a huge glob was sliding down his chin and about to slither down his neck.

He was holding the Roti against his mouth hoping to prevent more curry from spilling out, while he pathetically tried to chew the piece already in his mouth. His usually confidently proud eyes betrayed a humbling that bordered on desperation.

She quelled her first impulse to double over laughing, feeling she had been amused enough at his expense for the day and in actual fact, was responsible for the poor man's predicament. Giving him the sweetest smile, she carefully took the remaining Roti out of his hands and rested it on his plate. Without realizing what she was doing as it seemed the most natural thing to her, using her fingers, she gently started pushing the messy curry into his open mouth. This action took him by surprise, but he was pleased by her attentiveness.

She was just about to move her fingers away, Michael having licked off the last remaining traces of curry from around his mouth, when he clamped her fingers between his lips.

She tried to pull them out but he held her hand, clamped his lips tighter, and sucked on her fingers. This felt extremely amatory to both, and sent shivers down their spines to their most private of parts. His eyes gleamed mischievously.

She attempted to sound annoyed but he could see the smile in her eyes, "Are you enjoying yourself, Your Highness?"

Taking her hand away from his mouth he held it in his lap, "Actually, I don't know when last I've had such fun. I haven't relaxed like this in ages." His face grew serious, "I enjoy being with you, Elizabeth Angelique Richardson."

She could not ignore the thrill she felt at his compliment or the fact that the feeling was unnervingly mutual, "I've enjoyed being with you too Michael Alexander Stephen. But I'm afraid I should be going back to the hotel soon. I've an early business meeting tomorrow and I must be sharp and alert to deal with these people."

His interest was aroused, "Oh, what's it about?"

She replied with forced insouciance, "I'm trying to get a grant from an international body that's based here."

He waited for her protraction and when it was not forthcoming, he pressed, "What do you want the money for?"

She replied slowly, and he could tell reluctantly, "For a voluntary organization I co-founded in Trinidad." Seeing his look of expectancy for her to continue, she added modestly, "Actually, I'm the president. It's a non-for-profit home for mentally challenged children. We've been experimenting with different exercises, especially in the water, which has been very successful. But it's a highly specialized field and we need funds to build another type of pool, and bring in foreign instructors to teach our people."

"You'll get your grant," he said simply.

Her jaw set, she looked at his eyes, determination sparking out of her own, "Michael, I didn't mean to bring this up. You asked so I gave you the explanation, but I don't want any help from you. This is my problem, I can handle it myself. Please don't interfere."

Surprised at this admonition, yet greatly admiring her for it, he thought for such a beautiful and sweet young woman, she certainly has a strong independent spirit. Anyone else would have jumped at the opportunity to have him use his influence to get them what they wanted. He squeezed her hand, "You know you're a very remarkable, unusual person. I'm not quite sure how to read you, though. Sometimes I feel I can see what's clicking inside your gorgeous head, other times you're like a closed book, I can't read you at all. It's very disconcerting."

She laughed lightly, "We seem to share the same opinion of each other, Michael."

"Really? I couldn't possibly be as perplexing as you. In fact, I think I've been very open with you," he looked at her out of the corners of his eyes flirtatiously.

Elizabeth flushed, realizing he was referring more to his actions than his words, and she knew that he knew that she knew exactly what he meant. Deliberately diffusing the sensuous moment she looked at her watch, "Goodness! It's ten-thirty, I was hoping to be asleep by ten. I really must go, Michael."

Standing up, he gave her his hands and helped her up. They stood still for a moment holding hands, eyes locked, taking each other in, until Elizabeth reluctantly, slowly, let go of his hands, and walked to the car.

They drove along in silence awhile, Elizabeth looking out the window, Michael staring straight ahead, both wondering what the other was thinking. He spoke first, "Would you like to go to the ballet tomorrow evening? There's a rare performance by the visiting Sarasota Ballet of Florida from the U.S. I hear they're quite wonderful. I'm sure you'd enjoy it."

Her face lit up excitedly, "They are fabulous! I saw them once in Sarasota, my aunt and uncle have a winter home there. I've been dying to see them again-"

"Great!" he interrupted, pleased that she was so enthusiastic about his invitation. "We'll have an early supper at a little French restaurant I think you'd like. I'll pick you up at six. Alright?"

She didn't answer, remembering she had promised herself she would not see him again. That she should not. It was not right, not fair to him, or her, or anyone else. She chastised herself, *Elizabeth, you've always been forthright and honest, and this particular man deserves nothing less. Not because of his royal status but because he's just so unique, so precious and endearing…and he touches me in more ways than I felt I could be touched again. Tell him now. Tell him everything.* She searched her mind for the right words but they were elusive.

Nervously, he picked up her hand in both of his, "Elizabeth, haven't you heard me?"

Not looking at him, she pulled her hand away slowly, "Michael, I cannot see you again. I want to, but I cannot."

He frowned perplexedly, "Why, Elizabeth?"

Her mind filled with reasons she thought he would appreciate even though they would be far from the truth. She wet her lips, the action causing disquietude in his loins, "It wouldn't be fair to either of us to get involved. I'm not for you, Michael, surely you know that. You'd just be wasting your time. Anyway, aren't you dating that beautiful foreign princess that everybody's hoping you'll marry, Teresa? She seems to be perfect for you. A marriage with her will bring more unity in Europe, and it'll make everyone very happy."

His jaw tightened, "Who's everyone, Elizabeth? Doesn't *my* happiness count? Listen Elizabeth, I've spent my whole life doing the right thing for my country, but when it comes to choosing a woman to spend the rest of my life with, I'm going to do the right thing for *me*. If I'd met that woman before I would've been married already! I'm under constant pressure from my family to get married. My father and aunts are continually bringing it up. My father's health isn't good and he wants to abdicate. But he, and the government, are traditional, old-fashioned, and don't think it's 'right' that I take over without a wife. *I* want to rule desperately! There are so many changes for the betterment of this region that I know I can influence. I have so many plans for this country, for my reign. But I'll be dammed if I'll get married to the first 'suitable' woman that's available, just to please everyone else. That is *one* decision in my life that I'll make on my own. I'll marry only for love."

Elizabeth was taken aback by the angry tone of his voice, the vein in his neck that started to pulse, and the hard look that transformed his handsome face. Her heart went out to him. She contemplated how difficult it must be for someone as intelligent and, though famously sensitive, as strong-willed as he, to have to live his life to suit the needs of his country and family. She wanted to grab him, shake him, scream to him, "*Be free, Michael! Be free!*" Instead, she pressed his hand tenderly, "I hope you get your wish, Michael."

His expression remained serious but his voice softened, "Would you like to go to the ballet tomorrow, then?"

She could not bear to hurt him now, she had inexplicably, rapidly, built up strong feelings for this special man, who was exhuming a blissfulness in her that had been too long interred; but how could she see him again? It would just be prolonging the agony of the inevitable parting they must face.

Her voice filling with tenderness, she held his hand, "Michael, I want you to know, I've not met anyone like you in my entire life before, and believe me, I've met all kinds of wonderful interesting people, but you're way up above the rest, and that's where you'll always be. I'm just a commoner, not aristocratic, not even very wealthy. You can't afford to get involved with someone as lowly as me at this stage of your life. You're thirty-two now and your father's right, it's about time you got married and started a family. Unfortunately the government and society will take you more seriously then, you'll get more cooperation to implement the changes you want to make. I understand how you feel about choosing your own wife, marriage is difficult enough when you're in love, but, you've got to be realistic about your esteemed position. You must choose someone who everyone can accept. After all she'll be Queen one day, she must be someone who commands respect-"

He interrupted her with his teasing smile, "I don't think anyone cannot respect you. Why, even *I* respect you."

"Michael please, I'm being serious-"

His smile rapidly disappeared, "So am I. Elizabeth, you're hedging. None of this has anything to do with the reason you don't want to see me again."

Adamantly she raised her voice, "Yes it does! Can't you see? I'm nobody in this country. What if our relationship became serious? People will be trying to find all sorts of 'dirt' in my background, hoping to 'fix the common little upstart.' Think of all the scandalous rumors that will be heaped upon you and your family, especially as I'm from 'little Trinidad' in the Caribbean. What if, say, I had black blood in me. How will your family handle that? There is still so much ignorant prejudice-"

He interrupted lightheartedly, "Black blood is probably exactly what the country needs right now. That'll help to stabilize our relationships with our dark-skinned cousins in other countries." His mouth still smiling, his eyes narrowed unintentionally, "Do you have black blood?"

"No, maybe not genetically, but all humanity started in Africa anyway. But you see what I mean. What if-"

He grabbed her hands regarding her skeptically, "Elizabeth stop it! You're just running me around in circles. What are you afraid of?" Turning away, she didn't answer and he shook her hands, "Is there something in your past that you're ashamed of? Have you committed a crime? Murdered somebody?"

She was appalled, "Don't be ridiculous! Of course not!"

Shaking her hands again he asked with more than a hint of impatience, "Well, what is it then? Have you had a botched abortion, can't you have children?" Though surprised at this question she simply shook her head firmly.

His demeanor softened, "Have you got a bastard child then?"

She shook her head again, "No." She emitted a deep sigh, "Michael, why can't you just accept that I'm wrong for you, and leave it at that?"

His impatience growing as he found her inability to know what he already knew absolutely maddening, he said emphatically, "No! Because *you* are right for me! *I* know it and *you* know it!"

Elizabeth was aghast at this remark. *Surely he's being melodramatic? How could he possibly mean what he's saying? He hardly knows me. Does he have deep feelings already that he can speak with such conviction? For heaven's sake, love at first sight doesn't exist anymore, except in romance novels and movies. We're adults now, not kids anymore. This feeling I have for him must be just a passing infatuation, therefore that's what he has for me too, nothing more.*

The car stopped in front of her hotel. Jenkins got out and waited for Michael's signal before opening the door. "We're here," she said, relieved and grateful for the distraction.

Staring hard into her eyes, Michael held her arms, "I'm picking you up tomorrow at six. Be ready. That's a Royal Command, if you disobey, I'll have you beheaded."

Looking into his eyes, she saw a yearning there she had not seen before, and surrendering to his charismatic and humorous persuasion, and, her own true feelings, she sighed in acquiescence, "I'd like to hold on to my head for a few more years yet, Your Highness. I'll be ready at six tomorrow."

Elizabeth decided she must look simple but dignified. She pulled her hair back with a plain barrette, applied a light peach lipstick, a touch of blush on her cheeks, a soft brush of mascara to her already thick lashes, and that was as much as she felt was necessary. She didn't want to appear frivolous, or lacking in need, to the foundation board with which she had the meeting. Neither did she want to give the impression she was some poor incompetent 'hat-in-hand' begging for crumbs.

She chose to wear a simple navy-blue suit by a lesser known designer she had been friendly with when she lived in the States, rather than one of the new more outstanding ones from Paris Ruth had purchased for her. It looked smart and businesslike but still complimented her curvaceous figure.

As she hung up the phone from calling for the Granger's car to meet her at the front entrance, Olga knocked on her door, "Mees Eleezabeth, sometheeng come for you. The man no geeve eet to me, say you moost take eet youself."

Quietly, so as not to awaken the Grangers, she walked with Olga to the penthouse foyer where a man in a security type uniform stood at attention, holding a large, long box, "Are you Miss Elizabeth Angelique Richardson?"

"Yes." she answered, hiding her surprise at his formality and the use of her full name.

"I'll need to see identification please."

She fished in her bag, pulled out her American passport, and showed it to him. He nodded in recognition, handed her the box, gave a quick bow, and left.

Olga took the heavy box from her, rested it on the foyer table and ran to the kitchen for a knife. The box was double taped and it took a minute for Olga to get it open and when she did, the perfume of the most perfect two dozen long-stemmed yellow and white roses filled the foyer. Lying under them was a large hand-cut Waterford crystal vase wrapped in gold and white tissue, with an artistic yellow, white and gold silk bow tied around it. Nestled next to the vase were two small boxes which Olga excitedly handed to Elizabeth. Opening the smaller gold velvet one first she gasped, then laughed.

Olga looked at it and was puzzled, "What ees eet? A charm? But how you hang eet?"

Elizabeth glowed, "It's a Bindi, from India. Ladies wear it on their forehead, like this," she placed it above her nose between her eyebrows.

Olga was now impressed, "Eet beautiful, but so small."

"That's what makes it so special," Elizabeth said as she admired the delicate piece of jewelry. The Bindi was a small oval-shaped flat ruby surrounded by the tiniest white diamonds and encased in the most intricate gold filigree, truly a miniature work of art.

Bored with it already, Olga handed Elizabeth the other box, "You don't want be late. Open thees."

She opened it to find an ornate sterling silver frame, and in it, written in calligraphy, was the poetry Michael had composed about her eyes and hair, and her "*beautiful soul*," when they were in The Park yesterday. Her full name was its title and he signed it with the symbol of two intertwined hearts and his first three initials, *M.A.S.*

Olga rummaged in the box and became perplexed when she came up empty-handed, "But, there ees no card?"

Elizabeth replied dreamily, "There's no need for one, I know exactly who it's from. Now, come along, let's put all this in my room, and keep it between us for now, alright?"

Olga, thrilled to be the only person privy to Elizabeth's romantic secret, nodded and scooped up the large box. Elizabeth placed the framed poem on her bedside table, put the jewelry box with the Bindi in her handbag, called out instructions to Olga to fix the roses in the vase with water and put it on the desk in her room, and dashed out the suite.

After thirty minutes of talking to the board about her detailed presentation of what was needed for The Children's Home expansion, Elizabeth knew she had created an excellent impression with her convincing proposal. She was confident she had a strong case and put it forward with enthusiasm and sincerity. The austere four men and three women listened carefully, asked many pertinent questions and were very attentive to her answers. After making additional notes on their individual copies of Elizabeth's proposal that they had received two months earlier, they asked her to go to Reception and have a cup of coffee while they deliberated over her request.

Too anxious to risk the additional caffeine in the coffee offered by the receptionist, she already having had green tea and nothing else back at the hotel, she accepted an apple, and nervously sat down to await the verdict.

The smiling faces that greeted her when she was allowed back in the room told her that her angst was unnecessary. She was informed that her cause was worthy of the grant her project needed, and she would have it in her hands within a month.

The Grangers were having brunch in the dining room of the suite when she rushed in and excitedly gave them the good news. Knowing how important this project was to her and her country, they were genuinely thrilled for her, and inwardly proud of her, especially as she had intrepidly turned down their offer to fund The Children's Home in its entirety from its inception. This had proven to them that despite her having been raised with all the luxuries money can buy, they had not failed in instilling in her the importance of self-accomplishment, and the value in earning assets for oneself, while contributing to the welfare of others.

Ruth's hazel eyes glowed with pride, "I wonder if your date last night with the Prince had anything to do with it being so easy, you were so worried about being turned down," she motioned Elizabeth to the empty seat beside her and continued eagerly, "sit, tell us about the date."

Elizabeth felt a little peeved at not being given full credit for her accomplishment, but hid her feelings and calmly, succinctly, told them about her dinner date with Prince Michael, not mentioning any of the intimacies that took place, or the gifts that arrived early this morning.

CHAPTER 4

*R*uth looked at Robert, "Well, can you believe this Robert? A Royal Prince falling for our Elizabeth?" Not waiting for an answer, she turned to Elizabeth, "Imagine him asking *us* if he could take you out, as if you were some young debutante. He was so proper and old-fashioned. It nearly floored me, I didn't know what to say. I'm sorry we left you like we did, darling, but there didn't seem to be any other diplomatic way to handle it."

Ruth looked upset and Elizabeth felt sympathetic toward her aunt and surrogate mother whom she adored, "It's alright, not your fault. Anyway he hasn't 'fallen' for me. He was just curious about me, what with my mixed-up accent and the exotic sounding country I come from. Actually he's invited me to supper and the ballet tonight. I just don't know how to get out of it."

"Why on earth would you want to do that?" Ruth asked incredulously.

Elizabeth looked at Ruth then Robert, "Look, you know my position. I can't just date someone, especially a Royal Prince of his status, and act as if it's the most natural thing in the world. Because it's not. To me, it's unethical. I feel it's wrong at this…crazy, stage…of my life."

Robert was silent. He didn't think he belonged in this conversation. After all, he was only the uncle-by-law, and felt it was not in his place to give this kind of advice to Elizabeth anymore. She was a grown woman now and no longer in his charge. He also knew his wife was one powerful lady who, as she had told him several times with a put-on exaggerated Trinidadian accent, had *"no license to mih mouth,"* and was going to say exactly what she wanted anyway. He backed out and left it up to her.

Ruth's expression became parentally stern, "Elizabeth, you're being very childish. Here you are being given a once in a lifetime opportunity, on a silver platter, to get the top influences in this great country to assist you in getting whatever you need for your own small country, and you want to cast it aside because of some stupid Victorian principles. You haven't taken after your aunt, girl, that's for sure. Besides, aren't you being a little selfish? Think of this as doing something for the children, and your country, not to please yourself, and I'll bet you'll soon lose all qualms about it." Ruth softened, held Elizabeth's hands and shook them gently, "On top of that, darling, you've been going through the most hellish time of your life with what happened. It's made you fearful and indecisive. We didn't raise you to harbor those insecurities. Stop being so uptight about everything. Now that you've been able to, at last, lift out of your terrible depression since I took you back home to the States, away from all that…tribulation…in Trinidad, you have to forget that awful… stuff. You deserve to have fun again. Just go and relax. You need to get back to being your old care-free happy self."

Elizabeth said nothing. How could she tell them her trepidation about going out with Michael had nothing to do with his position or even her situation, his influence and wealth were not even an issue for her. She was not intimidated by him, but was weakening with him, and had become unaccustomed to that feeling with someone else. She knew she must fight it, what with the uncertain circumstances that had thrown her life into turmoil, but it was proving to be increasingly difficult, because deep within that *"old care-free happy self,"* she knew she really didn't want to.

Dressing unhurriedly, she hoped her physical speed would help to slow the racing activity in her mind. It seemed to work, because she calmly came to a decision. She was not going to feel guilty about seeing Michael again. Surely there could be no harm in it. She did so much enjoy his company, and as Ruth pointed out, it had been too long since she had some fun. Perhaps Ruth was right, maybe she could get him to use his influence to obtain the best personnel and equipment for The Children's Home, surely there was nothing wrong with that. Anyway, she'll be back in Trinidad in four weeks' time with the grant, get back to her busy life, and, formidable decisions, and her 'interlude' with him will soon be forgotten. Hopefully.

Olga came in and told her, "Meester Jenkeens ees waiteeng een the foyer."

She picked up her shawl and gold crystal Judith Lieber evening bag, kissed Ruth and Robert goodbye, and walked with Jenkins to the car. He explained that Prince Michael apologizes for not picking her up at her door himself, but due to security reasons, it was not advisable for him to do so at this time.

Elizabeth assured him she understood perfectly and did not expect it. Although always very proper, polite, and respectful to a fault, Jenkins unnerved her. She felt he was criticizingly judging her. Despite his impassive expression, she could feel his black eyes penetrating through her, seeing beyond her façade, and warned herself to be very careful when around him.

Michael watched her approach, and for the first time since his early twenties, a burgeoning desire flamed up in him, and his mind struggled with his body in an attempt to cool it down. He felt like a sex-starved teenager again. An amusing thought flitted across his psyche that whenever he was to be in her company, he might have to revert to wearing tighter underpants to try to keep his manhood contained like he used to in those lusty youthful days. At least for now.

He didn't consider that because he had unusually, deliberately, kept himself celibate the past few months, to possibly be the reason for these present stirrings. He had many stimulations while dating Princess

Teresa, but none had the profundity of this desire that overtook him now. His celibacy was encouraged by the younger Teresa insisting she must be a virgin for her husband. Strangely, he had no inclination to change her mind, as he had, successfully, with numerous ladies in the past. He simply took himself in hand whenever his manhood grew too painful, convincing himself he could wait; although he was unsure of what, or who, he was waiting for. Until now.

Elizabeth seated herself close to the door, smiled at him and said, "Good evening, Your Royal Highness."

Michael responded with a warm admiring smile, "You look absolutely stunning."

She flushed slightly in appreciation but knew she looked quite lovely in her gold silk gown. It was a perfect color to show up her suntan and flawless complexion. The neckline was flattering to her bust though discreetly décolleté, but the back dipped all the way down to just past her waist, hence the reason for the shawl. She wanted to be attractive for him but didn't want to look too seductive or appear to be deliberately tempting. She felt a flutter in her chest as she took in how debonair he looked in what she recognized to be a Gianluca Isaia black evening suit, and told him he looked very handsome.

On seeing his gold silk tie she exclaimed, "It's the same color as my dress!"

His delight was obvious, "Great minds think alike."

She teased, "Fools seldom differ," then she pointed to the Bindi on her forehead, "thank you for the Bindi, it's absolutely exquisite. You really shouldn't have. But honestly, I love it. It brought a smile to my face…and to my heart…a wonderful and humorous memory of our Roti fiasco. Where did you find it?"

He was pleased with himself, "I had it made for you."

Impressed, she said, "Had it made? So quickly?"

The teasing gleam in his eyes appeared, "Perquisites of being a royal personage."

With a shy smile, she thanked him for the roses, the Waterford crystal vase, and the framed poem, ending with a sincere remark, "I'll cherish them forever."

He teased again, "That might be difficult, the roses are sure to die."

She laughed, "You know I meant the Bindi, the vase…and poem."

Becoming serious, he fixed his eyes on hers, "There's a lot more where that came from."

Wanting to change the subject, she quickly asked him what his day had been like. He described parts of it to her in his effortless unpretentious manner that she liked so much. He asked her about hers, and she told him of her success in getting the grant. Keeping the conversation light and relaxed, she was determined they should have a cheerful non-confrontational evening this time, steering clear of anything that could turn serious or bring about any unpleasantness. He sensed this and fell right in with her gay easy mood.

On entering the restaurant, Michael shook the fawning maître d's hand and told him softly, "Play Edith Piaf."

Elizabeth noticed the man pocketed the money Michael surreptitiously slipped him, and after seating them in the quietest darkest corner of the room, rushed to change the music.

She was delighted with Michael's taste in music. Despite being born and spending her early years in Trinidad, the 'Land of Calypso and Steelband,' she grew up exposed to every genre of music by her well-traveled, refined, sophisticated parents.

Her family was of mixed ancestry from Europe, her mother's being mostly French, and the late Edith Piaf's mournful haunting voice was much loved and played in her home and that of her maternal relatives. She mentioned this to him, teasingly asking if perhaps, between their matching colors tonight, his taking her to the ballet that she absolutely loves, and his choice of music, that he was able to read her mind.

He put down his menu and gazed sensuously into her eyes, "Nothing would make me happier than to get into your beautiful head." She could feel her cheeks heating up in a blush as the thought

of him getting into other parts of her entered that beautiful head. She
suspected the thought might be occurring to him too. It was.

The dinner was a gourmet's delight and everything perfection, as
one would expect when dining in a five-star restaurant with royalty. A
few people stared at them at first, most simply thinking, *what a beautiful couple.* Michael wore tinted glasses which changed the look of his
face slightly but did not diminish the glow in his eyes and the way he
absorbed her. Ignoring everyone around them they acted as if they
were just an ordinary couple dining alone.

They conversed freely about the arts, travel, sports, and philanthropy, but were brief about any subject that accidentally came up
that could get too personal, intense or controversial. Neither was surprised that they had many similar interests and a great deal in common. Elizabeth felt the closeness building up between them again and
reminded herself to be on guard, yet not do anything to spoil the evening. Several times during dinner Michael rested his hand on hers, but
that was all. He too was being cautious and she was thankful for it.

Michael was finding it difficult to contain his emotions. He knew
he should not risk upsetting her again by demonstrating any serious
affection toward her, having realized she found his kissing her yesterday to be audacious behavior. Yet he felt vibrations coming from her
that told him she was feeling the same as he. When he first met her he
conjured up visions of the beautiful goddess creature gyrating fervidly
under him, on top of him, and all over him, giving him the ultimate
pleasure he knew he would give her. Except now, the visions have
expanded, become more involved, more detailed, more entrancing,
with more serious emotions than lust, creating an unusual and disturbing yearning. He was beginning to see the beauty within.

He observed his enjoyment of her had become more than just a
primal physical desire. Everything about her excited and interested
him. The more they talked, the more he wanted to hear her talk, and
to talk himself. This verbal dance of 'getting to know you' was proving
to be more rhythmically exciting than any he had ever participated in
before.

The ballet performed by the Sarasota Ballet Of Florida was quite different from what Elizabeth had seen them render previously. Based on Robert de Warren's concept of 'Madame Butterfly,' it was not traditionally classical nor outrageously contemporary. It was extremely beautiful, faultlessly executed, and both she and Michael, and judging from the lengthy standing ovation, everyone else in the audience, enjoyed it immensely.

Chatting nonstop in the car, they both felt completely in accord with each other, neither wanting the evening to end. Becoming aware the car had stopped at her hotel and Jenkins was waiting outside for a signal before he would open the door, Michael held her hands and spoke softly, "Am I correct in believing that you've enjoyed this evening as much as I have?"

She smiled shyly, "Yes Michael, it was just perfect." Pleased, he returned the smile, but then became serious, "Elizabeth, tomorrow I have to go to the West Country until Thursday. The next few days are going to be hectic, putting it mildly. My father and the government have asked me to intervene in…a potentially volatile situation over there, because negotiations have reached a stalemate. Anyway, I can't go into details but I'm confident I'll sort it out." He saw a concerned look cloud her face and continued quickly, "I don't think I'll be getting much sleep while I'm there, so by Thursday I'll be in need of a little rest and relaxation. My cousin Susan Jamestown and her husband, John, have invited me to spend a few days with them to 'recuperate,' so to speak, at their country estate. It's very peaceful and private there, more than my own family's country estate, and I don't need an entourage. It's the perfect place to relax, get back to nature. I'd love you to come with me. Would you please come?" Michael saw the disturbed look that settled on Elizabeth's face, mistook it for virtuous embarrassment and added quickly, "I assure you, we'll be well chaperoned. Susan and John will both be there, along with a houseful of domestic staff. And you'll have your own suite, of course. It would be a lovely change from the city."

Seeing Elizabeth's look not shifting he realized this was going to be a harder sell than he originally thought. Putting on his most convincing smile he continued with even more enthusiasm, "I know you'll enjoy it. They've got great horses, tennis courts, a huge heated pool, amazing gardens and grounds, fully equipped gym, it would be fun to work-out together. There's a wonderful winery and vineyards nearby, and the country scenery is an artists' dream. Actually, Susan's a famous artist, you'll love her work. And you'll love Susan and John, they're two of my favorite people, and I had to tell them about you. They're dying to meet you. Will you come, Elizabeth, please?"

She didn't know how to answer, he had taken her completely by surprise, she had not bargained for *this* type of invitation. She chose her words carefully, "It sounds very tempting, Michael. But, I don't see how I can. Grangers are leaving to go back to America next week and I really should spend the rest of their time here with them. They've been so wonderful to me all my life, and now, having me stay with them, getting me invited to the Royal Garden Party, spoiling me in so many enjoyable ways. The least I can do is be with them until they leave, you know, they're not getting any younger. Then, I have to move as well. I'm not even sure where I'm going to stay until I've…completed my…eh…business…here. One of my friends is hopefully getting her cousin's apartment for me. I'm sorry, but it just doesn't seem possible, Michael."

Holding her hands tighter he spoke with an element of desperation, "Elizabeth, I can't wait a whole week to see you again! You mentioned you'll have to go home in four weeks' time, that doesn't leave us much time to be together, to get to know each other. You can see the Grangers almost anytime, they must visit your family often enough. Surely they'll understand. I'll speak to them, alright?"

Nervousness entered her voice though she looked calm, "No Michael, I'll have to discuss this with them myself."

"Will you come, then?" he asked softly, his eyes pleading.

She knew Ruth and Robert would tell her she should go and enjoy a little R'n'R, Ruth would probably give her the "*lost opportunity*"and "*get back to your old care-free happy self*"lecture again, so that was not the reason for her hesitancy. She hesitated because she was afraid. Afraid of this venerable imposing six-foot-three-inches tall Adonis' continuous presence. Afraid of these mesmerizing silver-sparked blue eyes that penetrated her very soul. Afraid of these luscious lips now imploring, "If you feel at all uncomfortable, we'll return to the city the next day." She was afraid of *him*.

And now, most scary of all, she was afraid of *herself!*

Fear was not an emotion she had previously allowed herself to submit to for any length of time, and she decided that she had to cast it out, immediately. *I'm a strong confident woman. I'm in charge of my emotions. I'm in control. Can handle anything. Despite what happened to overturn my perfect world, I will not be scared anymore. Of anything. Of anyone. A relaxing sojourn in the country is probably just what I need to help me make my tough decisions. I need to feel normal again. I need to feel like* me! "Alright, Michael, it does sound quite wonderful, and as it's just for a few days, I accept your invitation."

"Great!" He smiled happily, "I'll pick you up around six-thirty Thursday evening. I'd like to give you my private mobile number. But you must keep it confidential, you can't give it to anyone or record it."

Astonished and honored by his trusting gesture, she said quickly, "I wouldn't dream of it, I'll memorize it." He gave it to her, she repeated it once to him, then, closing her eyes, repeated it to herself, storing it in her memory.

He took his phone out of his jacket pocket. Elizabeth had not seen such a strange looking mobile phone before. It was more compact than hers, encased in platinum, and its entire face was a screen with just one tiny button on one side. "May I have yours?" he inquired hesitantly.

She jumped in surprise, "Oh…yes, of course," and trying hard not to show her reluctance, gave it to him.

"Do you text?" he asked.

"Not much really, usually to my offices. Honestly, I prefer to speak directly to someone."

"Really? Do you know I feel exactly the same way." His expression softened and he looked at her lovingly, which both thrilled and scared her. He touched her hand, "Do you mind if I record your number?

I promise nobody else will get it from here, but I'd like to put it on speed-dial, although I'm going to be extremely busy the next few days and may not get a chance to speak to you."

"Alright, and you needn't worry, I'll not disturb you." There was a hint of disappointment yet haughtiness in her voice as she quickly repeated her number for him to record it.

He smiled flirtatiously, "Elizabeth, you already disturb me, in more ways than you can imagine."

She blushed and turned away thinking to herself, *You obviously have no idea as to what I can imagine*. She thanked him for a lovely evening, said she looked forward to seeing the countryside with him on Thursday, and turned toward the door.

He held her arm and she stiffened, not knowing what to expect. But he merely thanked her for giving him a lovely evening too. Leaning forward to open the door to let her out for Jenkins to escort her back to her suite, he brushed against her. Though this light touch brought heavy amatory feelings to both, he did nothing else. Elizabeth was unsure of if she felt relief, or disappointment.

Ruth and Robert had to return to America prematurely; two of the alternative energy companies they had invested in called for emergency meetings. When it came to expanding into ecologically friendly technology companies that used safe, healthy, and renewable resources and methods, Robert dropped everything that was of lesser importance than the sustainability of the planet. That included having more fun in Europe with his precious wife and her niece who was more like the daughter he never had. The frightening undeniable truths about the precarious condition of Earth made him, and Ruth, nervously aware that *all* fun on the planet could soon be brought to a disastrous halt, if faster and drastic actions were not taken. Even though his family had made their fortune in oil and its byproducts, like most knowledgeable and intelligent people, Robert knew that not only would the crowded planet be running out of oil, but more significantly, humanity's waste-fulness of it was contributing to Earth's rapid demise. Ruth and he now made it their mission in life to do everything they possibly could to, "*save planet Earth.*"

Their goodbyes were lengthy, tearful, and filled with regret. Though Elizabeth was much saddened to see them go, she was also relieved to have some quiet time alone. She was disturbed by thoughts of incompleteness. She still had to do further investigations into the equipment needed for The Children's Home, research the necessary personnel to bring to Trinidad to teach locals, make many personal and work related phone calls and e-mails to her family and others in Trinidad, the United States, and several other countries around the world, as well as fine-tune her upcoming important speech.

Olga had packed most of her clothes before leaving, separating what Elizabeth would need as a guest in the country from what she would leave in the hotel's storage. She had sworn Olga to secrecy about her trip, although she didn't say who she was going with, think-ing it best the Grangers not know of her plans. She didn't want to attempt explaining things she herself had no explanation for.

She tried to immerse herself in work but thoughts of Michael kept taking away her focus. Struggling to put him out of her mind, she kept seeing his handsome face with intense serious eyes and sensuous mouth smiling flirtatiously, boyishly, teasingly, hearing his voice saying all those sincerely ardent words that took her by surprise. She imag-ined the touch of his luscious lips on hers again, the sweetness of his taste and the succulent feeling of his tongue enveloping hers; and her heartbeat would quicken. *If this is how I feel when he's not around, what's going to happen when I'm with him again!*

CHAPTER
5

On awakening the next morning, Elizabeth's phone told her there were fifteen voicemails, four from family, two business related, the rest from Michael. She skipped through the six and went straight to Michael's. His calls the next few days were made late at night and in the early morning hours when she was asleep and her phone on its charger. He was obviously too busy during the normal hours of the day. The messages were short and sweet but what surprised her and tugged at her heart, was that he played love songs, mostly by their original recording artists and often just snippets of them. The first snippet he played gave her a good giggle. It was sung by The Merry Men of Barbados, "*Island Woman, island woman, making me forget who I am-*" Then Michael's voice came on, "Hi, my island woman. I don't care if I forget who I am but I want to make sure you don't forget me." Immediately after that he had her dancing and singing to the whole of 'Brown Eyed Girl' by Van Morrison.

Next came Jon Cedaca lamenting it was, "*Just another day without you.*" Following that was the first chorus of Bruce Springsteen's 'Brilliant Disguise' which had her suspecting his message there was to inform her that he was aware she had many mysteries which he was waiting for her to reveal. Then he played two lines of The Beatle's 'All You Need Is Love,' and ended that snippet medley with Cheap Trick's 'I Want You To Want Me.'

In a message he left at five-thirty the next morning, a voice she didn't recognize gleefully sang a chorus of 'You Are My Sunshine' and followed that romantically crooning "*Beautiful Beautiful Brown Eyes, I'll never love blue eyes again.*" She observed there was no background music but she could not believe it might be Michael singing to her, the voice was too polished, professional. He then played Eurhythmics chorusing, "*There must be an angel playing with my heart,*" and later that night, Roy Orbison crying, "*Only the lonely, know the way I feel tonight.*" In another message, he brought back memories of their perfect evening at the French restaurant and ballet by playing Edith Piaf's 'La Vie En Rose.'

Another voicemail had just one song in its entirety, Brian Adam's 'You Love A Woman,' and it was not just the connotation of the words that made her heart flip, but to hear Michael say at the end of the song, "I really want you." The last voicemail that day was the most suggestive of all, Elvis Presley was seductively convincing as he pleaded that she must, 'Surrender.'

After she completed her numerous phone calls and e-mails, she gave up working on her speech as Michael's songs kept repeating in her head, causing constant distraction. She went for a long speed-walk in The Park, worked-out in the hotel's gym, got dressed, and went shopping, all the while unintentionally day-dreaming about Michael.

Thursday morning arrived with another batch of singers' voice-mails from Michael. Most of the songs were in the same vein as the previous days, but there were two that stood out which she found unsettling. The first was John Denver's haunting voice letting her know that she "*filled up*" his "*senses*" in 'Annie's Song.' This particular song was more than deeply romantic, it was expressing an everlasting commitment. To "*let me always be with you, let me die in your arms*" was beyond the sweet wooing and romanticism of the other songs.

The one that nearly floored her though, actually scared her somewhat, he was getting too close to home and she could not imagine *how* he got it, was an old Trinidadian calypso by the late Fitzroy 'Lord Melody' Alexander. It went, "*Your crazy, crazy love is what I'm dreaming of.You're haunting me, and my heart starts to beat, darling love me or let me be free. Any time that I ring you on the telephone, girl like you never home,*" and right there in mid verse, Michael hung up.

At six-thirty Brian arrived at the luxury suite to collect her. He explained that he was to drive Prince Michael's personal sports car behind the Rolls Royce she and the prince would be in, he was too tired to drive today but wanted to have his car while they were in the country.

On seeing Michael her heart literally missed a beat, a strange fear gripping it. She almost didn't recognize him, gone was his usually impeccable condition. His tie was unknotted, clothes in disarray, hair disheveled, there were dark circles under his eyes, his eyelids drooped, and his normally salubrious handsome face looked sickly and drawn.

He gave her a tired smile, grabbed her hand and clasped it, "I missed you."

"Michael, you look awful!" she cried, "What happened?"

Kicking off his shoes he slumped his shoulders, too exhausted to show his excitement at seeing her again, "Sorry, I'm too tired to talk now, will talk tomorrow, be fine then. I just need some sleep."

"Haven't you slept at all, the last three days?"

"No," he mumbled groggily.

Without another word she gently, slowly, pulled his head down onto her lap. Appreciating her gesture he smiled up at her, raised his shoeless feet onto the other end of the seat and snuggled against her, falling asleep immediately.

She spent the entire journey taking brief glimpses at the picturesque countryside and long compassionate looks at Michael. Completely fatigued, he hardly moved at all, but when he did, he groaned softly as though in pain. This disturbed her. She wondered what he could be dreaming of that would cause such a reaction. *What the heck's going on in theWest Country? There's nothing in the news about the "potentially volatile situation" he mentioned, just suggestions of negotiations to avoid the usual strikes, nothing about his involvement either. I'd think something so serious that warrants his intervention would be big news.* Deep concern about his condition mingling with disinterring feelings scared her. She wanted to hold him tight and cradle him in her arms, but contented herself with stroking his hair and back every time he shifted, soothing him back into deeper slumber, and ignored impinging flashes of foreboding.

Night had already descended when they arrived at last. Looking out the window Elizabeth was astonished to see the estate home was not even a mansion, it was a castle, and enormous. The exterior walls were made of thick square stones, several towers spearing upwards beyond the four stories visible in the darkness. Three leaded-glass windows on each side of the heavily carved front door were all lit up for their arrival.

It looked nothing like the picture she had in mind of the "*estate home*" Michael had so casually described. A couple in their forties and two servants came out to greet them. Michael didn't stir. She decided against waking him, he was deep in sleep and she knew that was all he desperately needed right now.

The car door opened and a woman's voice called out gaily, "Well, hello there!"

The woman's head came into the car and Elizabeth put a finger to her own lips and whispered, "Hello, I'm Elizabeth, you must be Susan. I'm very pleased to meet you." She pointed to Michael, "I don't want to wake him, he's exhausted. He hasn't slept in three days. Could you ask Jenkins to bring another blanket, please? He might get cold, now that we've stopped."

Susan stared at Elizabeth, "Oh. Why yes, certainly. But you can't stay like that. What if he sleeps through the night?"

Whispering still, Elizabeth shook her head, "I'm alright. If I could just have a small pillow for my neck, I'll be fine."

Susan withdrew and instructed her butler standing nearby to get what Elizabeth requested. He returned quickly and helped Susan spread the blanket over Michael and over Elizabeth's legs. Elizabeth put the pillow behind her head and tried to appear comfortable, "This is lovely, thank you. We'll come in when Michael wakes up, alright?"

Susan stared again and whispered, "Alright."

Michael did not move for over two hours. Elizabeth's neck and back were hurting terribly and her legs were totally numb. When he eventually stirred she attempted to shift into a more comfortable position and this awakened him. He squinted at her and mumbled, "Aren't we there yet?"

"We've been here over two hours. You were sleeping so soundly, I didn't have the heart to wake you."

He sat up, looked out, and looked back at her, "You mean you've been holding me on your lap the whole time? You must be hurting." She made light of her discomfort and asked if he was ready to go in. He regarded her with appreciative admiration for some time before he finally said, "You're the superlative one who's way up above the rest, Elizabeth Angelique Richardson."

Jenkins, who had not taken his eyes off the car, came forward and opened her door. Elizabeth's legs could not move, "I have cramps, Jenkins. Could you help me please?"

"Wait a minute," Michael said, getting out on his side.

He leaned forward to lift her out, but she put up her hands protesting, "No Michael, are you crazy? You've been lying down too long, you could hurt yourself. Just walk on one side of me and let Jenkins walk on the other. It's poor circulation, I'll be alright once I start moving."

They helped her out, and half walked, half carried her up the steps where Susan and John stood waiting. Michael introduced them hurriedly and Elizabeth smiled weakly feeling somewhat foolish, but she was still aching. Susan kindly suggested that taking into consideration their conditions after the long journey, she would send their dinners up to their rooms as soon as they were settled. Elizabeth's cramps ceased but Michael still held her closely, and they leaned heavily on each other as they followed the servants with their luggage up the carved mahogany grand staircase to their suites.

Arriving at her door, Michael asked, "Will you be alright?"

"Of course," she said, and with a half-smile, joked, "It must be old age catching up with me. Will you apologize to the Jamestown's for

me, I'm not hungry and don't want any dinner. Do you think they'll
be insulted if I just went to bed?"

"No, course not, darling. I'll do the same myself. We'll both feel
better tomorrow. Goodnight Elizabeth and, thank you." He kissed her
softly on her lips and slowly walked to his suite.

"Quite a girl you've got there, Michael." It was Susan's voice.
Elizabeth walked over to the room it was coming from and knocked
on the half-opened door.

"Here she is now." John smiled at her, standing as he beckoned her
in.

After they all exchanged greetings Elizabeth apologized for her
condition last night and turned to Michael, "I'm surprised to see you
up already, I thought you'd be sleeping all day."

He gave her one of his teasing smiles, "There was no need, I feel
perfectly rested. I had the best, most comfortable sleep in years, on
the journey here."

Susan observed Elizabeth's blush at his remark and started making small talk to make her feel at ease. By the time they sat down to
breakfast in the formal dining room under the unseeing eyes of several
Royal ancestors framed in gilt, the atmosphere was totally relaxed and
they all chatted like old friends.

After breakfast, Susan suggested they all go riding. Elizabeth had
a few qualms about that as she had not been astride a horse in several
years and said so. John assured her she would be given a very gentle
but good riding horse and she agreed to give it a try. Arriving at the
stables, the groom brought out two magnificent already saddled chest-
nut horses, a mare for Elizabeth and a stallion for Michael.

Michael helped her onto her mount and seeing an anxious look
flash across her face as she tried to settle herself in the saddle, held
her hands as he gave her the reins, "Don't be afraid, darling. I'll take
care of you." Feeling reassured and appreciative of his concern and

protectiveness, it occurred to her this was the second time he called her 'darling,' and she ridiculed herself for enjoying a silly little-girl thrill.

"You two go on," John called out, "We'll catch up. We're going to check some crops behind the stables, we'll meet you at the beginning of the woods."

"Alright," Michael called back, and he and Elizabeth took off at a slow trot, four of six excited estate dogs in the lead. They rode for some time in silence, Elizabeth aware that he was casting glances at her every so often. Her mare had a soft mouth, was easy on the bit, and responded willingly to Elizabeth's light touch on the reins. This helped to restore her confidence in what she had thought might be a forgotten equestrian ability.

"Can't we go faster?" she asked Michael who was setting the pace. Smiling at her renewed confidence he spurred his more powerful horse into a gallop. They went at a steady pace and arriving at the woods, he dismounted, walked over to Elizabeth who was now breathing heavily, helped her dismount, and held her in his arms on the pretext of steadying her.

He leaned in to kiss her when John called out, "Oh, there you are!" Michael released her slowly, gazing seductively into her eyes the entire time. She flushed under his meaningful look and also in embarrassment at being caught by Susan and John in this position. It didn't seem to faze Michael in the least and as he helped her remount, he kept looking into her eyes with a smoldering stare, sending thrilling waves up and down her spine.

The four cantered along, stopping occasionally to admire the natural beauty of the sometimes celadon, sometimes emerald green, rolling hills and shallow valleys, which were interspersed with bubbling streams cascading gently into several serene ponds, where many species of wild ducks could be seen feeding and frolicking. John promised a guided tour of the rest of the estate tomorrow in a Land Rover and they headed back for lunch.

Luncheon was al fresco on the ground floor terrace which was lacily shaded by stately ancient oaks and evergreens. During lunch,

Elizabeth's phone rang in her bag. She quickly apologized for the intrusion saying she was compelled to take calls that came through because of the time difference between this area and the other countries with which she had to communicate. The royals were understanding as she excused herself and went into the garden, away from inquisitive ears, and eyes, as loving faces lit up her screen.

After dessert had been served, Michael excused himself saying he was still a bit tired and needed a nap. He squeezed Elizabeth's hand and left. John immediately excused himself also, Elizabeth thought a bit sheepishly, saying he must check on some new cattle. Susan asked Elizabeth if she wanted to nap as well or would she prefer to keep her company in her studio, where she was in the midst of painting a still-life in acrylics. Elizabeth said she was fine and would be delighted to see Susan's talent in action, Michael having told her that she was an accomplished artist and had several paintings hanging in museums, the Royal Palace, and other less prestigious institutions.

Although Susan's manner was overly polite yet somewhat reserved, Elizabeth sensed an underlying warmth and quiet strength. She was an attractive, petite woman, the daughter of Michael's aunt, Anne, who lived at the palace with her older sister, Claire. Her father had been killed in a hunting accident when she was three years old. Her mother never remarried.

Susan was an only child and grew up in the palace with Michael, taking him under her wing as her "*baby brother,*" she being fifteen years older than he. Unable to have children due to damaged ovaries, a result of being thrown from a spooked horse as a teenager, she and John chose not to adopt, but instead focused their parental capabilities on Michael, his siblings, and their own numerous and diverse pets.

In the conservatory-studio, with an aviary full of multihued budgerigars, a bubbling saltwater aquarium filled with exotic tropical fish, six dogs at their feet, and a purring obese cat in each lap, they talked about Susan's work awhile, after which Susan asked Elizabeth about her own interests.

Elizabeth described some of the things she was involved in, particularly her charities and participation in a group that educates people about their endangered planet Earth and what could be done to stave off disaster. Responding to some questions, she mentioned her love of music, dance and languages, and was surprised to discover Susan already knew quite a bit about her, "Has Michael spoken to you about me?"

"He didn't stop talking about you the day I phoned him," Susan replied.

Putting down her paintbrush, she turned to Elizabeth with unabashed directness, "Elizabeth, I hope you care for Michael as deeply as he cares for you. I've never seen him like this with another woman, never so open about his feelings. I don't really know you, but I must tell you that you're obviously very special to Michael, and I've always respected his judgment of people. But, he's very special too, not only to our family and this country, but in fact the whole world. I know you're very new in his life, and I sincerely hope you're deserving of him."

Elizabeth was taken aback at Susan's candor and didn't know how to respond. Guilty feelings returning, she wanted to run outside to escape Susan's searching gaze. Susan read her discomfort and apologized for interfering.

Elizabeth assured her she was not offended and appreciated her concern for Michael, because right now, he was all that concerned her too. Susan smiled, relieved, and politely changed the conversation to more artistic topics.

At four-thirty, the ladies, having entered into varied and often serious conversations all afternoon in which they assessed each other with mutually growing veiled respect and affection, joined John for tea, finger sandwiches and dark chocolate cake, in the library. Michael didn't come down. Elizabeth asked John to check on him to see if he was alright. John was gone a long while and on returning alone, informed them that Michael was still asleep. Elizabeth again noticed sheepishness in his demeanor but didn't dwell on it as he began to attempt to pry information out of her on the pretext of being interested in her ancestry. Answering his questions with circumspection she strived to appear relaxed, skirted around more probing questions about her life in Trinidad, simply talked a little about her parent's companies and her work with mentally challenged children, and steered the conversation back to her ancestry, "I'm French and British, some of my ancestors went to Trinidad a couple hundred years ago." She gave some stories about how her ancestors ended up there, until Susan, unintentionally, saved her from further reluctant divulgences by saying it was time to get dressed for the evening as Michael will probably be down shortly.

Elizabeth was on her way back downstairs when Michael caught up with her. She told him he looked so much more rested and asked if he was feeling better. He held her hand and smiled, "Better than ever, now I'm with you."

Susan and John were not down yet and Michael suggested a walk in the gardens. She told him how much she liked the Jamestowns and was extremely impressed with their property. He described some of their additions, and changes they had introduced, praising them for their work ethic and all their achievements despite a very difficult global economy.

He explained that he felt more relaxed here than at his own family's country estate, "People hang around outside our property hoping to get a glimpse or photo of one of us, but nobody knows I come here to get away so it's very private for me. Of course, I've put in top of the line electric fencing, security cameras, etcetera, for John and Susan. That's how I could send Jenkins and the men away." He decided against telling her they were staying at a bed-and-breakfast in the nearby village. He stopped walking, held her arm and looked at her, his eyes narrowing, "You haven't said anything about the voicemails I left you. Didn't you like them?"

Looking steadily back at him, she responded, "I was just about to bring that up. Yes, they were quite…lovely…actually." She looked down shyly at his hand holding her arm, "Some of the songs were…interesting."

She heard the disappointment in his voice, "Interesting?"

Looking at his beguiling eyes, she wet her lips nervously, "Well yes…they were…complimentary, and…romantic."

His face lit up with delight, "So you did like them?"

She felt pleased that he was so pleased, "Very much."

There was a long uncomfortable pause, Michael hoping Elizabeth would elaborate on her feelings about his messages, Elizabeth knowing that was his expectation. Then, remembering one of the songs that had negatively disturbed her, she eyed him scrutinizingly, "I'm curious, where did you find that calypso, 'Crazy Love?' I know it couldn't have been from your cousins, it's very old, since my parent's or even grandparent's time."

Looking mysterious, he unnerved her, "Someone I know from Trinidad gave it to me years ago, but you probably wouldn't know him, he's black and is-"

Interrupting him, she didn't conceal the anger rising in her, "Michael, you'd better tell me right now, do you have a problem with people of color?"

He was astonished, "No! Why would you ask me such a ridiculous question?"

She exhibited a contentious mien, "Well for one thing, the day we first met and I remarked that *what if I had black blood in me*," your eyes got really serious and looked like if I did, that might be a major concern for you."

Smiling facetiously, he put on a solemn voice, "I wasn't concerned. I was just surprised that *you* would have brought that up, someone looking as lily white as you. But then I thought it was your way of trying to put me off-"

She interrupted again, a little less angrily this time, "Then this remark you just made, that I wouldn't know your Trinidadian friend because he's black, makes it sound like you think I don't associate with black people. Michael, I spent the first part of my childhood and now my adult years in Trinidad. I want you to know, more than three quarters of my friends are either black, Indian, or of mixed races. I also have family who are married to dark-skin people. So, if you have a problem, any kind of racial bias, tell me right now, so I can get as far away from you as possible!"

A mélange of emotions hit him all at once. He felt shocked, amused, pleased, and relieved. He could not suppress his delight and smiling, reached out to embrace her, but she backed away from him, anger still apparent in her face as well as her body language, and he knew she needed to hear convincing words.

He lost the smile and said somberly, "I have no racial prejudices in me whatsoever. My parents made sure of that when I was growing up, and I've traveled and learnt too much since that has confirmed everything they taught me. I thought you might have heard in Trinidad, it being a small island and I understand from my friend, a gossipy place, that my roommate when I was at Harvard was a black guy from Trinidad."

He saw her expression change to shock, but continued, "He wasn't just a roommate, we became like brothers. We thought so much alike, enjoyed so many of the same things in sports as well as the arts and sciences, he joined me for a year after I moved on to Oxford. Sadly, both our lives took separate paths after university, the last time I heard from him a few years ago, he was touring Africa." He subdued the teasing smile that was twitching at the corners of his mouth, "I was going to tell you, before I was so chastisingly, undeservedly, interrupted, the reason you may not know him is because he's black and is researching the roots of his ancestors and has been living in Africa. His name is George Alfred Davis. Do you know him?"

She looked away and dropped her head, frowning, pretending to be contemplating as to whether she knew his friend. In actuality, she was trying to hide her face because his saying his friend's name had turned it truly "*lily white*" as the blood drained from it.

Several years ago George Davis returned to Trinidad from Africa. He was not only a close friend and a major part of her social circle, but he and his wife Jennifer were active members on her board for The Children's Home. George was a man of great integrity and ethics and never divulged the name of his famous roommate from when he was at Harvard and Oxford Universities. Although knowing Royalty around the world often clandestinely sent their heirs to universities in America and Britain, it still had never occurred to Elizabeth that the "*famous person*" whose name George kept secret, was this Prince Michael.

She fought to compose herself but still stammered, "I...I'm sorry...I...I...misunderstood you. It's just...I know there's still so much ignorant bigotry in this world that we all struggle to get past... I...I know *of* your friend, but I believe he's still traveling." She was not being dishonest about George's traveling; he and Jennifer had taken sabbaticals from their professorships at The University of The West Indies, where Elizabeth was working on getting her Master's Degree. Having completed a book on African tribes that were taken to the West Indies during the slave trade, they were revisiting Australia for about a year to do more research for a new book they were writing about the Aborigines there.

Determined to change the subject she turned to Michael abruptly with a sugary smile, "I *did* love all the songs you left on my voicemail, particularly the way you composed the medleys and played snippets of pieces. That was very creative, especially for someone with no spare time to even sleep."

He knew she was deliberately distracting him from their original subject but chose to ignore her manipulativeness, too pleased to see how much his voicemails impressed her, "It wasn't difficult to do on my phone, and you kept disturbing my thoughts when I had some quiet time, usually late at night when I knew you'd be asleep and I wouldn't be able to talk with you."

Looking away quickly, gesturing outwardly with both hands to intentionally move the conversation onto something else, she enthused,

"This estate is absolutely fabulous, more amazing than you described. I can't wait to see the rest of it tomorrow."

They were now quite far from the castle and it started drizzling. Turning around to walk back, the rain suddenly started pelting down huge drops like daggers.

He grabbed her hand, they began to run, and were halfway there when they realized they were almost soaked to the skin, and ran to shelter under a large Sycamore tree.

Huddling together, senses and emotions in conflict with propriety, they watched the torrent come down around them. Michael was longing to kiss her but thought he should take it slower this time, he didn't want to turn her off by his being so turned on by her. Little did he know, she had the same thoughts and longing. Looking at each other's condition, they burst out laughing. Their hair and clothes sticking to their bodies, they looked like a couple of half-drowned monkeys. Their amusement at themselves was shortened by a flash of lightning and a deafening thunder clap.

Elizabeth shivered, "Oh no, Michael, lightning! We'd better get out from under this tree and dash for the house." They ran to the castle, holding hands and laughing all the way.

Slamming the front door shut behind them, they collapsed in a soaking wet heap on the foyer marble tiles, still laughing, and holding hands.

CHAPTER
6

Having changed again they met Susan and John in the library where everyone had a cocktail before dinner. Following dinner in the formal dining room, they proceeded to the sitting room where they were served Irish coffees and had the butler light a fire as due to the storm, the evening had become chilly.

Michael stretched out on a couch facing the large stone fireplace and motioned to Elizabeth to sit next to him. Resting his head on her lap, he gave her one of his boyish grins, and continued sipping his coffee. Susan and John exchanged knowing looks, pretended drowsiness, said goodnight, and departed. Michael lay still with his eyes closed. After a while Elizabeth said softly, "Michael, you asleep?"

He murmured, "No."

She nudged him gently, "You're tired. Come on, upstairs."

Not budging he said softly, "I want to be with you."

"You're tired, you ought to be in bed."

"Alright, if you say so." He rose, placed his cup on a coffee table, held her hand, and they walked upstairs. The door of his suite was before hers and on his opening it she leaned over to give him a goodnight peck on his cheek. He pulled her into his room closing the door.

"What're you doing?" She asked, taken by surprise.

A twinkling gleam in his eyes surfaced, "Why are you so surprised, you said you'll come with me."

She feigned coolness, "What're you talking about?"

"When I said downstairs I wanted to be with you, you said I ought to be in bed, so I thought that's where we were heading," his teasing smile appeared.

She simply smiled back at him and turned towards the door to leave. He pulled her into his arms and kissed her softly, first on her lips then all over her face, then lower, on her neck and shoulders. She began to feel panicky, what he was doing was too delicious. She didn't want him to stop, but was afraid for him to go further. She knew what he wanted, needed, and felt the same want and need, but knew they could not afford for it to happen, neither of them, and pushed him away gently, "Michael, we mustn't. Please, don't let's do something we'll regret."

He released her slowly with a crestfallen expression clouding his face, and she darted out the door to her suite.

Just coming out of a dream of Michael, naked, playing hide and seek with her, naked, Elizabeth thought she heard knocking coming from somewhere in the large suite, opened her eyes, and listened. There it was again, coming from the hallway door. Slipping on her dressing gown she wondered who it could be at this hour as glancing at the window, she saw it was pitch black outside. She opened the door to see Michael, wearing a sweater, windbreaker, jeans, boots, and the sweetest smile, "Good morning, beautiful. Get dressed quickly. Let's go up to the big hill and watch the dawn come in. I'll bring my car round to the front door, okay?"

"Okay, Your Highness," she replied in a mockingly obedient tone and ran to get dressed. Knowing it would be cold for her this early in the morning she donned lined woolen trousers, sweater, fur-lined suede jacket and boots, and ran quietly downstairs and outside.

Michael had put the top down on his car. She hopped in beside him. Placing a blanket over her legs, he sped off.

"How come you're up so early?" she asked.

He wanted her to know how she affected him, "I couldn't sleep anymore, I kept waking up thinking of you."

"Oh." Hoping to discourage him from giving details of his thoughts she played it cool, glancing around the car at its stainless steel space-age looking interior, unique cockpit-like dashboard, and pleasing sleek lines, "What kind of car is this?"

He smiled proudly, "It's a T.V.R."

"Really? I've been in a T.V.R. before and it didn't look anything like this. This is incredibly gorgeous."

Wondering whose, jealousy encroached, "Oh? Um…they're all custom hand-made in England, I had this one specially designed for me," he looked at her and grinned, "perquisites of being-"

Smiling, she finished the sentence with him, "'a royal personage.' Of course."

Delighted with her humor he laughingly mimicked, "Of course."

Parking the car on top a small hill, he helped her out, "We'll walk down into the meadow, up the other side and sit on the crest of the highest hill under those trees," he pointed, "we'd get the best view from there."

Holding her hand as they walked she began to feel cold, her teeth chattering. On observing it he put his arm around her and drew her close, "Cold, little girl?" She nodded and he pulled her in even closer, "It'll soon warm up when we get to the top and the sun rises. Hey, I've an idea that'll warm you up fast. We'll have a race to the top. Game?"

She gave him a slightly cynical smile, "I was a pretty good runner at school but all I've done since is speed-walk, some tennis, and swim," she looked down at his long legs and let her eyes slowly wander up his well-toned body to settle on his amused eyes, "you're a lot more athletic than I so I don't think I stand a chance."

He faked petulance, "Well, this isn't fair to me either. *I* wasn't a runner at school, and, apart from the gym, my athletic pursuits the last few years have been mostly equestrian, and some tennis. So if you want to compare, I think *I'm* the one who doesn't stand a chance."

"You have longer legs than mine," she argued.

"Not running legs like yours," he argued back.

They stared at each other and began to laugh.

"Alright," she agreed, "you're on. Let's go."

They took off up the hill, he letting her take the lead. She held that position until they covered a quarter of the hill but as the cold air got to her warm weather acclimatized lungs her breath began to run short, her pace slowed, and he sped past her, laughing. She followed him quite closely, studying him.

His long muscular sturdy legs striding easily up the hill. His firm full buttocks moving rhythmically in his jeans. His broad shoulders upright, even when running uphill. His handsome head with his digni-fied straight nose that she loved, so unlike her perky one, upright too, his shiny light brown hair blowing wildly in the breeze. She thought to herself, *Even while running he is so regal but, God, sooo sexy.* She felt stirrings in her genitals but knew she had to dismiss this trend of thoughts. She was troubled by the direction in which they increasingly kept turning, and concentrated on getting up the hill faster. Squatting on the hilltop, smiling and lightly panting, he put out his hand and helped her up her last few steps. She collapsed beside him, her labored breathing coming out in short gasps.

He grew concerned, "Are you alright, darling?" Nodding, she put a hand up indicating she needed a minute to catch her breath. Despite the warming run she still felt chilly and snuggled closer to him. Opening his jacket, he pulled her in against his heated body and began to rub her icy hands, "Gosh, you *are* cold." She felt his heat, everywhere, but her hands.

They sat in silence until she could finally speak, "I told you it would be unfair, I've become unaccustomed to cold air. I could hardly breathe. I am, after all, a child of the tropics."

"Hmmm," he said, his tongue in his cheek, "I never thought you'd be such a poor sport."

She pouted, "I'm not! You took advantage."

The pout of those sexy lips sent a tremulous motion to that part of him on which he envisioned them, "There are a lot more things I'd prefer to take advantage of with you."

She gave him a cautionary look but he saw beyond it to her true feeling, the same one he had been fighting to repress. He saw, desire. Holding her tight against his body he pressed her down to lie on the grass and kissed her hard, his tongue pushing her lips open, seeking her tongue. Feeling his body on hers, weakening to her long suppressed innate animal instincts, she could no longer resist, responded willingly, and let him in. Leaving her mouth, he kissed her softly all over her face.

This action, though sensuously satisfying, brought her back to her reality, "Michael," she whispered, "we can't go on like this, we're getting in too deep."

Looking longingly into her eyes, he kissed the tip of her nose, "We're already in deep, darling. I've fallen in love with you Elizabeth. I want to share my life with you."

Shocked at his words, she eased herself out from under him and sat bolt upright, "Michael! No! That's impossible!"

He pulled her back down and said softly but firmly, "Nothing is impossible. Some things may be difficult, but nothing is impossible." He kissed her mouth again, even harder this time, his breath quickening, causing hers to do the same.

Feeling his maleness harden against her crotch her womanliness quivered as her mind fought for control. She murmured between intense kisses, "No, Michael, not like this." She backed the lower half of her body away from his, still clinging tightly to his upper body, returning his kisses with equal passion. He understood her meaning and knew he must respect it, this was neither the time nor the place to fulfill their desires. They lay on the grass, embracing and kissing, drinking each other in. Forcing their nature to cool down, as the warming sun came up.

Arriving back at the castle they were served a huge breakfast of pear juice, fruit salad, various breads, pastries, steaks, and eggs.

"All home grown," Susan and John informed them proudly.

Following breakfast, with John at the wheel, Susan as tour guide, they took off in a Land Rover for an extensive tour of the estate. It soon became evident to Elizabeth that the property was efficiently run and expertly organized. The fields were cultivated with rotating crops, some plots left fallow to rejuvenate for a year. Everything looked lush and healthy. She concealed how much it affected her, not in a comforting way, that it looked so similar to an estate of relatives in France, knowledge of whom she could not reveal.

"We are completely organic now that we have more cattle to make manure to add to the compost for natural fertilizer," John said as he stopped the vehicle at a cattle pasture. The animals came running up to the fence hoping to get treats. Rapidly dismissing a disturbing thought flashing through her mind that the delicious steaks they enjoyed for breakfast probably came from one of their relatives, Elizabeth apologized to them that she had no treats, and patted every one she could reach over the fence. The royals were thoroughly amused at this although Susan and John could see the proud adoring gleam in Michael's eyes. John thought to himself, *It might be too late to talk to Michael, he's already completely smitten with this one.*

On returning to the castle Susan and John excused themselves from staying for lunch saying they had some business to attend to in the nearby town.

Climbing the grand staircase, Elizabeth said to Michael, "I must have a shower before lunch."

Giving her a playful look he said agreeably, "Me too."

"I'll meet you in the dining room in thirty minutes," she smiled, pushing him away from following her into her room.

Their suites had connecting doors and she made sure the door on her side was kept locked. The bathrooms were constructed back-to-back as was often necessary in older mansions with limited plumbing whenever they were remodeled and updated, and newer, thinner walled bathrooms were added, making each bedroom *en suite.* Consequently, the guest in one bathroom could hear muffled activity coming from the other. Michael was stepping into the shower when he heard Elizabeth's singing through the new thinner wall. He sat on the toilet seat, leaned against the tank, and listened. *Wow! She can really sing! Somehow, I'm not surprised, I just knew this woman was perfect for me.* Her sweet voice grew louder. He leaned back against the toilet tank and gasped on recognizing the song. It was Abba's 'I Have a Dream.'

His eyes misted over as the memory of his mother singing that song to him as a child came haunting back. The shocking loss of his mother when he was barely nineteen put a void in his life he had been unable to fill. She was to him not only "*the best mother*," as he would often lovingly tell her, she was his unflagging motivator, best friend, and devoted confidant.

The year she died was tumultuous and life-changing for him. Immediately before her tragic death, he committed the most regrettable infelicitous act of his entire life that threatened to destroy him, and his whole family. The worst of it was that she was not there to advise and assist him in handling the devastating situation, and in his grief, confusion and fear, he had to reluctantly surrender to the demands of the senior members of his family. As if the damage caused by the impulsive act of his passionate youth was not bad enough, to have to simultaneously go through the profound sorrow of losing the most loved and important person in his life, especially at his young age, made everything seem unbearable. For too long afterwards he wallowed in grief, self-deprecation, and guilt, which gnawed away at his ingrained self-esteem and confidence. Only time and his impending maturity into manhood, facilitated by positive advice, words of encouragement, and unconditional love, from his father, aunt Anne, Jenkins, Susan, and John, managed to gradually lift him out of his melancholia and despondency.

Now at last, his heart was full again, in fact overflowing with love for this woman, so new in his life yet he felt he had known and loved always. For the first time in many years, not even during the serious two-year relationship he had some time ago, he experienced a loving joyful comforting security that had been eluding him for too long. That she would choose to sing this particular song actually shocked him, he had not told her anything about it and what it meant to him.

Though he was a man devoid of superstition, his romantic side saw this as a perfect omen for their lasting relationship. Her voice rose when she sang the line "*I believe in angels.*" Smiling, he thought, *you are my angel.* Her singing stopped. He heard her turn off the water, the shower door open, then close.

She started singing again, a totally different tone and beat this time, "*come on baby, light my fire.*" He envisioned her perfect naked body reaching for the towel, drying her full perky breasts, gently massaging them till the nipples turned raspberry red, then moving the towel down to between her legs, slowly rubbing it back and forth, the motion causing her body to rock rhythmically, sexily. His thoughts were interrupted by a sudden jerk of his own body as his penis rose up straight and hard, so quickly and with such force it slapped his relaxed abdomen. He straightened up and operating on automatic reflexes, grabbed it. Looking down at it, he chuckled. His phallus with its foreskin pulled right back, the hole open and his hand around it, looked like a face smiling up at him. His instinct to masturbate was quelled by his desire to ejaculate in her, not in his hand. She was what he wanted. Forcing his hand away, he decided he must save it for her. He knew then that this was an occasion for him to have a deflating, extremely long, freezing cold, shower.

Thirty minutes later Elizabeth walked into the dining room. Michael was not there. Except for a tall crystal urn filled with fresh flowers and two oversized silver and crystal candelabras, the dining table was empty. She heard soft chattering voices coming from the kitchen. Opening the richly carved door leading into the butler's pantry, she walked through that small room and pushed open the swing door leading into the kitchen.

The cook and two maids, packing two large baskets, looked up smiling. The rotund cook, nicknamed Cookie, said, "Good morning, Miss. Everything's ready."

Elizabeth greeted the servants cordially and pointed to the baskets, "What's all this?"

Cookie answered, "Prince Michael told us to pack a picnic lunch for you to have in The Vineyards, didn't you know, Miss?"

Elizabeth smiled shyly, "No, actually."

Cookie responded with a warm reassuring smile, "You're going to love it there. There's a beautiful gazebo in the middle of the grape fields surrounded by flowering shrubs and a moat with fountains. It's magical."

The youngest maid, her head down, giggled, "And…romantic."

Michael literally bounced into the room through the backdoor, his idling car parked outside. Elizabeth's heartbeat quickened on seeing him. His handsome face had a special glow. His muscles bulged under the close fitting blue-grey polo shirt that matched his sparkling eyes. Tied loosely around his neck was a slightly darker blue cashmere cardigan. White linen drawstring pants and navy-blue Mantellassi leather loafers on sockless feet completed his ensemble. She envisioned the godlike mortal stepping out of the cover of a G.Q. magazine.

Michael took in all of her with just one look. Her face was devoid of makeup except for light mascara and pink lipstick that matched the blush of her cheeks. Her hair was pulled back softly with a pink and blue ribbon that she had taken off her dress. The dress, a white cotton Embroidery Anglaise halter that tied behind her neck, had pink and blue ribbons intertwined in loops just under the bust-line. She carried an old-rose colored Pashmina shawl and a small white eyelet cotton handbag, her feet shod in white flats with a front opening that exposed pink polished toenails. He thought possessively, *here's my angel.* Suddenly, less than angelic thoughts flashed back to the earlier bathroom occurrence and his penis rose into another erection.

Grabbing a basket in each hand, he held one directly in front his crotch to hide his bulging tumescence. Winking at her, he tilted his head towards the back door, "Let's go, angel."

The drive to The Vineyards seemed much shorter than he said it would be. He was no longer tired but excitedly energized, loquacious and happy, and she too felt joyful to see him this way. It also put her at ease that he stopped questioning her about her past but readily gave information about his own, describing events in his life and that of the royal family that were totally unrecognizable from what was published in the media. By the time they arrived at their destination, she felt even closer to him than she would have believed possible at this juncture of her life, and, more disturbingly, than she needed.

CHAPTER 7

On entering the winery, they were greeted by a very excited vintner, who promptly ordered five bottles of his rarest reserve wines, two whites, two reds, and a dessert wine, to be placed in their baskets. He handed them a glass each of the coldest champagne, told them to make themselves at home, go wherever they pleased, their baskets would be taken to the gazebo, promised they would have it to themselves, and he will instruct his employees to keep their visit a secret from other visitors.

They strolled leisurely through the vineyards discussing different types of wines. Stopping occasionally at rows of grapevines, they read signs that stated their names, the type of root stock, date of planting, and in some areas, descriptions of the soil mixture, insects, and molds, that affect the vines and infuse the grapes. He was surprised and impressed that her knowledge of wines was more extensive than his.

He asked her about this and she proceeded to explain how it came about, "After I finished boarding school in England and other European countries, I was still too young to go to college and live on my own, barely sixteen. So, my Aunt Ruth and Uncle Robert offered for me to

) to New York University, and my parents agreed.

:d their only child should be given every oppor-

_ . would have the tools to create the best life possible.

κuth is my mother's younger sister and they were very close. Mummy was heartbroken when, at twenty-three, Ruth went to live in New York to "*seek her fame and fortune.*" But Daddy came along and patched up Mum's broken heart." She smiled at this and he joined her.

"Anyway, Ruth married Robert who apparently was quite the catch. He was a confirmed bachelor, handsome and charming, old money, and twenty-six years her senior. Every socialite in the country was after him. But he, in his middle-aged wisdom, fell for my aunt. Well you can see why. She's not only beautiful charming and gracious, but extremely intelligent, yet very sensitive, loving and caring." Michael, though having met Ruth for such a short time, nodded in agreement. It occurred to him how strongly her aunt must have influenced the young Elizabeth.

Elizabeth took a deep breath and continued, "For three years they practically took over my parenting. They had no children of their own so were thrilled to have me. Of course my parents visited several times a year, usually traveled with us, and I went home for one Christmas, and a Carnival. But, because I wanted to get my degree in three years, I stayed Stateside and took extra credit classes at nights. In between that I traveled with my family and, oh, I had a temporary job as a linguist at the United Nations. I'm fluent in Spanish, French, Italian-" Michael interrupted, "Wow! Pretty impressive. But it sounds like you took on far too much for a kid."

She responded defensively, "Oh but it wasn't hard at all. In fact, compared to most people, I had it extremely easy. I was living in the lap of luxury with my loving, very wealthy aunt and uncle in their Fifth Avenue penthouse in the most vibrant city in the world. They had as many maids as my parents in Trinidad, who all spoiled me completely. I didn't have to do a domestic chore, all I had to do was go to school, study, occasionally work at the U.N. and travel. Ruth and Robert taught me so much. They took me on most of their trips. Apart from the Manhattan penthouse they have a mansion in The Hampton's, another on Sarasota Bay, Florida, a ranch in Texas, and traveled overseas often. By the time I was twenty-one I'd pretty well been around the globe with them and my parents twice-"

Michael interrupted again, excitedly, "Wow! Tell me about that first. Where'd you go?"

Elizabeth breathed even deeper than before, she had not planned to divulge this much but had gotten caught up in his enthusiastic interest. Realizing it would draw too much suspicion for her to stop now, she continued truthfully, but succinctly, "We toured and explored every continent except for Antarctica. We safaried and gallivanted all over Africa, toured the Orient, climbed The Great Wall of China, dove in the Great Barrier Reef in Australia and trekked around Uluru Rock and The Olgas. We cruised every ocean, sea, river, and through the fiords in Norway, Montenegro and New Zealand. We barged down the Nile in Egypt, canoed up the Amazon, whiteriver rafted in the States as well as Central America. We rode camels in Arabia, elephants in India, visited every holy shrine, every vortex, every ancient ruin and pyramid on this planet. You name it, I believe we did it. They just wanted to expose me to as much of the world, its history and different cultures, as possible, before I went back to "*save*" my island, as they would teasingly say whenever I talked about going back to Trinidad after I got my degree. They never said anything, but I think they wanted me to stay in the States." She looked at him apologetically, "Gosh, I hope you don't think I'm being boastful or snobbish, I'm simply telling it like it was. I assume you've probably traveled more than I-"

With loving eyes he interrupted again, "Don't be silly, darling. I could never think of you as boastful or snobbish. Anyway, you sound like you had a lot more fun than I had, my trips were often just duty trips. Go on. Tell me everything."

"Well, Robert is quite the wine connoisseur, every country we visited that had even the smallest wine industry, he would take us to their wineries. It's his third great passion, Ruth being the first, the saving of planet Earth coming in a close second." They both smiled and she became silent.

Touching her hand gently he spoke encouragingly, hoping at last to learn more about her and her past, "This is so interesting. Go on."

Wanting to end her unintended long soliloquy she shrugged, "Well, that's how I learned so much about wine. Robert was my wine teacher, and Ruth my teacher in many other aspects. They, and my parents, afforded me to have many amazing experiences that I wouldn't have had otherwise. More importantly, they didn't just give me material things but lavished me with love and attention. I hardly ever felt homesick. I just adore them. I'll be eternally grateful for all they did, still do, for me," she grew silent again for a moment, then added, "that was who I was speaking to on my phone this morning. We speak every day." She half-lied. Although she did speak to them often that was not who she spoke to every day, several times a day. He didn't tell her he overheard her talking on her phone the day before. He could not discern what she was saying, but the tone in her voice was so loving and tender, he actually felt jealous of whoever she was talking to. They sighted the roof of the gazebo on a rise in the distance and made their way toward it.

Just as they rounded a bend of rows of very old and tall grape vines, the gazebo came into full view. Elizabeth gasped softly, "Michael, it's so beautiful, it really is magical."

Holding hands they stood transfixed, taking it in slowly. To see such an unexpected sight in the middle of old gnarled grape vines on the crest of the highest hill in the vineyards was breathtaking. The gazebo was magnificent.

The building was round in shape, there were four pairs of tall white marble Corinthian columns supporting an ornate iron domed roof, and between each pair of columns stood life-size white marble Goddess statues representing the four seasons. Hanging from transparent wire all around the base of the dome were small white papier mache cherubs and doves, moving in the wind as though in flight. Surrounding the structure ten feet away, numerous towering Cypresses swayed gently in the breezes, guarding the privacy of the romantic oasis.

Flowering pink and lilac rhododendron bushes peeping out from under the Cypresses, and rambling red, yellow, and white roses on trellises nearby, added the perfect amount of color to enhance the heavenly scenery. Encircling the gazebo was a seven-foot wide moat from which fountains shot up playfully every six feet. A cobblestone path led to an arched stone bridge which had iron railings in the same intricate pattern as the dome.

Hand in hand they walked over the bridge, excited to discover the interior of this magical place. On entering, their eyes were drawn upwards to the center of the dome where, despite the brilliant sunshine outside, someone had lit the candles in a huge grape-and-vine patterned iron chandelier that hung from the ceiling. The ceiling was covered in white canvas fanning out from the center to the sides in swaged widening pleats. The same material cascaded down from the ceiling as drapery on either side of the double columns. It was tied in a relaxed swag with heavy leaf-green colored silk cords with tassels, allowing just enough daylight in to keep the ambience duskily romantic.

Hidden behind four large marble urns in which grew graceful Areca palms, were stereo speakers from which they were fittingly serenaded with international romantic classics by The Three Tenors. There were six round wrought iron tables placed around the perimeter of the room, with a seventh in the center under the chandelier. Each table had four chairs except the center one which had just two. This table was set with a leaf-green cotton table cloth, matching napkins, silverware, two sets of three different appropriate sizes of wine glasses, and a silver wine bucket with ice and a white wine already ensconced within.

Seating themselves at the center table they said in unison, "Isn't this romantic?" laughed, and proceeded to unpack the picnic baskets. Out came Michael's favorite foie gras, a tub of Beluga caviar with toast tips, crackers, a handmade cheese from the Jamestown's estate, a mixed lettuce and nuts salad, various estate fruit, and some prettily decorated petits fours. When they saw the huge tasty-looking roast beef, lettuce, pickles, and tomato sandwiches Cookie had made for them, they decided to forego the already chilled white wine and drink the more full-bodied red. Michael opened it immediately to allow it to breathe. They heartily tucked into the foie gras and caviar, shared one of the large roast beef sandwiches and a salad, and washed it all down with the entire bottle of red wine.

Michael was about to open the bottle of dessert wine when Elizabeth held his hand to stop him, "Do you really think we need more wine?" she giggled, "*I'm* already feeling a bit tipsy, and *you* still have to drive us back."

He laughed, and grasping her hands in his, hooded his eyes seductively, "Does this mean you'll be easy to take advantage of?"

"No." She giggled again, somewhat coquettishly.

The Three Tenors became silent and the soothing, timeless, romantic voice of Andy Williams took over singing 'Love's Theme.' Eyes lustrous with a combination of love and lust, Michael pulled her out of her chair and danced her around the room, swaying in-between the tables and chairs, pressing her closer and closer to him. She got a whiff of his scent, a mixture of subtle cologne and masculine passion, and inhaled deeply. He breathed her in. She smelt like roses, exotic cattleya orchids, and sensuous femininity. Their breathing became labored, whether from their emotions or motions, or both, it didn't matter, they were beyond caring. Resting her against a column he pressed his lips to hers. Then flicking his tongue lightly over them he kissed her softly at first, then harder as she relaxed and opened her mouth to let his tongue ravish hers.

He left her mouth to breathe in her ear, "I love you."

"I love you," she murmured dreamily. He kissed her neck and bare shoulders with moist sucking kisses, gently caressing both her arms, slowly working his way down and back up again.

Passion overtaking her reasoning, her ability for self-control rapidly disintegrated. His manhood grew hard against her thigh, and succumbing to curiosity, and surfaced desire, she opened her legs. Centering himself between her legs, he pressed harder against her.

Sighing softly she let herself sink into a sensuous fantasy, banishing all thoughts of reality.

Reaching behind her neck, with one quick pull, he untied the bow of her halter dress. The top fell forward exposing braless voluptuous breasts. His eyes widened on seeing her pointed pink nipples and the contrast between her white breasts and the golden tanned skin above her bikini line. Cupping her left breast with his right hand, he massaged it, then gently twisted her nipples between two fingers elongating it. Lingering on her tan lines, he kissed the top of her right breast then worked his way around the nipple, kissing and softly sucking alternately. Placing his mouth full open on her puckered nipple, he began a soft, then hard sucking motion, repeating it over and over till she moaned, "Michael, stop…no…don't stop."

He saw the skin on her breasts rise into goose bumps as his phallus rose into something much more formidable. Reaching down between her legs, he lifted her skirt, felt her stiffen, and realized she was unknowingly holding her breath.

He bit softly on her left nipple and whispered, "Breathe."

Reality returned to Elizabeth in a flash. She removed her hand from holding him and reached down to push his hand away from her skirt; but something stronger than she held it back, and helplessly, she let it drop. Reality left in an even quicker flash than it had come as she sank back into erotic bliss. Her sexual senses heightening, her body trembled with a long denied desire. Revelation came to her that what was once an unobtainable fantasy was fast becoming a living sweet reality, and she gave up the fight, surrendering to indulge in its pleasures. Her clitoris vibrated to the point that she experienced mild pain and she unintentionally groaned aloud.

Instinctively he knew what was happening to her and pulled her lace panties down past her knees. His exploring fingers found her swollen labia, "You're wet," he whispered hoarsely as he gently massaged the soft fleshy lips that had been denied the touch of another for far too long, "you're as ready as I am."

"Yes," she whispered, pushing out her pelvis toward him and opening her legs wider. Venturing gently, he inserted one finger into the opening of her vulva, found the erect nodule that was the center of her pleasure, then added another finger, and slowly stroked his way through her vagina. Moving his fingers unhurriedly deeper he felt her thick cream surround them. The love and reverence he felt for her overshadowed his lust, and wanting to satisfy her in the most uncompromising, respectful way possible, he moved his fingers in and out, leisurely at first then gradually faster as she sighed and moaned in ecstasy. He skillfully masturbated her till she screamed his name as she climaxed into full orgasm, "Michael! Oh God! Ooohhhh!"

She felt her legs weaken and knew he needed to hold on to her or she would collapse on the floor, so she grasped his pleasuring hand and placed it around her waist. He held her tight, kissing her all over her face, happy and pleased at his accomplishment of altruistically obtaining from her a complete sexual release. Gratified, filled with love and passion, she grabbed his face and kissed him forcefully on his mouth, pulling his tongue out with hers, sucking and gently nibbling his full lips. Feeling his hardened manhood quaver against her still throbbing genitalia she instinctively knew what she must do.

Spinning him around to stand against the column, she deftly tugged on the drawstrings of his pants causing it to drop to the floor. Kneeling, she bent forward till her face lined up with his now reddened fully erect phallus. It was so engorged, she hesitated when she saw the length and girth of it. Even though she had seen many phalluses in her young life, thanks to her frequent trips to the theatre and her enjoyment of every type of play, including those where she could safely get firsthand knowledge of the great variety of male genitalia that existed without her being physically involved, she had only ever been up this close to one other. This having been some time ago, and for the fact that she had shut out that part of her life so as to avoid more pain and anger, she could not remember if the other phallus she had experienced was as enormous as this one. Regarding the impressive erection now pulsating before her, she was certain of one thing, this prince was extremely well-endowed. Literally, '*A prince of a man.*'

With her left hand, she gently caressed his full testicles in his scrotum, now slightly recessed upwards behind his distended penis. She licked them with her saliva filled hot tongue, at the same time feeling for the tiny ball under her fingertips, then pressed softly on finding his perineum, while holding his penis firmly with her right hand. For an instant she wondered if it was too big for her mouth, but it looked so ripe and enticing, and with an overwhelming desire to pleasure him as he had her, her trepidation quickly vanished. She opened her mouth wide and slowly began to take him in, and just as slowly, withdrew from him. He groaned disappointedly, but on reaching the head, she circled her tongue around it several times, teasing him. Then suddenly, animal instinct overwhelming, she plunged her lusty mouth over his shaft again.

Still gently massaging his testicles with her left hand, she placed her right hand around the base of his penis pulling the foreskin further back, and began moving it up and down, her ravenous mouth following the same rhythmical motion. Sucking hard on it, she dragged on him hungrily as if she were an infant feeding from a bottle.

Stopping for a few seconds to lick all around it she let her tongue slide over its head, then pointed it into the open hole, and swirled it around several times. Michael moaned as his legs trembled in unison with his penis. Holding his quivering phallus steady she again engulfed him, this time even deeper than before, suckling him in earnest, pulling on him, drawing out his viscous fluids. Taking her time, she let her teeth scrape against his penis gently, then harder, and began to alternate dragging her teeth then her tongue on each side, gradually increasing speed as she felt his body begin to spasm.

Holding her head, he shuddered violently and groaned loudly, "Oh God! Oh God!"

His ejaculation exploded into her mouth almost choking her. She swallowed some of it but the amount of semen was excessive and she carefully spat some out down the sides of his penis while still suckling it, pulling out everything he had held in for far too long.

Weakened, he slid down to the floor grabbing her, and sated, kissed her tenderly, with more the emotion of profound love than sexual passion. Tasting the saltiness of his semen in her mouth, he kissed her deeper with the added emotions of gratitude and admiration. After a long tender kiss, she moved her head away to nestle it against his neck. They cuddled like this for some time while their breathing returned to normal.

She spoke first, "This was crazy. Fantastic, but crazy."

Michael sat up and looked adoringly into her eyes, "If this was crazy, I hope we never go sane."

He held her as they stood up, embracing her lovingly. Beginning to feel embarrassed she said quickly, "We should go. It's late and we have a long drive back." He agreed, they hurriedly fixed their clothes, repacked the baskets, and left.

They drove in silence awhile, glancing and smiling at each other occasionally, that special shy but knowing smile of new young lovers. The volume on the radio was low and not disturbing to their thoughts, which were as diverse as they could possibly be. Michael suddenly turned up the volume, turned to Elizabeth, and joining Neil Diamond, sang, "*You are the sun, I am the moon, you are the words, I am the tune, play me.*"

Elizabeth was astonished. Not only at his unexpected burst into song but that he could actually sing beautifully, his voice strong and masculine but at the same time sensitive and sensuous. She recognized it as the same voice that sang love songs to her on his voicemails, "You have a lovely voice, Michael, very polished. Where did you learn to sing like that?"

"My mother," he replied softly, "we sang a lot."

Knowing a little about his mother's tragic death from malaria in Africa, she observed a touch of sadness in his voice, thought to brighten his mood, and reached into the compartment that held the Compact Discs, "Let's see what else you have here. Ah, Tina, I love Tina Turner. Shall we play it?"

"Definitely. I remember Mama playing that particular C.D. over and over, she loved it. So did I." He slipped it into the player and they both started belting out song after song with Tina Turner. They sang, and laughed, and sang again. Tina's sexy guttural voice slid into Elizabeth's favorite Tina song and knowing all the words, she began to sing it with innocently sensual actions, "*I call you, I need you, my heart's on fire. You come to me, come to me, wild and wired...*" she sang the entire verse seductively, unknowingly getting Michael literally wild and wired; but he controlled himself and meaningfully belted out the chorus with her and Tina, "*You're Simply the Best, better than all the rest. Better than anyone, anyone I've ever known-*"

Taking too long a look at her, unable to contain himself anymore, he pulled off the road, stopped the car, and kissed her passionately. He reached inside her dress for her breast but she gently pushed his hand away, "No, not here." Fighting for control he bit his lip and drove back onto the road, as Tina sang on. Twice more he pulled off the road to kiss her, twice more she pushed his hand away from caressing her breast. On his third attempt she said softly but firmly, "Michael, you've got to stop, at this rate, we'll never make it back." He desisted and they drove in silence awhile, lost in dissimilar thoughts.

It was dark now, the unpolluted country navy-blue night sky brilliantly lit by billions of twinkling stars, a full harvest moon ascending to join them. Michael pointed to the moon, "Look, a rising full moon, approving of our love."

It impressed her that with all the adulation she knew he received all his life, all the girls and women, probably boys and men too, that absolutely worshipped him, he remained unjaded, was simply a natural born romantic. She laughed softly but said nothing. With the arrival of the darkness of night, her thoughts were illuminating to the immensity of what happened sexually between them at the vineyards.

CHAPTER 8

Becoming fearful and riddled with guilt, Elizabeth began to deprecate herself for weakening her resolve and impetuously succumbing to him, felt ashamed of her lack of strength and inability to resist him. Her behavior was the antithesis of the standards she always upheld for herself. Trying to dissect her feelings, her mind went back and forth between the immense pleasure she enjoyed from what they did, and an overshadowing feeling of ignominy, that she had cheapened herself by giving in so easily and willingly. Not that he acted disrespectful in his advances afterwards. On the contrary, he was very loving and understanding when she rebuffed him; in fact, acted as if everything was perfect and the way it should be, as if their sexual encounter was not only normal behavior but was their right. She pondered over this, but it failed to comfort her. The guilt from thinking she had no right to even the feelings she had for him, far worse her actions with him, was overwhelming.

How could she let things go so far? Why did she allow this huge complication to come into her already calamitous no longer perfect life? She should have known better than to have accepted his very first invitation because she knew she had a strong attraction to him. Why didn't she fight harder to resist, to escape from this compelling affinity to him? What kept drawing her back to him?. She searched her mind for an attribution but it evaded her. She was certain it was not just a sexual primal force, it was something inexplicably deeper.

He had taken possession of her every thought, every fiber of her very existence. It felt as though they always had some special bond. Looking at his perfect profile now outlined in the risen moon, her heart skipped a beat and her body shivered. An ache developed in the pit of her stomach as an odd sense of foreboding overtook her.

Not realizing it, she sighed loudly and Michael became concerned, "What is it darling, are you alright?" She could not speak. He looked at her, saw the anguish in her eyes, pulled off the road and stopping the car, reached out for her. She put up her hands in protest as her eyes filled with tears which tumbled onto her cheeks. "Oh God, what's wrong?" he asked, bewildered.

Looking away from him, she blurted, "Michael, I feel so embarrassed and ashamed."

He reached over and pulled her into a tight embrace, "Why my darling, why?"

"Because of what happened between us in the gazebo," she mumbled against his chest.

"God, my darling, what happened was wonderful! Actually, fantastic, like you said. Why would you be embarrassed or ashamed with me? It was the most perfectly natural thing for us. I love you Elizabeth. I thought you loved me. I feel it from you. Am I misreading you? Don't you feel the same way I do?"

"Yes, I do...but I shouldn't...I...don't have the right-"

"Nonsense. Don't say that. Why do you keep saying that?" Not answering him, she sobbed softly. He held her tight saying nothing, waiting patiently for her to speak.

Eventually, ignoring his question, she spoke slowly, "I've never done anything like that before. I don't know what came over me...I... I just lost control. The way I feel about you...I couldn't help myself."

Feeling suddenly fearful, he held her away from him, trying to see her face which she kept turned away. After a moment, he asked incredulously, "Elizabeth, are you trying to tell me you're a…a…virgin?"

She looked up but not at him, "No. I'm not. But I've only had sex with one man, and that was only after a long courtship."

He tried to sound understanding, "Oh, I see," he said, not seeing at all. He was totally confused as to why that even mattered, what bearing it had on her feelings for him, or what happened between them. Querying his judgment, he wondered if he rushed things too early in their relationship, and maybe, was a little forceful. He knew in the very depths of his heart and soul she was the one for him at last. He had waited a long time for her to come along, so very long to feel like this.

Mentally and physically he had wanted her so badly, but she wanted him too, he could tell, all the signs were there. She said she was ready. By God, she *was* ready! He thought he had shown her how much he loved her, he knew women needed that, and she said she loved him, confirming what he felt all along. *So, what's the problem?* Unaccustomed as he was to being so incognizant about a woman in his arms he persevered as gently as his capability would allow to try to pry more information from her about her only other serious relationship, but to no avail.

She simply assured him her tears were not because of him, Michael; and even though he became convinced he was not their cause, he knew they still involved him. Knowing a woman of her great beauty, sensuality, sophistication, well-traveled, educated, *and* twenty-eight years old, would have had to have had *some* sexual experiences, he was surprised that, comparing her to others in his past, she had known only one man. In this day and age, a rare thing indeed. Pangs of jealousy raced into his thoughts, *Who is that man? What's so special about him? Was he a great lover? Does she still love him? No! She definitely loves me! I know it deep inside. She tries to restrain her feelings but I see how she looks at me, acts with me, the things she does. Yes! She loves me. I know it! Then why does she regret our lovemaking? We didn't even have intercourse, for crissakes! And she enjoyed it as much as I did. She had an orgasm! And what she did to me! No woman has ever done it like that before. It was incredible! So, what do I do now? What do I say? And here I was planning for us to have a perfect romantic evening tonight, to consummate our lovemaking, to know and enjoy each other completely. Well, abandon those plans, buddy, the mood is gone for her for sure. Geeze, what do I say? How do I handle this?* He took a deep breath and plunged in, "Elizabeth, all I can say is, I love you. I didn't mean to rush you into something you weren't ready for. You gave me the impression you were ready, but it seems you weren't, and if I hurt you in any way, I'm truly sorry. It's the last thing I wanted to do. Please forgive me?"

Frowning, she stared at him, her mouth open. She shook her head, then spoke, "Michael, there's nothing to forgive you for. How I feel isn't your fault. I'm sorry I upset you but I feel so guilty that I didn't control the situation." She took a deep breath and looked into his eyes with intensity, "Michael, I do love you. I think I fell in love with you the moment we…bumped, into each other, and I looked into your eyes-"

Thrilled and relieved, he interrupted, "Me too. That's when I fell in love with you. From that moment I knew we belonged together," holding her face, he wiped her tears away with his thumbs, "darling, what happened between us in the gazebo is natural with people in love, we're only human. Please don't regret it, it was beautiful. There's nothing to be ashamed or embarrassed about. Can't you see that my darling?" giving her a tender peck on her lips he looked at her questioningly.

She was obstinate, "You don't understand. I've only ever had sex with one man. My behavior was totally out of character. Certainly I've been attracted to other men, even fantasized about…him…them, but always kept my sexuality under control. This is the first time I lost it, and the *way* I did it-" she turned away and murmured, "I thought you'd think me such a slut."

"What!" he raised his voice. "Don't be silly! Of course not! I could never think such a thing of you, never!" Grasping her arm he turned her to face him again, "Elizabeth, for God's sake! We're in love! People in love should be able to do whatever they want with each other as long as they both enjoy it. I so much enjoyed what you did for me. I've never been given fellatio the way you gave me. It was phenomenal! Didn't you enjoy what I did for you?"

Hiding her face in his chest she smiled, "God, yes!"

He lifted her chin making her look into his eyes, "Elizabeth, listen to me. The way I feel about you, I've never felt about anyone else. Sure I've come close, once, but it was nothing like how I feel now. Just being in your company gives me such great pleasure, I look at you and feel like my heart's going to burst with joy. I can't remember ever feeling this happy. But that doesn't matter one bit if I can't make you happy too. Your happiness is more important to me than my own. That's how much I love and cherish you. Please don't feel embarrassed about anything with me ever again. You're the most wonderful thing that's ever happened to me. You have this amazing aptitude for appropriateness that astounds me, you epitomize the perfect lady. Hell, you're a million times more regal than anyone in my family. Yet you exude this extreme sexuality that just drives me insane. Your inner beauty radiates to your outer beauty. These feelings I have for you are all encompassing, I can't get you out of my mind, day and night. This isn't lust, Elizabeth, this is love. I want you always in my life, I want to share my life with you. You are the soulmate I've been searching for, my perfect angel-"

Though feeling awed and elated by his outpouring of love and reassurances, guilt got the better of her. She interjected, "Please Michael, don't put me up on such a high pedestal."

He smiled adoringly, "Why not? It's where you belong."

"The fall sounds like an awfully long way down," she said somberly.

"I won't let you fall," he responded with determination.

She thought dolefully, *You may already be too late.*

Seeing a look of fear return to her expression he felt he had not yet convinced her that everything was the way it should be, and that they would have a wonderful future together, "Elizabeth, we're made for each other. Don't you feel it?"

In the heart of her heart, she could no longer deny it, she had felt it from the very beginning, "Yes, I do." They kissed tenderly, and clinging to him, she whispered, "Just hold me Michael. Hold me, and don't let me go."

He held her tightly in his arms while she buried her head in his chest, and sobbed softly. Although he wanted to say more about their relationship and his desire for the permanency of it, he realized from her fragile condition, this was not the time. He knew she was going through some sort of turmoil that was beyond his comprehension, and having been through his own turmoils before, he thought that right now it was best to just comfort her, give her silent loving support, until she was ready to open up to him, which he anxiously hoped would be soon.

Elizabeth's mind was reeling. She knew she needed to control her emotions, stop crying so that she could collect her thoughts, cogitate everything that had happened, and all the wonderful things Michael had said. Her attempts to ignore her true feelings so that she could look objectively at the situation proved futile. Michael handed her some tissues, she wiped her face, blew her nose, and he started to speak, but she stopped him, "Please Michael, don't talk right now, just hold me, darling." Nestling in his arms, she thought back to their first meeting, how he affected her from the very beginning.

Becoming introspective, she questioned her judgment, then tried to justify it. *How could I not fall in love with this man? He's perfection. I love everything about him, his mind, spirit, passion, humor, face, body, mannerisms, smell, taste, the way he treats me, everything! In many ways, he's so much like...NO...I will not compare them! I will not think of the beast! My heart now belongs to Michael. Now and forever. Like his, my own heart fills to overflowing with joy whenever I see him, just think of him. He's revived emotions I thought I'd never have again, stirred up feelings I've been suppressing for too long.* A brief smile entered her thoughts, *As for that Trinidadian saying about 'women who haven't had sex in a while growing 'cobwebs' down there,' I've proven it's a big lie, there were no cobwebs on me, that's for sure.*

She felt her lingering sadness magnifying again, *I thought repressing my feelings would help me get over the devastating betrayal I've endured. Yet the sense of loss continues to haunt me, like I'm grieving a death. I can't bear the depth of the pain anymore. I need to heal. I must get past this hurt, get rid of bitterness. Memories of what happened must be erased. Who am I kidding? I may not ever get over it. Forget the most horrific thing that's happened to me in my perfect life? Get through it, yes, but get over it? Or is Michael my savior, my salvation? But is it fair to put this burden on him? To expect him to have patience and understanding while I ride through this emotional rollercoaster that I'm on? And I can't even tell him about it? I never thought I could love a man this way again. My love for him is so overpowering. God, it frightens me! I cannot go through another heartbreak! I know he loves me. I see the adoration in his eyes, the way he treats me, things he says with such emotion and passion. But how will he feel when he learns of my past? Will it be too much for him to handle? There's no precedent for my situation. What will he put first, me, or his country, his kingdom? What will be sacrificed? Does there need to be a sacrifice? This love between us is so strong already, happened so fast! I know he's a man of great strength and resolve, but when it all comes out, will he stand by me? I myself feel so strong again when I'm in his arms. When he holds me I feel reborn. Even though he's so tightly wrapped around me, I feel free at last. He's healing me and doesn't know it! Doesn't know I need healing! It's been tough hiding it from him, I feel he knows I'm going through something, but hasn't a clue as to the enormity of it! God, I wish he'd never have to know…but that's impossible. Our relationship's too involved, we're in too deep already. I, am in too deep! I'm going to have to tell him…but can't face it now, can't even think about how to do it, have to regain my strength, my confidence. My self-esteem had been ripped from me along with my heart. I've been functioning in a dark fog too long. Michael has entered my life just when it needs re-illuminating. I feel the burden of sadness lifting off me. Is there some spiritual meaning to this? Is he my destiny? I feel his heart beating in rhythm with mine, it's as though we are one, my prince and I. He really is the ultimate cliché, my 'Knight in Shining Armor!' He's come to rescue me from the depths of despair, resuscitated feelings of hope for happiness I'd lost completely, aroused my carefree spirit from dormancy. He fills all my most profound desires. Why should I deny myself the wonderful*

feeling of renewal he gives me? Why get into a mental battle of suppositions and
'what ifs' about the future? Why not go back to my old philosophy of 'que sera,
sera, what will be, will be?' Why not accept and absorb the healing power of our
love? I've been through absolute hell! Now with Michael I can be in paradise.
I deserve this! I'm entitled to it! I adore this man! He adores me! I'm going
to put the past behind me. I'm going to live only in the present. I'm going to
be happy! Happiness is a decision, I decide to be happy. Deserve to be happy.
I'll make Michael happy. He deserves to be happy. To hell with everything else!

With a tender smile she caressed his face, "I'm sorry if I'm confusing you darling, but all I can tell you right now is that I've gone
through the most traumatic thing of my life and I've been struggling
to forget it. Please be patient with me-" she paused a long pause then
blurted, "I adore you. I just want to make you happy. I want *us* to be
happy."

Overjoyed and relieved, Michael beamed his widest smile, kissed
her tenderly on her mouth and said emphatically, "We *will* be happy, I
promise."

Their embrace was disturbed by a strange buzzing sound. "What's
that?" she asked, having not heard it before.

"It's Jenkins, on my phone. We have special rings for each other.
Sorry darling, I must take this. He wouldn't call unless it's important."

Reminded of Michael's position she said quickly, "Of course. Do
you need privacy, shall I get out of the car?"

"Certainly not," he patted her knee as he took the phone out of a
hidden compartment, "yes, Jenkins?"

"Can you talk?"

"A little. What's up?"

"Have you checked your messages?"

"I haven't even looked at my phone since I'm here."

"His Majesty called me, frantic. Said you haven't responded to over
a dozen messages he left since you returned from the West Country.
He's very worried about you."

"What does he know?"

"Everything."

"What! How did he find out?"

"The new bodyguard, Frank, he blabbed everything that happened to your father, hoping to gain his favor."

"Fire him."

"Already done."

"Good. Do me a favor. Call Papa for me. If I call, he'll want me to come home right away, and I'm not ready yet. Say I'm out of reach now but I'm doing well and will call tomorrow."

Jenkins chortled, "*You!* Out of reach to the *King?* Your *father?* That's one for the books. Anyway, alright. I understand. I'll make something up. But call him tomorrow. Call me too."

"I will. Thanks buddy." Michael turned off the phone, placed it back in its secret compartment, punched in numbers on a combination lock and a cover slid over the lock, causing everything to blend and disappear again into the trim of the car. He kissed Elizabeth tenderly, started the car and pulled back onto the road, "Darling, I hope you don't mind but I must do some work tomorrow morning, return calls, check e-mails, etcetera. Could you entertain yourself until lunch?"

She became amused at his overly courteous and considerate manner, "Of course, silly. I myself need to catch up on...some things. Also, Susan said tomorrow's going to be awfully hot so I think I'll go swimming. She lent me one of her swimsuits but she's shorter, more petite than I so I hope it fits. Anyway, I can also get back to my book."

Hoping for more insight into a secret area of her psyche, he asked, "What are you reading?"

"It's called 'Welcome To America,' written by my Trinidadian best friend who immigrated with her family to the States. It's been described as a very different immigrant story. It's not available in stores yet. She gave me an advance copy."

"Hmm, interesting. True story?"

"She won't say, been very evasive about it. Actually, I only just started it."

"Sounds intriguing. I'd like to meet your friend sometime."

"I'll be sure to arrange it. I know she'll love you."

Arriving back at the castle after dinnertime, Michael parked the car in the garage nearest the kitchen and Elizabeth and he entered through that door.

Susan was in the kitchen quarrelling with the cook, "It's not working Cookie you must get somebody else. She doesn't speak enough of our language and I don't speak enough Spanish. We're running out of time. The prep work should've been done for tomorrow already!" Seeing Elizabeth and Michael, her demeanor shifted and she smiled at them, "Oh, there you are, we were getting worried about you two."

"Sorry about that," Michael said jovially, "we got lost. What's going on? What's the problem?"

Susan now looked distraught, "Cookie hired this new assistant from Spain, Maria, but her vocabulary is limited, my Spanish is abominable, and Cookie speaks no Spanish. Oh, by the way, we're having a dinner party tomorrow for twelve people. Our cousin Henry called. He's coming with his new girlfriend, and I've invited some of our friends from neighboring estates. Don't worry, I've told everyone you're just passing through, they're very excited to meet you, Michael, I hope you don't mind."

Michael displayed a benevolent smile, "Course not. But what's the problem with Maria?" He gestured toward the pretty young woman cowering behind the cook.

Susan pointed to a cookbook on the counter, "She doesn't understand the recipes I've chosen and Cookie doesn't have time to do everything. Apparently Maria is a fabulous cook and she's nice enough but honestly, she's useless to us. Wait…Elizabeth, Michael said you're quite the linguist, can you speak Spanish?"

"Fluently. Let me help." Elizabeth stepped towards Maria, shook her hand introducing herself and rattled off a quantity of questions in Spanish with such ease, one would have thought it was her native tongue. Maria regained her confidence, became animated and pointed out the words she didn't understand. Susan proffered a pen and notebook, Elizabeth wrote down the translations and gave them to Maria who immediately started working.

Susan, relieved and filled with gratitude, gave Elizabeth a warm hug, "Thank you, thank you."

Elizabeth smiled, "You're most welcome. Fortunately, I've spent some time in Spain so I'm familiar with the dialect of the area Maria's from. But, may I make a suggestion, a little change to the menu?"

Appreciativeness made Susan adaptable, "By all means."

"I see you have beautiful fresh pineapples, oranges, and lemons, I know a fabulous recipe for the Cornish game hens, it's sort of sour-sweet, very easy, absolutely delicious. Would you like to try it? The cooks will find it simple, and so is the stuffing. I could stick around a bit, make sure it'll come out alright. What do you think?"

Susan became not just grateful but impressed at this genre of talent in someone such as Elizabeth. Looking at Michael, she teased, "You got lucky with this one." Turning back to Elizabeth she smiled, "It sounds wonderful, would be a nice change. But surely you'd like to have dinner now? You two must be starved?"

Elizabeth replied, "Actually, I can wait an hour or so." She looked at Michael questioningly.

He agreed, "Me too," grabbed an apple from a bowl, and hoisted himself up to sit on the granite counter in a quiet corner of the room.

Susan said, "Alright then. Cookie made a wonderful osso buco, spinach pasta, and Cesar's salad, let her know when you're ready. I'm going to choose the linens and table settings for tomorrow and get started in the dining room with Betty, the butler's off tonight. See you in a bit."

Susan left the room with the youngest maid following, Maria put an apron on Elizabeth, and the three women got busy with preparations for the upcoming dinner party.

Michael watched Elizabeth intently, not taking his eyes off her. There was such fluidity in her every movement. She chatted, laughed, and giggled with the two women constantly, effortlessly moving from one area of the kitchen to the other, her speech rolling easily back and forth from one language to another, occasionally flashing Michael a demure smile.

He was totally entranced; *This woman is full of endless surprises. She's so capable in this area, I'd never have believed it had I not seen it for myself. For someone raised with servants all her life and not having to do domestic chores, she sure handles herself with amazing pragmatic competence.*

Having finished helping Maria and Cookie grate, cut and chop all the fresh ingredients needed, Elizabeth explained how to make the marinade for the hens, and also the wild rice, dried blueberries, and pine nuts stuffing. She then donned a pair of rubber gloves and zestfully pulled lumps of fat off the Cornish game hens, tossing them into a container across the room as though it were a basketball hoop, not missing once. The two cooks laughed uproariously at her little game.

Michael smiled to himself, *She makes fun out of even the most mundane of tasks. I love her sense of humor. It's admirable how she's taken control of this situation, yet without antagonizing the others. On the contrary, they treat her with endearment and at the same time great respect. She knows how to handle people to get what she wants, a great asset for me to have in my life's partner. The way she multitasks with such vigor and dexterity exhibit's youthful energy, yet with the experience of a woman much more mature than her twenty-eight years. Even in this messy place she has such grace and poise. I love this woman!*

Susan came in and leaned against the counter next to Michael, "You having fun?" she teased.

He kept looking at Elizabeth, but spoke to Susan with a strange serious inflection to his voice, "She's the one. The one I've been searching for. She is to be my queen."

The kitchen clock rang its first toll of midnight causing the four in the room to jump simultaneously.

Cookie said apologetically, "Oh my, it's so late, and Miss Elizabeth you and Prince Michael haven't even eaten yet. I'll see to it, Maria will set you up in the outside north terrace. It's a nice warm night with a beautiful moon." She thanked Elizabeth profusely ending with, "We'd never have gotten ahead so well without you. You're a wonderful, kind, and talented lady." Taking back control of her kitchen, she practically pushed Elizabeth and Michael out the door.

The night air was warmer than it had been for the past week, summer was definitely making itself felt. The moon, looking smaller than it had earlier, was now directly overhead, causing the shadows of the surrounding tall trees to dance like fairy ballerinas in the soft wind that blew. They ate half of what Cookie had served them but drank most of the deliciously robust Spanish red wine Elizabeth and Maria had chosen from the castle's extensive wine cellar. Michael had heard of the wine but was not as familiar with it as was Elizabeth.

Loving and attentive throughout the meal, he touched her often on her face and hands. She reciprocated every touch, every feeling, their eyes meeting with intensity.

Pushing his plate aside he said, "I enjoyed watching you operate in the kitchen. You never fail to amaze me, you handled that situation like you were accustomed to that role. Where did you learn to cook?" Humor mixed with curiosity in his question.

"I'm totally self-taught," she replied seriously, "I've always believed cooking is intrinsically instinctive in everyone. Who taught the first person that some things taste better when cooked? Or for that matter, that some things are no longer poisonous when cooked?"

"Interesting concept…so you think I can cook then?"

She leaned forward seductively, and giving her best imitation of Tina Turner's sexy, throaty voice she sang, "Baby, you were cookin' since the day you were born."

He laughed gleefully, squeezing her hands, but did not take the bait to switch the conversation away from her and on to him, he was determined to find out more about her past tonight. Recollecting what she said in the car about having had sex with only one other man, the envy of this mysterious person was beginning to gnaw at his insides; he was becoming obsessive.

He *had* to find out who it was, and what happened to him. "This is a lovely wine. Very special. How did you find it?"

"In the wine cellar," she replied with a jesting smile.

He became serious, "You know what I mean."

"Oh, someone from Spain introduced it to me."

His eyes narrowed, "Who?"

"I can't remember. Why?" She suddenly became aware that he was actually interrogating her.

He put on a casual voice, "Oh, I just wondered. You spent a lot of time in Spain it seems. I mean you're not only as fluent as a native, but to have learnt other dialects is no mean feat."

She was silent for a moment, then spoke just as casually as he, "Yes, I guess you could say I spent a lot of time in Spain, that's the best way to become fluent in Spanish. I've always felt knowing another language is like having an extra arm or leg to help one through life. It's opened many doors for me." She paused contemplatively, then added pointedly, "Remember, I speak three other languages and I'm learning Portuguese and German."

"Yes. You embarrass me in this area. I can barely get around Europe with what little I know of the many languages, and as for Spain, that's even worse. You'll have to accompany me on all my travels from henceforth." He gave her his broadest smile, and suddenly, taking her hands in his, he became serious and changed the subject, "I feel I need to reassure you of something." There was a long awkward pause before he continued. "I have a complete physical every six months. It includes testing for HIV and other diseases. I'm always given a clean bill of health. I'm very discriminating about who I have sex with, I haven't had sex without a condom for many years. I…um…I felt it important for you to know."

Although taken aback by this intimate confession of sorts, she looked at him with deepening respect and spoke just as frankly as he had, "I also have regular checkups, actually had one just before I left

Trinidad, and was as usual, given a clean bill of health. And…I'm… on the pill." They both looked down at their hands, still locked in each other's, a certain shyness having crept up between them. She broke the uneasy silence, "It's been a really long day, we should get some sleep."

Michael assented with coy formality, "Yes, certainly."

They stood up, he rang the silver bell Maria left on the table, put an arm around her waist, she put an arm around his, and they strolled to their rooms.

CHAPTER
9

Arriving at her door, they embraced and kissed tenderly. She said softly, "Thank you, Michael, for one of the most special days I've had in a very long time."

"And I thank you, for the very same reason." He kissed her again, more passionately this time.

She felt a tingling sensation in her vagina as his manhood grew hard against her crotch, but she knew it was too soon for them, and, too late in the day, "Goodnight my darling, sweet dreams. I look forward to enjoying tomorrow afternoon with you."

She pushed him off gently as he responded softly, "Me too, sweet dreams, my darling…I love you."

She whispered, "I love you too," entered her room and closed the door. They both went immediately to their respective bathrooms and each had an extremely cold shower.

"Good morning, Jenkins. How're you?"

"Fine thanks. Good morning, Michael. More importantly, how're *you?*"

"Brilliant, actually. It promises to be a great day. I need you to do another check for me."

"Yes? On who this time?"

"Elizabeth."

"Ah…you want me to reinstate Standard Procedure?"

"No. She'd never forgive me if I did, and she's too smart not to find out. She mentioned a man she had a relationship with before, it's gnawing at my gut. I *must* find out who it is. I've a hunch he's in Spain. She spent a lot of time there and I sensed evasiveness about it. Check Spain first. Call as soon as you know something."

"Of course. And Michael, take it easy will you?"

"I will. Thanks, buddy."

Elizabeth, Susan, and John had already started breakfast when Michael jauntily joined them on the terrace, "Good morning all. Sorry to be late, but I had to deal with important calls."

Susan, who was nearest to him, he kissed on her forehead, John, who was seated at the head of the table between Elizabeth and Susan, he patted on his shoulders, and saying, "Hello, darling," he kissed Elizabeth on her lips. She lifted her napkin to her mouth trying to hide her blush.

John stood up, "Michael sit here between the girls. I must get started on paperwork but I'll see you in an hour for…our…appointment."

"Right. Thanks, John," Michael said as he took John's seat.

Betty rushed out with a clean place setting. Maria followed with a tray of fruit salad, a lit chafing-dish filled with steaming hot scrambled eggs with cheese and turkey sausages, and a basket with whole-wheat toast and freshly baked muffins. Michael attacked it all ravenously, squeezing Elizabeth's hand often. She loved that he was so openly affectionate with her, although she felt a little embarrassed sometimes, depending on who was around to see. Swallowing his last mouthful he said, "Darling, we should warn you about our cousin Henry who's coming to dinner. He's the son of my oldest aunt, Claire, who lives at the palace with Susan's mother, Aunt Anne. He lives outside the palace, is my age. You might not like him. Frankly, he's a pompous snob-"

Susan interjected, "I think he's an obnoxious ass. Anyway, we only have to suffer him through dinner. He's driving on afterwards to his family's estate, apparently wants to show off the new girlfriend to everyone, claims she's absolutely gorgeous and extremely smart."

Michael chortled, "Not too smart if she's with Henry. And nobody's more gorgeous than my Elizabeth."

Elizabeth spoke quickly, "Could we please act as if I'm Susan's friend and you and I have never met?"

"Why, darling? Hey, I want to show you off too."

"I...I think it's too soon. I'm sure everyone coming will be discreet but people like to boast they are 'in the know,' and could slip up and say something to the wrong person. Next thing we know, this place will be surrounded with paparazzi and we'll lose our privacy. Our lives could become a nightmare."

Susan nodded in agreement, "She's right, Michael."

Michael reluctantly conceded, "I know. I didn't think about that. I just want Elizabeth and I to be like any normal couple in love. Alright, so we'll put on a big act as if we're 'Strangers in the Night'," he sang the title of Frank Sinatra's famous song, "but I still want Elizabeth seated next to me."

Susan agreed and Elizabeth teased, "Only if you behave yourself, Your Highness," turning to Susan she asked, "How would you like us to dress?"

"I would've liked to have had just a casually elegant evening but unfortunately Henry feels this is a special occasion and said he's going to be formal. So, for peace's sake, formal it is. He obviously wants to impress the girlfriend. I'm going to wear a long black gown. Do you have something suitable?"

Elizabeth smiled, then looked at Michael with concern, "Yes, but do *you* have a formal suit here?"

Appreciating her caring, he smiled lovingly, "Definitely, my valet always packs a tux or two no matter where I go."

Finishing breakfast, they all agreed to meet at noon for lunch. Elizabeth and Michael went to their respective suites to get caught up on neglected work.

Michael and John had their meeting in Michael's room and after they concluded their business, John looked at him squarely, "Michael, please don't take this the wrong way, I'm only looking out for you. I can see how you feel about Elizabeth, believe me, everybody can. We've never seen you like this, not even with Priscilla. And it's evident she feels the same way about you. But, I'm concerned you might be moving too fast. Look, Elizabeth's fabulous. It's obvious she's very special, not only stunningly beautiful, but intelligent, sweet, charming, and all the social graces come naturally to her. It's apparent she's well-bred and educated, but what do you really know about her? About her past, I mean?"

"We're still getting to know each other, John."

John became agitated, "Wait! Are you saying you haven't ordered Standard Procedure on her?"

"Ah…I had. But I felt compelled to tell her. She was terribly upset, said it was demeaning and cheapening among other things, actually walked away from me. I felt she was justified. I feel she's trustworthy. So I promised to stop Standard Procedure adding that I expect she'll tell me what I should know. She's too smart John, I can't betray her trust now."

John stood up, his face and neck turning a deep red, the veins bulging. Every blood vessel looking like they would burst, he shouted, "Trust! Fuck that, Michael! This is your future we're talking about! Your *life*, dammit! You *cannot* go through something like what happened with Priscilla again! Or *worse*, the situation in Greece! For God's sake, man! Listen Michael, your responsibility goes far beyond just to yourself. You've the monarchy to think of! This country! You know the monarchy's in jeopardy with what's going on in the West Country. And, *you* cannot risk a personal disaster again! These are different times, the whole world would know now. You must be extremely cautious, put the monarchy and the country first. Remember *who* you are! Put yourself, your position, first. Before *any* woman!"

Michael stood up, towering over John by a foot, but feeling very small and childlike at this moment. Though his elder by sixteen years, John and he had always been close, and apart from Jenkins, he and Susan had become his most trusted confidants since his mother died. He admired their relationship with each other, their ethics, courage, and all their hard-earned successes through the years of a difficult economy. Moreover, they knew him well, and loved him as much as he loved them. He had the utmost respect for them and their opinions and often sought their counsel on many subjects. However, Elizabeth was one subject that was not open to debate or analysis. He felt extreme loyalty and responsibility towards protecting and defending her at all costs. Knowing every word John said was true, and well-meant, he appreciated his caring and candor. Yet he resented being given a lecture in this manner about someone who had become the first priority in his life. Nevertheless, he did not want to argue with John. His first thought was to change the subject but he knew John would not let him off the hook, John could be relentless. So he bowed to the wisdom of his elder, decided to continue the discussion, and explain himself.

"John, what you say is true. The situation in the country, and the precariousness of the monarchy greatly concerns me, you know I'm working on it. You know my plans, as soon as I'm King, with what modicum of power the monarchy still has, I'm going to work diligently to implement them. With the help of the government and the backing of the majority, I'll be influential in bringing peace, prosperity, and stability, to the whole region. To do it, I need stability in my own life. I need love, I've been too long without. You know I've been through a lot, and, I've searched a lot. At last I've found the perfect person to share my life with. The way you described Elizabeth, she's all that and so much more. She has a strength of character and intelligence mixed with a caring, loving, sweetness I've not experienced in a young woman before. When you get to know her you'll see her inner beauty is as apparent as her outer beauty. She possesses my mind, my soul! I can't think of anyone else. I'm completely in love John, like never before. I know she feels the same way about me. She's the only one for me."

John calmed down, his color returning to normal as an unexpected tenderness came into his voice, "Michael, that's wonderful. I'm happy for you. And from what little I've seen, Elizabeth's perfect for you. But, you need to protect yourself...as well as her. You can't just go blindly into a relationship not knowing too much about a woman who'll one day be Queen. I strongly recommend that you reinstate Standard Procedure on her immediately."

Michael shook his head firmly, "No, John. I'll have to tell her, and she'd never forgive me. There has to be complete honesty in our relationship if it's to survive and flourish. I did do something this morning that I'm already feeling guilty about. She mentioned she'd had a serious relationship before. It ended badly and she didn't want to talk about it, said she just wanted to forget it. But I can't forget it. It's still affecting her, and, it's eating at my insides. So I called Jenkins, asked him to check on a hunch I have about Spain. He'll call me as soon as he knows something. So you see, I'm not some naïve fool rushing in where angels fear to tread. Honestly though, I feel guilty about it."

"Don't!" John said emphatically, "You need to know as much as possible as soon as possible."

"Yes," he agreed, "but I'd prefer Elizabeth to tell me."

Elizabeth had difficulty getting through to Trinidad on many of her calls, and Skype would not function. Probably because of a stormier than usual rainy season in the Caribbean, there were malfunctions of satellite connections for the mobile phone systems in that area. Due to its southernmost position in the Caribbean, next to the South American mainland, unlike the other islands, Trinidad was spared of hurricanes; but because of global climate change, it had recently been deluged with frequent and unusually prolonged severe thunderstorms. Finally, in disgust, knowing she could not risk being overheard on a land phone in the castle, she threw her phone into a bag with a towel, donned the, on her, skimpy swimsuit Susan lent her, slipped on a robe, and went down to the pool.

It was a glorious day. The sun was shining as brilliantly as if she were back in the tropics, except the air temperature was just pleasantly warm, not yet hot, the sky colored in that perfect deep blue one would usually see on a clear summer's day in Provence, or a clear winter's day in Florida.

She dipped a foot in the water to test its temperature; it was not as warm as she would have liked but it was tolerable and she dove in. She swam nonstop for twenty lengths, changing her strokes from freestyle to breast stroke to back stroke at every turn, paying close attention to perfecting her strokes and turns, wanting to, just for a while at least, take her mind's focus off her trepidation about speaking to Michael.

She tried in vain to convince herself that the decision she made yesterday when she was in his arms was the only option she had, to live in the moment, forget the past, say 'que sera, sera' to the future, let it take care of itself. Except for the fact that her conscience kept being pricked by her early strict Catholic upbringing - she could still hear the nuns at school, "*Always tell the truth!*" - she would have been able to rely on her once care-free spirit to 'live in the now.' On the surface, she knew she could continue to dwell in her fantasy world, her belief that everything always works out for the best. Yet, deep inside her soul, and her heart that kept her functioning in spite of the still bleeding wound which it had sustained some time ago, she knew she could not continue to live a lie. She dreaded that she could cause Michael pain when all he ever brought her was hope and happiness. How could she hurt this man who saved her from drowning in an ocean of sorrow and despair? Who gave her faith in her ability to love unconditionally again?

She determined that he should not have to suffer in any way because of her, he must never experience a heartbreak like what she had endured. He loved her so much, and she loved him too much.

Nevertheless, he will have to learn the truth about her sometime in the near future.

She wondered if facing something difficult sooner rather than later would make it less painful. *How will it diminish his hurt by knowing about my past now, rather than at a more convenient time in the future? And will it really be that bad after all, when he hears my story? He has this unshakeable belief that some things are difficult but nothing's impossible. We're already so much in love. Why shouldn't we just enjoy basking in this wonderful new rejuvenating love that is enriching both our lives, creating such passion and joy; and extinguishing my long-held destructive anger and bitterness?*

Deciding to stop debating the dilemma that confounded her, she determined that to procrastinate in this instance could do no harm. This was their time to revel in the exultant love that was now enveloping their lives.

The conversation he had with John stirred up Michael's curiosity about the mysteries of Elizabeth's past. What caused the anomaly of her usually joyful loving eyes' occasionally pained expression? Is it a serious risk to forbid Jenkins from continuing Standard Procedure on her? He could not renege on his promise to stop investigating her, scrupulousness was entrenched in his essence, he never broke a promise. *Anyway, what harm could someone like Elizabeth do to the monarchy? She's obviously an intelligent woman of impeccable integrity, generous spirit, and, deeply passionate. Her Granger family is venerated internationally, but more importantly, she's the most extraordinary woman I've ever met. She's done what no other had been capable of, she captured my heart and soul.*

He knew he would accept anything about her, he was completely and irrevocably in love, positive she was the only woman he wanted forever in his life. He believed there was no obstacle so insurmountable that could block their path to the wonderful journey of the life they would share.

However, the necessity to find the missing pieces of the puzzle to her enigmatic secretiveness and occasional unexplained sad emotional behavior kept haunting him, taunting him. He convinced himself that to check The Children's Home website and Google her family's business in Trinidad would not be breaching his agreement with her about stopping Standard Procedure. In point of fact, if they are on the internet, they are open to public scrutiny, and who is more public than he.

The Children's Home website came up as a Non-for-Profit Organization. Elizabeth Angelique Richardson, the founder, headed the board as President, Jane Mary Thompson was Vice President and there were eight other members. One name stood out making Michael's eyebrows touch his hairline: George Davis.

He wondered if it could possibly be his friend from university, then decided it was not, because surely Elizabeth would be thrilled and proud to tell him that his George was on her board and her friend too. Also, George was particular about always using his full three names on anything official, and anyway, this George was attached to a woman's name, Jennifer. George's sister was Margot and his mother was Helen. There was no way Jennifer could be George's wife either. George and he had made a pact that when they both eventually decided to settle down after they had enough of sowing their wild oats, they were definitely going to dance at each other's weddings. George, like the rest of the world, knew exactly where Michael lived, and Michael had never received a wedding invitation. Besides, George came from an extremely large family and had told him Davis was a fairly common name in Trinidad. George also was a popular name worldwide so there was no reason to think this man could be his George Alfred Davis.

There was a lovely picture of Elizabeth with a brown-skin woman whom he presumed was Jane Thompson. They were surrounded by about fifty children of every color of flesh that humanity comes in. Both women were holding small babies. The rest of the children were of varying ages up to late teens, all their faces displaying the widest and most beautiful smiles. Somehow, none looked retarded. A happier picture Michael had never seen. Visible in the background on either side of the group was a rose garden abloom with a large variety of colors.

Below the photograph was a poem composed by renowned and cherished Trinidadian poet, Barnabas J. Ramon-Fortune.

GOD'S COLOUR SCHEME
Within a garden scented sweet
I walk at morning tide;
The new-moon grass was at my feet
And Angels by my side.
I lingered near one dainty bed
Adorned with roses fair,
In colours-pink, white, cream and red-
True harmony was there.
Then spake the Angels unto me
In accents full of meaning:
"What shade of rose appears to thee
The bloom at fairest seeming?"
I watched the roses once again;
Each had a lovely hue,
And each diffused a sweet perfume,
Full-mellowed by the dew.
"I cannot tell," I said at last,
"No matter how I try,
Each rose seems comely as the rest,
As pleasing to the eye,
The pink is fair, and so the red,
And so the cream, the white;
Each helps to beautify the bed
And make it wondrous quite."
The Angels smiled a knowing smile,
And softly whispered them:
"As with these roses here, you see,
So with the sons of men,

Each shade of skin beneath the sun,
From tropic clime to cold,
Is part of God's Great Colour Scheme,
And glorious to behold.
The ebon black, the copper brown,
The gold, the ivory white-
Each shade is perfect in itself,
And precious in His sight,
Man judges blooms, not by their hues,
But by the scent they give,
God Judges Men, not by their skins,
But by the way they live."

Michael sat back after reading Fortune's poem, pondering on the profundity of it. It dawned on him why Elizabeth would not say she had a favorite color rose while walking in The Park the day they met, only conceding that she preferred yellow and white after he pressured her to choose. He realized she said those two because he pointed out the two in those colors that were named for his mother and father. Appreciating yet another side of this extraordinary woman who had taken possession of his heart and soul he felt his chest swell, not only with love but a peculiar sense of pride. Both these feelings magnified as he continued reading about the humble beginnings of The Children's Home, the difficulties Elizabeth and her friends had to overcome, the trials and tribulations they struggled through to get it going. It seemed that were it not for their tenacious perseverance and the generosity of mostly private companies, it would never have happened. He wondered why the Trinidadian government, the little country being rich with oil and natural gas and having one of only two pitch lakes in the entire world, didn't just fund the whole thing. Then, suspecting Elizabeth to be fiercely independent, and resourceful, and knowing her great capacity to be passionate and emotional, he thought perhaps it was her choice to be in control, and to not ever have to answer to an impartial, objective, and perhaps unemotional, power.

He was extremely impressed to see how much it had expanded in such a short time, just three years, from a tiny concrete boxy building to a huge complex of five attractive modern structures, with well-maintained grounds surrounding a fenced pool and playground. *What an incredible accomplishment!* His admiration and respect for Elizabeth increased tenfold. Turning his attention to Google her family's business he realized he didn't have a name and punching in just her last name simply showed a furniture store. The information on it was minimal, so, temporarily pushing ethics aside, he punched in her full name. To his surprise and disappointment, the only thing that came up was a reference to her founding The Children's Home and information on its website. The phone rang, and thinking it was Jenkins, he shut down the computer to focus on the call.

It was John calling to give him some information he just obtained on an adjoining property Michael was interested in acquiring. Hanging up the phone, he walked over to the window that overlooked the pool and smiled when he saw Elizabeth in Susan's swimsuit, her bosom barely covered. There was a hint of areolas peeking out when she leaned forward to place her bag on a chaise, and when she turned around to dip her foot in the pool, half her bottom was exposed. *Wow! She has the perfect figure for childbearing, small waist, full shapely hips, great round bottom, and those exquisite voluptuous breasts I so much enjoyed. I must have her tonight or I'll go crazy!* He developed an ache in his groin as he watched her stretch her shapely golden-tanned body before diving in the pool, the too small swimsuit completely exposing one nipple. He felt his penis rising, looked at his crotch and said aloud, "Down boy," thinking to himself, *If I don't have real sex soon I'll burst!*

Picking up the house phone, he pressed the button for the kitchen, "Maria, is that you?"

"Yes, Prince Michael, you need something?"

"Yes, can you please come to my room immediately?" he asked in perfect Spanish.

"Yes, Sir, but you speak Spanish well."

"Yes but don't tell anyone let's keep it our secret, okay?"

"Okay, Prince Michael, I'll be up right away."

After Maria left his suite, concerned that he had not yet heard from Jenkins, he paced back and forth. Finished making the necessary phone calls, sending off the e-mails he wanted to handle today, it was nearly noon, and he wanted desperately to go to Elizabeth at the pool. Impatiently picking up his phone, it rang in his hand, "Yes Jenkins."

"Your Spain hunch was right. She was engaged."

"Engaged?"

"Old Spanish distant nobility. His name's familiar, Don Frederico Carlos Pablo Del Rico. Know him?"

"Yes. Many years ago in my wilder youth I'd been to parties at his home. Remember? He has a palace outside Madrid? He gave great parties. But had a wife, Carmen, if I remember correctly."

"They divorced. Already divorced when he and Elizabeth became engaged. Anyway, Elizabeth broke it off, a complication about a long-time mistress. Apparently the mistress was the reason for the divorce too. That's all we've been able to learn so far. Our people had a tough time getting information. Those aristocrats over there are pretty close-mouthed about protecting their own, and everybody else has to be heavily bribed. Actually we got most of this information from an old almost senile aunt of his. I'm afraid somebody might talk about our investigation, Elizabeth has friends there, it might get back to her."

Michael became nervous, "Pull everybody off immediately. I can't risk Elizabeth finding out, not now."

"Right. By the way, it's not of major importance, but she has two passports, American and Trinidadian."

"Oh? That legal?"

"Yes. Both countries have dual citizenship."

"Hmm…she did live and get her degree in the States, and she has family there, so I guess it makes sense. She'll have to relinquish one. Thanks Jenkins. I'll call you tomorrow."

Michael sat and deliberated over what he just learnt. *So, this is, was, my rival, Frederico Del Rico. It's obvious Elizabeth's accustomed to move in our kind of circles, so I expect they would've met. Any man would go after her, especially someone like him. He's typical of our class, loves beauty, culture, intelligence, sophistication, she exemplifies those attributes. I'm not surprised she fell for him either, he isn't just handsome, he has an effusive charm that wins everyone over. Hard to dislike him, even now when I'm envious he was her only other lover. He's quite the ladies' man, suave, debonair, dark green eyes contrasting with jet black hair, really a handsome devil. Tall too, for a Spaniard, almost my height. Plenty older than Elizabeth. So, it seems he wasn't willing to give up the mistress he had during his marriage. What an idiot! Imagine not giving up another woman for Elizabeth! What planet is he on anyway, women don't put up with that sort of thing anymore. His wife didn't, and knowing Elizabeth's ethics, sure as hell she wouldn't. That must've been tough for her to bear, that the stupid fool didn't think she alone was enough for him! This obviously was a tremendous blow to her self-esteem as well as her breaking heart. So, this, is the 'traumatic' thing she wants to forget. Well, my darling, I'll do everything in my power to make you forget, starting now!* He glanced out the window to make sure Elizabeth was still at the pool before going down. She was talking on her phone, and crying. He was nonplussed, *Good God, what now? Why is she crying?* Suddenly, tears still streaming down her cheeks, she threw her head back laughing. Bewildered, he thought, *What the hell's going on?* and dashed down to the pool. By the time he got there Elizabeth had already shut off her phone, collected herself, wiped her tears and donned her robe. Not wanting her to know he had been watching, he walked up casually, "Hello, darling," and embracing her, kissed her with the utmost tenderness.

"Thank you," she said softly, "I needed that."

"Is something wrong?" he enquired in a concerned voice.

"No. Not anymore. Not with you in my life."

CHAPTER
10

Lunch was served again on the outside terrace, Susan having already set up the formal dining room for the dinner party. Besides, the weather was so perfect, it would have been foolish to waste such a day by eating indoors in the castle's lovely small family dining room just off the kitchen.

Susan asked John and Michael how their meeting went to which they both replied quickly and somewhat dismissively, "Very well," and Michael, wanting that subject ignored, asked Susan if everything was shipshape for the dinner party.

Susan replied, "Yes, thanks to Elizabeth the food's going to be wonderful. The only thing we have to worry about is saving our guests from our boorish cousin's insults."

He patted her hand, "Sit him near me, I'll handle him."

"I'm putting you at the head in my place across from John at the other head, Elizabeth on your right, me on your left and Henry on my left so I can keep him in check. I'll put the girlfriend next to him so at least I won't get any complaints."

They all agreed that was a good plan and John turned the conversation to enquire about Elizabeth's morning. She responded that it was extremely relaxing as well as gratifying as she was eventually able to conclude some business she had neglected to finalize yesterday, hastily adding, "All to do with The Children's Home in Trinidad for the mentally challenged."

This aroused the interest of the others and Michael asked, "What attracted you to get involved in that particular charity? It seems heart-rending to handle kids like that."

She saddened, "It is. But a good friend had a baby with severe Down Syndrome. It not only devastated her, but her husband wimped out on her and the baby and divorced them. She became so distraught she had a nervous breakdown. So her best friend and I had to step in to help. Cut a long story short, we got help for her to get well, and co-founded The Home for all degrees of mentally retarded children, calling it simply The Children's Home. You see, too often these children are just dumped around to any family member who'll handle them in small doses. We saw the necessity for them to have permanent structure in their lives so they can develop into more whole and often productive human beings, not just some 'useless retard' as many seem to think of them. Hence the name, The Children's Home, we wanted them to feel secure that they did have a home of their own, where they are valued and cherished. We're experimenting with new concepts and exercises, primarily coming out of America and Germany. The majority of kids have progressed amazingly." Turning to Michael, she continued, "Yes, Michael, it is heart-rending for a so-called normal person to be with these kids sometimes, took me awhile to get accustomed to them. But when you spend more time with them you appreciate how sweet, innocent, and special they are, they epitomize unconditional love. What still breaks my heart is when I have to leave them after a session and they cling to me, grab my hands, skirt, bag, legs, whatever they can hold on to, begging me, in whatever way they can vocalize, to stay with them. That still upsets me even after all this time."

Elizabeth's voice cracked and they saw her eyes were watering. Susan and Michael each put a hand on her hands, his voice sincerely sympathetic, "I'm sorry you have to go through that, darling. What you're doing is so commendable, courageous. I'll help in any way I can."

Also touched, Susan joined in, "Me too."

Not wanting to be left out, John said, "And me."

"You're all so kind and sweet," she responded, dabbing the corners of her eyes with her napkin, "thank you."

Maria and a housemaid arrived to take their plates away in order to bring the dessert course. Elizabeth said she'd eaten enough and did they mind excusing her as she wanted to speed-walk around the grounds.

Michael asked, "Would you like some company, or do you want to be alone?"

"I'd love you to join me, if you want."

He smiled that boyish smile she loved, "I want."

She smiled appreciatively, "Okay, we'll need to change into track-suits. Give me twenty minutes, alright?"

"Alright," he said, standing to pull out her chair.

They thanked Susan and John for yet another lovely meal, Michael took her hand, kissed it, and placed it around his waist. Placing his arm around her waist, they strolled inside, gazing at each other, smiling that special smile of lovers.

As soon as they were out of earshot John said to Susan, "Our boy has fallen hard this time. He's beyond besotted. Do you know he even stopped Standard Procedure on her? I told him he's taking a hell of a risk."

Susan said reassuringly, "Drop it John. I've had long chats with Elizabeth, I've good instincts about her. She's very special, is deeply in love with him. When she talks about him, she lights up like a pubescent girl with her first crush. She'd never do anything like Priscilla did, it's not in her. She's perfect for him. It's great to see him so happy again at last."

Michael teased Elizabeth about the fast pace she set, "Hey, I thought we were *walking*, this is a jog."

"We are *speed*-walking. We're here to do aerobic exercise, not some lazy stroll. So move it, Your Highness. Keep up!"

He laughed at the unsolicitous manner in which she spoke to him, loved that she was so unintimidated by him and his position that she not only treated him as her equal, but could actually reprove him without any sign of discomfort, yet with caring respect. Regarding her from a few paces behind, seeing her perfect figure, perfect posture, and even through her tracksuit, perfect bottom, he felt himself swelling with love in his chest, and lust in his loins.

She turned her head around and feigned castigation, "Excuse me Prince Michael, but I believe you are committing improper protocol. I don't agree with it but as I understand it, Sir, *I'm* supposed to be the one walking behind, not you. So you think you can bend the rules a little and at least walk beside me, or is it too difficult for you to catch up and keep my pace?"

Laughing again, he ran forward, grabbed her hand, and fell in with her stride, "Excuse me, Princess Elizabeth," he came back at her mockingly, "are we allowed to talk, or is that bending any of *your* rules?"

She responded with pretended condescension, "Talking is permitted, but only if you don't slow the pace."

He faked petulance, "Oh no, Your Royal Highness, I wouldn't dream of slowing *the* pace."

It was her turn to laugh, and swell, in the same places he had, but she managed to ignore the latter area, "So, what would you like to talk about?"

"Religion, politics, money. All the topics polite society considers taboo."

"Ah, my brave and intrepid knight, plunging fearlessly into dangerous and forbidden territory."

"For you my lady I'll happily plunge, and risk everything."

Even though she read an adianoeta in his facetious remark, Elizabeth decided to discontinue their humorous banter. Particularly after conversing with Susan, she had recently wanted to delve deeply into these serious subjects with him. She glanced at him with just a hint of a smile, "Well, we can take money off the list. Compared to you and your family, I practically don't have any."

"Oh, I don't know about that, I think the Grangers are right up there-"

"They're my aunt and uncle, Michael. My immediate family is still building wealth through our businesses. Certainly we're not struggling, we don't want for much, but we all work pretty hard," she grinned, "mind you, in true Caribbean tradition, we also play pretty hard."

He smiled encouragingly, "I always knew you would fit right in with my family. What are your businesses?"

"We've several. A recycling plant, four factories and an import-export company to handle our products. We're also the agents for other products, we've a few exclusive lines." She raised a hand to indicate she needed to stop, bent down, and made a big show of having to retie her sneaker's laces while she tried to think of a quick and undetectable way she could get away from this topic.

However, Michael was thrilled to at last be getting more information about her, from her. Being more attuned to her than he let on, he sensed her reluctance to discuss her family's businesses, but was not going to let that deter him from learning more. Remembering he could not Google them earlier, he told himself, *Get a name,* so with a small degree of nonchalance he persisted, "What's your company called?"

She stood up and resumed her fast pace. Undesirous of being mendacious, she was extremely proud of her family's businesses, but not wanting him too know too much about them, at least not yet, not until she makes her decisions, she replied evasively, "They have different names. But everything operates under the mother company, Richardson Enterprises. My grandfather started the original company but Daddy greatly expanded it, he's grooming me to take over when he retires." Hoping to terminate the discussion on this subject she added quickly, "But I'm working on getting my Master's Degree so I'm not too involved, don't know much yet, so let's move on to topics I do know something about. Which do you want to discuss first, religion or politics? Though, quite frankly, the way much of the world has been operating, unfortunately, often the two go hand in hand."

His expression turning solemn, he nodded in agreement, "Yes, I'm afraid you're quite right about that. One of the greatest disservices mankind has done to itself is to allow organized religions to dictate the way nations should be run. With all the immense strides we've made scientifically and technologically, we're still so backward, barbaric even, in our treatment of each other. You'd think by now world leaders would've wised up enough to figure out how retarding man-made-up religions with their discriminating practices have been to the advancement of peaceful unified, respectful, civilized behavior. Obviously some religion has its place in providing help to some people's spiritual needs, but in regards to its responsibility to bring out the best in human behavior on the world stage, it has been sadly lacking. When you consider that all the major wars and conflicts on our planet have been influenced by religious beliefs, one group wanting to force another to succumb to their way of thinking, any intelligent person can't help but lose respect for organized religions, their historical beginnings *and* their current leadership. Our only hope for the stupidity and greed to cease, actually for our very survival, is that humans get educated and knowledgeable more rapidly so we can have the courage to at last evolve into peaceful, unselfish intelligent beings, coexisting freely and contentedly on a healthier, better nurtured planet."

He became aware that their pace, which she was controlling, had slowed down considerably. Glancing at her with the intention of apologizing for monopolizing the conversation with his monologue, he was taken aback to see her jaw had dropped open and she was staring at him, her eyes widened like demitasse saucers. He smiled meekly, "Oh...oh, it appears I've shocked you."

She responded softly, "You certainly have."

"I'm sorry darling," he did not sound apologetic to her, "but I thought you being a sophisticated educated world-traveler, and... female, would understand what I'm talking about-"

She interjected, "Michael, I'm shocked because I understand completely. I think exactly the way you do, I too am disenchanted with organized patriarchal religions."

He eyed her cautiously, "Oh…I thought your being raised staunchly Catholic might cause you to disagree."

Taking in his look she commented without caution, "Being raised Catholic didn't close my mind and stop my brain from functioning, Michael. Fanatical indoctrination only thrives if one is too fearful, or too lazy, to explore other fundamental principles. I was very fortunate to have been raised in a family that believes our contribution is greater if we are shepherds not just mere sheep, leaders not followers, unenlightened benign acceptance being unacceptable. And I'm certain you were raised with the same advantageous attitudes and principles. You were raised staunchly Protestant and yet you've come to the same conclusions I have. So why did you think my being raised Catholic would make me disagree? It isn't by any chance, because I'm a woman, the 'weaker meeker sex?'" She scrutinized his face.

He walked in front of her, turned around and stopped, his eyes narrowing, though she detected a twinkle in them, "You! 'Weaker meeker sex'!" He began to laugh so hard he scared a flock of birds out of trees nearby. They protested with loud screeches and whistles that startled Elizabeth making her jump. He stopped laughing and held her shoulders, "Do you hear that?"

"Of course."

"Good. Do you know what that sound is?"

"Birds, silly."

"No. That is the laughter of God."

She became irritated, "What! What do you mean?"

"That's in response to your remark about being a woman and the weaker meeker sex. You're making God laugh!" He gave her a broad smile and squeezed her shoulders.

"Oh, very funny, Michael." She shrugged his hands off her shoulders playfully and speed-walked away.

Running forward he fell in step beside her, "Elizabeth?"

She didn't look at him, "Yes, Michael?"

"You're not annoyed with me are you?"

Looking at him, her love was undeniable, "No. Why? Should I be? I've become accustomed to your teasing and-"

He read her look correctly, "I love you, Elizabeth."

She stopped. He stopped. She looked deep into his eyes and said simply, "I love you, Michael," and resumed speed-walking.

They were silent awhile until Michael started whistling the Jamaican-American singer Shaggy's 'Strength Of A Woman.'

Elizabeth smiled, "I see you know Shaggy's music."

He grinned, "A little. I know *that* song. Word for word."

"Sing it for me."

He began to sing, "*So amazing how this world is made, I wonder if God is a woman. The gift of life astounds me to this day, I give it up for the woman-*" he stopped singing, looked at her seriously and spoke slowly, "What do you think God is, man or woman? Or androgynous? Or do you still believe in God? What do you *really* think of the possibility of God's existence?"

She was silent for a while contemplating how best to answer without giving too much of herself away, "I believe all things are possible. Anything the human mind can think up, it's possible. Like most people, I *want* God to exist and I do believe in God, but differently to the way I was taught by the Church. Most humans have the need to feel somebody or something greater than us is looking out for us. It's not the most practical way to think and let's be honest, probably perpetuated by religions promoting fear to keep us, and our money, bound to them. Most intelligent people go through doubts at some stage I'm sure. Even today when I pray, and I pray often, sometimes when I'm finished I say, *God, you'd better be there. Otherwise you're making me waste a hell of a lot of time praying to you!*" She looked at him with a teasing smile and a saucy pout of her lips.

He spoke in a disturbed voice, "Please don't do that."

Surprised at him, but smiling, she retorted, "Why? You like to tease me, but you can't handle my teasing you?"

Searing her with a passionate gaze, he said, "No. It's the way you look. We're having a very serious conversation, and all I can think about right now is how much I want you."

"Oh." Elizabeth looked away as she felt a blush warm up the cheeks on her face and work its way down her body to in front of her other cheeks. She fought a wild urge to grab him right then and there, throw him down on the grass, and ravish him. Instead she held her shoulders up, looked straight ahead with calm comportment, and suffocated her carnal desires.

Striving to distract them both she sped up the pace, "I'd love to hear more about your plans for this country, things you want to influence. Can you talk to me about that comfortably?"

With smiling eyes he said seriously, "Elizabeth, I think I can talk to you about anything. You're the only woman I feel will understand what I'm about. I want to share my dreams and hopes with you, my very life, you're the perfect partner to help me achieve my goals for my reign."

With these words coming out of him so matter-of-factly, yet lovingly, she felt an avalanche of emotions fall on her: love, pride, respect, guilt, fear, joy, and, lust.

Oblivious to the impact he was having on her he continued to impart his most private secret plans, taking her into confidences that more than surprised her, she was astounded.

Going into some details about his shocking intention of convincing the government to give back more power to the monarchy when he ascended the throne, which he felt would bring more stability to the region, he finally took a deep breath and asked for her views on his ideas. Although she felt flattered and honored but thought not qualified to have her opinions taken seriously, she gave them anyway, because with what little she knew about the country and its politics, she agreed with almost everything he said. The conversation drifted into philosophical debates on a great variety of topics as they vacillated between serious issues and frivolous subjects.

After they got into an intense discussion about philosophies and psychiatry he surprised her by saying more as a statement than as a question, "Well of course, except for his ideas of God, you know in many ways Freud was a fraud," he grinned, "'Freud the Fraud.'"

She showed she was amused but still responded cautiously, "Well, I've never understood that concept about 'penis envy'-"

Michael grinned interjecting, "Me too! Why would women envy something that men have no control over and is often embarrassing them by showing their most intimate thoughts unintentionally. If there should be any envy of one gender of the other, to me, it's more likely that men have 'womb envy.' You women definitely have the more important parts, and roles, for the continuation of humanity."

Elizabeth gave him an impressed look but teased, "Spoken like a man who knows where his bed is made and how to lie in it," though she wondered, *Is he hinting he knows about my speeches? No. He's so open, he would've told me if he knew.*

They both remarked how wonderful it was that they disagreed on nothing major. Speed-walking and talking for more than an hour, they came upon a large wooden pergola covered in flowering vines with wood and wrought iron benches beneath, in the middle of an apple orchard. Stretching, they gulped down two bottles of water Cookie had given them.

Elizabeth sat down, and feeling an exhilarated sense of relief after their revealing conversations, she patted the bench next to her, "Michael, I have something important to tell you."

Michael sat, thinking to himself, *Oh good, she's going to tell me about Frederico del Rico.*

She watched him guardedly, "I've been putting off telling you because I wanted to wait until you got to know me better. I didn't want you to get the impression that I was some kind of crazy radical feminist, you know the 'burning the bra,' castrating 'down with men' type."

What is she talking about? He wondered, totally perplexed, but said nothing; he was now completely intrigued.

"Getting the grant for The Children's Home isn't the only reason I came to this country. I've been invited to give a speech as a result of one I gave in Trinidad and other Caribbean islands. A nondenominational group heard about it and asked me to repeat it here. They're paying me an exorbitant amount of money to do it, which we need for The Children's Home. It's next week Thursday at five-thirty, in Davidson Hall."

He was extremely impressed, "Davidson Hall, that's very prestigious. It fits over a thousand people."

She shivered, "Two, actually. I'm a bit nervous about it, they said it's sold out. I've not spoken in front of such a large crowd before, I've only done events with three to four hundred people. I want to add more facts, I need to do more research and fine-tune my speech a bit-"

Michael interjected excitedly, "Let me help. We have access to the best speech writers in the world. They could make it a lot easier for you-"

Elizabeth quickly interrupted with a firm inflection to her voice, "Michael no. Thank you, darling, but no. I must do this myself, use my own words to come across as credible and sincere. Also, in the latter part of the lecture I introduce a university professor. He does a slide presentation, mostly historical, then we do questions and answers from the audience. So I have to ad-lib, be extemporaneous, simply just all me, no ideas or words from uninvolved speech writers. But I appreciate the offer." She leaned over and pecked him on his lips.

More than a little impressed by her sagacity and courage, he smiled lovingly, "Alright. I understand. So, what's the subject matter?"

"It's titled 'God Has No Gender.'"

"No agenda?"

"No. Gender. As in male or female."

"Wow! That is extremely profound. I love it."

"I knew you would."

"I can't wait to see you do it."

"Wait a second Michael, you can't come."

"Why?" He frowned disappointedly.

"You'd only make me more nervous."

"No I won't darling, I'll be there to support you. If you're worried I'll detract from the impact of your talk, I'll wear a disguise. I believe in your subject. With all I've learnt through the years, and travels, I'm positive God has no gender, that patriarchal tribes chose God to be male. Please, darling, let me share this with you, I want to know everything about you, to be involved in everything you're involved in. I love you, Elizabeth."

Deciding against divulging the concerns Davidson Hall's managers had in regards to her safety, she touched his cheek, "I love you too darling, but I'm already nervous, no, terrified, of doing this speech in front of so many strangers. In Trinidad, anyone who didn't know me knew my parents or grandparents and even though it was controversial for most of them, the audience was still warm and friendly towards me afterwards. I know this is going to be tougher. Knowing you're in the audience would just exacerbate my fears. I'll be a wreck. And I cannot mess this up. It's too important, don't you see?"

"Yes," he responded, looking hurt and somewhat dejected, "but I'm sorry you think I'd have an adverse effect on you, I want to be the opposite, sort of a cheerleader."

Seeing the look on his face a surge of guilt came upon her, "I'm sorry darling, I didn't mean to upset you. But I'm so moved by you, just thinking about you stirs up…things inside me, far worse being in your presence. Knowing you're there would be even more unnerving for me. I know I'll get distracted. Please don't be upset with me. I can't help how I feel."

Although disappointed, he simultaneously felt thrilled to hear her describe the effect he had on her, and took her hands in his, "It's okay, I'm not upset with you. I only want to be a help to you, never a hindrance. I'll settle for watching it on a D.V.D. I trust it'll be recorded?"

"Yes. You'll have the first copy. We'll watch it together and you can critique me to your heart's content."

With a doting smile he said convincingly, "There's nothing you can do that I will ever criticize."

"Michael you are the most wonderful man. I just adore you." She stared into his eyes for a long time before she leaned over to kiss him with the intense passion she could no longer hide. Hearing his breathing quickening, knowing what was happening to her was also happening to him, she said softly but emphatically, "Michael, we *have* to take it slow."

He gave her a solemn but loving look, "Elizabeth, I've waited a lifetime for you. I'll do whatever it takes." He pecked her nose and stood up, stretching, "Let's go to the gym. I've missed my weight training these last few days. You mind?"

She stretched with him, "Not at all. I've missed mine too."

They speed-walked again all the way back to the castle and down to the basement where the gymnasium was located, both needing to burn off more energy to abate the sexuality they were denying. Standing at the door, smiles lit up their faces on reading the sign above, 'Gym Dungeon.'

An hour raced by as they each did a round with the weight machines then Michael lifted some heavy free weights, Elizabeth lighter ones. Then they did stomach crunches together side by side, chatting all the while. They went back to previous subjects, introduced new ones, and again agreed on almost everything, remarking how much "*in sync*" they were with each other. He sat on the spin bike and pedaled slowly as he watched her slide from difficult looking Yoga positions into Pilates stretches as she hummed 'Getting To Know You.' Appreciating her flexibility and skill he translated her movements into interesting sexual positions and thought to himself, *I don't know how much longer I can wait to get to know you completely.*

At six-fifty, Michael knocked on Elizabeth's door and called out, "Are you ready, darling?"

She called out back to him, "No darling, go on down. I need more time. I'll be down shortly."

Elizabeth needed more time not to finish getting dressed, but to collect herself. She was fully coiffed, made-up, perfumed and dressed when she picked up her necklace to put it on. Memories of who gave it to her came haunting back along with the extreme pain he had caused. Fighting an impulse to throw it back in her jewelry case she reminded herself of her resolution to live in the here and now, enjoy each new moment as it comes, and cast aside the painful old ones. Additionally, the matching sapphires and diamonds necklace and earrings set was perfect with her royal blue gown that she designed and Ruth had had made for her in Paris.

The gown was strapless except for a thin strand of Swarovski crystals crossing from the far right top of the bodice to over her left shoulder, and down the center of her bare back to a brooch of more Swarovski crystals in the shape of a crown, which was attached to the top of a deep 'V' below her waist.

Earlier that day when sorting out what she would wear, she noticed the shape of the brooch for the first time. She was startled to see it was a crown, the couturier had told them it would be a flower. He changed it without consulting them. *Is this an omen? Here I am wearing a gown in Royal blue, with an unchosen Crown brooch, a Regal looking train, and having dinner with three Royals, in this Palatial castle. On top of all that, my father never calls me by my name, only calls me 'Princess'. Could this all be coincidence, or…destiny?* She clasped the choker around her neck, hooked the earrings into her pierced ears, took a deep breath, and made her way down the corridor to the stairs.

Standing at the top of the staircase she took in the scene in the entrance hall below, the guests all arriving at the same time, Susan, John, and Michael greeting them. The first person she sighted was Michael, not because she was naturally drawn to him but because he stood out prodigiously from the rest. Certainly she had seen photographs in the mass media of him in a tuxedo with his royal accoutrement many times, but to actually see him in the flesh in his impressive formal regalia raced her heartbeat for an instant. She studied him care-fully. *He's so incredibly handsome, could be a movie star or a model. The way he stands, carries himself, so regal, charismatic, easily charming everyone. So natural, ironically, royally earthy. His movements, lithe-full yet so masculine, so damned sexy. I wonder if he realizes he has such strong animal magnetism.*

The incident in the gazebo flashed through her recently healed mind, sending a vibrating wave commencing in her brain, running down her spine, and terminating in her too long deprived vagina. She knew she could not continue denying her desires much longer, *I love him, I want to make love to him. I want him to make love to me. I want to make love* with *him.*

She proceeded down the stairs. As though Michael read her mind he suddenly looked up at her, his mouth dropping open. Everyone's eyes followed his star-struck gaze. A sudden silence fell upon the room followed by soft gasps.

Elizabeth's statuesque form appeared to be an apparition of a god-dess floating down the staircase, an ethereal air about her astonishing everyone as they beheld the celestial vision. Some of her hair was held together on top her head with Ruth's diamond clip, tresses of curls hung around her neck, shoulders, and down her back, some wispily curling onto her beautiful face now radiantly smiling at the mesmer-ized group. The royal blue silk-satin gown clung tightly to her breasts, waist and hips, then gradually flared to a flowing train up the stairs behind her, completing the stunningly regal angelic picture.

CHAPTER
11

*B*ursting with love, Michael, remembering the little ruse they had planned, to act as if they had never met, restrained himself from running up the stairs to escort Elizabeth down. Susan broke the awed silence, "Here comes my friend Elizabeth now. Elizabeth, may I present you to my cousin, His Royal Highness, Prince Michael Alexander Stephen-"

Michael interjected, "Please, tonight I'm just Michael." He took the hand Elizabeth offered and instead of shaking it firmly and quickly as was customary, he kissed the back of it with a slow but surreptitious wet kiss. Looking up at her, he smiled, a playful gleam in his eyes.

Susan carried out the rest of the introductions, and to everyone's surprise when it came to their cousin Henry's turn he copied Michael, taking Elizabeth's hand and kissing it, but with a longer, not at all surreptitious, wetter, kiss. This gave her a feeling of repugnance toward him, the opposite emotion of what he intended to elicit. It startled her that Michael's first cousin, with a resemblance to several features of the beautiful man that she loved so completely, could revolt her so deeply.

Susan and John ushered everyone into the drawing room for cocktails and hors d'oeuvres. Almost immediately, Henry cornered Elizabeth on the pretext of being, "intrigued by your lovely accent with the occasional singsong Trinidadian inflections."

Likewise, Henry's girlfriend Linda cornered Michael, gushing with compliments, among them the overly used and overly heard, "You are even better-looking in person than in pictures."

Elizabeth and Michael kept glancing across the room at each other, a 'rescue me' look on both faces. Eventually, Michael, his tolerance threshold much lower than Elizabeth's, tactfully guided Linda towards Henry and a now blushing Elizabeth, the obnoxious Henry having just propositioned her by suggesting she stay with him when she returns to the city.

Seeing her expression, Michael knew Henry said something to disconcert her and remarked half-jokingly, "I hope Henry's been behaving himself. He has quite a reputation with the ladies."

It was Henry's turn to become red-faced, not only at Michael's insinuation but because Linda was staring fiercely at him and he realized she had caught him lecherously glancing at Elizabeth's face and cleavage. The butler saved an embarrassing situation by announcing, "Dinner is served."

Michael held Elizabeth's elbow and guided her towards the dining room saying loud enough for Henry and Linda to hear, "I understand my cousin has seated you next to me, I'm very honored to have you as my dinner partner."

She smiled demurely at him and said, "Thank you, Prince Michael. I too am honored, to be your dinner partner."

He smiled provocatively, "Please, let's drop the formalities, just call me Michael."

"Oh. I don't know that I should. It seems to me that would be improper etiquette seeing that we've only just met," she said with a twinkle and affectatious haughtiness.

Enjoying their little game, he persisted, "Please, I insist. It would make me feel more comfortable."

She replied with a hint of sarcasm, "Oh. Alright then, I wouldn't want to cause Your Royal Highness any discomfort."

The maids brought out the first course of escargots ensconced in their shells in a truffle and garlic butter sauce while the butler acted as a sommelier, authoritatively describing the white wine he poured.

Michael squeezed Elizabeth's knee and whispered, "So, you want to play? I'm very good at this game." He took off his right shoe, put his foot under her gown, and proceeded to rub the naked calf of her leg up and down and up again.

She put her head down and whispered harshly between her teeth, "Michael, stop that! People will know."

"Really? How? And I still have a way to go," he whispered back, smiling impishly, raising his foot higher.

"Michael you're upsetting me, please stop!" she whispered, now angrily between gritted teeth.

He dropped his foot and she turned her attention to answering Henry's question about her ancestry, "My mother's family is French, my father's British."

Henry, attempting to look intellectual, sat back in his chair, pompously held the lapels of his tuxedo, and began to pontificate, "Ah, yes. A bunch of French nobility escaped to the West Indian islands in the Caribbean during the French Revolution, to save their necks from the guillotine. You do know, of course, that all royalty in Europe is related, it's more than likely that you have a bit of blue blood in you, Elizabeth. In fact, we might even be cousins. Now wouldn't that be nice," he leaned forward at an angle towards Elizabeth, obviously hoping to avoid Linda hearing him, smiled smirkingly, and said softly but roguishly, "kissing cousins."

Turning to Elizabeth, Michael jumped in, speaking louder than necessary to make sure Linda could hear, "That *would* be nice. That would make you my kissing cousin too."

Elizabeth felt the foot return, this time up the middle of her gown, between her legs. She put her head down pretending to look at the Lalique crystal finger bowl of warm water and floating lemons that

Maria had just placed on the table to her left, and whispered jarringly, "Michael! I told you to stop!"

"I did!" he whispered back, surprised.

The foot kept moving up her leg making her seethe, "Michael! It's not funny! Stop it!"

His whisper increased in volume, "I did! I swear!"

She looked up at him, saw the dismayed somewhat hurt look on his face and realized he was indeed innocent. Paying closer attention to the angle of the foot she determined it came from someone sitting obliquely across from her to her right. She turned to Michael with an annoyed whisper, "It's Henry!"

Michael took his napkin off his lap, dropped it on the table and no longer whispering, said, "I'll kill him!"

As he attempted to rise Elizabeth gave his knee a painful squeeze under the table which pulled him back down and said in a firm whisper, "You'll do no such thing! I'll handle this!" She clamped her legs over the foot which was now below her knees, squeezed them together tightly, and with all the force she could muster without moving her upper body so that her actions would not be obvious, she twisted the foot sharply to her left.

"Ow! Shit!" Henry exclaimed aloud.

"Henry!" Susan cried out, shocked at his obscenity, but being the well-mannered lady that she was her voice quickly altered to concern, "What's the matter?"

Squirming in his chair, his face distorted from the pain Elizabeth inflicted on his foot, Henry blurted, "Sorry. It…it's a terrible cramp! I think I'd better walk it out." He rose, and Linda rose grasping his arm as he pushed away from the table, and clutching her, limped out of the room.

Elizabeth and Michael giggled under their breaths. "What did you do?" Michael asked amusedly intrigued.

"I'll tell you later," she responded conspiratorially.

"I'll give that relationship maybe one week." he sneered.

"Two days, if it were up to me," she said, looking at him with a mysterious smile.

He repressed his risen annoyance, "Ah ha! I knew he was hitting on you. In the drawing room I could tell something was happening. What did my debauched cousin say?"

"He made me an offer I had to refuse…he offered for me to stay with him in the city."

"How dare he! This time, I'm really going to kill him!" Michael said resolutely.

Observing the vein in his neck pulsing, she grasped his right arm saying softly, "Darling, calm down. Remember, he doesn't know you and I have any connection, he thinks I'm free, single, and disengaged."

He looked at her lovingly, "We'll have to alter that soon."

Wanting to change the subject quickly she said reproachfully, "And by the way, you don't have any right to get your peacocky feathers all ruffled up, I saw you in the corner of the drawing room, all enthralled with Miss Linda."

"You've got to be joking. That woman was practically attacking me! I was hoping you'd come and save me."

She laughed, "I was hoping you'd come and save me!"

"I did. And just in time it seems. Before you got suckered in to a stay of debauchery with my debased, loathsome cousin, whom I shall disown from henceforth."

Unaware that Susan was hearing their humorous banter while pretending to listen to her neighbor, the elderly soft spoken gentleman seated on Elizabeth's right, Elizabeth and Michael continued to tantalize each other until the main course was served. Believing she knew her cousin exceedingly well, Susan came to a very surprising conclusion.

With much fanfare and pomp, the stuffed Cornish game hens sitting on nests of fresh arugula and haricots vert were served on individual platters of Royal Worcester fine bone china. Everyone dug into them voraciously, stopping only to effuse compliments about the different but absolutely delicious flavor, for whish Susan gave all the kudos to a blushing but pleased Elizabeth.

Two more courses later, Henry and Linda still had not returned to the table. Susan sent the butler to fetch them twice, each time he returned alone saying they were nowhere to be found but their car and chauffeur were still in the driveway.

Michael assured her they were alright and she should not be concerned as he was quite sure, knowing Henry, they were off somewhere private, "Where he was having Linda lick his wounds."

Elizabeth's suggested dessert of Bananas Foster flambéed tableside with the Angostura 1919 Select Rum from Trinidad that she brought the Jamestowns as part of a gift, served over homemade vanilla ice cream, was also a big hit with everyone. After dessert the butler announced, "Coffee and liqueurs will be served in the library," and the happily stuffed diners repaired to that room.

Susan came up to Elizabeth and Michael while they were sipping their Grand Marnier liqueurs, "Elizabeth, I hope you don't mind if I steal Michael away for a minute but I need to consult with him on a private matter."

"No, certainly not," Elizabeth replied politely.

Taking his arm, Susan took Michael into the family sitting room, looked around to make sure they were alone, and turned to face him, "Michael, you two haven't had sex yet, have you." It was a definite statement, not a question.

Stunned, Michael stammered, "Wha...what do you mean?"

She was abrupt, "You know what I mean, coitus."

"No, Susan, we have not had sexual intercourse yet. What business is it of yours, anyway?" He was nonplussed.

"You are obviously madly in love with Elizabeth. You mentioned to me in the kitchen last night that she's the one to be your queen. Well, this monarchy needs heirs if it's to survive. Male heirs too, I'm afraid, as we still have that ridiculous archaic tradition the government and your father insists on continuing. So, *you* need to produce an heir to the throne. God forbid, if something happens to you before you produce an heir, it'll be the end of us. We can't rely on your brother, you know he's gay, don't you?"

Michael raised an eyebrow, "Well, it's been rumored-"

"Oh wake up, Michael, he's as queer as they come, just look at his mannerisms. And that's fine, whatever makes him happy-"

Michael interjected impatiently, "What's your point exactly, Susan?"

"My point is, you need to make sure you and Elizabeth are compatible in 'that' area. You two are going to have to make babies, Michael. Lots!"

Michael laughed, "Don't worry cousin, we're compatible in 'that' area, as you call it. The opportunity just hasn't come up yet for us to... go all the way."

Nervous and uncertain, she persisted, "Well, you need to create the opportunity as soon as possible-"

He took her hand to escort her out of the room, "Stop worrying, cousin. I assure you, I have it all arranged."

"Is everything alright?" Elizabeth asked Michael as he walked up to her.

"Everything's fine. Susan just needed assurance about something of great importance to our family. Dance with me?" He held out his hands as he saw Susan instruct the butler to change the music.

Susan came up to them and smiled at Elizabeth, "This music is in your honor, Elizabeth."

The sweetest classical music filled the room. The mahogany paneling on the library's walls vibrated gently as the unique melodious sound of the drums crescendoed, and then abruptly softened again into a flowing lilting rhythm. Elizabeth gasped, "Oh my gosh! I can't believe it! Where did you get this Susan?"

"I didn't. Michael brought it with him."

Elizabeth turned to him, a surprised thrilled expression lighting up her face, "I'm amazed. I never thought I'd hear this music again. My parents had it on an L.P. record years ago but between being played too often and the humidity in Trinidad, it got badly scratched and warped. We couldn't find a replacement for it and eventually gave up. The Pan Am North Stars Steelband disbanded, I think, before I was born. I thought we'd lost this music forever. It's among the most exquisite Steelband classical music I've ever heard. How did you find it?"

With a mysterious twinkle in his eyes and smiling in delight at seeing her so thrilled at his, to her, unbelievable accomplishment, he said, "One of the perquisites-" she joined in "of being a royal personage."

He pulled her close, they began to sway and she looked up at him, "You do realize this is not really a piece for dancing?"

Knowing it full well, but reveling in the feel of her body against his, swaying more, he said amorously, "With you, every piece is for dancing."

Out of the corner of her eye Elizabeth saw Henry approaching them, Linda tagging behind, and was relieved to see him walking normally. Even though she found him repulsive, she hated that she may have done severe damage to his foot, for she was truly a pacifist at heart.

Henry called out in an obstreperous voice, "Dancing? To classical music? Only you two would do such a stupidly weird thing!" They stopped dancing and turned to face him, Michael intending to give him a quiet dressing-down, but Henry continued in an unnecessarily loud scornful voice, "Oh, I hear it now! Steelband! From your little Trinidad, Elizabeth. Of course YOU people would dance to anything! It must be a big thrill for someone like you to come here, be entertained so extravagantly-"

Moving to stand in front of Elizabeth, Michael stopped him, "Henry, Elizabeth comes from a noble family, was educated in Europe and America and has traveled to more countries all over the globe than you even know exists-"

Henry sneeringly interrupted him, "Oh yes? And how did she do that-" Elizabeth sensed that something foul was about to leave Henry's mouth and instinctively wanting to protect Michael from being upset by it, quickly stepped in front of him as Henry snarled, "did she do it on her back with her legs wide open-"

Appearing in a flash as if by magic, John, the butler, and the youngest male guest, grabbed Henry and literally dragged him out of the room, into the front hall and down the steps to his car, Linda following, both screaming profanities at everyone.

Michael began to run after them when Susan grabbed his arm, pulled him back as she ran past and shouted, "Michael, no! The guards'll handle this! Look after Elizabeth! She's crying!" and she raced after the three vigilantes with their captive in tow.

Michael turned around to see Elizabeth surrounded by the three women and the two older men from the neighboring estates, Maria holding her around her shoulders while another serving maid was handing her a tissue. They were all talking simultaneously to Elizabeth, trying to comfort her, "Drunken fool," "Obnoxious bastard," "Egotistical moron," "Embarrassment to the Royal Family," "Should be outcast," "A black sheep," were among the remarks Michael could discern.

He pushed his way through the group and took Elizabeth in his arms, "I'm so sorry, darling. So very sorry."

Wiping her eyes, she said self-consciously, "I'm sorry to be such a cry-baby...but he was so crude and disgusting...I was so shocked...it was so embarrassing."

The vein in his neck pulsed, "I should have dealt with him earlier, it's my fault. I promise you, you'll never have to be around him again. I meant it when I said I'm disowning him."

Elizabeth showed her dismay, "Michael, no. You can't disown your family, your blood. Especially *your* family-"

Elizabeth was interrupted by shouts from the group around them as they pointed to the window behind her.

Everyone walked over and looked out to see Henry violently flailing his arms in the air, angrily screaming obscenities at Susan, John, the butler, the guest, and two security guards who materialized out of the bushes nearby. Suddenly, Susan gave him a solid slap across his face. The group gasped collectively as Henry spat at her and raised his hand to hit her back.

"That's it!" Michael shouted, his rage apparent to everyone, "He's dead!" He turned to run from the room, but Elizabeth and one of the men grabbed an arm each, and the others blocked him from leaving.

The oldest gentleman spoke quickly and firmly, "Prince Michael, don't go out there! You're much too angry and this could turn out badly! There are more than enough men there to handle the situation. Look!" the man pointed to the window and Michael turned around to look.

Elizabeth and the group ushered him back to the window to see the compact but furious John pummeling the much larger Henry with both fists. Henry fell through the open backdoor of his car, on top of Linda who was already seated in the car. John tossed his legs into the car like they were a sack of manure, slammed the door shut, and slapped the roof of the car telling the chauffeur to take off, which he did at a roaring speed.

John, his hair disheveled, his clothes in disarray, and his face bright red but smiling proudly, with Susan on his arm, led the vigilantes back into the library, "I believe a stiff brandy is called for. What say you, everyone?"

Everyone applauded and laughed saying, "Hear! Hear!"

After the butler and Maria served the brandy, the group sat around discussing the events of the evening. Elizabeth and Michael chose to forego the offered brandy and finish the Grand Marnier they had been sipping before all the drama transpired.

Michael lifted his glass to John, "A toast...to my hero."

Everyone joined in a rousing 'For He's A Jolly Good Fellow' after which Michael knocked his signet ring against his crystal liqueur glass to indicate that he wanted silence as he had more to say. He bowed to Susan and John, "I believe I speak for everyone when I say to the Jamestowns how appreciative we are to have been invited to this absolutely superb dinner party this evening." Various guests made different remarks of agreement and gratitude but Michael tapped his ring again for attention, "And, I understand we also owe a debt of gratitude to Elizabeth for her culinary talents in providing us with the major courses of the delicious repast we so enjoyed. Here's to Elizabeth."

The room filled with copious compliments and blandishments which Elizabeth accepted graciously while turning several shades of pink as the proudly smiling Michael continued, "For the protection and privacy of everyone present, I suggest we swear to complete secrecy about the events that took place here tonight. Do you all agree? Why don't we swear?"

Immediately everyone, with camaraderie, raised their right hand and said, "I swear."

John raised his glass smiling conspiratorially, "A toast. To good friends, who share secrets." Many repeated his words, all sipped their drinks.

CHAPTER 12

Elizabeth and Michael sneaked away from the group and went out onto the terrace. The moon was still full and lit up their surroundings with a soft blue light. With one arm around her waist he stood looking at the moon, sipping his liqueur, lost in thought. She regarded his handsome profile, taking him in with silent admiration, not just for his exterior beauty, but for the extraordinary man that existed inside. She knew deep in the center of her being she was totally captivated, and regardless of whatever happens in the future, she would love him forever.

Realizing she was staring at him, he turned to her, "What? What are you looking at?"

She said solemnly, "You. God help me, but I've fallen so totally in love with you Michael Alexander Stephen, I feel as though I'm possessed by you, body and soul."

Resting his glass in the hand of a vert-de-gris Venus statue, he embraced Elizabeth, "And I by you. I've never loved anyone, anything, this much."

They shared soft sweet sensuous kisses until Elizabeth, bothered by the way she had shown such weakness by breaking down and crying so much in front of Michael, released him, "I hate that you've seen me crying like some weak damsel-in-distress these past two days. I don't want you to think that I'm a fragile crybaby that has to be coddled, looked after, handled with kid gloves. Because I'm not. I'm actually a very strong person and can normally handle any situation without falling apart. It's just that my emotions have been on a rollercoaster for some time now because of…a traumatic event in my life that shocked me so badly, it left me deeply wounded, vulnerable and unsure of myself. But I'm working through it, and I'll come out of it even stronger than before."

Lifting her chin, he gave her a serious look, "Elizabeth, I never thought of you as anything but an extremely strong and amazing woman of great courage and spirited independence. You had every right to be upset with what happened tonight with Henry. And as for yesterday-"

She put a finger to his lips, "Yesterday was perfect. Let's not rehash anything about it, please?"

"Alright. But I wish you'd talk to me about the 'traumatic' thing you're struggling with, let me help you get over it." Having made the assumption that what he learnt from Jenkins about her ex-fiancé Frederico del Rico not giving up his longtime mistress to be the reason for her trauma and pain, he resolved to do everything possible to reassure her that she'll never have to endure another heartbreak over an infidelity.

She returned his serious look, "Michael, my darling, I don't want to talk about it and spoil everything, and you have already helped me, more than you'll ever know."

The seductive powerful voice of Elvis Presley wafted over them from an artificial rock speaker in the garden as he sang, 'It's Now or Never.' Michael held her in a tight embrace and they began to sway eurythmically in time to the music. Their bodies rubbing against each other sensuously, their breathing quickening, each felt consumed by love, and desire.

He kissed her ear and whispered "Let's ditch this party."

She felt a rush of exultation, "And go where?"

Kissing her ear again he pressed against her, "To my room."

Not looking at him, without speaking, she took his hand; they walked into the castle, and slipped upstairs to his suite.

Arriving at his door Elizabeth seemed to hesitate. Michael got a sinking feeling as he knew he should not force the situation. Despite the inferno raging inside him that he desperately needed to extinguish with her, he wanted her to know that he was not pressuring her, that it had to be her choice. His consideration for her feelings, his ability to put them before his own, implicitly convinced him as to how deeply and everlastingly he loved this woman. He looked at her earnestly, "Darling, I want you to be sure. If we go ahead, there's no turning back. We're making a serious commitment here."

Elizabeth clung to him in a tight embrace, practically squeezing him, her voice barely above a whisper, "Love me."

He kissed her tenderly, "Elizabeth, I loved you from the moment I met you, and I'll love you for all eternity."

Although feeling elated and secure to hear him say these marvelous words with such deep emotion, she realized he mistook her statement for a question. So that there would be no misunderstanding of what she meant, she took his face in her hands and with an amatorial gaze said passionately, "Make love to me."

Michael swept her up in his arms and carried her to the door, "Close your eyes."

"Why?" she murmured dreamily.

"Do you trust me?"

"Completely." She closed her eyes.

He opened the door, walked into the room and kicked the door shut behind them, "Open them."

Opening her eyes she caught her breath, wonderment flooding her face, "Michael, it's so beautiful! It's like a fairyland. How did you do this? Who did this?"

"Maria. I arranged it with her this morning."

Elizabeth gaped, looked around slowly, glancing at every nook and cranny in the room. The entire suite was ablaze solely with candlelight and a roaring fire in the marble fireplace. There were scores of flickering candles in candelabras and candlesticks of every size, shape and material. They were gold, silver, brass, bronze, iron, crystal, and porcelain, and were scattered all around the room, placed in every corner, on every table, nightstand, chest of drawers, desk, the mantelpiece, and even taller candelabras directly on the floor. The four-poster bed and antique furniture in the suite, though actually mahogany, walnut, and rosewood in color, all glowed in hues of gold and amber from the reflection of hundreds of fluttering flames; as did the white silk sheets on the bed and the pale green silk damask draperies that were drawn over the windows and balcony doors. The air was pungent with the sweet aroma of dozens of roses in every color in vases placed around the room.

Having taken it all in, her eyes rested on Michael adoringly, "You're amazing. It's the most romantic thing I've ever seen...I...I'm speechless."

He kissed her softly while still carrying her, walked over to a compact disc player, pressed a button, and the sexiest most emotional voice of any singer that ever romanced the planet serenaded them. She was not surprised that he would choose this music to make love with her. Despite Julio Iglesias being of an older generation, his music was timeless, and also universal as he sang in every popular language, and no other singer could touch a lover in the right places like Julio could; and somehow, Michael knew exactly how and where to touch her.

Michael gestured to the bottle of Clos du Mesnil 1995 chilling in a silver bucket, "Champagne for my lady?"

She smiled nervously, "No thank you, don't think I should."

Giving her a reassuring smile he put her down gently to lie on the bed, "I'm not going to either. I want to be completely alert to savor every moment of this first night with you."

He kicked off his shoes, knelt down at the foot of the bed, took off her shoes and began to kiss, then suck her toes, one by one. He wanted to experience and make love to every single part of her. Her entire body tingled with shameless desire. She sat up, eased herself toward him and kissed him quickly on his mouth, her tongue darting in and out, hardly touching his.

Although reveling in the romantic moment, an overwhelming sense of erotic urgency came upon her. More than a desperation to end her long abstinence, it felt strangely like a foreboding that they had too little time. Untying his bowtie, she pushed his jacket off his shoulders. He helped take it off completely and threw it on the carpet. She removed his onyx and diamond studs from their button holes, kissing him softly on his lips after each one came off, and dropped them on his jacket.

Opening his shirt, she fondled his breasts, leaned forward, and sucked his nipples. He remained on his knees enraptured with her, with this new pleasure she was giving him, his mind and body feeling strange things he had not felt before. He had the sensation that he was floating, flying, weightless. It was as though nothing existed but Elizabeth and he, nothing else was of solid matter. Time was at a standstill. They were in forever.

Standing upright he peeled off his shirt. She looked at his completely naked torso for the first time in the flesh, and her clitoris felt like her heart was beating down there as well as under her breasts.

Unbuttoning his trousers, she could see the bulge of his erect penis under the fabric, and was anxious to touch it but she had difficulty with the zipper. Impatiently, he ripped it open, dropped his trousers, pulled off his underpants and socks and threw them aside.

Bending over with her mouth open she was ready to enjoy, and give joy, to his tempting engorged phallus, but he whispered, "No."

Pulling her up to stand he turned her around, unzipped her gown and unhooked the crown brooch holding the crystal strap. He pulled her gown down to the floor and as he did so, she shimmied her hips to help him. He was delighted to see she wore no underwear. Looking at her round full buttocks moving tantalizingly in the shimmy, he could not resist it, knelt down and started kissing and sucking her flawless cheeks.

She turned around, pulled him up and whispered, "I want to look at you," and stood back away from him. Gazing at her, he stood motionless as her admiring rapacious eyes meandered from the crown that was his magnificent head, to all over the realm of his majestic naked body. Taking in the beauty of his exemplification of male perfection, she feasted her eyes on his squared broad shoulders proudly erect above his well-developed muscular chest, that she was pleased to see he left unshaven and natural with a fine soft mat of blond hair. This confirmed for her that, like her, his attention to physical fitness was more about the depth of health rather than the shallowness of vanity. She observed his nipples were as puckered as her own and almost as pink, his muscles on his abdomen firm and just defined enough to show he was well-maintained but not obsessively conceited about his body. She held in a smile when she saw his navel, it was recessed and had a cute look about it that made her want to tickle it with her tongue. Settling her eyes on his enticing phallus standing at attention in a most noble manner, her mind told her body or her body told her mind, she could not decide which seeing that the yearning was now rampant, that her waiting was over.

Looking at his glistening eyes she stepped towards him and said almost demandingly, "I love you. You are perfection. I want you in me. Now."

Michael put up his hands, and smiling sexily, gently pushed her away, "It's my turn to look at you."

She stood still, holding herself straight and stately, unashamed in all her naked womanly glory. She didn't take her eyes off of his, following them as they traveled all over her. He looked gluttonously up and down at her frontal nudity, absorbing every curve, every mound and valley of what he saw as the personification of the female form.

His eyes dwelt on the roundness of her full voluptuous breasts, their nipples flushed and protruding so enticingly, he had to hold himself back from suckling them so that he could first let his eyes drink in the rest of her.

Checking out her flat abdomen, he startled himself with a flashing vision of it rounded and filled with their unborn child, verifying for him that his instincts were right from the very beginning, 'She is *the one.*'

As his eyes settled on the brown tuft of hair she left growing on her pubic mound the anticipation of looking inside it, uncovering all its sweet mysteries before tasting, climbing, and entering to at last conquer the yearned for arduous mound, was more than he could bear.

He unconsciously licked his lips, his phallus now throbbing; but wanting to sustain the pleasure he was experiencing from seeing his love in the nude for the first time, he forced a control he never knew he had and said amatorially, "You, are the perfect one."

Looking down the length of those long and shapely legs, he envisioned them wrapped around him from top to bottom, literally. He turned her around to take in her back. Letting his eyes roam over her curvaceous torso, small waist and shapely hips, and settle on her voluptuously feminine buttocks, his control began to wane. Instinctively she knew it, backed up against him, and opened her legs. He placed his penis between her legs and she closed them over it, slowly gyrating her hips, causing her buttock cheeks to move titillatingly against him.

Stretching her arms up behind her to wrap them around his neck, they brushed against the sapphire and diamond choker still on her neck, *No! The beast will not be in my life tonight!* "Unclasp my necklace," she said quickly.

He was surprised, "But it looks so beautiful on you."

"Please Michael, it's…uncomfortable." He took it off, she put her hand back to receive it, unhooked the earrings, and swiftly threw the jewelry on their clothes on the floor as though casting away an unhappy memory.

Picking her up in his arms again he laid her on the bed. They kissed each other hungrily, both equally burning hot with rapacious desire. Kissing her inside her ear he whispered, "I love you." She whispered it back, caressing his body everywhere she could reach. He moved slowly down her body wetly kissing and sucking every part of it, neck, shoulders, breasts, navel, abdomen, and at last, that part of her she needed so desperately for him to get to. He kissed the insides of both thighs, deliberately unhurriedly working his way to her core.

As he licked then sucked on her vulva, her head began to swirl as though in a whirlpool. Plunging his tongue deep into her vagina, she suddenly felt as though all her blood was rapidly coursing through her veins heading for only that place, and she heaved her hips upwards to him in ecstasy.

Skillfully, he thrust his tongue in and out, his lips enveloping her lips, performing cunnilingus on her till she was close to orgasm. Knowing what was about to happen, she didn't want it that way for their first coupling of complete love. She wanted to feel all of him, and for him to feel all of her.

She called to him, "Michael stop, come into me." He didn't stop. He could not. For the first time he was tasting the delicious nectar of his goddess. She sat up, lifted his face and looked in his eyes pleadingly, "I want your penis in me, your body on me, your tongue in my mouth. I want all of you."

He kissed her open mouth. Her excitement heightening on tasting herself, she fell back on the bed as he moved to lie on top of her. But suddenly, as though some other entity took possession of him, he stretched over to the side, opened the drawer in the night table, and started rummaging in it.

Astonished at this unbelievable and unwelcome interruption, she said quickly, "What's wrong?"

He murmured embarrassedly, "I'm trying to find a condom."

She held his face and looked into his eyes, "Why?"

Incredulity hit him, "You don't want me to wear one?"

With absolute trust she said, "I want everything you have to give me. I want to feel your juices pour into me."

Appreciating the faith she bestowed on him and the special eroticism of her, he said passionately, "God, I love you."

He mounted her and entered her slowly, inch by delicious inch, feeling the warm moisture inside her vagina surrounding the head of his penis in a sea of rapture.

She felt the strength of his rock hard phallus and the thickness of it beginning to stretch her insides willingly to receive it, *God, even though I want him more than anything, this hurts, it's been too long, and he's so deliciously big. Ah, but how sweet is the pleasure that comes with the pain.*

Michael felt her tightness, saw her suddenly wince, and backed off slightly, knowing his exceptional size and recalling what she had said about knowing only one man. Wondering how long ago that might have been, he whispered throatily, "Am I hurting you? You tasted so ready, shall I stop?"

She clung to him, pulling him back in, "No! Don't leave me. Just go slowly…it's been…a while…for me, but you have me more than ready, give me everything. I love you, Michael."

Kissing her mouth he murmured, "I love you," and continued his unhurried lengthy journey into perfect paradise.

As she fervently accepted his all, she squeezed her buttocks tightly and began to move under him. He felt her vagina cling onto his organ in a tight grip, every now and then relaxing slightly with each rise of her hips, each deep penetration of his phallus. They moved rhythmically together, synchronized in harmony as though of one body one mind one soul.

She felt herself get wetter with his pre-come which spurred her on closer to orgasm. He wanted to wait for her to climax with him but could not contain his any longer. His body began to shudder as his orgasm started; she felt her vagina filling with his semen. Feeling the texture of her vagina change around his penis, they both recognized they were actually climaxing together, sped up their movements, and as the full force of their orgasms peaked, each cried out, "Oh God! Yes! Yes!"

They sighed and moaned, their ecstasy overflowing. She kissed his chin, "Sweet, Michael, so sweet."

He slowed his movements, going in and out of her slower while still supporting himself so as not to lie heavy on her, and covered her face with soft kisses.

She clung to him when she thought he might get off her, "Don't leave me, darling. Stay in me."

He stayed, tenderly kissing her face all over and whispering, "I love you," with each kiss.

"I love you," she repeated after him each time, meaning it with all of her now unbroken heart.

Knowing his penis would not become flaccid while he remained inside her, and as much as he wanted to make love to her again, he thought it might be too soon, so he kissed her softly saying, "I want to hold you."

Wrapped around each other, they profusely declared confirmations of undying love.

CHAPTER
13

Needing to go to the bathroom, Elizabeth quietly eased herself off the bed as Michael seemed to have fallen asleep. His eyes flew open and he grabbed her hand, "Where're you going?"

She smiled with shy adoration, "Bathroom."

"Oh. I'm right behind you." He sounded relieved and she realized he was afraid she was leaving him to go to her room. He didn't know her well enough to know that she was not done yet. Loving him with all of her essence, now that she had seen all of him, felt him, smelt him, tasted him, knew him, she insatiably wanted him more than ever.

The bathroom was softly lit by six votive candles creating just enough light for vision. The sweet scent of roses in vases on the tub and vanity was pervasive, making her feel even giddier with desire for her precious passionate prince.

Finishing washing her hands at the marble sink, he came in and rested against her. His phallus felt as hard as velvet iron, and as hot as a poker in use. He moved over to the toilet and stood away from the bowl holding a huge erection down with both hands so as not to spray outside the bowl. She was fascinated by this and moved over to stand behind him. Something inexplicable compelled her to experience as much of him as quickly as possible. Acting on an incomprehensible impulse, she stretched her arms forward on either side of him, placed her hands above his, and helped to hold his penis downwards.

Incredulous that she would do this, his erection became even more turgid. Turning around when he was finished she surprised him by jumping up onto him, flinging her arms around his neck and wrapping her legs around his hips. His penis found her opening immediately, sliding in fully with little effort this time, she was already wet and willing. Grabbing her buttocks, they clung tightly to each other, their mouths bonding. He took control of their actions, moving in and out at a leisurely pace, trying to prolong their pleasure, to delay his ejaculation, wanting them to climax together again. Intuitively knowing his intention, her sexual senses became even more heightened. She loved that he was not only an extremely hot-blooded sensitively passionate lover, but was also a romantic fool like herself.

Her orgasm was close and she felt she must let him know. Just as she started to say, "Faster," he sped up his movements. He already knew, he could actually feel the change in her vagina. As their fluids joined together, they moaned and exclaimed in unison, "I love you."

They lay in bed whispering sweet words of endearment, arms and legs wrapped around each other, contentedly dozing from time to time. Eventually, Elizabeth murmured, "I have to bathroom."

Michael said quickly, "Hurry back."

She did, to find him lying on his back with his erect penis seemingly, unbelievably, more swollen and elongated than before. *Wow! He's limitless!* "My God! You're insatiable!" she teased.

He smiled seductively, "I suspect I'm in equal company."

Wetting her lips she looked at him lasciviously, "Don't move, until I tell you." She straddled him, and on her knees, crept up to his face. Open-mouthed, she kissed his chin, cheeks, forehead, eyelids, ears, and lastly his mouth, whereupon he embraced her.

Removing his arms from around her she placed his hands to grip onto protruding carvings of cherubs on the bed's headboard. Wishing she had something with which to tie them on, she reproached, "I said don't move, remember?"

He moaned in delight at her expectation that he could be submissively under her domination. She worked her way down his front, kissing and sucking on almost every inch of it.

She stayed her tongue in his navel for a long time swirling it around. Sensing his excitement, his tumescence increasing, she knew he was going wild with desire, his anticipation driving him crazy as he squirmed under her. She reprimanded softly but demandingly, "Do... not...move." Seeing her reach his blood-engorged phallus he moaned loudly, expecting her wet mouth to relieve his pain, delivering the satisfaction he desperately needed. She ignored it, went straight to his testicles, and lavished them with wet gentle kisses, caressing his buttocks simultaneously. He squirmed again. Again she reprimanded, "You...are...moving."

Writhing, he gasped, "Sorry! You're making me insane!"

"Hush, no moving," she commanded, knowing he was now totally under her control, mind, body, soul. She rubbed her breasts up and down between his inner thighs and over his phallus. He sighed and moaned softly. Unpinning her long silky hair and taking it in her hands, she wrapped it tightly around his penis and proceeded to rub her hair up and down over it, tightening the hair every few seconds, then releasing it again.

Barely able to speak, gasping, he begged, "Oh God, woman, I'm going to explode! You're torturing me! Take me! Please!"

Knowing he was almost past his limit, and wanting him to know that she was really about pleasing him, she asked in a beguiling voice, "How do you want me?"

He gasped, "On top me, I want to be in you! Now!"

She mounted him, and as his covetous penis plunged into her depths, she ordered, "Now you can move," and as he did, she gyrated on him, her own body overly stimulated by all the intense pleasure she had been giving his.

They climaxed in unison again, for the third successive time; a first for both. This time, Michael called her name, "Elizabeth, oh God, I love you. Say you'll be mine forever."

She panted in return, "Michael, I love you. I'm yours forever." Kissing him tenderly, she slowly rolled off him.

Turning onto his side he faced her, his face glowing, reflecting her glow, "We came together three times consecutively, isn't that awesome?"

"Amazing," she responded shyly.

Propping his head up on an elbow he held her face with his free hand, "This has never happened to me before."

"Nor to me," she said demurely. "Michael, do you think it's that important? That we come together?"

"No, not at all. I just found it so unique, that's all. Things are happening with us that haven't happened before. It's like something's confirming we're meant for each other. Don't you agree? Don't you feel it?"

"Yes," she replied, then added, "But Michael, I want you to know, I don't care when you come. Regardless of if it's quick or slow, don't worry about me, I always come."

His face lit up, "Really? How do you manage that?"

"I don't know," she giggled, "just lucky I guess."

He leaned over and kissed her, "I'm the lucky one."

Pulling her back into his arms he whispered hoarsely, "I like what you did with your hair."

Rubbing his chest hair she giggled, "Something new to you?"

He wished he could ask where she learnt to do that but knowing he shouldn't, said seriously, "Definitely. Someday I'm going to tie you up and torture you like you just did me."

She wriggled out of his arms and sat up to guardedly look in his eyes, "Oh? Your Royal Highness does kinky bondage?"

Grinning wickedly, he pulled her back down to rest her head on his chest, "I'll do whatever I have to, to keep you satisfied. And I'm going to make you love it, and beg for more."

She suddenly felt fearful and unsure, "Really?" She paused a moment, "But just making love with you will keep me satisfied, Michael. I…I hope I'll always be enough for you."

He read her surfaced insecurity, held her chin and said reassuringly, "Just having you in my life is enough, my darling. You in my arms is all I really need."

Regaining her confidence she stroked his now flaccid penis, "Oh really? I don't agree. And I know *he* doesn't either. Neither is that all *I* need." She slithered her body down against his, and as her sex-swollen lips lined up with his swelling penis, she swathed it with her hot wet talented tongue and mouth. Suckling and nibbling on it until it elongated to touch the back of her throat, she had to ease away from him slightly; but without stopping, she alternated between sucking hard and soft until he burst forth with sweet release, screaming her name.

Holding in a mouthful of semen she rose and kissed his open mouth, filling it with his semen, and said, "See how delicious you are? This is why me in your arms is not all we need."

He swallowed, and grabbing her with a salacious grin, went down to her core, "Right back at you, babe."

Massaging her clitoris with his full lips, thrusting his tongue in and out of her depths, he masterfully brought her to another orgasm. Not swallowing her fluids as he loved to do, he deposited them in her mouth, murmuring, "I agree. I'll always need *your* delicious juices to sustain *me*."

Michael awakened first and stared at his angelic sleeping beauty for a long time. He felt himself overflowing with love for this incredible woman, yet he also felt fearful. He told himself this sense of foreboding that came over him sometimes was simply a reminder of past hurts in his life and therefore should be ignored. He could hardly believe how lucky he was to have at last found his precious angel, his soulmate, his perfect match, in every way. Pondering on all their profuse lovemaking throughout the night he smiled to himself in delight and gratitude. Then, thinking of some things she had done to him, the fangs of that green-eyed monster called Jealousy were bared as it crawled into the erotic scene in his head. *Where did she learn these things? Damn! Did Frederico teach her? He was older, more experienced, not only married before but had a mistress on the side. No! Elizabeth is such a loving sensual woman I'm sure sexuality comes naturally to her. Anyway he's out of her life now, permanently. Screw you Frederico, she's mine now. All mine.*

Sensing his eyes upon her, she opened hers and looked at him, "Bonjour," she said, smiling sweetly.

"Bonjour," he responded, similarly smiling sweetly.

"Did you have a good sleep?" she enquired shyly.

"The absolute best ever."

The early morning light peeped through slits of the drapes drawn over the windows and doors to the balconies, allowing them to barely see each other, all the candles and the fire having long since burnt out. Turning to fully face him, she felt the bed wet under her thigh.

Wondering how their fluids could have soaked that area so thoroughly she pushed the sheet down to have a look, and cried out, "Oh no! I got my period. It's not even due for weeks. Gosh, this is so embarrassing! The bed's wet with it." She grabbed the sheet again, pulling it up to hide her almost bloodred face.

Pulling the sheet down from her disconcerted face he chuckled, "This is momentous. To think I've such power over you I changed your menstrual cycle."

Though grateful he could jest about something so mortifying to her, she hid a smile, "Not funny Michael."

The love in his eyes was convincing, "I think it's awesome. I can't wait to share this new experience of you. Don't move. I have to go to the bathroom, I'll be right back."

He pecked her on the tip of her nose, stood up to leave, and that's when she saw it, "What's that? Michael, you have blood on the back of your thigh, it's a cut…no, a gash!" She pulled the sheet down again, looked at her genitalia and saw no blood there, "Michael, it's *you* who's bleeding, not me!"

He twisted his body and looked back at his thigh, "Damn! The dressing came off. Not surprising though, with all the vigorous sex we had."

"Dressing? You mean it's that bad? Come here, let me look at it." She sat up on the edge of the bed as he reluctantly backed up, "My God, Michael, this is a huge wound! It looks really deep. How did you get it?"

He faked nonchalance, "Oh, it happened in the West Country. A madman stabbed me with a…a…table knife, but he was quickly apprehended…returned to the lunatic asylum he escaped from. Um…he didn't even know who I was, seems was just jealous of the attention I was getting."

He was proud of himself that he could concoct this story so quickly, he never thought he would have to explain it to her, he thought the damned thing would have healed by now.

Elizabeth's voice shook as that strange foreboding entered again, "A knife! How could the guards allow someone to get so close to you with a knife!?"

Seeing the fear in her eyes he continued in an even more flippant manner, "It was just one of those freak situations, a crowded area with outdoor cafes. He grabbed it off a table when I was passing and lunged at me through people's legs. Anyway, he was caught and is safely back in an institution."

Horror overtook her, "Jesus, Michael, that's frightening! They must make sure you are never, ever, put in that kind of situation again! We must get this attended to immediately! Let's get you to a hospital. You need a bunch of stitches."

"Oh no, darling, no hospital. We've done everything possible to prevent the media from learning about this. Elizabeth, if it gets out there was any kind of attack on me…we could have a revolution on our hands. Jenkins, and now John, have been cleaning the wound and dressing it with steri-strips, butterfly stitches. John'll put more next time."

She stood up, tears moistening her eyes, and spoke with determination, "Michael, no! This wound is much worse than you think. It can't possibly heal without proper stitches! Already it looks like it's going to leave an ugly scar. A royal prince should not have an ugly scar. Now, call somebody to get a doctor over here immediately!"

He wanted to laugh and make a joke in reference to her remark *"a royal prince should not have an ugly scar,"* but thought better of it. He knew by the look on her face, the tears in her eyes, and the tone of her voice, it would not at all be appreciated. "Yes ma'am," he said quickly, and punched in John's personal number on the house phone, "John, this thing has opened up rather badly. Elizabeth says I need some real stitches. You know a doctor we can trust who'll come out here?"

John thought for a second realizing what must have happened for Elizabeth to have seen the wound, then said slowly, "I know just the man. He knows all our family secrets. I'll call him immediately. Incidentally, he's Susan's gynecologist."

"Oh…" Michael mused over that last bit of information, "but…he *can* stitch me up, right?"

"Of course, Michael, he's a doctor. I'll call him now."

Hanging up the phone, Michael turned to Elizabeth, unmistakable humor lighting up his face, "Guess who's coming to stitch me up?"

"Who?" she asked, wondering, in light of the seriousness of his wound, what he could possibly think was so funny.

His smile broadened, "Susan's gynecologist."

"A gynecologist!" she exclaimed, and burst out laughing, falling backwards on the bed.

Michael fell back on the bed beside her, also laughing hilariously at the ludicrousness of the entire situation.

After they caught their breaths Elizabeth turned to him grinning wickedly, "We'd better get showered and dressed before *your* gynecologist gets here." They laughed uncontrollably again.

Eventually, realizing time was running short, they got up to get ready for the doctor's arrival. Michael took her hand, "Shower with me?"

She smiled modestly, "That could be dangerous, Sir, I don't think it's wise."

He didn't return the smile, "Please? I don't want you to leave me."

She too became serious, "I don't want to leave you either. But you must promise to behave."

"I promise."

They poured soap on washcloths and began rubbing their bodies. Unable to resist her, he dropped his washcloth and pulled her into a tight embrace. She could feel his manhood rising against her and said softly, "You promised to behave."

He replied, not softly, "I *am* behaving. I'm behaving like a naked man in a shower with the most incredibly beautiful naked woman." Standing under the hot shower, their hot bodies entwined, with Michael's hot blood running down his leg to join the hot water, they pleasured each other for the fifth time.

Michael walked through the door that joined their two suites without even knocking. Elizabeth had unlocked her side on returning to her room to get dressed. Gone was the need for coy formalities between them. They now shared the most intimate bonding that exists between a woman and a man, all barriers were down, forever demolished.

He thought out carefully what he would say to get rid of her before the doctor arrives. He knew the doctor, being a professional, when he saw the wound, would see through the story he had fabricated for Elizabeth. He would have to tell the truth, especially to describe the actual kind of knife with which he was attacked. Remembering the fear and tears in her eyes when she saw the wound, he knew she was not ready to handle the dangers and perils of his position, and he wanted to spare her any more anguish, at least for now. "Darling, do you mind going down and ordering a huge breakfast while the doc's stitching me up? I'm famished."

"Oh? Don't you want me to stay and hold your hand?" She smiled, but was deadly serious and he knew it.

He faked a laugh, "I can handle it alone, I'm a big boy."

Glancing down at his crotch then up at his face, she teased, "That indeed you are, a big boy."

Reaching out he grabbed her, "I'm not sure if to take that as a compliment or a complaint."

She fastened her eyes on his seriously, "Michael, there's absolutely nothing about you that I could ever complain about. You are perfect for me."

His eyes reflected hers, "And you for me. You realize we are the perfect match. The perfect fit, in *every* way?"

"Yes." They kissed, a soft, sweet, slow, sensuous kiss.

John's voice could be heard coming up the stairs.

Michael said quickly, "Do you mind if the doc stitches me up in your room? Unlike mine, it's neat and tidy," grinning, he added, "besides, mine reeks of sex."

She giggled, "Not surprisingly."

Still holding her, he said, "After breakfast, I'm going to give you the thrill of a lifetime."

"More thrilling than last night? That's not possible."

"True. But this is a different kind of thrill. An adventure you haven't mentioned you had before, and I'm really excited that I could do something different for you."

"You've already done many things different for me."

"Great," he smiled, "but not like this. And don't eat too much breakfast."

"But you just said you're famished."

"I am. It's you I'm concerned about."

"You have me completely intrigued. What is it-"

"It's a surprise."

"Oh, oh, I don't like the sound of this."

"You'll love it. I know you will."

Michael ate an enormous breakfast but reminded Elizabeth not to do the same. Like little children in a sugar rush, they raced each other up the stairs to brush their teeth and wash up. Having finished first Elizabeth walked boldly into his room. She too did not feel the need to knock. She already felt she was a part of him, his body, his soul, his life.

He smiled his impish smile, "Sorry, you'll have to change, you look too good for what we're about to do. Put on stretch jeans, and just a comfortable sweater. And...don't wear any underwear, it'll make you...uncomfortable."

Underwear will make me uncomfortable? Elizabeth was about to question him as to what the heck he was up to, but changed her mind. She felt she could trust him implicitly, even when she felt somewhat skittish, as she did right now.

CHAPTER
14

Brian and his portly partner Eric arrived at the front door. Elizabeth looked at Michael, "What are they doing here?"

He was succinct, "They're going with us."

"Okay. So tell me now, where're we going?"

"Nope, don't want to spoil the surprise." He hustled her onto the backseat of Eric's car.

Driving out of the gate she noticed a car with Jenkins, Tommy, and another body guard, pulled up behind and followed.

They drove for nearly an hour, Michael and Brian talking nonstop, Michael questioning Brian about the latest 'goings-on' at the palace and the outside world. Elizabeth observed that in the privacy of the car, away from the watchful eyes of all the other guards, Michael, Brian, and Eric no longer had the formal relationship of prince and commoner employees but instead acted like best buddies. She stayed silent listening attentively, hoping to catch a slip-up, at least get an inkling, of what was about to happen. Frustratingly, the men often spoke in a sort of code. The only thing she got from them was an occasional smile, and a squeeze of her hand and wicked winks from Michael.

The cars drove straight up to what looked like an airplane hangar and everyone got out. She heard the drone of a small plane, looked up and saw two brilliantly colored parachutes floating high up in the sky, two bodies dangling from each.

She shouted at Michael, "Skydiving! We're going skydiving?"

His face lit up mischievously, "Yes! Supri-i-i-ise!"

A nervousness crept into her, "You're crazy. And what makes you think I haven't done it before?"

His disappointment showed, "Well, with all the other things you mentioned you'd done, that's the one thing you didn't talk about. Darn, I hope you haven't?"

"No, actually. I was going to. In Sarasota, Florida. One winter we were at Granger's house for a weekend, I was sixteen and begged them to let me do it but not tell my parents in Trinidad. They eventually agreed and we drove all the way out to the site, I got suited up with my instructor and everything, but Auntie Ruth got scared for my safety and called my mother, who nearly had a stroke. The jump was cancelled. I was furious. I didn't speak to them the rest of the day."

He grinned, "Well, you'll definitely be speaking to me, because there'll be no cancellation today."

Elizabeth looked timorous, "I don't know, Michael. I was so much younger then, with no responsibility for anyone else. And I *know* I'm not invincible now, like I *thought* I was back then."

He spoke determinedly, "Darling, it's perfectly safe, you're with me. We'll be strapped together in tandem-"

Prudence joined her hesitancy, "Then we could both get killed. What if the parachute doesn't open?"

Pulling her to him, he teased, "Well, we'll just die together. What better way to die than in each other's arms." She pushed him away but he pulled her back, "Come on, you know I'm kidding. I promise we'll be perfectly safe. Brian and I have been jumping for years. We got certified together, have our own chutes, double check them ourselves. Darling, you think I'd risk our lives just as we've found each other and have an awesome future together to look forward to? Don't you want to feel what it's like to fly? That ultimate feeling of freedom?"

"Yes, of course. I always wanted to, and bungee jumping in New Zealand and parasailing in Mexico were both a bit disappointing. I know this would be more fun, more freeing…okay. But promise you'll hold on to me."

"I'll never let you go," he kissed her tenderly, "now come on, let's get suited up, then I'll double check the chute."

"Is Jenkins jumping too?" she asked, showing surprise.

He gave her a playful smile, "No. He stays on tierra firma so he can report if anything happens."

Her eyebrows shot up sharply, "Anything happens?"

Wickedly, he suppressed the smile, "You know, like if you and I end up looking like scrambled eggs on the ground."

"Michael! Don't tease. I might change my mind."

Grabbing her hand he said encouragingly, "No you won't. You love me too much not to experience this with me."

Looking at the elderly bearded obese pilot as the plane taxied for takeoff, Elizabeth whispered nervously to Michael, "He looks older than Santa Claus, and twice as big."

Michael's booming laugh filled the small plane.

He said reassuringly, "Don't worry, he's been flying before we were born. Anyway, if he decides to conk out, I learned how to fly during military service, mostly jets, but I could easily fly this small plane."

Elizabeth said simply, "Me too."

Michael gaped at her, "What? You fly?"

"Yes. I have a turbo-prop Cessna. We…my family…use it to go to islands in the Caribbean."

Michael caressed her face with his ungloved hand, "Woman, you just continue to amaze me. I can hardly wait for whatever surprises you're going to hit me with next."

Brian called out, "I think I should jump first. Agreed?"

Michael yelled back over the noisy drone of the plane, "Roger." He stood up, pulled Elizabeth up, and Brian and he strapped her to him and the harnesses, her back to him.

Michael spoke in her ear with more calm than he felt, "Now darling, the free-fall is going to be the most exciting part of the jump." Not wanting to put pre-suggestion in her head he decided against telling her that, especially to a skydive virgin, it is also the scariest. "I want you to relax, enjoy the freedom of flying on our own, so stretch out your arms with me and absorb the feeling, the most free you'll ever feel, totally liberated. After I pull the cord to open the parachute, you're going to feel a strong jerk as it unfolds and pulls us up higher. But the motion smoothes out and we just float in the air and enjoy the peace, and the views, which are incredible. Don't worry about the landing, if you think you can't run with me just lift your legs, I can run for both of us."

With the mention of legs, Elizabeth was reminded of Michael's stab wound, "Wait! What about your stitches? Michael, I don't think this is a good idea, what if-"

Grinning, he hugged her over the strappings, "Oh no, you're not going to chicken out on me now. I won't let you use me as an excuse either. I told the doctor what we were going to do and he put a special bandage around my leg to keep everything in place. He said it'll be fine, so stop worrying, let's just enjoy this."

Brian opened the door. Stretching his body out like a giant bird, he shouted, "Liberty!" and jumped off.

Standing at the edge of the opening Michael said in her ear, "Know I love you more than anything more than life itself." With a strong push with both his feet, they were airborne.

Elizabeth could not believe her heart rate could increase more than it already had when Michael dove off the plane with her, but it did, and seeing the ground rapidly coming towards them she began to scream. Grabbing her hands he stretched her arms out to emulate wings, shouting, "Don't look down yet! Look at the far horizon! Relax! Think you're a bird! Fly baby! Fly!"

Quickly obeying his instructions, she relaxed for a few moments, and felt an exhilarated feeling of freedom unlike anything she had ever felt before, anything she could ever have imagined. She started to look around but made the mistake of looking straight down again. The realization that the ground was thousands of feet closer than it was just seconds before, and with the wind loudly whistling past them as they hurtled downwards, she became gripped with terror and screamed, "Pull the cord Michael! Pull the cord!"

He screamed back, "Not yet, it's too soon!"

Fear enveloped her, "No it's not! Pull the damn cord!"

He shouted his assurance, "It's too soon, darling! We'll end up tangled in the chute in those trees! We must clear that area! I know what I'm doing!"

She believed he did, but seeing the ground now even closer, she pictured them "*looking like scrambled eggs on the ground*," and screamed hysterically, "Oh God! We're going to die!"

Hearing the hysteria in her voice and thinking they had reached a good spot, he pulled the ripcord. They jerked violently upwards as the parachute unfurled and the strong wind swept them higher into the unending blue space of the heavens, the proverbial dwelling place of the gods.

Michael felt her rigid body relax at last against his and said, "I love you. You did great. You're my hero."

She shouted with more relief than anger, "Well you're not mine! I love you too, but I'm going to kill you when we land. You terrified me, taking so long to pull the cord."

He hugged her, "Honestly, I didn't darling, I did it at the right time. I wasn't going to pull any daredevil stunt with your life in my hands. I'd never do anything to put you in harm's way. I want you to know that."

She did not respond verbally but instead pressed her body against his, pulling his arms tighter around her to show she was reassured. Releasing all the tensions of her mind and body, she concentrated on appreciating the magnificent views.

As they floated slowly downwards Michael spoke softly with reverence as though they were in a holy place. He described the topography, flora and fauna within their range of visibility, pointing out and sometimes naming different mountains and hills, meadows and valleys, lakes and rivers, cultivated fields and those of wild flowers. He directed her attention to scattered mansions and houses, farms and barns, ant-size people, animals, birds, anything he thought would be of interest to her.

Taking in nature's verdant mosaic of dense forests and open fields interspersed with wildlife and evidence of humanity's touch, Elizabeth filled with awe. To see the earth for the first time with her body suspended openly in the sky was phenomenal. Even the thrill she experienced the first time she looked out the cockpit window of her plane at a higher altitude did not compare with the unconfined feeling of enjoying this panoramic view of the creation of the gods. Despite her protective goggles there was no restriction to her vision, she felt she could see beyond perpetuity. Relishing the endless vistas, the elated lovers reveled in the serenity and breezy quietude.

Eventually finding her voice Elizabeth said gratefully, "Michael, it's truly the most marvelous, breathtaking view I've ever seen. Thank you darling for the thrill of a lifetime."

"You're welcome, but I plan to get paid."

"I'm still going to kill you when we land, putting me through the scariest experience I've ever had in my life."

"Okay," he chuckled, "and how do you propose to do that?"

She smiled to herself, "I don't know yet. I haven't thought it out. But I promise you, it'll be slow…and painful."

He licked the back of her neck, "I look forward to it."

"You're a pervert."

"Takes one to know one."

"You've corrupted me."

"And how sweet it is.'

Knowing where this banter was heading, knowing they could presently do nothing about it, she squeezed his hands affectionately, "Shush, let's just enjoy the views."

They floated along in silence, lost in the angelic feeling of flying freely in the heavens, each with a tranquil sense of complete peace neither had experienced before. In all his years of skydiving, the jumps he made, whether for a thrill or to sort out his thoughts, or both, never before had he felt this totally uplifting sensation of absolute peace combined with ultimate joy. At last he found what he had been searching diligently for, his perfect mate, the woman who will be his life's partner, who will always be at his side to support him in the life and role he was destined for. The woman he loved beyond measure, who made him feel secure that she loved him the same, who made his life complete, now flying with him, cradled in his arms, his angel.

Elizabeth envisioned their souls soaring in fusion with the cosmos. Her feelings of weightless peaceful freedom transported her thoughts to a world without cares or fears, a life of endless loving contentment. Now at last she had a man who loved her as much as she loved him, who would be faithful to her, never betray her or let her down. A man she could rely on forever, truly, a prince of a man. Her thoughts of love, stability, and happiness, were interrupted by a disturbing reminder of the difficult decisions she still had to make, the unavoidable unpleasantness that yet lay ahead. She pressed his hands against her body, "Michael, no matter what happens in our lives, wherever the winds may blow us, I'll love you forever."

Michael stayed silent, mused over what she said, cogitated her meaning, and became discomposed. He hated being incognizant of whatever it was that troubled her from time to time, bringing an enigmatic sadness to her usually felicitous eyes. Convinced it involved Frederico Del Rico in Spain he wondered how bad the situation had been, but knew he had to be patient and give her time to overcome the "*traumatic*" thing. He was confident he could assist her in that endeavor but wished she would communicate with him about it. He felt he could get her to open up soon, but for now, must bide his time.

Not getting a response from him, his silence was now making her uncomfortable, "Michael, I don't care if you may hate me one day, I will always love you. Always."

It saddened him to hear her say he could ever hate her, but gladdened him to hear her say she will always love him, "Elizabeth, I could never hate you. I'll always love you. The winds will blow us wherever *we* want to go. Wherever I go, you will go with me, wherever you go, I will go with you. We'll be together forever, blowing our own winds."

She pressed her body against him, "You've brought me back from the depths of emotional hell and literally raised me up to a heavenly place. You've brought richness to my life that I never knew it was lacking. You're embedded in my very soul."

Feeling her body press against him more than before, the erection he had been trying to not take notice of from the time the parachute opened and he hugged her tighter became impossible to ignore. He strived to focus on returning her loving words, grateful of the heavy jumpsuits they wore and all the strappings that would not allow her to feel his physical when he wanted to be spiritual, "My darling you'll always be embedded in me, every aspect of my existence, in this life, and whatever lies beyond."

She sighed elatedly, "This is all so perfect, darling. I wish we could be like this forever."

He pecked the back of her neck, "I'm sorry darling, but we'll be landing soon, the wind's dying and I want to make it to our landing site. But I'd love to come back up with you, after we have some refreshments. You game?"

"Yes!"

Their landing was perfect, the steady breeze making it slow and smooth with little running necessary. Brian helped them get unharnessed and Eric and he picked up the parachute and took it back to the hangar to be examined and re-rigged. Elizabeth and Michael each drank some juice, then visited the two restrooms adjacent to the hangar.

Coming out of his first Michael pulled Jenkins aside, "Elizabeth and I are going to jump again, alone. We'll do it on the other side of the lake. Everything organized with the boat and picnic?"

"Of course, here's the key. The food's already set up in the refrigerator and on the table."

"Thanks. I'll call and let you know when to pick us up. Now, I want you to collect the men's binoculars, I don't want anybody looking at us for this jump."

Jenkins showed perplexity, "Why not? Michael, you know we need to watch you in case of an emergency."

"Not this time. And we'll be fine. But we'll need our privacy. You can have your binoculars if it'll make you feel better, but I'm warning you, you'll need to turn away at some stage. You'll find it too embarrassing."

"Michael, what the hell are you planning?"

Grinning wickedly, he winked at an edgy Jenkins, "After the freefall, which is going to be short, Elizabeth and I are going to make love while floating in the sky."

Jenkins wondered why he was surprised at his playful concupiscent charge, "Oh yes? She agreed to that? She was a bit nervous before. You had to talk her into the first jump."

"She doesn't know yet, but she'll agree."

"Huh! If she agrees to that, she's definitely for you."

"She *is*, Jenkins, she's my queen."

CHAPTER
15

Only after they were settled in the plane did Elizabeth notice Brian was not suited up and asked Michael why. He smiled seductively and said softly in her ear, "We're jumping alone, because we're going to make love while floating in the air."

"What! Are you crazy! That's impossible!"

"No it's not. We're going to do it."

"Oh? Have you done it before?" She looked at him accusingly.

"Course not, I've been saving it for you my love."

"You are nuts! I'm nervous enough about the free-fall-"

"I promise it'll be a very short free-fall, and you'll be facing me so you can't look down. Think how exciting it'll be, darling. Captain Santa Claus will fly to where we'd get the best upwind, we'll be on the other side of the lake where it's private, no one will see us. Brian's coming over shortly to strap you to me." He embraced and kissed her softly, "This is going to be something really special. Are you with me in this?"

She giggled nervously, "You crazy fool. Yes. You're lucky I'm so madly in love with you, with emphasis on the word *mad*-ly. So explain, how's this going to work?"

"Quick, Brian's coming over. Let's unzip our jumpsuits and push our pants down as far as possible, then cling to me before he gets here."

Brian followed Michael's instructions on how to attach them together to the harness facing each other instead of in tandem. He had a knowing smile which Michael kept distracting Elizabeth from noticing with idle chatter, certain that she would be mortified if she knew Brian had any idea of what they were about to attempt and would probably change her mind; and he could not hold out, or more correctly, hold in, much longer. Pecking the tip of her nose he whispered, "Don't be nervous darling, it'll be wonderful. I hope you're as excited as I am."

"I'm excited *and* nervous. I still think we're nuts, but I'll try anything with you Michael, I love you so much."

"I love you so much too, babe. Talking about nuts, you have me so flaming hot for you right now, my nuts feel like they're ready to erupt." They giggled, kissed, and giggled.

Brian opened the door and guided them to it. Michael said in her ear, "I promise the free-fall will be very short but if it makes it easier for you, close your eyes and kiss me," and immediately dove off shouting, "I love you my angel!"

Elizabeth could not close her eyes and her angst would not allow her to kiss him, too distracted by the tremendous speed at which they were falling; but true to his word, he pulled the ripcord much sooner than he had on their previous jump. They rose jerkily into a vertical position. She laughed with relief and delight. Michael looked deep into her eyes, "I want you."

Elizabeth riveted hers to his but said nothing vocally, she had her hands do the talking. She grabbed his fully erect penis with both hands and attempted to insert it into her, but she was too low down for him to be able to enter, "Michael, you're going to have to raise me up higher."

"Alright, but don't touch me there right now," he shivered, "I'm so darn hot for you I might come all over your stomach."

She giggled but chided, "Don't you dare. I'm not going through all of this to be left out. I'm going to pull up on the straps, lift me as high as you can."

As she hoisted herself higher, he grabbed her buttocks and pulled her upwards with all his strength, so determined was he to succeed in getting and giving this heavenly pleasure. The gods were definitely blessing them because even in this almost impossible position, they managed to make a complete connection as his penis slipped into her vagina, already moist with expectation. They clung to each other, she wrapping her legs around him as much as the strappings would allow. He groaned as he felt his orgasm coming on much sooner than desired. Feeling him spasm, she murmured, "Go for it babe, don't wait for me," and pressed against him as his ejaculation spurted into her.

He moaned, "Damn. I'm sorry darling, I just couldn't wait any longer. I wanted you since the first jump."

"Don't you ever apologize to me about that, my darling. Just hold me tight, stay in me."

"I'm not going to leave you until you come."

"I'm not sure I can Michael, I'm still a bit jittery."

"What? Remember, you told me you always come."

"I know, but this is a whole different thing-"

"We're not going to land until you're satisfied."

"But I am satisfied, I'm satisfied you came."

"Well, I'm not satisfied. I won't be until I make you scream." Still hard, he proceeded to move in and out, slowly, cautiously, making sure they stayed connected, whispering loving, sexy words in her ear, sucking it after every seductive sentence, every thrust of his pelvis. Elizabeth paradoxically became both stimulated and relaxed, taking him all in, his wordage, his manhood, his love. She clung to him, barely moving, fearful of losing their connection, she let him do all the work.

After he thrust his tongue deep inside her ear and murmured a particularly explicit graphically erotic sentence she whispered, "You are so devilish. Yet I feel as though we're two copulating angels, making love in flight while being watched over and blessed by the gods."

He whispered, "We are my darling. Now, let's take it to the most heavenly place, the highest of the highest. Come with me." Screaming each other's name, calling out to their creator in unison, they ecstatically reached the desired pinnacle.

They landed on the other side of the lake as planned.

Their landing was anything but smooth this time because Elizabeth could not run backwards; he had to carry her and run, causing them to take quite a tumble, ending up with half the parachute on top of them. With their spirits elated despite the clumsy return to tierra firma, they lay on the ground, arms and legs intertwined to the point that one could not tell where one body began and the other ended, laughing hysterically.

Calming to chuckles, they disentangled themselves from each other and the parachute. He led her onto a speedboat that was moored at a nearby jetty, taking delight in her delight at yet another one of his fun surprises. They assisted each other out of their jumpsuits and clothes, and observing that he was already beyond half-mast, she playfully shoved him over the side and dove in after him. Cavorting and splashing gleefully and tantalizingly, they heated up their bodies and desires in the cool waters of the lake, until they both knew it was time to curtail the amusing preliminaries and change their actions into something serious. He pointed to some shallows with mossy rocks jutting out of the water, told her there were hot springs over there and they swam to it.

He sat her on a submerged rock where she could rest her back against a taller rock, allowing her body to be exposed above the water from her breasts up. The water's surface was smooth except for gently lapping waves caused by the gushing of the underground springs, but it was crystal clear in the shallows. Becoming buoyant, Elizabeth's legs stretched out in front of her almost lifting her off the rock, but Michael leaned into her between them and held her down from floating away.

She wrapped her arms around his neck as his hands slipped down her back, one cupped a cheek of her buttocks, the other settled in the crack between them. He pulled her to him, the tips of her distended nipples brushing against his as a soft current of water rose up between them, and she clung tighter to him. He sought her mouth hungrily through the flowing wet strands of her long hair that floated like sea grasses swirling around them. Eventually releasing her from their fiery kiss, he bent his upper body backwards and thrust his hips forward.

She felt an inrush of warm water and hot muscle enter the part of her that was waiting for him to fill, and be fulfilled. With no sound but low loving sighs and the soft thrashing of the water as their two bodies joined in a synchronized water ballet, the lovers, their heads struggling to stay above water to keep from drowning, lost themselves in each other as their body's liquids intermingled with the body of liquid all around them.

Alternating swimming and floating, they made it back to the boat and heartily partook of the delectable picnic Jenkins had Michael's favorite restaurant in the village prepare for them. They took a thrillingly speedy spin around the lake, and then, seeing the inviting queen-sized bed in the boat's cabin, again heartily partook of each other.

Elizabeth was about to walk out of the ladies restroom adjoining the jetty when she overheard Michael talking to Jenkins, "Pick us up at eleven tomorrow to escort us back to the city. I must get back to work and Elizabeth needs to work on her speech. Remember, it's on Thursday."

She immediately phoned her friend Andrea who was supposedly getting her cousin's apartment for Elizabeth to stay in while he was away on business. She disliked relying on the scatterbrained but sweet Andrea for a place to stay, but felt it was her only option, apart from "*wasting*" money on a hotel, money she could use for The Children's Home. After her second date with Michael she decided against visiting her own paternal cousins who lived in the city. She had not told them yet about her speech, knew they would affectionately monopolize her time and attention, and she wanted to give it all to Michael. After the Grangers left she had phoned them to say goodbye, giving the impression she was rushing home for important business reasons.

The decision held some regret. Her cousin James, who she nicknamed 'Jamie,' and who she grew up with during her early childhood in Trinidad, but who left at eighteen along with his two siblings to be educated in Europe, was due back from a business trip momentarily. He was her favorite cousin, knew she was his favorite, and missed him a lot, since, after finishing university, he got a wonderful engineering job traveling all over Europe, and hardly visited Trinidad anymore.

Michael approached as she was arguing with Andrea, "But sweetie, I was really hoping to get my own place. Sure I would've loved to stay with you if I was vacationing, but I've work to do that requires deep concentration, no distractions. That's why I needed to be alone at Harry's-" Michael waved at her and made a time-out sign. Frowning at him, she said into the phone, "I'll call you back, something's come up."

Michael looked at her quizzically, "What's going on?"

"That was my friend Andrea who was organizing the loan of her cousin's apartment for me. She says he's postponed his trip for a couple weeks and I'm to stay with her till then. I'm not keen on that because, even though I love her dearly, she's a very nosy gossip, and I'm afraid you and I won't be able to see each other until I move out, so-"

Becoming puzzled, he interrupted her, "What're you talking about, you're staying with me."

"With you? At the palace? No Michael, I can't-"

"Of course you can, and you will."

"No Michael. It wouldn't be right-"

"What do you mean, what's more right than us being together"

"Not at the palace, with your family there. No Michael, I'll get a hotel room."

He drew her into his arms, "My family's all excited to meet you. I told them I have a new girlfriend who'll be my guest-"

Frowning, she pushed against him, "You told them about me!"

"Of course darling. The twins are thrilled about spending more time with you, and my father and aunts remembered you being presented to them at the garden party. You made quite an impression, not surprisingly. So you see, you'll be right at home, welcomed with open arms."

Her frown deepened, "Gosh Michael, no. I…I couldn't. It's too soon, too much…exposure…for me, right now. I…I don't want to shock my family about you yet. I…I have to tell them in person. Surely you understand, we must keep our relationship secret…private, for now-"

He interrupted with a reassuring smile, "Alright, we will. Remember, I have my own apartments, we can be as private as we want, we don't have to see anybody but trustworthy staff if we don't want to. If you're concerned about decorum, you can stay in your own suite adjacent to mine. The situation is similar to what we have at Jamestown's except a bit larger." He gave her his special persuasive smile that didn't make her feel manipulated and controlled, but instead desired and secure, "I assure you, my lady, I will take every precaution to ensure full propriety will be adhered to, at least in the presence of anyone you might feel uncomfortable with."

Her reticence wavered, "Michael, I don't know…I want to be with you, I can't stand the thought of not being with you. But to stay in your apartment at the palace just seems too…audacious, forward. You know what I mean."

Michael lost his smile, "I certainly don't. Darling, you *have* to stay with me. We've only a few weeks before you have to go to Trinidad, which already I'm dreading although I'm only letting you go for a short stay, just enough time to tell your family about me in person. But you can't leave me now, darling. What little time we have together is too precious to waste on even this discussion."

"But Michael-"

"No 'buts.' We belong together, now and forever. Please don't let's argue about this darling. Look, let's do this, my immediate family is having an intimate dinner party for us tomorrow, if anything happens that gives you the slightest bit of discomfort, we'll leave immediately and go to a hotel. Alright? Agreed?"

She sighed in surrender, "Alright. But you must know, I'm holding you to this agreement, Michael."

He found his smile again, "I never break an agreement."

There was a burning question at the back of Elizabeth's mind that she had to bring forth and voice, "So, how many of your 'girlfriends' have had this honor before me? Of staying in your apartment?"

Michael raised a surprised eyebrow, "None."

Astonishment shook her, "None! I don't believe it."

"I would not lie to you about this. Of course I've had sleepovers, but never before have I asked a woman to stay with me. You are the first. And the last."

Their last evening with the Jamestowns' was filled with fun and laughter. The two couples went from taking turns telling jokes they had heard, during dinner, to telling true humorous but embarrassing tales, after dinner, and another good bottle of wine. Wishing to give themselves a respite from shaking with hilarity, they then played Scrabble, which turned out to have the opposite effect as each person kept making up the most absurd non-existent words hoping to gain points, and that led to even more squeals of raucous laughter. By the end of the evening the strong bond that had developed between the four was undeniable. It was further cemented by the Jamestowns not simply insisting that Elizabeth and Michael return soon for a longer stay, but by Susan saying to Elizabeth in front of Michael, not jokingly, "God forbid, if things don't work out between you two, you know you're always welcome here."

Michael was slightly upset but at once immensely pleased by her words. It pleased him that two of the most important people in his life had not only accepted the love of his life but had become quite enamored with her and now understood why he was totally so. On the other hand, he felt disappointed there was even a thought that "things" would *not* "work out" between them, seeing that he was certain that his God was definitely forbidding that, not so long as God was with him and in him.

On returning to their suites Michael led her to his bed, but she said quietly yet firmly, "No, come with me."

He followed as she walked into her suite, and shifting from disappointment when she rejected him, to excitement at her taking him there, he said, "Ah, I see you like variety, my lady, you want a new venue…your bathroom this time. Alright, how do you want me-"

Standing behind him she said abruptly, "Drop your pants."

Surprised at her attitude but thinking she was going to give him a new and perhaps kinky treat, he hurriedly dropped his pants and grinned, "Are you going to painfully kill me now as you promised on our first jump? I meant it when I said I'm looking forward to it."

She bent down, "I plan to do that when you're perfectly healed, but nothing more is going to happen between us until I'm sure you can handle it."

Excited with anticipation, he became befuddled, "What do you mean? I can handle anything you do to me…Ow!"

She dug her index fingernails under the end of the two inch wide waterproof plaster the doctor had wrapped around his leg over his stitches, and swiftly ripped it off to expose the wound. She examined the stitches carefully, satisfied herself, and the surprised Michael, that everything was still intact, and after changing the bloodstained piece of gauze that was on the wound, she pressed the sticky plaster back onto its old place.

"Thank goodness," she said showing her relief, "it's alright. I was worried the stitches may have opened up…because of…what we… you know-"

Michael grinned, "The only thing I was worried about was keeping you satisfied, and happy," and he proceeded to do exactly that, all over again.

Arriving at The Palace the next afternoon they were greeted enthusiastically by the twins Megan and Mark, all Michael's personal staff, and, his 'mini menagerie.' This consisted of two overly-excited and rambunctious Great Dane dogs who, based on their unruly behavior, were ridiculously and inappropriately named Duchess and Duke; and, rescued from the pound, two cats of indeterminate breeds, the male suitably named Sampson as he was of a shorthaired variety and looked as though he had been given a bad haircut because he was balding in several areas, but the female's name, Delilah, was undeserved as she turned out to be the sweetest and most dignified of the bunch.

After the introductions were completed, during which Elizabeth felt the staff's eyes examining her scrutinizingly as though appraising her on an auction block to be bought as a slave, Michael dismissed them all, took her hand protectively, and led her to his apartments. He gave her a quick tour of his living and dining areas, study and kitchen, then led her towards the bedroom wing, watching her carefully as he opened a door, "This is my bedroom, darling. Yours is adjoining through that door, but I'm hoping you don't feel you have to use it. I want you to feel like this is ours, yours and mine."

Beginning to feel more comfortable and secure again, Elizabeth smiled, let go of his hand that he was aware she had been tensely clinging to, and started to look around, "This is absolutely beautiful, Michael."

"Yes? Do you really like it, not too masculine for you? Change anything you want to, I want you to feel at home-"

A boyish nervousness had crept into his voice and Elizabeth now felt she had to do the reassuring, "Don't be silly, darling, it's perfectly gorgeous, I wouldn't change a thing. As for being too masculine, not at all. In fact, it's quite androgynous, despite the male dominating colors, it has a sensuous softness to it. I really want to say, a certain femininity."

Michael raised an eyebrow, "Oh? You see that? Interesting. I did have some help from Susan and Aunt Anne in decorating but mostly I enlisted the talents of the palace decorator, a very masculine heterosexual man I might add. Of course, we had some constraints with the furniture, had to use historical pieces. I'm glad you don't find them too heavy, dark and overpowering."

"They are exquisite, very elegant, dignified and befitting your station. I absolutely adore the silk brocade fabric of the drapes and bedspread, the color blue with greenish hues in it. Does it have a name? I would call it 'peacock blue.'"

He smiled in surprise, "That's exactly what it's called. How did you know?"

She smiled back at him seductively, "Because it's perfectly titled for you, most appropriate."

He pulled her to him, "I want nothing more than to stay here with you and substantiate why I have this color. But unfortunately, I promised Papa I would go to see him as soon as I got you settled in, he's anxious to see my 'war wound,' and I know his spies would have told him of our arrival. So I hope you don't mind if I leave you for a short while in the capable hands of Celia, your personal maid. I'll send her in to help you unpack after which you should have a soak in the hot tub. I'll join you as soon as I can. Just ask Celia for whatever you need. Will you be alright without me, my darling?"

Kissing him softly on his lips, she murmured, "I will never be alright without you. Hurry back."

Celia was very efficient, and quickly had Elizabeth's clothes neatly ensconced in her dressing room in the dresser drawers and hanging in the richly carved and mirrored antique wardrobes, resting wrinkled articles on a chair in the main hallway to be ironed later. Although she treated Elizabeth with the appropriate amount of deference, Elizabeth got a distinct impression the respect was given begrudgingly. This set her to thinking there had been something between Michael and the woman he assigned to be her personal maid. She became determined to accost him with her suspicions on his return. Apart from the disdainful attitude she discerned from Celia, Elizabeth's distrust of her was fed by a tiny twinge of envy. Celia was not only very pretty but had a sexy shapely figure although she was a good bit shorter than Elizabeth, was young, though mature, and Elizabeth thought probably closer to Michael's age than she was. She was obviously totally familiar with everything in Michael's private space, moving around his apartments with haughtily proprietary comportment.

Additionally, she spoke to Elizabeth without looking directly at her and only concisely. Elizabeth realized she was subtly trying to make her feel like an intruder, someone not worthy of being in the royal household clique.

Her first inclination was to tell Celia to leave and never return. Then rethinking she should be dignified and calm, not let, *That woman,* have the satisfaction of knowing she could unnerve her, she smiled sweetly, thanked her for her help, and told her she was dismissed for the rest of the day as her services would not be required, because Prince Michael would be only too willing to assist her with getting dressed for the evening.

Celia glared at Elizabeth contemptuously, turned on her heels disdainfully, and nostrils flaring but her nose pointed to the ceiling, strutted out the door, violently slamming it shut. Elizabeth became more than unnerved, she heated to a simmering anger, and decided to take Michael's suggestion and 'cool down' in the therapeutic waters of the hot tub.

His Majesty, King Alexander the Fourth, was indisposed. Unsure of what ailed him, he put his indisposition down to feeling rejected. By his own son no less. He had literally been worried sick about Michael ever since Michael was put in charge of negotiating with the dissidents, at their explicit request.

Then to know his worst fears for Michael's safety had taken form in the stabbing attack on him, and his son did not even see it fit to come home immediately, or at the very least, return his father's frantic phone calls, made the King fill with dubiousness and regrets. The information he garnered out of Jenkins was inadequate and did nothing to allay his anxieties.

On the contrary, it exacerbated them; he became even more concerned that he had erred grossly in allowing Michael to be placed in the dangerous position in which he was now stuck.

Not for one minute did he believe that cock-and-bull story Jenkins conveyed that Michael was off on a romantic interlude. Michael was long past that sort of thing, he not having had a serious relationship since Priscilla's disloyalty, and instead, chose to only indulge in discreet inconsequential sexual dalliances. That, in of itself, created yet another worry for the ailing King. Having ostensibly failed to convince Michael of the imperativeness of his acquiring a wife as soon as possible to secure his future position on the throne, and therefore the permanency of the monarchy, the king's terror at his family losing it all had become a constant companion, especially while striving for sleep at the end of each wearying day.

When Michael eventually deigned to speak with him on the phone, his tone was much too flippant, almost dismissive, making light of the attempted assassination and changing the subject to something ridiculously frivolous about having a lady guest coming to stay with him at the palace. The king could not recall Michael ever having done that before. Apparently he had taken up with the stunning young lady that was presented at the Garden Party. This added further annoyance to the King's emotions as he remembered her, and it was obvious the girl was much too young for Michael. He was again just wasting his time on a piece of fluff. *To be fair, the girl does come from a very upstanding, and wealthy, family, is well traveled, educated, and cultured, according to Jenkins's investigations, and she is exceptionally beautiful. To be sure, Michael and she would make gorgeous healthy offspring. However, my heir must be made to realize the necessity of focusing on finding a mate with more maturity who can be a proper partner to support him in the important work ahead, not some pretty little doll to play house with.*

CHAPTER
16

The King, long ago, having assessed that his heir had developed into an intelligent, empathetic, passionately headstrong young man, accepted that Michael would never agree to an advantageous arranged marriage, but would choose his own wife. Just as he was reflecting on how best to broach that subject with his son, the young man himself knocked on the door, entering at the same time.

The King rose quickly but walked unsteadily toward Michael, his arms outstretched in expectation of a hug. Taken aback at not only his father's now unusual gesture of familiarity but at his surprisingly feeble condition, Michael abandoned all previously planned bravado and rushed into his father's waiting arms. This was the first time Michael and his father had been in a full embrace since he was twenty-two years of age. Naturally they had given each other the customary respectful quick hugs and back pats when one of them had been away and not seen the other for a while, but they had stopped holding each other in a tight warm embrace, ever since a coolness had developed between them because of a serious disagreement ten years ago.

Two years after Michael's beloved mother was laid to rest in a crypt in the cathedral, the King summoned Michael to his office to discuss a private matter. Concealing his exhilaration, he calmly and as delicately as he could, informed Michael that he had been extremely lonely, and since the proper amount of mourning-time had passed, he had recently secretly been seeing "a lady," and wanted to introduce her to his children at dinner that evening. Stunned by this totally unexpected news, Michael was dumbstruck. Seeing his son incapable of conversing for the first time ever, realizing he was severely shocked, the King himself didn't know what to say to alleviate the damage.

The prolonged palpable silence in the room seemed to shout at them both, until the real shouting began.

Michael's voice was the louder, and angrier, and reverberated through the thick paneled office door.

Jenkins, who had been privy to the King's secret and was previously instructed by His Majesty to stand watch outside the door, had to chase away two guards, the office staff, and several servants, who came running to see what the commotion was all about. He forbade anyone from entering the surrounding offices, locked the hallway doors, and stood sentinel outside the door of the King's office. Knowing the great and abiding love Michael had for his mother, Jenkins knew he would not take the news well, and was ready to be a buffer between the two bull-headed royals, if need be. Except that he was not fully prepared for the shockingly passionate argument that ensued.

He could hear the heated fury and emotion in Michael's loud voice as he accused his father of treachery to his mother, that he was besmirching her memory, and bringing shame, and pain, to the entire royal family. His majesty strived for control but in an abnormally raised voice, tried to reason with Michael that it was never his intention to replace the Queen, she would always be uppermost in his heart, but she moved into heaven a long time ago, he was still a young man, and deserved to have a compatible female companion for both his emotional and physical needs.

His reasoning only added fuel to Michael's fire. Shouting at an even higher volume, Michael proceeded to question his father's morals, and integrity, in a most denigrating manner.

This was the impetus that caused the King to lose control, and although he stopped short of slapping Michael across his face which was his first impulse, his voice raised to a deafening shrill when he reminded Michael that he of all people should be the last to judge anyone, considering the playboy way in which he had run his life that nearly brought down the entire monarchy. Seeing Michael blanch then redden, the King realized his words delivered an even harder blow than if he had physically hit him, and he became immediately filled with regret; but no more so than Michael. Without another word, Michael yanked open the door, angrily brushed past Jenkins, and took off to places unknown, for two days and nights.

His Majesty became panicked. Jenkins tried to calm him by reminding him that though Michael was still young and headstrong, he was too intelligent and pragmatic not to get over his anger quickly. This had no effect as King Alexander had never been able to forget how fragile Michael's emotions were for such a long time after his mother's death. In addition, the King knew he was wrong in letting his own emotions get the better of him, when he angrily threw it in Michael's face about the stupid mistake of his carefree youth that could have jeopardized the monarchy. What worried him most was that Michael disappeared in such a hurry, there had been no time for the customary tracking device to be placed on his person, and he didn't take any of the cars which were already so equipped.

A month before their argument, Michael, without 'Royal Permission,' purchased a Harley Davidson motorcycle. Annoyed at not being consulted, fearful for his safety, the King made sure Michael was kept too busy with studies and royal duties to be able to take it out on public roads. Therefore Michael was only able to take quick spins around the palace grounds. As a result, no one had thought to outfit it with a tracking device. This was the mode of transportation he chose to get to his hideaway.

The day after his disappearance King Alexander had to leave on a preplanned trip for an international conference in Saudi Arabia. Overwrought over the situation with Michael, he debated cancelling his trip, but was reminded by the government that to do so would create an international upset of astronomical proportions. Even so, the only reason he stuck with his schedule was because Jenkins, falsely, assured him he had learnt of Michael's whereabouts and as soon as he could get to speak to him, he knew commonsense would prevail and he would come home.

Michael did come home but not until the following day, and not because he had been found and convinced to do so, but totally on his own volition. The time away allowed him to rationalize his father's situation. He realized how difficult it must have been for him after his wife passed on to have led a life of celibacy, knowing the loving relationship his parents had shared, and especially as his father was still quite young, in perfect health, and obviously virile.

Thinking about the pleasures of the flesh his father had been denied, he felt an extreme sympathy for him as he knew he, Michael, could not go without sex for two weeks, far worse two years. Determining to apologize and give his father his blessing by agreeing to meet his girlfriend, Michael said thank you and goodbye, and sped on his Harley out of Jamestown's Estate.

On his return, Jenkins gave him first a thorough dressing-down about his disrespect towards his father, and his selfishness in worrying everyone by not letting them know of his whereabouts. Then he presented him with a new Breguet watch saying it was a gift of apology from his father. Reading the inscription on the back, Michael was moved to tears, '*Nothing more important than my love for you, Pa.*' Wiping away his two escaped tears he accepted Jenkins's reprimand with an appropriate amount of humility, and promised to make amends on his father's return.

Jenkins responded, "The perfect way to prove you mean it, is to put on that watch and never take it off."

Assenting, Michael immediately slipped the Breguet onto his left wrist saying, "This will always be with me."

Without showing the relief that flooded him, Jenkins reinforced Michael's resolution by saying seriously, "Make that a promise to yourself as well as your father."

With a rueful smile, Michael agreed, "I do. I promise I'll never take it off."

Jenkins relaxed a little knowing that, at last, he had a permanent tracking device on his precious charge, and Michael would never know it.

After the king's return from yet another unsuccessful conference on equal rights for women in Saudi Arabia, father and son had a long discussion, and forgave each other.

When Michael asked his father if he was planning to move his girl-friend into his mother's suite His Majesty became visibly perturbed, "Elena is a widow with two grown sons older than you. I don't know the boys well, to have her family live here is too risky. I would never do anything to jeopardize the monarchy. So no, she'll live in her own home not far from here."

The subject was never raised again and even though Michael, his siblings, and most other members of the royal family, grew to love and respect Elena, she continued to live outside the palace. Through the following years, Michael often wondered if his initial reaction to her existence could be the reason for his father holding firm to his original decision. Though he felt some guilt about it, he was unable to force himself to bring it up again. Consequently, a lingering reticence remained between father and son. This saddened them both, but as in the way of proud men, it was ignored and never discussed.

Seeing his father's weakened physical condition today shook Michael in his soul, and he resolved to rectify all previous hurt and negligence. He knew he would have to come up with a creative expla-nation as to why he took two days to return his father's desperate calls after he was attacked. When he eventually did call him, he could not but help pick up on his father's tone of disappointment and hurt, which the King had attempted to disguise with restrained annoyance. Twinges of guilt had nagged at him whenever he thought about it, but these were easily erased when he was with Elizabeth. Taking in his father's current fragility, the guilt and regret revisited him, and he vowed to himself that he would do whatever was necessary to make the King's life easier, and restore him to good health.

His Majesty reveled in the long missed warmth of a full embrace from Michael, it felt as if the *'prodigal son'* had indeed *'returned.'* When father and son eventually released each other, Michael hastily apologized for his negligence in not immediately returning his calls. Now unable to be mendacious, he admitted to him that he had been preoccupied with Elizabeth Angelique Richardson, with whom he had fallen hopelessly in love. Seeing his father's dubious, almost censorious expression, Michael knew His Majesty was going to need some serious convincing, so he laid it all out for him with more detail than he originally intended, his joy and exuberance uncontrolled.

He described Elizabeth's personality, intelligence, caring sweetness, and capabilities, as only he knew how, with such passion and devotion, his father was pleasantly astounded.

The King's reaction was a relief to Michael as he saw his father's face soften and a happy gleam return to his eyes, although he still had a look of uncertainty and spoke cautiously, "She sounds wonderful, son, but I found she looked a bit young for you...for what you need."

"Pa, she's twenty-eight years old, and is immensely more mature and wiser than others her age-"

"Really? Twenty-eight? Are you sure? Sorry, stupid question. I know you would've had her checked out with Standard Procedure. Well, this is all quite exciting, son. I'm overjoyed for you." *And for me,* he thought wearily.

Thrilled with his father's response to the news about Elizabeth, Michael also felt shame-filled relief that the King did not question him further on information about Elizabeth that should have been obtained through Standard Procedure; he obviously assumed that Michael knew everything possible about her, and trusted his judgment.

His Majesty's face took on a nervous look, "Have you told her about...the Greek...situation?"

Michael's hesitancy was detectable, "Ah…no. Not yet."

The King spoke with understanding, "Michael, you know, if you're as serious about her as I feel you are, you're going to have to tell her. And the sooner the better."

Concealing his discomfort, Michael said quickly, "Yes, I know. I just haven't had an opportunity to do so yet. I…I plan to tell her as soon as she's fully settled in."

Having turned down the heat in the hot tub, Elizabeth rested her back against a jet to enjoy its soothing massage while inhaling the lavender infused aromatic fumes that rose up from the bubbling swirling waters. Becoming hypnotically relaxed, she fell into a meditative doze. Her trance was suddenly disturbed by a rustling sound in the room. A horrifying thought sped into her mind that Celia returned to drown her.

Her heart racing, she flung her eyes open, planning to jump up and do battle with Celia and fight for her life. She was shocked to see Michael, in all his naked beauty, already sexually aroused, about to climb into the hot tub.

Anger combining with fright, she shouted, "Stop right there Your Highness!" Bewildered by her frightened look and angry voice Michael froze, his entering leg suspended in midair as though in a game of Simon Says. Feeling her heart rate return to normal, she suppressed the urge to laugh in relief at Michael's comical stance and confused expression. Observing the rise of his outstanding phallus between those long well-defined muscular legs, despite the desire she felt in her risen wet and heated hidden clitoris which matched his outwardly visible craving, she decided it was necessary to postpone their mutual satisfaction.

It was presently more important for her to get satisfaction of a different kind, "So! *That's* how you are around here, prancing around naked for your servants to see?"

Dropping his leg he placed his foot on the edge of the tub, his legs no longer open but held self-consciously close together, he said defensively, "Certainly not. I locked the doors. What's the matter?"

"I want to know what happened between you and Celia."

"What? Nothing. What're you talking about?"

Elizabeth described everything that transpired after he left her with Celia. He became quite disturbed, apologized for her being subjected to such behavior from someone he entrusted to take care of her, promised it would never happen again, and she would be given a different maid, of her own choosing.

This assurance was not what Elizabeth was looking for and she asked demandingly, "I still want to know what happened between you, Michael. I know something did."

He looked ill at ease but spoke without delay, "The only thing that happened was just after she came to work here a year ago, she offered me…er…any "*extra services*" that I may require. I politely refused her, told her it would not be proper and I was only interested in a working relationship. Thankfully, a few months ago she told me she had a new boyfriend, so I thought she was fine with everything. She's extremely efficient, I didn't see the need to fire her."

"Hang on. She only got a boyfriend a few months ago, after a year in your employ? Someone looking like her? Didn't you find that strange? Didn't you realize she was hoping you'd change your mind and agree to accept her "*extra services*" eventually?"

"Call me naïve but that never occurred to me."

"Well, even though she had me freakedout I now feel sorry for the woman. I think she was, maybe still is, in love with you, and was living in hope. I'll bet anything when she's having sex with the boyfriend she's fantasizing it's you. And who can blame her. Michael, I will not have that woman lose her job because of me-"

He shook his head, "Do not concern yourself about it, I'll see that she gets a position in a far wing of the palace. But after what happened and what you just said, we certainly can't have her around here from now on." After that episode, Celia was not seen anymore, anywhere in the palace.

Having had a doubly satisfying hot sexual session in and out of the hot tub, Elizabeth and Michael lay in each other's arms on a chaise where they had ended up, discussing the dress for the evening's intimate dinner party.

He squeezed her gently, "I'd like you to wear the blue gown, you look amazing in it and it evokes the most wonderful memories of our first night of love-making."

Giggling, she pressed her body against his, "Anything to please you, my lord. So, we're to be that formal?"

Michael kissed the tip of her nose and sat up, "Darling, you'll have to forgive me, but things have gotten a bit out of hand, it's not just my immediate family for dinner tonight. Unfortunately the word is out, a bunch of the family who live in the palace and the city want to meet you. So, it's going to be a more formal affair than I was planning for your palace initiation. I'm really sorry, but it appears my excitement about you is contagious, my father and siblings have invited all my aunts, uncles and cousins. Please don't get upset with me, it was all done before I found out."

Elizabeth paled as she sat up and faced him, her voice tremulous, "Michael…I…I told you I wasn't ready to…go public with…our relationship…my own family knows nothing about us, I can't shock them. And you promised to ensure that I wouldn't be made to feel uncomfortable when I agreed to stay here. Now your whole family knows about me, are probably coming armed with phones, cameras, video recorders-"

Michael steadied her wringing hands, "No, I won't allow it, there'll be no photos, I won't let anything happen to make you uncomfortable. I made you a promise and I always keep my promises. Listen, it's just going to be the palace and city family who haven't left yet for their summer residences, only twenty…or so. And you needn't worry about anyone revealing us, my family has learnt, by bitter experience, how to be close-mouthed. Our secret's safe until *we* decide otherwise."

She furrowed her brow doubtfully, "Are you sure? I can't have my family find out about us until I go home and personally explain it to them. This…us, is just too big. After all our discussions and your agreements, I thought you understood that?"

He tenderly kissed the frown lines that appeared on her forehead and spoke soothingly to her, "I understand perfectly, darling. The outside world will not know about us until you've spoken to your family in person, and you tell me you're ready." Seeing her still tense and hoping to placate her, he jumped up from the chaise and picked up his jacket that he had tossed on a chair earlier, when he had been so anxious to join her in the hot tub. From the inside pocket, he removed a long blue velvet jewelry box and presented it to her with a flourish and a low bow, "Jewels for my Princess."

Raising her eyebrows, she stared at him before she put out her hand to accept his unwrapped gift, "What's this?"

"Open it so you can find out," he coaxed, looking somewhat pleased with himself.

Opening the box gingerly as if something having life would jump out at her, she gasped when it sprang open to reveal its contents, "Oh my gosh! They are absolutely exquisite, Michael. I have never seen this kind of detailed work on such pieces."

Placing the box on the chaise, she lifted the ornate sapphires and diamonds bracelet and rested it on her left wrist, not clasping it.

Michael reached into the box and took out the sapphire and diamonds ring Elizabeth left there, "Don't you like the ring? They were made to go together."

Her eyes widened, "Like? I love it! But I can't accept this from you. It's much too extravagant, darling. They're obviously rare pieces, I suspect historical. It's a fabulous gesture but I can't accept them. Here." Attempting to hand the bracelet over to him, he grabbed her wrist, slipped the ring on her ring finger and deftly clasped the bracelet onto her wrist.

Lifting her to her feet he embraced her, "My great-grandmother will be most insulted if you refuse her jewels. She'll rise out of her burial chamber to haunt you forever. So you have no choice but to accept them from the heir to her throne."

She wriggled in his arms, "These were hers? I knew they were important. All the more reason I can't accept them. They should be worn by your daughters, eventually."

His lips turned up softly at the corners but his eyes were serious, "And so they will, my darling, so they will."

CHAPTER 17

The formal introductions completed, the reserved polite conversation in the opulent official drawing room rapidly warmed to mirthful chatter after the second round of champagne had been imbibed. Elizabeth surveyed what could be her future in-laws and residence, and was relieved and pleased at how comfortable and at home she felt. Everyone had been quite friendly and welcoming. She experienced no insecure strangeness but instead a powerful sense of familiarity and belonging.

The butler announced "Dinner is served." Michael, who had not for one instant strayed from her side, took her hand and led her to the chair on his beaming father's right at the head of the long banquet table in the formal dining room. He then stood behind the chair next to her intending to sit there after all the ladies, his father and the older gentlemen, were seated.

From the other end of the table, the King's elder sister, referred to as 'Aunt Claire' by all younger royalty and considered the matriarch of the family since the Queen's death, called out in a commanding voice, "Michael bring your young lady here, she'll sit next to me."

Michael looked at his father questioningly. The King simply smiled, nodded, and patted Elizabeth's hand, "Go ahead. Take her to your aunt, anything for peace," he widened his smile at Elizabeth, "we'll have lots of time to get properly acquainted in the coming days."

After Michael seated Elizabeth on his aunt's right, he was about to sit next to her when Claire flicked her hand at him as if shooing away a fly, "Go sit with your father. We ladies will have a tête-à-tête."

He bent over and whispered in Elizabeth's ear, "I assure you her bark is worse than her bite. I know you can give as good as you get. Remember how much I love you." He kissed Elizabeth on her cheek, then leaned over to her other side and kissed Claire on hers, whispering in her ear, "Be kind. This is your future Queen."

As soon as Michael left, Claire immediately launched into an interrogation of Elizabeth that would have made any Intelligence Agency proud. Fortunately, having had much practice in evasion in recent days, Elizabeth was able to sidestep and fend off most of the probing advances of the inquisitive dowager's attacks with impressive diplomatic skill.

By the time the salad course was served, having triumphantly survived Claire's omniscient onslaught, with her confidence and good temper still intact, Elizabeth struck up a conversation with Michael's cousin and his young wife sitting across from her, whose one-year-old firstborn nature had chosen to burden with autism. The baby had been crying incessantly in the playroom, until one of his older cousins who was unable to tolerate the wailing any longer, against the protests of his nanny, brought him into the dining room to his parents. She put him on the floor next to them to play with their silver napkin rings. The infant cooed and jingled his new toys contentedly, until an enormous diarrheal bowel movement escaped out of his supposedly waterproof diaper, the stench permeating the air.

Mortifyingly embarrassed, the young parents were confused as to what to do. Elizabeth excused herself from the table, went over to the distressed family, and instructed the hovering butler to have a maid clean the floor. She then told the mother who was holding the screaming feces-dripping baby away from her clothing to accompany her, a footman showing the way to the nearest bathroom. After helping to clean and re-dress the child, Elizabeth comforted the humiliated tearful young mother, as she had done for so many others in the past.

She picked up the baby and with her head held high, led the way back into the dining room whispering to the mother some now famous words of advice, "Never let them see you sweat."

Elizabeth sat the now sweet-smelling and immaculate baby on her own lap, rested his back against her chest, and smiling down at his dribbling but cherubic face, she took his hands in hers and began to gently clap them together, softly singing the ancient nursery rhyme, '*Clap Hands for Mummy.*' The baby rocked back and forth in great delight, and with vacuous eyes, gurgled and drooled copious bubbles of spittle.

To all at the table, save for Elizabeth and the child's parents, he was not a pretty sight. Not wishing to embarrass the parents further, all at the table smiled politely, except for Margaret, Michael's fifteen-year-old cousin, a beautiful black-haired, gray-eyed spoilt brat. She was seated obliquely across from Elizabeth and for much of the meal, often rudely interrupting someone else's conversation, had complimented Elizabeth on her beauty, makeup, hair, dress, jewelry, and excellent taste. All superficial attributes.

Seeing Elizabeth's unexpected actions, she pouted and stuck her nose up in the air exaggeratedly as though the baby's foul smelling excrement was still in the room. Looking at Elizabeth with unguarded effrontery she said in a haughty loud voice, "I don't know how someone looking like you can stand to be playing with such a disgusting looking mess of humanity."

Without stopping her clapping play with the baby, Elizabeth looked squarely at Margaret, and in a clear but kind voice, said to the girl at the now hushed table, "Margaret, when all is said and done, and I mean finally done, we're not going to be judged by our beauty or even the quantity of our trappings," she glanced quickly around the ornately decorated room and sumptuously adorned table, "but by the quality of our deeds." She stopped speaking to wipe the baby's face with her napkin, then continued, "I hope not to be too harshly judged when the time comes."

At the other end of the table, in a daring move, Michael spoke loudly, "Elizabeth, you need have no fear of harsh judgment, your place in Heaven is definitely assured, for you have already taken me into Paradise."

Seeing his serious expression, yet with a mischievous glint in his eyes, the double entendre was not lost on Elizabeth. Nor on other adults in the room. Not wishing him to stand alone with his bold remark in front of his family and servants, she returned his serious look but held his eyes seductively, "I'm most elated to hear it, Sir, for you too have brought me to a Heavenly place."

Observing the adianoeta exchanged between the lovers, and remembering, not just the many admirable things Michael told him about her, but the devoted and enthusiastic manner in which he had, the King felt a relief he had too long been waiting for. *Ah yes, she's the one for him, at last. And, she will make him happy. Thank you God.*

Claire on the other hand was not so easily convinced. Ever since, what she filed in the cabinet of her mind under, *'Michael's Grecian Misadventure,'* she had taken it upon herself to be the watchdog of Michael's romances. She scrutinized every woman Michael dared to bring in her presence, in such an obviously censorious manner as to run off very quickly the weaker ones who, "*didn't shape up.*"

Watching every move Elizabeth made, taking in the tiniest details, she was reluctantly warming to Elizabeth's possibilities. Claire habitually categorized people by their manners, and was pleasantly impressed by Elizabeth's. *Well, at least this American from Trinidad knows how to eat properly. Not like those nouveau riche others he dated in the States when he was at Harvard. Why, most of them hardly ever touched their knives, cutting their food with the side of their fork! Pointing with their forks while speaking! Talking with food in their mouths! And elbows on the table! Disgraceful!*

After ordering a footman to take the baby back to his nanny in the nursery, she impudently touched the ring and bracelet on Elizabeth's hand, "These are beautiful. They look familiar."

Not waiting to fence off any more embarrassing questions, Elizabeth said quickly, "Probably because they belonged to your grandmother, Michael lent them-"

Michael interjected firmly, "I've *given* them to Elizabeth, Aunt Claire, with Papa's blessing."

Claire made a "*harrumph*" sound, then quickly rested her eyes on Elizabeth's sapphires and diamonds necklace and earrings, "Well, they do go quite well with your other pieces, and who gave you those, do tell?"

Out of the corners of her eyes Elizabeth could see Michael at the other end of the table straining forward to hear as she said softly, "An old friend."

Claire dropped her eyes censoriously to Elizabeth's dress with an acidulous critique, "Well it all matches with your lovely dress but you should've had the good sense to have kept this outfit for the Ambassadors Ball on Saturday."

Unable to hide her ignorance of the event, Elizabeth responded with honesty, "I'm sorry, but I don't know anything about it." She sneaked a quick look at Michael and observed he seemed just as surprised as she.

Michael looked at his father, then back at Elizabeth, "I had totally forgotten about it. I'm sorry, darling, I'll tell you all about it after dinner."

King Alexander rang the Baccarat crystal bell that stood on the table in front of him. The attending servants dotted around the room standing against the walls rushed toward him, puzzled expressions on their faces as they knew they had performed their jobs in their customary perfect manner and didn't see what he could possibly need. He stood up and waved them back to their assigned places, raising his Merlot filled Lalique balloon goblet indicating he was going to make a toast. Everyone was taken by surprise. The King had a consistent reputation amongst his family for being parsimonious with his words at their social gatherings, he being best known as an attentive listener, and only when asked, would give sage, concise and pertinent advice. No one at the table could bring to mind The King ever standing for a toast on what they all thought was just a little more than an ordinary occasion, the introduction of Michael's new and perhaps serious girlfriend.

Knowing this action to be unprecedented, at least in his experience, Michael shifted uncomfortably in his seat, nervous about what his father might divulge from the private conversation they had earlier that day. He hoped his father would be true to form in his predilection for succinct speeches and say nothing about Elizabeth that would make her want to leave the palace. He looked at her. She was staring at him apprehensively. He gave her a false reassuring smile, she returned it with an honest unsure smile.

He held his breath as his father began to speak.

His Majesty scanned the eager faces around the table, smiled benevolently at Elizabeth and lifted his glass to her, "I'm sure you all join me in giving a warm welcome to Miss Elizabeth Richardson, Michael's... friend, and wish her an enjoyable and memorable stay at our home in the palace. Elizabeth, welcome. Here's to your health and happiness."

Most at the table called out "Hear, hear," all directed their glasses toward her, she nodded and smiled graciously to everyone who caught her eye, the King sipped his wine, his family followed, and Michael breathed again.

With the majority of the family gone to their respective homes, including Elena, Claire, and her kindlier younger sister, Susan's mother Anne, the King, his children, and most of their cousins, repaired to the family's private drawing room.

Elizabeth returned from a trip to the powder room to see Michael entertaining his family at the grand piano, playing Andrew Lloyd

Webber's music from 'Phantom Of The Opera,' one of her favorite plays. He continued playing with one hand as he beckoned her to sit next to him with his other, gave her a loving smile and began to sing 'All I Ask Of You,' not taking his eyes off her face. Reaching the part for 'Christine' to be sung by the female of the duet, he nudged Elizabeth, and without hesitation she joined him, her sweet voice in perfect harmony with his. They finished the song to gleeful applause from the enchanted audience. Michael took Elizabeth's chin in his hand and gave her a soft but slow kiss on her lips, turning her cheeks as red as the roses next to the piano. The clapping increased, along with wolf whistles from some younger members of the group, Mark's being the loudest. When His Majesty eventually left the young people to carry on with their singing and dancing, he knew that tonight, and hopefully from henceforth, he will get a good night's sleep. His son and heir was at last truly in love, with the perfect woman to be his Queen.

Michael reclined on his bed totally nude, feeling blissful and blessed, waiting eagerly for Elizabeth to finish her nightly bedtime toilet ritual. The evening had gone off smoothly for her, despite his forgetting to warn her about Aunt Claire, named clandestinely by the younger royals 'The Family Bitch,' who was rightfully feared by them all, with the exception of Michael. He filled with pride at how diplomatically polished Elizabeth handled the occurrences of the evening, especially the messy situation with his poor cousin's retarded infant.

Pangs of pity for his cousin and his wife because of what they would have to deal with for the rest of their lives were genuine, but fleeting, as he knew in his soul that Elizabeth and he would never have to face such grief. They would only have perfect babies, and he wanted to get into the act of starting to make those immediately. He was watching her through his open door as she stood with her back to him at the sink in her bathroom, wearing a short silk negligee.

His lustful thoughts working his body into a sexual frenzy, he called out impatiently, "Elizabeth please, come to bed darling, don't brush your teeth, I want you now."

Unaware that he could see her, she giggled and called back, "Patience darling, I just have to finish brushing my teeth." She rinsed out the toothpaste and bent over to spit. The negligee rose up to expose the lower half of her ivory smooth round bottom, and below the cleft of its cheeks, he got a titillating peek at the object of his desire.

In a split second he leapt from the bed and was upon her like a bull elephant in musth. Grabbing her arm, he spun her around and lifted her up in one swift motion. Searing her with a predatory look, she dropped her toothbrush, widening her eyes in shocked fear mingling with desire as she herself reeled from a rush of passion. He dropped his mouth hard onto hers, giving her a bruising kiss as he thrust his tongue in to lash against hers. Falling on the bed with her still in his arms, he nuzzled, nibbled and sucked her neck, then did the same to each breast, making her shudder with the pleasure and the pain.

He worked his way rapidly down to her inner thighs with wet hot nips and kisses. Licking at the outer lips of her labia voraciously with long hard strokes he growled in-between, "You kept me waiting…too long…woman. Now…I'm going to devour you."

She did not comprehend what she had done to incite him so. She had not experienced this kind of forcefulness from him before, and although extremely aroused, she felt suddenly afraid, *Oh God, how rough is this going to get!*

Feeling her stiffen, he laughed hoarsely, which did nothing to alleviate her fears. She called to him soothingly but he ignored her, his tongue diving deeply into her more savagely, making guttural animalistic sounds of feasting enjoyment.

Tasting her salty moisture turn to sweet cream he increased the suction on her like a human milking machine, lapping at her very core, intent on emptying her completely, milking her to his fill. Elizabeth let out a cry of pleasured anguish, then begged him to stop. The throbbing liquid heat he had elicited from her became delightfully painful but now she needed to take a break, if only for an instant, to recover, and breathe again.

In no condition to be reasoned with, he ignored her, he was all animal instinct and lust, his mind functioning only on the lowest level of rationalization, his innate desire to mate overpowering all reasonable thinking.

She tried to sit up but he raised his head, grabbed her hands, and pinning them down against the sheet, crawled over her and stuck his throbbing, bobbing penis in her face, "Suck me baby," he commanded, "but don't make me come."

Unsure of how that would be possible given his uncontrolled state, but grateful of the chance to give her own genitalia a respite, she steadied his as he released her hands, inserted it into her salivating mouth and closed her eyes to savor it.

"Look at me," his voice more demanding than before, she opened her eyes quickly. The first thing coming into her vision was his scrotum, ripe, reddened, and ready to release.

His voice deepened, "Look into my eyes," she opened her eyes wider and looked up at his, darkly penetrating hers, her mouth half stuffed with his core, "You belong to me. You will never do this with another, ever again. Neither will I. We are one forever. Do you understand me, Elizabeth?"

Aghast at this scenario, her mouth incapacitated for speech, not understanding what he was thinking, if indeed he was thinking, all she could do was nod her head in agreement, shaking his scrotum comically as she did so. His eyes looked wild, like an animal in the throes of mating, its carnal appetite still to be satisfied. He cupped both her breasts, his fingers digging into her soft skin. She yelped and dug her nails into his back causing him to groan and shake his head violently.

His expression changed radically as it softened to a caring sweetness, back to the man she thought she knew, the man she knew she loved. Slowly, he slid himself out of her mouth, slid his tongue in its place, and slid himself into her now hungrily awaiting portal, she opening her legs wide and granting him access. "I love you, Elizabeth. You are my life. Tell me you feel the same way about me." He began to move slowly, tortuously, as he waited for her to answer.

She whimpered as he dragged against her insides, now as greedy as his, her patience running out, "Yes...yes. I love you. You are my life."

He began to stroke her strong and long, attacking and retreating with a vengeance as she moaned with each forceful descent. She held on tight to his buttocks and rolled her hips in an upwards grinding motion, seizing every delicious inch and creamy morsel of him as he continued to ram into her, all the way to her uterus. Feeling her walls beginning to pulsate as her second orgasm rolled into a crescendo, she clenched onto him, milking him as he had her. Michael screamed like a caged beast being released as his orgasm ripped through his body ferociously, pounding into her as he pleasurably, painfully, emptied his seed. With a low growl and a loud groan, he collapsed on her, sated. Bearing his full weight for a second she felt the air rush from her lungs but she managed to gasp, "Michael, you're crushing me." He rolled off quickly and begged forgiveness for his ungentlemanly conduct. She laughed softly, "You were a wild animal tonight, Your Highness."

He sat up, "Too wild for you? Was I too rough?"

His face became pathetically concerned and she broke into a sympathetic laugh, "No, my darling. You could never be too anything for me, except too wonderful."

He kissed her lips tenderly, gently pulling them into his mouth, then releasing them, "I felt we could've made a baby tonight, we were both ripe for it."

She caressed his face, "No doubt, I could feel you touching my womb. Good thing I'm on the pill."

Tracing an index finger over a pale blue vein under the white skin of her breast he said excitedly, "I can't wait to see these beautiful mammaries engorged with milk to feed our babies."

Looking very serious she sat up "Babies...sss?" she placed strong emphasis on the plural, "how many are you talking about, Sir?"

Taking in her look, he thought to reduce his desired number but then decided, *Oh what the hell, go for it,* "Six. I've always wanted six... you'll be the best mother...I'll be an amazing father...it'll be so much fun...they'll be so gorgeous...we can afford it...we'll get all the help we need...and, I'm rambling, and, you look...surprised? Upset? What? Tell me what you think, darling?"

She drew in a deep breath, "Michael, I already have...dozens of children...that I'm responsible for-"

"But these will be ours darling, our flesh and blood-"

Solemnity registered in her mien, "Talking about flesh and blood, it's mine that's going to have to suffer through the making of these six you're wanting, mister man, not yours! And too besides, the world is already over-crowded, we're running out of resources to support the people we already have. It would show gross irresponsibility on our part to procreate like a couple of wild rabbits. People like us have to set the right example for the more ignorant-"

"Ah...ha. That's exactly why two intelligent people like us, strong and healthy, and beautiful," he kissed her quickly, "should make it our responsibility to bring more like us into the world. Alright, I can tell by your face that I'm never going to win this argument. I know the initial hard work falls on you, but I'll support you in every other way possible. I'll be your coach, go to classes with you, be with you for the deliveries every step of the way, and, you'll always be waited upon hand and foot, I promise, not just by me, by everyone. But darling, I always wanted a big family. My mother had three miscarriages between me and the twins, due to overwork, and in my early childhood I felt like a lonely, only child, until some cousins grew old enough to be playmates. I'd hate my children to go through that. Would you settle for four? Can you handle four?"

Elizabeth looked at his beautiful puppy-dog entreating eyes and knew she was being manipulated, but loving him so deeply, she presently didn't care, "Alright, my darling, I'll settle for four. So, four it is." Drawing her to him, he kissed her forcefully as if sealing a bargain.

Wanting to get away from such a serious subject, she pushed him gently and teased, "So, when were you going to tell me about this Ambassadors Ball, weren't you going to invite me?"

Apology dominated the tone of his voice, "I honestly forgot all about it, you are such a distraction. Actually, it would be the perfect event to introduce you as my-"

Her glowing tan turned an insipid ivory as she stood up, "Michael, no! You promised you'd wait until after I've been home and spoken in person to my family, and I can't go until I've done my speech and secured the grant for The Children's Home-"

"Alright, alright. Excuse me for being so excited about wanting the world to know I've fallen in love with the most incredible woman, who claims to feel the same way about me, but is apparently embarrassed to publicly say so-"

She affected a patient mien, "Darling, you know that's not true. I thought you understood my reasons for waiting-"

"Yes, yes, but I'm anxious for us to get on with our lives together. Okay, let me tell you about the Ambassadors Ball. It's an annual event that's held in the palace banquet hall and ballroom at the start of every summer, before all the diplomats start taking off for their summer holidays. It's very grand and elegant and, yes, you're going to need a ball gown. I'll call my mother's main designer first thing in the morning and have her come over to meet with you. Don't worry, it'll be ready in time. Choose red. I'd love to see you in red." He kissed her now red nipples quickly and continued, "Oh, by the way, two days after the ball, we're going to Geneva. I'm addressing a U.N. conference about the ecology and climate change. You can wear wigs in public. After that we're going to gallivant incognito all over Europe for a couple weeks and have some fun. What do you think, you game for adventure?"

"Anytime. It sounds wonderful. Hopefully the grant for The Children's Home will have come through by the time we get back. Since we're gallivanting, can you arrange for us to be in Germany and go to the World Cup on the fifteenth?"

Pleased surprise manifested a twinkle in his eyes, "Oh? I'd no idea you were that interested in football. Great. You can join us in our family matches this summer. I've been too busy trying to take over more of Papa's workload to keep abreast of who's playing, why the fifteenth?"

Choosing to ignore his subtle raillery she smiled proudly, "Trinidad's playing against England-"

His surprise increasing, he interrupted her, "What! Your little island made it to the World Cup?"

She gave him a sulky but sultry smile, "Plenty of varied talent in my 'little island,' Your Royal Highness."

He returned the sultry aspect of her smile, "Yes. You prove that to me every wonderful, blessed day. And night."

She laughed, but then suddenly became serious, "Gosh, so much is happening, and I still have a lot to do-"

Michael picked up on her sudden nervousness, "You're not to get flustered about anything. You'll be given every assistance to handle all these events, and your speech. Just tell me what you need."

Hiding the tension that had left her groin and risen up to her chest, she kissed him softly, "Thank you, darling. Mostly what I'm going to need is some space, peace and quiet, for the next couple of days, to finish my research and perfect my prose and delivery."

"You'll have it. I'll instruct everyone to not disturb you in a private room that's attached to the library, it'll be your own personal office. Just use the phone when you need something done. But, can I at least pick you up to have lunches with me? You have to take a break, to eat?" There was a hint of seductive wickedness in his smile.

She responded with a similar smile, "Yes, We have to eat."

CHAPTER 18

Every day at twelve-thirty, Michael arrived at the library to escort Elizabeth to eat lunch on his balcony, and then each other in his bed. When their 'matinee' was over, he'd escort her back to the library, where they would kiss goodbye with the passion of frustrated lovers who had been denied each other for much too long. He would drag himself away back to his large office, she would drag herself away back to her small office.

King Alexander, Claire, Anne, Megan, and Mark, informed Michael and Elizabeth that they were expected to accompany them to the Opera House to attend a Royal Command Performance of Mozart's 'The Magic Flute.' Knowing that particular opera focused on spirituality and its lovers having to literally go through 'the fires of hell' before they could finally be united, Elizabeth wondered about the possibility of it being a presage for Michael and herself. Casting aside thoughts of premonition of their fate, she agreed to go only on the condition that she would wear a black wig and sit between Michael and Mark, inferring to the public she was Mark's friend, not Michael's.

Claire took issue with her requested arrangement, and Michael had to patiently explain that Elizabeth wanted to tell her family about him in person on her return to Trinidad, and not have them shocked by learning about him in the media.

In typical Aunt Claire fashion, she cross-questioned Michael as to why Elizabeth had to wait to claim him to her family in person, when every young woman on the planet would be thrilled and honored to immediately proclaim such a relationship to the whole world. He did his best to assuage Claire's suspicions, and criticisms, but while trying to defend Elizabeth's reasoning he unnervingly developed some suspicions of his own. Certainly he knew how difficult it was for one unaccustomed to the limelight to have to adjust to it and to one's loss of anonymity, and worst of all, to have to fight for every modicum of precious privacy; yet, he was aware that Elizabeth was not without her fair share of more than the statistically allotted 'fifteen minutes of fame.' What with her amazing work with The Children's Home, and, her courageous speeches on the contemporarily controversial topic about the gender of God, she was surely no stranger to fame, even to some extent, notoriety. Granted, she was extremely close with her family, as he was with his, this being one of the many things he loved about her, her capacity for boundless love.

Smiling as a vision of their lovemaking flashed into his head, *Boundless love of every kind,* he decided not to put Aunt Claire's questions to her until after her speech, or maybe after the ball; he will postpone adding to her stress.

Although he found Claire's persistence with him about gaining more detailed information about Elizabeth, her full history and family pedigree, thoroughly annoying, he knew, despite his knowledge of Claire's secret deep-seated resentment, it was well-intentioned, and justified. Especially, as Claire was quick to remind him, her mouth twisted in censure, "We must not have another Priscilla or Greek Misadventure happen again."

At four-thirty Elizabeth looked at her ten-year-old *"old faithful"* Baum & Mercier watch feeling her brain was overloaded. She shutdown her laptop computer, gathered up her notepads and books with it, and found her way back to Michael's apartments. There was a note from him on her vanity saying he was with his martial arts instructor in the gym, would be finished at five, and would love if she came down after that to work-out with him. He drew a map to the gymnasium and signed with his first three initials, M.A.S., and two intertwined hearts. She donned her exercise shorts and top, track suit and sneakers, snatched up his map, and followed his directions to the gym.

Observing the gym was as well-equipped as any private club or public gym she had ever been in, she snuck in quietly, took off her track suit and hung it next to Michael's on hooks near the door. Seeing him still with the instructor at the other end of the long, large room, she started working-out at the ballet barre, doing stretches, steps and positions. After awhile she surreptiously looked at the far corner of the room.

The two men were positioned in what looked like a stand-off, on a large rubber matted area, both wearing white Tae Kwon-Do outfits, and black belts. *Interesting, Michael never told me he does martial arts, and, has a black belt. What a relief, he's doing self-defense. I have such great fear for him after what happened in the West Country. But he mustn't know, can't let him see my weak side, I suspect he didn't tell me the whole truth about what really happened over there.*

The Tae Kwon-Do Master raised his voice, sternly lecturing Michael, "You've lost it, Sir. You're going to have to work harder on getting power back in your kick."

Elizabeth accidentally knocked the ballet barre with her watch which made a loud echoing noise, causing the men to look in her direction. Michael smiled at her, bowed to the Master, and beckoned her over. "Darling, this is Master Huan. Master Huan, meet my girl-friend, Elizabeth Angelique Richardson."

Master Huan gave her a snappy bow from the waist, bending so low his handsome Korean head hit his knees. Regarding the striking beauty before him, he now understood why he had such a difficult time today to get Prince Michael to be aggressive. With such a goddess in his bed, any red-blooded male would lose his killer instinct. He would want to make love, not war.

Observing Master Huan openly admiring his woman, Michael put his arms around Elizabeth's waist proprietarily, smiled smugly and said only half-jokingly, "Take it all in now, buddy, because the next time you see her, she'll be covered up in a long white gown."

After Master Huan left, they made a valiant attempt at working-out on some machines but seeing each other's beautiful bodies temptingly beginning to glisten with perspiration, they unitarily agreed they would prefer to expend their energies working-out on each other. Pulling two yoga mats onto the rubber floor, they followed Master Huan's thinking, and oblivious to the warring activity the area was designed for, they made love.

Ecstatically lost in each other, they lost track of time, and had to make a mad dash for the shower to get dressed for the opera. Racing down the corridors to the rest of the family long waiting outside in the car, they helped each other with zippers, studs and jewelry, the final touches of being appropriately dressed, giggling like tykes caught in an act of mischief.

As expected, Claire was infuriated at their tardiness, making it blatantly obvious with a barrage of chastisements, despite their profuse apologies. The others simply smiled in sympathy, although the lovers detected a knowing gleam from the King and Aunt Anne, and a comprehending wink from Mark.

Heading back to the palace in the limousine, having thoroughly enjoyed the humorous yet melancholy romance of the opera, the four young people, Michael as maestro, bellowed into their favorite amusing aria dramatically, exaggeratingly stuttering "Papa...pa...pa...pa...pa...gen...i...o...o," their hands and upper bodies moving jerkily in their seats, comically imitating the tenor and soprano who had entertained them. His Majesty and Anne, sitting with Claire across from the young ones, became caught up in their fun and began to conduct the amateur chorus.

The querulous Claire, on the other hand, found it all an abomination. Making more than her usual noises of disapproval, and irked at being disregarded, she eventually pointed to Megan and Mark, "You two can't even hold a tune. You should shut up and let Michael and Elizabeth finish it!"

Overly sensitive Megan looked crushed from the insult. Her twin quickly put his arm around her shoulders protectively on seeing tears well in the corners of her eyes. Elizabeth and Michael heard him mutter in her ear, "Ignore the frustrated old bitch. She's like this because she hasn't been fucked in eons."

The car stopped. The door was immediately opened by two palace guards and Claire huffed out, King Alexander and Anne hard on her heels to give her the scolding she deserved, in private. Michael pulled the door shut and the four young people stayed in the limousine. They spread themselves out, played music, drank wine from the mini-bar, nibbled on olives and nuts, and talked for hours about every subject they could think of, the least of which was the bitterness of Aunt Claire. Elizabeth pondered on the archaic tradition of the country excluding a primogenital female from being the monarch if a male sibling followed, giving Claire cause for her attitude, she being older than the King; but sensibly kept her speculations to herself.

She observed there was no sibling rivalry amongst these young royals, only an enduring, caring, familial love, of which they desired to make her a part.

Resting in each other's arms after a particularly slow and tender session of love-making, looking thoughtful, Michael suddenly asked Elizabeth, "Do you think he's homosexual?"

Although having not spoken about anything other than how much they loved each other, and loved making love to each other, since their orgasms, she knew exactly who he was referring to. Still, she tread carefully onto the subject, "Who?"

"My brother, Mark."

"No."

"No? Come on. He has some very feminine mannerisms. I'd bet anything he's into guys, no pun intended."

"I didn't say he's not, but he's into girls too. He's bisexual."

"Oh? What makes you think that?"

"I saw how he is with women. It's not different from how he is with men. He's definitely bi."

"You noticed it too." He kissed her forehead which was near his lips, "You're so smart. I swear, I'm the luckiest man alive. Thank you, darling. I feel relieved to know that my brother will enjoy the sweetness of woman." Kissing her forehead again, he decided he would have another candid brotherly 'birds'n'bees' conversation with Mark tomorrow, and fell into a peaceful sleep.

Morning brought Elizabeth emotions of extreme fears of incompletion. The speech at Davidson hall was tomorrow and she had not finished her additions, learnt them by heart, or practiced speaking them aloud. She was confident of her content, phrasing and prose, but was nervous that she had not yet rehearsed physical delivery of the new material.

And, although she didn't want to face it, nagging the back of her mind was Davidson Hall management's fear for her safety.

Staring into the diffused light of dawn in Michael's perfect, handsomely decorated regal bedroom, she envisioned an ugly contrast of herself on the stage tomorrow, blundering, bumbling and blubbering, making a complete fool of herself, being an unsuccessful communicator, a failure to her gender, a failure to humankind. A panic took hold, she began to shiver and shake involuntarily, and spooned her body against Michael's, needing his warmth and comfort.

Awakening to her condition, he knew immediately from his own long past experience what was happening with her. Placing a warm leg and arm over her he held her tight against him, "Let me help. You cannot do everything on your own. What do you need, my darling? What can I do to make it easier?"

She let her fears spill out, felt ashamed at showing such weakness, but knew he would not judge her, only love her.

He offered to clear his calendar and spend the afternoon working with, listening, and coaching her, "Whatever you need, darling, just tell me, I'll do it."

She looked at him with cautious but loving eyes, "I need to practice in front of an objective person, Michael, which you are not. Do you think I could ask Aunt Anne? Would that be too much of an imposition?"

He kissed the tip of her nose, picked up his phone from the bedside table and called Anne.

By the time Michael came to get her for their standard lunch and 'matinee' date, Elizabeth was in harmony with her calm spirit, with no more attacks of fear or panic. She had completed her research and additions to her own critical and analytical satisfaction, imprinting them in her memory with just a few minutes to spare, which she used for meditation.

Clearing her mind of worry, knowing that Anne was thrilled to come at three o'clock to critique her delivery, that Michael was always going to support her in this work, as he had promised numerous times, she felt reassured of success at Davidson Hall.

Their dinner that night was a more intimate affair in the King's private dining room with just King Alexander, his girlfriend Elena, the twins, and Anne, Claire being noticeably absent but not at all missed. Sitting in the more casual family drawing room after dinner, listening to music and chatting, all in the group felt a camaraderie amongst themselves that was both stimulating and satisfying, that special feeling of endearment one only experiences with others of like minds.

Mark suddenly walked over to the C.D. player and announced with a grin, "Enough chitchat and onto more important activity. Elizabeth is going to teach us to dance Calypso."

The room filled with the strong baritone sweet and emotional voice of the long ago declared 'Calypso King Of The World,' The

Mighty Sparrow, his real but hardly used name being Slinger Francisco. He was born on the smaller island of Grenada but came to live in Trinidad when just a year old, where he was inspired to develop his immense talent, climbing easily to the top of Calypso Land to deserve his given title. Prolific with his compositions, producing over seventy albums, the phenomenal genius was honored with numerous international awards including honorary doctorates from universities, and Trinidadians were only too happy and proud to claim him as their own.

Elizabeth recognized the medley of old calypsos from Sparrow's greatest hits, most dating back to her parent's youth, all beloved classics. Although she was by nature moved by the music and wanted to get up and dance, she stayed seated, her demeanor turning shy and reserved.

Michael stood and pulled her up to stand, "Come on, darling, I've been dying to see you do your native dance. And you have to teach us. The twins and I don't want to look like idiots at Carnival next year."

Elizabeth looked apprehensively at The King, "Oh dear. Sir, I'm sorry, but some of the...movements, are...quite...eh...seductive. Sexy, actually. I wouldn't want to offend-"

The three young royals who were standing beside her, eagerly awaiting instructions, collapsed on the couch next to their father and Elena, laughing hysterically.

His Majesty exhibited his regal diplomacy with an assuring smile at the bewildered Elizabeth, but an irritated 'calm-down' wave of both hands to his ill-mannered offspring, now sprawled out on either side of him laughing uncontrollably.

Shaming them into polite and considerate behavior, the King stood up and held her hand saying, "I beg you to please forgive the rudeness of my children. What they really mean to convey is there's nothing you can do that will shock me. In fact this music happens to be mine. I purchased it when The Queen and I sneaked into Trinidad for Carnival many years ago. It was the most fun we'd ever had. But, if you don't mind excusing me from the lesson, seeing I'm ahead of my foolish children and already know the steps, I'm rather tired tonight, and will leave you young people to have more fun without me." He kissed Elizabeth on both cheeks, shook his head in feigned disgust at his now chastened smiling progeny, took Elena's hand, and they departed.

The three younger royals stood up with faces and words full of apology, and encouraged by support from Anne, begged Elizabeth to teach them how to "dance Calypso."

She gave them a condescending but forgiving smile, "It's not really a specific kind of dance. Basically you let the rhythm guide you and move in time to the music, sometimes shuffling your feet slowly, sometimes picking them up, and putting one leg behind the other like this, your hips swaying." She demonstrated the simple steps and continued, "Now, when you really 'catch the spirit' as we say, you have to lose your inhibitions, and wine-"

The group looked at her with ridiculous incredulity and Michael interjected, "Oh, you drink wine at Carnival? I thought the drink of choice was local rums or beers?"

Taking in their look and Michael's silly interruption before she could explain, Elizabeth now enjoyed a good laugh, to the bemusement of the others. Eventually catching her breath, she explained that 'wine' had nothing to do with a drink but was a Trinidadian mispronunciation of 'wind' as in winding of the hips, which she proceeded to demonstrate expertly, sexily.

The twins and Anne giggled gleefully but Michael's eyes widened, he turned an embarrassed pink, and mumbled, "I hope *you* don't do that in public. You have to keep that movement just for me, in private."

She glared at him with pretended annoyance and exaggerated the winding of her hips defiantly, thrusting backwards and forwards, side to side, and around, gyrating wantonly, seductively moving her hands in the air.

Then ignoring him, not stopping, she addressed the twins, "Once you get the hang of this, which we call 'moving your waist' or 'bum-bum,' you can do other steps. At Carnival people really go wild, doing all kinds of fun things, sometimes making up new steps depending on the words in the song they're dancing to. Anyway, I think I'd better stop now. I don't think your brother can handle more of this tonight. The poor thing's sensibilities have been heavily taxed, it would seem."

They all laughed at her teasing. Michael squeezed her hand saying with a mock threat, "I'll show you my 'sensibilities,' later."

On their return to his apartments, Michael magnanimously informed Elizabeth that in view of her nervousness about her big day tomorrow, and for the fact that they had already made love twice that day, although he was dying to make love to her again tonight, he would make the supreme sacrifice and deprive himself by giving her instead, a relaxing, stress releasing full body massage. Knowing his unrelenting concupiscence, Elizabeth gave him a demurely cynical smile but graciously accepted his offer, remarking that she missed her weekly massages back in Trinidad. Michael promised he would more than make up for that with his great expertise, and they both proceeded to undress.

Lying down to receive his ministrations, through closing eyes she caught a glimpse of him. His face looked professionally serious as he rubbed his hands together with what she could smell was lavender oil. However, when her eyes dropped to between his naked legs and saw a seriously unprofessional arousal there, she smiled to herself in the knowledge that her initial cynicism was not unwarranted, and started to amusingly make bets with herself as to how long he would last.

To her great surprise he actually got through the whole of her frontal massage, and did a fine job of it too, although he did dally long on her breasts and inner thighs.

Starting on her back, his breathing began to deepen when he vigorously kneaded her buttocks, and she smelt a totally different oil. He had changed the oil to one with a spicier, sexier, scent, and then, she recognized it, *It's Ylang Ylang!* That, is when she knew he was undone, and so was she.

She murmured under her hair, now spread out over her face and back, "Enough, darling, stop torturing yourself-"

Breathing harder, he mumbled, "No. I promised you a full body massage...and I'm going to give it...to you...out and...in." He hurriedly rubbed the back of her thighs and calves, "And now for your 'happy ending,' you want it in the front or in the back?"

In less than a second she flipped over onto her back and pulled him to her, sending the bottle of Ylang Ylang oil flying in the air. Michael caught it just in time to stop it from falling on Elizabeth, but not quickly enough to stop it from spilling its contents on her. Sliding, literally, on top of her, and inside of her, he more than managed to hold up his end of the bargain and completed her full body massage, out and in, with a 'happy ending' for both.

CHAPTER
19

*M*ichael banged the entry door to his apartments shut as he rushed into Elizabeth's suite, "So sorry I'm late, darling, but something I'd ordered for you only just arrived."

Standing in front of the full-length mirror, she looked at his reflection complimenting hers and her face softened as the tension she had been feeling left her, "You're not late, my darling, and I was well attended to by Pamela."

"I'm sure. Thank you Pam, you can go now, I'll take over," he gave Pamela, Elizabeth's new and idolizing maid, a polite smile, and began helping Elizabeth into her jacket, "you look absolutely beautiful, darling."

She had pinned the sides of her hair behind her neck hoping it would make her look more mature, which it didn't, but she looked elegantly professional in a beige Oscar De La Renta suit over an emerald green silk and lace blouse. Having worn the same outfit to her first speech in Trinidad she was sentimentally attached to it feeling it to be somewhat of a lucky charm. *Nobody pelted me with rotten eggs or tomatoes then, so hopefully that won't happen this time either!* She allowed herself a nervous half-smile at the thought.

Michael noticed the smile, "I hope this is going to broaden your smile and give you the positive energy you need," he pulled something out of his jacket pocket, "lift your hair please."

With an expression of surprise, she obeyed, "Darling, what have you done? The gorgeous roses and lilies on my dresser are more than enough-" her eyes took in what he had done and her mouth froze in a gasp.

Finished clasping a choker around her neck, Michael's own smile broadened, "Don't say anything until we get the earrings on, I'm going to need your help with this." He handed her one earring, then managed to successfully hook the other into the hole in her right earlobe.

Hooking hers into her left she said softly, "Michael...I...I can't-"

"I designed them for you myself, do you like them?"

She stared at the jewelry in amazement. Her initial intention was to refuse yet another extravagant gift, but his intuitive interruption of her words gave her the realization of how insulting and hurtful that would be, considering the love he demonstrated in the effort and trouble he had gone to for her. She knew her lover was a man of numerous creative talents, but had never thought of him in the artistic sense, at least not as a designer of jewelry.

The earrings and necklace were extraordinarily beautiful. The thick gold chain was similar to a Cartier design. In its center hung a two-inch round gold medallion which held the face of a cherub with the most angelic smile. Its eyes glowed with two of the darkest emeralds she had ever seen. The entire face was encircled with a wreath of tiny roses in the centers of which were minute white diamonds.

Each earring was an inch-wide gold rose, and in its center were similar miniature white diamonds to the ones in the cherub medallion, encircling an emerald as deep in color as the cherub's eyes, with similar lush *jardins*.

She put one hand on the medallion, the other on an earring, "Michael...I'm shocked...it's the most beautiful thing anyone has ever made for me. I can't believe you designed them yourself. They are incredibly beautiful. I don't know how to thank you. What inspired you? I...I'm in awe."

He glowed love and pride, "You, are my inspiration, angel, will be forever. You inspire me to create great things. And the best is yet to come." He kissed her softly on her lips so as not to remove her lipstick, "Let's go angel, your public awaits."

The Rolls-Royce pulled into the private celebrity entrance at the back of Davidson Hall an hour before the recommended time. Even though she had previously been to Davidson Hall, met and rehearsed with everyone who was associated with the production of her event, Elizabeth insisted on giving herself extra time to de-stress and pray in the dressing room, alone.

Just before Jenkins opened the car door to escort her inside, Michael embraced her gently, "Darling, if you change your mind, feel it'll help to have me there, I'm a phone call away. I'll stay nearby in the car, working at my laptop."

"Thank you, darling. I'll be fine. I'm looking forward to seeing the D.V.D. with you later." She gave him a quick tender kiss and moved to the now open door, "Thanks for convincing me to allow Aunt Anne and Megan to be in the audience, it does make me feel like I'll have some family support."

He took her hand and kissed her open palm, "You'll always have it. Aunt Anne is extremely impressed with you, and what you're doing. You're going to be awesome. Bowl them over. The genderless God is with you. I love you."

"I love you too. See you later."

Standing alone on the huge stage in front of two thousand strangers, Elizabeth had to call on every ounce of bravery she ever had in her entire life to stop herself from running hysterically back to the dressing room. The meditation and affirmative prayers she thought would assist in calming her seemed to have been for naught. She now felt totally deserted, her trembling legs useless, and wished she could just sprout wings and fly away. She fought for focus, said a silent prayer to the Universal Spirit and that of her paternal grandmother, to give her the fortitude to carry on in the crusade against eons of ignorance and injustice, and instantaneously, she became aware of her legs. They were steady, no longer shaking, she was grounded. A serenity came upon her and she became extremely present, a spiritual being having a human existence.

Picking up the microphone from the table where a water jug and two glasses stood alongside her cue cards, notes, a slide projector, and a vase of multicolored roses mixed with white lilies and curly willow sent by Michael, she smiled softly, turned slightly, and saying its words clearly, she pointed to the banner that hung high on the velvet curtains behind her:

"GOD HAS NO GENDER"

"I suppose you are wondering, who is this Elizabeth Richardson you so politely welcomed when Dr. Norton introduced me. You're probably speculating as to who this woman is that's so presumptuous to think she can give a new insight about the gender of God, is so bold to dare think she can teach something new. Well, honestly, that's not me. Nothing I'll say here tonight is anything new, though maybe to some, but not to all. Much of the information I'll be giving has been around since the beginning of recorded time. I'm simply hoping to impart it concisely and believably. What you choose to do with it is entirely up to you. I've no desire to control your minds and lives as others have. What I say may elate, or deflate, or motivate you. Or free you, or bound you tighter, or…anger you. Or you may even fearfully try to ignore and suppress the emotions you'll feel. Whatever way you handle your emotions, I humbly beg of you to hear me out, just listen to the message, don't shoot the messenger."

She gave a little smile, which she noticed was returned by very few people in the first several rows as she heard soft murmurings dispersed throughout the audience.

She felt both pleased and nervous to see although females in the crowd vastly outnumbered males, there were many more males here than had ever attended her speeches before. "As you may have read in your programs, there'll be a slide presentation by Professor Dr. Daniel Thomas after my speech, after which he and I will strive to answer your questions. But first, I would like to ask *you* a question, which I'd like you to answer simply by a show of hands. Who among you knows that before men decided God was male in the newer religions of the last two-plus millennia, that God was worshipped as female?"

There was stirring in the audience as many hands shot up all around, but following some harsh murmurs, several were dropped. Elizabeth stretched her neck slightly shaking her head, "Oh, I see some people aren't sure of their own knowledge and have put their hands back down. Perhaps I can help those people get clear in their knowledge, but I certainly don't want to force them to change their minds, as others around them do. My only wish is that everyone knows it doesn't matter what *people* think of what *you* know, just that *you* think, and *you* know.

Before I attempt to communicate what knowledge I have gained on the true gender of God, I'm going to answer the question that I'm sure is on everyone's minds...I was raised in a Christian religion, my family is devoutly Catholic. So, this starts you wondering, how is it that a woman indoctrinated practically from birth in one of the most fanatical patriarchal religions of all time, could come to the conclusion that God is not male and has no gender? I'll abbreviate the answer. The most obvious reason would be that I am, after all, female, and what *thinking* female would want to live under the yoke of a religion that strives to deprive her of one of the most basic of human rights, the right of gender equality. The right to fully serve its Christian people during worship and in everyday life; to be respected as equally intelligent and capable as her male counterpart, treated accordingly, and not considered to be "*subservient*" to him, to use a Biblical metaphor a mere "*rib*."

Then there's the right to decide what she can handle in her own life with her own mind and body, when she alone is faced with a, to her, devastating unwanted pregnancy. All these rights denied simply because of being female, when Christ himself according to the male propounded Bible, loved, respected and surrounded himself with females, not *just* males.

He preached and practiced equality of men and women, something perhaps unprecedented in those times and even more remarkable, written about in the New Testament Gospels during the rule of male dominated imperialistic Rome. You can peruse the Bible and find passages that corroborate his love of females including his three miracles resurrecting people from the dead, all involving females. One because he was touched by the weeping of a mother for her son; another, the twelve-year-old daughter of a synagogue elder; and, Lazarus, brother of two special women in Jesus's life, Mary and Martha."

Elizabeth picked up a paper from the table and read, "In the Gospel of Philip, he refers to 'Three Marys.' "*Three Mary's walked with the lord: his mother, his sister, and Mary of Magdala, his companion. His sister, mother, and companion, were Mary.*" In another passage of Philip's he writes: '*The companion is Mary of Magdala. Jesus loved her more than his students. He kissed her often on her face and they said,*"*Why do you love her more than us?*" *The savior answered,*"*Why do I not love you like her? If a blind man and one who sees are together in darkness, they are the same. When light comes, the one who sees will see light. The blind man stays in darkness.*"

She looked up, "Obviously Jesus elevated this particular female, Mary Magdalene, above all other disciples. So much so the 'rock' on which he supposedly built his church, Peter, was jealous of her esteemed position, according to what's written around the second century in the Gospel of Mary. Actually, brother Andrew was the first to question Mary's words of enlightenment given her by Jesus when he said to the men, "*Say what you think about what she said. I do not believe the savior said this. These teachings are of strange ideas.*"Then Peter asked, "Did he *really speak to a* woman *secretly, without our knowledge, and not openly? Are we to turn and all listen to her? Did he prefer her to us?"Then Mary wept and said to Peter, "My brother, Peter, what do you think? Do you think I concocted this in my heart or I am lying about the savior?"Levi answered, saying to Peter, "Peter, you are always angry. Now I see you contending against this woman as if against an adversary. If the savior made her worthy, who are you to reject her? Surely the savior knows her very well. That is why he loved her more than us. We should be ashamed and put on the perfect person and be with him as he commanded us, and we should preach the gospel, without making any rule or law other than what the savior said."When Levi said these things, they began to go out and proclaim and to preach.'* End of verse.

Another story, this one from the New Testament, is that Jesus's first miracle was changing water into wine at the behest of a female, his mother, for, of all things, a celebration of a marriage. Marriage being something the Bible skirts around when it comes to the spousal bonding of Jesus and Mary Magdalene, and which the Church chooses to ignore altogether.

Both Jewish and Christian Biblical scholars know the Hebrew word 'Messiah' means "The Anointed One" as does the Greek rooted word 'Christ.' Research shows, in the ancient rituals of the Near East, the King was anointed by the Royal Bride.

Though details are varied, there's only one story recorded in the canonical Gospels of the Christian faith of an actual anointing of Jesus, by a woman at a banquet feast in Bethany.

In pouring the unguent of nard over Jesus's head, the woman traditionally identified with 'The Magdalene' performed an identical act to the marriage rite of anointing the Bridegroom or King. Many scholars believe the account of the anointing of Jesus by The Magdalene proves this woman he so loved and kept close, was actually his Goddess Bride in a Sacred Marriage.

It makes one wonder why the Church focused on giving Jesus's mother Mary all the glory, down-playing Mary Magdalene's role, though she was obviously of great importance to him. Similarities of the story of that anointing from the four Christian Gospels are found in myths of celebrations in so-called 'pagan' fertility religions of the Middle East that worshipped Tammuz, a shepherd God originally King of Erech; Dumuzi, Sumerian God of vegetation; and Adonis, a handsome youth under the patronage of Zeus, supreme God of the ancient Greeks.

It makes sense that Jesus who was of the royal lineage of the dynasty of King David would be anointed in the regal manner of ancient Jewish tradition, by the woman he loved above all others, Mary Magdalene, in a ritual performed during a marriage ceremony. Because at that time, according to Jewish law derived from the Torah, males were married before their twentieth birthday. For Jesus to have been unmarried and celibate as suggested by the Church, he would've been considered a heretic and certainly would not have had a following. He himself declared that he came "*not to destroy the law, but to fulfill it.*" He also acknowledges this type of rite in his role as sacrificed King, in Mark, chapter 14:verse 8b: "*She has anointed me in preparation for burial.*" The Bible states Mary Magdalene was prominent among the women disciples who went to Jesus's tomb the Sunday after his crucifixion and found it empty, the male disciples already in hiding. She was the first person he appeared to after his death, not his mother.

The New Testament records that Jesus had women as companions, *disciples*; was generous with his time and attention toward them, preaching of a society where all are equal, encouraging Mary Magdalene to sit at his feet to absorb his words of wisdom alongside other disciples, educating her equally. Thus, the question begs to be asked, why then did the Church choose to ignore the importance of Mary Magdalene, and for centuries actually besmirched her calling her "*prostitute*" and "*whore,*" these abhorrences only now, thousands of years later, being revised?

Why too would the founding fathers of Christianity propagate denigration of the female of the human species, the gender that suffers the most to continue it, relegating her to be just a "*hand-maiden,*" "*subservient*" to her husband, created from a mere "*rib of man,*" when the man for whom they founded the Christian religion with which to worship him, never preached or practiced such abominations!

Notably, throughout the entire New Testament there is not one word credited to be uttered by Jesus that his disciples, preachers, should be *only* males. Yet, in the Bible we read in Paul's letter to the Corinthians: "*For the man is not of the woman, but the woman of the man. Let the woman keep silence in the churches, for it is not permitted unto them to speak, but they are commanded to be under obedience, so saith the law. And if they learn anything, let them ask their husbands at home, for it is a shame for women to speak in the church.*" And again in his letter to Timothy he states: "*Let the woman learn in silence with all subjection. But I suffer a woman not to teach or to usurp authority over the man, but to be in silence. For Adam was first formed and then Eve, and Adam was not deceived, but the woman being deceived was in the transgression-*"

Mr. Paul certainly epitomized male chauvinism with the discriminatory stories and concepts he and or Church patriarchs composed, and dishonestly attributed to Jesus, their "*Son of God.*" It is incomprehensible and atrocious that some men today, knowing the equal intelligence of women, still believe, preach, and practice, this diatribeous oppressive patriarchal nonsense!

In order to control and shut-up women, and destroy the power they had as Goddess worshippers, the writers of the Bible even ridiculously chose to ignore the biological fact that the man is of the woman and not the other way around!

Most religions claiming to be Christian propagate the most un-Christian of practices: blatant discrimination of half the human population: females! If these religions truly believe Jesus to be The Son of God, how is it that they can indulge in the most un-Godly of practices: disparagement and belittlement of the half of humanity who carries the heaviest load to continue its very existence? Why do men still continue to this day to preach of the outrageous blaming of Eve who represents women, for the downfall of Adam who represents mankind, when the whole world has been thrown off balance and suffers because of this ridiculous fairytale of man not being held accountable for the carnality in his own head? Surely it's time to, making better use of Paul's Biblical words, "*Put away childish things.*"

Of course, some people don't believe Jesus was the Son of God, saying he actually confirmed his simple humanity when he said, "*These things that I do, so shall* you *do, and greater!*""

Elizabeth paused for effect then continued, "Luke tells us in chapter 17:verses 20-21 Jesus said, "*Behold, the Kingdom of God is within* you!" And also-" she paused again, raised her hand and her voice, and pointed to the audience, ""*Ye, are Gods!*""

She smiled as many startled people jumped, then she continued, "Jesus Christ gave us many great perfect teachings, yet men prefer to follow ridiculous nonsensical teachings of unenlightened lesser others in so-called 'holy books.' Jesus was obviously telling us not just *he* alone, but *all of us,* are part of the Divine. Mind you, many scholars will point out that he simply said pretty much the same things that Buddha, another great mystical teacher, said, five hundred years *before* Jesus!

However, the fact remains that whether you believe he was the *only* Son of God or not, he's been the most influential man of our times, with numerous religions or cults founded in his name in the last two millenniums. Just two thousand years.

So, seeing there's evidence of human existence on earth in fossils that are more than a *hundred thousand* years old, numerous more millenniums than two, it stands to reason there must have been more claims of being sons and daughters of God, or Gods themselves, *before* the God of Abraham, or Jesus's Father in Heaven, or Allah, came along.

Let's face it, anybody with a modicum of intelligence today knows the Bible is comprised mostly of fairytales, fables, folklore, myths and metaphors, not meant to be taken literally, but was an easy way to keep under control, the simple people of a more ignorant, scientifically uneducated world, at that time."

There were stirrings and loud murmurings from the audience and Elizabeth took a sip of water but remained silent until some people started shushing the others and everyone became quiet again. "That's not to say that *all* the people and events written of in the Bible did not exist or happen. It means they probably didn't exist or happen *exactly* the way in which the stories were told and much later written down. We all know how stories get embellished, changing their original content when passed on from person to person. So why should scriptures passed on hundreds of years later not be filled with *miss*-understandings, *miss*-quotations, *miss*-conceptions, *miss*-interpretations, and, alas, *miss*-takes? Additionally, the knowledge that early clerical leaders censored, chopped and changed, various translations of scriptures when they didn't like what they said, makes it difficult for open-minded, intelligent, educated people, to know *what* they can believe of what is left!

The fact is, there is really no *physical* evidence of the existence of things that most of today's religions tell us to blindly have faith in.

But, there is much irrefutable evidence of other, *older,* religions which are deliberately ignored by many historians, and usually sullied as being "*pagan,*" primarily because they worshiped the *female* God, the Goddess.

In checking innumerable books on the history of religion, I found too few that even mentioned the first religions of the Goddess. And those that did, usually relegated her to just a few lines or pages.

Yet, the earliest statues or figurines of *deities* unearthed in excavations are, *female*! Some later referred to as 'Venuses.' Many have small heads, all are voluptuous with large breasts, some have seemingly pregnant bellies symbolizing fertility. An enormous amount of Goddess sculptures and plaques have been found, in areas as widespread as France, Spain, Germany, Austria, Czechoslovakia, Russia, the Mediterranean, many other countries, spanning a period of more than 10,000 years!

Even in the Bible, passages report "*idols*" of the female deity Asherah were found on every high hill, under every green tree, and next to altars in the temples. Museums worldwide have objects and relics of the Goddess religion, though they are seldom properly displayed, and even when they are, often not objectively described in detail, but instead inconsequentially and irreverently referred to as "*pagan*," or God-less.

Why most of the Goddess information and artifacts unearthed, and corroborated, though obscurely by primarily male authors in archaeological accounts, are so deliberately minimized, often ignored, sometimes hidden from public, shoved to the back of archives, is a question that needs to be answered. Could the answer lie with the blind belief in the *male* God of today who has been constantly promoted by dominating patriarchal societies these last two millennia?

Now that we have so much overwhelming proof that God was worshipped as female before, and even *after* male deities by force became popular, it must make you wonder why the Bible and other so-called 'holy books' were so determined in their efforts to try to convince us that God is male.

For those of you who are incognizant of the Goddess religion, I'll give a brief history, which is difficult because the Goddess was around a lot longer than just two millennia. Actually, based on archeological findings, she existed from the beginnings of human development, *millenniums* before the concept of the male God came in to play!

The 'Great Goddess' was worshipped in prehistoric *and* early historic times. Some authorities date her beginning in Neolithic periods of 7,000 BCE. The last Goddess temple was closed down around 500 CE. Others extend Goddess worship even further back to the Upper Paleolithic Age, about 25,000 BCE, when 'Venus-of-Willendorf' was discovered. In fact, traces of Goddess worship were found in France on a site settled by Neanderthals dating back, according to radiocarbon tests, 32,000 years! 'Venus–of-Hohle-Fels' is dated to be between 35,000 to 40,000 years old!

Take into account that Abraham, the first prophet of the Hebrew-Christian God Yahweh or Jehovah, Bible scholars believe lived no earlier than 1,800 BCE.

Remember, the three leading religions on our planet today: Judaism, Christianity, and Islam, *all* stem from Abraham!"

There were more murmurings from the crowd but softer than before as Elizabeth picked up another sheet of paper, glanced at it and continued, "Okay, let's take a look at this Goddess who had been around a lot longer than the present God has been. Firstly, what was she called, and what was her name? Among many other titles, she was called Creatress of the Universe, The Great Goddess, Divine Ancestress, Mother Goddess, Queen of Heaven, Earth Mother, The Throne. But, she did have a long list of names, depending on the part of the world where she was worshipped and the language spoken. Some of her names were Anat, Anahita, Artemis, Asherah, Ashtart, Ashtoreth, Astarte, Attoret, Au Set, Baalat, Hathor, Inanna, Innini, Ishara, Ishtar or Eostre, Istar, Nina, Umm Attar.

The Bible briefly mentions her as Ashtoreth or Asherah. Not surprisingly, the Old Testament has no word for Goddess but refers to her in the male gender, usually derogatorily, sometimes as Elohim. It simply ranks all peoples who didn't worship the new male God as "*pagans*."

In Syria her name was Athar or Baalat or Isis-Hathor. In Cilicia, southern Turkey, it was Ate or Atheh. To the Egyptians she was Isis. They also had Nut known as 'The Heavens' whose husband-brother Geb was known as 'The Earth.' The Libyan warrior-Goddess called Neith was also revered in Egypt.

In Mesopotamia the Goddess Ninlil was credited for the development of agriculture, while in Sumer in the country we now know as Iraq, the Goddess Nidaba was honored for inventing clay tablets and the art of writing; that honor proven to be deserved according to archaeological evidence of the earliest examples of written language over 5,000 years ago, at the temple of the Queen of Heaven, in Erech. Sumer also had The Creatress Queen Nana-Glorious One-Mighty Lady.

The Egyptian Cobra Goddess is believed to have been involved in the development of early medicines, which included extraction and use of venom from serpents. Not coincidently, the symbol of serpents was not only one of the Goddess symbols of ancient times, but is *still* used as the medical symbol today!

In parts of Arabia she was Umm Attar, Mother Attar. To the Vikings she was Freya, to the Canaans, Anthirat. To the Celts she was Nerthus, the Earth Mother of the Germanic tribes. In Celtic Ireland the Goddess Brigit was the divine patron of language, and Cerridwen was the Goddess of Intelligence and Knowledge. Later Celts, who preferred Goddesses over Gods, even had Goddesses for horses, in France she was Epona, in Britain Riannon, in Ireland Macha. Celts revered the Goddess Cybele who was also worshipped by the envious Romans as The Great Mother of the Gods.

All over the known world throughout the Mediterranean and as far as India, the Great Mother Goddess reigned as the supreme deity. There were also other smaller religions that worshipped Goddesses along with Gods, some still do in our time.

In Hinduism, which started around 4,000 BCE, the oldest religion that still exists today, there are many Goddesses, alongside Gods, that are still worshipped. Among them are Saraswati, the Goddess of Knowledge, the inventor of the original alphabet, the inspiration for music, poetry, drama, and science. There's Shakti, the Great Divine Mother Goddess who has two other characters known as Kali and Durga. Also Lakshmi, the gentle Goddess of beauty, prosperity, good health and joyful family life. Also, Sita, Parvati, and many others. There are about ten Goddesses who are worshipped by yogis and mystics, under the heading of Dasha Maha Vidgas. Many different areas have their own personal versions of the Goddess.

The Japanese have the Sun Goddess Amaterasu Omigami, as in ancient Anatolia, now Turkey, existed the Sun Goddess of Arinna. To the Ashanti in Africa she still is Mother Thursday. The Ibo tribe honors the earth spirit Ala who is depicted in her temples cradling or suckling an infant, a common 'pagan' symbol. This symbol, adopted by the Christian religion as Madonna and Child, helped immeasurably with the converting of 'pagans' to Christianity. So too did the adoption of other Goddess symbols, rites, and practices, dates of celebrations and festivals, including using near the solstice date for Christmas Day. We all know how much easier it is to follow that which is familiar. Forcing conversion is less difficult when the seed of brainwashing has already germinated.

Even though the Goddess of the Near and Middle East went by so many different names, the *worship,* of the Great Goddess in *numerous* areas of the ancient world, *vary only slightly* in their basic religious beliefs. As is proven by the similarities of statues, artifacts, plaques, symbols, titles, texts, rites, and rituals. I've given you just some of her names, there were others, more probably unknown to us today.

As the worship of the Great Goddess was so widespread for thousands of years, then for thousands more existed simultaneously with the newer male God religions, *how,* and *why,* did she eventually die?

For several views written on this subject, those of you who wish to pursue this and other things we discuss, we've a list of books and literature that you can take from the table by the door when you're leaving. Of course, the Bible's one of the best sources, but, you need to learn about the Goddess *first*, and then re-read the Bible with an open mind, and often between the lines."

CHAPTER
20

*E*lizabeth sensed, rather than heard or saw, a disturbance taking place in the audience somewhere to her left, and took a few cautious steps over to better see what was happening. Looking past the middle rows she saw a man attempting to stand, but the woman sitting next to him was tugging at his jacket sleeve trying to make him sit back down.

Her heart rate speeding up but her words slow and calm, Elizabeth called out to him, "Sir, you wish to leave? What have I said that offends you?"

On hearing Elizabeth, the woman dropped her hand. The man stood up and addressed Elizabeth angrily, "Everything! Everything you said offends me! What're *you* suggesting? We give up on God and start worshipping some ancient Goddess we know nothing about! How's that going to benefit humanity today? How's that going to get us out of the mess we're in? You some kind of crazy feminist? And what the hell's going to happen-"

Realizing the man was not only angry because he felt his gender power to be in jeopardy, but was also intent on using her forum to take his 'five minutes of fame,' she determined to put a stop to his tirade and interrupted him loudly and firmly, "Sir, you've asked me some questions, and even though they were premature, it's only fair, if you understand the concept of fairness, that you allow me to answer so I can get on to the heart of the subject I'm here to discuss."

Voices all around the room, both male and female, directed a variety of remarks to the man. Some said simply, "sit down, shut up!" Others were more detailed and less polite in what they thought of his lack of manners and intelligence, but then many others shouted to Elizabeth above the din, "Yes, I want to hear your answer."

She walked back to the table in the center of the stage and spoke authoritatively, "Alright, I'll give in just this once to answer a question before the designated time, and only once. Please save your questions for later. If we succumb to interruptions we could be here all night, and neither you nor I have time for that; apart from which, none of us wants to embarrassingly be thrown out of Davidson Hall because we've overstayed our welcome."

Many in the crowd laughed and some clapped. She took another sip of water and waited until they became silent, "Firstly, I do not propose that anyone worship the ancient Goddess. I'm merely trying to educate you about her existence and the power she once held, how and why she was destroyed and how all of that, unknowingly, affects societies today. And it's apparent, based on your outburst, this is absolutely necessary. My intention is to enlighten people that God has no gender by showing that it's humans who made up Goddesses and Gods, not the other way around. So, you need to bear with me until I can get to it." She fastened her eyes on the man's eyes, "Secondly, as to my being *some kind of crazy feminist* as you put it…I'm not crazy, but most definitely and proudly, a feminist. Which brings me to ask you a question, sir…who is that lady sitting next to you?"

The man bent over pulling the woman's hand but she refused to stand, "My wife of thirty-five years." He declared proudly.

Elizabeth smiled, "Sir, do you love your wife?"

The man became indignant, "Of course!"

"And sir, do you believe your wife, who you've lived with and obviously loved for the last thirty-five years, to be of equal intelligence and capabilities and deserving of the same equal rights as you?"

He sneered at Elizabeth, "Naturally! In some subjects, she's even smarter!"

"I see. Sir, the definition of a 'feminist' is one who believes females should have the same rights as males. So, I have news for you, sir... *you,* are a 'feminist'!"

The audience burst into thunderous laughter and applause, startling not only the man but Elizabeth, but she hid it well, with dignity. The man dejectedly flopped down onto his seat.

She raised her hands then slowly dropped them in a polite 'please be quiet' gesture, and the crowd courteously obeyed. "Alright, let's get back to the subject and examine *how* the Goddess religion met its loss of power and final death. According to expert authorities both Biblical and archeological, she expired because of much tortuous and oppressive violence over many, many, generations. Much of this is stated in the Bible in great detail, with several accounts of merciless slaughters and heartless massacres of those who refused to give up the worship of the Goddess, and convert to the new God Yahweh. At the back of your programs we've listed chapters and verses for whomever wishes to look them up, I don't have time to read them now. But I'll give one example of the harsh laws composed by the Levite priests that commanded Hebrew worshipers to murder their own if they refused to worship Yahweh. This is in Deuteronomy chapter 13:verse 6, '*If your brother or son or daughter or wife or friend suggest serving other gods, you must kill him, your hand must be the first raised in putting him to death and all the people shall follow you.*' This was obviously directed to male heads of households.

The general consensus amongst historians and archeologists alike is that the Near and Middle East was invaded by patriarchal warlike tribes from the north, beginning around 2,400 BCE. Although, it's suggested that small invasions of those and other tribes took place periodically as far back as 4,000 BCE. The patriarchal invaders saw themselves as superior based on their ability to violently conquer and subjugate the more culturally developed peoples of the Goddess religion. Though motivated by political ambition rather than religious fervor, they promoted their myths of a male God creating the universe when none previously existed. Yes, you heard correctly, *none previously existed*!

A male God solidified for them the justification of a kingship, and their patriarchal society, the Goddess society having been matrilineal and in some ways matriarchal.

How and when the northern invaders from mostly Russia and the Caucasus regions decided their deity was male is unknown, as, unlike Goddess societies, *no* cultural centers, temples, or tablets, of their earliest development, have been discovered. *None!*

Archeologists and historians determined them to be aggressive warriors, probably hunters, fishers, shepherds, dominantly warlike, patriarchal, and expansive. By all accounts a barbaric people. Uncivilized and brutally cruel.

Bear in mind these northern invaders were larger in stature, fairer in color, already learnt how to make iron weapons, and used their horse-drawn chariots for war; unlike the smaller, darker, civilized southern people they conquered who had no iron weapons, but gold, copper and bronze, and used their donkey-drawn chariots for transporting produce and people.

It's apparent the more cultured conquered were militarily outclassed by the armed, uncivilized, larger, violent, patriarchal northern tribes collectively called Indo-Europeans.

The transition from the 'death' of the Goddess religion to the 'birth' of the God religion was achieved, to borrow a description from Genesis chapter 3:verse 16, in reference to how females, because of the so-called 'sin of Eve,' must suffer through "*childbearing*," the God birth was endured with much "*pain.*" Again, mostly on the female's part.

By the way, I'd like someone to explain how it would be possible for an animal to expel an object that's much larger than the area it has to pass through, do so without some degree of pain. That's just not rational, but then, when it comes to female issues, there is certainly not much rationality in most of the male propounded Bible. And surely, the more intelligent way to handle the female who has to endure this "*pain*"as she alone is physically given the supreme responsibility of carrying and delivering the babies to continue the human race, should be with love, care, respect, admiration, and devotion! And not as a curse, as Genesis in the Bible declares, which still causes females in many parts of the world to be denigrated and abused, when the human race will undoubtedly *die,* if females did not courageously and heroically go through "*pain*" while delivering."

Elizabeth heard dispersed clapping coming from the audience and along with it ubiquitous loud murmurings. She was disappointed they did not react with more passion, but assumed it was because of their European conservative politeness.

With calmer actions than feelings she took a sip of water, slowly replaced her glass on the table, and waited for quiet to resume, "The invaders, with their more advanced iron weapons, were able to rule, literally with an 'iron fist.' Many new laws were imposed, and gradually, over millenniums, the Goddess was deposed, destroyed.

The conquered were ruled by fear. One Hittite law stated, "*If anyone opposes the judgment of the King, his household will become a ruin. If anyone opposes the judgment of a dignitary, his head will be cut off.*" They were forced to become subservient while the invaders became leaders and royalty. Overtime in different areas the invaders acquired legitimacy and acceptance of their kingship by marrying Goddess priestesses, who most likely had rights to the throne because of matrilineal descent. Later in Egypt, after two Goddesses were demoted, the king wore both crowns that were their symbols, one inside the other! The Goddess Maat was allowed to retain her nature and qualities *only* as long as she was the *possession* of a God! For millenniums after waves of invasions started, the Goddess religion assimilated male Gods, but remained the popular religion. In some areas the male deity was attached to the Goddess as either a husband, son, lover, or brother.

There're accounts of the Goddess grieving over the untimely violent death of the same male relative, much like that in the Bible about the Marys grieving for Jesus.

Some legends portray the male deity as a hero destroying the Goddess because he was promised supremacy in the hierarchy of the Divine. When the God Horus was brought in as the son of Isis, the priests introduced a new concept of God the Father. They called him Ptah, describing him as the creator of everything, who, while masturbating, produced all the other Gods, causing elimination of the need for a Goddess!"

Though some in the audience burst into laughter, most people giggled softly while a few called out remarks like, "*ridiculous*," "*crazy*," and other indiscernible mumblings.

Again Elizabeth waited for absolute silence before continuing, "As an aside, in one of several contradictions in the Bible, this one ignoring the 'only one God' propaganda, the book of Genesis, chapter 6:verses 1-4, says there was a time that a *bunch* of male deities came down and mated with attractive females when they, "*went into the daughters of humans, who bore children to them*," declaring of the offspring: "*these were the heroes of old, warriors of renown*." Interesting how monotheism is used as a convenience, isn't it?

Anyway, more male Gods kept being introduced as decades and centuries went by. They're all known to most educated people like you, as many were worshipped in more recent historical times and written about extensively.

In texts of certain tribes there are descriptions of various myths of rapes and murders of female deities. The victims were serpents, dragons, or animals, all symbolic of the Goddess. Gradually, Goddess worshippers were forced to submit to the aggressive conquerors who foisted their newly invented God upon them as they wrested control over their lands, property, lives. Eventually, priests of the God worshipping invaders replaced the priestesses of the Goddess."

Elizabeth proceeded to describe the Luvians or Luvites who may have been a priestly caste of the northern Indo-Europeans, from which originated the powerful violence preaching Levite priests of the Hebrews. They claimed the new male God Yahweh commanded the people provide them with all manner of 'gifts' including food, gold, silver, livestock and property. She explained these ruling-class priests composed patriarchal laws to effectively subjugate and control the ordinary Hebrews and conquered peoples, persisting in destroying the Goddess religion.

She quoted a passage from the book of Jeremiah chapter 44:verses 15-19 that showed as late as 600 BCE, a Hebrew colony in Egypt refused to give up their ancestral Goddess worship for the new God Yahweh, declaring that when they used to worship her, '*We had plenty of food then, we lived well, we suffered no disasters. But since we have given up offering incense to the Queen of Heaven and pour libations in her honor, we have been destitute and have perished either by sword or famine.*'

She gave a brief explanation of the Hebrew tribes, their priest's methodical and violent methods of ensuring the eventual complete destruction of the Goddess religion and with it the equal rights of females, then the imitating Christians jumping on their 'bandwagon,' with the Mohammedans to follow. She reminded the attentive audience that the three patriarchal religions that dominate today's global societies, Judaism, Christianity, and Islam, all had their beginnings in the Abrahamic tradition of the Hebrew Bible.

She gave just two short quotations to further show the contempt that was, and in some religions still is, felt for females. The first was one that Hebrew males are taught to say every day: "*Blessed art thou O Lord our God, King of the Universe, who has not made me a woman.*" and the second was from Mohammed: "*When Eve was created, Satan rejoiced.*"

She then quoted from Paul's letter to the Ephesians chapter 5:verses 22-24: "*Wives, submit yourselves unto your own husbands as unto the Lord. For the husband is the head of the wife even as Christ is the head of the Church and he is the savior of the body. Therefore as the Church is subject unto Christ, so let the wives be to their own husbands in everything.*"

Picking up one of her notes she glanced at it briefly and spoke slowly, "Alright, let's look at *why* the Goddess was deliberately, systematically, destroyed, which, incidentally, helps to prove God has no gender.

Many anthropologists and scholars presume the initial worship of a female deity as opposed to a male, was influenced by the ignorance of people in humanity's early days in regards to the male's role in pro-creation. They assume the female was more revered because her body was obviously the one honored with the continuation of the species; but, even *after* the physiology of the male's contribution came to be understood, females were still held in higher esteem. Respected not only for their ability to conceive, endurance and forbearance during pregnancy and delivery, but valued for their intuition, wisdom, coun-seling, care-giving, healing, and creative talents. These were evidenced in their developments in agriculture, medicine, formal education, business, the arts, prophecy, and other natural talents, not the least of which was their...sexuality.

Ah yes, their sexuality. This later was used to play a major part in their downfall.

As appreciation of the attributes of females grew so did the basic human need to feel secure in a mystifying, frightening, constantly changing world. Without scientific knowledge and understanding of the planet on which they lived, it was only natural that early humans looked to the adoration and appeasement of things that elated, intimi-dated, mystified, and controlled their lives. Such as the moon, sun, earth, rain, mountains, volcanoes, rivers, oceans, etcetera.

It appears an extraordinarily wise female, or females...s, fell into that category, and thus the Goddess was 'born.' Possibly. In actual fact, nobody knows how the Goddess was born. Or just as importantly, *exactly* how the newer God was born. But, if you are to put credence in parts of the Bible and so-called holy books, what is blatantly obvious is that the patriarchal men who wrote them were determined to kill off the Goddess, and force their vengeful God on humanity in order to control the people, their production, their property, and most of all their women. Why was it important to control the women? Because the women appeared to be in control!

There are numerous accounts of legends and fragments of prayers and texts that suggest the Goddess was the personification of sexuality, not monogamous, and through her incarnation in her high priestess, annually chose a new mate in a sacred marriage. Thought to be a younger man as he was often referred to as her 'son,' the 'husband' assumed the role of consort or king. In earlier times when his year was up, he was ritually sacrificed in autumn and then 'resurrected' in glory in the spring. One Sumerian legend says that although the Goddess Inanna grieved her youth's death, it occurred because of her wrath at his arrogance in attempting to equate to her.

There are texts from Isin, a flourishing city of Sumer, that confirm the young kings were *not* the dominant partner, but their dependence of being the God was totally upon the Goddess. Even the invading patriarchal Hittites adopted the Sun Goddess of Arinna, praying to her as '*She who controls* kingship *in heaven and on earth.*'

The custom of marriage to the high priestess was later forcefully used to legitimize a man to the top royal position for the subjugated people to behold.

In Babylonian times the king was no longer sacrificed but instead humiliated. In other legends, because he was forbidden from copulating with another after the Goddess, he chose castration rather than death. All over the ancient world there are texts and legends describing similar events of the ritual of a divine marriage and a dying God. In all cases the Goddess through her high priestess *still* remained in power!

It's understandable why the patriarchal northern invaders were intimidated by the institution of hereditary royalty that came by divine right only, through the Goddess, and therefore the *female* lineage. The role of high priestess juxtaposed with that of Queen. Her esteemed political position and power was a huge hindrance to the patriarchal invader's designs on kingship and control of the government, lands, and property.

Some experts believe the castration ritual replaced the husband-king sacrifice, castration is evident in several ancient accounts of the

Goddess religion. Others suggest that as men began to gain power, they replaced priestesses, this right achieved by imitating the female clergy that had the power originally, by the 'priestess wannabees' divesting themselves of their male organs in a castration ritual, then donning women's garments. In Anatolia, now Turkey, alone, classical texts report the number of eunuch priests serving the Goddess religion in certain cities were as many as 5,000! In some areas it appears they gained total control of the Goddess religion. Emasculation, in return for domination, shows their desperation!

The temple complex of the Goddess was the heart of the community. It was customary for many women to live there. It controlled not just religious matters and counseling, but all essential activities, including employment of farmers, gardeners, shepherds, hunters, fishermen, artisans, traders, etcetera, and the ownership of land and domesticated animals. It maintained the cultural and economic fiscal records, functioning as the central management offices of the society.

The women took their lovers from among the men who came to worship the Goddess. The sexual act was thought to be so sacred, it was even performed in the temple, one of the Goddess aspects being the patron deity of Sexual Love and Procreation. Human sexuality was considered a reward from the Divine, not associated with shame and sinfulness as later promoted by some patriarchal religions.

Highly respected women from wealthy and royal families along with ordinary women of the community participated in the sexual customs. They lived in the temple sometimes, free to come and go as they wished, could marry at any time, and as late as the first century CE, were regarded as exceptionally good wives, considered "*sanctified*," "*holy women*," "*the undefiled*."

The sacred sexual custom was an integral part of the religion, described as a 'gift' to *civilize* the people of Erech, in Sumer, now Iraq. The women were not forced to be faithful to their husbands but instead had sexual independence, could make love to various men of their choosing.

The children were communally raised, remember the old African tried and true saying, '*it takes a village to raise a child*.' They would have questionable paternity, presumably inheriting their mother's titles and properties, matrilineal descent being the inherent social structure of the community.

So, let's put this in perspective from the patriarchal invaders point of view: They've come down from the ice-cold harsh primitive north to a "*land of milk and honey*," to find a fairly peaceful, intelligent people, smaller and darker, with no iron weapons with which to fight, who use their chariots for nonviolent transport with smaller donkeys, not with powerful horses for warring like the barbarians.

These smaller people have gold, silver, bronze, agriculture, animals, food in abundance, are developing medicines, are smarter, talented, industrious, and, loving. They have flourishing communities, in some cases even walled cities, and temples where they communally worship and celebrate. They have festivals, feasts, fun. Obviously the barbaric uncivilized tribes would covet such a well-organized advanced people, their property, and riches.

The invaders, with their superior weapons and equipment, larger physical size and violent, patriarchal attitude and ego, were able to conquer the physical…but the mental and spiritual presented more of a problem. The conquerors realized that in order to control the conquered so they could enjoy the fruits of their labors, they needed to control their minds. You control the mind, you control the purse! Unfortunately for the conquerors, the conquered already had their own mind-control, the Goddess religion!

To make matters worse for the patriarchal northern bullies, this religion worshiped a *female*! And, to top it off, was *run* by females! Females were in control of the society! They not only had the freedom to do as they pleased but property and title were passed down from mother to daughter, not father to son! Naturally, to a patriarchal mind, females should not have all this power, property, and, reverent respect. So, having killed off masses of the southern people initially, again, check the Bible for accounts of the slaughter and massacres of "*pagans,*" the invaders realized they needed to destroy their Goddess religion to gain full patriarchal control.

And of course, this business of a woman having the freedom to have sex with various men of her choosing had to be stopped, so that men could now claim paternity of children and therefore all rights to property. So thus, the natural sexual customs practiced for thousands of years, were now being turned into a new "*morality*" issue by the uninvited immigrant 'priests.'

Laws were composed to control women and deprive them of the same rights as men. *Only* women, were forced to comply with pre-marital virginity and marital fidelity. Females were cut out of inheritances. Many became chattel, relegated to virtual slavery at the hands of men. Men were encouraged to degrade women, forcefully take as wives, rape, beat, and, if they so desired, treat them like slaves, they could divorce them simply by saying the word, throw them out when they tired of them, and allowed to have many wives, concubines and lovers.

Women lost their sexual autonomy along with their independence legally, economically, socially, reduced to being completely powerless.

But, despite the harsh one-sided laws, it took many generations, *millenniums*, before the destruction of the Goddess religion came to finality."

CHAPTER
21

"The male God, which, remember, unlike the Goddess, there is *no* discovered evidence of its original existence, was forced upon the people. But, for millenniums it struggled for acceptance alongside the still worshipped Goddess. Only through forceful, fearful, unwavering violence, constant threats, and aggressive indoctrination, was the patriarchal God able to triumph and eventually become the unmitigated supreme deity.

The Old Testament is rife with passages of denigration and debasement of Goddess worshipers, along with commands to destroy the people of her religion, referring to them derogatorily as '*pagans*,' her symbols as '*idols*.'

Well, do you still wonder why I believe God has no gender? From the beginning of time people have been making up religions for Goddesses and Gods, rationalizing it was the best way to control and supposedly 'civilize' humanity, literally by putting "*the fear of God*" in them. Still today, most religions, and nations, control people by fear, threatening some form of violence, "*If you don't behave, God is going to get you!*" Or "*military might*" will!"

Elizabeth walked over to the table, put down the paper she had been glancing at periodically, picked up another, took a sip of water, and walked back to the front of the stage, "My conversion to a genderless God came about after years of searching, researching, and major soul-searching. I did this through years of global travel, visiting shrines, holy places, archaeological sites, traversing ancient ruins, and museums, digging in their archives, whenever I was allowed.

Believe me, my investigations were thwarted at every turn by the men who ran the various institutions but I persevered, and triumphed. I spent countless hours in science, natural history museums, and planetariums, read thousands of books and literature. I attended innumerable lectures given by both male and female scientists, international historians, archeologists, and various sages of great knowledge. I interviewed them, and respected experts, spiritual, clerical and secular, and, through prayer, meditation, I was eventually blessed with enlightenment.

The more knowledge I absorbed, the more I wanted proof of it. You could say I was sister to the proverbial 'Doubting Thomas.' Truth came to me slowly, painfully. My childhood indoctrination was so well ingrained, it held steadfast through my early journey on the path to Truth. It took a lot more courage than I knew I had, to persevere with my quest for Truth. My battle against my brainwashed demons was eventually won, not only by studying the damaging effects of the ignorance of our ancestors who bowed down to archaic retarding beliefs and acceptances, but by my continuous observation and study of life around me. I realized I needed to get realistic new answers to my doubting old questions. Interestingly, it was my father, not my mother, who first told me about the earliest religions of the Goddess, then advised me to read the Bible and study world religions, so that I could better understand why humanity is still suffering with old problems today, despite all our new scientific knowledge and technological progress.

As a questioning pubescent girl, what struck me as odd was why did God who created everything and everyone, have to have a gender, and how come it's male? Why is God King, not Queen? When even in nature, life fails to exist without the Queen bee or Queen ant, not the King? And males of most species are more colorful and beautiful so they can attract the reluctant female, and not the other way around?

Understand, I hadn't yet begun to travel, investigate, and educate myself. I thought, if God indeed has a gender, *why* would it be male? Why 'Our Father who art in Heaven?' Shouldn't it be 'Our Mother who art in Heaven?' The female is the gender whose body goes through the sometimes difficult process of carrying, and *always* painful process of delivering, of the babies to continue the existence of the human race.

What's of more importance, the few minutes of male pleasure to ejaculate the sperm that connects with the female's egg, or the female's nine months of discomfort growing that sperm and egg into another human, then suffering the utmost agony to deliver it into this world? And, is usually expected to carry the larger burden of its upbringing.

Which gender is the most tested here? Exhibits the most strength? Has the most tenacity, patience, courage, or to put it more bluntly in modern-day terms, 'has the most balls?'"

Elizabeth paused, she knew that some people would find the last remark distasteful, but she also knew it was important that it be said, and dramatically. There was a second of completely dead silence as though the audience was trying to grasp her meaning, or recover from yet another shock. Then suddenly, every woman was on her feet, applauding vigorously, many calling out "Yes!" "Yeah!" "Yah!" and other comments she could not discern.

Gradually a few men, probably husbands or lovers who wanted to ensure a warm bed tonight, stood up as well, some smiling but clapping less enthusiastically. Elizabeth could barely suppress her pleased smile and thought, *At last, they're getting it, some passion at last,* but didn't show the full smile she inwardly filled with, reminding herself to stay objectively professional.

Again she made a sign for quiet but this time the audience was much slower to react, taking several minutes to stop applauding, talking, and reclaim their seats, before she could speak again, "Strangely enough, it wasn't just my discovery of the gender biased ancient matri-lineal Goddess religion and the patriarchal barbarians creating a male God to destroy it, that began to convince me of a genderless God.

It was mainly through my dissecting the very so-called holy books that I was taught to respect and believe that promoted God to be male! Reading the Bible was the biggest shocker of all! You see, having learnt about the Goddess religion, I began to understand why various sto-ries in the Bible were composed. I saw parallels of the symbols of the Goddess, and the myth of Adam and Eve in the Garden of Eden and the loss of Paradise. The serpent Goddess worshippers used for good became the evil tempter. The forbidden fruit from the tree of knowl-edge was sexual consciousness which the Goddess was revered for, but now its use was declared sinful by men who wrote the Old Testament, mostly on the woman's part, her seductiveness, while the man was considered almost blameless when he willingly participated.

Then the severe punishment that was meted out by the male deity was directed solely at the woman: "*I will greatly multiply your pain in child-bearing, in pain you shall bring forth children, yet your desire shall be for your husband and he shall rule over you.*" The only suffering imposed on the man was he would now have to work to get food instead of just lazing about.

I realized the Levite writers composed this story to convince peo-ple of the 'perils' in worshipping the Goddess, and of the omnipotence of the male God in his ability to inflict pain in childbirth; also to ensure patriarchy would be triumphant by husbands being given the right to dominate and "*rule over*" wives. By the male divinity himself, no less. Likewise to brainwash women into being faithful to husbands saying their "*desire*" will be only for them, therefore forcing the loss of sexual independence and choice, making that to be sinful and harlotry, for women only.

Then to see the terrible violence the northern invaders inflicted upon the Goddess people! The abominable way the priests of their newly invented God instructed men to treat women was absolutely horrifying. And why did they do it? To control their possessions! It was all about *greed and power!*"

Elizabeth demonstrated pensive cynicism, "Greed and power…two thousand years later, and how little things have changed! Other so-called holy books may have a different spin on things, but most convey pretty much the same message: shameless violence for men to achieve omnipotence, and women to be subjugated and controlled by men."

She heard many gasps followed by murmurs. Focusing on the nearest rows to better see the expressions on people's faces, she was not surprised at the widened eyes and opened mouths as many people were suddenly hit by their epiphanies.

She did a dissertation on observations and theories of societal experts, psychologists, and psychiatrists, as to how these ancient religious writings and practices have damaged humanity's rapid advancement to globally civilized behavior and world peace. She gave details of cultures that still practice abominations as regards to the equal rights of women, thinking that their backward ignorant religions gave them permission to continue these atrocities; the bigger disgrace though, in intelligent experts eyes, being the way more educated and advanced cultures allow the men in power in the guilty societies to think their barbarous behavior is tolerable, if not acceptable, because of their so-called 'culture,' which in fact, is molded by their antiquated discriminatory religions.

Pointing out that even in modern societies, too many men still violently take out their frustrations on smaller females and children, she said the vicious effect the promotion of violence in ancient religious books and the subsequent brainwashing it has on their psyches, is undeniable.

Taking advantage of agreeing murmurs from the audience, she sipped some water before continuing, "In learning the ancient history of the Goddess and her matrilineal worshippers, and then of the invading barbaric patriarchal tribes who created a male God in order to control her people, take their lands, produce, and possessions, I began to look at humanity in a new, enlightened light. I noticed humans basically come in three categories: those who are full of confidence and want to lead, those who lack confidence and want to be led, and the rest fall in different degrees in-between, not brave enough to lead, not meek enough to follow, but just go with the flow, leading when they are forced to, following when they tire, but most of the time just conforming, oftentimes ambivalently, with society's accepted 'norms.' I realized I was struggling to get out of the latter category, because I felt I belonged in the first, I wanted to lead. But how could I lead when I didn't know where I was going?! That's why my journey to find Truth began. I had to discover it first before I could lead others to it.

I began to pay closer attention to the natural laws of physics and noticed they reflected my own laws of spirituality, not that of man-invented religious laws. I observed there's a continuous unfolding of the mysteries of the universe, everything's in an evolutionary pattern, and synergistic, interconnected, reliant on the other. The universe is participating in all our lives, but through ignorance, religious brain-washing, fear, or greed, too many humans are too slow to accept and use its natural creating power in a calm, productive, positive, sustaining manner. What was most surprising was, on my studying the works of mystics, ancient and contemporary, they had already figured this out. Yet this has not been taught in patriarchal religions. Then I started to re-notice my sixth sense, the intuitive clairvoyance I had been ignoring ever since I was told by clerics that not to do so was blasphemous, only their God was allowed to have psychic powers. Remember, 'you control the mind, you control the purse.'

It dawned on me that the patriarchal societies we live under since men invented the male God have not advanced spiritually. The religions they created haven't kept pace with the newer knowledge of the scientific realities of the universe. They ignore the evolution, growth, and understanding of the real, natural, universe we live in.

We now have sophisticated scientific knowledge of how things really are, how once mystifying things really work, in many cases advanced technology to go with it.

Yet, many religions are still telling us to believe in archaic, retrograde, retarding and damaging, usually unproven concepts and fables; some still believing their antiquated religious doctrines and not even admitting, despite scientific proof, that the Earth is millions of years old!

They teach that we must agree with the thinking of simple, domineering, egotistical, chauvinistic, greedy, scientifically ignorant minds, whose primary function was to frighten, subjugate, and control people, so they could take what those people had for themselves, feeding their power driven egos. And in doing so, destroying the equal rights of half of the human race! Setting the planet on a collision course for disaster!

Of course these people threw in the odd awesome, usually male, character, in their stories, to keep us hooked and give us hope. But mostly they told us how bad our ancestors were, what shameful sinners all humanity is, especially the women. And, as if that wasn't bad enough, the afterlife is limited to just two obscure places, heaven and hell, and we are rewarded or damned forever to one or the other depending on our behavior.

Then I looked at the matrilineal society and presumed practice of matriarchy of the Goddess religion, along with the sexual freedom and indeterminate paternity of children, and knew it wasn't fair to the males, or their children. Fathers should be able to know who their children are as mothers always do. Not because of being able to control and have males inherit property, although that matrilineal practice of mostly females controlling property was also unfair, but to be involved and share in their upbringing and nurturing. Children, like adults, need gender balance to feel like confident, productive, humans.

But in the ancient religion, sexuality and procreation was part of Goddess worship in a time of human under-population and high infant mortality. Scientifically, paternity tests didn't exist. Also, men weren't necessarily faithful to one woman either. And, it appears this was not an issue for either gender. Actually, we don't know if the men took issue on anything in that society until the barbarians invaded and commanded a different, patriarchal lifestyle. Certainly to a fair and honest way of thinking in our modern world it wasn't right that children not know who their fathers were and vice versa; and the women shouldn't have had total control of the society and its enterprises, even if those societies were flourishing, as is proven in various texts, relics, and ancient ruins.

No one human gender should have more control over the other. Animals may do that but humans are way above that, mentally, spiritually, and should know better. Should.

But, those were simpler ignorant times and the belief, of both genders, in the Goddess who was around for so very long, gave the women the upper hand, allowing them to indulge in and be revered for their intuitive and psychic powers, using all their mental faculties as they wanted. Respected and admired for bearing the physical, painful, responsibility of populating. Enjoying the freedom of economic and sexual independence. And based on the extremely long reign of the Goddess compared to that of the newer invented God, apparently the men had no problem with it. Not until greedy patriarchal, *godless,* violent invaders came along and forced different indoctrinations.

The intelligent thing to have happened was for the men to say, "*Both genders are equally important, one cannot exist without the other. We're in this world to sink or swim together, so let's share everything equally, respect each other's equal rights.*" But, these were not intelligent men, and, though physically powerful and fierce, they were fearful of things they didn't comprehend. And, they had no formal education. They were barbarians, primitives accustomed to bullying to get their way.

So, the pendulum swung from one side all the way over to the other when it should've rested in the middle where there would've been the proper, fair balance, of gender power. Instead, the greedy barbaric male-controlled invaders used their superior weapons and brawn to slaughter masses of people, subjugate and oppress the females, destroy the ancient Goddess religion, and endeavored to control the minds of her people. It became a battle of brawn against brain. Brawn won... or...did it?"

Elizabeth took a deep dramatic breath, "Let's look at the situation on our planet today. Males mostly control governments and nations. In some countries females are still denied basic human rights, not just to vote and have a say in who rules their countries and thus their lives, but even to get an education, choose a job, and independently look after their needs for survival. In so-called 'advanced countries,' even when they achieve these things, they're often not paid equal wages for equal work."

CHAPTER 22

"Some countries and religions still dictate that women be ruled by men, merely treated as sexual playthings, slash baby-makers, slash domestic servants "*man's helper*," usually all combined; relegated to do just the men's ideas of "*woman's things*." With all we know about female and male brains having the ability to learn equally given the same opportunity, females are still often deliberately kept back, oppressed, in patriarchal societies. Many men putting the blame on motherhood! Or menstruation, or menopause, claiming the dangers of 'mood swings.' Mind you, the men are yet to come up with excuses for their own abundant mood swings!"

There was more applause and laughter from the audience, and Elizabeth took advantage of the break to take more than a few sips of water to moisten her now parching throat before continuing, "One biological difference discovered scientifically in recent times, is that the listening part of the male brain is smaller than the female's. When that was announced with an explanation that confirmation of that information took much time and expense, many a wife and girlfriend declared the scientists would have known it from the beginning, saved time and money, if only they had asked them!"

The crowd went into more laughter and applause and surprisingly, even some of the men joined in, but Elizabeth did not smile this time, "I'm afraid this isn't funny. In fact it's extremely serious. Could destroy us all. We've a planet that's governmentally under the control of the gender that is lacking in full listening ability. The dictionary describes '*listening*' as '*making a conscious effort to hear, to pay attention to something, and to take it into account.*' Added to less listening skill this gender is loaded with the more aggressive, some experts say "*violent*" hormone, testosterone. Well, based on the track record of how things have been run, and the direction in which they are going, this appears to be a lethal combination.

Now please know, I'm not about any kind of 'male bashing.' I want you to know I love and respect males as equally as I do females. I'm simply giving you the observations of many, of both genders, who have much more expertise than I. One just has to look at how little has been learnt by humans in how to peacefully coexist with one another. With all the advances we've made scientifically and technologically we still haven't figured out how to properly treat one another.

When they have major conflicting views too often the men in control still resort to violence, war, and all its accompanying dangers to life and our planet. It's obvious that working things out with conversation and negotiation is not yet perfected.

Could it be that the majority of people involved are just not *listening?!* As well as filled with a hormone that creates 'The Three Pesky P.s': Pomposity, Presumption, and Posturing?!

Another thing, biological anthropologists and scientists have ascertained the two hemispheres of the brain in men are less well connected than in women, which allows men to focus on one thing at a time and be very goal-oriented.

On the other hand, the build of the female brain allows her to assimilate many feelings at once. Hence the reason for females being famous multi-taskers, not as prone to tunnel-vision. Doesn't this further confirm why we need gender balance to share the power of controlling countries and societies on the planet? Imagine the heaven on earth that is within our reach if people in power were multi-faceted because of gender balance!

Why do leaders still react to irresponsible, ignorant behavior from others by threats then violence, fighting destructive wars, hoping to get them under control and perhaps toward intelligent behavior? Haven't they noticed, after all this time, those methods aren't beneficial to humanity? Hasn't it occurred to them the only way you get rid of ignorance and its attending behavior is to educate? Teach the better way, usually by example? Why's it taking so long for men to understand this? Surely it's not just because of a couple of physical conditions of those in charge?

Or…could it be, they are subconsciously letting themselves be guided by backward, unfair, destructive teachings of ancient stories in so-called holy books and religions that promote them? Thus allowing societies to be molded by them?"

There were cacophonous ubiquitous remarks from the audience but Elizabeth, knowing her speech allotted time was close to infringing on Professor Thomas's slide time ignored them and raising her voice, pressed on, "Let's look at how these attitudes and policies stemming from patriarchy are damaging *all* humanity. Consider, not only the unconscionable disregard for the equal rights of females who are half of its inhabitants, but disrespect for our planet Earth, the only planet we presently know that we can live on, our only home.

But because of domineering and possessive ego, *greed*, putting immediate financial gain before future reality, governments and companies are allowing the rapid depletion of many of our natural resources, to the point that masses of us could soon be without the most ordinary conveniences we presently take for granted. The abuse of fossil fuels could put us back in the dark ages. Not just because we are wastefully using too much, but also because of the damaging poisoning emissions they put into the very air we breathe! Threatening not only our health and lifestyle, but the life of our planet! Therefore our very existence!

Yet, most governments are not taking strong and speedy actions to develop, promote, and make mandatory, the use of the non-polluting, natural, sustainable alternative energies. Such as the sun, wind, tides and flows from bodies of water, geothermal from the earth's core, biomas from biodegradable waste, etcetera.

I could go on about the destructive practices that are continued despite expert's warnings about the dangers to our planet and its ability to sustain us, the damage to our ozone layer, its resultant effect on our sunshine, climate change, and ultimately, our health and life. But that's a whole other speech. And you are smart people, I'm sure you already know this. Then to add to abuses and pollution damage, there's still continuation of nuclear development and use, despite its ability for widespread destruction!

Consider also pollution from discharges of bombs and weaponry used in the conflicts and wars men childishly indulge in. Big men still playing little boys games! With our lives! And those of our precious children! That *only* women's bodies suffer to bring into this world! Besides domination, is that the other reason why so many men and their patriarchal religions still seek to force women to go through unwanted pregnancies? Is it no longer just to have more worshippers to control, and get rich from, which they disguise as morality? Or is it for them to have more unlucky naive people to fight their preposterous egomaniacal battles? Unconscionable destruction of women's lives and that of their already born children!

Or…can war be a confused method of handling the severe overpopulation problem our planet faces today? By killing off people with violence, instead of limiting population with practical caring prevention, widespread availability of 'morning after pills,' and medically safe abortions, thus allowing females to have control over their own bodies *as men already do?*

Don't these men realize they are also killing our planet, humanity's only home, with their stupidity? Would men continue to try to resolve conflicts by killing if it were their bodies and emotions that have to go through making more humans?

Would they continue to have such a flagrant, flippant disregard for human life, and the planet that sustains it, if *they* were given the sole responsibility of growing, nurturing, and birthing the fetus so that humanity can continue to exist? Why can't they see their behavior still reeks of primeval barbaric cavemen!"

Elizabeth heard more, louder, indiscernible remarks coming from the audience but acted as if she didn't and continued without signaling for quiet, raising her voice which got everybody's attention, "For thousands of years, most of humanity has lived in fear and peril continuously, with little hope for permanent peace and security. Why? Why is that, when the alternative is to live peacefully in the paradise the Universe's Creator gave us? Why is this, after all our scientific and technological advances, not been figured out? Some experts have given a variety of reasons, even solutions, but few have been acted on and aren't having widespread effect. Too little has changed to make a difference."

She struck a pensive pose, "Which leads one to think, hasn't *anybody* wondered how the patriarchal religions and societies that we've been living under the last two millennia affected the destructive decisions that humans make?

How many have come to the realization that the imbalance of gender power on our planet is *most* responsible for our demise?

How many think deeply enough to admit that this damaging imbalance continues in spite of all we know about the equal intelligence of the sexes, *because* of the major religions, their patriarchal indoctrination and invented male God?!

How long must we wait before those in power realize that backward man-invented religion's sensitivities, and *not* advanced realistic science, prevails, to the detriment of all humankind? When will humanity open its eyes and see the terrible damage that eons of ignorance and injustice against one gender has done and continues to do to *both* genders, *all* humanity? When all our eyes have been permanently, unintentionally, irretrievably closed?

We cannot let that happen people. *This,*" Elizabeth swept her arms outwards in quarter circles, "is the only life we're sure of. It's a mistake to think it's a '*dress rehearsal.*'

That thinking stops people from developing to their full potential, achieving great things for themselves and humanity. That thinking only serves to make people careless, abusive, in their treatment of others, thinking they'll be easily forgiven and get another life in which to redeem themselves. That thinking stops people from being accountable for their mistakes, blaming them on "*the will of God.*" That thinking allows certain religious leaders to contradictorily forbid their followers to *write* or *say* the name of God, but encourages them to *kill* God's children in the name of God!

That thinking allowed thousands to turn a blind eye to the Nazi atrocities against the Jews in the holocaust.

That thinking convinces Moslem terrorist youth that it's alright to kill off innocent fellow humans who may disagree with their indoctrinated philosophy, and destroy their own life in suicide bomb attacks, thinking when they get to their "*heaven*" they'll have seventy-plus virgins. Though why anyone would want all those virgins is beyond logic, sounds boring. You'd think after a while they'd want somebody experienced who knows what they're doing and could give them real pleasure."

Many in the audience squealed with laughter but Elizabeth put her hands up and said seriously, "Or maybe, again, that's only about oppressing and controlling females.

That thinking is what caused such fanatical religious fervor for domination of disagreeing religions, and sanctioned two hundred violent years of the Christian Crusades against "*non-believers,*" and, the horrors of the Inquisition. Simultaneously, that thinking allowed atrocities and massacres of anyone considered "*infidels,*" in the name of Islam.

All of that and more, because of the unrealistic belief in an unproven God and better afterlife!

The obvious solution to many of humanity's problems is to expose and learn the facts about women and men creating anthropomorphic Goddesses and Gods and their doctrines and not the other way around. People need to know about the Goddess religion to understand this and to know *why* the male God was created by despotic patriarchal invaders. There's too much danger in the belief that we must worship some mysterious detached anthropomorphic entity who is responsible for whatever happens to us. It makes us lazy, selfish, even destructive, when we believe we alone are not culpable for our actions, thinking we can throw the blame on an invisible God when things go wrong.

Any intelligent person given the knowledge of the, for that time, civilized society, of the Goddess and the barbaric men who created a male God to dethrone her, should realize that the patriarchal manner under which the world has been controlled, and has for two millennia been considered and accepted as the right and natural way, is not only wrong and unnatural, but is heading humanity down a path to extermination!

We must have more respect for this planet and *all* its life-force, which the genderless Universal Creator gave us and put in our care. We have to acknowledge and respect the divinity that is in each and every one of us. Even the prophet Mohammed told us, "*If you would know God you would know yourself.*" Jesus also pointed this out when he said, "*Ye are gods,*" and, "*The kingdom of God is within you.*" He didn't instruct that he should be worshipped as God, he merely taught if we'd follow his teachings and emulate him we would lead a good life.

Now, I know many have lost faith in what has been left in the Bible by the men who censored and changed it. But if we believe *half* of what there is of Jesus's teachings, you must admit, he gave us some important lessons and guidance, as did Buddha before him, and other mystics of both sexes.

It's obvious Jesus's quotations that are contradictory were changed to suit the patriarchal writers who were hell-bent on destroying any remnants of Goddess worship, in their determination to enforce patriarchal societies. Think of it, there is no way the superior mind of a mystic would promote a "*father* in heaven," and second-rate the *mother* who bore, nurtured, and raised him, and not put *her* in heaven first.

Unfortunately, most religions and doctrines men invented in the last two-plus millennia have lost the true meanings of the mystics that inspired them. Most tell us God is loving, forgiving, and merciful. Yet they say that *same* God will punish us mercilessly, damming us for all eternity, if we don't do what they say! Most are rife with contra-dictions, more concerned with physical needs and our contributions rather than our *spiritual needs*, the very reason religion was supposedly invented in the first place! Religions must start living up to their true meaning: to bind and unify humanity in nurturing its *spirituality*, but while appreciating *factual scientific knowledge*, physics and the evolu-tionary process that's constantly unfolding. They cannot divorce scien-tific physical fact from an intelligent belief system!

They must start serving humanity properly by preaching Truth, destroying fables, and promoting facts; culling from doctrines the destructive, barbaric teachings that create disunity, hate, and anger, between peoples and genders. Even an American patriarch, Abraham Lincoln, gave us a profound unifying message when he said, "*Am I not destroying my enemies when I make friends of them?*"

Humanity must be courageous and open its minds to reality, look beyond the biased indoctrination of their man-made-up religions. We must make our leaders, both secular and religious, accountable for the damage they've done and are still doing to our lives, by the perpetua-tion of false, restricting and oppressive ideas about the female gender, her intelligence, roles, and capabilities.

Men, *and* women, must educate themselves about their igno-rance in their blind obedience to religious doctrines that domineering greedy unintelligent patriarchal barbaric men had composed, in order to destroy a religion they were afraid would deny them the power to dominate the people practicing it.

Women, particularly, must learn the true history of religions, so that they can stop buying in to the need for patriarchy, regain their strengths, trust in themselves, their intelligence, their abilities, and stand up for the equal rights of *all* women, globally. They need to real-ize that once they regain the confidence that had been stripped from them because of patriarchal societies, they must stop participating in the degrading of other women and desist with the common think-ing of them as a threat, whether to a marriage, a relationship, or a job. When a woman has her full independence, economically, socially, spiritually, and sexually, she doesn't have to feel helplessly reliant on, jealous of, or intimidated by, *anyone*.

In fact, as humans get to learn the truth about how the predom-inantly global patriarchy came about, put the blame where it truly belongs, forgive, and rise above the ignorance, all women and men will develop even stronger bonds of love and respect for each other than the smarter ones already have.

We must all open our minds and hearts to more possibilities of the Divine. There is only one Divine power in the universe, the Infinite Creative One that makes everything out of itself of which we're all a part.

God loves us all equally, a superior Creative Divinity will not divide, judge, or condemn, its own creation, as some religions will have us believe. Unenlightened finite humans think that way, not the Infinite Creative Essence.

There're many who already know that God has no gender who feel the spelling of the Supreme Divine should reflect that and be changed to something with a genderless connotation, perhaps G-o-d-d-e. It may help humanity to forget the atrocities of the past, but it might take some time for people to adjust.

Our purpose on earth is to evolve and grow spiritually, and con-tribute to the growth of others if even in the smallest measure. *If* our souls can choose to return after these bodies expire, we must ensure it will be to a better world because of us having been here before. No one knows what happens after we leave this life. Most of us hope for another, superior, one, but nobody has proven its existence to us, it's simply a *belief*, a hope, not a *fact*.

Some people feel fortunate to have had what they believe to be a 'visit' from a departed loved one which is seen as proof of an afterlife, but that's an individual personal thing, and, we all know the human imagination knows no boundaries.

At this time I'd like to introduce Professor Dr. Daniel J. Thomas with his amazing collection of slides, which will help to corroborate that God has no gender. Here is Professor Thomas."

The audience burst into thunderous applause, much more than was warranted for the introduction of the professor who was unknown to most of them, making it obvious the applause was primarily for Elizabeth. Professor Thomas gestured towards her, smilingly looked out at the audience, and the applause increased. She bowed graciously to the audience, gestured towards Professor Thomas, and quickly stepped to the side of the stage so the professor could start his slide presentation.

This turned out to be the most impressive and comprehensive collection of international photographs anyone in the audience had ever seen. First came images of the various idols, statues, plaques, artifacts, and relics of the Goddess that had been unearthed, not just from archeological digs but, metaphorically, from the 'burial grounds' of many a museum's archives.

Then came slides of numerous archeological digs worldwide. The Professor was quick to point out they were all run by men. He showed scientific tests that were performed on the excavated objects to garner information from them.

Next came prehistoric drawings and carvings from caves, rocks, tombs, and pyramids, all the while explaining their meanings in that clear, calm, monotone voice that Elizabeth had grown to love and respect along with the man.

Then came drawings of the evolution of the human race, and photographs of skeletons of the earliest humans unearthed in various parts of the globe, which he explained scientifically, unemotionally. Next were photographs showing similarities of humans to chimpanzees, and DNA tests proving their relationship. He went on to show, describing in detail, various ruins and relics from the ancient world; jewelry, tools, and their uses, crockery and vessels, and the art that adorned them.

As the slides rolled on, he did a dissertation on churches, syna-gogues, temples and mosques, while pointing out similarities and dif-ferences to both their religion's designed methods of worship and the designs of the actual buildings of worship.

He did the same with clerics and leaders of various religions, show-ing texts and sculptures of when popes and priests had mistresses, and used to marry, until that practice was stopped as the Church did not want fortunes leaving it when children inherited after fathers died, though the Church expounds a different, discriminatory reason.

After showing sculptures and paintings while giving descriptions of the nature of several Goddesses and Gods before and of the Greco-Roman era, he showed recent history of newer religions and cults, including media photographs of violent events that involved some of them. He touched on the power of indoctrination and brainwashing, showed slides of old drawings and paintings pertaining to the violence of the Christian Crusades and of that to spread Islam.

Then, to a loudly gasping audience, he showed horrifying photo-graphs of the Nazi holocaust against the Jews, the Branch-Davidian murders/suicides at Waco Texas in the U.S.A., and the mass suicide of the American Jim Jones's koolaided-brainwashed following in Guyana.

Next he did a synopsis on philosophies and religions that believe God has no gender, while sliding pictures of the people who inspired them. Showing book covers that promoted various beliefs of the gen-der of God, then several quotations along with art both ancient and contemporary, he remarked on similarities and inconsistencies in vari-ous depictions and texts.

Following these were slides of several scientists and philosophers with brief accounts of what they were credited for. After that were several geographic photographs which explained their relevance to the incredibility of different religious myths. Next were old and recent comparison pictures, of problems and pollution on planet Earth relat-ing to climate change that occurs because of the abuses of mankind.

He closed with photographs of awe-inspiring displays of planets, meteorites, stars and solar systems, accompanied by his enthusiastic descriptions of them, along with experts' theories about their creation and evolution.

Stopping the projector on a vividly beautiful photograph of the Earth which had been taken from a spaceship, he faced the audience, "In conclusion, I hope if you leave here tonight with only one truth in mind, it is that if religions and societies stop the unfair, destructive, practice of patriarchy, make sure matriarchy too stays obsolete, and accepts that God has no gender, we stand a better chance of saving humanity and our planet and at last of having 'peace on earth.' Now, let's see if Ms. Richardson is ready for Questions and Answers."

Elizabeth walked over to stand next to the erudite professor, took his hand and smiled as the audience applauded, many standing to show their appreciation. The professor and she bowed in acceptance of the accolades, and after almost a minute, when she felt enough time had passed, she raised her hand politely in the manner of asking for quiet, which was quickly granted; though many people stayed standing, waving their hands frenetically trying to get her attention.

Elizabeth gestured to four attendants walking down the aisles with microphones as the house lights were brightened, and announced that Dr. Thomas and she would now be answering questions, adding politely but firmly, "One at a time, please." Tensing at seeing the two security guards Davidson Hall's management insisted on positioning on either side at the bottom of the stage, take a nervous step forward, she quickly added, "Please stay seated until it's your turn."

CHAPTER
23

Both Elizabeth and Professor Thomas felt enormous relief that everything had gone so well, thus far, but she knew she must brace herself for the onslaught she was certain was forthcoming. Surprisingly, the first batches of questions were simple and polite, mostly about her and her research, some people making complimentary statements. Questions were asked about her unusual accent, ancestry, and education, despite a synopsis describing the latter two things in the program.

She deliberately made no mention of Trinidad as she didn't want people digging into her personal life until she had time to sort it out, and, more importantly, explain it to Michael.

A group of four young women stood up together and declared that she made such a strong case for the Goddess, they were going to do some further investigations and then revive a Goddess religion. This astonished Elizabeth and she felt compelled to give more detailed explanations of how frightened and ignorant humans invented the Goddess as well as the God, and for them to contrive yet another religion would be an enormous backward step for humanity. With much sensitivity she was able to convince them of their folly. They thanked her for the knowledge she had imparted which boosted their self-esteem, with a promise they were going to devote the rest of their lives to educating, and saving the planet.

Just as Elizabeth began to relax, thinking how easy this was, the attacks started with a vengeance. The first came from a middle-aged man who stuck out his chest pompously and loudly attempted a rebuttal of her subject. She cut him off in the middle of what was turning into vitriolic semantics that made no sense, so much so, people began booing telling him to sit down, which he did when she told him to start researching and educating himself to learn the Truth. Two people accused her of *"pure conjecture"* to which she asked, "Were you asleep? Didn't you hear anything we said?" this got a smattering of laughter and she added, "Read just a few books on our list, then read the Bible, it will definitely awaken you!"

Two nuns in the fourth row she had not previously noticed as, though dressed in matching garments, only seconds before donned their habits, stood up. The younger one lambasted Elizabeth about being raised Catholic and promoting abortions and the killing of souls, half probably female like herself.

Elizabeth argued, "I'm not promoting abortions but female's equal rights. Males don't have to worry about unwanted pregnancies, why should females not have the same privilege? Are you saying females must be denied equal rights, shackled and punished, because they possess a womb? Females know better than males what they can cope with in their own lives. And by the way, no one knows when the soul enters the body, some believe we don't even *have* souls, and as it is, *all* fetuses start out as female for the first six weeks of gestation." Then she asked, "What's more important, the chance at good quality of life for an already living female, or, that of an unwanted one not yet born who very likely will have poor quality of life in an already over-crowded harshly discriminatory world?"

Without giving an opportunity to answer she stared directly at the young nun and continued, "I would think someone looking as smart as you would've realized the whole anti-abortion issue is fueled by religious fanatics who seek to control women, deprive them of equal rights under the guise of 'God's wishes.' Abortion is a female's *medical* health issue, whether it be *physical, mental,* or, *emotional*! Patriarchal religions have turned it into a moral issue. If Godde and nature was against a female's ability to abort, abortion would not be possible!"

There was ubiquitous applause from the audience and Elizabeth noticed an unusually soft knowing smile on the older nun's face as she quickly sat, the younger one following with a contrasting look of confusion. Elizabeth was tempted to tell the young one she needed to go out into the world and see what real life was about, but realized the advice was not to come from her. She felt certain the older, wiser nun, would do that job.

A couple in their mid-forties, the man wearing a clerical collar, accused her of lacking in morals, voicing their assumption that she disagreed with the stopping of females having sex with men other than their husbands. She retorted that she should not be so harshly judged, she herself not judging the ancient rituals but simply stating what they were, and, she did agree that the promiscuity should have been stopped, but for both sexes. Reminding the couple the men were not necessarily faithful to their wives either, she conceded, "When you think of it, for all we now know, we should be grateful for the disbanding of the females' multipartnering. This probably cut in half the spread of venereal diseases as that risky behavior became only the males' domain. But, other risks were taken. Although it's been kept hidden from the pages of most history books, not just religious but secular, some ancient societies thought nothing of sexually vacillating between both sexes. And, not just in the past but actually today, clerics who want to enjoy only the pleasures of their own gender, many beleaguered by guilt and shame do so under the guise of "*celibacy*," using it to excuse themselves for their sexual orientation, because it doesn't include participation of the opposite sex."

Three different people questioned her reasons for promoting a genderless God, stating that much of what she said was unbelievable, and questioned not only her judgment, but again, her morals. She then had to defend, it seemed convincingly, not only her and Professor

Thomas's research, but her own integrity, ethics, and honesty. She warded off a few more females' stabs at her about her "*jabs*" and "*accusations*" against "*The Holy Bible*" by telling them to first educate themselves about the ancient Goddess religions, then re-read the Bible with open minds.

Two different women, and a man, reprimanded her with varying statements about her "*sacrilege,*" and threats of "*burning forever in the fires of hell,*" if she didn't "*repent.*" She smiled condescendingly and simply reminded them that no Divine Creator would condemn its own creation, only ignorant dominating humans think that way.

Two male political pundits castigated her for her "*misleading remarks on the disregard the men in power have for the planet,*" to which she simply replied, "You gentlemen need to wake up from your sweet dreams and educate yourselves as to the nightmare we're facing because of apathetic, ignorant attitudes such as yours." Several others asked questions about things she already covered but wanted more details.

She included the professor in some answers as no one directed any questions to him. Both she and he referred to the list of publications people should take when leaving, and read to convince themselves of the information given.

Just as she began to feel the tension that had returned leave her, six rows from the back, three men, two bearded, stood up and started shouting, violently shaking their fists at her.

She could not discern what they were saying but their anger was unmistakable. Professor Thomas rushed to her side, grabbing her hand as the two stage guards moved towards the men, but they quickly ran up the aisle and out an exit, accompanied by loud boos from the crowd.

Shaken, Elizabeth had to force a calm demeanor for the audience, and whispered to the professor, "Thank you, I'm alright, are you alright, shall we continue?"

The elderly professor's face transformed into that of a much younger man as he smiled, squeezed her hand gently and released it, "Of course my dear, ignorance must not be allowed to intimidate."

Elizabeth looked back at the audience with a soft smile, "Unfortunately, some people felt it necessary to physically corroborate some of the things we've spoken about. Any more questions?" There was widespread laughter in the crowd and several people stood up waving, trying to get the attention of the microphone attendants. Suddenly, a constant murmur rolled towards the stage from the back of the room. People started turning their heads around and the murmur increased in volume. Elizabeth and the professor stretched their necks to see what everyone was now looking at, but could not see all the way to the back, the stage technician had neglected to put on the lights over that area. She could see him at the side of the stage and made a sign telling him to turn on the back lights, but he shook his head and shrugged.

Puzzled, she walked offstage and asked why he could not turn on all the lights. He looked sheepish and said he was instructed not to, by a higher authority. The audience started speaking excitedly louder and Elizabeth began to distinguish some words, "royal family…" "leaving…" "wonder why…"

She glared at the man, "This is *my* show, *I'm* the highest authority here tonight. Turn on those lights. *Now!*" The man took in her redoubtable demeanor and thinking better about disobeying her command, flicked on all the switches in front of him.

She walked back onto the stage, looked towards the newly lit area and gasped. There was Michael, standing in the aisle, directing almost his entire family out of the back row. The only ones missing as far as she could tell were the King, Claire, and some cousins. Even Susan and John had made the long journey from the country to attend. She simultaneously became thrilled and annoyed. She stared at Michael, hoping to force him to look at her. It worked. He looked directly at her but not her eyes. He seemed to look right through her and as the last royal exited the row, he walked out after them.

She was mystified, disappointed, hurt. Knowing the show must go on, she must act professionally like nothing unusual happened, she began clapping and shouted into the microphone above the clamor,

"Let's thank the royal family for coming and honoring us with their presence." The audience joined her in clapping until six armed guards who followed Michael were out of sight, then many resumed gesticulating to the microphone attendants.

The barrage of questions seemed unending but she answered each one convincingly, unwavering in her convictions.

Many questions pertained to the oppression of one gender over the other. One elderly couple argued in vain for its necessity to keep order on the planet, even the need for wars. Elizabeth ended that debate by stating emphatically, "As long as we have oppression, discrimination of anyone, for whatever reason, gender, race, religion, age, looks, financial status, we are contributing to the eventual destruction of a civilized planet. Oppression is the basic reason for wars. Wars kill precious people and other living things. It pollutes the mind as well as the air we breathe, and if not stopped, will eventually destroy everything. The insanity of war must cease, or we'll all die."

An intellectual looking young man with thick glasses stated that although he agreed religions' patriarchal domination was retarding humanity's chances for world peace, it was so deeply entrenched, he didn't believe global gender equality was achievable, at least not for many generations.

Elizabeth pointed out that, again, another intelligence, him, was letting his *belief* get in the way of progress, reminded him that if ancient beliefs were not abandoned for realities, there would be *no* future generations to reap the benefits of eventual gender equality. She then challenged him to join other enlighteners in educating the ignorant so that world peace could be achieved in his lifetime. Smiling, he nodded agreeably, and sat to back-pats from colleagues around him.

An elderly priest with a censorious expression asked her pointedly, "So, what do *you*, really believe in?"

She smiled benevolently, "I believe all things are possible and until there is proof of something, I keep an open mind." Then she added seriously, "Only a fool questions "*Who is God?*" and it's an even bigger fool who thinks he knows the answer."

With every question answered patiently, intelligently, realistically, the general mood of the audience gradually changed. They became more than just polite but friendly, some actually addressing her affectionately. Many asked where she was speaking next as they wanted to bring family and friends, causing her to feel confident that she had gotten through to a large number of them.

Eventually, Professor Thomas, seeing their Questions-and-Answers had gone over their allotted time by an hour, feeling convinced of their success, and thinking Elizabeth must be exhausted, because he certainly was, stepped back onto center stage. Visibly touching his watch, he announced they had gone over their time limit. Many in the crowd jovially shouted "No, no!" "Stay, stay!" "More, more!" and other friendly entreaties.

Elizabeth smiled in appreciation, then became very serious, "If you can't take our word for anything we've said here tonight, I encourage you to do the research yourselves, and I'm confident you will come to the same conclusion we have: God has no gender." She thanked the professor for his outstanding contribution, he did the same to her, and facing the audience, they together thanked them for coming, and bowed. She called out, "You were a most wonderful gracious audience," applauding them as she walked off the stage, the professor following.

The applause from the totally standing audience was thunderous and continuous. The professor reached out to Elizabeth to escort her back on stage for another bow when someone else's hand appeared from behind the curtains, grabbed her arm, and not saying a word, his lips shut tight, pulled her forcefully towards the back of the building, out a door she had not seen before, and into a waiting armored vehicle.

Still holding tightly to her arm, Michael vehemently pushed her down onto a seat near the door of the strange vehicle, dropping onto the seat beside her. A guard slammed the door shut and the vehicle sped off.

Stunned into silence by his appearance and behavior during their rush to the vehicle, on looking around and seeing, apart from Eric, there were eight fully armed military with weapons drawn in the van with them, she asked in a frightened voice, "Michael, what's going on?"

Michael did not look at her but dropped his head shaking it, "Jesus Christ, Elizabeth! You should've warned me what you were going to do!"

Aghast at his remark and attitude, she became defensive, "What do you mean? You knew exactly what my speech was about, and you approved. Actually, you were encouraging."

He raised his voice, "I did *not* know *exactly* what you were going to say! I thought your speech was going to be about your observations on why God has no gender! I didn't know you were going to go into all those details and dissections of religions, and the Bible-"

She became infected with his emotional state and interrupting, raised her voice to his level, "And *how* did you think I was going to prove God has no gender *without* involving religions and their literature Michael?! Surely-"

He interjected agitatedly, 'I didn't know you would delve so deeply into it! And then the way you went on and on about the whole patriarchy thing-"

"So *that's* what this is about, your fragile male ego!"

He now, became defensive, and snarled at her, "Don't be ridiculous! My "*male ego*" has nothing to do with it! You should know me better than that! Elizabeth, you have to understand, what you're doing is dange…um…risky!"

She shouted, "I understand that perfectly well! But you better than anyone should know it's worth the risk!"

He glared at her, "But not for *you*!"

She glared back, "What do you mean, not for *me*?"

He raised his voice even higher, causing Eric and the eight military who, up until now were discreetly looking down at the floor, to look up and stare at them, "Elizabeth, people in our position cannot afford to be so blatantly outspoken in these matters-"

She was now fuming, "'Blatantly outspoken,' my eye! You mean blatantly honest! Are you saying your position requires dishonesty and hypocrisy? If so, I want no part of it!"

Michael's expression shifted radically with fear which she misconstrued to be judgmental anger, "For God's sake, Elizabeth, you can't be so naive as to not realize the ramifications of exposing… um…promoting this sort of thing! Have you thought of how this is going to affect people? Masses are going to consider this kind of thing as just downright blasphemous, absolutely sacrilegious! Surely you know there can be consequences to the bold concepts you're proposing? The average person doesn't want to deal with this, it'll turn their worlds inside out! Ordinary people don't want to question their belief systems that they've been indoctrinated with from many generations past. Even highly educated people can be afraid to touch the subject of brainwashing. Who wants to think, far worse be told, that they are so gullible that they've been suckered into false religious beliefs their whole life! Have you considered how those people will feel? What they could…resort to? What they…might…*do*? And then to be told about it by someone like *you*?"

Astounded, her eyes widened, "Someone like me?"

Seeing her innocent look, Michael became genuinely angry, "Yes! Like you, a woman! Strikingly beautiful, but female nonetheless, in this ridiculously male-dominated world. And on top of that, a really *young* looking woman! Do you have any idea how much that must go against the grain of older people who've been around so much longer than you, and feel they already have all the answers? And now you, a 'whipper-snapper' to them, comes along, and brings up these disturbing questions to turn their lives upside down, just when they thought that at last they had it all figured out!" Michael did not let up. Barely taking an occasional breath, he went on in a tirade, berating her for her unbelievable naiveté.

What was most unbelievable to Elizabeth was the radical reversal Michael's attitude and support had taken. She could not believe what she perceived as his censorious anger combined with a desire to control and dominate her. She saw and heard nothing but his unvarnished criticisms and denunciation, although she had become aware that everyone in the vehicle was staring at them and taking in the entire spectacle.

Her shocked feelings vacillated between anger, hurt, fear, *What happened to "I could never criticize anything you do" or, when I told you about 'God Has No Gender' how much you said you loved it? You bastard! Is this the real you I'm finally seeing? You bloody turncoat! Oh Godde, I can't believe this is happening! Another betrayal!* Her thoughts were interrupted by a scathing remark he made in reference to her stupidity in believing her audience was not taking umbrage at her speech, and probably left tonight more irate than impressed.

This felt like an arrow pierced her soul. So flabbergasted, she could barely get her words out, "Ho...how co...could you say that? You...you didn't even stay for the Q'n'A. You obviously didn't care what they thought about it! They were wonderful to me towards the end! Nicer than people in Trinidad who knew me! And leaving when all of you did was totally insulting to me!"

Taking in her deflation he felt sick, but was determined to succeed in his mission, "We...I...had to leave at that time, it...it couldn't be helped, but I left Brian and some men to stay to protec...um...to listen, and report back to me-"

"Well, have you spoken to Brian? And why did you leave at that particular time that you did?" she demanded.

He felt extreme guilt about what he was doing to her and thought he should give her a little something, "Jenkins heard there might be an attack on my family, I had to protect them."

"Oh." She looked concerned for a moment, and Michael determined he had to bring this discussion to a conclusion.

He grabbed both her wrists, his eyes searing hers solemnly, "Elizabeth, I have to forbid you from continuing with these speeches, you *cannot* do them anymore."

Her simmering anger flamed up into a boil. His words burnt her brain. Her face and chest turned red as she became inflamed. His grip on her wrists felt like a fiery vise. For the first time in her life she felt suffocated by a smoky claustrophobia.

She shrieked, "You *forbid* me!" She tried to pull away from his grip but feeling her recalcitrance he tightened it. She gave him a venomous look and her voice reflected it as she screamed at him, "Let me go Michael!" Shocked at her transformation he released her quickly. She turned away from him and screamed at the guard who was nearest the door, "Open the door! Let me out!"

The man looked at Michael who then grabbed Elizabeth by her shoulders, "Elizabeth, he cannot open it. It…it's too dangerous. We're not on palace grounds yet!"

"I don't care!" she shouted, "Don't touch me! Ever again!"

She pushed him away and reached for the door handle, but he grabbed her arm, "Elizabeth, stop! You can't get out now! We're almost there! Control yourself!"

She knew she was losing control, her breathing had become erratic, but she had to get away from him, from all these men staring at her as if she were a raging lunatic.

The vehicle stopped, she banged on the door and it was opened from the outside. She jumped out, slipped off her heels and raced to her suite locking the door behind her, her only thought to get away from him.

Michael knocked on the door, softly at first, calling her name in a loving voice; but getting no response, knocked harder, calling out louder, until she finally opened it and came out.

She brushed past him. He observed she had changed into her track suit and sneakers. "Where're you going? Wait, I'll come with you. I'll change quickly-"

Her fury was palpable, "No you won't! Don't even speak to me! Don't come near me! And *don't* have me followed!"

She ran through the doorway as he shouted a warning, "Don't leave the palace grounds, it's too dangerous!"

CHAPTER
24

Nervously, Michael picked up his phone, "Eric take two men, follow Elizabeth, don't let her see you. She just left my apartment. I guess she's going to speed-walk to calm down. I'll change quickly and catch up. Keep me informed of her location!" Tearing off his jacket and tie, he slipped on sneakers, dropped his phone in his pants pocket, and raced out the door.

Eric called to say Elizabeth ran out the palace gates.

"Damn!" he cursed, and ran faster as his phone rang again.

It was Brian, "Michael, you'll be so proud of her-"

"I am. But I also want to kill her, taking such a crazy risk, antagonizing all the people, and now I have a bigger mess to deal with-"

"Wait a minute, antagonizing all what people, what're you talking about?"

"The audience! I was there, remember. I heard the attacks, and rumblings of annoyance. It's a good thing I had to leave, I couldn't have handled seeing her take all the abuse."

"What abuse? There was no abuse, Michael, on the contrary, she had them eating out of her hands. By the time she was finished with the Q'n'A they wanted to adopt her and take her home. She had a standing ovation."

Michael was stunned, "What! What're you telling me?"

Brian gave him a full account of everything that transpired after the royal's departure, taking relish in Elizabeth's handling of adversities she changed into successes. When he finished, Michael remained silent. "Michael, you there?"

"Yes...I'm here. You're not going to believe the biggest screw-up I have ever made in my entire life-"

"I believe it, Eric just told me. Looks like you're going to have to do some major bowing and scraping, buddy. Well, you were frightened for her. You *have* to tell her what really happened now. Anyway, we'll talk later, you'd better check with Eric, find out where she is."

Michael called Eric who informed him Elizabeth was now running in the most isolated area of The Park, so fast that he, who was carrying more weight than he should, was having a hard time keeping her in sight and had to send the two other younger men in front; then he described what path Michael should take.

Michael asked in surprise, "You say she's... 'running'?"

Eric panted, "Faster than any cheetah I ever saw!"

Elizabeth felt she was in a nightmare fleeing from a gigantic two-headed forked-tongued monster. Her legs sped up as comprehension of what happened in the armored car sped into her psyche. The initial shock at Michael's behavior began to grow in volume, as did the bile in her stomach.

Her discombobulated condition caused her thoughts to run rampant from rage to pain, *Oh Godde! Not again! I'm such a fool! Entrusting my heart to another man. Opening my soul to him. Loving him with everything that I am. How could I have been so wrong about him? So easily deceived? With all his intelligence and education he still thinks of women like masses of ignorant men do! His love for me is secondary to his dominating macho ego! It's over! Close your heart if you want to survive woman! Never let another man in! They'll destroy you, the bastards!*

Michael willed his feet to speed up as his thoughts did the same. He recalled the events in Davidson Hall and how impressed he was with Elizabeth and her attention to detail. When he and his family had sneaked in after his orders were followed that the lights over the reserved back rows be turned off, he noticed even her choice of introductory music was perfect. He loved how she changed the words in songs and hymns to give God no gender. Susan pointed out to him that 'The Peace Song' referred to God as '*power*' instead of '*father*' and '*brothers*' was changed to '*companions.*' Even a traditional hymn that he loved as a child, 'How Great Thou Art,' referred to God as '*creator*' rather than '*my savior*' and the word '*Lord*' was changed to '*Godde.*' Her last two songs could not have been more appropriate, Gloria Estefan's 'Reach' and John Lennon's 'Imagine,' and they had played alternately in his head when he was dashing to the back of the stage to get her after he had gotten his family safely into their cars. Visioning her taking over the stage, he remembered how awed and proud he was of his Elizabeth, her intelligence, knowledge, ability, courage, charm, composure, confidence.

The same confidence he had sought to destroy. The only way he could, in his panic, think to save and protect her. He reviewed that terrible moment when, at the beginning of the Q'n'A, Jenkins tapped him on his shoulder and on looking up at him, saw he was accompanied by ten armed military guards.

He cringed as he heard again Jenkins whispering in his ear, "We must get the family out immediately, we've received a threat. I've ordered an armored vehicle to collect Elizabeth as soon as she's finished."

Michael remembered not moving at first, torn between getting his family out and staying with Elizabeth. Seeing his hesitancy, Jenkins had handed him a smoothed out crumbled piece of paper, "This was tied around a rock and thrown at the feet of guards outside, by two men who sped off on a motorbike."

It was a plain piece of white paper with a typed message in capital letters, and there was no mistaking its meaning:

PRINCE MICHAEL

IF THE INFIDEL BITCH DOESN'T STOP SPREADING HER POISIONOUS DISEASE SHE AND ALL WHO LISTEN WILL SUFFER THE CONSEQUENCES! If YOU CAN'T CONTROL YOUR WHORE WE WILL! TORTURINGLY! PERMENANTLY!

It was signed with the symbol of the most dangerous group of terrorists in existence: two long swords forming the shape of a 'V' piercing a heart that dripped red blood.

Michael had shuddered at the sight of it, but not as much as he shuddered now. *Who the hell disclosed our relationship to them!? Jenkins must find out! Heads will roll!*

He knew he must beg and plead for her forgiveness and started taxing his brain for the right words to convince her why it was necessary for him to act in the manner he had. His quandary was how to do that without divulging the entire terrorist's message. Apart from him being terrified she would leave the palace if she found out strangers knew she and he were connected, he didn't want to terrify her as much as she should be terrified.

Try as he might, the words didn't come to him. He felt nothing was contrite enough, and re-focused on getting to her as fast as possible. Before she did something regrettable.

The phone vibrated in his hand, "Yes, Eric?"

"Sir…you'd better hurry! Something's wrong with her!"

A strange fear flooded the panting prince, "Wrong?"

Eric also filled with fear, "She's stopped at the north end of the small pond, shaking and all bent over. I don't know if she's…we're out of her sight but I feel I should go help her-"

"No! Don't let her see you, in fact, back off, I'm here, just around the bend."

Michael's words repeated in Elizabeth's head, and echoed in the pit of her stomach. Visions of him wavered between the anger and hypercritical disapproval he exhibited in the armored car, to the love and security she had only hours before experienced in his arms. As the pain settled in her heart and soul, the bile unsettled in her stomach. She stopped running as she felt her stomach then chest constrict, her throat followed, and, shaking, she began to gag on food that was involuntarily ejecting.

Feeling a loss of support from her legs as her knees buckled, she was suddenly held up at her waist from behind, by the two familiar arms she only moments ago vowed to herself she would never feel again.

The contents of her stomach rose up and spouted out her mouth, spewing regurgitated food all over their hands, clothes and sneakers. Even Michael's Breguet watch and cufflinks got a solid dousing. When he saw she had finished retching and there was nothing more forthcoming, he sat her on a bench.

Kneeling in front of her, he held her hands and began earnestly, "I'm so sorry, my darling. I didn't want to hurt you, but you were included in the threat to the family and I was afraid your speech provoked it, I was scared for you. I thought the only way I could keep you safe was by silencing...stopping, your speeches. When I saw how the audience attacked you I was upset, and after we got the threat, I became frightened for you...and the family. And those men who abused you...it was more than I could bear. We suspect they had something to do with the threatening note, the police are searching for them. I am obligated to protect you, Elizabeth. And my family. I'm sorry that I had to miss the Q'n'A, Brian told me you were phenomenal, they wanted to take you home with them, fell in love with you. I can't blame them. But nobody's more in love with you than I."

Her heart still racing, she could hear it pounding in her ears between Michael's words. As a result, many of them fell by the wayside, and her anger boiled up again. Her head hanging down, he could not see her eyes which she kept shut, not wanting to see him. Observing her heavy breathing and silence, he realized she had not absorbed his words and began repeating them with even more tenderness and sincerity than before.

She pushed his hands off of her, her anger not abating even though she could hear and feel the love and caring he had for her. The tears she was damming started to burn, forcing her to open her eyes to let them flow. Her head still down, she saw the disgusting vomit that coated them both and felt a surge of embarrassment, but her rage overshadowed it.

Trembling, tears streaming down her face, she shouted, "You doubted me! Questioned my knowledge! My integrity! My ability! My honesty! And in front of all those men in the car! You were disloyal to me! Nothing you say now can change that!"

"No! Don't say that," he pleaded in a loud voice, suppressing his temptation to shout back at her as he desperately wanted her to look at him, to see the sincere regret and repentance in his eyes, "I didn't mean it that way. I only meant to make you see how *some* people will react, it wasn't what *I* was thinking. I would never doubt your knowledge or integrity, ability or honesty. I will *never* be disloyal to you-"

She interrupted him, her emotional voice just one octave lower than before, tears still flowing from her eyes, "I feel an immense sense of betrayal!" and dropped her head to her knees, her entire body shaking with sobs.

Feeling her pain as though it were his own, he knew he must take it away from her or she would take herself away from him. Trying to get her to look in his eyes, he attempted to lift her face but she fought him, keeping her head down. He said loudly and firmly, "Elizabeth look at me!" She didn't budge. His voice softened, cracking as he pleaded, "Elizabeth *please* look at me?"

The crack in his voice tugged at the surface of her heart. Slowly, she raised her head a little, but still would not look at him. He grabbed her face in both his hands, forcing her to look in his eyes. They were wet.

Fear and regret causing him to be tremulous, he said with contrition and resolution, "Elizabeth, this is my promise to you. I will never, ever, betray you. I will always be there for you. I will always protect you. I will always love you. Till death, and even beyond."

Although Jenkins and two guards arrived in a car to drive them back to the palace, Elizabeth and Michael chose to walk, and talk, Eric and the other bodyguards following behind at a discreet distance. Finding a garden hose hidden in a flower bed, they gave each other a quick hosing down.

By the time they arrived back at his apartments, Michael having done more "*major bowing and scraping*" than was necessary, though not divulging the last sentence of the threat, Elizabeth had regained her confidence in his love for her; but she did not exhibit it, and Michael's own confidence in her love for him diminished. Entering his apartments, he saw shopping bags on his bed that reminded him of a trump card he could use to regain her full favor. Taking her in his arms, he asked sweetly, "Are you up to a Bruce Springsteen concert tonight?"

Her spirits lifted, "The Boss is here? You got tickets?"

Seeing delight return to her he laughed, "He is, I got."

She threw her arms around his neck and pressed her body against his wanting to kiss him, but remembering the vomiting episode in The Park, did not. He seemed to have forgotten it, or simply didn't care, because he held her tightly and kissed her deeply, his tongue licking hers.

When they eventually released each other she sighed and looked lovingly at him, "Michael, you're simply the best. I love you. I'll always love you," and stealing a line from him, "till death, and even beyond."

They kissed again, and slowly, she undid her arms from around his neck, "You're going to laugh at this cliché, but I honestly don't have a thing to wear. I didn't think I'd be going to a rock concert when I packed for this trip."

He smiled, pleased with his foresight, "Don't worry, it's been taken care of. Earlier today I sent Jenkins to buy you suitable clothes for the occasion."

"Jenkins! You sent *Jenkins* to buy me rock concert clothes?" She fell into a stuffed chair, laughing uproariously, both from amusement and tension release.

"Well, I told him to make sure they were cool and sexy," he said defensively.

She rose, still laughing, "I can't wait to see what he got, where're they?"

"I presume in those bags on our bed."

They dumped out the contents of the shopping bags onto the bed. She examined them carefully. The jeans were of a stretch material and seemed alright, although the cut-outs down the outer sides of the legs looked to be more revealing than she would have chosen. Then she checked out the two tops, "Michael, these are so brief, I can't even wear a bra under them. He really took you at your word about "*cool and sexy*." When I feel cold my nipples are going to stick out."

"Well, I shall just have to hold you from behind and keep my hands over them to keep them warm," he said jokingly, but she knew he was quite serious.

Taking her hand he led her into his shower. They removed their vomit stained clothes and dropping them in a corner, lathered their wash cloths.

Reading each other's minds, they wordlessly began rubbing one another clean. When they got to near the genitals Michael's stamen was in full bloom, as was Elizabeth's hidden flower.

They stared at each other, but to her disappointment, he didn't pull her to him as he usually would have but instead said shyly, nervously, "Turn around. I'll do your back, then you can do mine." Quickly rubbing the cloth over her back, he gave her his to receive her ministrations.

She could see and feel the tension in his body. His muscles more taut than usual confirmed what she suspected. She stepped around to face him, "You think I'm still mad at you?"

Wrinkling his forehead, he looked at her gravely and asked almost woefully, "Are you?"

She shook her head, "I could never stay mad at you. I know now that you were only trying to protect me. But Michael, I'm a grown woman, I know what I'm doing, I've confidence in my work. I can handle whatever comes up. You have to have faith in me."

"I do, my darling, I do," he said insistently though obsequiously as he moved toward her.

"Good," she said seriously, and dropped her eyes to his phallus, "Now, give it to me."

With a rush of relief, he bent his knees and thrust his penis so hard into her, she staggered back against the shower's glass wall. He grabbed her buttocks and she grabbed his. They gyrated wildly against each other until, with more than normal release, their orgasms came flooding down, joining the shower's water falling down around them. With still united genitalia, letting go of her buttocks and taking hold of her face, he looked earnestly into her eyes, "I love you Elizabeth. I'll never hurt you, not ever. I promise."

She knew he expected her to promise similarly to him but simply nodded saying nothing, for she knew it was already too late for her to keep that promise.

CHAPTER
25

Elizabeth zipped on five-inch-heel boots and walked out of her dressing room laughing, "Michael these jeans are so tight it's a good thing I don't have my period, there isn't even room for a tampon!"

He laughed at her intimate joke, then seeing her, his eyes widened as he blew a piercing wolf-whistle, this was the sexiest he had ever seen her look. Not only were the jean's cutouts exposing almost as much leg as if she had on a bikini, but were it not for spandex, she would never have fitted into it at all; it fit like another skin on her curvaceous body. The skimpy turquoise top had no back, only a tied string behind her neck and another behind her waist. Her nipples were already showing under the flimsy fabric and she was not even cold. She decided not to blow-dry her hair, crunching it up while it dried so it would curl more than it would naturally. She wanted to look wild tonight, in keeping with how she felt. She had a desperate need to let loose completely, and as Trinidad Carnival was not an option, a Bruce Springsteen concert was the next best thing.

"Wow!" Michael exclaimed, "You look absolutely scrumptious. I'm going to keep a tight rein on you tonight, every man there is going to want you. Maybe the women too!"

Giggling, she took him in and exclaimed, "They will be *my* worry, Prince Drop Dead Gorgeous! Look at you! Looking so hot in your 'The Boss' t-shirt, muscles bulging all over the place. Your jeans look as tight as mine! Do you still have a hard-on?"

He laughed, "Cut that out, you're embarrassing me," and dropping a cap on her head, pulled another out of a bag and dropped it on his own.

Reading what it said, her mouth fell open feigning shock then laughingly chided him, "'Born In The U.S.A.' I wonder what *your* father would have to say about *that?*"

Putting on his best imitation of an American accent, he tilted his head toward the door, "Baby, tonight, we are *all* born in the U.S.A. Let's go rock!"

Jenkins was waiting for them inside the door to the palace garages. Elizabeth removed her long jacket, wickedly thinking, *I'm going to have some fun with Mr. Prim and Proper.*

Walking straight up to him she said demurely, "Thank you for the clothes, Jenkins. What do you think?" she twirled into two pirouettes then posed sexily like a runway model.

Jenkins turned as red as beetroot, though she detected a hint of a smile at one upturned corner of his mouth. Looking away quickly, he said formally, "Very nice Miss, very nice," and ushered them hastily to the car, Michael repressing the internal laughter he enjoyed at Jenkins's embarrassment.

Six bodyguards waited near three cars, all dressed in jeans and t-shirts with 'Born In The U.S.A.' embroidered on their caps. Seeing them, Elizabeth burst out laughing, "Michael, we look like a Carnival band! If we're not careful they'll put us on the stage as part of the show!" The men overheard her, and suppressing what would have been disrespectful guffaws, simply smiled in agreement.

Michael's demeanor stiffened on becoming serious and authoritative, "Alright, listen men. I need everyone keeping the caps on. Don't worry, there'll be lots of people wearing caps, we'll look like a bunch of groupies, but I need to be able to see you around us at all times."

He looked tenser than she would have liked but she said nothing until they were alone in the backseat of the car, "Darling you need to lighten up, this is supposed to be fun."

His face softened as he looked at her, "I know, darling, but this could get dangerous, what with the big partying crowd. I want to make sure we're safe and protected."

She held his hand, "The best way we'll be safe is if we blend in, look like we're part of the crowd. So relax, let's go wild tonight!"

He threw his head back laughing, "Alright, let's see how wild you can get."

"You too, baby. You have to let loose, or you lose."

Sneaking their group in halfway through the opening act, Michael pulled his cap down low over his face in an attempt to be irrecognizeable. They had perfect seats for them, center stage, three rows back, they could see the stage perfectly but at the same time blend in with everyone else. The atmosphere was electric with excitement and anticipation, everyone wired up, impatiently waiting for 'The Boss.' When Bruce Springsteen and his band eventually lit up the stage the fired-up crowd went crazy. Every fan clapping, screaming, jumping, whistling, dancing and singing, their seats becoming redundant as no one sat for the duration of the concert.

Elizabeth was jubilant, she felt she was home again. Her years of living in the United States were some of her most carefree and happiest, and she desperately needed to experience those feelings again, especially tonight.

Michael stood behind her all night, holding onto her as she danced wildly against him, uncontrolled and unrestrained.

Seeing this side of her created a new excitement for him, not just sexually but mentally. After the emotionally difficult day they had been through it was a relief to see she could expel all her worries and fears, totally surrendering to the music to let it exult her. After Springsteen performed a few numbers and Michael saw the crowd around did not take much notice of them, everyone just dancing and singing with The Boss, having a great time, he relaxed and got into the swing of it all.

He started dancing uninhibitedly with Elizabeth, following her every move, singing the choruses with her, laughing, hugging, kissing her, the two of them completely joyous and exhilarated.

When Springsteen swung into 'Dancing In The Dark,' Elizabeth put her arms around Michael's neck and leaned against him, "Thank you for this night, this day, for everything. You're the most precious man and I adore you. You've filled the hole in my heart with your love. I'll cherish you forever." Michael was relieved and ecstatic to hear her say these words, he could actually feel them emanating from her body against him.

The magical moment was shortened by Brian whispering close to his ear, "Sir, couple guys heard some people saying Prince Michael's here and he's with a…ahem…really hot chick."

"Damn!" Michael's annoyance evident to his people, he added quickly, "We'd better leave."

Overhearing their exchange, Elizabeth said firmly, "No way. We're not leaving. Just tell our group to speak with American accents, act like tourists, that'll fool people."

"Good idea." Michael readily agreed. The last thing he wanted was to cut their fun short, it was especially important for Elizabeth to release and disencumber all the tensions of today, because tomorrow, he had to be the messenger of what he knew would be disturbing bitter-sweet tidings.

The bodyguards chose whatever American accents they best identified with from movies or television shows they had enjoyed. The accents ran the gamut of the U.S.A.

They tried the Wild West, the Mid West, the South, Texas, Boston, and New Jersey, among others no American would have been able to recognize. Elizabeth was highly amused at their unusual but enthusiastic attempts at what they thought to be "American;" but did not criticize and instead gave words of encouragement, "cool," "good job," "brilliant," "authentic," being among them. She and Michael flowed easily into the accents they had once perfected from when they had been at school in the U.S.A.

After awhile two strange men approached while they were hugging and dancing. The always alert bodyguards still surrounding them moved in cautiously closer.

The bigger man stared at Michael and shouted, "You know Yank, you look just like our Prince Michael."

Michael held Elizabeth even closer and with his American accent more pronounced than before, responded without looking at the man, "Yeah, I get that a lat."

Elizabeth chimed in with a Southern Belle drawl, "Nah, ma guy is bedder lookin'," and grabbing Michael's face, kissed him hard and long, for both desire and the desire to hide his face.

The men shrugged, and walking away, the big one mumbled, "Don't know about that. Our Prince is a very handsome fellar."

After that incident, they were left alone with no upsetting disturbances to their enjoyment of the concert.

Springsteen roared into 'Born In The U.S.A.' and the royal group joined in with gusto. Singing louder than everyone else, they stuck their hands up in the air with victory signs and index fingers or fists pointing jovially towards The Boss, in acknowledgement of their 'birthplace.'

On the way back to the palace, kissing hungrily and with exploring hands, Elizabeth teased Michael about how they were, "Making-out like horny teenagers," in the backseat of the car.

He teased her back gutturally, "But we are *not* teenagers, and I have something all grownup here to give you that's bursting to get out." Seeing his bulging crotch, knowing the discomfort he felt due to the confines of his tight jeans, she unzipped him, unwrapped his grownup gift, enveloped it in her mouth and began to savor it. Not wanting her to be left out and with a desire to feast on her as she feasted on him, he pulled her down onto the carpeted floor.

They hurriedly helped each other struggle out of their jeans, lay on their sides, and with heads to each other's genitals, formed, and performed, a perfect sixty-nine.

After Pamela left the balcony with a tray-load of empty breakfast dishes from their huge repast, Michael reached over and held both Elizabeth's hands, "Darling, there's something we must discuss."

His demeanor unnerved her and he could see it, but in spite of his fears, knew he had to give her all the information, it had to be entirely up to her what she did with it. "You had a call from your American agent, Gloria Goldman, last night when you were getting dressed and left your phone on our bed. Seeing what...had occurred earlier, I knew the call was important, but knowing we were running late for the concert I answered it...don't worry, I told her I was your favorite cousin Stephen and you were staying with my family. I didn't tell you about it before for two reasons. Firstly, Gloria said it could wait till morning. Secondly, more importantly, I knew you needed to relax and release your tensions from the...events...of the day; what she said would have caused you to think excessively, maybe not enjoy yourself as much at the concert. So," he smiled, "you're going to have to forgive me, I was only thinking of you, as usual."

Not returning his smile she said nothing, she just wanted him to get on with it, wondering, *What now?*

Getting serious, he continued, "Gloria said that an equality group from the United States wants you to come over to give your speech, in two weeks."

"What?" The surprise in her voice pleased him. "Where?"

He smiled broadly, "New York City."

She became contemplative, "Oh...I guess that's not surprising. That it's New York, I mean. America probably has more man-made-up religions than anywhere else in the world, such is the price of 'Liberty for all.' So it would have to be in a sophisticated, worldly city like New York, or Chicago, or somewhere in California. Not long ago a survey claimed that more than a third of Americans surveyed still believe in Genesis and all that nonsense. Can you imagine? I wonder where they lived. What else did she say?"

"They're going to pay first class return flights for two, you and a bodyguar...companion, your stay in a suite at The Plaza for four nights, and-" he paused deliberately, "pay you a quarter million dollars."

She caught her breath, "Wow! That's double what I got here in Europe!"

"I know. But…there's a contingency."

"Contingency? What kind of contingency?" there was an edge to her voice, she obviously did not like the sound of that.

Michael took a deep breath, "They want you to… change…modify…some of your theories, and…some facts."

Elizabeth became furious, strode over to the balcony railing and turned to face him, her voice raised in indignation, "What! Are they crazy! One doesn't modify facts! They are what they are! And as for my theories, they are mine, based on extensive research, I'm not going to change them for anyone! Look Michael, I've spent *years* researching all that material, traveled the globe collecting data, read thousands of books and literature on the subject, spoken to hundreds of people, theologians, scholars, educators, archeologists, curators, and ordinary intelligent people. I've already sacrificed too much of my time, not to mention *emotions*, on this. Have you any idea what I went through *emotionally* while doing the research? To learn what I suspected is the Truth, *is* the Truth!?"

He eyed her sympathetically, "I know, I went through the same emotional upheaval when I learned the Truth."

His look and words making her feel justified she said emphatically, "I'm not going to change one damn thing! They can bloody well go to hell!"

Seeing her confidence return in her fighting spirit, although feeling a little afraid, inwardly he smiled thinking, *That's my girl, you tell them babe,* but outwardly he remained serious and calm, "Gloria anticipated that would be your reaction, so she got them to agree that if she could get you to elaborate, basically to provide more detailed support for some of your facts and theories, they'll have to pay you another quarter million dollars." He didn't dare divulge that, stressing the "*danger aspect,*" it was actually he who had negotiated the extra quarter million during a conference call with Gloria and the organizers, and made them all swear to never tell Elizabeth, or anyone else.

Falling back into her chair she let out a breath, and said softly, "Are you kidding me? Is this for real?"

He allowed his internal smile to become visible, "It is."

She was quiet for a while, pondering the situation, the ramifications and complications that could arise from such a venture; although it remained in the forefront of her mind as to what a great honor this was, besides being an equally great opportunity to educate, spread Truth. And, expand The Children's Home. Feeling Michael's searching eyes on her, eventually she looked at him enquiringly, "What do *you* think, Michael?"

He looked at her lovingly, flattered and appreciative that she wanted his opinion on something so important to her, especially after his, though pretended but painfully censorious, behavior, yesterday, "Darling, it's really about what *you* think, if you feel to acquiesce to their request is compromising or depreciatory in any way."

She deliberated on what he said, then spoke unhurriedly but definitively, "Elaborating on my theories is easy. I could go on about that for days, no problem. Giving more details on my, no, *the* facts, that's going to be tricky. One can only do so much with facts, something either exists or doesn't, either occurred or hasn't. So, I'm going to have to scrutinize my research and draw from that how I go about further substantiating what they're concerned about. Did Gloria give specifics?"

He pointed towards Elizabeth's laptop on the desk in the next room, "She was e-mailing you as soon as she had details. You need to check immediately. The organizers now have a mad rush on their hands to put it all together in time. They're celebrating their silver anniversary and are changing their program to make you their keynote speaker, star presentation. They'll have to get new ads out, programs reprinted. If you agree, that is. This is a very big honor for you, darling."

She leaned forward in her chair, new excitement beginning to build on an old foundation of fear, "Gosh, now you're scaring me. Where're they doing it?"

His face beamed, his eyes gleamed, "Canterbury Hall."

Her mouth fell open, "Oh my Godde!" Sitting back against her chair, she sucked in a deep long breath, letting it out with a loud, "Whew." Knowing Canterbury Hall to be the most eminent of such institutions, having been there many times for a variety of events, all prestigious, she knew there were different sizes of rooms, and wondered in which one the event would be held.

Telepathically reading her mind, Michael said impressibly, "It's in the Stein Auditorium. It has the largest capacity, about three thousand seats." Elizabeth stared at him.

He perceived she was struggling to hide the fear that had descended upon her and said encouragingly, "Darling, it doesn't matter how many are in the audience whether it's two or three thousand. They're just people, no better or more important than you. Besides, *they* are paying to hear what *you* have to say."

She gave a troubled sigh, "But, it's a lot of money, Michael. Half a million! The responsibility is huge. I'm petrified. But…I can't possibly turn it down now. With that money I can do so much more for my children. We can build the additional dormitory we desperately need. I *have* to do it. I've no choice." Rising from her seat, she gave him a peck on his lips, said, "Thank you," and walking inside to check her e-mails, reminded herself to be more careful, never again to leave her phone where Michael could get to it.

Jenkins strode into Michael's office and dropped a newspaper on his desk, "How do you want to handle this?" In the boldest print on the front page the headlines screamed, *ROYALS RUN FROM GENDERLESS GOD SPEECH.*

Michael let out an expletive, then read the account of him and his family leaving Elizabeth's speech before she was finished, how it, '*disrupted the event, creating an uproar, and why would they leave when they did? The people deserve an explanation.*' Very little was said about Elizabeth or the actual speech. The focus of the article was on the royal's premature departure and speculations as to the reasons why, the most detailed one being, '*they must have disagreed with the subject.*'

He shook his head in disgust, "Everything we do is always blown out of proportion. And you'd think the guy who wrote this would've given Elizabeth and her speech more exposure, he sure had enough there to scandalize '*the people.*' Just goes to show how right she is about the patriarchal mentality, eh? Alright, I'm going to have to deal with this. You know if she hasn't seen it yet somebody'll make sure she does. Any info on who disclosed us to the terrorists?"

"None yet. It's going to be difficult to find out. The staff knows they'll not only lose their jobs but will be blacklisted from getting a decent one elsewhere, so that leaves family. Someone broke the silence code. I have my suspicions, I'll let you know if…when…I get confirmation of them."

Michael was correct in his assumption. Susan, Megan, Mark, and Anne, sought Elizabeth out thinking to comfort and reassure her. They found her in her office in the library, going over her research for the speech in New York. Having spoken to Gloria earlier, she was relieved to learn what the organizers of the event in Canterbury Hall wanted was for her to speak more Biblical quotations rather than give out lists of where to find them; plus divulgence of her sources for some of her research, even though this could add a quarter-hour to her speech.

The four royals entered with feigned enthusiasm, Anne shaking the newspaper telling her bad publicity is better than no publicity, and nobody important is going to take it seriously anyway. Seeing the puzzled look on her face, realizing she was unaware of the article, they apologized for their "faux pas" and had no choice but to show it to her.

Elizabeth's calm reaction on reading the article gave the impression she was being professionally dignified. In actuality, she was greatly relieved that so little was said about her, her last name was spelt incorrectly, and she hoped the significance given to the royal family would take the spotlight off her, and the article would not make it to the international press.

However, at lunchtime, Michael, fearing it would have an adverse effect on her and perhaps their relationship, before making the tenderest most unselfish love to her at their 'matinee,' assured her that he had taken steps to appease the journalist, and to inform 'the people' that his family having to leave early was 'much ado about nothing.'

The following morning over coffee, the happily smiling prince presented the newspaper to Elizabeth. A small article had been circled in ink in the middle of the front page. He was particularly pleased that for once the newspaper got everything right and actually printed his press release as he had written it, with just a minimum of embellishments.

It was headlined '*Royals Explain*,' and stated that the royal family had to leave when they did because had they stayed, they would have been extremely late for an important family engagement, Ms. Elizabeth Richardson's intriguing event having run longer than expected. It went on to say that their leaving was in no way a reflection on Ms. Richardson and her speech, and in fact they found it powerful and gave much food for thought.

Though concerned that Michael had the spelling of her name corrected not once but twice, she was nevertheless more than appreciative of his daring and courage, to have his family defend her and her speech in this manner. She was well aware of the risk he was taking, stepping out on a limb for her.

Wanting to show her gratitude in the modus operandi she knew he would most enjoy, she took his hand, led him to the bed, removed her dressing gown to tantalizingly expose her naked body, lay down on the bed seductively, and beckoned him to her.

As he lay his naked body beside her, she said, "It was so wonderful and brave of you to defend me. I'm forever grateful, darling, but I sincerely hope this is the end of it, and you'll never have to defend me and my speeches again."

He responded solemnly, "Darling, I'll always come to your defense, on every subject," then he grinned teasingly, "at least in public. But in private, I'm going to let you know what I really think and you'll always agree with me." Taking in his wicked grin and provoking words, even though she assumed he was being jocular, she was not going to let him get away with that remark. She sat up, picked up a pillow and hit him so hard he fell off the bed, the pillow bursting open sending feathers flying all over the room. Jumping onto the bed he stood over her, his hardening penis dangling and swaying enticingly.

With mischief in his eyes he grabbed a pillow, "So you want to fight? You can't win. I'm bigger and stronger than you."

Grabbing another pillow, she scrambled out from under his long legs, stood up and hit his side even harder than before, bursting that pillow also, sending a mass of feathers all over the two of them. Laughing hard, he hit her retreating bottom with his pillow, but too softly for it to burst.

She turned and teased him about being "*a wimp*" and not as strong as she. Taking up her challenge, he hit her bottom with force this time, the pillow bursting wide open sending even more feathers all over them and the room. They both overbalanced and fell on the bed, Michael halfway on top of her. Lying in their feather bed, covered with a blanket of feathers, they laughed so hard they breathed in some tiny down feathers and had to sit up and slap each other's backs to stop from choking. Catching their breaths, they looked around at the "*royal mess*" they created, and fell back on the bed laughing hysterically all over again.

Turning to face her he managed to say between gasps, "Alright, you win. This time."

She blew feathers off his face and responded pluckily, "No, every time, ducky."

Slowly, he blew feathers off her face, causing stimulation in both their genitals. Very slowly, they blew feathers off their appropriate and necessary parts, and wordlessly agreeing to a ceasefire, surrendering to their innately pacifistic desires to make love and not war, they both won.

CHAPTER
26

Elizabeth's proclivity for domestic orderliness took over and pulling out a corner of the sheet, she industriously began an attempt at cleaning up their feathery mess, when Michael stopped her, "Leave it, darling. You don't have time for that. Pam'll take care of it."

"But darling, how are we going to explain this?"

He shook his head grinning, "No need she'll figure it out."

Her sex flush deepened, "Precisely. It's embarrassing."

Laughing, he pulled her into his arms, "How many times must I tell you nothing you do with me is embarrassing." At that moment, the knock on the door indicated that Pamela had arrived to do her morning tidying up and check on Elizabeth's requirements for the day.

Letting her in, Michael said with a straight face, "Good morning, Pam. Sorry, you've a bit of a mess to clean up. Oh, and you'll need to get us some new pillows. The old ones just couldn't take any blows at all."

Pamela surveyed the battle-scarred room and looked at Elizabeth in surprise. Elizabeth grinned and shrugged embarrassedly. Pamela suppressed a chuckle, simply nodded, and sedately began to clean up the lover's nest mess.

The day of the Ambassadors Ball arrived with much excitement and anticipation. However, the frenetic hive-like buzzing of the palace staff the previous five days metamorphosed into an organized confident calm. Elizabeth's gown was delivered mid-morning. She tried it on immediately, Michael calling at the same time to check if it had arrived. On hearing it had, he said he was coming to see it. She hurried out of the gown and hid it in her dressing room. After he greeted her with a long passionate kiss he asked her to model the gown for him, he was dying to see her in it. He said his day was an extremely busy one with preparations for "*seriously diplomatic 'casual' talks*" with various Ambassadors, he was going to be dashing in at the last minute to dress for the ball, and would not have leisurely time to admire her in it before having to face a night of serious diplomacy and formality, and being "*on*" all night.

Smiling flirtatiously, she denied his request, "No. You'll have to wait until tonight. You're always surprising me, now it's my turn to surprise you."

He returned the flirty smile, "I'm assuming you're going to make the surprise perfect and allow me to introduce you tonight as my ladylove, my bride-to-"

Her smile faded as she interrupted, "Michael, please don't start again, we've already been through this a dozen times."

He kept his smile, "I know, but I thought you'd change your mind today, it being such a special event tonight. We could at last stop the nerve-wracking hiding, we'd Skype your parents as soon as we're dressed, then announce our engageme-"

She interrupted again, shaking with obvious controlled anger, "Absolutely not! We cannot shock my family! We're not going to discuss this again until I'm ready, Michael!"

He didn't control his own risen anger which was bolstered by his overwhelming disappointment. He had felt certain that with all they had been through she would feel confident and comfortable in his everlasting love, and finally agree to go public about it, after he asked her parents for her hand on Skype. He didn't see this method of asking to be unorthodox and a problem. After all, this was an electronic age, they were sophisticated people, surely they would understand his position, how busy he was at this time and unable to ask in person.

Showing his dismay and displeasure at her outright rejection of his idea he turned his back on her, stalked towards the door and shouted, "I've had enough of all your drama! Now I have to change the seating at the banquet table and put you to sit away from me! Far away! I'm fed up with all this damn crap!" With that retaliatory salvo, he slammed the heavy door so hard it caused a strong vibration in her as well as the room.

She sat on the bed, bewildered. She could not fathom how, after having convinced him with her fabricated explanations, and with everything they had been through, he could behave this way. He had assured her many times that he understood the reasons she had given him for waiting to publicly announce their relationship, but now, today of all days, he is mad at her and wants to renege on his agreement.

Then the way in which he spoke to her was shocking. That was no pretend act like in the armored car, that was from the heart. Not only was he truly furious but it was the first time she had ever heard him use foul language, and it forced her to the realization that his patience with her situation was rapidly running out. The time had come, she could not procrastinate any longer. As scared and as unprepared as she was to do it, she had to tell him everything; but not until after the ball.

Hands trembling, she punched in his number but it went into voicemail, and she forced a steady voice, "Michael, I'm sorry I upset you. I need to talk to you tonight, I have to explain…everything. Can we please meet after the ball to discuss…everything, please? I love you. I always will."

The day dragged for Elizabeth as she waited for a response from Michael but none came. With an anxious heart, she went into the shower to prepare herself for the ball. Walking out of the bathroom she noticed the phone message light blinking. Grabbing the phone she played Michael's message.

His voice was stiff, polite but not unkind, "Got your message. I'm extremely busy, couldn't return your call earlier. Yes, we'll definitely meet to talk after the ball. I'm looking forward to at last hearing your explanations about 'everything,' as you put it. By the way, I've rearranged your seating at dinner. You'll now be sitting between the Trinidad and Tobago ambassador and her husband. Hope that meets with your approval. See you later. Goodbye."

Pamela having secured in Elizabeth's hair, a diamond and pearl tiara Anne lent her, answered a knock on the door. Brian rushed in, looked at Elizabeth in her gown, smiled and bowed, "You look perfectly regal, Your Highness. Prince Michael will be blown away. But, I'm afraid he won't be able to escort you to the ballroom, he's been swamped with last minute rearrangements. Jenkins will take you there, he'll be here shortly. Actually, I've come for Prince Michael's clothes and whatever his valet set out for the ball, he'll have to dress in his office," seeing disappointment cloud Elizabeth's sweet smile, he looked regretful, shrugged and added quickly, "he's sorry, but it just couldn't be helped, it's been a crazy day."

Elizabeth could see Brian was sincere in his apology for Michael, but wondered how genuine Michael's own apology would be. She walked over to her dresser and took a beautifully gift-wrapped small box out of a drawer, "Please give this to Michael for me, I…I hope he likes it…enough to wear it."

Fifteen minutes later Jenkins arrived carrying a black leather briefcase from which he unpacked four red velvet jewelry boxes. She noticed he snatched up the smallest one and put it in his trouser pocket. Opening the largest box he took out an exquisite necklace of rubies diamonds and pearls set in gold, and with a shy smile addressed her a little less formally than he usually would, "Elizabeth, Prince Michael asked me to assist you in putting these on. May I?"

Simply nodding as she could not think of anything to say, she lifted the tresses of hair that had been left to trail down her back, the rest of it having been pinned up on top her head behind the tiara. The necklace secure, Jenkins silently handed her the matching earrings for her to attach, then he clasped the matching bracelet on her wrist. He stood back appraising her, "Perfect. You look every inch a Queen. Now, shall we go?"

She hesitated, looked at him sadly and said softly, "I don't feel like going. Michael and I have quarreled, he left this morning very angry. I'd rather just stay here and talk with him after the ball-"

Jenkins shifted his feet nervously, "No, Miss. You must go. Everyone would be upset if you don't. Your absence would be insulting, actually damaging. Remember, you're sitting with the Trinidad and Tobago ambassador and others from your embassy. It's imperative that you attend. Don't worry about the quarrel, Prince Michael never stays angry for long," he offered her his arm, "now come on, chin up. You're going to a ball."

Standing at the entrance to the ballroom still clutching Jenkins's arm, Elizabeth, old memories made new, regarded the beauty and splendor of a Royal Ball. The room sparkled from the brilliantly lit crystal chandeliers combined with the bejeweled and elegant expensively bedecked guests, everyone in evening dress, many men in tuxedoes with tails, all the ladies in full-length designer gowns. Their Excellencies, wearing their colorful silk sashes with medals and ribbons prominently displayed, stood out proudly from the rest of the crowd, and there was no mistaking who was honored to be an ambassador.

Jenkins gently unclenched her hand from his arm, "Prince Michael said when you're announced you're to walk in alone as you don't want to be connected with anyone from the palace."

Observing the liveried dressed men calling out people's names as they walked in, she asked nervously, "Must I be announced, can't I just sneak in at the side?"

"No Miss, that would be improper, it wouldn't be allowed, you'd be stopped, and embarrassed. You're going to have to get accustomed to this sort of thing. Don't be nervous, it only takes a few seconds. Just give him your name and after he calls it out, give a big smile and walk to the left side, your embassy's people are there. Do you know what they look like?"

"Yes," she replied with relief but still unsmiling.

"Very good. Now, go and," Jenkins smiled at his pun-like attempt at humor to lift her spirits, "have a ball."

Her heart beating rapidly, she barely heard her name being read aloud from the guest list after she gave it to the liveried man. She looked to her left hoping to walk quickly to the sanctuary of her Trinidadian people, but her eyes could not find them. She became aware of murmuring, noticed she was being stared at by people nearest the entrance, and said nervously to the liveried announcer, "Is something wrong?"

The man didn't look at her but said formally, "No, Miss. They are dazzled by your beauty. Please continue in."

Her eyes lit up on seeing Michael. He was standing next to her ambassador. Her racing heart seemed to do somersaults as she absorbed him. He was adorned with more royal insignia than she had seen him wear before. His chest was practically covered with a red silk sash, gold braids with tassels, ribbons, sparkling medals and pins; all looking even more outstanding and imperial against a black tuxedo, white pleated shirt and bowtie. His regal bearing set off the impressive ensemble admirably. His lush light brown hair was combed back more formally and shone brightly under the crystal lights along with his stunningly handsome smiling face, as he reveled in his natural element.

She noticed he did wear her surprise gift, the cufflinks she had his jeweler secretly make, fashioned after the design of the Bindi Michael had had made for her but larger, white diamonds surrounding oval rubies set in gold filigree.

Relieved, she wanted to run and embrace him, proclaim her love for the whole world to see, but her feet could barely move as he turned away from speaking to her ambassador and gazed at her. He stopped smiling and took her in painfully slowly, his eyes wandering leisurely from her tiara down to her red satin shoes. His heart racing at a faster pace than hers, he absorbed her with an enormous rush of love, desire, pride, and, possession. *Here is my Queen.*

Elizabeth was resplendent. Her majesty was declared by her prefect posture, beauty and grace, in the regal red satiny peu-de-soie gown, and she looked every bit a stately Queen.

The bodice was fitted and had tiny gathered horizontal pleats, with a sweetheart neckline at her bosom, just high enough to discretely cover her areolas. The top and center of the bodice was heavily beaded with tiny red and clear crystals, gold beads, and white seed pearls. These cascaded past the waistline, narrowing to a point at the bottom of the first large frill of the skirt. There were two more similar beadings descending from the waist on each side of the one in the center, and three more in the back.

The back was open to the waist from where hung a padded large bow that created a subtle bustle. The skirt was comprised of three billowing blouson-type frills that flared out at the bottom, the last one touching the floor. The design gave the impression Elizabeth was floating on air as she glided towards Michael and the contingent from the Trinidad and Tobago Embassy.

He held her eyes for an instant, smiled softly, and turned away to talk to some people who came up to greet him, then, walking away with them, disappeared into the crowd.

Elizabeth had no appetite for the delicious feast that was set out and the observant ambassador remarked, "Child, now I know how you keep that skinny figure, but you must eat, you've a long night ahead."

Thinking how prophetic those words were she was tempted to say, '*you don't know the half of it,*' but simply smiled and enquired about the health of the ambassador's children and young grandchildren.

Ambassador Amelia was fairly typical of Trinidadian aristocracy, well-bred, educated, and traveled, with more worldly sophistication than the average outsider imagined a small-islander would have. She was multi-racial, an unequal mixture of African, East Indian from India, Carib Indian, English, Spanish, French, and Chinese. With high Indian cheekbones, Oriental almond-shaped eyes, a small flared West African nose, the smooth complexion of an English peach, and a full-lipped French pout, she was a beautiful representation of her various ancestors. Though somewhat thick around her torso, as is most older females who have had children and neither time nor inclination to spend the necessary hours exercising, she still retained a comely figure, with high breasts and buttocks. Her face had a smooth serenity about it which disappeared quickly when she was amused; then it would crease and light up like the tropical sun she grew up in but no longer missed.

Her complexion was light brown and contrasted interestingly with that of her strikingly handsome husband's, his being the darkest brown that human skin comes in, which covered a tall muscular physique and intelligent face that immediately made one think of an African tribal chieftain.

After a polite amount of small talk, including a variety of compliments about both her looks and accomplishments with The Children's Home, Elizabeth was relieved that nothing was said about her speech. She had more than enough seriously difficult things to deal with tonight. As it is, she was forcing a charm she did not feel. She could see Michael at one end of the banquet table twelve seats away, sitting next to a pretty platinum blonde blue-eyed young woman, and he seemed to be totally engrossed in her, and she in him.

Elizabeth hoped from his exaggerated actions and laugh he was trying to make her jealous, thought two could play at that game, and looked around for a suitable handsome young man to flirt with. There was none. Michael had deliberately placed her in the middle of the geriatric section of the long table, *The bastard,* and she became determined to get even with him later.

The ambassador closed her knife and fork and looked seriously at Elizabeth, "If I didn't know better, I'd think you and Prince Michael have something going on."

Elizabeth hid her fluster with a little laugh, "Why would you say such a ridiculous thing?"

Amelia smiled, "Well, I notice you sneaking looks at him all the time, and he's doing the same to you too."

She feigned a giggle, "That's absurd, look at how he's flirting outrageously with that beautiful blond on his right."

"Yes, but only when you're looking. When you're not looking his way, he ignores her and just stares at you."

The banquet portion of the evening completed, the cheerfully chatting crowd were ushered back into the ballroom to dance every silly dance that was ever created to the music of a full orchestra, and drink themselves silly at cocktail bars situated in the four corners of the enormous room.

Elizabeth did not sit once. Every man from her embassy's party and other West Indian islands danced with her, some for several songs, and there was an unending line of other gentlemen waiting for their turn. But Michael was not one of them.

She saw him only twice in the ballroom, both times dancing with ambassador's wives, wondered who he was with the rest of the time, and why didn't he come to surreptitiously check on her. Feigning fatigue, she begged off dancing with the remaining waiting gentlemen, and engaged the ambassador and her husband in an involved debate about the descending quality of true Calypso with its evolution into 'Soul-Calypso,' abbreviated to 'Soca.'

She was facing the couple with her back to the dance floor so as to discourage any more invitations, when the ambassador suddenly smiled at her interrupting a serious sentence, and said quietly, "Oh… oh, don't look now, but he's coming for you."

With her heart speeding up she asked innocently, "Who?"

"Prince Michael."

"Why do you think that, he's probably coming for you."

"No child. It's definitely you. I saw him speaking to the singer, now listen to what's playing, 'Lady In Red.' You're the only one here in red. I knew he had the hots for you."

"That's too bad because I have to leave, I've an early-"

The ambassador grabbed Elizabeth's wrists nervously, "No child, you can't leave. It would reflect badly on our country. Come on, you can't let the side down. What's one little dance, and with such a beautiful man," she winked at her husband, "he could put his shoes under my bed anytime."

Michael's hand rested on her bare back. He placed it at the top and suggestively dragged it slowly down to her waist, "Excuse me, beautiful lady, I believe this is our dance, they're playing our song," he pulled her quickly into his arms swirling her onto the dance floor, and began to sing the song looking deep into her eyes.

Enraptured with him and his romanticism, she didn't notice they were alone on the dance floor until the music stopped and everyone applauded them. Becoming flustered, she acted as if she didn't know him, said in a loud voice, "Thank you, Your Highness," curtseyed, and turned to leave.

Michael held her arm, digging his fingers into her flesh, "No, my lady, we've only just begun," and swirled her back onto the center of the dance floor, the band playing 'Love's Theme,' as he had previously instructed. Holding her close and swaying with her as sexily as he had that day at The Vineyards in the gazebo to the same song, she was aware they were still alone on the dance floor, the crowd watching with full attention.

Fearing his purpose was to reveal their true relationship, she said through a gritted smile, "Michael, stop. Escort me back to my ambassador at once." He responded without words, twirling her rapidly instead, then dipping her gracefully to the floor several times, to admiring applause from the crowd. More than a little annoyed she repeated her demands, adding, "You're making a fool of yourself, we're becoming a spectacle-"

His laugh was full of mischief, "Alas, you got it right. I am a fool. A fool in love. And as for us being a spectacle, frankly my dear, I don't give ten damns."

In the middle of a floor touching dip, they were suddenly blinded by flashbulbs going off all around from banned cameras. She called to him in a panic, "Michael, we're being photographed! Please stop! You promised you would hear me out after the ball! Please don't do this now! Please!"

Seeing the near hysteria on her face and hearing it in her voice, he felt remorseful about tormenting her, though he really was about just being playful, and he apologized, "Alright. Sorry. I only wanted us to at least have a little fun together tonight. Forgive me. We'll meet in the south corridor after the ball and go to our apartments for you to tell me 'everything,' like you requested, alright? You probably won't see me for the rest of the ball, you do realize I'm on duty, I have to 'work the room.'" He escorted her back to her Trinis, kissed her hand and bowed. Turning to face the ambassador and her spouse, he could not help himself, flashed them a big sparkling smile, winked twice, and walked back into the crowd.

Leaving an engrossing conversation with the Chinese ambassador and his aide-de-camp about nuclear energy, with a promise to continue the discussion in a more appropriate place in the near future, Michael spied Henry walking towards Elizabeth. She was standing with her back to him, enchanting a group from the Spanish Embassy with her beauty and extensive knowledge of their country and language.

Michael strode up to Henry, grabbed his shoulder and spun him around, "Don't you even go near her! This time, *I'll* kick your sorry ass all the way to your car!"

Henry put up his hands, palms facing outwards to protect himself, but gave his smirky smile, "Whoa! Hold on cousin. Actually, I was going to apologize. So, I see you two hooked up, eh? You always got the best ones, Michael. Come, let's have a drink to celebrate and let bygones be bye-gones."

Michael's instinct was to wipe the smirk off Henry's face with both fists but reminding himself where and who he was, he contained his anger, which allowed Henry to take advantage of the situation. He put his arm around Michael's shoulders and cajoled, "Come on cuz, we're blood. You've got to forgive and forget. Look at a bunch of our boys doing justice to the bar, let's join them and toast to your and Elizabeth's happiness."

Michael looked over at the north bar that Henry was trying to lead him towards. Several of his male cousins were gathered, drinking and laughing, including two of his favorites, his Uncle Patrick's younger sons whom he had not seen in a while, and they were waving him over. He aggressively shrugged off Henry's arm from his shoulders and made his way over to them. After much pyramid-style hugging, back slapping, hand shaking, and fists bumping, he relaxed for the first time for the day, unthinkingly accepted all the drinks the maliciously smiling Henry plied him with, and enjoyed catching up with his cousin's private lives.

Seeing the last batch of hard core party-goers about to leave through the main door, Elizabeth slipped away to the south corridor to wait for Michael whom she had noticed in the distance with a group of men at the north bar. He didn't turn up for nearly an hour. She didn't mind for the first half-hour as it gave her some time to rehearse in her head, the least upsetting way she could tell him what she was about to divulge.

Nothing she tried sounded palliative enough and eventually she gave up trying, deciding to just tell him everything as it comes, *And que sera, sera*. In some ways, this decision brought relief, she was tired of keeping secrets and it was against her nature to be mendacious; in other ways, she felt fearful that Michael would not understand and she would lose his love forever, and she knew she could not live without it.

When an hour was up she thought he didn't care enough and, disheartened, readied to leave to try and find her way back to his apartments, when he staggered in, grabbed her roughly and propped himself against a wall. He attempted a clumsy kiss but getting a strong whiff of his alcohol soaked breath, Elizabeth turned her head away revolted, "Oh my God, you're drunk!"

"Drunk as a skunk," he drawled with a vacuous grin.

"Michael how could you! You knew we had important things to discuss and this is what you do! Obviously you don't care-"

His tongue heavy, his speech dragged annoyingly, "But I do care... baby...I care about making love...to you...right now...right here. I know you want me too...so let's get it on."

She tried to wriggle herself free but he held her in a tight squeeze and she glared at him, disappointment mixed with disgust, "Let me go Michael. You're despicable."

His drawl turned to slurring, "Aw, com'on, I love you woman. And you know you love me. Admit it. Despite the golden bullets of hate shooting at me from those gorgeous eyes right now, I can feel it from your body, you love me. You want me. As much as I want you, admit it."

Her disgust and hurt churned into anger, "I'll do no such thing. And how dare you think I can be so easily swayed after the outrageous way you flirted with that blond bimbo!"

He chuckled, "Didn't mean anything. Incidentally, that 'blond bimbo' happens to be Her Royal Highness Princess Teresa, the same princess you once suggested was suitable for me to marry. Whaddya thinka that, Princess Elizabeth?"

Anger intensifying with her surprise, she sneered, "Then you should go find her and you can both go to hell! Now unhand me you... you bloody royal bastard!"

His glassy eyes gleamed wickedly, "Whoa! My lady doth cuss me. Something new. What other somethings new am I to enjoy this night, my one and only love?"

"Not one damn thing, Michael! There is nothing more disgusting than trying to have sex with a drunk man. Let me go!"

She struggled to liberate herself from his arms, but despite his inebriated state he had her in an unyielding clinch, and pressed his pelvis against hers, "You will not be disgusted, baby, I promise. You can beat me after, if you want."

She could not believe the solid erection he accomplished that was discernible even through her billowing skirt and crinoline. That he could be like this in his drunken condition was both maddening and exciting to her, *How the hell did he do this anyway, doesn't he know too much alcohol kills libido? How dare he go against this law of nature! Damn his sexy mind. Damn his sexy body. Damn mine for loving and wanting him as angry and hurt as I am.*

Recalling the pain and despair over a lost love from which she had only recently been able to heal, ironically, thanks to the 'royal bastard' who was now bringing her renewed pain and disappointment, future king notwithstanding, she knew she must lay her standards out for him. He must know that she won't be taken for granted, played games with, or used against her will.

Too intoxicated to realistically appreciate her angry demeanor, and having had thoughts of making love to her for much of the evening, and now feeling his loaded erection, he persisted forcefully, one hand groping her buttocks, "If you don't give yourself to me, I'm just going to take you."

That remark set her aflame, but not with the kind of fire he desired. Balling her hands into fists she pounded on his chest and pushed against him, "Are you crazy! Are you saying you're going to rape me!?"

He broke into a stupid grin, "I doubt I'll need to, you hot bitch, I know you always want me-"

She pounded him again, "You're wrong! I'm revolted! You're repugnant to me!" Calling on her hurt and anger to boost her resolve she snarled at him, "If you don't let me go *now*, I'll never feel the same way about you! And I'll never forgive you!"

Having mistakenly thought, in his inebriated condition, that she was just playing with him like he was playing with her, he was taken by surprise at her words and attitude, and in his befuddlement, slackened his grip on her. Taking advantage of that action she used her enraged strength to successfully push away from him, quickly picked up her skirts and turned to run. He stepped toward her making a grab for her arm, but in his drunken stupor he overbalanced, stumbled, and his shoulder hit the wall with a thud. The wall bracing him, he barely avoided falling over fully to land face down on the marble floor.

Without a backward glance, tears stinging the backs of her eyes, Elizabeth hiked up her skirts and crinoline higher and raced down the corridor. Michael leaned against the wall, his arms open, and empty, as was the feeling in his soul.

Blindly rounding a corner with tears obscuring her vision, she ran headlong into Claire and Anne. Claire took the brunt of the blow, toppling onto Anne as she shrilled at Elizabeth, "Are you mad? Why don't you watch where you're going!"

Elizabeth could barely sob out the words, "I'm sorry," and reached out to help Anne steady Claire.

Seeing the reason for her blind assault, the aunts said simultaneously, "What's wrong? Why are you crying?"

Elizabeth swallowed and sobbed softly, "Michael's drunk, and we had a fi…argument."

Claire snorted censoriously, "Probably the first of many. Pull yourself together, girl. Someone in your position can't afford to fall apart over a silly drunken quarrel. You're going to have to deal with a lot more serious situations in your life ahead, I can tell you that."

Anne reached into her evening bag, and pulling out a lace-edged monogrammed handkerchief, handed it to Elizabeth saying sympathetically, "Don't worry dear, it'll be alright in the morning. Dry your tears. Keep the hankie."

Elizabeth thanked her, did as she was told, asked for directions to Michael's apartments, said goodnight, drew her shoulders back, and held the rest of her tears in until she rounded another corner and was out of sight.

CHAPTER 27

Michael shook his head, pushed away from the wall and started after Elizabeth, when Jenkins came up to him, "Your father sent me to find you. Something important about following up a discussion you had with the Chinese ambassador-"

Michael looked at him with one bleary eye, his shoulders drooping, and slurred, "Not now, Jenkins, I must go to Elizabeth, she's really angry at me."

Jenkins rightly assessed his condition, "Oh, oh. You've obviously over-imbibed."

"Yah. A bunch of the guy cousins, spear-headed by Henry, really did some serious damage to the bar."

"That scoundrel Henry always brings trouble."

"Yah. I screwed up, Jenkins. Henry had his revenge tonight, that's for sure," shaking his head again, he leaned back against the wall for support, "Elizabeth's really angry at me."

"You said that already."

His stupid grin returned, "I told her she could beat me. Might've been fun," his slurring became more indistinct, "she refused, me."

"Go sleep it off, Michael, you can apologize and grovel in the morning. Let me escort you to your-"

"Nah, I know my way around my own house…palace… home… whatever."

"Alright. Don't forget your meeting in the morning with your father to discuss strategy for your next visit to the West Country. Elizabeth will wake you, I told her about the meeting-"

Michael straightened, ostensibly suddenly sobering up, "What! You told her about *that* meeting?"

"Just that you had a ten-thirty meeting, not its subject."

He slouched again, relieved, "Oh. G'night. Hasta manana."

Jenkins watched his charge saunter, sway, stumble, and bump the wall several times, as he made his way down the corridor, realized there was no way Michael could make a morning meeting, and called the King to suggest a time change to after lunch. Shaking his head, he mused over the complexities of relationships, *Lover's quarrels, thankfully, those are ancient history for me now."*

Calling Elizabeth's name, Michael stumbled through his living areas to his bedroom. The room was dark and he assumed she was already asleep. Feeling his bladder about to burst, in order not to awaken what he now perceived to be an angry sleeping giant, he didn't put on a light, attempted to quietly stagger to his bathroom, and made an inebriated judgment error in trying to do so on tiptoe.

His vestibular nerve apparatus already gone awry from alcohol immoderation, he hit and knocked over every chair and small table on his way, some not even in the path, telling each item, "Shu…uu…ush, you're going to wake up Elizabeth."

With enough racket to awaken ten sleeping giants, he just about managed to make it to the toilet in time, not that this difficult achievement did any good as his stream landed everywhere except in the toilet bowl. Staggering to his bed, he sat down and felt around for Elizabeth. Alarmed to find the bed empty, he switched on a lamp, pushed himself up and made his way to her bedroom in the same calamitous manner as before. Seeing a light on in her bathroom he started to head that way but his eye caught a large splash of blood red on her never used bed, and kicking off his urine soaked shoes, he flopped down beside her.

Dropping a dead-weight arm over her he sang a snippet medley from famous songs with a tuneless drunken voice, "*I'm sorry, so sorry, that I was such a fool…A fool am I, a fool am I, in love…Fools rush in where angels fail to tread, and so I come to you my love, my heart within my head…*" He stopped singing, sloppily kissed the back of her neck and slurringly rhymed, "Elizabeth and Michael, made for each other, meant to be together, always and ever, together forever."

Planting another sloppy kiss on the back of her neck, he dropped an uncontrolled leg on top of her, and passed out.

With her face buried in a dead queen's three-hundred-year-old petite-point pillow, now newly stained with teary make-up, Elizabeth could not help but smile at his maladroit musical apology medley, and sweet poetry of never-ending love.

"Michael, you've got to get up *now* or you'll be late for the meeting with your father!" Elizabeth had been trying to rouse him for the last fifteen minutes. She tried every method she knew, shaking, pushing, tickling, prodding, stopping just short of a few hard slaps which was her original temptation, to no avail. His only response, and that was just in the last minute, was a couple grunts followed by some groans, and now she was beyond fed up. Debating whether to throw the orange juice she was holding in his face, he already looked a mess and stank to high heavens anyway, his intuitiveness about her functioning in spite of his drunken stupor, he opened one eye just in time to save himself as she had made the decision to douse him.

"Get up! You have to get ready for your meeting."

He groaned, "My head's splitting. What's the time?"

She put on a school principal's demeanor and spoke sternly, "You have thirty minutes to shower, shave, get dressed and eat something.

Here, take this." She handed him the orange juice and, being well pre-pared from past experiences in her other life, two headache pills.

Rising laboriously, he drank the juice and pills, muttered, "Thanks," and as he took his last swallow, made a dash for her bathroom, where he vomited everything that had entered his mouth in the last twenty-four hours. Elizabeth phoned the housekeeper and gave a brief discreet explanation of the need for a clean-up maid immediately. Having slept under Michael's leaden appendages she was still in her ball gown. She removed the crinoline, swung the red velvet-lined cape that matched her gown onto her shoulders, and quietly left his apartments.

Michael found her lying on the banks of the farthest pond in the pal-ace gardens, her red gown spread out around her as though in depiction of a 'Stop' sign, her angelic face staring expressionlessly at the graying sky. His voice was emotionally apologetic, "My fortune for your thoughts?"

"Your fortune won't cover it," her voice was toneless, ethereal. No amount of money would have bribed her to share her thoughts with him. They may devastate him, and she had sworn to herself to never intentionally hurt him, she loved him beyond reason. However, with what happened yesterday plus the daily communications from Trinidad becoming more upsetting, tugging at her heart, and her con-science, she had to rethink her entire position. She thought the deci-sion she had made in Michael's arms the first time they committed to each other was conclusive, but after yesterday, dubiety had begun to seep into her determination. *Where is this going? How is this going to end? Is this going to end? I've no choice now but to tell him everything anyway, my secretiveness is putting too much strain on our relationship. But with all my intelligence and education, I still can't find the words. How do I conquer the fear? The one person I could usually look to for sage advice and assurance in this type of circumstance is the one who has hurt me the most!*

Sitting down on the grass beside her, unable to look at her he looked at the water, his voice full of contrition, "I don't know where to begin. How to say I'm sorry, again. In my defense, I've never been that drunk, I suspect Henry must've slipped me something. I have to be honest, my memory of our contretemps is somewhat vague."

She was blunt, "We didn't have a mere contretemps, we had a fight. And it didn't start with your drunken stupidity, it started in your apartment in the morning with the rude and disrespectful way you spoke to me."

He shook his head several times as though to clear it, "Oh, yes. I'm sincerely sorry about that, it'll never happen again. I was as angry at myself for pressuring you as I was at you for not giving in. I was trying to figure out my motivation and emotions when I was in the meeting with my father-"

"How did the meeting go, with your doozey of a hangover?"

"Actually, Papa and I started talking about you and me, our…situation, and when he saw how…upset, I was, he cancelled the meeting."

Elizabeth sat up quickly, "You discussed our fight with your father?"

"He's a very intelligent man, he figured out that I was…distracted, and came right out with the reason. So, I told him…some… of what happened. His take on my emotions is that I'm still insecure in our relationship, but I also have a need to make you feel more secure. I know you've been holding back something important from me and you weren't ready to discuss it until you felt forced to. Well, I don't want you to ever feel forced to do something against your will. And…in fact…I've been holding back something important from you too. I've had a hard time trying to figure out how to tell you, but-"

"Why? Michael, I thought you knew you could tell me anything. Is it about what happened to…with…Priscilla?"

"Elizabeth, please, don't interrupt me…this is the most difficult thing I'll ever have to say to you, it affects our entire lives. So, let me just get it out."

Elizabeth could see he was actually suffering to tell her his big secret. She became gripped with fear and foreboding, wondering how much worse than hers it could be.

He shifted to face her but didn't touch her, "The summer I was nineteen, six of us, all guys, cousins and friends, took the family sailing yacht and cruised the Greek isles. During the first week I hooked up with a beautiful eighteen-year-old local girl living on one of the smaller islands. We had a torrid romance, she was my first virgin, and I felt a certain pride and responsibility for being her first. Two weeks into it, I had to rush over to Africa where my mother had become deathly ill with malaria while on safari. I got there just in time to have her die in my and Papa's arms. Six weeks later, I was still in extreme shock and grief, Papa insisted I get away, go back to meet the others on the yacht and finish the summer there."

He drew in a deep breath and she noticed a tremor in his hands, making her even more fearful of what was to come, but he continued in a steady voice, "On my return, her parents sent for me at the yacht. When I got to their house, they informed me she was two months pregnant."

Michael looked away, Elizabeth looked at him intensely, but he continued almost in a monotone, "I had run out of condoms and naively believed her that it was alright, that she would take care…of…things. Anyway, I offered to pay for an abortion and for her and her mother's stay on the mainland where it wouldn't get out to the islanders. Her mother was Italian, her father Greek, both Orthodox-Catholics."

He sucked in another deep breath, "Her father attempted to throttle me, then tried to stab me with a kitchen knife. I had to run for my life. The boys and I set sail immediately for Santorini, though I didn't tell anyone why I was in such a hurry to leave. Anyway, I felt terribly guilty, knew I had to do something, even marry her, but was so confused, still grieving over my mother, I called Jenkins, told him what happened and my thoughts on going back to marry the virtual stranger I impregnated. He flipped out, told me I must absolutely not go back, he would have to tell my father, and for me to stay in Santorini for word from him. Jenkins, Aunt Claire, and Aunt Anne arrived the next day, with instructions from Papa on how the situation was to be handled. They went to her island and negotiated with her parents. I was forbidden to get involved, forced to stay in Santorini until their return, to learn of my fate. Mine and hers." His expression saddened on continuing, "It was a terrible time for me. The grief for my mother was fresh, and then to have been so stupid and careless as to cause a girl, a virgin, that I hardly knew, to become pregnant, was the ultimate sin. Especially someone in my position, as I was often reminded by some of my elders for many years afterwards."

Michael's voice succumbed to the tremor visible in his hands. Elizabeth reached over and grasped them, "But darling, you were just a teenager, a boy with raging hormones just like any other-"

Michael pulled his hands out of her grasp, "But I was *not* like any other, I was the future *King*!"

Seeing him becoming self-deprecating she sought to comfort and reassure him, for, as yet, his 'sin' was not as great as hers, and she reached for his hands again.

He pulled them away again and looked at her, "I need you to focus on the seriousness of what I'm about to tell you. This decides if we are to have a future together. But, we have to always be honest with each other, you must know everything."

Elizabeth shivered, *Oh God, don't tell me his family used their power to force her to have the abortion…or, something worse, got rid of her, permanently!*

He noticed her shiver and his own increased knowing his future would soon be in her hands; but he braced himself for her reaction as he strived to sound calm, "Her parents wouldn't allow an abortion but agreed to a settlement, a very large sum, for their silence, they'd already found out who I was. To save her reputation, they decided to force her to marry a cousin who was in love with her, not tell him about the baby, he'll raise it as his own, and they'll never speak about me to anyone. That was supposed to be the end of it. But not for me. The whole thing haunted me for a year. When I eventually regained my self-confidence, or you might say, grew up, I went to my father, told him I was unhappy with how the situation had been handled, and Jenkins and I were going to see my child and negotiate a different agreement."

Elizabeth's words were almost inaudible, "So…she…had…the baby?"

"A girl. A beautiful girl. Katherina. She has her mother's olive complexion, and my eyes and hair."

Making a quick mathematical calculation Elizabeth's voice was incredulous, "You're telling me you have a…teenage daughter?"

Hearing her incredulity, Michael looked away and swallowed, "Yes. But, that's not all. I knew to have her existence become public knowledge at that time would put the monarchy in jeopardy, my family had already had to give up most of the power to the government, we were all under censorious scrutiny, by a very judgmental society, so I couldn't just do what I wanted. Anyway, I told her mother and her parents that I wanted my daughter to be raised with all the comforts and advantages I was raised with, she should want for nothing. I added a large wing to the already huge home they had built with part of the original settlement. I furnished it luxuriously, hired extra staff, a tutor, and a governess, all of which I still pay for."

She reached out to touch him, "That's so commendable-"

He backed away from her touch, "Let me finish. This is the most important part…that affects us…you and me," he looked back at her and swallowed again before continuing, "I drew up a written agreement, a binding contract, in the presence of their lawyer, which they all signed except her husband. He was not involved, he still believed the baby was his, and fortunately, was away on business when we were there. The contract stated that I was giving another large lump sum immediately, and would cover all my daughter's expenses through her life until she finished her education and settled in a lucrative career or became happily married. She was to be raised like royalty and groomed to be a princess, we gave them a list of what that entailed," he swallowed again, "and…after I married, within a period of marital adjustment, she was to be told who she was. Her mother would bring her to the palace, leave after settling her in, and after my wife… my ready-made family, had all adjusted, when I felt it would be more accepted because of my now stable lifestyle, announce the situation to the world." Michael sucked in a deep emotional breath filled with relief yet fear. He looked in Elizabeth's eyes, "You do understand what I'm saying to you, Elizabeth?"

Elizabeth nodded, then amazingly, stated unemotionally, "We're going to have a ready-made family."

Shocked at her composed reaction, he scrutinized her face, looking for disapproval, contempt, flight. *No! Do I see...relief?* "I need to hear how you feel about this, Elizabeth. But...you must know, I can't change this, not any of it."

Elizabeth grasped his hands again, needing to steady her own as well, "Michael, I love you. I always will. She's part of you. I'll love her as if she's ours."

He reached over and, embracing her, lay them down on the grass, gratefully kissing her all over her face, "Thank you my darling. I always knew you were perfect for me. I would've died if you couldn't accept the situation I have to put you in. You know I can't live without you."

"Nor I without you."

"I'll love you forever, and beyond. I promise not to pressure you any more about your secret, you'll tell me when the time's right for you," he suddenly looked at her pleadingly, "will you still give me those four babies you agreed to?"

"Of course, my darling. I'll even give you the original six you wanted, or seven-"

He grinned teasingly, "Whoa! Let's not go overboard now, I need to have you alone with me too."

"Don't worry, as you said, we'll get the best help."

He smothered her with passionate kisses, which she returned with grateful passion as he had given her a reprieve. Actually, it felt more like a stay of execution. If he thought his secret was 'life-threatening,' hers was 'earth-shattering.'

The following day they flew to Geneva where Michael delivered his speech titled 'Climate Change: Man's Fate Or Folly?' with, according to the media, "*eloquently controlled enthusiasm, an art only he has perfected.*" The speech was publicized worldwide, many of his words later to become mantras for those concerned about the future of planet Earth.

Elizabeth was so impressed and in awe of him, she felt a pride that surpassed even that which she had experienced when any of her children accomplished an "*impossible task.*" *Godde, how I adore him, he has every quality I love. He's so intelligent, confident and in control. He's taught me so much. He has conquered fear. He has conquered me!* Once more, she became firm in her decision, knew no matter how Michael handled her 'big secret,' her love for him was eternal, and she would do everything possible to ensure his for her would be the same.

She started making plans for reorganizing her life, cleaning up the mess she left back in Trinidad, and handing over the presidency of The Children's Home to Jane Thompson after hiring her an assistant; then dealing with the formidable task of giving up the family businesses. However, no plans could be implemented until she returned to Trinidad, and as yet, she still had not secured the grant. Moreover, the speech in New York loomed in two weeks and four days. An additional concern was that although his actions were loud and clear, Michael still had not said the actual words she needed to hear.

The next fortnight was a whirlwind filled with loving, exciting, tornadic activity. They traveled incognito, sans visible bodyguards, all over Europe and the Mediterranean, staying mostly in exclusive boutique hotels. They hiked, biked and skied in the Alps, swam in and boated on many country's rivers and lakes, danced beside them, and in various city's discothèques; went to numerous museums, historical sites, and music, film, and arts festivals, taking in all the amazing sights and sounds, and each other.

Making and declaring love in the language of every country they visited- "I love you," "Jeg elsker dig," "Ik hou van jou," "Je t'aime," "Te amo," "Eu te amo," "Ti amo," "Ich liebe dich," "S'agapo"- they confirmed their unending love.

Wherever they went, they could not keep their hands off each other, Michael doing everything he possibly could in atonement for his 'sins' to ensure he could hold on to the love of his life, Elizabeth holding on to him for dear life.

They were an inspiration to all who observed them, everyone assuming the beautiful and devoted young lovers were on their honeymoon, and would be perpetually.

There were a few opportune moments when she felt she could broach the subject of her secret, but lacking confidence in her ability to say the words in a manner that would be the least upsetting, she procrastinated, then some distraction would come up, and the opportunity would be lost.

The morning of the fifteenth, they arrived in Kaiserslautern, Germany. They dropped off their luggage at one of Michael's friend's apartment where they were going to spend the night, after seeing Trinidad play against England in the World Cup. Finding their seats in the Fritz Walter Stadium, Michael looked around for the Trinidadian flag, hoping they were sitting near to Elizabeth's friends who she had mentioned flew all the way up just for this event. Suspecting his thoughts she copied his actions hoping for the opposite, that they would be on the other side of the field. But she wore a black wig and large sunglasses in case Michael's hope would be the one to be fulfilled. As luck would have it, she was the fortunate one, spying her flags, friends, and others, in a couple of surprisingly large groups obliquely across from them.

Relieved in one way that she didn't have to worry about further hiding Michael and herself, in another way she regretted she could not be with her Trinis to unifyingly cheer their team on, and at the same time proudly introduce her precious prince. *Ah well, not yet, but soon?*

The game turned out to be nail-bitingly exciting as both teams fought equally hard, and it was tied zero to zero up until there were only seven minutes left. When England scored a goal, it was obvious to Elizabeth, Michael, and a bunch of people around them, that the scorer had fouled the Trinidadian defender. To everyone's surprise, and in some cases annoyance, Elizabeth's in particular, the Japanese referee did not call it. Elizabeth was tempted to 'boo' the referee's inattention to the foul but reminded herself that she was not surrounded by her Trini friends but mostly by 'enemies.' She clamped her mouth, and hands, shut, boycottingly refusing to clap for the goal that was sending three-quarters of the stadium wild. The match was won by England shortly after with a score of two nil, to the great disappointment of all Trinidadians and West Indians present, and those glued to televisions around the globe.

In the guest room of his cousin's apartment that night, Michael, sympathizing with Elizabeth's letdown feelings, did all he could to lift up her spirits, apologetically making love to her with selfless tenderness. She was soon elevated, as she reveled in Michael's substantial elevation.

Their other major sporting event was the men's final tennis match at Wimbledon in England. This was equally exciting, but both Elizabeth and Michael were disappointed by not being able to experience it completely together. After they entered their box she observed cameras and phones of all descriptions pointed at them, despite Michael wearing a cap and sunglasses.

Although she wore another wig, she felt uncomfortable, told him, and exchanged her seat next to him for one four seats over, with an older aristocrat from Denmark who Michael vaguely knew. The woman was ecstatic and grateful to be able to sit next to "the handsomest prince in the whole world."

In Holland, they childishly giggled their way through several sex shops and bought a bunch of interesting-looking toys. After having fun playing with them, on and in each other, back at their hotel room, they put them aside, to seriously play only with each other.

CHAPTER
28

*D*uring their second week of gallivanting, on their first night in Rome, Elizabeth was awakened in the middle of the night by severe cramps in her lower abdomen. Although she knew her period was due momently, she was unaccustomed to painful menstruation, and became concerned as the strange pain intensified when she pressed the area. *Oh no! Appendicitis! Not here! With Michael!* Dragging her bent over frightened body to the toilet she breathed a sigh of relief to see the welcome sight of menses blood. *Thank Godde. Darn, I don't have tampons, I'll have to get in the morning. Hopefully the pains'll be gone then. This is weird, I've not had cramps since my teenage years.* Wrapping a huge wad of toilet paper in a tissue she stuffed the crotch of the panty she donned and crawled back into bed.

Michael woke that morning in his usual manner with a substantial erection, and the desire to relieve and reduce it in the sweetness of his Elizabeth. Stretching a leg over her and thrusting gently so that she may feel the extent of his protrusion, he pushed her hair away from her ear, sucked on the lobe and whispered, "Ti amo, mi bella amore, your Italian stallion is ready to mount my willing filly."

Lying on her side with her back to him, she gave a little moan, pulling her knees up in the hope the pain would lessen in a new position. The innocent prince took this as an invitation to proceed with his equestrian mating intentions, and pulled at the strange panty, "Why're you wearing this, mi amore? It's going to take a lot more than this to deter me, mi bella amore."

She murmured against the arm of his hand now fondling her breast, "Sorry, Italian stallion, but you're going to have to forget this willing but not able filly, and either rein in, or take things in hand, I got my period."

"Oh?" his hand and hip actions stopped but he didn't back off, "and this affects us how?"

Chuckling, she turned slowly to face him, "So, it's not enough to deter you, eh?"

His face brightened, "I'm more excited than ever. I've been looking forward to experiencing this with you."

"But mi amore, I'm having painful cramps. I haven't had them since I was a teenager. I've a feeling it's because with all the traveling I haven't exercised properly this last week-"

Nibbling on her ear, he chuckled, "Surely you jest, that sweet thing has been exercised at least twice a day-"

She giggled, "Not down there silly, my whole system. I'm sorry mi amore, but I'll feel better after I get pain medicine. And I need tampons. I noticed a Farmacia down the street. Can you send someone to get them for me please?"

His concern was sincere, "Of course, my darling. What else can I do to make you comfortable?"

Kissing him softly on his lips, she murmured, "Nothing. Just the menstruation medicine and tampons. Then, you need to leave me alone so I can sleep till the pain goes away. I hardly slept last night."

She turned away, unintentionally groaning softly as the cramping pains stabbed at her insides. She pulled her legs up into a fetal position, totally confusing the now worried prince. This was the first time it occurred to him that his strong Amazonian goddess could possibly weaken and be vulnerable to any kind of physical malady. He determined that he was going to make her robust and healthy again in no time.

Not trusting a hotel employee to be as quick as he to get the necessities for his ailing love, he ran to the Farmacia himself.

Allowing no show of embarrassment at the male pharmacist's smiling enquiries as to what strength or size tampons his "wife" requires, Michael hid his ignorance and replied with overstated confidence, "Give me thirty boxes of each."

The omniscient pharmacist became even more amused at the bravado of the naïve foreign lover, who was returning to his girlfriend with several years supply of tampons.

Arriving back at the hotel, he ordered hot milk, oatmeal and herb tea for Elizabeth, and a hearty breakfast for himself, tipping the desk clerk extravagantly to have the kitchen hurry and send it up quickly. He vaguely remembered whenever Priscilla was menstruating she wanted only hot liquids in her body, and not Michael, until it was over. *But it's going to be different with my Elizabeth.* Without the necessary patience to wait for the slow elevator to descend, he bolted up the five flights of stairs to their suite, two large shopping bags stuffed with tampons swinging from two proud hands.

Impressed with his perception, speedy efficiency, and loving attention, Elizabeth took the pain pills and herb tea from her adoring "Prince Florence Nightingale," not having the heart to burst his proud bubble with a teasing admonition about his ridiculously exorbitant purchase of tampons.

He took his nursing duties more seriously than she needed, or wanted, staying in the small room adjoining the bedroom to do his e-mails and phone calls, rather than doing them in the larger outer salon. He kept the bedroom door ajar so that he could easily hear and rush to her assistance should she need it. Unfortunately, the sound went both ways; she was unable to sleep as she could occasionally hear his deep voice on the phone, even though he made considerate efforts to speak softly.

When she eventually called out to ask him to close the door, before she could finish her request, he raced in and embraced her, "What do you need, my darling?"

With a miserable sigh, she eyed him wearily, "I need you to shut the door and be quiet. And, leave me alone." Observing a hurt look taking over his eager face she felt badly but her pain took priority in her sympathies. However, she did manage to mumble, "Go work in the salon. All I need is sleep, and the pain pills to work. I love you. Thank you. Go away."

Closing the door, disappointment mixed with his hurt feelings; her attitude brought back shades of Priscilla. He resigned himself to never experiencing every kind of sexual situation he wanted with the woman he loved.

Remembering his mother having warned him that some females could become moody at certain times of their monthly cycle, it surprised him that his stalwart and stable Elizabeth could be amongst that category. *But then, true, she is in pain, and, she hadn't slept last night. So maybe, I can still hope-*

Elizabeth slept the entire day, awakened free of pain, had a refreshing shower, donned her bathrobe, and greeted Michael sitting at his computer with a grateful kiss, "Thank you for being the best, most understanding nurse a girl could have. Forgive me for being bitchy? It was the pain, not me." She sat on his lap and nuzzled his ear, one hand around his neck while the other reached inside his shirt to caress a breast and play with his nipple.

Michael stiffened, everywhere, and looking at her eyes, said cautiously, "Oh, feeling better?"

She took her hand out of his shirt and placed it on his bulging crotch, "Perfect. Except for being in the red, of course. But then, you gave me the impression you wanted to be in the red too."

Still feeling unsure, despite her implication, he said hesitantly, "I assumed you wanted to be left alone, for the duration-"

Eyeing him seriously, she started rising from his lap, "I want whatever you want, Michael."

He stood up with her, took her hand, and led her back to bed, *Thank you, 'hope springs eternal!'*

On their return to the palace, life took on an even more hectic pace as they attended family functions amidst preparations for the New York trip in four days. Arrangements had been made for their stay as a married couple under a pseudonym, in the very appropriately titled 'Royal Plaza Suite,' at The Plaza. In her youth Elizabeth had stayed at that hotel with her parents a few times when the Grangers were overbooked with important house guests, making it her favorite New York hotel with the fondest memories of youthful carefree days.

She was relieved the Grangers were away on an unusual selectively arranged trek in the mountains of Tibet, as she was not ready to reveal her relationship with her prince. She also wanted to make this visit to one of her 'hometowns' exclusively special for Michael. She intended taking him to some of her favorite old haunts and had Gloria Goldman make the necessary reservations, including an exclusive private tour of The Statue of Liberty, a meaningful symbol dear to her heart.

The plan was to take a night flight to the U.S., spend the first day meeting with the organizers of her event, then some rehearsal. The following three days would be spent incognito, taking in plays, wonderful dining, clubbing, sight-seeing, shopping, and just having fun. The fifth day would be devoted to rehearsals, that evening her actual speech, then fly back that night before, as Michael put it, "things get dangerous."

After organizing Michael's disguises for various events and sorting out their wardrobes for Pamela and Michael's valet, Roger, to pack, they got into a heavy discussion about the number of bodyguards that would be necessary, Michael having stated his concerns about their, mostly her, safety.

Already nervous about all the additional exposure her speech in America would cause, Elizabeth wanted them to keep a low profile before the event, "I don't want you to bring your usual entourage. Jenkins, Brian, Eric, Tommy, fine, but no more. And please instruct them to be invisible to us and everyone else." Her voice was as firm as her facial expression.

Not wanting to upset her further as he thought her irritability was fueled by fear about the event in Canterbury Hall, he appeared to relent and pulled her into a comforting embrace, "Alright. Look, if it makes you feel any better, we could even fly in coach with the plebeians."

She pushed him away, "Are you mad? No way. Michael, I haven't flown coach on a long flight since I was fourteen going to boarding school."

He pulled her back to him with a teasing grin, "Well, aren't you the little princess."

She grinned back, "Darn straight, Your Highness. Have you ever flown coach? Do you have any idea what it's like?"

He looked at her shamefacedly. "I must admit I haven't."

"Well," she smiled condescendingly, "let me educate you. Nowadays with the exorbitant cost of running airlines, they pack people in tighter than sardines. On a long flight with our long legs it would be unbearable. I hate to sound like some high maintenance princess wannabe, I'm simply telling it like it is."

His expression turned serious, "Sweetheart, if a commercial flight is going to be a problem and cause you any stress, I'd rather we take the family jet like I'd planned-"

Her irritation returned, "What! And draw even more attention to us? Absolutely not! End of discussion."

Elizabeth sighed and punched her pillow twice, trying to reshape it for the third time. Michael opened his eyes and whispered, "Still can't sleep?"

"Oh, sorry darling, I didn't mean to wake you."

"I wasn't totally asleep, just dozing."

"It's these damn seats. Why can't all airlines put in the same first-class seats as South African Airways? Those things virtually turn into beds," she punched the pillow again.

He gave her a mollifying smile, "Shall I get you a sleeping pill from the guys, they'll have something."

"No thanks, don't want to be like a zombie when we land. I'll fall asleep eventually," she sighed again.

Sitting up, his eyes twinkled, "Actually, I've something better. Go to the restroom, I'm right behind you."

She giggled, "You're not thinking-"

He smiled lustfully, "We're joining the 'Mile High Club.' Go prepare yourself fully to make history."

Sneaking past the men in their entourage who seemed to be sleeping soundly, not knowing Brian and Tommy were pumped up with caffeine but had been instructed by Michael to fake sleep if she should pass by, she thought, *Fat lot of good they are, someone could kill us in our sleep and they wouldn't even budge.*

On opening the restroom door he was pleased to see she took his words literally. Fully prepared, she was stark naked and had hoisted herself up to sit on the stainless steel sink-counter, her legs wide open with full exposure. That was all he needed. Dropping his pants, he grabbed her bottom as she wrapped her legs and arms around him, and his already primed penis entered her already primed vagina. The slight sway of the plane assisting their motions, and with the naughty thrill of knowing where they were, they achieved orgasms quickly. Instinctively, each placed a hand over the other's mouth to muffle the sounds of ecstasy when they reached their highest peaks. At that moment, the plane hit an air pocket and Elizabeth's teeth dug in to Michael's finger, drawing blood, "Ow! You bit me Princess."

"Oh my Godde! I'm so sorry," she took his hand and sucked on the minimally bleeding finger. This action and the embedded love he felt for her caused another stimulation as he hardened again. He began to move in and out repeatedly, causing her own stimulation to intensify.

Again reaching the summit of coitus, this time they could not care less about disturbing the sleepers, and as the moans and groans of their highest pleasure reached the ears of Brian and Tommy, the two men gave each other high fives and whispered, "She's definitely the one for him."

Feeling her still moving, although already sated, Michael managed to hold on to his erection, continuing to move with her until she accomplished a third orgasm. They hobbled back to their uncomfortable seat-beds, but thoroughly spent, cradled each other and immediately fell into infant-like deep sleep.

Elizabeth's agent, Gloria Goldman, met them in a luxury limo at the airport, excited to see Elizabeth again but even more excited to meet the sexy sounding 'cousin' she was bringing whom she had never spoken about.

Michael and she took to each other immediately.

Relaxed by her friendly spunky personality he inadvertently slipped out of his American accent.

Gloria boldly reached over and pulled off his sunglasses, "Prince Michael! I thought it was you! Miss Elizabeth, you owe me one hell of an explanation!"

Elizabeth widened her eyes in warning, faked a tight smile and surreptitiously pinched Gloria who was sitting next to her, "We'll talk later but 'mums' the word. Understand?"

Gloria smiled and nodded concurringly.

Although sorry they had been discovered, Elizabeth was not overly concerned because if anyone could keep a secret, this agent could. Because of the caliber of her clientele, her mental vault most likely was larger, more sophisticated, and secreted a greater amount of confidentialities than that of a confessional priest's, she probably having heard it all.

Meetings with the equality group who organized the event in Canterbury Hall, and rehearsals, went smoothly, and Elizabeth, knowing she could rely on the high standards of the work ethic and efficiency of her people in "the good ole U.S. of A." felt confident that it would all go well despite her initial trepidations. Helping to reinforce her confidence was Michael's insistence in humorous cowboy lingo, that immediately her speech was over, they, "high-tail it outta here for the airport."

While she was involved in conversations with organizers, he looked around the foyer where various items were displayed for sale. He was amused by most of the sayings on t-shirts, bumper stickers, posters, and coffee mugs, though Elizabeth was surprised and a little perturbed by some of them when he described them to her. The ones she liked most were: *MORE SPIRITUALITY LESS RELIGION; FEMALES FIRST FETUSES SECOND; RELIGION=DOMINATION SPIRITUALITY=FREEDOM; RELIGION=MANMADE SPIRITUALITY=GODMADE,* and the classic Sanskrit for *"The divinity in me acknowledges the divinity in you"- NAMASTE.* Though she saw humor in some others she thought they might be considered sexist and even antagonistic by those with a narrower sense of humor, and was surprised they were being sold at an 'equality' event. One stated that God was female and was only joking when '*She*' created males. Another said that God is coming and how '*She*' is pissed. Another declared that all women's problems begin with '*men*,' such as '*men*-struation,' '*men*-tal breakdown,' and '*men*-opause.' Michael thought they were hilarious, was tempted to purchase something for Megan, but felt it improper for someone in his position to purchase something that could be construed by the humorless as inflammatory.

Gloria took Elizabeth to a wonderful sushi lunch at Nobu downtown and proceeded to cross-examine her in what Gloria thought was a subtle manner that was anything but. Elizabeth in turn subtly evaded divulging the information Gloria was after, simply assured her that Michael and she were, "just good friends, but please don't talk to him about my family and my past," to which Gloria, the stereotypical 'celebrity confidant agent,' simply nodded that she totally understood.

While Elizabeth was rehearsing, Michael sneaked out to do some secret shopping at Tiffany's, Bloomingdales, Macy's, and finally, Victoria's Secret.

Elizabeth just narrowly missed him coming out of the latter as she herself snuck in to do her own secret shopping, right after she had taken a taxi to a slightly sleazy part of town. Afterwards, she had a productive visit with old friends at Bergdorf Goodman while purchasing several gifts.

That night the lovers luxuriated in an elegantly romantic and sumptuous feast at 'Le Grenouille,' one of their favorite New York restaurants from their separate pasts. Experiencing it together made it even more memorably special. Finished sampling two delicious deserts, Michael took her right hand and pressed a Tiffany ring box tenderly into it, "It doesn't match perfectly with the necklace and earrings I designed for you but I don't think that matters as it's beautiful and stands on its own. I wanted you to have it for your speech, as a good luck charm if you will. I'm assuming you're going to wear my jewelry again, with the pale green Vera Wang suit you brought?"

"Yes, but," gingerly opening the box, Elizabeth exclaimed, "Oh my Godde, it's gorgeous! But Michael, I can't accept this," she rested the box on the table, "your gifts have all been too extravagant, I can't reciprocate-"

Kissing her palm, he interrupted, "Darling, every moment you're in my life is reciprocation." He removed the ring from the box and placed it on the ring finger of her right hand, the one on her left still occupied by his great-grandmother's sapphire and diamonds ring at his insistence that she not take it off, "At least, not yet."

Staring at the largest emerald she had ever seen with the deepest most lush of jardins, surrounded by fourteen quarter carat diamonds, *It's larger, but so similar in style to the one that beast gave me!* she shook her head in double disbelief. "Nothing I give you can compete with this, it's absolutely the most beautiful ring, I'll cherish it always. Thank you, darling. I do have some little presents for you back at The Plaza. They can't compare, but I bought them with my heart full of love for you, I hope you'll like them."

Impatient to get back to the hotel to make love, Michael balked at Elizabeth's insistence on taking a hansom cab ride in Central Park complaining, "It's too touristy."

Acquiescing only because she promised to do "something special" for him, they ended up having more than the predictable romantic ride around the park. Undercover of the blanket in the horse-drawn carriage, and again under the lights of a Plaza elevator, they both enjoyed the promised "*something special*."

The following morning she awakened him with a face-full of kisses, "Come on, lazy bones, let's eat some fruit so we can go speed-walk in Central Park."

Michael groaned and just missed grabbing her as she retreated from the bed, "Woman, you're a sadist. Forget the park, come practice your sadism on me."

Observing the reason for his request standing at full attention, she laughed and saluted, "Oh no, Sir, reveille has not been sounded for that. You need to put that thing 'at ease.' It's now time for exercises of a different nature." She threw him his shorts and t-shirt followed by an apple. "Come on, Your Royal Laziness. We're in New York!"

It was a typical New York kind of day, everyone hustling and bustling purposefully, all heading for somewhere of importance in different directions.

Walking into the serenity of Central Park, the oasis of sanity in the midst of the usually maddeningly hectic world of one of the busiest, most exciting cities she had ever been in, Elizabeth became emotional with a feeling of homecoming, *Godde I miss this city.* With misting eyes, not looking at him, she took Michael's hand and slow-walked into the park.

Attuned to her more than he previously revealed he held her chin, "I promise we'll visit often," and kissed her teary eyes. She nodded in gratitude, and started them off speed-walking.

Central Park sparkled under the summer sun, the sunlight through the recently greening trees dappling everything under them with shimmering dots of gold.

Evidence of the enjoyment of this jeweled atmosphere was everywhere: lovers holding waists or hands, joggers and cyclists smiling at strangers, people on phones twittering alongside twittering birds, squirrels vying with birds for crumbs thrown by laughing mothers and nannies, babies in strollers squealing in delight at the mini-battles, toddlers stumblingly joining in the fray temporarily scattering nonhuman contenders, older children on bikes, scooters, skates and skateboards, ignoring the whole scene thinking it beneath them.

Elizabeth and Michael took it all in with wishful smiles, both envisioning their life to come. Wanting him to experience the overall riches of her park, she steered them in zigzagging directions, taking them through The Mall of poets and authors, past the reservoir, Bethesda Fountain, and numerous important statues, to various locations where they enjoyed the entertainment of the moment, and he could get a different feel for her city. Granted, she knew he had been to New York many times before, but not like this, and never with her.

Remembering an area of the park that had previously moved him, knowing it would do the same for her, Michael gave her a melancholy smile and took her hand, "This way."

"Oh?" she questioned in surprise at his interference of *her* tour of *her* park, but lovingly and curiously obeyed. Comprehension came to her, not just as to why he led her this way, but also as to how well he understood her, when she saw the familiar sign, 'Strawberry Fields.' Circling the 'Imagine' medallion in the ground of the garden honoring the late, much loved and admired John Lennon, her eyes misted again. This time, not for the loss of her daily walks through Central Park, but for the loss of an icon of music, a beacon of peace, a loss for the world. A dozen people sat around listening to a sad-looking young man strumming a guitar and singing 'Yesterday' with an unusual but sweet voice. Not wanting to speak in this hallowed place, Michael simply squeezed her hand.

Elizabeth squeezed his hand back whispering, "Thank you."

Their cardiovascular exercise became intermittent as they kept stopping to relish the variety of entertainment. On one corner there was a saxophonist playing Abba's 'Dancing Queen,' while children danced jerkily in front of him under the watchful eyes of their swaying mothers and a few fathers and nannies.

In front of The Boathouse, 'Fascination' could be heard from an old man playing a harmonica. Next to the Bethesda fountain a budding actor covered with a white sheet, his hands, hair, and face sprayed white, performed a mime that made no sense to passers-by who took a minute to watch, then shook their heads in bemusement and amusement, and moved on.

On the other side of the fountain another saxophonist was playing 'Mona Lisa,' and a little further down the path a plain-looking young girl with blond dread-locks accompanied herself on a beat-up old guitar to an unrecognizable mournful folksong.

Approaching another corner, Elizabeth grabbed Michael's arm with a thrill as they spied a lone Steelband man. He was playing a chrome-plated perfectly pitched tenor pan, making a valiant effort at Strauss's 'Tales Of The Vienna Woods,' bringing back memories of their brief romantic time in Vienna, when they waltzed beside the Danube during their two-week jaunt in Europe. Feeling her excitement, Michael bowed low to her with a flourish, took hold of her and waltzed them flawlessly around the Steelband man. The man laughed and shook his head at the contradiction of the two weird white people dancing so elegantly but wearing exercise clothes and copiously covered in sweat.

Seeing how he laughed, hearing how well he played, Elizabeth called out above the music, "You're a Trini, aren't you?" the man simply nodded in acknowledgement and kept on playing. Elizabeth called out delightedly, "Me too."

The man stopped playing, smiled, and blew her a kiss, whereupon Michael proprietarily took hold of her hand, dropped a twenty dollar bill in the man's upturned hat on the ground, smugly waved to him and whisked them away, back into the park.

Climbing some small hills, Michael noticed a gate ajar to a fenced-in area that seemed to be isolated as no one could be seen or heard.

Grabbing Elizabeth's hand, he pulled her through the gate and behind some tall bushes.

He proceeded to cajole her into permitting him to, "Feel you up, as, seeing you denied me your pleasures this morning, I'm now suffering through a relentless erection and deserve some small compensation for my pains." Observing the area around them empty of other mammalian life, she allowed herself to journey into his guilt trip and let his hands travel all over her curves and mounds. The agreed to molestation only served to put him into more agony, and Elizabeth additionally, with her clitoris now throbbing in her own erection. Pulling her further in behind some lush bushes he begged her to, "Go all the way."

Giggling, she warned him he needed to behave in the country's accepted norms of morality, "This is America, if we're caught we'd be arrested for 'lewd and lascivious behavior' or 'indecent...' something or other." However, feeling him decently protuberating hard against her pelvis, she forgot about the threat of incarceration. Standing behind a large tree she pulled down his shorts to release the guilty culprit, happily freeing them both to indulge in lascivious behavior.

For three fun-filled days and nights Elizabeth and Michael ignored the cares of the world and dwelt only in the cares of each other. Days were spent sightseeing, museum hopping, selective shopping, leisurely lunching, and sometimes a 'matinee,' not always of the theater kind. Nights were spent at bars and clubs, early dinner and the theater, or the theater and late supper. The night before her speech, they took Gloria and her latest beau to the latter. The play was an off Broadway revival of 'I Love You, You're Perfect, Now Change,' which had them all in stitches.

Afterwards they dined splendidly at Le Bernadine, another special favorite restaurant of the entire group. At the end of the meal Gloria suggested Elizabeth and she go to the powder room to which Elizabeth agreed.

Immediately Elizabeth went into a cubicle Gloria raced back to their table to speak privately with Michael.

CHAPTER
29

Gloria excitedly told Michael about her plans for Elizabeth to be on some top television talk shows, "I've already made overtures to agents for Oprah, Barbara Walters, Diane Sawyer, Piers Morgan, Fareed Zakaria, Christiane Amanpour, Bill Maher, even NPR, and others. It's all very promising. I know when they see the D.V.D. of Elizabeth in action they'll want her. My dilemma is how to get her to agree. It requires more traveling than she's done in recent years. So I'm hoping to get your support when I tell her and you'll help convince her-" she saw Michael blanch then vigorously shake his head.

Michael spoke with more vehemence than she felt was warranted, "No! I will not! Elizabeth has already been put into extreme danger in Europe. I…we…my family, will not allow that to continue! You have no idea what I've had to…. Look, my advice to you is to shelve these ideas. At least for now. The world is too unstable at this time. You cannot expose Elizabeth to any more risks of having violence damage her life. People have to get more educated about the origins of religions and the resultant societal behaviors before-"

Gloria slapped the table, her face reddening, "Exactly! That's exactly what Elizabeth is going to achieve if she-"

Michael banged his fist on the table causing the glasses, silverware, and Gloria's beau, to jump, "Stop! Gloria, understand this! I, and my family, are responsible for protecting Elizabeth! We'll not allow *any-one*, and I mean *anyone*, to do anything to endanger her. So, I'm warning you, you are *not* to bring any of this up to her. Not now, or anytime in the near future. If you really care about her and not just about filling your own pockets, you'll promise me right now to shelve future engagements until I…we…tell you it's safe for Elizabeth. Do I have your promise?"

Gloria took in this European prince's determined demeanor and quickly digested his words. She knew she could not fight a royal battle with Elizabeth's 'knight in shining armor' and win. Not even while on her own turf. At least not this time around. However, she also knew she would devise her own battle plan, believed she was more determined than he, and she would eventually be the victor.

Michael hardened his penetrating glare at Gloria's eyes as he saw Elizabeth striding towards the table, "She's returning. I want your promise, now! Do I have your word? Are you going to put Elizabeth's safety before your own affluence?"

Gloria forced an agreeable smile, "Of course, Your Royal Highness, you have my word."

Entering their suite back at The Plaza, Michael stood just inside the locked door, "This is killing me, because I want you so badly, but I know you need to get a good night's rest to handle tomorrow, so I'm going to sleep in the other bedroom or I'll be waking you in the middle of the night-"

"You must be crazy! I'm never going to sleep without you again, not while we're under the same roof!" She smiled seductively, "And, you know better than anyone, what the most effective sedative is for me. Now, stay here. Sit. I have a surprise for you. Prepare to make history!"

Wiggling her bottom she sashayed into their bedroom. Not trusting his anticipatory excitement to stop him from coming in after her
and spoiling her surprise, she locked the door. Pulling out sexy purchases from her shopping expedition, she slipped into some things uncomfortable: a black lacy see-through bustier with unnecessary push
up pads for her breasts making her look top-heavy as if she might fall
over, its matching thong, and garter belt, to which she affixed black
fishnet stockings. Around her waist she added a half-skirt made of black
transparent nylon that fell to the floor only in the back. She zipped on
six-inch spike-heeled black patent leather knee-high boots. Next she
donned black elbow length gloves, black sequined headband with a red
ostrich feather, black leather with silver studs choker, and finally, with
only a moment's hesitation, she picked up what the woman in the sex
shop referred to as "*the completion of the ensemble*," a long black leather
whip.

Fighting back the urge to giggle, she put on a wanton face, and
in the C.D. player, the striptease C.D. the woman said was the most
appropriate. Turning up the volume, hoping it would give her the
courage to complete the task ahead without collapsing into embarrassed ridiculous laughter she unlocked the door and, leaning sexily
against the door frame, slithered out.

Michael was sitting where she had instructed, his own shopping
expedition bags on his lap and around his feet.

On taking in her unpredictably sleazy shocking entrance, the bags
he held dropped to the floor, his mouth dropped open, his gleaming
eyes widened, his erection instantaneous.

Her years of studying dance holding her in good stead, she did a
professional looking bump-and-grind routine towards one of the slender columns separating the foyer from the living room. She proceeded
to rub her body erotically against it, dancing around it, occasionally
clinging to it upside down, her legs in near impossible positions, performing her version of a pole dance, periodically snapping the whip
against the marble floor. Winding the whip suggestively around the
column, she hid behind it, though he could see her hips swaying sexily

on either side in rhythm with the music. Stretching an arm out, she took off its glove with her other hand and flung it towards him. She repeated the same action on the opposite side, this glove landing on his head. Snaking from behind the column, she did more bumping-and-grinding and slowly, rhythmically, began divesting herself of the non-garments in a seductively slutty striptease, throwing each item at him provocatively.

He was beside himself with desire. Even though he had been to striptease clubs with buddies while on overseas tours of duty during military service, he had never been this moved by any strippers. Not that he was undesirous of partaking in pleasures of the flesh afterwards like his buddies did, but aware of not only health risks but of blackmail because of his position, he had always ignored temptations.

He watched for a few frustratingly enticing minutes more, but on her removing the boots, garter belt and stockings, seeing her volup-tuous bottom for the first time in a thong, he was no longer able to hold himself down, and joining his phallus, rose.

Shaking her head, she gave him a sternly sexy glare, gestured he sit back down with an index finger she wet with her tongue, and using her nubile flexible body for some long-practiced yoga and Pilates moves, she slithered on the floor, painfully slowly, towards him. This proved to be more than he could take and he began to rise again.

She stood, sauntered rhythmically over to him, pushed him back down aggressively, sat astride his legs, and pressing her crotch against his, began winding and grinding against him in a lap dance. He tried to kiss her but she bent over backwards, swiveling her hips against his bulge in time to the music, her head following the same rhythm, her long hair wildly lashing against the floor. Barely able to control a bodily function as she uncontrollably moved against the part in ques-tion, he stood up, taking her with him.

With her legs clinging around his waist, he shuffled over to the thick rug in the living room. Laying her down not very gently, he quickly unwound the whip from around the column. Sitting up she grabbed it from him, "No Your Highness, it's not for me!"

Staring hard into her eyes, he spoke gutturally, "So, it *is* for *me*?!"

She showed a twinge of fear, "No, no. I was just playing-"

He smiled challengingly, "You mean intimidated. Coward!"

She was befuddled, "What! You don't mean you want-"

"I don't know. I've not experienced it before. You make the decision. Surprise me."

So she did, and history, again, was very definitely made.

The morning was taken up rehearsing, organizing, and tweaking, not just Elizabeth's speech, but the equality event itself. By lunchtime, with dark glasses always firmly affixed to his face, Michael, who occasionally sat watching the activities at a distance but mostly roamed around with Brian, Eric, Tommy, and the head of security, making observations, saw Elizabeth needed a break and approached her, "Darling, everything's under control here. Why don't we take a couple hours for lunch?"

"Definitely. After lunch, I hope you don't mind, but Aunt Ruth had Olga call to tell me she left something for me at the apartment, an unnecessary apology for not being able to be here. It's Olga's day off but the other maids'll be there. We must be discreet towards each other in their presence, no touching. Okay?"

Giving an agreeable smile so as not to unnerve her on this important day, he let go of her hand that he was holding, "Okay. From now on, touching is verboten."

On their way out of the auditorium they were stopped by three organizers who invited them for lunch. A refined elderly gentleman that everyone simply referred to as Mr. Schwartz was soft-spoken, "Seeing that we only just learnt you have to leave right after your speech and will miss the celebration party, it's the least we can do." Put like that, Elizabeth and Michael felt forced to accept, but did explain up-front they only had an hour as they had to attend to important family matters.

Lunch ended up taking two fleeting hours. Three more organizers joined them along with Professor Thomas and Jenkins, and with the high degree of intelligence of every individual in the group, the conversation was continuously stimulating, educating, provoking, enlightening, and inspiring.

Introducing Michael as an, "Old friend from school," Elizabeth was amused by the way the Granger's two pretty young maids openly flirted with him, and shooed them away saying in Spanish, "Forget it, he's happily engaged." After they retreated to the kitchen giggling childishly, she showed Michael around the Manhattan penthouse that was as big as a wing in his palace.

Impressed with the extensive collection of museum quality art and important antiques that were complimented by rare relics and souvenirs from the owners' world travels, he commented, "It's all very beautiful and tasteful. Now, I want to see your old bedroom." He had been looking forward to this visit, to at last be able to get some small view into Elizabeth's past.

Opening her bedroom door she was not surprised to find that except for personal items, everything was the same as when she lived there. Ruth and she had worked with a famous interior designer to redecorate it when she moved in at sixteen, and though it had cost a small fortune, she knew that was not the reason it was left intact; her aunt and uncle, her surrogate parents, wanted to keep a part of her constantly in their lives.

Michael saw her becoming emotional, and sat down with her on the bed thinking this the perfect opportunity to extract information about her past. "Why don't you talk about some memories, darling? Why, this room still smells of you. It's wonderful. It even makes *me* feel nostalgic," he sniffed and kissed her neck, "I just love your perfume."

She swallowed the lump in her throat, "On one of our France trips we went to Grasse, I had this scent formulated for me. Actually, we all had scents made exclusively for us individually that time. Mine's a blend of cattleya orchids and roses."

"It's perfect for you, romantic, sexy but lady-like, yet almost child-like, but intriguing and mysterious. Aunt Claire remarked about it, suspected it was designed just for you."

"Oh? Has she been questioning you about me again?"

"Every time we cross paths."

"I'm sorry darling. I hate putting you through that. I'll relieve you of that problem soon. After we get back, alright?"

"Alright, but I didn't mean to pressure you."

Elizabeth kicked off her shoes and stretching out on her old familiar bed asked Michael to hold her, "Just for a while."

They lay quietly locked in each other's arms for several minutes, then without warning, she began to sob. Not understanding her emotions he said nothing, but held her close, both their bodies shaking gently with her sobs. He knew she needed to release something, but what? What was the unwanted burden she could not let drop? Was it from her childhood, or more recently? Or was it some regret, maybe because of a childhood lost, of having to grow up too soon?

She stopped sobbing and kissed him. Feeling his jacket lapel damp from her tears, with just three words, "Take everything off," they were soon naked and made intense love.

She needed to do it here with Michael, as though in an exorcism ceremony, on the very same bed she had made love with another, in times past.

Still giggling, the maids handed her a card with a box, and again retreated to the kitchen.

Opening the shoe-size wooden box, Elizabeth was shocked to find inside, lying in padded faded green velvet, a small, crude, clay statue. Its shortened head had no discernible features, the arms and legs were mere suggestions, but the full-bodied figure emphasized bountiful motherhood with an ostensibly pregnant abdomen, pendulous breasts and ample hips.

Caressing it with both hands she exclaimed, "Oh my Godde! It's the Goddess! Michael do you realize how rare this piece is? It's millenniums old!" She glanced around the opulent living room, "This is more rare, more expensive, than any one item in this entire home!"

He smiled in agreement, "I know. I can't imagine how they came by it, just goes to show how much your aunt and uncle love you. But not as much as I," he grinned, then teased, "perhaps you should've opened the card first?"

Still in shock, she hesitated, "What? Oh, of course." With an index finger, feeling a little foolish at her childish impatience in opening the present before the card, she tore open the envelope in one swift action. The note was written in Ruth's hand but she noticed Robert had signed it also.

Our Precious Princess,

Despite all the heartache and unwelcome changes in your life that you've been through, know that you are completely loved and always will be. Stay true to yourself and your primary purpose in life, to enlighten and improve the lives of others, to love and be loved. Never forget the power and influence only one person can have over millions, billions. Let her be your inspiration to ensure you spread the Truth that will eventually lead to world peace. Our love and thoughts are with you always,

A. Ruth & U. Robert

P.S. Certificate of Authenticity and Insurance papers are under velvet in box. Put them in safety deposit box at your bank.

She smiled at the P.S. thinking, *Still being my parents with sound advice,* and handed the note to Michael.

Checking the estimated value on the prepaid insurance papers, she drew in a long breath, *Twenty Million U.S.dollars!*

Hidden behind heavy drapes at one side of the stage, Michael stood with Jenkins and two visibly armed guards. Brian, Eric and two more guards were on the opposite side.

Tommy was in the audience with six more guards in plainclothes carrying concealed weapons, who were dispersed throughout the packed auditorium. Although knowing the ten extra bodyguards he brought with them, without Elizabeth's knowledge, were well supported by the organizer's security, Michael still was unable to shake off the tension he felt all day.

Hearing and seeing Elizabeth deliver her message again reinforced the pride he felt the first time he saw her on stage, but today, it combined with guilt and regret. He had made a decision that tonight would be her last speech on this subject.

He was not going to allow her to risk her life anymore. He was going to do everything in his power to stop her, he was not chancing losing the love of his life. He began devising a plan to enlist Anne, Susan, and Megan, all the women in his world he knew cared for her, to help him achieve his goal.

Because of her extreme, unreasonable, inexplicable dislike of Elizabeth, Aunt Claire could not be relied on for her assistance. In fact, due to her incessant lecturing, "*You should marry a real princess!*" he worried that she would do something to sabotage their relationship, including contriving a diabolical plot to have Elizabeth 'removed' from his life, permanently.

Succumbing to the ingrained male-ego-power caused by thousands of years of patriarchal religious and thus societal indoctrination, he had not taken into account the indomitable spirit of womankind who had endured, survived, and triumphed, over eons of various forms of domination and discrimination in their patriarchal-religiously-brainwashed societies.

Feeling afraid and responsible for Elizabeth's life and safety, and therefore to his loving-obsessive mind, that of his own, he ingenuously ignored that she was a woman fully and fortitudinously aware that she alone was accountable for her own life, and how she lived it.

Elizabeth could not believe how smooth and uneventful the entire evening went. Not only surprised at no interruptions during her longer speech she was shocked no one verbally attacked her during the

Q-and-A. She had expected the worst, considering this is America, '*the land of the free*,' and naturally therefore, of 'free speech.' She had prepared herself, and Professor Thomas, for fending off all kinds of abuse, but none came. People were more than polite; they were friendly, agreeing, encouraging.

Then she remembered why, *Most of us here share the same opinions. That's why I was invited in the first place. I must keep that in mind when next I do this speech in a different environment. I must be wary and not sit back on my laurels.*

Safely airborne for the journey home, Michael, and Elizabeth relaxed, revisited the restroom, and blissfully reinstated their membership in the 'Mile High Club.'

CHAPTER
30

"*D*arling, I hate to wake you but I couldn't leave without saying goodbye."

Elizabeth opened her eyes to see Michael fully dressed sitting on the bed next to her, and it was still dark outside, "What? Where're you going? What time is it?"

"It's early, go back to sleep. Something's come up, I've meetings in the West Country, be back in a couple days. I love you," he leaned over, kissed her on her lips and stood up quickly.

His words rapidly came into focus along with his situation. A vision of his fresh scar flashed through her mind. She sat up reaching for his hand, "The West Country! Oh no, Michael! I'm coming with you."

As she jumped out of bed he walked swiftly to the door, "No! You can't come with me. Get back into bed. Bye darling."

Walking to him she pleaded, "Please darling, let me come?"

He smiled teasingly, "No. You're too much of a distraction. Look, everything's fine over there, nothing to worry about, and the sooner I leave, the sooner I'll return. Now, go back to sleep, I'll call you later."

She looked forlorn and frightened and he felt bad but knew he needed to get away quickly before she got to him.

She sprinted across the room, "At least give me a hug and a proper kiss." Putting her arms around his torso, she felt the stiffness he was trying to avoid her feeling, "What's this? You're wearing a bulletproof vest! No! Michael, no! You're *not* going! I won't let you go!" Shaking, she squeezed him tightly.

Wresting her arms from around him, he held her hands, "Elizabeth, I *have* to go. Important meetings have been set up and I have to negotiate-"

She shook her head, "Not you! Send somebody else!"

"I can't. This is my responsibility. The…people, I'm meeting with will not negotiate with anyone else, only me. You have to understand, in my position, there are certain things I must do myself-"

"Yes, but not this, not there! I can't forget what happened the last time you were in the West Country-"

He shook her hands, "That was just a freak accident, darling. Nothing's going to happen this time, every precaution has been taken. I'll be alright. I promise you. And you know I never break my promises." Kissing her, he let go of her hands and quickly opened the door, "I love you," he blew a kiss and hurried out the door.

Finding her voice a little late she called out, "I love you," and hoped he heard her, which he did.

Fear enveloping her, she knew it was impossible for her to recommence sleep and decided to take for a walk, the two rambunctious dogs who had raced in the door when Michael opened it, and were now romping all over the room and on the bed.

Between unceasing attacks on her by long wet tongues, their tails slapping each other's excitedly, she managed to don underwear, track suit, sneakers, and lastly, Michael's 'Born In The U.S.A.' cap. She needed to have his scent not leave her.

Trying to get Duke and Duchess to stand still long enough to be leashed proved to be more of a challenge than she thought it would be, and although grateful for Brian's help when he came along, she was also annoyed, and suddenly even more afraid, "Why didn't *you* go with Michael?"

Though well practiced in the art of deception, Brian could not help looking sheepish under Elizabeth's accusatory glare, "Michael insisted I stay here and…keep you…company."

She showed her annoyance and fear, "More like *watch* over me. I would've preferred you to have gone and watched over *him*."

Attempting to appease her he smiled sweetly, Elizabeth noticing for the first time under his tousled mop of coarse red hair and bountiful freckles how good-looking he was, and handed her Duchess's leash, "You mustn't worry. Eric, Jenkins, Tommy, and all our best men are with him, he'll be fine."

They tried to get the energetic and unruly dogs to follow the path through the rose gardens, but eventually gave in to Duchess and Duke's dogged desire to head for the ponds. It became obvious these dogs were incapable of adhering to the normal disciplines of being taken for a walk, their understanding of the protocol of this exercise being that the canines are to drag the humans through the human's walk.

On their arrival back at the palace's private back doors, Elizabeth, feeling her two arms had been pulled out of their sockets, gratefully handed over Duchess's leash to Mark who greeted them, Megan running up behind him.

Giving them both a hug, Elizabeth chuckled somewhat cynically, "So, I see, the gang's all here, to "*keep me company*." Michael sure has control over you people-"

Megan and Mark piped up with one voice, "Not at all, we're looking forward to spending this whole day with you."

Elizabeth smiled through the feeling of foreboding that intensified within her, "All we need now is the King, Aunt Anne, definitely Aunt Claire, *and* the Holy Family, to complete Michael's little 'Protective Party' for me-"

Megan gave her the sweet innocent smile that endeared her to everyone, "You forgot Susan. She came last night. She's staying with the aunts."

Elizabeth's smile disappeared as the seriousness of Michael's trip settled in. *He even had Susan come to be with me in case...oh Godde! Please keep him safe! Protect him from all harm, better than he's trying to protect me!*

Having given the dogs some biscuits to calm them down, Mark read her tension and holding her around her waist, pulled her off to the side, "Don't worry, he's got the best protection, he'll be fine."

Not gently, she pushed him away, "Don't worry?! Everyone keeps saying that! But it's not working! And nobody will tell me what he's doing over there! He was stabbed the last time, Mark!"

The blood drained from Mark's face and she regretted her outburst, "Oh gosh, I'm sorry, I thought you knew."

His shocked response was barely audible, "Nobody told me...us. Thanks for telling me. I'm tired of all the secrets. I don't know what he's doing over there either, no one will tell us. All we know is he's in charge of...serious negotiations."

Taking in his frightened look, their roles reversed and Elizabeth now sought to comfort him, and hugged him, "It's no consolation that we're all in the dark about what he's doing, but at least we have each other for company until he returns to us, safe and sound."

The day that she thought would drag slowly and tensely turned out to speed by with non-stop fun activities Michael and his family had planned for her. It started with a sumptuous breakfast at Claire and Anne's apartment, followed by a game of tennis doubles. Elizabeth and Susan teamed up against Megan and Mark. The twins won by just a few points, the King joining the aunts to cheer everyone equally from their over-looking balcony. Passing the pool on the way back indoors to shower and change, Mark wickedly shoved all three ladies into the pool fully-clothed, then took a running leap to land in the middle of the surprised group with a bombing splash, soaking also, the two gardeners working nearby. Everyone took the watery trickery in good spirits, the girls dunking Mark several times until he begged for mercy with reluctant apologies.

Divesting themselves of waterlogged shoes and socks, the tennis players transformed into competitive swimmers. Swimming almost every day living in the tropics and therefore with more practice than the northerners, Elizabeth beat them shamelessly in every race, regardless of their chosen stroke.

Lunch was at a downtown restaurant considered to be a hotspot by the 'in crowd,' most likely because it was owned and managed by one of the royal cousins, Paul. Elizabeth was grateful that apart from large sunglasses she wore a short blond wig for this excursion as their group, consisting of Anne, Susan, Megan, Mark, Elizabeth and Paul, were soon joined by two more cousins, and, what the royals whisperingly referred to as, "*the plague-a-razzi*," the paparazzi. After posing with dignity for the annoying cameramen the royals asked to be left alone.

Their polite requests fell on deaf ears, two of the newsmen persistently asking for Elizabeth's name; whereupon the royals started hamming it up, deliberately blocking Elizabeth from being further photographed. Paul eventually gave a false name for Elizabeth saying she was his friend, gave the photo journalists a beer to go, and saw them out the door, which he locked, so that the rest of the lunch crowd could dine in peace.

Accompanied by great conversation, anecdotes, jokes and much laughter, lunch stretched into afternoon tea. By the time they all sneaked out the back door to their cars where Brian waited with two bodyguards, the frustrated paparazzi had gone from in front of the restaurant.

The still laughing group decided to chance going to shop in a trendy boutique owned by yet another royal cousin. There they continued making jokes and fools of themselves, trying on every unsuitable outfit each could find. The girls dressed Mark and Paul ridiculously in ultra-feminine frilly scarves, outrageous costume jewelry and feathery hats, to peals of laughter from them all, including thankfully, the amiable owner-cousin, Laura.

Feeling a little guilt but mostly gratitude for their boisterousness, though she suspected some of it to be forced, Elizabeth bought handbags of their choice for each of the ladies and neckties for the two men and Michael.

For herself, she bought a pair of sexy outlandish but comfortable boots with next year's Carnival in mind, totally bewildering the others who questioned where she would wear them, to which she simply stated, "They're for a costume."

Piling the merry group back into their cars, Anne declared, "Dinner and movies is on me!" and took them all back to the palace's home theater. After discarding shoes and bags at the door they got comfortable. A butler served hot dogs, cheeseburgers, popcorn, nuts, chocolates, plain Coca-colas or Cuba Libres. Elizabeth, as designated 'guest of honor,' was allowed to choose the first movie, which was '*Dangerous Beauty*' and was thoroughly enjoyed by all.

Anne, as designated 'senior clown of the day' was given the choice of the second movie which was '*Walk The Line,*' a surprise to everyone except Elizabeth who had observed the dignified dowager's adventurous fun-loving streak throughout the day.

It occurred to Elizabeth that Michael's family was filling his time away in the West Country with distractions not just for her, per his instructions, but were doing so out of necessity to distract themselves also. After cautiously questioning each member singularly during the course of the day, she came to realize they were as incognizant of Michael's activities in the West Country as she, all of them knowing only that he was negotiating with "*dangerous people.*"

Everyone kept their mobile phones on their person, each jumping nervously whenever a phone rang, the others quietly listening when the call was answered, then breathing sighs of mixed feelings of relief when it had nothing to do with Michael.

He did call Elizabeth three times but simply played more love songs, including Enrique Iglesias's 'Hero.' *Michael, you'll always be my hero, you don't have to prove anything to me. Please don't take any risks! Just come back to me safely.*

The second song he played made her wonder if he realized more about their past than he acknowledged. It was Savage Garden's 'I Knew I Loved You Before I Met You.' He spoke only once, during Stevie Wonder's 'I Just Called to Say I Love You,' repeating the title melodiously in tune with Stevie. In his last voicemail he played a song that had his family staring at her with wonderment. Considering all the many romances of Michael's they knew of, the only other woman that he held in such high esteem was his mother. In this song, he had Josh Groban praising Elizabeth on his behalf, that she "*raised him up so*" he "*could stand on mountains.*"

Because of the tense situation she felt compelled to share her phone calls with the family and Brian to somewhat alleviate their worry. After listening to, and censoring some of them in private first, she played them back on speaker for the group who crowded around. Everyone was delighted to hear this unknown side of Michael, a prince in love, except for Paul.

He had been making flirtatious advances, though cautiously, towards Elizabeth throughout the day, to Mark's and Brian's extreme annoyance, inwardly amusing Elizabeth no end.

The second movie finished after midnight. Elizabeth politely turned down Paul's invitation to lunch again tomorrow, which he sensibly also offered to the whole group, saying she had to catch up on some neglected work as she felt Michael would be returning tomorrow. Just as she was about to ask, Susan offered to spend the night in Michael's apartments with her, both knowing this was not a night for her to be alone.

The anxious ladies indulged in girltalk until after two in the morning when Susan suggested Elizabeth needed, "To get some sleep, be energized for Michael's return, hopefully tomorrow."

Susan slept in Elizabeth's suite, Elizabeth in Michael's bed as usual; but having made a pact to share all information pertaining to Michael's situation, both kept their doors open in case either should receive a call during the night. Neither slept well, Elizabeth waking almost every hour to look at her phone in case she had slept through a call, but there were none.

Megan came to wake them at eight, unnecessarily, as they had been sipping tea and chatting on the balcony since seven. She announced that her father was expecting them to breakfast with him and the rest of the family, adding quickly, "Nothing's wrong. Papa just thought it would be nice for us all to have breakfast together for a change."

Elizabeth and Susan dressed quickly and walked with Megan to the family dining room where the King, uncharacteristically informal, greeted all the ladies with a smiling kiss, and Mark with a warm hug, totally unnerving everyone. The initial conversation was forced and strained until the King put everyone at ease by saying he had spoken with Michael earlier and things went well, and he'll probably be home later today.

The King obviously read Elizabeth's concerned countenance and surprised her with a hug, saying consolingly, "Don't worry. Everything's fine. He'll be home soon."

Michael phoned as she entered the apartment, "Where've you been party animal? I've been calling day and night. And what's this I hear about you flirting with my cousin Paul? Looks like I'll have to put a leash on you when I return in three days."

"Three days! Your father told us probably today-"

"Don't try to change the subject, I'm not going to, until you explain what's going on with you and Paul. He's a very straight up guy, he'd never flirt with my woman. You must've instigated it. So you'd better fess up."

He was unsuccessful at hiding the tease in his voice which para-doxically both relieved and irritated her, "Michael, cut the B.S. Are you alright? When are you returning home?"

"Not for three days, like I said."

"But your father said-"

He interrupted with a wicked laugh, "Pack your bags, sweetheart. You're going to meet me halfway. We're going to spend a few days at Jamestowns' estate, Susan's already heading there, Brian will drive you in my car."

Elizabeth was unsure of how to approach Brian to be her accom-plice in some mischief. She knew Michael and he had a special relationship which, according to what she had gathered from a few things said occasionally, existed since childhood. She also remembered the bonhomie she witnessed between them during, and since, the journey in the car when they were driving to the skydiving site. She knew that Brian's feelings toward her went beyond just respect for her position as Michael's girlfriend. He appeared to look upon her as not simply a woman whose safety he was entrusted with in the line of duty, but more as someone special with whom he wished to develop a lasting friendship. She felt comforted, and amused, that he stuck to her like a tick to a newborn lamb in Michael's absence.

So, with these things considered, she decided she could rely on him to join her in a prank against their beloved prince.

She looked serious but her lips twitched, "Brian, I'm going to play a trick on Michael, and I need your help. I want to pay him back for all the 'suffering' he's put me through."

Taking his eyes off the road for an instant, he looked at Elizabeth and laughed, "Not going to happen. Prince Michael is the 'King of Tricksters.' The men have given up trying to catch him, he's always figured us out. I would've thought you knew by now what a teaser he is?"

"Oh yes, but all the more reason why you have to help me catch him this time. Please? You could boast to the men later?"

Brian didn't hesitate, "Okay. What's your plan?"

His entourage in three cars pulled up to the previously selected rest stop. Michael exited the middle car immediately. Thinking Elizabeth was sitting in his car, he could barely control his excitement at being with her after his ordeal, and practically ran to his waiting T.V.R. with Brian and a guard standing beside it. Seeing the car empty as he approached, he frowned, "Where's Elizabeth?"

Brian returned the frown, "Sorry, Sir, but Susan came back to pick her up. She wanted to go with Susan, I don't know why. I sent a car with two men to escort them."

Michael's happy excited demeanor shifted instantly and he became crestfallen, which made Brian feel guilty, but only for a fraction of a second. He was now convinced that at last his best friend since boyhood, the 'King of Tricksters,' was finally going to be thoroughly tricked.

Michael mumbled an expletive, turned on his heel and walked toward the driver's side of his T.V.R. saying agitatedly, "Well, let's get moving."

Brian called out, "Wait. I think you should use the restroom here, the next stop's a long way off. The men have all gone already, except for Sam here. Sam, you'd better go ahead of Prince Michael, check everything's okay."

Michael turned around to see who this Sam was standing behind Brian, he knew of no bodyguard named Sam, when Sam, his cap low on his face and his head down, bounced into him forcefully throwing him off-balance causing him to stumble.

Sam brusquely muttered in a deep voice, "Pardon me, Sir," and strutted off to the restrooms.

Michael was aghast, "Did you see that?"

Brian turned to face him with a dumb look, "What?"

"What he just did! He almost threw me over! And he didn't apologize properly. Actually, he was disrespectful. He must be new. I don't like his attitude. And he's much too scrawny to be effective, on top of that he's clumsy. You'd better get rid of him when you return."

Brian was straight-faced, "No can do. I understand he has some very special talents that you need. And, he was recommended by the highest authority-"

"Who? Not my father-"

"Oh yes. Michael, you're the one with an attitude-"

"What else do you expect? You just told me, after I risked my life for everybody, my girlfriend would rather travel with my cousin than with me!"

"Well, I'm sure she had a good reason, you'll find out soon. I see Sam's already out of the restrooms, talking to Tommy, you'd better hurry and go so you can get your explanations sooner."

Feeling his stomach upset, Michael sat on the toilet to see if he could get relief, but none came. He could not understand Elizabeth's actions, he felt both hurt and angry and was going to let her know in no uncertain terms. He flushed the toilet and stood pulling up his underpants when the cubicle door flung open violently hitting the wall, and Sam jumped on him.

Staggering backwards he shrieked, "What the hell-"

With one arm clinging around Michael's neck, Sam grabbed Michael's exposed penis with his other hand and began massaging it, at the same time sticking his tongue in Michael's shocked open mouth. For an instant Michael froze, perplexed at his arousal and strange enjoyment of the attack on him. Fear mounting, he began pushing Sam off him, *Is that perfume?* but Sam clung to him and pressed his body against him, *Breasts! The bugger has breasts!* Recognition coming to him, he tore off Sam's cap. Elizabeth's hair fell out.

"Elizabeth! You bitch! You scared me! You tricked me!"

She grinned wickedly, squeezing his phallus, "Gotcha!"

Shaking slightly he began to laugh, "You planned this with Brian! Conniving bitch! I'm going to make you pay, both of you."

Laughingly she teased, "What part scared you the most, Your Highness, the assault, or getting turned on by a man?"

He spluttered, "I...I was not turned on by a man! It was your soft and talented hand that did it, you bitch! I'm going to make you pay, right here, right now."

Pulling off the over-sized leather jacket she wore, he ripped open her shirt and pushed her against the wall.

He sucked hard on both breasts, then bit a nipple causing her to cry out, "Michael don't hurt me!"

Putting a hand over her mouth his voice was softly gruff, "Shh, we don't want the men to hear. You should've thought of that when you were plotting to trick me. Now, you have to pay."

With that said, he made her pay in the most rewarding manner for them both.

Feeling as well-compensated as he, she decided she would not admit to Brian that Michael was fooled and their trickery worked, in order that her precious prince could not be dethroned and therefore would remain forever, the 'King of Tricksters.

CHAPTER
31

$\mathcal{I}$t was a perfect sunny warm summer afternoon. The sky looked like a tourist's postcard, clear baby-blue with just a few aesthetically pleasing interruptions of tiny white cottony clouds, unhurriedly floating across the interminable heavens.

Settling Elizabeth and himself in his T.V.R., Michael, wanting to savor everything about this special day made even more perfect with the wonderful weather, put the top down on the car, when Brian attempted to stop him, "Not a good idea, Sir. Because of having to meet you here the route we must take to Jamestown's wasn't thoroughly checked. We'll be going through many small towns, narrow, winding roads. You should wait."

Michael stuck his tongue in his cheek, "First off, friend of 'Sam' and no friend of mine, you don't have to use the 'Sir' when we're alone with Elizabeth, especially after what you two put me through."

She grinned, "For which he's already made me pay big time."

Michael grinned back at her with complicity, "Oh no my lady, you'll be paying for the rest of your life," then turned back to Brian, "and you, mister, can start paying right now by making sure the road's clear. Jump in the front car to guard us with your life. I want to show

Elizabeth what this car can do on these kinds of roads. The day is too gorgeous, I'm not putting the top back up. Nobody knows I'm in the area anyway. Now snap to it. You drive. I'll give you a head start, put on some speed or I'll rear-end you. Tell Jenkins and Tommy in the car behind they'd better be sharp and keep up."

Michael was exhilarated from the certain success of his negotiations, which before yesterday, although not abject failures, the agreements he previously obtained from the adversaries had always been capricious; but not this time. This time, with the higher intelligence and ethical reputations of their new leaders, he knew the covenant would be honored.

Knowing that everything was right in his world at last, he felt confident that with this loving, passionate, exciting and intelligent woman always by his side, he would achieve his highest goals, now that the region was on its way to lasting peace and stability. *Next on the agenda, world peace!*

Dangerously speeding round sharp narrow bends, precipitously climbing steep hills and pelting down from their crests at a hundred miles an hour, for fifteen minutes, was all that Elizabeth could tolerate, and she finally pleaded, "Darling I'm impressed enough, slow down! Please quit while we're still alive! Could we please talk? I want to hear how it went in the West Country, and I'm sure you'd like to hear about my day, at least what hasn't already been reported to you."

Laughingly he obeyed, "Anything for you, angel. I must say, I'm very impressed with how calm you were just now."

She punched his arm softly, "Calm! I was dying inside! I thought you wanted to commit suicide, and take me with you!"

He laughed again, "I can't tell you about yesterday yet, but I want you to know how happy I am today. Mostly because of you. I'm so completely in love with the most wonderful woman in the world. You've made me so happy, beyond my wildest dreams. If I should die today, I would die the happiest man on earth!"

Talking and sharing for over an hour, the lovers became filled with similar feelings of pleasurable contentment. Their relationship, though intensely passionate and still filled with mysteries, had taken on a com-forting dependability and stability fortified by an all-consuming caring love for one another.

Elizabeth was still mystified by Michael's reluctance to tell her what really happened between him and Priscilla, his only other seri-ous girlfriend. She felt, because of the way the media had made such a fuss about their very public breakup, speculations running from the ridiculous to the macabre and then abruptly stopping com-pletely, that the royal family used their power to silence everyone concerned, including Michael. From then on, Michael had kept a low profile with his romances, his reputation went from 'Prince Charming' to 'Prince Conservative,' and Priscilla was made to 'dis-appear' into oblivion.

After Michael recovered from the shock of Priscilla's betrayal, which he eventually partially blamed himself for, he kept a stringent control over his heart's emotions. Suppressing his instinctual open-ness and closing off any feelings for potential serious relationships, he became determined to never again allow himself to be vulnerable to the possible sufferings that come with unconditional love. Until now. Until Elizabeth. She was the special angel he had been waiting for, to open his heart again to a true, complete, everlasting love.

Elizabeth resolved to ask him to clear up the Priscilla mystery tonight, thinking that discussion and his explanation might give her some leverage in softening the blow of revealing her own mysteries. Feeling her old strengths renewed, due in part to Michael divulging his 'big mistake' in fathering an illegitimate child in his youth, and, relying on his present ecstatic mood, combined with the happy and tranquil atmosphere they would have at Jamestown's, she decided she would tell him about her past after dinner. She hoped he would handle the shocking revelations the way she wanted.

Having passed through several quaint quiet villages and towns with only occasional cars, trucks, and a few villagers visible, usually with friendly waves, they became totally relaxed, basked in the joy of the day, and planned their future.

Brian phoned from the car in front, "We have to slow down some more. There's a local celebration in the village we're about to pass through, but to be safe, let's go as quickly as possible. That's without hitting anybody, Prince Speed Racer."

Smilingly, Michael put the T.V.R. in forth gear.

Passing through a large group of people standing on either side of the narrow street it became apparent Michael had been recognized. Both adults and children started madly waving flags, cheering and clapping, all with excited smiles, many having not seen their prince this close up before. Some children threw firecrackers on the street as they passed, *Bang! Pop! Bang! Pop! Bang! Pop!*

Startled, Elizabeth jumped, "Lord! You'd think their parents wouldn't have allowed those kids to throw firecrackers so near to us," she said, turning her head to look back at the group on her side and give them a disapproving stare, in her Trinidadian mind, *A really strong 'cut-eye!'*

Michael accelerated the car so rapidly she was forcefully jerked back into a forward-facing position, the seatbelt digging into her shoulder painfully. Looking up, she opened her mouth to chastise him about his speeding again, when she saw the wall. She screamed, "Michael! What the hell are you doing! You're going to hit that wall!" The car was heading straight for a ten-foot-high concrete block wall. "Turn! Turn!" she screamed, mesmerized by the wall that appeared to be speeding toward them.

Michael ignored her, the car speeding even faster toward the wall. Her survival instinct kicking in, she grabbed the steering wheel, yanked it away from his grasp, and swiftly turned it as hard as she could. Michael fell over to the side and hit his door with a heavy thud. She flashed a look of dismay at him which turned to horror, "Oh my Godde! Oh my Godde!"

His head, face, and torso were covered with blood. Blood was oozing out of the left side of his head above his ear, rivulets trickling down his neck, to join with more blood that was streaming out of wounds in his upper left arm. His sunglasses fell to one side clinging to an ear, his eyes were closed, his mouth hung open, and his limp body was slumped against his door. Fascinated, she stared disbelievingly for an instant. Then it sank in. *Those were shots! Michael's been shot!*

She was snapped out of her shocked stupefaction by the jolt and crunching noise of the side of the car hitting the wall, sparks flying in all directions from the friction of the heavy metal violently scraping against the concrete wall.

Barely slowed by the sideways collision, the car kept going as if driven by a deathwish. She knew she must stop it somehow but Michael's two feet, now dead weight, were firmly pressing on the accelerator pedal. Steering with one hand, she unbuckled her seatbelt and tried to pull up the emergency brake with the other but could not get it to budge. Swiftly exchanging hands, she pulled on it again with all her strength, to no avail, it was jammed. She knew she had to get his feet off the accelerator pedal but could not figure out how to do it without hurting him.

Something whispered to her, *Pain him now or he'll not pain forever more.* Gritting her teeth, she swung a leg toward his and with all the force she could muster, kicked his legs away from the accelerator pedal toward his door, crying, "Sorry darling!"

Hoisting her body over the gear shift box, she slammed a foot down on the brake pedal. The car skidded from side to side, hitting against the wall three times before it came to a screeching halt, and stalled.

Elizabeth turned to hold Michael when Jenkins, driving the car that was following them, sped up alongside and shouted, "Elizabeth, keep on driving!"

"No!" she screamed, "Michael's been shot!"

"I know!" Jenkins shouted, "But we've got to get him away from here! It's not safe! Follow Brian!"

Brian reversed to ten feet in front of them. She could not fathom why Jenkins was behaving this way. To her loving but panicked way of thinking the most important thing was to attend to her precious love, now crumbled up in a ball, bleeding his life away. She thought the only thing to do was make him comfortable, hold him until help arrives, *Where's that damn ambulance?!* Her heart was pounding so hard, it felt like it was trying to escape from her chest.

Tasting the bitterness of adrenalin in her mouth as she looked at the blood gushing from Michael's wounds, she cried, "He's dying! Call an ambulance!" and caressed his bloodied face.

Jenkins screamed at her, "We're in the middle of nowhere! There's no ambulance! Start the fucking car and follow Brian!"

Startled by Jenkins' belligerent manner and crude language, she caught herself and turned the key in the ignition. The car sputtered and stalled.

Bang! Pop! A bullet whizzed past her head hitting the clock on the dashboard shattering the glass, scattering splinters everywhere. "Oh my Godde! We're being shot at!" she screamed.

Jenkins screamed back, though he tried to sound calmer, realizing Elizabeth was in shocked panic and had not fully grasped how danger-ous the situation still was, "Elizabeth, just turn the key harder this time! Let's go!"

She fought for her sanity, *Don't panic! Do as he says!* Hearing Jenkins's words echoing in her head in-between incessant gunshots, talking to herself, "Start the fucking car," she turned the key with determination. The car started. Pressing the accelerator, she forgot about balancing the clutch and tried to shift the gear stick. She had become unaccustomed to a non-automatic car, having not driven one since she was a teenager in Trinidad and Spain. The car bucked and stalled again.

Jenkins and Brian simultaneously opened their doors to get out intending to take over, when she remembered what to do.

Quickly pressing the clutch with her left foot, her right on the brake, she started the car, changed the gear into first, pressed the accel-erator with her brake foot as she released the clutch, and the powerful car leapt forward as though it was a wild animal speeding after prey. Brian's car sped forward in front, Jenkins's car taking up the rear.

Though still completely dazed Michael's dying condition was the impetus she needed. Hearing the echo of Jenkins's words "*We've got to get him away from here! It's not safe!*"in-between her heart hammering in her ears, she was given even more motivation to speed faster by the sound of gunfire all around them. *Bang! Pop! Rat-a-tat-tat!* She rammed the accelerator to the floorboard, almost hitting Brian's car.

Brian immediately sped up his car to skillfully lead the terrorized group round the sharp bends in the undulating narrow country road, the bodyguards in Jenkins's car, led by Tommy hanging out the window, shooting at their pursuing attackers.

Elizabeth was now running on automation, like a puppet with some unknown force pulling her strings.

Leaning over the steering wheel trying not to crush Michael, she handled the speeding car, smoothly changing gears, as if she were a professional race car driver.

Her mind seemed to have left her body, her thoughts whirled and raced but though motivated by urgency, her panic was gone.

She prayed more sincerely than she ever had in her entire life, *Oh Godde, please save Michael! Godde, whatever you are, wherever you are, hear me! I beg you, save Michael! Blessed Mother and Father of the Universe, save Michael, my love, my life! Please Godde, save him, heal him! I beg you!* Unknowingly, she began to pray aloud, repeating her entreaties to Godde and the Blessed Mother and Father over and over like a stuck CD.

Winding around a particularly sharp downward bend, she barely managed to precipitously skirt the edges of a deep drainage ditch filled with water from heavy rains the day before. The near miss jolted her mind back into her body.

She glanced quickly at the speedometer. It read one-hundred-sixty-five kilometers. She gasped as a wave of panic hit again, *Shit! This is dangerous! If I screw up I'll kill us both!*

Struggling for control over the terror that had gripped her once more, she prayed aloud again. This time she invoked every deity she could think of, and all her deceased relatives and friends, to pray for

Michael, and herself. Then she said a prayer her grandmothers and mother had taught her from the time she first learnt to speak as a toddler. *"Oh angels of God, our guardians dear, to whom God's love comest thee here, ever this day be at our sides, to love and guard and be our guides."* Taking in a deep breath, she exclaimed aloud, "Guardian angels of Michael and Elizabeth, protect us! Take us to safety! Amen!"

A surprising calm came over her. An unexpected tranquility taking over, she heard a voice whisper, *"Focus, Elizabeth. Focus on your driving. It's all up to you."*

Tightening her grip on the steering wheel she deftly turned it to follow the unending sharp curves and undulating rises and dips in the narrow road as they careened at breakneck speed.

Although she had never driven this road there was a familiarity about it. Her memory flashed to a similar type of road to this she had once driven before, *Italy's Amalfi Coast!*

She was eighteen years old that summer and traveling in Europe with her parents, Aunt Ruth, and Uncle Robert. They were touring Spain, France, Switzerland, and Italy, by car that trip. Robert had done most of the driving, only letting Elizabeth take the wheel for short periods if he felt tired. The other three adults were too nervous to drive in foreign countries.

Her Trinidadian island parents were horrified by the tremendously high speeds driven on the highways in Europe.

Driving through the Alps in Switzerland, they were forced to notice if they got into the fast lane to get a better view of the breathtaking valleys, lakes, and majestic snowcapped mountains, and happened to slow down a little, the car behind would deliberately, frighteningly, come up to their tail at top speed as though to push them off the road.

After the initial scare from the first time it happened, it became obvious that Europeans considered slower driving in the fast lane unforgivable, and American Robert learned in a hurry to swerve back to the slower lane or else. Elizabeth's father remarked with some jocularity that he thought Trinidadians were the craziest drivers when it came to taking risks, but after this trip, he would have to reassess his thinking.

The drivers in Italy were even crazier. The road on the Amalfi Coast (although it did resemble in certain precipitous areas one in Trinidad through the mountains to Maracas Bay built by Americans during World War II) was the most treacherous Elizabeth had been on, up to that time. Apart from drivers and passengers alike having to cope with constant climbing up steep hills, plummeting down deep valleys, and swaying through numerous sharp bends, the winding road was also unnervingly narrow for certain large vehicles that traversed it regularly. For much of the route there were sheer rising tall cliffs on one side, and on the other, plunging precipices down to jagged rocks and the deep blue waters of the Mediterranean Sea.

The five adventurous travelers had partaken in a hearty, lengthy, late luncheon at San Pietro Hotel, overlooking one of the most amazing blue water views in the world. The adults had drunk far too much wine, Elizabeth only a quarter glass, not caring for alcohol in the middle of the day. On the other hand, the adults had made quick work of four bottles of Chianti, plus an entire cello-shaped bottle of the region's famous liqueur, Limóncello, and were now feeling no pain.

It became obvious to all that Elizabeth was the only one capable of driving them to their next stop, their hotel two hours away. She took the wheel with glee, excited to be able to drive the powerful car on this particular "*fun*" road.

With the fearlessness of youth, she drove bravely into the speeding endless traffic. Between the excessive imbibing and cradle-like swaying of the car, the adults were soon in slumber-land, the men snoring louder and more melodiously than the women, but the women closely holding their own.

Although the road was not as narrow as others she had driven, there was only one lane going in each direction, therefore passing a struggling slower vehicle was out of the question. The traffic moved along continuously for a while but then abruptly halted in the middle of a steep incline. Peering out the window to better see the cause for the unusual stop, she saw that beyond the four cars in front of her there was a huge coach filled with tourists, and it was having difficulty making an extremely sharp uphill bend. With little room between him and the car behind, the coach driver started to reverse so that he could maneuver differently in order to attempt the steep tight bend again. It looked like the coach was about to hit the car behind, the steep hill causing the heavy vehicle to slide backwards faster. The screams of its terrified passengers penetrated through its closed windows.

The driver of the car about to be crushed reversed and swerved quickly into the other lane which had become empty as oncoming traffic had been blocked from coming through because of the changed position and large size of the coach.

The nervous driver behind that car also started reversing, planning to do what the car in front was doing, to swerve into, what was just a few seconds ago, the empty lane beside him. Unfortunately, an impatient ignorant idiot had sped up from way behind, flew past the line of waiting vehicles, and almost hit him. In breaking and swerving to avoid him, the idiot's car spun around and skidded towards Elizabeth's car. Knowing that she was only a few feet away from an insignificant low wall and the edge of a precipice which plunged down more than a hundred feet to the rocks and deep waters of the sea, she rammed in the reverse gear, narrowly avoiding crashing into the car behind. Thankfully, that driver had the good sense and reflexes to reverse into the empty lane just in time, right after the idiot passed him and he envisioned what was about to occur.

Horns of every description were now blaring, trumpeting and beeping. Gesticulating angrily at the impatient idiot, annoyed and disgusted drivers and passengers alighted from their vehicles, emitting a cacophony of the worst insults and obscenities of every major language spoken on the planet.

Hearing loud noises of a different kind, Elizabeth was shaken out of her flashback by the grating clangs of metal against metal, as Brian crashed through a large half-opened iron gate. Following him, she observed there were two military men on either side of the gate who had to jump out of the way, Brian not waiting for them to fully open the gate.

He headed for an open field and just as she began to question his judgment, wondering why he didn't go to the safety of the large barracks-like building with armed soldiers running out of it, she heard the thunderous reverberation of helicopters.

CHAPTER
32

The roaring noise of two landing bulbous flying machines was deafening to everyone, except the two lovers. Michael was unconscious, Elizabeth was conscious of nothing but Michael.

Four paramedics carrying bags and all manner of medical paraphernalia jumped out the first helicopter and ran to Michael, now cradled in Elizabeth's arms. Jenkins barked orders to everyone including dozens of armed soldiers running to surround the cars and the loudly whirring aircrafts.

The paramedics gave Michael a brief but expertly executed examination. One checked his vital signs while another attended to his wounds in an attempt to stop the bleeding, at the same time the other two were attaching him to various tubes and wires of life support emergency equipment. After strapping him onto a stretcher, two of them hopped into the first helicopter.

The other two with Jenkins and Brian lifted the stretcher in, and the two inside locked it down securely. The four men outside hopped into the aircraft. Brian turned to help Elizabeth in when the pilot shouted, "No! We can't take more!"

Jenkins called out to her, "Go in the other 'copter with our men. Brian and I have to stay with Prince Michael-"

Ignoring him, she hopped in and grasped Michael's free hand, "No, Jenkins, please-"

Jenkins looked at her with regret in his eyes, his characteristically formal demeanor metamorphosing into one of caring fatherliness, "Elizabeth dear, I'm sorry, but Brian and I are duty bound to stay with Prince Michael in this situation-"

Looking down at Michael's lifeless bloodied body, tears welled in her eyes for the first time as she begged, "Please Jenkins, I *must* stay with him! Please don't separate us!"

Jenkins noticed, even in his unconscious state, Michael's right hand was squeezing Elizabeth's.

Brian's eyes followed Jenkins's, "Jenkins, I'll go in the other chopper. Don't worry, we're right behind you." Jenkins nodded, put a hand out to Elizabeth and helped her to a makeshift seat next to Michael. Brian jumped out and slammed the door shut.

The long helicopter ride was a blur to Elizabeth. Her mind's focus entirely on saving Michael, she was unaware of Jenkins's compassionate and grateful, though frightened, arm, around her shoulders for most of the journey, as the paramedics worked on Michael. The ostensibly star-crossed lover's fingers clung to each other's as though in appendages of additional life support, the air pungent with the scent of blood and death.

With no access to his lips now occupied by an oxygen mask, Elizabeth kept kissing his blood spattered forehead whispering repeatedly, "I love you. You're my life. Don't leave me. Stay with me darling. I can't live without you. Stay with me."

The instant they landed on the roof of the nearest major hospital, the door was flung open from outside by orderlies accompanying a large team of doctors and nurses, anxiously waiting to try to save the life of their much loved prince. Placing him on a hospital gurney, the throng of medical experts rushed him to the elevator and down to

X-ray and Surgery, everyone running, some in front, some alongside, the royal party and soldiers immediately behind.

Jenkins and Brian had to restrain Elizabeth from following Michael into the Operating Room. Jenkins, unfamiliar tenderness in his tone, held onto her hands, "Elizabeth dear, you've done all you can. The doctors must take over now. It's up to them to save him. We must get *you* some medical attention immediately."

"Me?" the sad numb expression on her face was replaced by puzzlement, "I'm fine." Silently, they led her to a mirror in the hallway. Seeing her reflection, she staggered backwards against Brian, "Holy Mother!"

The swollen red stranger in the mirror looked like she had been severely beaten and thrown through a glass door, while being afflicted with the worst case of Chickenpox.

Her entire face, neck, upper chest and forearms were speckled with red dots of blood, tiny glass splinters still sticking to many of them. Abrasions covered her naked forearms, two inch-long shards of glass stuck out from her right forearm just below her elbow, and her body was splattered with her and Michael's blood. Her originally pure white linen dress now displayed an artistically abstract Batik-like design in shades of maroon, red and pink.

Jenkins called forward two nurses who had been hovering expectantly. Stunned into compliance, Elizabeth let them help her into a wheelchair.

Treating her with gentleness and care excessive of her physical injuries, speaking little and softly, they wheeled her to the Emergency Room Surgery. Numbly, she let the nurses remove her bloodstained clothes. Only her panty escaped being soaked with blood, though even that had a sprinkling of Michael's blood; but she refused to take it off, needing to feel any kind of physical connection to him, no matter the morbidity of it.

Tying a strapless hospital gown on her, the nurses sat her on a surgical bed and instructed her how to hold her forearm upright so as not to puncture her wounds further with the shards of glass sticking out of it, "Those have to be removed by a surgeon. We'll do the splinters."

They gently sprayed her face, neck, upper chest and arms with an antiseptic and proceeded to carefully remove the clinging splinters with tiny forceps. The younger one remarked, tactlessly but without malicious intent, that it was a good thing Elizabeth had on quality sunglasses in the car which protected her eyes, because without them, the situation would be much worse. The doctors would not only be having to try to save Prince Michael's life, but would be having to try to save Elizabeth's eyesight. The older one gave the novice a reprimanding look that said 'I'll deal with you later.'

Just as they were gently patting a healing antibiotic ointment on her now splinter free skin, an elderly doctor walked in and introduced himself to Elizabeth, saying he had come to remove the pieces of glass from her arm and give her, "Just a few stitches" to ensure she "will have nothing more than two small scars, which should fade in about a year."

Though noticeably emotionally shaken, she had sat in motionless shock throughout the nurses' extraction procedure. But now, seeing the doctor outfitted in surgical attire, she was jolted into the realization of what his associates were doing with her precious love at this very moment. She began to shake and tremble uncontrollably, her teeth chattering noisily.

The doctor spoke gruffly to the nurses, "She's going into delayed traumatic shock. Quick, get warm blankets!" then turning to Elizabeth, in a surprising kindlier voice, he said, "Miss, you need to lie down for me to tend your wounds."

She appeared not to hear him, simply sat there staring at him, vacuous and trembling. He knew it would be impossible to extract the pieces of glass and suture her cuts the way she was shaking, and decided he had to treat her shock aggressively, "Miss, you're going to feel a little pin prick-"

Seeing the syringe coming toward her, she was startled into focusing on her own current circumstances and glowered at him, "Don't put me to sleep! I must be alert when Michael wakes up!"

The doctor smiled calmly, but suspecting Elizabeth's relationship to the Prince, and taking in her rapid and radical transition, he was perceptive enough to foresee the consequences of disobedience, and exchanged the syringe with one the older nurse handed to him, "Don't worry, you'll be awake. This is only going to relax you a little and help stop any pain," with well-practiced speed he stuck the needle in her arm, "there. All done. Now, let us help you to lie down, alright?"

Wordlessly, she lay down obediently like a sleepy child as the nurses placed several warmed blankets over her from her breasts down, keeping her wounded areas exposed.

Staring at the bright fluorescent lights in the ceiling above, all the events of the past weeks illuminated in her mind, flashing through her slowing consciousness. Visions of blood, seeping out of Michael's lifeless head, flowing out of his arm to wash over his body, kept interrupting her loving ruminations. She became consumed with fear and remorse, *Is this what I've done? Is this what we have ahead of us, a prelude for the rest of our lives? The price we have to pay for my convictions? And forbidden love? For this man I adore to suffer this way? Is this Godde's way of punishing me, by punishing him?*

"I don't want Prince Michael to see me in a hospital gown. Could you get my bags please?"

The nurse looked at her sympathetically, "You didn't come with any bags, Miss."

"Oh…I see." Far in her awakening mind she heard a ghostly roar of helicopters, *Wonder what happened to our luggage?*

The nurse looked at her with unabashed admiration, "Don't worry, stay lying down till I return, I'll get some clothes."

Returning with another nurse and clothes on a hanger, the older nurse helped Elizabeth to sit up, then slowly stand. They assisted her into a white silk shell, navy flared skirt, and her own recently cleaned shoes. The borrowed clothes fit quite well though the skirt's waist was loose. In a still dazed voice she asked, "Where did these clothes come from?"

"From our senior nurses, Bettina. You don't mind, do you?"

"No. This is so generous of her. I must thank her-"

The older nurse interrupted, "No need, Miss Elizabeth, she's very honored to have you wear them, after what you did, saving Prince Michael's life. You're everybody's heroine."

Brian was waiting outside the door with two royal bodyguards and two visibly heavily armed soldiers.

Elizabeth's worried look mirroring his she asked anxiously, "What's the latest on Michael?"

He responded glumly, "A nurse just came out from the Operating Room to say the surgery's almost over, the doctors will be out after to give us a full report. This part of the hospital's been cordoned off, there's a private waiting room for us down this hall, let me hold your hand and escort you there."

She was calmly defiant, "No. I'm going to wait outside the Operating Room," and started walking in the opposite direction.

Brian sighed loudly, not in frustration at her stubbornness but in relief, that was exactly his wish. Taking her by the elbow of her undamaged hand, he escorted her down the corridor to the Operating Room, and sat them both opposite its doors on two chairs a royal bodyguard hastily commandeered from another room. Supporting her sutured bandaged arm in her lap with her other hand, she observed Jenkins, Eric, and some royal bodyguards standing with their backs to them, immediately outside the closed doors of the Operating Room.

Jenkins was speaking with uncharacteristic animation to, judging from his abundantly decorated uniform and affectedly erect bearing, a high-ranking military officer.

Looking around, fear and foreboding refilled the largest part of her psyche as she studied the eight strange military guards who stood on either side of the Surgery doors, with ten more at each end of the corridor. They were in full battledress, complete with black Kevlar helmets and automatic assault rifles held at the ready. A small pistol and two magazines of ammunition sat in shoulder holsters on opposite sides of their chests, Gerber knives and radio phones attached to their belts. She shuddered, *Good Godde! They look like they're ready for war!*

Her fearful thoughts of violence and death lost precedence to the health and life of Michael as the doors slammed open, three doctors with two nurses entering the hallway.

Elizabeth and Brian immediately jumped up and joined them, the head surgeon already speaking to Jenkins. Jenkins quickly suggested they all go to the private waiting room that was assigned to them to get the doctor's full report.

"Please sit down everyone." The Chief Surgeon motioned to chairs around an oval shaped coffee table on which someone had thoughtfully placed a vase of multicolored flowers alongside a tray with a jug of water and glasses, in an effort to bring warmth and cheer to the cold sterile room; and perhaps the news to come. The otherwise starkness of the room was overridden by the fullness of it with tension and fear.

Accustomed to always being the most powerful person in a hospital room, but well aware of the prestige of his patient and now before him his frightened royal entourage, the young surgeon spoke with a certain degree of deference, though authoritatively and straightforwardly. He decided to spare no detail but be as positive as possible, "Prince Michael was very lucky."

Elizabeth was taken aback by his incongruous opening remark, *Lucky! With what I've caused to happen to him! You call that lucky!* Immense guilt came rushing back, which she struggled to ignore, so she could concentrate on the surgeon's report.

"We've checked His Royal Highness thoroughly with all the necessary X-rays, Cat-scans, M.R.I.'s etcetera. Emergency surgeries performed on him were as a result of our findings. He sustained damage from two gunshots, one to the left side of his head, one to his upper left arm. We can't be certain as no bullets were lodged, none embedded, but we suspect the weapons were revolvers of some sort as the wounds were quite clean, that's to say not spread out, although in the case of his head, that could be because, thankfully, that assassin was not a very good shot. The forensic department of the police will determine the type of guns from their examination of his car, but that information is not important to his healing. Fortunately, the bullet that hit his head did not penetrate his skull, though it did skim off a small fraction of bone, but that should cause no future problem. Not unless," the surgeon paused, forcing the smile he felt internally to show respectfully as only a slight softening of his serious expression, "Prince Michael decides to take up the skin-head fashion. Because he will have a tiny dent and scar. The cut in his scalp is approximately two inches long, slightly jagged, but he's young, has good skin, it should heal nicely. The dent and scar will be completely hidden when his hair grows back. Of course, the area had to be shaved around the wound for surgery. He has an egg-sized lump at the back of his head, presumably from falling back and hitting the metal on the car door when he was shot. Between that blow and the bullet to his head he suffered a concussion, which has become a coma. This is always a concern. He may take days or even weeks to recover full consciousness. But fortunately, there is no apparent bruising of the brain, no internal bleeding of any kind." The Chief surgeon looked at the other surgeon, "Why don't you explain your part?"

The younger surgeon nodded and spoke with a trifle more emotion than the Chief, "His upper left arm's my concern. The bullet went through the back and out the front. It missed bone but tore through the outer layer of the triceps muscle, I had to repair the muscle and surrounding tissues. After healing, he'll need therapy to avoid atrophy and ensure the return of full mobility and strength. But we don't anticipate any permanent damage. There should be no lasting effect on future activity, providing he's consistent with his exercises. Though the paramedics pressure bandages did help, he still lost a lot of blood. Unfortunately, because we were instructed by Royal Orders he was not to receive blood transfusions from what we had available, he'll be weak for a time while rebuilding lost blood. That'll be helped with diet, lots of protein, various vitamins, iron shots. You'll be given a list of our recommendations," he looked at the Chief, "that's all I have for now."

The Chief reclaimed his position of superiority and continued in his calm voice, "He has a large bruise on one leg in the lower calf area just above the ankle, from some sort of blunt force severe blow, but no broken skin or bone. It'll take a couple weeks for the blood to dissipate but there'll be no permanent damage." Elizabeth felt a sharp jab on her own calf in remembrance, *that's where I kicked him! I'll have to explain later.* "We'd like to keep him here at least until he recovers from the coma. But we understand you're making arrangements to take him to City Hospital to be nearer to Royal doctors and his family. We advise against moving him for the next few days until we see how well he's progressing. Any questions?"

No one spoke, everyone slowly processing the information, still in shock, feeling helpless and ineffectual.

Understanding their silence, the Chief turned to Elizabeth and asked softly, "I presume you're Elizabeth?"

Suddenly happy to be of some kind of use, the entire royal group chorused, "Yes!"

The Chief allowed himself a half-smile, "Prince Michael's mumbled your name several times. We've found it helps the unconscious to recover faster if loved ones try to communicate with them, talk, even sing, as if they're awake. We're still unsure how much penetrates, if anything even does, but it can hasten the healing process. I'd like to take you to the Intensive Care Unit so you can try it," his eyes made a rapid examination of the still beautiful woman's battered condition, "are you up to that?"

Elizabeth stood up immediately, "Let's go."

Before leaving the room, the Chief quickly surveyed the nervous faces of the men now standing, and said with a hint of acerbity and condemnation, "You people need to take better care while guarding him. He's our best chance for bringing some stability to this crazy world we live in."

Walking to the ICU, the Chief started instructing Elizabeth on how to speak to Michael when she interrupted him, "Don't worry, I know what to say. Can I touch him?"

The doctor suddenly looked embarrassed, "Er, where?"

It was Elizabeth's turn to be embarrassed, and confused at his embarrassment, *What else did Michael say?* But she continued seriously, "Anywhere that won't hurt."

He looked even more embarrassed at his previous embarrassment as he punched in a security code and opened the ICU door to let her in, "Oh? Yes, of course. I'll leave you here. The nurses will be around but I've instructed them to be respectful of your privacy. I'll be in periodically, and I'm always a phone call away."

Approaching the formidable contraption that housed Michael with two nurses standing guard beside it, Elizabeth's heart constricted on seeing the moribundly immobile figure that was imprisoned in the bed with bars on either side and strapped to endless wires and tubes.

Not reflecting her dignified calm demeanor, her mind became hysterical, *Oh Godde! The doctors are lying! Trying to give us hope! I see it! He's dying!* Michael's elated voice of just hours ago resounded in her ears, "*If I would die today I would die the happiest man on earth!*" The constriction in her heart raced to her throat as she struggled to keep herself from fainting.

Sprinting forward, she gently held his right hand, carefully avoiding the life-support systems of needles, tubes and wires, and spoke near the ear that was not covered by the bandages surrounding his head, "Michael my darling, I'm here with you, now and forever. I love you. I need you. I can't live without you. Please stay with me. Don't leave me. You have so much to live for my love. All your dreams to be fulfilled. Fight hard my darling. The doctors say you're going to heal perfectly. You'll always be perfection to me. My perfect love."

The hope she harbored that her voice and words would affect him and he would exhibit some kind of reaction was dashed as he lay deathly still. No longer able to contain her fears and sorrow, she lost control of the tears she had been intentionally damming; they came rushing forth in a torrent.

Jenkins, who had sneaked in quietly behind her and observed everything was filled with similar emotions, but his stoic persona would not allow public display of them. Grabbing a chair on seeing her knees buckling, he placed it next to her and helped her again trembling body to sit. Still holding Michael's hand, she rested her head next to his torso. Aware of Jenkins' and the nurses' watchfulness, hearing an echo of Aunt Claire's prophetic warning admonition, *"Pull yourself together girl…someone in your position can't afford to fall apart…you're going to have to deal with a lot more serious situations in your life ahead…"* she forced herself to cease weeping.

CHAPTER
33

"Elizabeth?" his voice so soft, she lifted her head and looked up at his face to make sure he had really spoken. "You need to eat. Let me take you to the cafeteria-"

She eyed him disconsolately, "No thanks Jenkins, I can't eat…can't leave him. I want him to feel me always with him."

He half-knelt beside her, knowing there was one sure way he could appeal to her to use commonsense, "You haven't eaten since yesterday. You've got to keep up your strength, if only for Michael. You're no good to him if you weaken and get sick. Now come along. The nurses will call us if there's any change."

Reluctantly, she rose with his assistance, and with a long frightened look at Michael, walked out the door. Passing the empty waiting room, she grabbed Jenkins by an arm and pulled him into it. Her face twisting with fear and despair she cried, "Jenkins, the doctors are lying to us! Michael looks terrible! All those tubes…wires…things… attached to him! It looks like he's dying!" She began to tremble again. Her eyes widened as if in a sudden confirmed revelation, "Oh Godde, Jenkins, he *is* dying!"

Jenkins could see she was bordering on hysteria, tried to get her to sit down but she refused, pushing his hands away, and he thought it best to exhibit calm and patience, "Elizabeth, the doctors can't lie to us. They have to tell the truth. Michael *will* recover. It's going to take time and he'll go through some difficulties, but he'll recover." Taking a breath, he hoped he sounded more convincing than he felt. "As for all those tubes and wires attaching him to the different equipment, they're just typical normal life-support for someone in his condition who's had surgery. They're simply there to help him get through… this rough patch, his unconscious state. Haven't you seen someone in a hospital who's had surgery before?"

Unconvinced, she argued, "My uncle Robert had surgery for his sinuses, but he didn't have anything looking like Michael has!" Hands shaking, she raised her voice even louder exclaiming her disbelief in his assurance, "He's dying I tell you!"

Realizing the shock of everything was now rising from where she had buried it in her psyche, Jenkins held both her hands in his and continued to try to reassure her, and him, that Michael will eventually be alright. But she interrupted him shaking her head, her eyes widening again, "It's all my fault! I'm to blame for what happened to Michael! They meant to kill *me*! Not him!"

Jenkins was astounded by this outburst, "What? What are you talking about Elizabeth?"

She grasped the lapels of his jacket, "Don't you see? It's *me* they're after! Because of my lectures, 'God Has No Gender!' The crazy religious fanatics! The ones calling themselves 'the far right! That I call 'the far wrong!'

Jenkins was beginning to lose his patience and shook her hands hard with only a small degree of restraint, "Elizabeth that's nonsense. Listen to me-"

Shaking her head vigorously in obstinate disagreement, her eyes rolling upwards to show more white than normal, she cried out hysterically, "*I* did this to Michael! *I* should be suffering! Not Michael! My precious love! I should be the one to die!"

Seeing her hysterical condition escalating he thought he had no choice but to do something radical. As slapping her injured face was not an option he swiftly took her by the shoulders and shook her violently several times, her head jerking back and forth, saliva flying out of her shocked open mouth. When he stopped she stared at him, aghast at not just the shaking but at the normally controlled and restrained person who had done it. He looked at her embarrassed, but relieved to see she had regained a semblance of calm. Holding her hands again he spoke with little visible emotion, "Sorry, I hope that didn't hurt but I needed you to control yourself and listen carefully to what I have to say. Sit here." Still alarmed by Jenkins' actions, she mutely dropped into the chair he held out for her, and sought to retrieve her dignity as he watched her austerely. Pulling a chair to face her he sat heavily, his shoulders hunched wearily, the weight of the tragic event bearing down on him as a contemplative expression wiped away his austerity.

Eventually sucking in a deep breath, he began to speak, "Elizabeth, what I'm about to tell you is highly classified information. As you know, Michael's been involved in top secret negotiations in the West Country. It's nothing to do with a proposed strike as has been rumored, but something a lot more serious with far-reaching consequences. There's a powerful group over there who have for many years been pushing for secession from the rest of the country, which would lead to civil unrest and chaos. Affecting not only this country but the whole region, probably the world." Shifting in his seat he breathed deep again as he sorted through his thoughts to be able to speak them in as concise a manner as possible, though honestly, but with only the most necessary details. Knowing Michael's plans for her and their future, he knew she should no longer be kept in ignorance of what it will involve, "The subversive group became clandestine, for a while went underground, primarily due to lack of financial support for their cause. Unfortunately, in recent months they started getting funding from foreign terrorist organizations. This has given them the ability, and courage, to resume and expand their disruptive activities and increase their…forces. Government has sent their top people to

PATRICIA D'ARCY LAUGHLIN

negotiate to try to resolve the conflict, even King Alexander has tried, but they won't talk to anyone but Michael. He's the only one whose opinions they respect. There was a coup in their leadership recently and it was taken over by more intelligent reasonable men, who were willing to sit down and negotiate a settlement, with a promise to cease all violence. That was who Michael met with, and, got an agreement from them to stop all terrorist activities, providing certain provisions were taken and conditions met. The details of which doesn't concern you…at least not at this time. Unfortunately, there's still a small faction that disagrees with the new leadership's agendas and their willingness to settle the conflict, and who keep fighting for control of the group. Michael's efforts for bringing a peaceful resolution to the situation has antagonized this faction. They are the ones who tried to assassinate him. This time, and when he was stabbed before."

Jenkins took another deep breath hoping his uncertainty was concealed as he continued with reassurances, "The people who made those threats the day of your speech have been rounded up. They were just a minor independent group of extremist religious fanatics, not connected to the conflict. Do you understand now that you are not responsible for the attack on him, that it had nothing to do with you whatsoever?"

Elizabeth was dumbfounded. Shocked at this information, to learn what happened to Michael was not her fault but that of secessionists and terrorists, she didn't know if to feel relieved or further terrified.

Sensing her thoughts, Jenkins sought to further reassure her, "Don't worry, the assa…would-be assassins, have already been handed over to the police by the honorable new leadership of their group," he closed his eyes for an instant and upon opening them stared at her, his austerity returning; but taking her hands in his he spoke with a certain sadness, "Elizabeth, I've devoted the better part of my life to Michael. To his safety, comforts, and when it's in my power, even to his happiness. But, there are times that things are taken out of my hands. Michael's his own man now. He must take responsibility for the risk he took in ignoring Brian's advice and driving in an unchecked area with the top down, causing him to be recognized. We who are responsible for his security will always do everything possible to keep him safe, but in his position, and with his strong-willed passionate personality, there will always be an element of danger. This is something you'll certainly have to face, and deal with. If you think you're incapable of handling it for the rest of your life, if it's beyond your scope of courage, as soon as Michael is well enough, you must tell him. And, get out of his life. Never see him again. Because your position can change, but his never can."

Elizabeth's composure had returned accompanied by growing anger as she took umbrage at his last remarks; but she quelled her first instinct to lash out at him and instead thought it judicious to defend her integrity and grit. She removed her hands from his and straightening her back, sat up exuding strength and pride, "So, is this what you think of me? That I'm a simple weakling who'll run away at the first sign of trouble? And how could you be so heartless to judge me as a coward when we see Michael's condition and have every reason to believe he's dying? Making me feel I'm going to lose him forever? And on top of that, I thought it was *my* fault! And what caused you to have such a low opinion of me, you don't really know me. Does this mean you have no respect for Michael's judge of character-"

Jenkins blanched, reached for her hand and opened his mouth to speak, intending a defensive apology with a clarification of what he really meant. But Elizabeth would have none of it, pulled her hand out of his grasp, and signaled for him to not speak, "You haven't a clue as to what my experiences in life have been. What I've had to endure, what I'm capable of, what's my *"scope of courage."* How dare you extrapolate about me based on what has occurred with Michael, deducing I'm some weak coward who is easily defeated and can't stand up to whatever adversities may come my, our, way, Michael's and mine. It appears you've never been in love, to know the feeling of total abandonment of oneself for another. Well I have. I love Michael. I'll do whatever I have to, to be with him. I'll face everything he has to face with bravery and undying devotion. Never doubt that everything I do is in his best interest. And right now, my whole focus is to make him well again. Now, excuse me." She stood up haughtily, brushed aside his outstretched hand as he tried to stop her, and strode to the door.

Jenkins caught her as she opened it and pulled her by an arm back into the room, slamming the door shut again, his tone apologetic, "Elizabeth, you misunderstood me, what I was trying to say. I just wanted to make sure that you know what living with...being married, to Michael, is going to be like. That it's not always going to be a smooth ride, there will be rough spots, perhaps many, despite all the wealth, and attention, and...love. I want you to be fully aware of what you're in for. Though we can take comfort in the fact that Michael, his family, and the Government, are bending every rule to ensure a lasting peace, it could be awhile before things settle down-"

A nervous edge entered her voice, "What do you mean, "*bending every rule?*" I can't believe the royal family would do anything illegal-"

Jenkins was too quick to come to their defense, "No, not at all. But they are having to use their wealth, in some instances...to convince... certain people-"

Alarm saturated her speech, "You mean *bribe* terrorists? That could eat up their whole fortune-"

Jenkins again defended his adopted family, "That won't happen. They are too smart. In any case, sorry, I don't mean to blaspheme, but they have more money than God."

A softening but not quite a smile appeared at her mouth, "You're not blaspheming, I've heard people say that about my aunt and uncle my whole life. Look, I appreciate your concerns about me, and Michael, but you mustn't worry, our love will see us through anything the world may throw at us. Let's hurry and go eat something so we can get back to Michael."

Jenkins could no longer keep up his disguise, his stoic face wrinkled to reveal his mental age, every crease deepening into crevices, revealing untold years of hidden anxiety.

For the first time ever, Elizabeth witnessed a distracted and uncool Jenkins, his stalwart demeanor heated to a pitiful meltdown, and she knew it was not as a result of her defensive abrasiveness, but because he was as afraid as she. Seeing his distressful expression, internally feeling the same, she held out both hands to him in a peace offering. Wordlessly, he walked into her arms, and they held on to each other, both allaying their multiple emotions, murmuring simply, "Sorry. So sorry."

The longest Elizabeth left Michael was to run up to the hospital's roof for fifteen minutes to make her daily calls on her phone, it being the only private location where it worked for overseas calls. Her computer and belongings had also been retrieved from Michael's wrecked car intact, and she was able to talk and correspond with her family and offices, but told them nothing about the latest tragedy she was enduring.

Her first call was to Miami. Years ago a cousin introduced her to Stella, a bioenergetic healer who becomes a translator for an individual's energy and with help from revolutionary technology, can usually connect to that person's physical and emotional condition and needs, no matter where they are.

Elizabeth and some family members had benefited from this marvelous gift on occasion, but she had had no serious reason to call on Stella's rare skills in recent times. With the teachings Stella had imparted to her she had been able to handle the little maladies that had touched her life, and had decided that she would no longer need to bother Stella, unless a desperate situation came up. There was no situation more desperate than this. She breathed with relief on hearing Stella's soft sweet Latin voice. Explaining the condition of her "*special friend*" in great detail, Elizabeth said nothing about her own.

Stella instructed her on things she should do to help Michael recover faster and completely, said she had already started an energy treatment on him, and she would overnight-mail all the vitamins, supplements, salves, and crystals he needed, to the address Elizabeth gave her, adding, "I'm sending you an excellent healing gel for your skin. It works miracles."

"My skin?" Elizabeth was only a little surprised. This was not the first time Stella knew something before she was told.

"Si. Follow directions, it'll heal quickly with no scars."

On her way back down from the roof she opened the stairwell door on Michael's floor just a crack, when she saw and overheard the younger surgeon speaking to Jenkins and Eric, "You know we did everything possible, but he had sustained too many gunshot wounds, we could not get to them all, I'm truly sorry for your loss, but we did our best."

Her heart stopped. Her breathing stopped. She felt like her very soul was trying to take flight from her body.

As she grabbed a handrail to stop herself from falling, she heard Jenkins say calmly, "Thank you, we knew it was a long shot, oh, I didn't mean to pun, I mean we knew how badly he was shot up. It's going to be difficult to tell Tommy's parents, he was their only son. Hopefully it will ease their pain a bit to know he died heroically saving the life of his beloved prince."

With her focus having been totally on Michael, no one had thought to tell her that Tommy also had been shot. She sat on a step, breathed again, and said a silent prayer of thanks to Tommy. To his generous, sacrificial, noble soul.

Elizabeth watched the nurses closely, paying attention to the gentle and meticulous care they took of Michael, especially how they sponge-bathed, shaved, and massaged him, and turned him onto his undamaged side from time to time. Certainly, she had some rudimentary knowledge of how to care for the sick from the odd occasion she had to look after an ailing child, but the detailed attention the comatose Michael needed was quite a revelation. The first time they sponged his genitals, despite his unconscious condition, he had an erection.

The youngest nurse jumped back and, looking at Elizabeth, giggled, "Ooo, Miss Elizabeth, you are a really lucky lady. Prince Michael is very well endowed."

Elizabeth glared at her cuttingly and said primly, "We don't have that kind of relationship. We've only just met."

The head nurse that everyone referred to as Matron Bertha, cast an even more cutting glance at the now chastened young nurse, and ordered her to leave the room.

Matron Bertha was Jenkins's age, fifty-two, a buxom, robust woman of Germanic origin, with a personality to match. All the hospital staff, doctors included, had great respect for her, perhaps combined with a touch of fear. It was evident this was not only due to her conscientiousness and admirable competence, but also to her intolerance of anyone possessing standards she considered lower than hers. She would make known her opinion of such a person to everyone by her 'no-nonsense' remarks and attitude, and pity the poor fool who would be on the receiving end of her wrath. In contrast to this demanding and often harsh persona, she was attractive to look at, but rather than call her pretty, although there was an undeniable sensual femininity about her, one would quicker describe her as 'handsome.'

After the disciplined nurse left the room Elizabeth stepped into the spot she vacated, looked steadily at Matron and said commandingly, "From now on, *I* will assist you and the senior nurse in attending to him, no one else." Matron glared at her like a ferocious guard-dog, not wanting to relinquish one iota of control over her Royal patient to this, '*Upstart novice.*' Unintimidated, Elizabeth glared right back with even more ferocity, "I'm not budging on this, so don't cross me." After that minor confrontation, Matron, having correctly evaluated the 'kind of relationship' existing between the lovers and observing Elizabeth's skills and her devotion to him, yielded to whatever she requested and occasionally demanded.

Two full days passed since the shooting and Michael still had not regained consciousness. The doctors assured the royal group that even though he was still critical, he was stable with all the normal signs of a sure recovery. Looking at the pallor on the thinning figure, lying motionless for most of the time, in his electronic cage, Elizabeth was still filled with dubiousity, but fortitudinously continued to hope, and pray.

The King, Anne, Susan, and John, had arrived the afternoon before, and joined Elizabeth, Jenkins, Brian, and Eric, in a loving vigil, everyone taking turns to communicate with Michael.

Elizabeth alternated between talking and singing, *His mother taught him to sing so beautifully, he said they "sang a lot." She'll help me bring him back.*

She spent most of the time in a chair at his bedside, often caressing his undamaged arm and hand. The few times they were left alone she would kiss him, in-between praying aloud to every deity and deceased family member to help heal him.

Once, when she was singing 'I Have A Dream,' she felt a soft squeeze from his hand, the King walking in from the restroom at the same time. She stopped singing and called his name, but got no further response. Then, telling the King what just occurred, she encouraged His Majesty to hold Michael's hand and talk to him. No sooner the King started speaking Michael shifted his legs, and, breathing on his own since yesterday and therefore unencumbered with oxygen paraphernalia, turned his head slightly, seeming to want to cock his unbandaged ear towards his father's voice. As though the effort exhausted him, he emitted a small sound that was neither sigh nor moan, and became still again. In the hours following his feeble actions, everyone stayed close, each taking turns talking to him hoping to get a reaction; but other than the normal reflex actions of a deep sleeping human, there were none.

At nine o'clock that night Matron Bertha informed everyone that it was time to let Prince Michael rest for the night and they needed to do the same, adding that she would call them if he should "do anything." With raised eyebrows at what they considered to be her ludicrous statement, that the prince with days of just lying down doing nothing needed to "*rest*," the group still filed out obediently, not wanting to risk antagonizing 'the Sergeant Major,' muttering their protests inaudibly. Elizabeth as usual did what she felt was best for Michael and stayed seated in the recliner beside his bed, in which she had unsuccessfully attempted sleeping the last two nights. Matron placed a large hand on her shoulder, "You too, Miss. I've had the bed behind the curtain made up for you. If you want to help him when he wakes, go sleep."

Too exhausted to put up a fight Elizabeth gave in, kissed Michael, and stepped behind the privacy curtain that separated his bed from the other one in the room which had been deliberately kept empty.

Hoisting herself up onto the ICU bed, she thought she would lie down for just a short while, and immediately sank into a fitful sleep. Entering a dream state, she saw Michael and herself flying at incredible speeds over the Caribbean islands, their arms and legs outstretched, alternately laughing and crying repetitively as they kept trying to grab each other's hands. When they were eventually successful in connecting, a ghostly figure flew in and struck their hands apart, separating them. Michael was whisked away by a strong gust of wind and she heard him cry out her name, "Elizabeth! Elizabeth!"

Shivering as she awakened hearing Michael's far away voice calling her name, she realized she was no longer dreaming, or sleeping. Jumping off the bed she ran to him, "I'm here, darling, I'm here."

Weakened eyes squinting in the darkened room, illuminated only by screen monitors behind the bed and numerous tiny dots of yellow, white, green and red lights from the medical equipment, he spoke in a hoarse, bewildered voice, as he saw her shadowy figure approach him, "Elizabeth…what happened…where am I?"

Keeping her face in the shadows, she picked up his hand with her unbandaged one, "You were shot darling, when we were passing through a village. You're in a country hospital. You've been unconscious for three days," looking around dazedly, Michael began to shift his body, "you've had surgery on your head and left arm so don't move around."

Alarm entered his raspy voice as he squinted at her, "Oh my God! Are *you* alright?"

Forcing a smile into her voice, she backed her head further away from his line of vision, "Yes, I'm fine."

He sighed and she could hear his relief, "Thank God."

CHAPTER
34

Having seen activity coming from Michael on her monitor at the nurse's station, Matron Bertha came bustling in accompanied by the younger surgeon, the senior nurse and Jenkins following closely on their heels. Elizabeth saw Matron reach out to flick on the overhead light switch and immediately turned away from Michael. As the others converged at his bed, she took advantage of the opportunity to steal away and duck behind the curtain.

After much fussing over and thorough examination of Michael and all the equipment he was connected to, the others stood around anxiously as the young surgeon asked him a barrage of questions while checking his reflexes. The Chief Surgeon came rushing in, having just finished delivering a baby girl mere minutes ago, and repeated the whole procedure all over again.

Michael having answered all questions correctly as to his name, birth date, status, royal position, and other mundane things, the doctors were finally pleased, and relieved. They left with Jenkins and headed to the King's room, leaving Matron and the senior nurse to continue attending to him.

Michael gave Matron a squinty questioning look, "Where's Elizabeth?"

Listening absorbedly the entire time she had sequestered herself behind the curtain, Elizabeth called out, "I'm right here darling. I thought it best to get out of the way so the doctors could examine you."

"They're gone. Come here. I need you with me."

"Um…as soon as the nurses leave…and turn off the bright lights…I'll be out."

"What? What's wrong with bright lights?" he asked puzzled, squinting at Matron Bertha.

Matron shook her head and directed an order towards the curtain, "You might as well get it over with, Miss. Come!"

Elizabeth walked out slowly toward him. On seeing the grotesque face of a stranger on an adored familiar body, Michael unbelievably paled further and cried out, "My God! Come here!"

He sat up, reached for her right hand, saw her bandaged forearm and screeched, "Holy Jesus!" grabbed her other hand and pulled her down to sit on the bed.

Wagging a finger at him Matron spoke sternly, "Now see here Mr. Prince, you don't go moving around and mess up your royal self you hear? Lie down until the doctor says you can get up!"

He quickly lay back down like a corrected child, not just because of the surprise at being spoken to in such an impertinent manner by the big bossy woman in white, but because of the painful throbbing that had developed in his head. Elizabeth stroked his good arm, "I'm alright darling. It looks a lot worse than it is."

Squinting again he looked closely at her face, "How did this happen? And why is your arm bandaged?"

Matron, looking at the heart, pulse, and blood pressure monitors, scolded him again, "Look here, Mr. Prince, you just calm your royal self, you hear. She's going to be fine. She only took seven stitches when they pulled the glass out of her forearm, and the little scratches on her face and body will soon heal, the swelling will go down in no time. She'll just have to keep applying scar healing gel and she'll soon be her old beautiful self. *You,* on the other hand, will need to discipline yourself a lot better. You have a longer road to recovery ahead of you!" Again wagging her finger in his face parentally, she turned to the door and motioned to the senior nurse that they should leave the young lovers alone for a while.

Michael immediately pulled Elizabeth closer to him, "Darling, I'm so sorry I failed to protect you. I promise I'll never put you in harm's way again-"

She put a finger to his lips, "Hush darling, you can't control everything that happens. I don't want you to start worrying about me or anything else. It's all going to be alright. Your focus has to be on getting well."

Michael caressed her undamaged hand limply with his own undamaged hand, told her how much he loved her, again how sorry he was that she got hurt, and then asked for details of what happened. Not wishing to upset him further, she gave him an abridgment of what had occurred, glossing it over as creatively as she could. She felt the horrifying details had to wait until he was stronger and could handle them, the last of which would be Tommy's heroic death while trying to save Michael's life.

Taking into account the King's fragile looking condition, it had been decided not to awaken him to inform him that Michael had regained consciousness. It was felt by all that His Majesty himself was in dire need of a good rest.

Walking into Michael's room after waking on his own, seeing him talking and holding Elizabeth's hand, the King almost collapsed on the bed beside Michael. Tears sprang to his eyes while he kissed his son's forehead. Unable to speak, he simply held the hand Elizabeth released and handed over to him, continuously bathing it with kisses and tears of joy and relief.

Eventually, after speaking with him briefly and noticing Michael becoming fatigued, the King, knowing of the great love between the two young people, left him with Elizabeth as she began to sing and hum softly about being "*in the arms of the angels.*" Michael slipped into a deep, healing sleep.

He slept soundly for over three hours, hardly moving, worrying Elizabeth and the King to the point of them wanting to waken him again. The doctors assured them this was normal, even a good thing, so they left him with Matron, Jenkins, and Anne, in order to have brunch together. His Majesty was profusely gratulant towards Elizabeth throughout the meal for saving Michael's life by, "driving like the devil while injured to get him to the helicopters and medical attention," her subsequent competence in handling the terrifying extraordinary circumstances, and her devotional care of him.

She accepted his gratitude and accolades for her strengths and bravery with total humility, modestly telling him her reason for doing what she did was completely selfish, because if Michael died, she would not be able to go on living without him.

Whereupon the King looked steadily at her, the genuineness in his eyes reflecting in his voice, "Elizabeth, Michael has assured me several times that you are the love of his life and the perfect woman to be his Queen. Now that I've gotten to know you, your mettle, and your love for him, I'm convinced of it. You two have my blessing. I know you'll make each other happy, regardless of what lies ahead."

When Michael awakened again, despite the copious remonstrations of the nurses, he insisted Elizabeth lie next to him on his undamaged side, saying he needed her body next to his for comfort and support. Although cautiously positioning her body next to his on the narrow hospital bed was anything but comfortable for her, she ignored the nurses and did as he asked. She was willing to do anything he wanted, anything to please and heal him. Interestingly, the doctors didn't agree with the nurses that Michael should be denied his "endangering demands," as they put it when they appealed to them that they "should not allow His Highness to further risk his recovery."

The male doctors totally relating to the prince's feelings, with an understanding smile, told the beleaguered nurses they saw no harm in it as long as the prince said he was comfortable and his health remained stable. Making a show of throwing their hands up in the air with frustration the nurses left the room, knowing full well in his debilitated condition His Highness was in no way capable of getting into any serious "trouble."

Alone again, relishing Elizabeth against him, Michael immediately had an erection and whispered in her ear, "I can't wait to get out of here. I want to make love to you so badly and this hard-on I'm nursing is really painful."

She sat up, "I'm sorry darling, but you need to put those thoughts aside for now or the pain won't go away, I'm sure it has something to do with the catheter tube-"

Michael sat up with a jolt, "What? Tube? Catheter?" He hastily pushed his cover sheet down and was alarmed to see that his now engorged penis was attached to a long tube sticking out of its hole, which in turn was attached to a plastic bag that was quarter full of his urine and hanging on a pole beside the bed. Agitation took over his dismay, "Take it off! Take it off!"

Elizabeth leapt off the bed, "I can't darling. You need it till you start being mobile-"

He raised his voice, "I'll be mobile in a heartbeat! Take it off, Elizabeth!"

She apologized sympathetically, "Sorry, I can't, darling. I don't know how, and I don't think it's supposed to-"

The volume of his voice grew with his frustration, "Call the nurse! Now! Please!"

Before Elizabeth had time to reach for the call button the always watchful Matron Bertha came bustling in, "What's going on in here? What's this commotion all about?"

Michael gestured towards his genitalia, "Take this damn thing off me! Right now!"

Matron, planting her powerful hands on her ample hips, her legs apart, her stance purposely intimidating, said defiantly, "No! Not until the doctor orders it, Mr. Prince! You're not the one in charge here, he is!"

Seeing the substantial and lively erection on this young man who just the day before was at death's door, and observing him holding Elizabeth's hand in a tight squeeze, Matron felt it her responsibility to set these two young people straight, "Now, listen here, you two. I can see what you're thinking, Mr. Prince, but it's not going to happen, not while you're in my care! That thing is going to need a good... two weeks...rest, after what it's...you...been through. Or you can do yourself some real damage that's going to have you on dry-dock for a lot longer than you can handle!"

Covering him with the sheet she glared at Elizabeth like a disgusted Reverend Mother, "And as for you, young lady, you should know better! You keep your hands off him or you'll *both* be sorry! You two should be ashamed, disrespecting my hospital this way!" With that final blistering salvo, she stormed out of the room mumbling, not quite under her breath, "Stupid children. Spoilt brats. No thinking. No control."

Elizabeth and Michael, taken aback at the frank and fearsome reproach from the imposing authoritative Germanic battle-axe, looked at each other wide-eyed, first with shock, then amusement. Both recollecting the infamous episode of the American television comedy series grasped each other's hands and said simultaneously, "Seinfeld! Nurse Nazi!" and doubled over laughing, almost to hysteria.

Jenkins walked in smiling, "You'd better share the joke, we sure could do with some laughs around here for a change."

In between hiccups of laughter, they, mostly Michael, told Jenkins what just happened. Elizabeth looked away uncomfortably as Michael asked Jenkins, "Do you think she's right, about the...abstinence...thing?"

Jenkins responded with the same amount of discomfiture that Elizabeth felt, "I really don't know, but with what little I know of 'Nurse Nazi,' I assume there's some truth to it."

Noticing affectionate amusement in his voice as he spoke of her, Elizabeth suspected there was a lot more to what Jenkins actually knew and thought of Matron, but put it aside in her mind as she also noticed Michael again beginning to tire. Fluffing his pillows, she helped him to situate himself comfortably, then lay beside him singing softly till he fell asleep again. From then on the three of them clandestinely referred to Matron as 'Nurse Nazi,' and Elizabeth and Jenkins enjoyed the private teasing of calling the reluctantly amused Michael, 'Mr. Prince.'

Brian handed Elizabeth the certified package that arrived from Stella in Miami, then sat down to chat with a more alert Michael while she unwrapped it. Michael bombarded him with dozens of questions, insisting Brian bring him up-to-date on events pertaining to the aftermath of the assassination attempt. They no longer spoke in their usual code in front of Elizabeth. Everything about Michael's covert activities with the secessionists and terrorists, and the subsequent attempts on his life, was now out in the open, splashed across every television, newspaper, and radio, around the globe. But Tommy's death was not mentioned. There were numerous conflicting reports about "*the mysterious heroine who saved Prince Michael's life,*" one C.N.N. anchorwoman referring to her as "*the guardian-angel who 'flew' Prince Michael's car to save him from death.*"

Everyone joined in a guessing game theorizing as to what her connection was to him, and where she was from. Her 'origins' ranged from England, Wales, America, Australia, Germany, Scandinavia, South Africa, and Switzerland, all places she had been to, but none of which could truthfully claim her.

Reading Stella's instructions to Michael as she showed each item they pertained to, she sensed trepidation from him, "Darling, I know all this is new and sounds a bit far-fetched. But I assure you, I've proven Stella's methods and supplements usually work. You'll heal and get your strength back faster. So, you're going to have to trust me on this. Do you trust me?"

He hid his dubiousity with a smile, "Implicitly."

Just then, the two surgeons, another doctor and Matron, entered, and cast interested looks at the array of strange bottles, boxes, and tubes spread out on the sheet at the foot of Michael's bed. Because of Michael's royal position and the great responsibility imposed upon them to make him well again, at the risk of being ridiculed, and perhaps outright refusal of being allowed, Elizabeth had nonetheless planned to show and explain Stella's supplements to the medical staff. She prudently decided against describing Stella's credentials factually, instead referring to her as a "nutritionist healer."

The three doctors at first acted as if they were humoring her by taking turns to read all the ingredients on the various items she gave them, handing them afterwards to Matron to read also. They soon lost their cynical condescending smiles, agreeing that most of the supplements and remedies were appropriate for Michael's healing, although they found some dosages to be excessive and should be reduced.

Though they were not familiar with several of the brands, they observed the ingredients didn't include useless fillers like many off-the-shelf vitamins do. Most supplements and vitamins were recognizable and included Calcium/Magnesium, mega doses of B, C, E, and D, B12, Glucosamine Sulfate, MSM, Chondroitin Sulfate, Manganese, Iron, Ginkgo Biloba, Luten, Co Q-10, fish oils, and capsules and liquids with combinations of Antioxidants, and Minerals.

Unfamiliar with five supplements, they told Elizabeth Michael must not be given them while under their care, even though Matron assured she knew the questionable ingredients and, "They could be beneficial or at the very least, do no harm."

The doctors remained traditionally steadfast in their opinions, picked up the disagreeable bottles and handed them to Matron with instructions that she lock them away, and not give them to Elizabeth until the day she was leaving.

The Chief Surgeon bent to pick up the largest box on the bed Elizabeth had not shown them, but she was swifter than he, whisked it up, and stuck it under her arm, "That's mine. It's personal." It was a box of special crystals that reportedly had healing energies, and she knew there was no possibility this group would agree to what Stella instructed had to be done with them, she herself feeling some dubiety about it; but going on blind trust, intended to follow Stella's instructions to the letter, anyway. She was determined to do anything that might help to heal Michael quickly and completely.

Within minutes after the medical experts left the room Brian walked back in and handed her a key, "Don't know what's this about but Matron dropped this in front of me. When I tried to give it to her she insisted it was yours, and whispered you must leave it in her desk drawer at her station. Then she winked and said to tell you the nurses are having a coffee break in their lounge."

Before leaving to retrieve Stella's banned five supplements now locked in Matron's drawer, she told Michael this was proof she was right and therefore was going to disobey the doctors and rely on Stella's expertise instead.

Michael started to argue on the side of proven medical methods to which she replied, "These methods have also been proven. By people with more open minds. You said you trust me. Now prove it. Here are your first doses, unreduced."

Timorously, he took it all from her, he was too weak to continue arguing, his head and arm were fiercely paining him and all he wanted was sleep; so that he could escape from the whole unmanageable, unpredictable, unpleasant, mess.

Enlisting a reluctant Brian to help her covertly hang crystals over the door in Michael's room, over his bed, and from the ceiling in every corner of the room, she had to use even stronger powers of persuasion to convince him to lift Michael's mattress so that she could slip more crystals under certain prescribed areas. Despite having lost five pounds the heavily sleeping Michael was still no lightweight. After much groaning and grunting, mostly on Brian's part, they were completing their unusual and, according to Brian, "*weird and freaky*" task, when Michael woke up, "What the hell are you two doing?"

Both out of breath, they sat on the bed laughing at his alarmed expression, and the ridiculousness of how they must have looked lifting and bending under his mattress.

Elizabeth patiently explained the concept and theory about the crystals to them both, whereupon they proceeded to chide her and make jokes about her indulging in "*Trinidadian Voodoo.*"

She handled the raillery in good humor but hastened to show their ignorance in such matters, "We don't call it Voodoo in Trinidad we call it 'Obeah.' So if you need to burn me at the stake with your childish accusations at least get the name right, 'Obeah.' Anyway, fools, this is not Trinidadian, it's international scientifically proven and all you people are going to eat your words when you see how well it all works together."

Within two days, Elizabeth not letting Michael miss a single dose of supplements, everyone's words were more than just eaten, they were choking on their cynicism, sputtering and stuttering to see the incredibly rapid improvement in Michael's energy, color, attitude, and overall health. Even his wounds were healing faster than those types of wounds normally would, and the pains felt lessened, and, Elizabeth's skin seemed to be healing by the hour with Stella's 'miracle gel.' The younger surgeon started writing down notes about the supplements on Michael's chart, adding at the bottom of the page in parenthesis (Got to research this business about the energy of crystals!)

On seeing Michael's amazing rate of recovery, sensing Elizabeth's "*curative powers*" and Stella's remedies to be primarily responsible, the King felt comfortable enough to leave his heir in the competent hands of the medical staff, the guards, and his son's devoted wife-to-be, Elizabeth, and return to the palace to attend to pressing affairs of state. Susan and John, thinking similarly, also left to return to affairs of their estate.

The day they left, Elizabeth walked in on Brian telling Michael he had sneaked a peek when she was on her computer while Michael was asleep. He saw an e-mail from Gloria Goldman in which she was pressing Elizabeth as to how to respond to the offers she had been inundated with from various organizations in countries around the world, wanting Elizabeth to do her speech. Michael became agitated at this information, and when she approached his bed she saw his eyes becoming misty.

He grabbed her hand, "You can't now, darling. It's still too dangerous for you. Please don't put any more stress on me. Not yet. Wait awhile before you consider doing any more speeches. Please?"

His words were pleading but his tone demanding. She could see fearfulness magnifying because of his weakened condition and hastened to propitiate him, "Darling, don't worry about that. The only thing I care about now is getting you well."

He still wanted clarification, "Does that mean you're going to... postpone...doing more speeches, for a while?"

She smiled agreeably, "Yes, my darling, for a long while." *As soon as you are well, and our lives stabilize.*

Feeling his strength returning, Michael discussed with Elizabeth and Jenkins, the possibility of returning home sooner than the doctors would allow. Jenkins surprisingly invited Matron to join in the conversation. She disagreed with Michael's intentions saying it was premature to move him at this stage, seeing that he only just started taking longer walks that morning and needed to build up his strength some more.

Michael was adamant that he was ready and ordered Jenkins to get it arranged, "Put a hospital bed in my room, whatever else I'll need, but I'm leaving this place in two days, discharged or not!"

Understanding his frustration at the vulnerability that had been foisted upon him and now not being in control of his own life, both Elizabeth and Jenkins were sympathetic, but despite his rapid healing, they were still a little afraid. Knowing how headstrong Michael could be, they worried that once out of the cautious and regimented rules of the hospital and its staff, he would rush into a normal routine and end up harming himself permanently. Jenkins argued that he agreed with the medical staff that it was too soon to consider going straight home instead of to the City Hospital as had been originally planned.

Pretending to look pensive while Michael kept arguing his case, Jenkins suddenly looked up, "Alright, Mr. Prince. I'll make the arrangements for you to finish your recuperation at the palace, but only on one condition."

Michael perked up even though he suspected he was being manipulated, "What's the condition?"

Jenkins smiled looking over at her, "Matron comes with us."

Seeing a guarded look of disappointment cloud his excited face, Elizabeth piped up enthusiastically, "That's an excellent idea. You'll need to have nurses around until-"

Michael practically groaned at the prospect of being bossed around by Nurse Nazi in his own home and interrupted Elizabeth pleadingly, "But I thought *you* could be my nurse, you seem to know as much as they do-"

She was apologetically compassionate, "Darling, I'm not properly qualified. You need a medical professional until you're on a permanent road to recovery. There're certain things that I'm not legally allowed to do…administer. Matron coming with us would be the perfect solution to get the doctors to discharge you sooner without creating a fuss."

Knowing the competent nurses that were on staff at the palace, Elizabeth was certain with their assistance she could look after Michael, but she doubted the gentle women had Matron's toughness and ability to control and even necessarily subjugate, the still healing but headstrong Michael, the way Nurse Nazi could.

Additionally, Elizabeth felt it would be very difficult for her personally to deny his concupiscence if they were too much alone, hers seeming to match his as it is; and if Matron's warning about the necessity for Michael's abstinence for as long as two weeks is factual, then she had better be around to enforce it.

With much debating and deliberating amongst the royal group and medical staff, the doctors eventually agreed to allow Michael to go home in three days, accompanied by Matron Bertha, who the hospital administration was reluctantly giving a leave of absence for just one week.

CHAPTER
35

*T*he next night, having moved over to her bed behind the curtain to sleep after Michael had fallen asleep cuddling next to her, Elizabeth was awakened by strange rustling and rumbling noises accompanied by loud whisperings. Fear gripped her, *Oh no! Michael's relapsed! What have I done!* Dashing off her bed to his, she was surprised to see him grinning blissfully sitting in a wheelchair, his wounded arm in a sling, a woolen cap covering his bandaged head, and Matron covering him with blankets.

Brian stood behind, his hands poised to push the wheelchair. Jenkins, Eric, and three other bodyguards whose names she could not remember, there were so many, were carrying her and Michael's belongings and all his medical necessities.

As she walked over to him, her fear visible, six soldiers in full battle gear entered the room. Her voice had a controlled tremor, "Michael, what's happening?"

His grin broadened into a child-like happy smile and he grasped her good arm with his, "We're going home!"

Relieved but puzzled, she asked, "But I thought not for two more days?"

There was an awkward moment of silence in the room, then Jenkins said quickly in order to save Michael from having to explain, "That's what we're hoping everybody else thinks, for safety's sake. You understand?"

Taking in Jenkins's anxiety, comprehension came to her immediately, "*there will always be an element of danger.*"

She held Michael's hand as Brian wheeled him out the door.

Lying with her head in the hollow of his right armpit, both tired from the helicopter ride and settling in at the palace, Elizabeth thought Michael had fallen asleep, when unexpectedly he said softly, "You know, I heard you.

She intuitively knew what he meant, "Heard me?"

"Yes, praying for me, in my car. And the hospital. When I was unconscious. To all kinds of deities, and other people. So-" he paused, then asked not accusatorily but with curiosity, "what happened to 'God Has No Gender?'"

She sat up slowly and faced him, "What better proof of the power of brain-washing and indoctrination, despite later more realistic knowledge gained." She gave him a wry smile, "You and I know Godde has no gender, Michael, because to an educated mind that makes the most sense. But, when humans are confronted with death, the worst fear, that of the unknown, and there seems to be nothing but helplessness and hopelessness, no matter how intelligent and knowledgeable we are, we still inevitably turn to beg for help from who we hope might have powers stronger than ours. Did you hear who I was praying to? What I was saying?"

He smiled conciliatorily, taking her hand to assure her that he was on her side and not being hypercritical, "Some of it. I kept going in and out. But I remember hearing the fear and despair in your voice. And you called out some strange names, and a lot of Gods and Goddesses, and mystics. You didn't stick to one or even a few. Why?"

Recalling her terrifying near-loss, she saddened, "I was in the depths of desperation. You were dying. I needed the help of anyone…anything…out there, that might be higher than me. I had to cover all bases."

For the next five days Elizabeth and Michael continued their rapid healings. Matron was in attendance during the day, the palace nurses taking turns sleeping in the infirmary with an 'on-call' duty at night. This arrangement suited Michael best as he didn't want any more from Matron than her assistance in hygienic matters, to tend to his wounds, and to reassure everyone, his father especially, that he was convalescing exceptionally well.

The second night they were home he argued with Elizabeth that she must sleep with him in his own bed, that he would not try to make love to her, but just wanted to feel her in bed next to him all night long, and wake up comforted by the sight of her angelic face in the morning. She didn't fall for his tempting persuasion, not because she was aware that her still healing face did not look anything like "*angelic*" but because she didn't trust either of them to keep their hands off each other, and she was not risking Michael's health in any way whatsoever.

However, she did agree to lie down beside him until he fell asleep and then go to her own bed, as she had done in the hospital and the night before. But when she unintentionally fell asleep with him, and was awakened by his hands fondling her breasts and a persistent erection rubbing against her bottom, she flew out of the bed, "Michael no! Don't you remember what Matron said? Do you want to have problems with…that," she looked down at his now protruding phallus, turned and ran to her room, ignoring his copious pleas as he begged her to come back.

When Matron came in the next day Elizabeth noticed Michael was rudely cold to her. After she left for a tea break Elizabeth tried to talk to him about it. He sulked and turned away saying that he did not need Matron anymore, messing up his life, and was going to tell her

on her return. Elizabeth was relieved that the palace doctor arrived
to remove Michael's and her sutures before Matron returned, and by
the time she did, the unstitched prince was in better humor and said
nothing to her.

That evening, shortly after Jenkins came to check on them and
collect Matron to take her out to dinner, Michael pulled him aside and
asked for the name and number of his urologist, Michael not having
his own, he never having had the need for such services before. He
became crestfallen when Jenkins informed him that unfortunately his
urologist had just left on a three-week holiday and he, Jenkins, did not
care for his replacement and would not recommend him.

Michael's disappointment turned to anger, "Well how the hell am I
going to find out when it's safe for me to…you know…have sex again!
I don't want to go to my father's doctor! This whole thing is insane!"

Jenkins commiserated with him, he himself going through some
frustration at having to deny his own renewed concupiscence, Matron
having stimulated it but not yet succumbing to it. He felt certain that
seeing how happy Michael and Elizabeth were in their love for each
other, they were his inspiration to risk loving again. After his young
wife died in childbirth delivering their stillborn son when Jenkins was
thirty, he was so shattered, he suppressed his sexuality and denied his
ability to love again, never wanting to have to endure another great
loss. Except for the odd dalliance with a nymphomaniac friend of a
friend when she was unoccupied, he had taken to masturbating to por-
nographic videos once or twice a week, and that was the extent of his
sexual pleasures.

To distract himself from his self-imposed celibacy, physically and
emotionally, of enjoying regularly the female touch, he immersed himself in the great responsibility of taking care of Michael and grooming him for Michael's own eventual great responsibility. Now, because
of Michael's near-death stay in her hospital, ironically, his charge had
brought Matron, and love, and the desire for its completeness, back
into his life.

Elizabeth walked in the room to see the two men involved in a tete-a-tete and instinctively knew what it was about. After Matron and Jenkins left she picked up the purring Delilah, placed her on a sulking Michael's lap, and kissed him softly on his forehead like she would a sick child, "Only a few more days, darling, surely you can handle that?"

He scowled at her, "I don't see why we can't do some things, I don't *have* to go in to you. Nothing's wrong with my mouth, and giving you pleasure would give me pleasure. Why are you denying me that? Have you no compassion, woman, considering what I've been through? How can *you* be so cold and heartless? I'm shocked! I would never have thought this of *you*!"

She knew what he was attempting and would not allow herself to feel guilty. After all, she was protecting his sexual abilities, that he was now willing to risk jeopardizing as he tried to convince her in which to now prematurely indulge. Knowing his high level of sexual concupiscence she felt it would not suffice him to satisfy only her.

There were times when she had been tempted to joke about him not being so royal, but just a typical male, thinking with his small head instead of the big one; but taking in his ugly mood that dominated recently, she knew he would not see any humor in it. He had lost his playfulness, it would only add to the tension that had grown between them. Though she suspected there was some exaggeration to Matron's warning, she was concerned that Michael had that catheter tube stuck in his penis for several days, and just in case there might be some kind of irritation he needs to heal from, he simply must handle the abstinence, no matter how hard it may get. She suppressed a smile at the pun and walked out of the apartment, away from his lamentations and continuing pathetic attempts at verbal abuse.

Throwing a ball for Duchess and Duke to fetch on the lawn below Michael's balcony, she looked up and saw Megan and Mark had dropped in to visit. He was enjoying their company, laughing vociferously, and she knew he would be in better spirits on her return. She had previously noticed the twins always had an uplifting effect on him, so great was his affection for his younger siblings. Handing the ball eaeaᵉ

over to Brian who came out to join her, she ran upstairs to see the twins and, hopefully, a less miserable Michael.

After greeting the twins with hugs and kisses, she looked over at Michael lovingly, "Feeling better?"

He smiled ruefully, "Much. I'm sorry to have been so cranky. Forgive me?"

She bent over and kissed him on his lips, "Of course, Prince Cantankerous, you've been through a lot."

The twins chuckled delightedly and he pulled her down onto his lap, "I didn't tell you but I read the possible side effects of the pain pills, those darn things could do more harm than help! So I stopped them this morning. It's not been easy. That's why I've been in such a bad mood. Sorry. And having nurses around in our private space is driving me crazy. By the way, I gave Matron the day off tomorrow. Jenkins is taking her to meet his cousins in the country. I hope you don't mind but I felt we could do with a break from the whole medical-sickness thing."

Beginning to feel a little depressed by it all, Elizabeth agreed wholeheartedly. Although she knew they were both doing well and would recover completely except for a few scars, it could not happen soon enough. Things appeared to be getting more difficult at home and she needed to get back, but she could not leave Michael until he was fully recuperated.

He slept badly that night. No matter what position he tried he could not get comfortable enough to stay asleep. His head hurt, his arm hurt more. In desperation at seeing him in such severe pain, Elizabeth tried talking him into allowing her to call the night nurse or doctor to give him a milder pain or sleep medication but he refused, saying he could "*tough it out;*" and he did, and with him, so did she.

That morning, the two of them feeling weary from the sleepless painful night, grunted at Pamela when she brought them breakfast, and grunted at each other during breakfast. After Pamela did the necessary cleaning and straightening, Elizabeth, at Michael's mumbled irritable demand on his way to the toilet, dismissed her for the rest of the day.

Coming out of her own bathroom feeling somewhat refreshed after her morning toilet routine, she heard a loud groan coming from Michael in his bathroom. She walked quickly toward it.

The door was pushed in but not completely closed. She could see him through the crack, sitting on the toilet, his damaged arm askew in the sling as he struggled to reach behind him with a wad of toilet paper in his right hand. His pained expression as he twisted his body to try to clean himself while the wounded arm kept slipping out of the sling, pulling at his wounds, tore at her heart; and she risked hearing more verbal abuse from his uncomfortableness, "Darling, do you need help?"

He was mortified, "No! Go away!"

Understanding his embarrassment, she stepped away from the door but quietly stayed to the side. He let out a loud shriek then another groan, and she knew she had to help him, "Darling, I'm coming in to help-"

He yelled, "No! Elizabeth, go away!"

"But Michael, you obviously need help-"

Frustration mounting, he yelled louder, "Call Matron!"

Patience thinning, she said firmly, "You gave her the day off, you were fed up with having nurses around, remember? I'm coming in."

His ashamed voice came out as a squeal, "No! Please Elizabeth, you can't come in here, it stinks! I can hardly stand it myself."

Despite the unpleasant situation she had to smile at his last remark, but said matter-of-factly, "That's the supplements, they're all-natural so they'll smell stronger. I don't care. Stop hurting yourself, I'm coming in."

He groaned with two different kinds of pain as she pushed the door open and stepped in. The stench hit her as if it was something solid and alive, so powerful and pervasive it was, she had to fight the natural impulse to stagger back and cry "Whew!"

Michael groaned defeatedly, "Oh God," and dropped his head, too embarrassed to look at her.

Trying not to draw in a breath, she fixed a fresh wad of toilet paper, rested her hand on his good shoulder and commanded, "Lean forward."

Hoping to hold on to his last vestige of dignity he said obstinately, "No. I can't believe you think I'd let you wipe my bottom."

Knowing of his mortification but loving him too much to allow him to suffer because of his macho ego, she sought to assuage his embarrassment, "Darling, I've wiped more bottoms than you can imagine-"

He groaned again, softly this time, "Maybe so, but children's, not mine-"

He heard an edginess enter her voice, "Stop being ridiculous. You're hurting yourself unnecessarily, now lean forward so we can get out of here," she pressed so hard on his shoulder it surprised him, and he involuntarily leaned forward a little, forcing him to realize this was yet another battle he could not win with her.

Knowing the strengths of this woman, now compounded with stubbornness, and all he really wanted right now was for them both to get to hell out of here, he capitulated. He leaned forward, she cleaned him, flushed the toilet, and left him to sit and collect himself, and regain his regal dignity.

With Michael feeling stronger, not always wearing the sling, he and Elizabeth had taken to going on long but leisurely walks around the palace grounds in the evenings after dining with the family, both putting off going to bed until too tired to succumb to what they desperately wanted with each other, real sex. Recently, though staying fully clothed in sleepwear, they had been doing more than cuddling when trying to fall asleep. Touching every orifice and erogenous zone like exploring pubescent teenagers, they would stop just short of coitus.

On their twelfth night back at the palace, Michael, feeling no pain anywhere else but between his legs, went too far and tried to mount her. Wanting him so badly too, Elizabeth had to force herself to push him away, closing her legs tightly. Michael could feel her heat matching his own but seeing her tightening, knowing to pursue his desires might tantamount to rape, altruistically felt the best he could do was to at least satisfy her, with cunnilingus, which he did.

The guilt she felt at allowing him to pleasure only her when she heard him masturbating in his bathroom afterwards vanished, when he walked out with an elated smile, "Everything's normal. I checked, nothing strange came out. So tomorrow, we're out of here, away from all this," he waved at the medical paraphernalia and hospital bed he used only once, "we're going, alone, to Venice."

Her joy equaled his, "Ooo I love Venice, but why Venice?"

"Because we have a secret romantic appartamento there. We'll wear hats and glasses, no one'll know us, we'll be free!"

It was lunchtime when they arrived in Venice. Michael's family's appartamento was, as he intimated, very private, in a tranquil and treasure-filled area of the precious, unhurriedly reluctantly drowning, waterlogged city. Romantically decorated, it was painted and wallpapered in soft pastels that somehow combined harmoniously in a marriage with ornately carved and gilded Venetian and Italian antiques, the rococo chairs upholstered with tapestries depicting scenes of Venetian lovers in eighteenth-century dress. The housekeeper greeted them excitedly jabbering in Italian that everything was ready in the appartamento, except for the groceries, as she was planning to go shopping after they discussed their desired menus with her.

Michael told Elizabeth he was going to explain to Lucia they needed only breakfast things, would cook it themselves, were going to mostly eat out, and she'll have the rest of their stay off after she goes to the market and unpacks their luggage.

Elizabeth offered to translate to which Michael responded proudly, "No thanks, you're not the only linguist here, I know some Italian." He made a brave effort in his limited Italian but Lucia looked totally befuddled, befuddling him as he thought he explained the situation perfectly. He looked at the beautiful, restored, amused face of his angel, and with a foolish grin, enquired, "Okay, what did I say?"

Elizabeth repressed a laugh, "Well Mr. Prince Linguist, you told her you and I are going to cook breakfast and eat each other inside our luggage, and afterwards she can go spend our time here unpacking our clothes in the market."

Elizabeth took over the rest of the translations between Lucia and Michael. Lucia's gratitude emoted with a deep curtsey to Michael and a relieved friendly but respectful hug for Elizabeth, after which they left her to unpack their luggage, and took a gondola over to the Piazza San Marco.

Looking like a couple of ordinary tourists in hats and sunglasses, they sat in an outdoor cafe and enjoyed a nourishing lunch, sticking as best they could to Michael's prescribed strengthening healthy diet. In lieu of treating their palates to all the rich foods they really wanted, their eyes instead feasted. Along with all the interesting people and sights of antiquity, they digested the breathtaking Saint Mark's Basilica, its gothic-like opulence and fantastical great domes decorating the sky as they reached upward to embrace the heavens.

Afterwards they took another gondola to the Riva del Vin, and strolled through the arcades of shops on the newer Rialto Bridge that was built in the sixteenth century. Having done enough sightseeing and people-watching, they hired a high-speed water-taxi to take them to Murano island, where shops fabricated and sold the historically famous blown glass of the same name. The exquisitely delicate pieces were sometimes made to order and created immediately in front of the waiting customer.

Thrillingly, the lovers designed a slender two-foot-tall vase. The main receptacle was transparent, with two gold colored cherubs at the top on either side stretching their arms around the vase to hold each other's hands, white glass ribbons flowing from around their bodies to form handles.

Watching their design being created right before their eyes, the lovers held hands and kissed frequently, inspiring the romantic Venetian craftsman to create his greatest masterpiece.

Both beginning to tire, not just from the journey and gadding about their beloved Venice, but also from the excitement of having been able to run away from the caring but invasive watchfulness of everyone back at the palace, they decided to return to the appartamento to nap. Alighting from the gondola that took them back to their area near Campo Santa Maria Nova, Elizabeth warned Michael he needed to "get a good rest and nothing else" before they headed out later for dinner, to which he smiled knowingly, but reluctantly agreed.

The pathways alongside the canals in their area were very narrow, one had to practically hug the walls of buildings to avoid falling into the canal. Grinning, Michael doffed his hat and bowed to Elizabeth in a cavalier's fashion, his right hand outstretched directing her to walk ahead of him, "So I can see you and save you if you fall in."

He watched her carefully, admiring her stride as she walked at a good pace, her two-inch-heel sandals on the cobblestones in combination with her pace and the narrowness of the path causing her hips to sway exaggeratedly, sexily. He scanned every part of her from top to toe, and then, literally, to bottom. He checked out her long gold-streaked auburn hair, curling at the ends from getting sprinkled on when a speeding private motor launch had passed too close to their gondola; her shoulders, square and always erect like a ballerina, even when she had to keep looking down being careful where she stepped; her small waist accentuating the curvaceousness of her hips and round firm buttocks; her long shapely legs that ended in paradise. He enjoyed looking at her, loved every inch, but his eyes kept reverting to her swaying hips and bottom, knowing only too well what she could do with those parts of her body, the pleasure she had given him, and he had given her, it seemed so long ago.

Too long ago. Rounding the corner into the private alley at the back of their building his erection happened at the speed of light. He put down the bag with the box of their carefully packed Venetian glass vase barely gently enough not to break it. Grabbing her wrist he spun her around, grabbed her other wrist and held her hands up above her head, pinioning her against the wall. They kissed more gluttonously than they ever had before. She felt his manhood like a rod of steel against her pubic bone. Her vagina and clitoris vibrated with anticipation.

Their sexual frustration had been fed for too long, they needed to put it into starvation mode. His breath coming fast, he looked hard into her eyes, "Elizabeth, we need to fuck."

If Michael didn't have her pinioned and wasn't pressing her against the wall with the lower half of his body, Elizabeth would have fallen to the ground in shock. In all the weeks of their wildest love-making, unadulterated, uncensored, unbelievably erotic sex, not once had Michael spoken or cried out an obscenity. She herself had come close to doing so a few times in the height of her orgasms, but contained herself because he never did and she thought he might find it offensive.

Reasoning that this new development was taking them to yet another level, she realized it meant there could be no holes barred. Catching her breath she said mockingly, "Why, Your Royal Highness, I'm shocked. I had no idea you knew of such words, let alone could use them."

"Only when appropriate," he half-smiled lasciviously, "and I'm so fucking hot for you right now, I want to sink my cock in your cunt. I want your bodily fluids to wash all over my body. I want to put my cock in every orifice of your beautiful body."

More shocked than before, his crude language becoming contagious, she exclaimed, "Shit, Michael!"

His voice turned guttural and he seared her with slitted eyes, "That too. I want it all from you."

Her shock increasing, she gasped and exclaimed louder, "Godde, Michael!"

Enjoying his ability to shock her like this, his stimulation intensified, "You think they have any laws in Venice against fucking in alleys?"

She giggled, "Possibly not, they're Italian after all! But there's no way we're doing it here, not in your condition. Especially not having done it for so long. Upstairs." He let go of her quickly, snatched up the bag, grabbed her hand, and they ran into the rear entrance of their building.

CHAPTER
36

*T*earing off her blouse before she could get to the first button he greedily sucked her breasts, going from one to the other purring in delight like a hungry newborn, she sighing with womanly enjoyment. Desirous of at last feeling his naked skin against hers again, she helped him take off his shirt, carefully removing the left sleeve off his wounded arm.

Taking in the still healing scar her eyes immediately lifted to the red scar on his now exposed scalp.

The suddenly visible reminders of the severity of what he had been through brought back a chilling dose of reality, "Michael, maybe it's too soon, I'm afraid of hurting you."

His voice sounded like a low growl, "The only thing you can do to hurt me now is stop me from fucking you." Pulling off her silk culottes he proceeded to go down to her core. Sniffing her already flowing cream he murmured, "You smell so fuckalicious."

She giggled, "Fuckalicious, Highness? You composing again?"

He dragged his tongue in her crease, "It's because that's what you are, 'fuckalicious'."

Thrusting his tongue deep inside her she fell back on the bed and into erotic heaven. With his hot enjoyable and enjoying talented mouth and tongue, her orgasm was almost immediate, so on fire was she. Pleased with what he had done for her but now wanting to further please himself, he whipped off his pants and commanded, "Turn over. Go up on your hands and knees."

She obeyed willingly, her vagina still tingling and wanting more. He stretched over quickly to his vanity case, took the bottle of healing massage oil she had been using on him at the palace, poured out a large amount in his hand and lathered his phallus liberally. She could not comprehend what he was doing, started turning to see what was causing the delay, and he mounted her from behind.

She relaxed as she felt his penis, like velvet iron, against her bare cheeks, but suddenly he was entering... *There! He truly meant it when he said he wanted to enter every orifice in my body!* "Michael!" she gasped, grabbing onto the sheet.

"Tell me if it starts to hurt," he said hoarsely, but caringly. She gritted her teeth as he persevered with a cautious but steady penetration. She moaned but uttered no words, the pleasure overshadowing the pain. He moved slowly in and out, wanting to prolong this new and gripping sensation, but his recent bout of dictated disagreeable celibacy proved too much for any kind of control. His ejaculation burst out like gushing water through a broken dike, filling them both with ecstasy as he screamed, "Fuck, Elizabeth, I'm coming! I love you!"

He stroked her plump cheeks with gratitude as he withdrew, and weakened and exhausted, flopped down on his undamaged side against her body. Feeling their fluids seeping out of her, she jumped up and dashed for the bathroom.

Tiptoeing back into the room as she saw his eyes were closed, she lay softly down beside him. He rolled over and caressed her, "Darling, I hope I didn't hurt you?"

"No," she said softly, then, rethinking, despite the lie she is now living in this fantasy world she had with Michael, there should only be honest in their love, and their lovemaking, she added, "well, just a little."

"I'm so sorry," he said sincerely, "let me kiss and make it better." And he did.

That night, foregoing their plan to dine in another favorite café from their separate pasts, they spent the evening dining on each other, in the literal sense, with a variety of foods that nature provides. Feeling stronger and hungrier, concupiscence no longer denied but magnified, Michael wanted everything she had to give. Relishing the shower of gold he insisted she wash him with, his mouth, body, and family jewels bathed in a new kind of glory.

The next morning Elizabeth awoke to the aroma of breakfast being cooked as it wafted into their bedroom. Thinking Lucia had ignored their instructions, she reached over for Michael to tell him, to find him gone. Donning her robe, she walked into the kitchen to see Michael expertly flip a large ham, cheese, garlic, and shallots omelet in a frying pan. Giving her a proud grin, he pointed to the dining table already set, complete with a steaming pot of coffee, a bowl of fresh fruit cocktail, sausages sautéed with onions and tomatoes, and hot rolls ensconced in a napkin-covered silver basket, "Breakfast is served Your Royal Sleepyhead, your slave is at your service."

The surprise in her voice was reflected in her widened eyes, "You did all this? But when we were at Jamestowns' you said you couldn't cook."

"No I didn't. I simply asked if you thought I could cook, and you said it was intrinsic in everyone. And you were right. I learned to cook during military service. Sit. Enjoy. Buon appetito, bella. Ti amo."

During breakfast they planned the rest of their day, intending it to be spent in the enjoyment of more fascinating places Venice has to offer, but after breakfast, and passionate love-making in the bathtub, the plans were postponed. They went back to bed and didn't leave it for the rest of the day, spending it in the fascinating enjoyment of each other instead. Trying every known sexual position they gigglingly created a few of their own. While resting and recovering in-between their insatiableness they talked about the future, and the past.

Michael asked if she ever fantasized about sex with someone else, to which she responded softly, "Not since I'm with you."

He eyed her nervously, "Well, when you were with someone else? Did you think about somebody else? Or somebodies…s?" he stressed the 's' to show he meant plural.

She mirrored his look and swallowed, "Yes, but only one person, and that was a long time ago. I don't need to do that now. What about you? How many did you fantasize about?"

He gave her a strange look that made her more nervous, "Hey, no throwing it back at me, I'm not finished with you yet. So, tell me who it was, and I'll tell you mine."

She forced nonchalance, "It was so long ago, I honestly can't remember." He knew she was not being honest, but decided not to press as he didn't want to spoil the concupiscent mood and he became silent. But she didn't want to spoil it either and said with a seductive smile, "Okay, I've told you mine, now you tell me yours. How many? And who?"

His voice held mystery, "Only one…and I don't know who."

She sat up and looked in his eyes with accusation in her own, "What do you mean you, *'don't know who,'* how is that possible? You don't want to tell me, do you?"

He looked at her with a hint of apology, "No, that's not it. *I* honestly don't know who it was. Anyway, it doesn't happen anymore, not since you've blessed my life. I'm sorry I brought this subject up. But, thankfully, it doesn't matter anymore, for either of us. Right?"

Smiling with relief she kissed him aggressively, "Right."

Two days later they managed to drag themselves out of bed to indulge in their preplanned sightseeing, but by the end of the day they barely made it back to the appartamento without publicly embarrassing themselves. Their desire for each other so strong and urgent, as though they were running out of time to make up for lost time, they almost had intercourse under a blanket in the gondola. The only thing stopping them was the inquisitive eyes of the gondolier. Paying more attention to what they were doing than what he should be doing, the man carelessly rammed into two other gondolas and almost capsized them twice.

Returning to the appartamento they ignored their phones which were deliberately left behind that morning so they would be free of disturbances that might interrupt their special day, and went straight to bed, to unknowingly fulfill the fantasies of their gondolier.

Elizabeth awakened before Michael the next morning.

Being careful not to outdo him but at the same time impress him with her equal culinary ability, she made a simpler but delicious breakfast of coffee, a citrus fruit salad, French toast, and a frittata with cheese, prosciutto, tomatoes, olives, mushrooms, peppers, onions, and garlic.

Michael's volubly expressed compliments of the frittata were interrupted by a phone call from Jenkins, "Michael, I left messages yesterday. Don't tell him I called but I'm concerned about your father. He's not looking well, grimaces sometimes as if he's in pain, but refuses to have the doctor check him. And I don't think he's getting enough sleep, he fell asleep during a business meeting yesterday. I'm not asking you to return, but I'd like you to call and convince him to see Doctor Martin. And insist on him slowing down a bit. I know he'll listen to you."

Michael called his father immediately, was unable to convince him to agree to see the doctor, did not like how he sounded, and within an hour, he and Elizabeth dressed, packed, said goodbye to their love nest, and headed home.

Having explained the condition in detail, the doctor looked almost as tired as the King as he spoke to Michael who was nervously clinging to Elizabeth's hand, she sitting beside him in the small salon adjoining the King's bedroom, his Majesty sound asleep in his king-sized bed next-door.

"It's called Angina Pectoris. Sorry to have to give you this news at this time Prince Michael, you still healing from your wounds, and therapy impending. But I'm afraid he's going to have to rest, take it extremely easy for a while. The pain is most easily precipitated by exertion, excitement, stress, which I know The King has more than his fair share of. I've given the nurses a list of instructions which must be followed without deviation, the medications taken exactly as prescribed. I'll be checking on him several times a day, and my phone's always on me should I be needed at a moment's notice."

The doctor, who had assisted at Michael's birth, looked sympathetically at the worried young prince he had watched grow into a handsome strong man, and rested his hand on Michael's shoulder as he stood to leave, "Unfortunately, you'll have to do some reorganizing of your own life and get help to take over his workload, until he's well enough to do *some* of it. Although his prognosis is good, if you want to have him around for a while, he shouldn't work as hard as he has in the past."

Taking in the doctor's pitying expression Michael deliberately replaced his worried look with one of stalwartness, "Don't worry, I'll have it under control. I've already enlisted my uncle Prince Patrick to assist me until I've trained-"

Dr. Martin's concerned face quickly developed alarm, "Oh!? Prince Patrick? I thought he had designs on the throne for himself. Be careful, son."

Michael was surprised, "Why? What do you mean? What have you heard? What do you know?"

Dr. Martin shuffled his feet as though he needed to leave to attend to more pressing matters, "Nothing really. Call it a gut-feeling," he unconsciously glanced at Elizabeth, "be careful who you trust. Put your own interests and your father's first, before all others."

Aware that the doctor was bound by an oath of confidentiality, Michael knew it was useless to insist he divulge more information. He decided he would have to uncover the doctor's "*gut-feeling*" from other sources.

Though disturbing, this new development made him even more determined to take over the role that was his birthright, "Thank you for the warn...advice. I'll keep it in the forefront of my mind. But I'm not going to allow my father to ever work as hard as he has again. And," he smiled at Elizabeth, "when I marry, he's going to abdicate and retire completely, to just enjoy playing with his grandchildren and watching them grow up."

The following days in the palace were filled with contradictions, there was an atmosphere of controlled confusion. Although people tread around stealthily like hunting jungle felines at night and spoke unhurriedly in hushed tones, everyone was busier and feeling more stressed than ever before; except for the resting King, his sudden and inconvenient illness being the cause of everyone else's additional physical and emotional strain. Yet through it all Elizabeth and Michael remained calm, confident and united, proving to the resident royals and palace staff, and to each other, that theirs was a match made in heaven for all time. As the still healing Michael took over the reins of his father's reign, Elizabeth worked alongside him at almost every task, doing everything she possibly could to help lighten his extra burdens, beyond the call of girlfriend duty, but within the realm of wife and partner.

Michael leaned heavily on her in most matters, excluding her only when royal public appearances were required, and this was not of his choosing but of hers. Only twice did she walk into his office when he was having meetings he had not previously told her about. He and the assembled acted guiltily when she entered, making her feel excluded and unusually insignificant. Strangely, these meetings comprised the very people who always made her feel welcome and important. Present were Anne, Megan, Mark, Jenkins, Brian, Eric, and, oddly, her maid Pamela. After they filed out smiling at her awkwardly, Michael would embrace and kiss her as if the preceding event never occurred. This puzzled her, but with everyone's recently frenetic schedules there was neither time nor opportunity to ask any of the group for an explanation, and none was volunteered.

With her bewigged, wearing large tinted glasses and conservative dark suits, he had her sit in on all his other meetings, including those of state with government officials, introducing her formally when unavoidable as his, "*business aide-de-camp*." She didn't sit next to his regular adjutant but unobtrusively off to the side, pad and pen in hand, silently taking in every detail of the proceedings, occasionally writing notes regarding her observations.

She would even jot down what she referred to as "*significant sillies*," idiosyncrasies Michael might miss that could be helpful in future meetings and decision-making: '*Sheik looks at his watch whenever unhappy with your response; American diplomat scratches ear when she's nervous; stout Japanese CEO blinks excessively when he disagrees but is too polite to verbalize disagreement; young entrepreneur nibbles top of pen when not fully understanding what's being proposed but is too proud to admit it,*' and so on.

In private, he included her in all decisions of major importance, even testing her acceptability when he asked her to check the recent maintenance bills of his secreted illegitimate teenage daughter in The Greek Isles. She passed that test by showing more tolerance and compassion than he thought possible for a woman who unwittingly will be thrown into the undesirable situation of having to accept and legally adopt, her husband's youthful 'mistake,' for the rest of her life.

Elizabeth handled the new and grave responsibilities of temporary and covert Queen as though she was born to it, gaining her unparalleled respect compared to that given to any of Michael's previous girlfriends, endearing her to all she came in contact with. Even the always disapproving Claire was forced to admit, though begrudgingly, "*she's not just a pretty thing after all,*" and, "*maybe has potential.*"

Because of the King's new illness overloading the palace's small medical staff, and with Jenkins' enthusiastic recommendation, Matron Bertha became a welcome permanent addition to the palace infirmary.

His libido now reinforced and being satisfied, Matron at last having succumbed to awakening her own latent libido with much persuasion, Jenkins, while everyone else had become nervous and worried, was ecstatic.

He eagerly obtained permission from a puzzled Michael - who could not envision the coupling of such a physically mismatched pair as the hefty tall Matron and almost scrawny, shorter Jenkins - and had her moved out of the sleeping quarters of the infirmary and happily ensconced in his personal quarters.

Almost everyone grew accustomed to the self-righteous, indomitable Nurse Nazi, the major exception, not surprisingly, being Claire. The dowager royal detested not only Matron's controlling disciplinarian manner but even the caring sweetness she displayed when attending to the King, or anyone with an ailment. This hatred went beyond a mere personality dislike. The royal matriarch secretly saw the competent and unintimidatable Matron as a threatening usurper to her own power in the palace.

On the other hand, Matron considered the haughty but assiduous Claire's much respected position of head monitorial supervisor to the smooth running of the domestic aspect of the palace to be, "*no more than a glorified royal housekeeper.*"

Claire could not contain her disapproval of Matron and her now continuous presence, making it quite clear to anyone who would listen. Eventually fed up with hearing more than enough unreasonable complaints from all sides, Michael summoned Claire and Matron to his office. He rebuked them for their childish selfish behavior, made more intolerable with the extra stress everyone had been recently put under.

Unflinchingly he looked from one to the other with equal annoyance, stating that even though both their positions were of great importance to keep the palace running smoothly through this difficult time, neither was indispensable. If their disturbing behavior continued he would regretfully have to bring in capable strangers to perform their functions. They must call a truce or be banished from the palace. He stared disappointedly at his aunt as he added, "Until His Majesty's well again."

This startling ultimatum immediately put a stop to the snide remarks and petty snubs the two adversaries had continuously exchanged, and a fragile peace ensued.

Inexplicably, both Claire and Matron felt a grudging pride in Michael and the 'King-Solomon-like' manner in which he handled the situation. But, Aunt Claire stored it in her memory file that when things return to normal, she and her nephew were going to engage in a royal battle about her humiliation in front of "*a mere servant,*" and she was determined to be victorious.

This latest ignominy he caused her made her feel forced into immediately acting on a decision she had been postponing, one which Michael had initially warned her she was never to consider. In response to her unremitting accusatory inquisitiveness about Elizabeth, he had dishonestly told her Elizabeth passed Standard Procedure with the highest qualifications to become a royal, and that was all she needed to know. She showed her anger at his "*insolence*" and threatened to institute her own investigation. Michal warned her that if she did, she would face dire consequences.

She now decided she was going to suppress her royal pride and clandestinely pay an associate in New York to hire a private detective to investigate Elizabeth. She thought that her exposing Elizabeth to be the fraud she felt certain Elizabeth was would be the perfect way in which to pull Michael down to where he belonged, below her, Claire.

Unknown to everyone except Michael, who had intuitively figured it out, Claire held a deep-rooted resentment against the antiquated tradition of the eldest male inheriting the throne ahead of the elder female who was firstborn. To her primogenital way of thinking, Claire felt she should be the reigning monarch, and her son, Henry, not Michael, heir to the throne.

Michael kept this knowledge secret, not simply because of his own ambitions, and also to not upset his much admired accomplished father, but because he felt to have the sanctimonious selfish Claire be Queen, and the pompous hate-filled and hateful Henry inherit the throne, would cause the inevitable downfall of the monarchy and his family. Though he understood Claire's feelings about the archaic unfair discrimination against her gender, and secretly sympathized with her, he knew in his soul that to have her and her misanthropic contentious heir in that high a position of power would not only be the demise of their entire family, but it would throw the country, perhaps the region, into terrible chaos.

Considering all he had achieved and the secret hazardous risks he and his father had taken to bring stability to the country, he was certain, and determined, that no person other than he was capable of ascending the throne to influence the world peace he believed was possible.

He conferred with Jenkins and Anne on ways to keep Claire extremely busy, socially and domestically, so as to stop her from creating more dissension. Based on what Dr. Martin had inferred, he was cautious with the duties he assigned to Prince Patrick, relegating him to only social functions such as the opening of a small business, and attendance at not very important parties but events that still required a member of royalty's presence so as not to insult anyone.

The young lovers became too busy to indulge in as much lovemaking as they had, and still wanted, as before. No longer did Michael's schedule allow for their regular after lunch leisurely 'matinees,' most lunches now becoming brief business appointments, or extended visits with the recovering king who insisted on being kept current on important matters. Working so closely together, there were times during the long workday that both their minds would wander in the same direction, and they would exchange that special look of lovers who yearned for each other. Once, Elizabeth took the initiative after a particularly difficult lunch-meeting with Government Financial Advisors, when she could see the stress beginning to weigh on Michael's unusually slumping shoulders as he returned to his desk.

Locking the outer office door, she took him by his hand and into the attached private bathroom, "Come, Your Majesty, you're in need of a de-stressing 'Royal Blowjob,'" and proceeded to give him a shorter but just as enjoyable version of the fellatio she performed on him the

first time, when they were in the gazebo in The Vineyards. The next
day he returned her thoughtfulness by de-stressing them both with
a *"stand-up quickie"* in the same bathroom. Not counting their normal
morning wakeup gratification, other than those two brief daytime
trysts, they were relegated to late-night but prolonged indulgences in
their loving sexual enjoyment of each other.

Seeing how well Michael adapted to the role temporarily vacated
by his father and at the same time was admirably able to continue carrying out his own duties, much of it with Elizabeth's assistance, the
rested King began to recover rapidly, to everyone's relief. Elizabeth's
in particular; she needed to go home. She recently noticed every time
she spoke to Trinidad on Skype, although the children looked as innocently happy as usual there was a strange tenseness on the adult faces.
Yet nothing was said to confirm her suspicions that things were not
going well. On the contrary, when she asked how things were everyone was quick to assure her that *"everything's great,"* that she should not
rush home until she had the grant, and she should relax and enjoy this
much deserved respite from all the troubles still waiting to be sorted
out on her return.

She felt greatly blessed to have the love, understanding and support of her family and staff. Though most of them didn't know the
details of her suffering, they knew of the depths, and loved her enough
not to demand she tell them but to demand she get away to heal from
'it,' whatever 'it' was that had caused her uncharacteristic sadness.

Now, at last, she felt healed and happy. Happier than she thought
she could ever be again. Thanks to her prince who dove into her sor-
row-drowned life and rescued her with his love. Thanks also to her
loved ones who gave her the opportunity to get to where she could be
saved by his love.

It was now time for her to reciprocate, show her love for them all,
return to the home of her birth to fix all their lives again, so that she
could come back to help fix everything in her newly adopted permanent home.

CHAPTER
37

Several times in past days Elizabeth would be on the verge of divulging her shocking secrets to Michael, when some royal disturbance or duty-emergency would occur, and she would have to shelve them yet again. The biggest familial disturbance, apart from His Majesty's illness, was caused by Mark.

He had recently fallen in love, headlong, for the first time. With a girl. She was the cousin of a school chum, sixteen, beautiful, precocious, and flighty. Although she declared to all and sundry how much she "*adored*" Mark her actions disproved her words. She flirted unashamedly with every male in her presence, regardless of their age or status.

It was obvious to his family how hurtful and embarrassing her behavior was to Mark, but when Michael and Megan told him he should not put up with it and should break up with her he became defensive, saying, "I love her. And she really loves me. She's just naturally friendly, doesn't mean anything by it." But they could tell he was uncertain of what he said and was blindly, painfully, besotted.

Her behavior was so outrageous, it even elicited whispered disparaging remarks from the normally uncritical conservative King, the first time he felt well enough to sit through a full palace-family dinner and witnessed her performances.

Seeing the King becoming upset, Elizabeth offered to speak to the girl and hopefully, "Talk some sense into her."

In the manner of men, The King and Michael immediately dissuaded her, saying that Mark would resent the interference, he's a big boy, and must sort it out himself.

She did not agree. She felt Mark was in over his head, too soft, sensitive and immature, to know how to handle the situation. She worried that he had been raised overly protected like she had been, and therefore was being set up for a devastating letdown; but, she knew she should not go against the wishes of the two most important Majesties, so she kept her own counsel.

Elizabeth's hands shook as she excitedly opened the official looking envelope from the International Foundation to which she had applied for the grant for The Children's Home in Trinidad. Pulling out a large Cashier's check, a rush of joy came over her. Seeing the typed in figure, her joy vanished.

The amount was half of what she had requested and was promised. Hoping it was just a first installment, she quickly read the accompanying letter, to discover it was the only amount that would be granted. The letter was apologetic but had a tone of finality. It stated concisely that due to the increasing and overwhelming requests for grants because of a slowing global economy, combined with a decline in donations from some of their more affluent philanthropists, The Foundation regretfully was unable to fulfill their entire commitment to The Children's Home. It even went so far as to suggest that seeing the Trinidad and Tobago economy is still strong with the rising prices of oil, natural gas, and asphalt, she should approach her government for assistance.

How little you know, she thought bitterly. She had so long ago made overtures to some top people in her government for aid in the expansion of The Children's Home and was bluntly told there was nothing left in the budget for such programs, the money having already been allocated to, "*improving roads, public institutions and utilities.*" Up until she left, she had seen no evidence of the start of said improvements, and aware of how slowly turned the wheels of government and bureaucracy, knew to go begging again would be another futile exercise.

Thinking the grant would be coming soon, and with the additional monies she received for her speech in America, just two weeks ago she had Jane Thompson give the Trinidadian contractor his customary fifty percent deposit, and he had already started on both the special pool and dormitory wing. The Children's Home would now be deeper in debt than ever before.

Michael looked at her, saw disappointment take over her excited expression and walked over from behind his desk, "What's wrong, darling? Bad news?"

Silently, she handed him the letter and check and slowly slumped down into an armchair, a sense of failure creeping in.

He read the letter, dropped it and the check on his desk and spoke with conviction, "Don't worry, you'll get the rest of the funding somewhere else."

Not looking at him she nodded as if in agreement, but felt hopeless. Her entire board had already tried every other possible source; the International Foundation was their last resort. One promise to herself she was never going to break was to not take advantage of an offer Ruth and Robert had made when she founded The Children's Home, to fund it completely.

She was already obligated to them for their enormous contribution in giving her the best childhood, and life, anyone could ask for, and felt to accept their offer would not only be an abuse of their love and trust, but would make them feel they failed in their manner of raising her to, "*be a provider, not a parasite.*" This was her undertaking, her responsibility, she had to do the mature thing and handle it on her own. Raising funds had always been challenging, but with her tenaciousness, abetted by her intelligence and beauty, somehow, someone always came to her rescue; until now.

Except, now she did have new options, dangerous ones, which she had recently promised her ailing frightened love when he was in the hospital to postpone using, indefinitely.

Sighing, she spoke her thoughts, "If I can't, I'll have to take up some of the offers to do my speeches in other countries. Actually I'd love to do it in China, Syria, Saudi-"

Michael whitened, "Absolutely not! It's just too dangerous. I...I can't let you do it right now. Too much...preparation, has to take place before you continue your speeches. And you promised me you would wait awhile till...things get...safer-"

She interrupted him agitatedly, "Yes I know, but I've exhausted all other avenues. Anyway, I really must go home now. Something's not going well down there, but nobody will tell me what." Looking at him, her serious face flooded with worry, "Do you think you can spend some time with me after your lunch with the King of the Zulus? I have to tell you...some extremely important things...what I've been putting off telling you. I'm going to book my ticket to leave in a couple days."

Michael fell into her agitation, "So soon? Can't you put it off until Papa's back at his desk in a few days? I'd like to come to Trinidad right after you've told your family about me-"

Her agitation turned to exasperation, "No Michael. I've put it off for much too long already. Sorry. But my instincts tell me something's terribly wrong down there and I won't know what until I get there. I'm beginning to feel I'm shirking my responsibilities, forcing other people to take up my slack."

Jenkins knocked and poked his head through the doorway, "Michael, you can't keep the Zulu King waiting. And your father, he's joining you. He's really made a remarkable recovery."

Michael held her hands, "Sorry darling, I must go. Meet me at our apartments in three hours," he smiled reassuringly, "we'll solve the problems of the world then." He pecked her on her lips and left with Jenkins.

I must be strong! Can't give in to tears! Or fears! Deal with reality! I've no alternative. I must go back! Elizabeth had spent the last three hours since Michael left speaking on Skype with her family and a member of her staff in Tobago. She was devastated by what she was eventually able to painfully drag out of them. The guilt and regret at what she had caused, and at the actions she must take to correct it, were unbearable.

She suddenly felt lost and alone, an incredible contrast to feelings that had ruled her these past seven weeks with Michael.

Michael opened his drawing room door to see her sitting at her computer, her hands hanging at her sides, not relaxed but lifeless, her eyes staring vacantly into space.

Despite the summer warmth wafting through the open balcony doors, a chill ran through him, and he knew. She had to go.

Surprised out of her shocked trance when he picked up her hand, she twisted her head to look at him. Stemming the tears wanting to flow she whispered, "Michael, I must leave tomorrow."

He knew there was no changing her mind, but with a renewed fear worrying him, felt he had to try, "Tomorrow? I thought we had a few more days, darling. We've been planning a surprise birthday party for you. It won't be a surprise anymore, but don't you think you can stay until-"

Still feeling numb by what she had learnt and what she dreaded she must do, it was an effort to speak normally, "That's awfully sweet of all of you. So that's what those meetings you excluded me from were about. I'll have to thank, apologize, to everyone, but I've put it off too long already, and there are...terrible problems. I must go tomorrow, I'm so sorry."

He refused to give up, "I understand. But I need to write a letter to your parents first and that's going to take me some time. Can't you wait another day at least-"

She stared at him with an uncomprehending vacant look, "Why do you want to write to my parents?"

He was taken aback at her question but then the answer hit him, "Oh. I've never really said the actual words. I just assumed, with everything we've discussed, all the plans we've been making…wait! Wait right here! I'll be back in a minute." He ran out the door.

Fifteen minutes later he returned to see she had not moved since he left, and this worried him further. *It's bad enough she has to leave in a hurry and miss the great birthday party we planned, but to leave because of some unknown problem in Trinidad that's upsetting her so terribly gives me a foreboding about how soon she'll return. I'll just have to go down there when Pa is back on the throne, help her sort it all out, and bring her back. We've a wedding to plan.*

He stood before her, "Darling, sorry to have taken so long but I had to run down to the vault, and then I was trying to reach your parents at their home, but I got this strange person who said something about them being in Tobago, but wouldn't, or couldn't, give me the number. I didn't understand most of what she said, she spoke some sort of patois." He took a deep breath, his excitement evident, and went down on one knee holding his mother's diamond engagement ring in his right hand. "I wanted to do this on your birthday, but since you won't be here, I'm doing it now before you go so you can hurry back to plan our autumn wed-" he stopped, then breathed deep again, "Elizabeth Angelique Richardson, the love of my life, my precious angel whom I shall cherish forever. Will you marry me? And be my Queen for life?"

Elizabeth sat frozen as though she had been hit by a bolt of lightning and struck dumb. Suddenly aware of what was happening, without thought to composition of her words, she blurted, "Michael I can't marry you now! I…I'm already married!"

Michael felt as if lightning had hit him also, but with a double bolt. His face turned white, then rapidly became suffused with color, but then he doubted himself, he must have heard incorrectly, "Wha… what did you say?"

She forced her eyes to meet his, "I'm already married."

"Al…re…ready…ma…married?" His tongue twisted on the words as if they came from a foreign language.

This is it, let it all come out, pain is inescapable now, "Yes. That's what I've been wanting to tell you. But we're separated, eight months."

He staggered up off his knee like a very old man, and faltering, stood to face her, his expression filled with incredulity, and fear, "You married Frederico del Rico?"

She was surprised for an instant until the name registered, "Frederico? No. Someone else."

Becoming more puzzled, he rested the Queen's engagement ring on a table, "But you were engaged to Frederico. You broke it off when he wouldn't give up his mistress-"

Wanting to get through this quickly, she interjected, "That was long ago, and he did give up the mistress. I was so young, it was just a teenage crush. I was infatuated with the idea of an older man of his distinction being in love with me. I broke it off when I realized. My parents and aunt and uncle also disapproved, he was so much older than me, and divorced."

His entire face frowning, Michael struggled to understand, "You're married. How could you not tell me something so important as this, Elizabeth? Who are you married to?"

Her mouth twisted with a hint of distaste, "A Trinidadian. Edward du Beauchamp."

His expression transformed as though everything was suddenly revealed to him, "I see. I suppose he's black?"

Seeing his look a pity took hold, "No. He's white. Of European origins like me. Except his mother's is British but with a quarter Lebanese."

A new puzzlement came upon him, "Lebanese? How come?"

She was beginning to feel more comfortable, at least this was quite civilized, "There's a pretty powerful Lebanese and Syrian community in Trinidad. I understand they started coming there during my great-grandparent's youth. Mostly Christians running from religious perse-cution in their own countries, from what I've been told."

Michael was not experiencing the civility she felt and said impa-tiently, "Well, you couldn't have been married that long. We'll get the marriage annulled. My family is friendly with a papal legate. All it takes is money to get an annulment from the Catholic Church."

She knew he was definitely going to get more upset so she spoke quickly, "It's not that simple, Michael. We've been married seven years and-"

Michael felt more lightning bolts hit his chest. A vision of Elizabeth stabbing his heart with a dagger turned real to him as the pain became immense, and he shrilled, "Seven years!"

Elizabeth could see what he felt, began to lose her nerve but knew she had to go the whole way, there was no turning back, and continued rapidly, "We married when I returned to Trinidad after university. I was twenty-one. We'd met when I was nineteen one Christmas when I went home, and had an intense though often long distance two-year romance-"

Becoming more confused than ever, he raised his hand, and his voice, "Stop a minute! You were married *seven years*, Elizabeth! For Christ's sake, why did you wait so long to tell me? You knew how I felt about you. You acted as if you felt the same way -"

She jumped in quickly, he thought, too quickly, "I do-"

He was uncertain of what to believe, he just wanted to get the facts, "So, what the hell happened, you said you've been separated for eight months. Why did you break up your marriage?"

She swallowed the saliva that had built up in her mouth, "I didn't. He did."

Michael winced like he'd been cuffed in his face, "*He* did? Why?"

She swallowed again, "Well, technically he did. He didn't want to break up, but caused me to want to. He...had an affair."

Incredulity flooded his face, "An affair! *Your* husband had an affair?! Did he go *insane*?"

She surprisingly felt as if she should make excuses for the cheating bastard, "In a way. He said he was drunk." She sighed but continued, "We'd both been working very hard building our businesses and taking over the running of some of my father's. And, I also had the added pressure of running The Children's home, and working on my Master's degree, and…we were overworked, stressed-out and tired. A tenseness had built up between us, but there never seemed to be a good time to address it. We were both traveling a lot, separately, for business. This particular time we'd been separated three weeks. He was in Jamaica overseeing the expansion of our company there, I was stuck down at home with…other responsibilities." She paused to take a deep breath.

Michael's impatience grew, "Marriages go through periods like that occasionally, that's no reason to have an affair."

Elizabeth now became impatient with his interruptions, could he not see how hard this was to tell him, "Michael, you must understand, we were very…close. And, we always had a very…affectionate…sexual, relationship." *Like you and I.*

Michael sucked in a breath giving her a bitter look, "Huh. With you? I'm not surprised."

She felt stung, yet strangely complimented, but hurried with her explanation, "We hadn't been…together, the week before he left. We'd been arguing a lot about my being too involved in The Children's Home, he felt it tired me out and I was neglecting his "*needs*." But I also felt neglected, that he let his power driven ego rule our lives. His whole focus seemed to be on building wealth." She could feel those blue-gray steely eyes steady on her, watching every expression, waiting. Breathing in deeply she exhaled slowly, "Anyway, apparently he got drunk one night after work, and the Canadian wife of our manager dropped him back to his hotel. Her husband was away. He *says* she helped him to undress, aroused him, and because he had been so stressed, sexually frustrated, and drunk, he gave in."

Michael eyed her with scrutiny, "I get the impression you don't believe him."

She looked away, "I don't know what to believe. He and I never discussed the details. Actually, I only found out because the woman called me, lording it over me. She always disliked me, and I suspected she wanted Edward. Edward said she was just envious of me. I was so shocked and horrified at what he did, I didn't want to hear any more about it. The betrayal was more than I could bear. I banished him from our bedroom immediately, couldn't even speak to or look at him. He begged and begged but I wouldn't, couldn't, listen. I started traveling even more to get away from his pleas. I told him I needed six months separation, he had to be tested immediately and again at the end of six months, before I would even consider any kind of reunion. But in my heart, I felt my marriage was over."

Hearing a strong, angry, intake of breath from Michael, she said reassuringly, "You're not to worry. He tested clean both times. So did I. I would never endanger you, Michael. Please believe me?"

For some unexplainable reason, in spite of her having kept secret from him things of this magnitude, he did believe her. "Well, where do *we* go from here, Elizabeth? From what you're saying, even though you're separated eight months, you've never even discussed divorce. In fact, you wouldn't even talk to your husband, and it sounds like you're not sure of what exactly happened. It seems you were afraid to find out, which is so unlike you-"

Feeling she had to defend herself from what appeared to him as cowardice she interrupted angrily, "I was devastated, Michael! In shock. My very foundation had been rocked. My world was disintegrating. We had it all, and I couldn't believe he would destroy what we had just for a few moments of pleasure. You don't know him...the amazing man he is. And he adored me...we adored each other. Everyone said we had the perfect marriage. And I believed it," knowing that her face would betray her sadness, she dropped her head, looked at the floor and said softly, "it *was* perfect, for seven years."

Not missing her expression, Michael staggered back as though hit by another lightning bolt, his voice coming out as a shriek, "Wait a minute! So what the hell was I Elizabeth! Some kind of fucking royal rebound?!

Startled by his accusation, she shivered and shouted, "No! No of course not-"

He was in enough pain, but he had to risk feeling more to get at the truth. Her truth. "How do you feel about him, Elizabeth? Tell me truthfully!"

Suddenly she was fighting back tears she didn't understand, "Truthfully, I don't know. I thought I hated him. I felt I could never let him…touch…me again. But, I've been speaking to Tobago for the last few hours and I've learnt…some things…I have to go back Michael, and figure this all out."

Michael's handsome face took on a cutting sneer, Elizabeth could see the vein in his neck bulging and pulsing, "Figure it out?! You've had *eight months*, woman!"

Taking in his look she began to feel a strange new fear and stuttered, "You…you don't understand Michael, there are…other people…to consider, and there are certain things I didn't know…and…and…you came into my life when-"

His sneer intensified, "Ah yes. I was your fucking diversion! A convenient fucking rebound, used as a fill-in, until you had the guts to make up your mind-"

Feeling the depths of his pain, she put hers aside, "I'm so sorry Michael, I never meant to hurt you like this. You were not a…a rebound. When we met I felt my marriage was over-"

"And now?"

She didn't have an answer and simply swallowed, unable to look at him.

His voice lowered acerbically, "I see. So these last months have been a lie. A magnificent deception on your part, my dear. You belong in Hollywood, you deserve every kind of award for your amazing performance. In fact, there isn't another actor who could touch your ability." He wished he could continue with more hurtful words with which to lambaste her, but his heart was breaking and his brain was depleted.

With her own heart divided, assuredly breaking again, she knew his true feelings, and had to try to prove to him that she was not a sham, "Michael, I did warn you that you might hate me one day, because of what I had to tell you-"

The pain and anger building, he interrupted, "It would've been easier if you'd told me at the start! Why did you continue with the charade? All the things we've done, been through. The plans we made. The confidences I took you into…I trusted you implicitly! I…I can't believe this is even happening! Why did you do this, Elizabeth? How could you be so evil? You knew from the beginning I was in love with you, wanted to marry you. Why didn't you just leave and go-"

She started to shake uncontrollably. Her legs weakening, she shouted, "Because I couldn't!"

He developed an additional fear. Was he the victim of some diabolical plot? Who is this hateful stranger destroying his life? His voice filled with pained sarcasm, "Why not? Were you having too much royal-fun? And did I service you well? What else did you expect to get out of me, Elizabeth? Glorification? Political power? Money? More jewelry? Why did you feel you had to stay all this time? Did you need it to be able to hurt me some more? Why Elizabeth? *Why!*"

She felt the sting of his words travel from her ears down to her heart then up to her eyes, tears forced out by them as she fell to her knees, "Because I fell in love with *you!* Godde dammit! *I fell in love with you!*"

Stunned, he stared at his once statuesque perfect angel now collapsed at his feet, her body suddenly tiny, frail and crumpled on the floor. A sad metaphor for his crumbling life.

Doubled over, her face in her hands, Elizabeth cried uncontrollably, her entire body shaking violently from heartbreaking sobs. The devastation Edward had brought to her, she brought to Michael, and, again, to herself; and, the worst was yet to come.

Michael stood motionless. Not that he was unmoved by Elizabeth's pathetic condition. His heart was being torn apart further to see the angelic love of his life reduced to the shattered human being on the floor at his feet. Her loud sobs became muted in his ears. What was distinct and thundered in his head were her words, "*I fell in love with you!*"

Slowly, wordlessly, gently, he helped her to stand, swept her up into his arms, and sat down with her on his lap in the overstuffed armchair. He remained silent, letting the room fill with her pain and sorrow, and with his.

CHAPTER 38

*E*ventually drained of every tear her eyes could produce, Elizabeth murmured in Michael's chest, "I never wanted to hurt you. No matter what happens, I will always love you. I know now we can't be together, you could never have married me. I guess I'm damaged-goods, in your eyes, and your family's. I'll never forgive myself for hurting you. There's something else I must tell you. Then I'll leave immediately."

She attempted to stand but Michael pulled her back down and wrapped his arms around her, "No. You're not leaving. We can work this out. Tell me whatever else you have to, then we'll decide what needs to be done."

She straightened up and looked in his eyes, her own becoming even sadder than before, "I have to stand for this."

He felt the fear that had subsided return, "What is it? Surely nothing could be worse?"

Her eyes gripping his, she stood away from him and said softly, "Not worse, but more important. I. . .Edward and I, have two children-"

Michael was on his feet in an instant, his face twisted in shock, "*Two children! My God!*" He felt her plunging the dagger deeper into his heart, twisting it savagely as she did so.

Elizabeth shook as she took in his reaction but steadied herself stoically. She had anticipated this would be his response when he learnt of her secrets, this was the reason she could never find the words to tell him, *Men are allowed their mistakes but expect women to pay for theirs.*

She thrust her chest out and said with careful but definite pride, "They are five years old. Twins. A boy and girl." Then, not knowing why she said it, perhaps hoping in some innocuous way it would help to soften the blow, she added, "Like Megan and Mark, but my son was born first. You told me Megan came first."

Michael was dumbstruck. Seeing his mouth open but speechless, she felt she should fill the void and continued nervously, "Their names are Zethan Edward and Zarnna Elizabeth."

Michael could feel his blood racing through his body as though he was running a marathon, yet he could not command any of his parts to move. He wished his mind could be as immobile, if only he could get his thoughts to at least slow down; he needed to concentrate on how he could fix all this. Intermingled with each speeding thought of despair was one of hope, her words resonating in his head, "*I fell in love with you!*"

Taking in his shocked frozen stance, she became suddenly fearful for his health, both physical and emotional, and touched him on his arm, "Michael, I think you should sit back down."

Startled by her touch and voice, he shook her hand off his arm, turned away from her and walked over to a window. Looking out onto the beautifully manicured palace grounds, with every flower bed, lawn, and pathway perfection, all he could see was the shambles his life had become.

Feeling the destruction of her own perfect life once again, thinking of dashed hopes and shattered dreams, Elizabeth despaired and weakened. She sank into the armchair she had tried to lead Michael to, her mind flying across the ocean and back, taking in the carnage that had been wreaked. With her heart breaking for them both, she succumbed to more profuse tears.

Michael cogitated on all he had just learnt, then tried to calculate the damage and what he could do to counteract it. He was trained practically from birth to think it was in his power to rectify most problems, and he had been able to correct and conquer many 'impossibilities,' but nothing as apocalyptic as this had ever been presented to him. The woman he loved beyond reason, who he knew in his breaking heart felt the same way about him, his pure angel who was to be his wife and Queen, was already branded, belonged to another. Compounding matters was the shocking revelation that two children existed from that union. Granted, he was bringing an unknown almost grown child into what would have been their marriage, and she had accepted it with incredible grace, but he never dreamed that he could be called upon to do the same. To accept *two* children, in fact. *Well, he reasoned, I always wanted a large family, and after all, they come from her, I'll grow to love them. When the situation's righted, I'll end up with seven children, because I know Elizabeth would not renege on the four she promised me. Especially after* this!

It concerned him less than he would have thought that there was no precedent for this situation. No monarch had ever married a divorced woman, much worse one with two children from another man. However, he had already started forming in his mind a public relations campaign blitz that would ensure the winning of everyone's approval of the match. He would expose all the wonderful and brave acts Elizabeth had accomplished, primarily her courageous driving to save him when he was shot, selflessly ignoring her own wounds. Then her devoted nursing to bring him back to health; her capabilities and willingness in assisting him when his father was ill and he had to take on the King's duties as well as his own. Realistically, he admitted to himself, his biggest challenge would be explaining her speeches to a still vastly ignorant and frightened world. He knew many would want them obliterated. He would have an international battle on his hands to defend them, and he would have to be triumphant, so the world can start to enjoy some peace at last.

What was most perplexing was her inability to say how she feels about the unfaithful husband now. What happened to make her suddenly uncertain about her feelings for him, she said she felt hatred and repulsion for him before. *The feelings, the times she and I had together were genuine, I know that, no one could act that well. I know her! She loves me! The things she's done for me, to me. And, I never thought I could love so unconditionally. This love of ours is for all eternity. We're made for each other. I'm not giving her up! I'll make whatever sacrifices have to be made. She's not leaving me, ever! I'll deal with all the adverse publicity her past will bring. When the public gets to know her, how special and precious she is, they can't help but love her. But why is she so convinced that she still has to "figure" things out? What binds her to him still after what he did and how it affected her so devastatingly?* He was jolted by a revelation, spun around and faced her, "Now I understand why you feel confused, why you have to go back, and your concerns about The Children's home. Your own children are retarded!"

Tears leaving her surprised eyes Elizabeth rose saying emphatically, "No! My children are normal. They're beautiful." Seeing his odd look, that of disappointment yet relief, she knew she must try to explain something she herself could not comprehend. Taking his hand she sat them on two armchairs that faced each other, a small delicately carved chocolate table between them. Wiping her tears with a napkin from the tray of the table she poured them each a glass of water from the crystal decanter that stood beside the napkin holder. Taking the glass from her, he clasped his fingers around hers for an instant. He saw something in her eyes he had not seen before, something that warned him he too was about to feel, excruciating pain.

Elizabeth held his eyes with hers while holding back more tears wanting to be shed, "Michael, you know in your heart how much I love you. You know I wanted to spend the rest of my life with you… and…" she sighed, "*all* of our children. When we met, I felt my marriage was over, that Edward had killed my love for him, that I could never trust or love another man again. Something inside me had died, I was in deep mourning. But you brought it, *me,* back to life." She emitted another sigh, "I tried to tell you about my past many times, but I didn't know how to do it without risking losing you forever. That's why I kept postponing it. I guess, stupidly, hoping with time it would get easier, that you'd be more accepting of the shocking truths." She brushed aside an escaped tear, "I was terrified of losing you Michael. You and my children became my whole life-"

He reached over and grasped her hand, "You'll never lose me Elizabeth. We're meant to be together forever." She clung to his hand, her nails digging into him, neither aware of this small pain, that of the heart being so great. Wistfulness clouded his eyes, "Damn, if only we'd met before you married."

"We did." Elizabeth said simply.

"What? We did?" He said in a puzzled voice.

"Yes. At a masquerade ball at Frederico's palace in Spain. When I was eighteen. I met Edward a year later."

"What? How could I not remember?"

She was mildly surprised. She had wondered about this before, becoming suspicious when he played Savage Garden's 'I Knew I Loved You Before I Met You' on her voicemail when he was away negotiating with dissenters. Now she *had* to jog his memory. "I was disguised as Elizabeth One. I wore a gold sequined mask."

Michael's eyes enlarged with more shock, "*That,* was *you?*"

"Yes. You were with Priscilla. You came across from the other side of the ballroom and asked me to dance. While we were dancing you asked my name. I said *"Elizabeth."* And you said *"Elizabeth what?"* And I said *"Elizabeth the First."* Then you smiled your teasing smile and said *"Okay, if that's how you want to play it, I won't tell you mine either."* To which I said, *"But I already know yours. You are Sir Walter Raleigh."*"

Michael looked disbelievingly at her, "My God, you remember it as well as I do."

She was now completely surprised, "You remember it?"

He dropped his head, then quickly looked up at her, "Damn you woman! *You,* were the reason I told Priscilla I wasn't ready for a committed relationship. Our romance went sour after that and then she… well, that's another story. We'd been dating two years, I knew my feelings for her weren't strong enough for the commitment she wanted if I could be drawn to you like a magnet."

Elizabeth said softly, "I thought you came to me because of our costumes and the history those two people shared."

"No!" Michael said forcefully, "It was because you drew me over like a hypnotized moth to a flame…even then, when I didn't know you." His memory sparked back to that fateful night, so long ago, "Why did you run away after I kissed you when I danced you out onto the terrace? The way you responded to my kiss I could tell you felt a connection with me too?"

She frowned, "It was all over the news that you'd secretly become engaged to Priscilla, and I would never do that to another woman… what the Canadian did to me."

He shook his head, "That was media fabrication. I'd never proposed."

Elizabeth similarly shook her head, "I didn't know that at the time, and I had such strong feelings for you. I fantasized about you since I was a pubescent girl-"

His face lit up, "You fantasized about me?"

She dropped her eyes, "You were my *only* fantasy, Michael."

He rushed toward her, lifted her chin and pulled her up to stand, "And you were mine! *You* were the mystery woman in my fantasies that I told you about when we were in Venice!"

Shocked, Elizabeth swayed on her feet, "Oh my Godde!"

His eyes misting, he grabbed her, and sitting in his armchair, drew her onto his lap and cradled her in his arms. They both began to silently weep, for their lost first love.

Elizabeth reached over to the chocolate table and picked up a napkin. She wiped Michael's tear stained face, then her own. Giving him a soft peck on his lips, she removed herself from his lap and sat down in her armchair, hoping it would help if there was some distance between them for what she was about to divulge. There was a battle raging inside her. She knew she must not stop now, not yield to cowardice and retreat; onward is unavoidable, regardless of the inevitable wounding that would be done to both sides. She must accept the outcome, but knew there would be no complete victory for either side.

Unable to disconnect from him she leaned over and held his hands, "I told you of my instincts about something being terribly wrong in Trinidad, but that nobody would tell me. Well, after you left for lunch, I spoke to my family and housekeeper on Skype, and I eventually got it out of them. It seems Edward has lost...hope...for life. He appears to want to die, only lives for the children. They and their nanny, my housekeeper, have been spending summer holidays with my parents at their beach house in Tobago. I've been speaking...seeing them, and my parents, on Skype, about two or three times a day. When you were working, or asleep. They think I'm staying with a girlfriend."

She felt a tremor from Michael's hands and wanted to cling to them but thought, considering what she still had to tell him, it would be best to release them, which she did, "My parents know...about Edward. At first they couldn't believe it, then they wanted to kill him. They agreed with me about the separation, but knowing what a great father he is, how much he loves...us, and said how much he regretted his infidelity and it would never happen again, they convinced me to let him stay in our guest quarters in order to give the children a period of transition. So they would not be as upset if...when, I finally decided to divorce him. I told my parents I couldn't forgive him. He'd become repulsive to me...I could never let him...touch me...again."

The lovers both shifted uncomfortably in their seats. Elizabeth looked away from Michael's eyes, she saw a new expression there that began to shred her heart further, he knew what was coming. He grasped her hands again, his eyes heating up, on the verge of more tears, "You don't have to go back, ever see him again. I'll send the plane for the children. And their nanny. And your parents-"

She pulled her hand out of his grasp, "No Michael. I have to face... the situation, myself. I see now that I've been running away from dealing with it. If you'd seen the faces of my parents and housekeeper when I finally coerced them into telling me what was going on...and afterwards, my children crying inconsolably when I asked them if they were missing me as much as I was eventually told. It was gut-wrenching. They'd put on such happy faces before because everyone had told them I needed a long rest to be able to come back happier. You see, when I first learnt about what Edward did I felt lost...destroyed. I became depressed, couldn't eat or sleep. The only thing that kept me going was love for my children, my family's love and support. And my responsibility to the children at The Home. Without all that I would've wasted away. So deep was my shock that...what happened, could happen to Edward and me. We had it all. Or so I thought."

Forcing herself to look at his eyes, she continued, her voice softer, "The six months Edward spent in the guest quarters was torture. I avoided being home when he was there but he tried and tried to get me to talk, and listen. I told him it was useless. I started traveling more to get away. Then the situation came up with the grant for The Children's Home and my speech. My family felt it best that I get a complete break, away from everything. They worried I was headed for a breakdown. I got too thin, was crying a lot, couldn't focus, was sinking into serious depression. So Aunt Ruth came to get me in their plane, spent a few days along with my parents convincing me to go to New York, and then Europe with her and Uncle Robert, for a long stay. At the time, I didn't think it would be this long. But then I fell in love with you, and the grant was so slow in coming through and-"

His jaw set, Michael grasped both her hands, "I'm coming with you. Uncle Patrick will take over until we get back-"

Elizabeth stood up, wringing her hands out of his grasp, "No! You can't! In any case, it's too risky for you to leave now. Remember what Doctor Martin said about Uncle Patrick having his eye on the throne-"

Standing to face her Michael was adamant, "I don't care about that, I'd rather lose the throne than lose you, Elizabeth." He saw a look of guilty horror come upon her and added quickly, "Anyway those rumors are just vicious gossip. That sort of talk comes up every so often, doesn't mean anything." He reached for his phone in his jacket pocket, "I'm calling our plane's Captain. We'll leave tonight."

She put her hand on his stopping him, "Wait Michael. I don't want you to come. I must do this alone, face Edward alone. *We* have to sort out our future, alone."

Michael was stunned. Taking in a breath, he said slowly, "What does *that* mean exactly, explain it to me please."

A frown covered her forehead, perplexity flooding her eyes, "I wish I could. I'm at a loss. I don't understand what I'm feeling. We should sit. There's more I have to tell you."

She sat again and he followed, not taking his eyes off her face as she looked away from him. His phone vibrated in his pocket and she heard its soft buzz. She hoped he would answer so that she would have more time to sort out her thoughts but he ignored it, still watching her intensely. Then his house phone rang, he ignored that also.

She worked at putting calm in her voice, "Earlier, when I spoke to my parents and accosted them with keeping things from me, my mother eventually broke down and told me she and Daddy were worried about the children, and, Edward. The twins had started acting up, throwing temper tantrums. Something they hadn't done since they were two, and then hardly ever. And every night waking up with nightmares, which scarcely ever happened before. They obviously sensed something was very wrong in their little lives." A sob escaped from her lips as she tried to contain more tears. "Mummy wouldn't say any more and walked away from the screen, I could tell she was starting to cry. I had to beg Daddy to tell me everything that was happening. He admitted that Mummy wasn't sleeping, worrying not only about the twins and me, but Edward. Apparently he flies over to Tobago after work every night, to read to the children and tuck them in. He sleeps in our room there. It's about a thirty minute flight from Trinidad in our twin-engine Cessna, more in bad weather. The weather's been terrible since I've been gone. Lightning storms every night. He's been flying in them, which is crazy. Suicidal in fact. My parents forbade him from flying when there're storms but he ignores them. He's been having dinner with them after the twins are asleep, and they've been talking. They say he's being destroyed by remorse for his...stupidity, is grieving terribly...over me. Says I never even gave him a chance to properly explain, and, make reparation, and *I* was the one who gave up on us." She shifted her feet and stifled another sob, "Then Daddy told me Edward had stopped drinking. This was always a bone of contention between us, too many Trinidadian men drink too much. He was drunk when...you know. Anyway, now he only has a glass of wine with dinner when forced by my worried parents, Daddy said the weight is just falling off him. He does another dangerous thing, he goes swimming in the sea for hours after dinner. Sharks have been sighted feeding at night recently and it's become extremely risky to swim at night. When exhausted he sits on the porch, staring at the sea until Daddy has to get out of bed and insist he go to bed. Daddy's caught him crying every time. I've seen Edward cry only twice, when I accepted his proposal, and when the twins were born. When Daddy told me, he looked like he was about to cry himself and he called Tilda, my housekeeper, to talk to me, saying he had to check on the twins in the tub. There're four other people in the house who could've checked on them."

Elizabeth became silent, she needed to focus on calming her heart rate, it was racing. As was Michael's. He hated hearing all this, dreaded what was still to come.

Softly, she continued, "Tilda corroborated everything, and began to cry, unashamedly. The only other time I saw her cry was when at eighteen, Edward and I put her and her retarded toddler on our plane after she'd written The Children's Home asking for help, and she had to leave her family, and homeland, the island of Saint Vincent. We became her family. She became our housekeeper and then a devoted nanny to the twins. She's indispensable. Her daughter is eight now and doing well at The Home." Michael shifted impatiently in his seat, wanting her to hurry and finish, but she was oblivious to this as visions of the distraught Tilda came back to her. Emotionalism rising, she continued, "She showed me a recent picture she took of Edward with her cellphone. I was so shocked, at first I didn't recognize him. He must've lost thirty pounds or more. His face looked gaunt, haggard. His eyes lifeless." A sob and tears escaped from her, "He looked like death, Michael."

She began to shake again, this time with fear exceeding the sobs, and Michael rushed to kneel in front of her. She held onto his hands and blurted, "He's dying because of *me*, Michael! Because I wouldn't listen to him, wouldn't give him a second chance! I have to go back and fix the mess my whole family is in. While I was here with you helping to keep your family together and strong, mine was weakening and falling apart!"

Michael squeezed her hands, his face filled with fear as the inevitable hit him, and he knew he must fight for his life, "Elizabeth, my family is yours too, you did a wonderful thing, what you did for us, for me. You and I are family, we are bonded forever. Even *before* you met him. Why would you want a man who almost destroyed you with his infidelities? I would *never* be unfaithful to you, my darling, you must know that-"

"He's the father of my children, Michael-"

"*I* will be the father of your children, yours, mine, and ours. I won't hold you to the four you promised if it's too-"

Tremblingly she blurted, "His *life* is at stake, Michael. My children's father, the man I married, shared my life with, and…love."

Michael's face became suffused in white then red color as he raised his voice, "Love! You can't still love him! Then what the hell do you feel for me?!"

She looked lost again, "I love you Michael. I always will."

Perplexity filled him, "And him? What do you feel for *him*?"

Michael's phone rang again, he ignored it again. The house phone rang again. He ignored it also and became infuriated, "Shit! Don't they realize I can't talk now!"

Elizabeth said soothingly, "Darling, perhaps you should answer, it may be important."

His irritability unabating he stared at her, "Nothing's more important than this! What do you feel for him, Elizabeth?"

"Michael, please try to understand. I was...am, married to this man for seven years, dated for two more, we have a history, most of it loving and wonderful. I'd put it out of my mind to escape from pain-"

He sneered, "Pain *he* caused-"

"I know. But I never gave him a chance to take it away, redeem himself, I was so immersed in my pride and grief I buried all the goodness. I thought I hated him, but now that I face the prospect of losing him forever, I realize I still love him."

Incredulity overwhelming him, Michael stood up and braved his fears, "So, what do you *really* feel for me, if you still love *him?*"

Elizabeth stood and faced him, her face pained and bewildered, "I love you too."

He winced as though she had slapped him rather than said what he wanted to hear. Befuddled, he said softly, "You love me too? What? More? Less? The...the same?"

Nervous about her response, she added two words she did not mean, "I think, the same."

He picked up on it, raising his voice slightly, "You think? You don't know? What would it take for you to know, Elizabeth?"

She reminded herself how much she really hated mendacity, "I do know. I love you both the same. I wish I could love you more than him. I can't comprehend it, but it's the way I feel. I'm sorry, Michael."

The vein in his neck bulging more, he exclaimed in disbelief, "Elizabeth that's impossible! You cannot love two men the same! It's incomprehensible!"

Her brow furrowed, her beautiful face looking waif-like, "I know. I can't comprehend it myself, I'm so sorry Michael, it's killing me to hurt you, I wish...I wish I could have you both." She dropped her eyes as they flooded again, "Let's hope in another life...you and I...but, in this one, I have to go back-"

There was a loud knock on the heavy door leading to the main hallway and Michael shouted angrily, "Go away! I can't see anybody now!" The knock was repeated, stronger and more persistent than before, Michael screamed toward it, "I said go away, leave us alone!"

The heavy door flung open, Jenkins rushed in, his face ashen, "Michael, you must come immediately! Something terrible's happened!"

Elizabeth and Michael walked toward him, both with the same thought but Michael put it to words, "What? Papa?"

Jenkins responded in a panicked voice, "No! Mark! The girlfriend broke up with him. Apparently she wanted to have sex, he told her he wasn't ready and she cussed him out, told him he's gay! And that all their friends think so! He went into your father's office, bolted the door, jammed something against it, broke into the gun cabinet and is threatening to shoot himself! The King, Megan, and I've been trying to talk him into opening the door but he won't listen, keeps singing some dreadful song to drown us out. I've phoned Brian and Eric to come break down the door, they're the only ones I trust to keep their mouths shut, but neither's answering. Doctor Martin isn't answering either. The King was eventually able to shout above the singing to tell him you're coming to talk to him, that you understand what he's going through and to wait until you get there, and he agreed. He's singing softer now, we hope listening to your father, he doesn't look good either."

Michael turned to Elizabeth, his eyes wide with fear. She hugged and kissed him softly on his mouth, "Go quickly. Mark trusts you. Only you can save him."

He kissed her again, "Wait for me here. We still can work it out. Promise me you'll wait here, Elizabeth."

She forced a sweet smile, "Of course darling. Go quickly."

Watching Michael's retreating figure as he raced out the door with Jenkins, she felt an overwhelming sense of loss, a great part of her very soul leaving with him. She said a silent affirming prayer as a fleeting thought came to her that Michael would save Mark. As he had saved her. Then the thought was gone, she knew it was her turn to be savior. She had to go.

Body shivering, mind quivering, Elizabeth gazed around Michael's apartments, the loving home they had shared, for the last time. She walked quickly to his dressing room, took out of the clothes hamper the shirt he wore the night before, and breathed in his scent. Rolling it into a tight ball, she stuffed it into her handbag. She had to take something of him; he was not an addiction that could be easily, if ever, cured.

Fighting the desire to weep she looked through the wet in her eyes and rummaged in her handbag. Locating her passport and wallet, she turned off her cell phone and zipped the bag shut.

She snatched up her laptop and placed it in its case and walked towards the hallway door. Catching her eye on the table where Michael had rested it was the late Queen's diamond engagement ring. She stared at it for a moment. Its exquisite dignified beauty notwithstanding, the symbol of Michael's everlasting love for her looked as forlorn and alone as she. She walked over to it, slipped his great-grandmother's sapphire and diamonds ring off her finger, kissed it, and placed it alongside the Queen's ring; yet, each still looked lonely, abandoned.

The pain in her soul increased as lost loves, shattered hopes, and forbidden dreams, invaded her thoughts, but she reminded herself of the reasons for her leaving, of the queenly thing she must do. *This is my sacrifice for a kingdom.*

CHAPTER
39

*W*alking hurriedly downstairs to the garages Elizabeth applied lipstick, then patted powder under her eyes in the hope of hiding evidence of her prolonged crying.

She gave a chauffeur a short story about having to go to Michael's cousin Laura's boutique to get something that came in that she had ordered and needed to try on. The man offered to pick it up and take it back if it didn't fit, so she added to the lie that Laura was expecting her to have tea. He still hesitated, saying there were no bodyguards around at the moment, and he was under strict orders from Prince Michael that she must always be accompanied by at least one. She was arguing with him that she would be quite safe when two bodyguards walked up. She chose the one she recognized who was happy to accompany her.

Being driven out of the palace gates for the very last time, against her better judgment, she turned around and looked at the impressive structures. They stood boldly magnificent as a paradigm of Michael's ancestry. She no longer saw the buildings but in their stead, her proud and loving Michael, fading away from her life, but living forever in her heart.

There was an empty parking spot directly in front of Laura's shop. Elizabeth jumped out, told the men she would be awhile so they should take a break, get some refreshments, and attempted to offer them money, which they adamantly but appreciatively declined, telling her to take her time.

Laura was thrilled to see her and offered tea, which she refused saying she had an upset tummy. Taking in Elizabeth's anguished face and washed out eyes, Laura believed the falsehood and was sympathetic. Elizabeth purchased stretch trousers, a blouse, and flat sandals. She then held her abdomen, gave Laura a pained look and asked to use the restroom, adding that she will probably be there awhile. Laura gave her a compassionate quick hug, told her to take as long as she needed, and she won't be disturbed.

Changing quickly into the new blouse, trousers and sandals, she felt a stab of guilt for having to use the sweet woman, Michael's own cousin, to unwittingly assist her in her escape from him, but felt she had no choice. In her confusion, it was the only way she could think of to get away.

She remembered from her previous visit, the day Michael's family kept her occupied in order to distract her from worrying about him when he was negotiating with "*dangerous people,*" that there was a small window at eye-level in the restroom. She had noticed it looked out on to a pretty little courtyard with multi-colored flowers growing in wooden tubs and clay pots, and leading out to the backstreet was a narrow tall iron gate.

She shoved her dress, pantyhose and pumps into the plastic shopping bag, knotted the bag, then knotted her long hair into a bun. Climbing on top the covered toilet seat she attempted to open the window but it was stuck from lack of use. She flushed the toilet hoping the noise would drown out the banging she knew she would have to inflict on the window's frame to get it open.

Banging softly, she managed to get it open only halfway.

Through the small opening she threw out the shopping bag, then her handbag, and flushed the toilet again. Banging harder and pushing simultaneously, the window suddenly flew outwards and she overbalanced hitting her elbow hard against the wall, on the same hand that was wounded during the assassination attempt on Michael. A sharp pain shot down and up her arm. An expletive escaped from her lips, and she took in three deep breaths.

Ignoring the lingering pain, she clambered onto the top of the toilet tank, slung her laptop bag's straps over her shoulder and clutched it to her chest. Hoisting one leg through the window she sat awkwardly on the sill, her back hunched, barely fitting in the opening. Her heart began to race as a sudden panic entered, *Damn! How do I explain if I get stuck here!*

Two more deep breaths brought a little calm and, dreading the fall, she looked at the ground outside. Relief came upon her as she saw a large tub of yellow chrysanthemums under the window, and knew the soil would be soft from the gray day's continuous drizzle which had only just abated. After another deep breath she straightened her interior leg and hurled her body over to the outside, landing on her side with a heavy thud in the middle of the tub. With her legs sticking out at odd angles, she held onto the side of the tub, righted herself, and sat for a moment in the center of the crushed chrysanthemums. Taking in her graceless position, and the undignified situation, she chuckled to herself, *If only Michael were here we'd have such a good laugh!* Then she began to cry.

Dusting herself off between sobs, she picked up her bags and stumbled towards the locked gate to attempt her next hurdle. Glancing from side to side through the vertical bars of the rusty iron gate, she saw four empty cars parked across the narrow backstreet but no one in sight. Swiftly, she hung her laptop bag on a spear at the top of the gate, flung her bags over the gate, and climbed onto the horizontal bar in the middle. She swung one long leg over the top and onto the outer side of the bar, the other leg in rapid succession, and caught the fabric of that trouser leg on a point of a rusty fleur de lis on the top of the gate. She heard the tear and felt the scrape concurrently. *Oh great! All I need now is to end up in hospital with tetanus!* Jumping onto the pavement she didn't take the time to inspect the damage, grabbed her laptop and bags and ran down the block to the cross street, away from the one where the palace car was parked. She walked hurriedly for five blocks before hailing a taxi.

On examining her latest wound in the taxi, she was relieved to see it was just a tiny scratch and wiped off the dots of blood with some saliva on a tissue. The tear in the fabric was visible only on close inspection. She had the taxi drop her off near a neighborhood park three miles away and after he drove off, walked into the park and sat under a tree behind rhododendron bushes, to formulate a plan.

Uppermost in her mind was the call she must make to Michael. She knew she would be traced if she used her phone or called from a hotel. Therefore she would have to call from a public phone, get a taxi immediately afterwards to take her far away from the area, then walk a few miles to some small hotel. Michael's detectives would be checking the taxi companies as to where she was dropped off. She could not face him again. She doubted she would have the strength to leave him again.

Arranging her thoughts, she decided she would tell Michael that although she would always love him, they could not have a future together, and though it may break his heart for a while, it may be of small comfort to him to know that hers is forever broken to have hurt him and from the loss of him in her life. In order to make it easier on both of them, they must sever all ties, she must go back and save her family.

Knowing the call must be brief, she jotted down some concise notes on the pad she always carried. They looked so cold and impersonal, not at all relating to their burning love and experiences together. She tore it up, deciding she could only come straight from her breaking heart.

Passing by a grand hotel with several taxis parked outside, Elizabeth saw through its glass doors, a bank of phone booths in the foyer with solid wood privacy doors. Walking in quickly, head down, collar up, sunglasses still attached, she chose the empty middle booth. She sat still for a minute trying to compose some words, and herself. Her heart racing and hands trembling, she put in the necessary money and punched in Michael's number. Although desperately wanting to hear his voice, she planned as soon as he answered to tell him to not speak but just listen, so she could empty her heart and soul quickly, and then hurry away before the call could be traced. There were five rings and his voice came on, pleasant but abrupt, "*You've reached Michael. Leave a message.*" It had not occurred to her that he may not answer and she would get his voicemail. After the first flash of disappointment came one of relief, she could leave a longer apology without the concern of being traced instantaneously.

An immediate fear took hold. What if he could not answer because things went badly with Mark? Looking at her watch she calculated that it was under two hours since Michael left the apartment. Obviously it would take some time to talk to Mark, and even more to settle him with professional help before he could return to his apartments to discover she was gone.

Swallowing, she spoke softly, "Hello Michael, it's Elizabeth. I...I hope and pray everything went well with Mark. I know you would've been able to help him. Please tell him for me that whatever his feelings, he's not a freak, and he should read more history that'll prove he's not. And I love him...he's extremely lovable, and he will find true love at the appropriate time." She took a breath and continued, a little more emotion than she had intended in her voice, "Michael, my darling. My precious perfect love. Please forgive me for all the wrongs I've done to you. I never meant to hurt you. It breaks my heart to know that I have, as much as it breaks to lose you." Holding in a threatening sob, she said emphatically, "You were my *first* love...and my *only* fantasy. But when we first met in Spain I thought you were bound to another, Priscilla. And so, in time, I fell in love with another, Edward. To whom I am now bound, legally and emotionally. And though fate may have played a cruel trick to have us meet again when I was suffering with a broken heart from...what Edward did, I will be forever grateful for your healing love, and that I had this precious, beautiful, time with you. I wish it could've been forever, I planned for it to be. But, discovering the love I was already bound to, not just legally but with two cherished children, would be forever lost to my children and I if I didn't give him a second chance, I was awakened to the love that I previously had for him. I cannot lose that love, I cannot let my children suffer…or him…anymore. I…I hope one day you'll understand, and forgive me."

She could contain the tears no longer, they came down in a rush and she gasped several times trying to stop them, with no success. Knowing she could be running out of time she continued through heartrending sobs, "You are a most extraordinary and wonderful man. In your life, and your reign, you will do many more great things that will positively impact the whole world. I wanted to be by your side to help you, but it's not possible now. You'll have to find another to be your Queen, to share your life. Please don't contact me in any way. It will only prolong the agony of our inevitable parting. I have to save… go back to…my family…my life. I will not change my mind. I cannot. I'll always love you Michael. You'll always be in my heart. 'Till death and even beyond.' Goodbye my perfect love. Goodbye."

The taxi-driver didn't know what to make of the blubbering pretty woman in the backseat of his cab. She gave him no address, simply ordered him to, "Drive! As far away from here as possible!" and proceeded with heartbreaking mournful sobbing.

He tried to talk to her, offering to, "Help in any way-did somebody break your heart-he's a fool-not worth wasting tears on the idiot-a beauty such as you should never have to suffer a heartbreak," and other compassionate remarks. He gave up eventually as she continued to ignore him, acting as if he didn't exist. Nothing existed but her overwhelming grief.

After twenty minutes of being driven around the city Elizabeth wiped her eyes and looked out the window, "How far away are we?"

The driver looked at her in the rearview mirror, "About five miles from where I picked you up. Where do you want to go?"

She pulled out some notes from her wallet and handed them to him, "Drop me here." Before he had time to give her the change she was out of the taxi and round the corner. Waving as he passed her he decided he had enough grief for the day, though now with a generous tip, and headed back to headquarters.

Walking endlessly, aimlessly, unseeingly, Elizabeth's feelings of guilt, shame, remorse, and pain, were of Biblical proportions. She wallowed in the grief of causing such tremendous damage to Michael, and for her own loss of such a great love.

In her distress, she lost track of time, and place. She was lost. In every sense of the word. Exhausted physically and emotionally, she wiped her eyes and looked up and around thinking she had better find a hotel, but didn't recognize anything around her in the city she knew so well. She had no clue as to where she was.

Daylight was long gone, streets empty of people but filled with parked cars. Lampposts were few and far between, and together with the dim lights from the occasional lit windows of otherwise gloomy homes, they cast eerie shadows all around. Taking stock of the situation, she became afraid and impulsively reached into her handbag for her phone. Seeing it was off, she remembered why and dropped it back in her bag.

A sinister-looking couple dressed all in black wearing nose and lip rings rounded the corner giggling, and her neck prickled.

She relaxed when she saw they had two black toy poodles on leashes, and walked up to them, "Excuse me, I'm afraid I'm a little lost. Can you give me directions to the nearest hotel?"

They looked her up and down and giggled some more, the dogs licking her sweaty ankles; then the man spoke, "You're more than a little lost, sweetie. There's no hotels around here. The best you'll get is a sorta Bed'n'Breakfast at Miss Nellie's three blocks down. Come. We'll walk you there. You shouldn't be walking alone here at night."

Arriving at Miss Nellie's, the woman ran up the steps ahead of Elizabeth, punched in a code on the door lock and let Elizabeth in. It turned out she was the day receptionist cum maid at Miss Nellie's. The exterior of the building was as depressing as others around it so it was surprising to see the contrasting cheerful interior, the walls covered in white wallpaper patterned with tiny pink and blue bunches of flowers tied with yellow ribbon. Elizabeth rang the brass bell that stood on the desk in the foyer, next to an enormous plastic vase filled with almost every type of polyester flower.

Down the hallway a door scraped open. A woman's voice called out gruffly, "Who's disturbing me at this late hour?"

Miss Nellie shuffled down the narrow hallway dressed in a flowery nightgown over which she was tying on a matching robe, flowered satin bedroom slippers on her feet, muttering all the way. The woman gave the old lady a quick wave and smile and bolted out the door. Elizabeth apologized for the late hour, explained she was unfamiliar with this part of the city, got lost, was flying out tomorrow, and would like a room for the night for which she would pay cash. Taking in the beautiful Elizabeth's red watery eyes and her measly luggage, Miss Nellie immediately assumed she was the victim of a domestic dispute, and discarded her irritated demeanor for one of compassion.

Accepting Elizabeth's money, she led the way up the rickety stairs, "Come dear, I'll give you a nice quiet room facing the backyard. Do you need me to wake you? You'll have to order a taxi. What time's your flight?"

She opened the door to a clean, small, but pleasant enough room with a double bed and yellow painted walls. The bed's comforter was almost the same color as the walls and patterned with bright blue flowers and green leaves. Attached to each corner of the walls were large paper appliques of blue dahlias and orange sunflowers. Standing on a table next to the bedside lamp was a blue vase filled with polyester sunflowers, another smaller vase with more sunflowers stood on a small chest. It was apparent Miss Nellie had an affinity for flowers.

Elizabeth forced a smile, "This is lovely, thank you. I can't remember my flight time but it's later in the day. Is there a payphone I could use?" She reached into her bag for her pad and pen, "And I need this address."

Miss Nellie gave her the address and led the way down the hall to the bathroom and payphone.

Pointing to the bathroom she said, "There're clean towels in the closet. Talk on the phone as long as you like, no one'll bother you. Only the old Colonel is on this floor and he sleeps like the dead, is as deaf as a doorknob anyway. Breakfast is from seven to nine. But it's after one now and you look like you need a good long night's rest, so I'll bend the rules for you. Just come down when you're ready. Sleep well, dear."

As soon as Miss Nellie was downstairs and out of earshot, Elizabeth phoned the only person she felt who could help her make sense of her incomprehensible feelings, the only other person to whom she could say just about anything. The moment she heard Ruth's voice, she collapsed into another crying fit and could hardly speak, "Aun...tie Ru... uth, hi. It...it's...me-"

Ruth went with her instincts as she didn't recognize Elizabeth's voice due to her incessant sobbing, "Elizabeth! Is that you?"

"Ye...yes."

"What's the matter? Why're you crying?"

She stuttered between the sobs, "My...my...heart...is...breaking, again...I...I need you."

Ruth was puzzled, "I don't understand. Did Edward do something else? *This* time I'll kill him! With my bare hands!"

Elizabeth fought back more tears in order to better explain, "No. It's Michael...Prince Michael. I fell in love with him...he with me. After you left. And...and now Edward is dying...and I realize I love him still...too." She lost the fight to tears, her words coming out in staccato as they gushed forth, "I feel...I must...go back...to Edward... my family...is in ruins...the children suffering, Mummy Daddy too.

But me too...I love Michael too...don't want to lose him...but I love Edward too...I don't know...what to do-"

Ruth could not make much sense out of her weepy ramblings but recognized from her condition that her 'child,' the niece she and Robert helped her sister and brother-in-law to raise, 'their' only child, that she loved as if she had been born of her womb, was in deep distress, and needed her immediately.

"I'm coming. Where are you darling, at our hotel?"

"No. Michael would look for me there. I'm afraid to face him again. Don't know what I'll do. I ran away from the palace...was staying with him. I'm at a Bed'n'Breakfast, somewhere on the outskirts of the city. Can't use my phone, he'll find me. I spoke to Mummy Daddy and the children this...yesterday...morning, told them I'm coming home. I booked a flight for today...but...I can't face it right now. I'm sorry to sound like such a fool, weakling. I'm just so confused. Never thought something like this was possible-"

Ruth spoke with her motherly voice, "Don't worry. We'll figure this out together. Give me the address and telephone number there. I'll call Captain Jefferson immediately. I'll be there in about seven hours. In the meantime, you rest and take care of yourself. When last did you eat?"

Sounding like the child she was feeling Elizabeth queried, "Eat?"

Becoming more worried Ruth snapped, "Food, Elizabeth. You know how you...forget, to eat, when you're upset. You need to eat and be strong to face...everything. Promise me you'll eat."

Not caring about promises being kept, so many had already been broken, she meekly, untruthfully, agreed, "Yes, alright."

Hanging up the phone she felt mildly relieved, help was coming from a source she could always depend on. Her stomach beginning to churn, she staggered to the bathroom and involuntarily regurgitated the only meal she had that day. She rinsed her mouth with mouthwash she found under the sink, urinated, and willed her legs to get her back to the bedroom.

Stripping off her clothes, she donned Michael's shirt. She could smell him all over her. Everywhere. Especially on her genitalia, the scent of his sperm sticking there as if to remind her that their hastily stolen lovemaking on the rug in his office, at lunchtime between appointments, was the last time they would ever make love. The last time she would revel in the inhalation of his special scent. The shirt was a poor substitute for the need to have him wrapped around her, but it was all she had of him, and would ever have again.

Dropping onto the bed, she curled her fatigued body into a fetal ball, and fell into a weepy restless sleep.

CHAPTER
40

King Alexander thanked God he now knew more about his disease, how to read the signs of an oncoming attack and when to take the nitroglycerin. Without it, he didn't think his poor heart could survive another turmoil, what with both his sons suffering with broken hearts. And in the same Godforsaken day.

Leaving Mark again in the professional capable hands of the psychiatrist and Doctor Martin, he walked briskly back to Michael's apartments accompanied by Elena and Jenkins. Opening the door, it disturbed him further to see Michael had not moved from where he left him hours ago, staring at his cellphone, its speaker on, playing Elizabeth's message repeatedly.

Gently, both the King and Elena laid a hand on each of Michael's shoulders. The King said close to his ear hoping to drown out Elizabeth's mournfulness, "Son, it's late. Let's eat dinner and get some sleep. We'll think more clearly in the morning, be able to handle…things."

Michael stared at his father with amaurotic wet eyes, "Leave me alone. All of you go."

Not retreating, the King bent down in front of his eldest son and heir, took in his defeated demeanor, one he had never seen before, and was beset by a moment's panic. Seeing the King's whitening complexion, both Elena and Jenkins stepped forward to stand on either side of him.

Elena held his arm, "Come, Alexander. I think Michael needs to be alone awhile longer. We'll have dinner sent to him. He'll eat when he's ready. But you are in need of some sustenance immediately." She rested a hand on Michael's knee, "Michael, please call us anytime, for anything. You know how much we all love you and want to help. Say you will. Please?"

Staring unseeingly, Michael gave a dismissive nod.

Jenkins rested both hands on Michael's shoulders demonstrating agreement with Elena's words, then said softly, "They're still searching. The taxi-driver was our best lead but the area he dropped her off was a dead-end. We have people watching the airports round the clock. I'll call you as soon as I have word." Michael gave another vacuous nod.

His Majesty kissed his son on both cheeks feeling more than a little afraid. The worrying group left the inconsolable prince alone, to wallow deeply in his sorrow. They all knew after hearing Elizabeth's heart-wrenching message earlier, and knowing her strength of character, that even when she was found, she would not agree to see Michael. Not ever again.

Ruth picked up the tray which held fruit, a thermos of coffee, milk and sugar, two hard-boiled eggs, a roll, cheese, and a jar of marmalade, that had been left outside the door, and knocked, "Elizabeth, I'm here, darling. Open the door."

The door flung open and Elizabeth threw her arms around her aunt almost knocking the tray out of her hands, bursting into a fresh batch of tears. Maneuvering the tray and a clinging Elizabeth over to the bed, Ruth managed to rest the tray on the bedside table and sit herself and Elizabeth on the bed.

She took Elizabeth's face in her hands and wrinkled her brow sympathetically, "You poor darling, you look a mess. And what's this you have on?"

Elizabeth could barely say the words, "Michael's sh…shirt."

Flinging her legs up onto the bed, she rested her head in her surrogate mother's lap, and began to cry more energetically into a bawling that reverberated through both women. Ruth let her wail until she thought Elizabeth must be depleted of just about every drop of water in her body.

Anxious to hear what had occurred she brushed Elizabeth's unkempt long hair behind her neck and spoke gently, "You need to talk about the situation darling so we can get it resolved. Come, drink a little coffee and eat something. Then tell me what happened."

Elizabeth sat up and shook her head, "No. If I eat anything now I'll be sick." she wiped her face and blew her nose in some tissues Ruth had been holding and kissed her, "Thank you for coming. I feel so lost, so confused."

Ruth returned the kiss, "Tell me everything, darling."

Elizabeth sat on the bed in the lotus position, faced Ruth, and synopsized what had occurred after Ruth and Robert left, glossing over the dangerous situations but detailing some of the romantic aspects of her and Michael falling in love.

Ruth kept control of her face, trying to not show emotions of shock or judgment, "Well, you haven't told me how far…okay, you stayed with him, so obviously you had sex. The question is, how much…how serious-"

Elizabeth interrupted, her dear aunt did not drop her own busy life to come all this way to help her and not be given the whole truth, "Very serious. In the seven weeks I had with Michael I did everything I did in the seven years I had with Edward."

Ruth could not contain her surprise, knowing how chaste Elizabeth had been before Edward but then how torrid was their sex life, and exclaimed, "Jesus!"

Suspecting Ruth's thoughts, and knowing how shocked she must be, Elizabeth could not help but see some amusement in the ludicrousness of the state of affairs and giggled, "Actually, I did more with Michael. I never had to wipe Edward's bottom."

Ruth held her chest as if hoping to stave off a heart attack, "What! You wiped Prince Michael's bottom?!"

Sorry to have so shocked her usually unshockable sophisticated aunt, Elizabeth quickly quelled her giggles and said seriously, "It was after he'd been shot, and the nurse wasn't there. He couldn't reach to clean himself without suffering extreme pain. So I barged in and did it. He was mortified. We never spoke of it afterwards."

Ruth herself fell to giggling, "I'm not surprised. How do new lovers discuss something like that!"

Elizabeth saddened again, "We discussed everything else possible. Did…everything, with each other. I love him so much. We made so many plans for the future. I really thought we'd be together forever." She emitted a deep sigh, "Until I found out about Edward, his remorse, his grieving, his condition, saw Tilda's picture of him. He looks like death, Auntie Ruth. You'd never recognize him. His eyes vacant. All his strength and power gone. It broke my heart to see him like that. It woke me up to how much I still love him. How much we had. Have. All the wonderful times, two incredible babies." She dropped her head back in Ruth's lap and began to sob softly, "I feel so confused. I love them both the same. How is this possible?"

Ruth's voice was wistful, her eyes clairvoyant, "Why not? The heart of a woman knows no boundaries. A woman will love ten children equally. Why not two men?"

Elizabeth sat up, "I never thought of it that way."

Ruth broke into a smile, "Look at the Mormons, when the men were polygamous. Of course a lot of people say they were probably just a bunch of dirty old men, but the men claimed to love all the wives equally."

Elizabeth smiled cynically, "Huh! Only *men* were allowed to be polygamous. I wonder how many women, were they financially independent, would've liked to have been polygamous?"

Ruth got serious, "Good question. We'll never know. The patriarchal religions that created our patriarchal societies would've never allowed it anyway. Which brings us back to your predicament. You are in love with two men. But you can't be married to both. You must decide on one." A deep frown transformed Elizabeth's entire face as though this information was new to her. Ruth correctly read it to be confoundedness and continued calmly with the wisdom gained from experiencing a quantitatively more challenging, longer life, "These are your two choices. You can stay here and start a new, different life, and family, with a prince you've been with for just seven weeks, and try to forget Edward. And hopefully forgive yourself for not allowing him to attempt atoning for what he did. But, know that he will fight you for your twins up to his last breath.

Or, you can forgive Edward, your husband of seven years who adores you and regrets his mistake, and save him from disintegrating further, and resume the loving life you once had together, with the two incredible children you already have. And maybe even increase that family with a cementing love-child. And, try to forget the prince."

Elizabeth stood up, held onto Ruth's hand for a moment, then walked over to the window that looked out onto the backyard. Staring out, she saw that the deathly gray depressing day that was yesterday had vanished, and today was resplendent with life renewing sunshine. Recollecting the wonderful times she had with Edward, the strong love that bonded them, and the two amazing children that came out of that love, she knew realistically she had no alternative but to go back. She had to be responsible, save her family, Edward, her marriage. There was much healing to be achieved, innumerable challenges lay ahead. The most difficult of which would be is, forgetting Michael.

Turning around to face Ruth, her old decisiveness returned, "I must call Edward. We have to meet somewhere alone, and talk, before we go home to the children. I must have it out with him. Find out everything. No matter how painful it is. Otherwise I'll always be wondering, may never be able to get beyond what happened. I always suspected there was more than he told me. The Canadian bitch started to give details when she called to tell me. I hung up on her, couldn't take it then. Afterwards, when I forced it out of him, he told me they might've done it twice. I need to know everything before I can get past it. He'll have to spend the rest of his life proving I can trust him again. I hope I can forgive him."

Ruth spoke with the sagacity garnered from her own experiences, "Remember, forgiveness is about healing you, not the other person. Though it often does heal you both."

Becoming pensive Elizabeth looked out the window again, "It'll have to. From the way Edward looks, he needs to heal as much as I do."

Ruth cajoled Elizabeth into eating some grapes and half a banana, then the women discussed getting Elizabeth onto Ruth's plane at the airport without Michael's people finding her.

Normally with a private jet this would not be a problem, these planes often have their own V.I.P. terminals where their passengers go through Security checks separately from those of the general public. Unfortunately, only yesterday the country had been put on 'red-alert' due to new bomb threats by terrorists, and all Security Checkpoints had been consolidated to only two now heavily guarded areas where the general public goes. In any case, Ruth pointed out, if Michael's people were any good they would have checked the private jets and would know Grangers' plane had come in, would find out when it would be departing, and to where. With this in mind, it was decided Ruth would go shopping for convincing disguises for both of them, while Elizabeth phoned Edward.

"Hello, Edward."

Relief was obvious in his excited voice, "Elizabeth! Your Mum and Dad told me you'd be calling. At last. I so desperately need to speak to you. How are you my lov…how're you?"

She had planned to be formal to the point of being acrimonious, but hearing his excitement and slip of calling her "*my love*," her own

excitement at hearing his loving voice again returned. Though he obstinately called every day, she had not heard his voice in months beyond
the first "*hello.*" She had been hanging up on him whenever she forgot
to look at the caller identification on her phone and had answered. She
also deleted his messages without listening to them.

Before she left Trinidad she told him he was not to call her, she
would talk only to her parents about anything that concerned the children, or the business, and he was to tell them if he needed her decision on any business matter. She would only go through them or deal
directly with the person in question. She knew this system would put
extra strain on him in running their business, but was too hurt and
angry to feel any sympathy.

She had developed an atypical bitterness that made her feel justified, *He has brought me such great suffering it's only right that he suffers too.*
Now, hearing the voice of the love that had for so long been her life, the
love that had helped her bring forth life, her once indestructible rock
that had started crumbling, she wavered, and felt a jab of remorse.

"I'm fine. How're you?" She was cool but polite.

There was no denying his desperation as he said in a suddenly
cracking voice, "I'm going through hell, Elizabeth. I'm missing you
terribly. Please come back to me. You *must* know how sorry I am for...
what happened. Nothing like that will ever happen again. I'm going to
spend the rest of my life making it up to you. I'll do whatever it takes.
Whatever you want. You know how much I love you. I'll do everything
to make you love me again. We're so great together. We'll be happy
again. I promise. I'll die if you don't come back. You are my life. I don't
care about anything else. Please, my love-"

His pleas paradoxically pleased and irritated her and she interjected, "We have to meet somewhere and talk. Before we...I, come
back to Trinidad, and see the children."

He hesitated, "Yes...of course. Where? Where would you like to
meet?"

She picked up on his hesitation, and a small degree of bitterness
returned. In the past, when one or both of them had been traveling

alone for more than a week, they would often meet in Jamaica before going home. That beautiful island and their gorgeous hotel was the most ideal and convenient location for them to rendezvous. They would not tell their Jamaican branch of their arrival for several days, and have a romantically torrid interlude intermingled with delightful conversations about their individual trips, before going in to the office for a few days. It was their special time and place for only each other, in which the world and all its stresses would be banished.

That could never be again. Not on that island. Not in that hotel. With the despicable deed Edward and the Canadian woman committed there, their sanctified place had been forever defiled, sullied beyond redemption.

Elizabeth was silent with remembering. Edward knew her reason for silence and it tore at his insides. Just as he started to make a suggestion to quickly break the awful silence, they said together, "Barbados. Let's meet in Barbados."

That exquisite tropical rock, rising solitarily out of turquoise waters, positioned defiantly away from the Lesser Antilles archipelago of other Caribbean islands, was the perfect meeting place for the estranged couple. It held only joyful memories for their entire family.

Before Elizabeth's parents built their spacious beach house in Tobago, Elizabeth and Edward divided the twin's summer holidays between Edward's parent's vacation home on the small island of Monos just off the Trinidad mainland, and renting a beach villa in Barbados.

When they were at Monos 'Down the Islands' as the area is called by Trinidadians, Monos being in a cluster of other small hilly vacation islands, Elizabeth, Edward, and his father Jean-Marc, would take one of their speedboats over to the mainland weekday mornings, collect their cars at Powerboats parking lot, and drive to their different offices to work.

The twins would be left with Edward's mother, Nadia, and her two sisters, Tilda, their nanny, three other female domestic staff, a boatman cum watchman and his wife, and a huge bunch of cousins, the offspring of Edward's three siblings and his aunt's grandchildren.

The cousins comprised of every age group from toddlers to teenagers, were equally of both genders, and a rainbow of colours from the mixture of many of humanity's races. Edward's older sister was married to a striking man of mostly white with a sprinkling of black and Chinese ancestry.

His younger sister was married to another handsome man whose ancestry was also black and white but no Chinese, but he had a Syrian grandfather. Edward's brother, the youngest, was married to a beautiful 'doogla,' a woman of half African, half Indian ancestry, and their contributions to the large brood of happy-go-lucky children were the youngest of the bunch, a one-year-old boy and a three-year-old girl.

Although the twins loved these carefree holidays with all their cousins, swimming and Marco-Polo, rafting and 'pirating,' playing every kind of children's game, hide-and-seek, cricket, football, tent and fort building, Star-Wars, Lego, dolly-house, board-games, school, and a host of other invented games, the highlight of their summer vacation was getting on their parent's plane and going to Barbados for two or three weeks.

That island was a complete vacation for Elizabeth and Edward as well, because they would take the time off from work. Apart from wanting to give their children this special fun time with their parent's undivided attention, Barbados was more than an hour's flying time from Trinidad in their plane, depending on head or tail winds. This ensured there would be no easy hopping over to Trinidad for any work emergency. The managers of the Trinidad companies would just have to handle any crisis that came up that could not be resolved on phones and computers.

Elizabeth and Edward would rent a two-story six-bedroom beach-front villa on the west coast of the island which was staffed by a cook, a maid, and a yardman. Tilda was off-duty from any housekeeping work. Her only job there was looking after the twins and their needs when their parents were not around. The cook would bring fresh fish, fruit, and vegetables, every other day. The rest of the shopping was done by one or both Du Beauchamps at a nearby supermarket. Having the well-trained Bajan staff in attendance for eight hours a day allowed everyone in the family to luxuriate in total relaxation and indulge in all the fun activities the tourist haven offers.

Sometimes the two parents-in-law would come either together or alternate spending a week in the villa. Other times they would take turns renting a condo just down the beach. Often, one or two, or all three, of Edward's siblings and their spouses, would come with their brood or just the adults alone, for a week or a four day week-end. Elizabeth's cousins, children of her mother's and father's brothers who still lived in Trinidad, would also sometimes come for a week or two with their offspring, either staying in the villa or renting their own place nearby, depending on accommodation availability. Although there was often a lot of comings and goings, everyone was so relaxed and carefree, all formalities and responsibilities of home and work temporarily put aside, no one was unduly bothered by the dramas of the revolving doors.

Nighttime was adult-time. After dinner and putting children to bed, Tilda would be left to stay in the house watching her favorite television shows, and watching out for errant children. The adults would sit out on the beach patio having after-dinner drinks, indulging in philosophizing, ole-talk, gossip, picong, risqué jokes, and playing music. The music would often come from a C.D. player; but there were special times, depending on what energy was left from the day, and on the partying mood, the music would be provided by members of the group who played instruments. Both Elizabeth and Edward played guitars, while Edward's father Jean-Marc, and Edward's older sister, Careen, played cuatros. Elizabeth's mother, Gabrielle, kept the rhythm on the tambourine, her father Anthony, equally rhythmical, doing so with an empty rum bottle and a spoon.

Whoever else was vacationing, and that included not just the visiting family but friends from Trinidad who happened to be there at the same time and would pop in to 'lime,' would join in with a variety of improvised instruments. Depending on the musician's creative abilities, these could be anything from an aluminum soup pot or plastic bucket substituting as a drum, or a couple of matchboxes doubling as a pair of maracas, or a grater and fork from the kitchen doing double duty as a scratcher; or even a collection of drinking glasses filled to different levels to make perfect sounding notes, from which the talented musician would play a tune with the assistance of a table spoon or knife being used to tap against the glasses. Every so often, depending on the song, Careen or Jean-Marc would flip their cuatros over and use the backside as a conga drum.

The songs ranged from love ballads to folk songs to pop and rock-n-roll, but would inevitably be intermeshed with calypsos old and new, and everybody gleefully sang along.

Sometimes different members of the group would compose rhyming lyrics to a well-known tune, filling the room with raucous laughter, as the witticisms and ribaldry that Trinidadians are famous for would take-over, and few would be spared from the extemporaneous playful 'picong' and 'fatigue' teasings. The hapless victims could be anyone in the group, but were often perverse corrupt politicians or any other disreputable person who was recently in the news.

Although these impromptu jam sessions were not a rarity with Trinidadians they somehow seemed extra special, with no one wanting to terminate them, when they occurred in Barbados. Perhaps it was because of the unhurried pace of the smaller island, so unlike that of their hectic metropolitan homeland. Tranquility aside, it is well-known that Trinidadians have an innate ability to create a fete just to celebrate living, whenever there is a friendly gathering. Whatever the reason, the stress-free holiday atmosphere always prevailed.

On quieter nights, usually during the workweek when there were not as many people around, Elizabeth and Edward would go out for a romantic dinner or a walk on the beach, or both. On occasion they would be joined by other adults. But whenever they were certain they were completely alone on the beach, under cover of darkness, they would slip out of their clothes, go skinny-dipping, and indulge in brief but intense lovemaking in the tropical sea. Their lengthy sessions of lovemaking would usually take place at night in their bedroom, and often also, after lunch, when they would use the accepted island excuse of needing 'a rest.' Tilda would keep the children quiet in the living room downstairs with board-games.

Whenever the adult vacationers were lucky enough to be in Barbados when The Merrymen or The Merryboys were in concert, the Trini group, being big fans of both, would be sure to go en mass to dance and be entertained by them. Whatever their activities, the magical fun times in Barbados always conjured up only happy memories for the Du Beauchamp family.

Thus, both Elizabeth and Edward automatically thought it the perfect place to make an attempt at renewing their loving relationship, and hopefully save their marriage.

Edward eagerly asked if she would be there tomorrow to which she replied, "No. I won't get there for three more days. I have to clear up some things. Where should we stay? What hotel?"

This time he didn't hesitate, "Sandy Lane. I'll make the reservation right away."

She was a little surprised at his choice at first, the exclusive hotel being the most expensive on the island, and they had not stayed there before; but then she realized he was going all out to please and impress her, so she pretended to be blasé, "I want my own suite."

He hesitated this time and was unsuccessful in hiding his disappointment when he did speak, "Oh? Of course. Will you let me know when you're coming so I can pick you up at the airport?"

She responded curtly, "I don't want you to pick me up. I'll take a taxi. I said I'll be there in three days, I'll see you then," and she hung up.

Speaking with him after such a long silence between them, an anxiety overtook her about seeing him again so soon. Ruth planned for them to leave around four the next morning, hoping that ridiculous hour would give them the advantage of being less detectable. She would drop Elizabeth off in Barbados, her plane would refuel, then immediately fly on to Trinidad for her to spend a few days with her sister before going back to America.

The three extra days Elizabeth told Edward she needed to "*clear up some things*" she really needed to clear her head. To try to clear it of Michael, so that it would be open once again to singularly receive Edward.

Despite the anger she harbored against him for destroying both her dreams of a perfect life, she knew she would always love him, as much as she would always love Michael. But, she required some time alone in Barbados to finish grieving the death of one love, so that she could begin to relive happily with the other.

Dressed as two businessmen in casual loose fitting suits, wearing salt and pepper wigs, heavily tinted spectacles, thin moustaches and differently styled goatees, the ladies made it through security and immigration without incident. Ruth was as nervous as her niece and became annoyed with Elizabeth when she stopped in at several airport shops to look for a children's book of her paternal cousin's, which had only recently been published. Eventually successful in obtaining the last four copies in a small bookstore, though severely burdened with sadness, she was elated to hear the saleslady say, "They're selling like hotcakes, such a unique children's story."

They were just about to open the final glass door to enter the tarmac where Granger's plane was waiting with its engines already running, when a man stepped out of the shadows and held onto Elizabeth's arm.

Elizabeth jumped back and shrieked, "Jenkins!"

He looked at her wearily, "I didn't mean to startle you-"

Ruth held her other arm as she started trembling, "Where's Michael? Is he here? I can't face him…I don't know if I can leave him a second time. And you know my leaving is best for everyone. Especially him. You know I have no choice, don't you? Oh Godde, where is he?"

Jenkins put on his fatherly persona, "It's alright, he's waiting in the car for word from me. The family convinced him you're doing the proper thing but he insisted on coming in case you'd agree to see him. He still feels he can get you to change your mind. I'm supposed to phone him when you're found-"

Elizabeth paled as tears sprung to her eyes, "No! Don't call him Jenkins, I can't bear to see him. Ever again. My heart is breaking. As I know his is. How is he?"

"He's in terrible shape. Just like you-"

Tears began to flow down her face like rivulets as her shaking increased, "Oh Godde! I never meant to hurt him like this. I never thought we'd end like this. End at all. I love him so much. But I have to go back to...my family. Please try to make him understand? Please do that for me? I have no choice. I must save my...family. It's the right thing to do. And it's the right thing to do for Michael...his position. You know that better than anyone."

Jenkins made a surprising gesture and tenderly wiped Elizabeth's tears with his handkerchief, "He'll never agree with that Elizabeth. Michael's willing to make the ultimate sacrifice for you, give up everything if-"

She grabbed his hand, "No! That must not happen. It would destroy him eventually. He's born to lead. He'll forget me in time. He must. As I must forget him!" and a gush of fresh tears came down to form new rivulets on her face. Swayed by her emotionalism and terrible sacrifice to do what is right, Jenkins pulled her into his arms and rocked her gently from side to side. She rested her head on his shoulder and let her tears have free rein.

CHAPTER
41

Captain Jefferson opened the door and raised his eyebrows, "I came to see what was the hold up. Do you need my assistance, Mrs. Granger?"

Ruth shook her head, "No. We'll be right there, thank you Captain."

Elizabeth lifted her head, kissed Jenkins on his cheek, stepped back and said softly through her tears, "I will always love him. We're just not meant to be. Take care of him for me. Keep him safe. Promise me."

Jenkins kissed her on her wet cheek, "You know I will. I promise. Oh, I almost forgot, Michael said I'm to give you these if you refused to see him," he reached into his jacket pocket and pulled out the velvet jewelry boxes that held the ruby Bindi, the emerald and diamonds ring Michael bought her at Tiffany's in New York, and the gold cherub emeralds and diamonds set that he designed and had made for her.

Elizabeth shrank back, "No, Jenkins, I can't take them. I don't deserve to have them-"

Jenkins' soft expression shifted to his usual austerity, "Elizabeth, Michael's heart is already breaking. Your refusal to accept these tokens of his love, which he had made especially for you, is only going to rub salt in the wound. You must take them, it's the least you can do."

She hesitated as she mulled over his words, but then reluctantly, slowly, put out her hands.

Ruth impatiently snatched the boxes away from Jenkins, "Say your goodbyes, darling. We need to leave. Goodbye, Mr. Jenkins. And, thank you, for everything." She nodded politely to Jenkins and went outside to wait for Elizabeth.

Elizabeth and Jenkins stared at each other awkwardly for a moment, then both stepped forward into an embrace.

Her voice coming out in sobs she released him, "I'll never forget. Thank you for everything you did for me, and Michael. Take care of him...and everyone. Oh, how is Mark? How did it go?"

His moistening eyes surprised her, "It took a lot of talking, but Michael eventually convinced him to let him in and hand over the gun. Then he kept him calmed down until the psychiatrist arrived. He's in therapy and will be fine. He just has to figure out who he is, that's all."

Elizabeth sighed, "Like the rest of us. Please give him my love... my love to everyone. Even though they must all hate me."

"You'd be surprised. Your actions, though terribly hurtful, seems to have gained a grudging respect and admiration. Especially from Duchess Claire. You have my mobile number, call me if you should need...anything, anytime. Alright?"

She gave him a rueful smile, knowing this would be the last time she would speak to him, "Alright. Thank you. Tell Michael I'm filled with remorse for hurting him, but though I'll always love him, I can't speak with him ever again, he mustn't call me. I'd change my number but I know your people would soon uncover the private new one. We'll both heal faster if we let go completely. You understand, don't you? Make him understand."

He nodded and returned the smile that was filled with regrets, "Goodbye Elizabeth. Be happy."

"Beautiful, beautiful, Barbados, gem of the Caribbean sea. Come back to my island, Barbados. Come back to my island and me"

Walking through the Grantley Adams International Airport, the mourning Elizabeth was forced to smile, as coming from nearby speakers she was welcomed by the sweet seductive voice of Emile Straker and the crooning Merrymen. Recollections of past visits and being entertained by them made her wonder if they might have reunited again, and were performing on the island or perhaps on tour. *Alright fellars, I'm back in your 'Beautiful Barbados.' I'm relying on it to help me patch up my life once more. It would be nice to see you guys back in action again. For me,* she sang an old song in her mind, *'You will never grow old.'*

Dismissing a brief debate in her head as to whether to rent a Minimoke, she decided against it, knowing Edward would reserve one, and she didn't intend to gallivant before he got here anyway, just swim, walk the beach, and think; so she took a taxi to Sandy Lane Hotel.

Michael's impatient voice belied his passive demeanor, "Tell me more. I want to know everything Jenkins. How was she?"

"In a terrible state, the same shape you're in. She was crying and shaking the whole time she was saying what I just told you. My spies told me even while walking through the airport in her disguise she had to keep wiping her eyes under her glasses. She did go into several shops though, asking for a specific book. She bought out the stock at the last store where she eventually found it."

Michael's lifeless eyes showed a small spark, "I know it. Her best friend wrote it. It's titled 'Welcome To America.'"

Jenkins hated contradicting, "No. That wasn't it. This was a children's book, titled 'A Pig's Paradise.'"

The spark left Michael as he slumped back in his chair, "Oh. Grieving for me, but still thinking of her children."

Jenkins tried to sound sympathetic in his rationale, "She's a mother, Michael. Her children will always come first. You know that was her primary reason for going back. And deep down you admire her for it, her caring and integrity. If she stayed with you, you would lose a certain respect for her. We know the husband would fight her tooth and nail for her twins, and with the not uncommon corruption in high places in those islands he probably could buy a judgment in his favor. She most likely would lose them. Neither she nor you could've lived with that."

A spark returned with a snarling remark, "I have more money than him. I would've fought for the twins for her-"

Jenkins shook his head exasperatingly, "Michael, she made the decision she felt was right. Most of the family think so too, as much as they love her…and you. It was the best thing all round when you consider your-"

Michael stood up and angrily swept two crystal glasses and a water jug off the table positioned between them. Jenkins jumped up as they violently hit the marble floor, smashing into minute pieces and scattering all over the balcony.

"Nobody decides what's best for me but me!" Michael shouted, and ran out of his apartment down to the gym and the waiting Master Huan, his Tae Kwando instructor. He needed to strike something, and knew it should not be Jenkins.

Sleep had been elusive on the queen-sized bed in Ruth's luxurious jet-plane, and again on the king-sized bed in the luxurious Sandy Lane suite. Elizabeth donned the white hand crocheted bikini and matching sarong she bought in the hotel and pensively, anxiously, walked the beach, and swam in the sea.

Wading out past the frothing waters that bubbled onto sparkling coral sands, she swam up and down parallel with the beach, resting only briefly to tread water and breathe deeply. She swam and cried, swam and cried, her salty tears flowing freely to mix with the salty sea; weeping over the confusion and disunity that once more encompassed her life, in the aquamarine warm healing waters, where the Caribbean Sea sought unification with the Atlantic Ocean.

Her tears at last emptied, she came out of the water and strived to put Michael out of her mind to focus on Edward, and on what she had to do before they could try to build a life together again. Lost in concentration as she walked, she was at first inattentive to the sudden abandonment of much of the beach as visitors and locals went indoors to cool off from the blistering one o'clock August sun, or for lunch, or a nap, or all three. Beginning to feel even more alone than she had in past days, she sped up her ambling pace intending to go back to the hotel to call her children, when for no reason she could fathom, the hair at the back of her neck bristled.

Looking into the distance, she saw a tall familiar figure walking down the beach toward her. She at first thought it might be a Barbadian friend she and Edward had made through business, or maybe Chris Gibbs of The Merrymen who, though much older than they, had befriended them many years ago at a Bajan fete.

As he came closer, she recognized, not the man, but the purposely wrinkled white linen shirt and matching calf length pants they had bought when on holiday in Saint Tropez, France, three years ago. *Oh no! He's here already. He wasn't supposed to come for two more days. I needed those two days alone to think!*

Edward's heart was racing faster than it had that unforgettable time he knelt waiting for her answer to his proposal of marriage, eight years and five months ago. He strode nervously toward her, the speed of his long strides deliberately controlled as he held back his true desire to sprint to her.

Elizabeth froze into a statue-like stance, watching the familiar gait of the man who now looked like a stranger, her husband of seven years. She was conscious of her flip-flopping heart, but anxiety, anger, hate, pity, love, fear, meshed in her psyche. Pity and fear dominated as she took in his unusually thin physique. He had needed to lose fifteen pounds, the weight he had gradually gained in recent years, not unlike many ambitious men in their society who had to work harder than others to pick up the slack of other's laziness, drank alcohol excessively as they became more stressed, and neglected exercising routinely as they had in the past.

Seeing her Alpha-male thirty pounds lighter, gaunt and some-what vulnerable, awakened an emotion in her she was not ready for, remorse. It annoyed her, and she suffocated it. She wanted her anger to be directed at him not at herself. She brought on a hardness unlike anything she ever thought she could possibly manifest.

Edward's dark brown hair shimmered in the sunlight, wayward strands of sunburnt auburn mixing with his first, though scant, signs of premature graying, which took her by surprise. He had no gray when last she held him close some eight months ago. His high cheekbones were sharper, more defined, as they contrasted with his now concave cheeks. Though unusually sunken, his bluish-green eyes sparkled out of his handsome tanned face as his full lips opened to a shy but loving smile, "Hello Elizabeth."

Serious-faced, she accosted him, "What're you doing here? You weren't supposed to come for two more days!"

He had expected some hostility but was stunned by her blatant aggression, yet he said lightly, "Well, neither were you. So I guess we were both anxious to see each other."

She responded defiantly, "No! I wanted more time alone. I'm not ready to deal with you yet!"

His left eyebrow arched upwards, "*Deal* with me? I thought we were meeting here to talk and, reunite-"

"We are here to thrash out your infidelities, and for me to see *if* there is a reason for us to reunite!"

Seeing him so calm, so handsome despite the subtle emaciation, strangely irritated her, and she strove to remind herself that she must no longer succumb to the malignant anger that once more was threatening to destroy her. She was a different woman now. Not the sweet innocent girl her parents and aunt and uncle raised with such love and devotion, making her naively feel protected from the possibility of ever being severely hurt by someone who loved her; not allowing it to enter her mind to be wary of the stupid weaknesses of the flesh of men that held the potential to obliterate a great love. Especially of this man who had absolutely worshipped her.

She suppressed the pernicious anger that had again begun to grow, and enforced her resolution to not feed it anymore. This time, she had the strength in her soul, the tools in her heart, and the skill in her body, and she was determined to cut the cancer out once and for all.

Edward's hands twitched nervously, "Alright. Let's go back to the hotel to my...or your suite, and talk."

She didn't want the enclosure of walls nor the sullying of their rooms by the depraved spirit of 'that woman.' She now wanted everything out in the open, to be swallowed up by the churning sea, blown away by the Trade Winds, "We'll talk here."

He looked around, "Here? But it's not very private Elizabeth. People may walk by and hear-"

She was obdurate, "I don't care. *I* have nothing to hide. We don't know them anyway. So start talking. Tell me what the hell happened in Jamaica with you and the bitch."

Edward shivered as his eyes narrowed, "Well...you know what happened. I...I told you."

Elizabeth's eyes hardened, "Not everything, and only after *she* called me. Otherwise I would never have known. You were never going to tell me, were you?"

He looked down at his feet, "No. I thought I would lose you. I just wanted to put it out of my head. I was too ashamed. The thought of it filled me with self-loathing."

She stared hard at him, willing him to look back up at her, which he did, "So, fill with more self-loathing. Tell me *exactly* what happened."

He hedged, "I don't remember much about it. I've worked on forgetting-"

She was not buying it, "You are super smart Edward Pierre Du Beauchamp, with a great memory. So you'd better use it, because if you don't tell me what happened, there's no way in hell I'm staying married to you! And you can say goodbye to the twins, because I'm taking them to Europe!"

Edward shuddered at the prospect of losing his whole life. One way or the other, he felt he was doomed, "Alright, I'll try. What do you want to know?"

She hid her fear and said with bravado, "Everything. Every *fucking* detail. And don't clean it up. Because the bitch will be only too happy to tell me everything if I call her."

She saw him cringe and it pleased her. No more miss nice sweet girl. No more the perfect lady. Thanks to him, she was experienced now, had been to hell and back, twice. She had grown up, grew a hard shell, and he had better get used to it.

Edward became not just afraid of her acting on her threat but was taken aback at her free use of obscenities. It had taken him years to get her to comfortably wrap her tongue around sexy 'dirty' words during particularly racy sessions of their salaciousness, so ingrained was her refinement. To hear her say some at this unstable point in time brought on a foreboding, a disturbing contrast to what it had done to him before.

He reached out for her hand but she kept it at her side, "Alright, Elizabeth. Come. Let's get in the shade under those trees and sit."

She followed him, watched as he pulled a dead coconut palm frond out of the bushes for them to sit on and dusted the stalk off with his hands.

She said coolly, "I don't want to sit. I can take whatever you have to say standing."

Looking up at her cold hard beautiful face from his bent over position, though a good six inches taller than she at his full height, he felt a smallness descend upon him.

He stood up to face her but not her demanding eyes, and kept his down, "Bill was in Miami on business for a few days. I was working late in the office, alone, when Helen came in to use the copier for some personal stuff. She suggested we go to a bar for a drink. It had been a long rough day and I felt in need of a couple drinks so I agreed. After we had a few Scotches, she began telling me she and Bill were having problems. 'Bedroom problems' as she put it. She went into a long story about him not turning her on anymore, and became quite upset. Well, I hadn't eaten much for lunch and all the bar had was soggy pretzels. I felt bad to stop her in the middle of her distress, so I let her talk, while I drank. And drank."

He took a breath, looked at her briefly then looked out at the water, "Before I realized it, I had become quite drunk. Too drunk to drive. She drove me to the hotel, walked me to my room. She...took off my shirt. Kissed me...on...in...my mouth. Then sucked my nipples." Edward shifted his feet.

His discomfort getting the better of his resolve to tell the whole truth to his sainted wife and convince her of his future faithfulness and undying love, he fell silent.

He could feel Elizabeth's impatience and heated eyes boring through him as she said coldly, "Go on."

He shook his head, "Well, as best I can remember, she...took down my pants...sucked me...I became aroused." His voice took on a sad pained tone as he pleaded, "Jesus, Elizabeth! Don't make me go over this?"

She was unmoved by his suffering, her own having never left, "Finish it Edward. I want the whole story or I walk."

Struggling to contain his fear he swallowed and continued with an attempt at an excuse, "Remember, I'd been traveling in the States on business for three weeks...you and I hadn't made love for days before I left, you were always so tired, I felt-"

Her coldness evaporated and a heat took over, "Oh no you don't! You're not going to put this on *me*, buddy! I'm not taking some kind of Eve-blame because you think you're bloody Adam and not accountable for *your* profane actions-"

He felt his own heat rising, wondering how he could possibly defend himself, "I'm not doing that, Elizabeth! I take full responsibility for my...stupidity. I'm trying to point out that I was...frustrated. And the whole trip had been very stressful, I had to deal with a lot of crappy people, and...and it felt good to be wanted, and with the alcohol and everything, I just weakened."

"How many times did you 'just weaken,' Edward?"

He shuddered, "A couple times."

"So, you weren't *that* drunk. A couple times as in, twice, or as in, two or more?"

"I'm not sure, I think twice. I had blocked the whole disgusting thing out of my head."

Twice! She wondered if she could believe him. He was desperate. Her father once warned her that even the most honest of men when they are cornered and desperate would lie unconscionably. If he could have hidden this from her for days before the bitch called to rub her nose in it, how much more could he hide? Men could block things out. Forget. Or at least think they could. Until it comes back to haunt them when they least expect it. Cynicism entered her voice, "If you could do it twice, drunk, you obviously really wanted her."

He raised his voice, "No! Not like I want you. I became...flaccid...after each time with her. I didn't stay hard like after I make love to you, always wanting more of you. Elizabeth, there was no love emotion, it was just physical sex. I had gone too long without. You and I made love every day before you got so involved with the expansion of The Children's Home and became so tired, and then I left right after on such a stressful long trip. I was bursting. I just needed to release-"

She shouted, "You should've done what any decent faithful husband would've and taken 'things' in hand!"

His head dropped, "It's not the same as having a warm body with you, to make you feel comforted. And, I was drunk! She had to...suck me...each time...to get me hard. It didn't just happen automatically like when I'm with you."

Unimpressed, her eyes hardened as she questioned, "Who was on top, the first time?"

His plea screeched, "Jesus, Elizabeth! Don't do this!"

Obstinately she persevered, "Who, Edward?"

He braved a cautious look at her, "She was."

Her eyes hardened even more, "And the second time?"

Squirming, he looked at the ground and mumbled, "Me."

Elizabeth shuddered, "Did you suck her?"

Braving another look at her eyes that sparked daggers, he questioned, "What do you mean? I may have sucked her breasts."

Trembling inside, she forced a calm voice, "Did you suck her *down there?*"

Astonished, Edward jumped, "What? No! I wouldn't do that with anyone else-"

Anger flirted with her controlled emotions, "You're lying. You love that. You always do it with me. For a long time."

Pleading reentered his voice, "That's because I love *you*. I love everything about you. You taste like heaven to me."

Skepticism joined her irritation, "Yeah, sure, a heaven you abandoned to go to hell with that she-devil."

Edward looked at her with pain-filled eyes, "And I'm going to suffer with that knowledge and regret the rest of my life."

Again Elizabeth looked unimpressed, "*She* told me she was on the pill so you didn't need a condom, and how you were so full of sperm, it was dripping out of her all next day. Why didn't you use a bloody condom, Edward! You could've picked up a fucking disease! And given it to *me*! And think what would've happened to our children if-"

Edward buried his face in his hands, "Oh God, I know! I wasn't thinking! And it was a spur of the moment thing, not planned! There was no condom available, no thought of it-"

Cynicism dripped from her words, "Not planned! I don't believe it. She was always flirting with you. And you flirted right back. I warned you that she wanted you. But you told me some crap about that kind of Canadian woman only comes down to the West Indies for black men, like Bill. And you knew she hated me. The flirting was very hurtful and insulting to me!"

He entreated, "But it didn't mean anything. I was just being friendly because of the business, she being our manager's wife. Believe me, Elizabeth, I had no intention of pursuing anything serious with her, or anyone else. Ever. I love *you*. You are my whole life. You and the children. I am incomplete without you. Just a shell. You are my substance, my essence. Please, my love. You have to forgive me. Nothing like that will ever happen again. I'll earn your trust. We belong together, soulmates. We're family forever. Please, my love. I'll make you forget… it… ever happened. You have to let me prove it to you-"

Interrupting him, his begging incomprehensibly vexed her, "Finish. What else happened?"

He looked confused, "Nothing. Nothing else happened. I swear. I passed out, when I woke up she was gone."

"Where is *she* now?"

"She's gone back home, left Bill. Actually, he's resigned. Said he needed a change, got a job with a cousin in Miami. He's training his replacement, leaves next week. I only started going back to Jamaica after she left. I wasn't able to face him before, though he doesn't act as if he knows…anything. He's been very conscientious, even found the new manager for me, is determined the company will have a smooth transition. I was so busy with you gone so long, your Dad had to fly up for the interviews and check everything out. After all, the Jamaican branch was his company before he had us take it over. He's very impressed with the new man."

He noticed her demeanor shift but could not read it as she said calmly, "Edward, I'd rather not talk about the business now. I have something important to tell you. Let's sit."

He sat beside her on the smooth stalk of the coconut branch but she slid away a few feet then turned to face him, "When I was in Europe, I met someone. And, I fell in love."

He was astounded, "Fell in love? What does *that* mean? Who?"

Elizabeth looked steadily at him, "Prince Michael."

Edward's face took on an incredulity, "Prince Michael? *The* Prince Michael? Who you told me you'd met in Spain when you were eighteen?"

"Yes. We met at a palace garden party the Grangers took me to. After they left, I stayed with him at his palace."

Edward jumped to his feet, his bronze-tanned face reddening, "What! *You,* had an affair?!"

She jumped up and leveled her eyes with his, her anger starting to simmer, "No! *You,* had an affair! *I,* fell in love!"

Edward crimsoned, "You *stayed* with him! What did you do with him? Did you screw him? We are married, Elizabeth!"

She reddened more than he, "You dare to throw that at me! I didn't *feel* married anymore! Because *you* screwed it up! Our perfect marriage! I'd wanted to die when you ruined my perfect life! I was suffering terribly, desolate, depressed, destroyed! He healed me. Made me alive again."

Edward looked away from her as his shock turned to disgust, "Shit! I don't believe this! You fucking with another man!"

Elizabeth's anger went beyond a simmer, "Don't turn away from me like I'm some whore! You're the one who went with a bloody whore! *You* became one! And caused me to believe our marriage was over. You repulsed me after I knew what you'd done with her! Defiled your body with her. The body you'd vowed was only for me! Risking my health! My life! And yours! Our family!"

His anger rose to match hers in intensity, "*I* only did it twice! And drunk! What did *you* do, *staying* with him? How long were you there?"

She kept her gaze steady, "The entire time I was over there."

"Shit! How serious was this falling "in love" business, Elizabeth? What did you *do* with him, he with you?"

Steady girl, keep strong, back to your honest self, "Everything. Everything you and I ever did, I did with him. I love him."

Edward's knees buckled and he doubled over, feeling as if a giant had punched him in his stomach and stabbed him in his heart with a sharp machete. He turned away, speechless.

Another man pleasured his Elizabeth. She pleasured another man. His virgin bride. Her sweet fruits meant only for him were plucked and feasted upon by another. *She feasted on his! This fucking prince! And now she thinks she's in love with him! Jesus God, this isn't possible! She's mine! Meant only for me! Never to be touched by another man! Never to love another! Only me! I'll kill the royal prick. Beat him to a pulp. Until he begs for mercy. Then I'll cut it off, and watch the motherfucker die!*

Elizabeth could see Edward becoming embroiled in anger, and felt some fear, but stood her ground. His rage frightening even him, Edward walked away from her toward the water's edge and stood there, looking out at the sparkling azure tides, seeing only his dreams darkening and being washed away.

Knowing how much he was suffering affected her less than she thought it would, her own suffering revisiting. She wanted to run away from it all, and sprinted down the beach.

He caught the swift movement in the corner of an eye and raced after her. Catching an arm, he pulled at her but she pulled back and he stumbled, falling to his knees in the sand. Her concerns for him from the past resurfacing, she turned, putting out her hands to help him up.

He gripped her hands pulling her down to her knees to join him, "Is this your way of punishing me Elizabeth? By giving yourself to another man? Saying you're in love with him?"

She hardened her look at him, "I *am* in love with him. And he with me. He asked me to marry him."

The plunged machete in his heart grew larger, sharper, went deeper. He dropped her hands. He could not bear to look at her, and looked away as his dejected voice came out in spurts, "So...you...want...a...divorce?"

She softened slightly "No. I don't think so-"

Unsure that he heard correctly he repeated her 'no' looking at her questioningly, "No? No? You don't want a divorce? Why?"

"Because I'm still in love with you. And we have two precious children that we both love and I can't hurt them."

He was happily befuddled, "You're still in love with me? But you just said you love *him?*"

"I do love him. I love you both. Equally."

His befuddlement saddened, his voice filled with disbelief, "You love us both *equally?* That's not possible Elizabeth."

His sadness weighed heavy on her, "It *is* possible. It's how I feel," then remembering Ruth's words of wisdom, she lightened, "and why not? A woman's heart has no boundaries. A woman can love ten children equally, why not two men? Men have gotten away in societies with loving more than one woman since Godde knows how long, probably before they killed off the Goddess and invented their God. You think millions of women haven't felt this way? Loving and wanting more than one man? You men need to come to the reality that you don't hold the monopoly on temptation. Women are no less tempted than men. But it seems that, so far, more women have evolved earlier than men and have come to the conclusion that to succumb to temptation and indulge in a sexual dalliance is, more often than not, going to result in an unhappy, painful, often permanent, unsettling outcome."

His entire face frowned as he processed her words, "But you succumbed to temptation, just like I did, Elizabeth. What you did was not lesser than what I did."

Her anger became aggravated, "The two situations are incomparable, Edward! *You* were unfaithful! *You* had a sexual dalliance! That made me feel belittled, insufficient, displaced, alone, and unloved! Unmarried! I would never have…been, with Michael, if you hadn't done what you did! You know it! You know how men were always coming on to me. I had no end of opportunities to do what you did. But *I* remained faithful to our vows. The vows that *you* insisted we say in Church before God and all our family and friends to "*make them more binding!*" But, *you,* gave in to temptation! *I,* fell in love!"

The shock at her startling rationalization in summation filled him with more consternation than he could handle. Taking in the beckoning and ebbing sea behind her he saw himself being dragged out, and felt like he was drowning.

Speaking rapidly he began grasping at imaginary lifelines, "Like you said, we have two precious children together, a perfect loving marriage before…I…screwed up. But that'll never happen again." Her indecisive words about divorcing resounded in his head, "*I don't think so,*" and he knew he had a royal battle on his hands. "Look, my love, you can't just throw it all away for some prince. We'll make a brand new start. We'll renew our vows. We'll do it in the same church we got married in. We'll have a ceremony exactly like-"

She snarled at him, "What good will that do, Edward, we broke them before! And you know I don't believe in all that Catholic brain-washing anymore! Neither do you!"

Edward stood up, pulling her up, "What do you want, Elizabeth? What do you want me to do? How can I make you forget the terrible thing I've done? How do I erase it? Tell me, and I'll do it."

She turned away from him saying bitterly, "You shouldn't have done the fucking terrible thing in the first place, Edward!"

Edward stared at her retreating figure as she walked down the beach, then held his head as he felt it swell with immense pressure, shaking it as he did so. No more words came to him, but he knew he could not allow defeat. He felt his very life was at stake, and the responsibility for it was solely his own.

The harsh reality was that his sinful actions could only be eradicated by saintly ones. Words alone would not suffice, he knew he would have to spend the rest of his life being above reproach. That is, if he could get her back. Win her away from, *That fucking son-of-a-bitch prince.*

CHAPTER
42

*T*he tropical night, always deprived of a long twilight once the sun had set, dropped like a stone, and suddenly, the beach was enveloped in pitch black darkness. Edward's anger turned to concern, then became infused with a high degree of panic. He had walked for ostensibly too many miles down the beach looking for Elizabeth and there was no sign of her. He knew she would not have gone onto the main road because she was barefoot and the asphalt might still be hot, and too rough for her feet, and he felt certain she would not go in the water alone after dusk.

He remembered the last time they were in Barbados how they had been impressed with the government clearing the beach of all the pesky beach bums who were basically male prostitutes, but that was years ago. He became frightened that the troubling situation may have returned, and she had been abducted.

He was about to turn back and run to the hotel for a security guard with a golf cart and flashlights to help him look for her, when he heard her voice coming from a nearby fisherman's house, singing. Walking towards the dimly lit porch, he saw her sitting on the steps surrounded by six small native children, leading them in a chorus of 'Yellow Bird.'

His heart leapt with relief, and love. *My Elizabeth. My love. Mother of my children. Light of my life. Always bringing joy, even in the midst of our sorrow. She's mine till death do us part, no fucking prince is going to take her away from me! I'll make sure of that!*

Elizabeth saw him approaching and stood up, the mother in the house shouting, "Dinner!" at the same time.

The children begged her to stay, but with a smile, she affectionately patted them on their backs and told them, "Scoot. It's dinnertime. Maybe I'll see you tomorrow."

Seeing the loving but sad look on Edward's face in the dim light softened her somewhat, but she determined that it would not daunt her from getting the complete cleansing she needed; she was not done with him yet, and she feared, now that he knew about Michael, he was not done with her.

She walked past him and headed in the direction of Sandy Lane. He fell in step beside her, "You frightened me Elizabeth, when I couldn't find you. I can't ever lose you, my love. You're my whole life. I know I can't take away the stupid thing I did, but I'll do everything in my power to erase it from your memory. You say you still love me, you have to give me a chance to be your husband again, you know I'll love you beyond this life and for all eternity. I'll make you happy again, you'll forget…him."

She swung around and faced him, "But will *you* forget him? Knowing what I did with him? Can *you* forget? Or is this something you will use against me every time we have an argument? Tell me honestly if you think you can live with that. Because I can tell you honestly, before I…had…time, with him, *I* couldn't live with what *you* did!"

Edward emitted a small groan, became too disturbed by visions of Elizabeth having sex with the prince, doing things he, Edward, had taught her, and he could not speak. She intuitively knew the reason for his silence, she having suffered through similar visions of him with the Canadian woman.

She took advantage of his thoughts to bring her point home, "You knew I was a virgin at nineteen when we met, and I stayed pure for you because you asked me to. And it wasn't easy. I met so many wonderful fascinating men that I was attracted to, in New York and throughout my travels. But I committed to you and kept my promise. But I never asked you to do the same, to wait for me, I thought it was a given, if you expected it of me, then I should expect it of you. I never thought I had to say the words. I know with all that you had to teach me, you probably learnt from somebody else, and I had assumed it was before we met. But since your...screw up, in our marriage, I started wondering if you continued doing it with other women while I remained frustratingly virginal throughout our courtship. Especially with us usually separated during semesters, you at Yale and me at N.Y.U. And now that we've been separated for eight long months, I'm again wondering if you became, and stayed, faithful, during that time. As I was not for the last two months, but then, again, I felt our marriage was over and I was not being unfaithful. But perhaps you felt so too. So did you? Did you screw around again?"

He looked directly at her, "I did not. I was determined to save our marriage, get you back. I knew how much I'd hurt you, us, and swore to myself I wouldn't again."

She retorted, "You expect me to believe that? You couldn't wait *four weeks* before!"

He was obstinate, "Well I did. I did what you said and 'took things in hand,' all the while thinking of you."

She was obdurate, "Huh! Eight bloody months too late!"

"Jesus God, Elizabeth! We've got to get past this! What else do you want? You want to know how many others I've been with? Two. Both before I met you. None after. I satisfied myself with our heavy petting and then would go home afterwards and jerk off. I did the same thing whenever I got a hard-on, always thinking of you, looking forward to our wedding night and the rest of our lives together."

Skepticism flooded her face again, "*If*...we try again, how're you going to handle the fact that I had...experiences with another man, whom I still love, as much as you? You've always been so jealous and possessive of me."

Grabbing her shoulders he said emphatically, "I'm going to put it out of my mind! I'm going to put the bloody bastard out of *your* mind! I'm going to make you forget the motherfucker son-of-a-bitch prince ever existed!"

She was shocked to hear him denigrate Michael this way. Michael who had saved her from despairing of ever being able to love again because of the damage Edward had done to destroy her, and her illusion of a perfect life. Michael who loved her beyond reason, who would sacrifice his kingdom for her. The old anger flared up inside her and she lost control of it.

Flaming mad, she pugnaciously pushed his hands off her and balling hers into fists, began to violently pound on his chest, screaming in his face, "Don't you dare speak about him that way! He's done nothing to you! In fact, *you* owe him! *He* taught me how to love again, after *you* became the 'bloody bastard' and nearly destroyed me! *You* are the 'motherfucker son-of-a-bitch!' You can just go to hell!" She gave him a vehement push, forcing him to lose his balance and fall backward on the sand.

Sitting lopsided in the sand, her belligerence shocked him. Who is this wild tigress attacking him, snarling at him, ready to devour his very soul? What happened to the most beautiful human he had ever known with the most perfect angelic disposition? Did he cause this horrible transformation?

She turned away as vicious tears burnt her eyes, and was about to run and leave him, when two black men came out of a house and walked toward them, the taller one shouting, "Aye, wha' goin' on here? Lady dis man boderin' you? We go fix him real quick. On yuh feet, pussy. Fightin' wid a woman? Shame! Get up and fight a real man yuh cowardly cunt! Off yuh ass!"

A sudden terror took hold of Elizabeth as she realized the men thought she was the victim in the dispute and Edward the aggressor. She quickly sized up the two men. They were about Edward's height, one slightly shorter but more solidly built, both perfect specimens of African masculinity. A once strong and muscular Edward of the past may have been able to defend himself till she could get help, or a big stick in the bushes to assist him, but this thinner weakened Edward was in no shape to take on one, much worse two of these obviously physically fit men.

Consequently, she knew it was up to her to diffuse the situation, "Wait! You don't understand. He's my husband. We were just having a difference of opinion, I pushed him and he overbalanced and fell in the soft sand. It's nothing serious. Just a little quarrel between married people. See," she bent down, kissed Edward hard on his mouth, pulled at his shirt trying to make him stand, and shifted into West Indian lingo, "we make-up already. Every ting good. Is awright, tanks fellars. We goin' now. Tanks again." She pulled the kiss-stunned Edward's hands and whispered, "Get up, dammit. Let's get to hell away from here. You're in no condition to fight these two men."

Edward stood up and turned toward the men, his hands clenched, his jaw tight, fight not flight in his eyes. Elizabeth's heart sank. She grabbed an arm, dug her long nails deep into his flesh and whispered angrily, "If you don't walk away with me *now*, we're through, for good!"

He stared at her for a moment, knew she meant it, and knew also, in that same frightening moment, she still did love him. Taking hold of her hand, blood blotching the sleeve of his white shirt where she had dug into him, he put his arm around her waist, she put hers around his, they gave a quick wave to the men, and made a hasty retreat back to Sandy Lane Hotel.

Out of sight of the men she removed her arm from his waist and stepped away looking at him with unrestrained ridicule, "I can't believe you thought you could fight those two huge men! You've lost too much weight. You're puny next to them. You'd better start eating and get back to the gym. Can't you see you look like hell?"

He laughed but was not amused, "So that's the thanks I get for my 'puny' self attempting to protect you from being ravished by two hulking black Bajan men. By the way, you look as ravishable as always.

And, the reason *I* look like hell, is because I've been pining for you, Elizabeth Angelique Du Beauchamp!"

She waved her hand flippantly, "I'll meet you in the main dining room for dinner in an hour," and ran up the coral steps of the hotel.

The delicious dinner they ordered in the dining room remained mostly uneaten, both of them playing with the food on their plates. Edward was hungry, ravenous. Not for food, for Elizabeth. Elizabeth too had a hunger, for neither food nor Edward. She didn't know what she hungered for, she only knew she hungered. He tried to converse with her but she was distant, unresponsive, somewhere else. His heart constricted at the thought of where she might be, not knowing that she herself didn't know where she was, or should be, in her life.

She knew she needed a new beginning, but was at a loss as to how to start, and who to start with.

He rested his hand on hers but quickly removed it when he felt hers stiffen, "You're not going to believe our luck, guess who's doing a reunion charity concert tomorrow night?"

She knew immediately, "The Merrymen."

He laughed, "I knew you'd guess. It's sold out."

"Not surprising, such a rare event."

He smiled proudly, "But you know I have the best connections, Chris sent over tickets for us."

She gave him a weak smile, "That's very sweet of him, but I'm not in a partying mood, Edward."

Edward hid his disappointment and said encouragingly, "We don't have to party, honey, we can just sit and enjoy the entertainment. The boys will be disappointed if we don't come, they're saving front row seats for us. Come on, sweetheart, they're good friends, and you love them."

"Alright," she conceded, then added quickly, "but don't expect me to dance."

He gave no attention to her remark but instead to the pink scars he suddenly saw on her right forearm, "Good God! What happened to your arm? How did you get those awful scars?"

Flicking a hand nonchalantly she muttered, "Oh, I stumbled... holding a glass, it broke when I...bumped into...something. Stella sent me a gel. It's healing nicely. I'm tired. Let's call it a day." She stood up and he followed, wondering.

At the door of her suite he bent over to peck her lips in a good-night kiss, but she turned her head and he caught her cheek, "I'm very tired, Edward. We'll talk more tomorrow. Goodnight."

He stood watching her closed door, wishing it would open again, she would come out, grab him, and take him inside to make the sweet love of their past that he had so long been denied. It was not to be. Elizabeth had thrown herself on the bed and began to cry. Upset by the numerous events that had brought turmoil to her life, causing her to no longer know what she wanted out of life, she bewilderingly cried herself into a sporadic sleep.

The next morning she awoke early and went for a long swim in the transparent Caribbean Sea, wishing it would wash away her fears and indecision, cleanse the reasons for it, and flood her with its crystalline clarity.

Edward sat on a chaise on the beach watching her, loving her, wanting her, all of her, mind, body, soul. He resisted the temptation to go in the water and swim with her. His intuition told him she needed solitariness. If he was to have her be his completely again, it could not be brought about by guilt or pressure, and, she would have to be the instigator to renew their old loving relationship. She would have to come to him of her own free will, wanting only him, always. In the meantime, the only thing he could do to influence her, regain her trust and win her back, is to show his love, understanding, repentance, and, strength. His strength in not ever talking about her having been with, *The fucking son-of-a-bitch prince.*

Elizabeth's thoughts swirled at the same speed as the waters around her. She had turned on her phone when she awakened this morning for the first time since she left Michael. It was over-filled with count-less heart-wrenching pleas from him as well as several from Jenkins, Susan, John, Anne, Brian, Eric, and a surprising brief one from the King simply asking her to call him. As soon as she had finished play-ing the messages, weeping through every one, the phone rang in her hand. The caller identification showed only a crown, *Michael!* and she quickly turned it off again.

The cool early morning Caribbean water refreshed her body, but brought no relief from the confusion that engulfed her mind. She felt the decision she had made to come back to her husband and attempt to start a new married life was the right one, not only because of her precious twins, but because she still loved him. *But I love Michael too, was willing to have four more children with him...but would've had to fight Edward for the twins and maybe lose them...then maybe not...but I love Edward too...I don't want to hurt him, any more...like he hurt me...but I'm hurting Michael who I love as much as Edward...and he hasn't hurt me... but my situation would hurt Michael's position...but maybe not...but there's no royal precedent for it so it probably would...and Edward needs me...he's dying without me...and I do love him...though I can't forgive him, yet...but I love Michael too...*

Coming out of the water, she immediately spotted Edward stand-ing next to a table and two chaises, his hands outstretched holding open a large beach towel for her. Wrapping it around her he kissed the back of her neck and said softly, "I adore you. And only you. I'll never hurt you again. I'll die adoring you."

Elizabeth shivered, dropped onto a chaise and looked at the table, "I see you ordered us breakfast. I'm not hungry. But *you* need to eat, Mr. puny."

He smiled teasingly, "Seems I'd better, It appears you're not attracted to me with this skinny body-"

She eyed him cautiously, "I never said that, I'm just concerned for your health."

"Oh? That's nice to know. That you still have some concern for me. Especially as all I'm concerned about is you." He picked up a plate with a slice of bright orange papaya and handed it to her with a fruit spoon, "Here, my love, you've got to try the pawpaw, it looks delicious. And we don't want *you* to start wasting away again, although *I'll* love *you* anyway you are."

She took the papaya from him and they both began to eat in earnest, continuing a comfortable somewhat flirtatious banter throughout the meal. Having finished eating they walked back to their adjoining suites both needing to go to their bathrooms, and agreed to go for a walk on the beach afterwards to talk.

Edward was waiting outside her door, mutely took her hand, and walked them out onto the beach.

Still holding his hand, Elizabeth stopped to look in his eyes and spoke first, "Tell me everything that's happened with the twins since I left. Every little detail."

The sunlight became reflected in his eyes as they lit up, and it did not go unnoticed by Elizabeth, her own eyes in turn reflecting the light in his. He knew she spoke to and saw the children on Skype twice or more every day while she was away, so it was thrilling to him that she wanted to know about them from him. He was determined not to use them as a pawn in his battle to win her back, even though he knew they would probably trump anything else he could offer, but knew in his soul, if she was to stay with him, it would have to be because she loved and wanted him, and only him. *Not the fucking son-of-a-bitch prince!*

The rest of the day was spent in deep conversations.

They talked about the children for hours, then went on to their parents, Edward's sibling's families, the business she and he built together as well as the ones they were taking over from her father and were in the process of expanding, The Children's Home, her speech, friends, fun times of the past, the world economy, many subjects significant and trivial, but, as if by an unspoken mutual understanding, shied away from discussing their future together. She thought it was too soon, he thought it could not be too soon. He sensed her thinking and kept his to himself. In-between their conversing and lunch they took several cooling dips in the sea. She felt guilty for teasing him about being puny as she observed he did not remove his T-shirt to swim, decided she would not bring up his insalubrious looking weight loss again, and felt relieved to see, at breakfast and lunch, a semblance of his old appetite returning.

"And now, a request from an adoring husband for his one and only love. She'll know who she is.

Every time I'm away from Liza, water come to me eye,-
I remember when love was new, water come to me eye,-
Come back Liza, come back girl, wipe the tear from me eye-"

Elizabeth looked blushingly at the Merrymen on the stage, all smilingly staring at her as they played their guitars while Emile Straker sang the plaintive calypso folksong to her in proxy for Edward. Then she glared at Edward, "You beast. You did this so I'd be embarrassed into getting up to dance with you."

A shy smile twitched at his lips, "Actually, the words of the song suited my sentiments exactly. But also, I couldn't stand to see you suffering anymore holding back from needing to dance. So, up, Liza, it's unhealthy not to follow your nature."

Edward stood and held out his right hand. Aware of more eyes on her than she cared for, she was forced to smile, nodded acknowledgement to the men on the stage, reluctantly took Edward's hand, and began to dance with him. They danced apart to the medium-paced song, touching only when Edward took her hand to twirl her every so often. Swiveling her hips in the traditional seductive Caribbean fashion, he followed her moves with his eyes, and his hips. The song ended and she went to sit, the Merrymen crooning into a slow love song; but Edward took her arm, pulled her to him, held her tight, and they began to sway, rhythmically in unity, as in years past. Her first instinct was to back away from him, she was not ready for their bodily closeness, but the floor became crowded with more dancers and they were pressed together by that circumstance and not by her choice. She wanted to resist the familiarity of his body moving with her to the music, but it brought an unexpected comfort to her, and she felt herself unwillingly melting into him, grudgingly magnetized to a love that had taught her how to hate.

Edward was ready to burst, with joy, love, desire. His psychological restraint competing with his physiological independence to be freed, the control he had been battling with got the better of him, and his body retaliated. She felt it immediately as his erection burgeoned against her pubis.

Pushing him away she said savagely, "No! Don't even think about it! No way in hell!" Forcing her way through the crowd she stormed out of the room and ran to the beach.

Catching up to her, he yelled pleadingly, "Jesus Christ, woman! Have a heart! I didn't plan it to happen. I love you, I'm mere flesh and blood, Elizabeth!"

She turned around snarling at him, "*I* have a heart! A heart that *you* shredded into little pieces when you let your "*flesh and blood*" take control of yours! Now you think I can so easily forgive and forget? Well I can't! I don't know if I ever can!" Walking towards her he extended his hands out in a plea and she shouted, "Don't come near me! Don't you dare touch me again!"

Edward was confounded. On the dance floor when she relaxed and leaned against him as she used to in the past, he felt certain she was coming round, feeling she was home again in his arms, that special sense of complete belonging. To see her so angry at his natural reaction that was once all she needed to flare up her desire for him, now disgust her so absolutely, deflated him in every way. His proud male ego came to the conclusion that her rejection could only be because of the hold *he* had on her, *The fucking son-of-a-bitch prince!*

He grabbed her arms, "It's *him,* isn't it? *He's* the reason why you won't even try at forgiving me! *He's* why you won't give me a chance to redeem myself! *He's* why you're determined to destroy *us* with your anger, why you've turned into this cold-hearted bitch! Allowing yourself to be overpowered by hate for me with love and lust for a manipulating, conniving, controlling, powerful, son-of-a-bitch prince -"

She broke an arm away from his grasp and gave him a resounding slap across his face, "Shut up! You're talking rubbish! He's none of those things! You're wrong about everything! I'm filled with hate not just for you but for me! Because he's the most wonderful amazing man and I broke his heart! Just like you broke mine! I thought maybe I could forgive you for breaking mine, but I could *never* forgive you for making me break his!"

CHAPTER
43

Elizabeth looked at her watch again. Two-forty and still no sign of Edward. She had been sitting on her veranda waiting for him to return since midnight, after leaving him standing stunned on the beach to return to her suite for yet another cleansing cry. She walked back onto the beach and a security guard with a flashlight approached her. She explained her concerns about her husband being gone so long and his inclination to swim at night. The guard walked with her at the water's edge, shining the wide beam of the flashlight at the water and at the beach alternately. Ten minutes later, they found Edward lying in the surf, foaming tides dragging his body in and out, and in again.

Elizabeth felt her heart leap from her chest. She collapsed over him, her screams stuck in her throat. Wet arms crept around her limp body to envelop her. His tear-filled voice cried out, "If you can't forgive me there's no hope for us! No hope for me! I love you too much to keep you trapped to a man you hate. I'll give you your freedom. You can have your divorce!"

Her breath coming back in gasps, she sat up and looked in his eyes, illuminated by the security guard's flashlight, "I've been a victim of the illusion of that fine line between love and hate. My hate should be spelt like 'hurt.' You'll have to spend the rest of your life proving to me that I can trust you. If you'll be patient, give me time to… get over Michael…hopefully one day, forgiveness will come. If you're willing to try again, to have me under those conditions, I don't want a divorce. I'll always love you." Evaluating the situation to be a momentous lover's quarrel, the security guard walked away and left them to the repairs of their damaged love.

Locked in each other's arms, they lay on the beach all night looking at the black tropical sky adorned with billions of silvery stars and constellations, the vividness of which is unparalleled with that of the light polluted skies outside the Caribbean. Excluding their infidelities, they talked of the past, the present, and the future, and all their hopes for it, for themselves, for their children, for the universe.

The sunrise as awe-inspiring as a sunset, they watched it in silence, until the risen sun's brilliance became blinding. Lifting her up in his arms, under her vigorous protests, he carried her to her door, "See. Your puny husband can still carry you, and always will." Putting her gently down to stand, he kissed her softly on her lips and whispered, "We should have a shower and get some sleep." He walked off toward his door, leaving a stupefied Elizabeth staring at his back as he called out, "Phone me when you wake up. I love you."

A great degree of clarity having come to her, Elizabeth slept with a soundness she had not experienced in many days, as did Edward. Awakening around the same time, they called each other, she on his cellphone, he on her room phone as he realized her mobile was off, and suspecting why, resolved to get her a new private number. He cautiously broached that subject after they lunched on his veranda, and she knew though many things would always be kept secret between Michael and herself, she would have to divulge certain things that happened with Michael to Edward, to give him some peace of mind.

She chose which things carefully and with much truncation, delicately avoiding completely any hint of their prodigious sexual exploits and the pleasures she derived from them. She spoke only of their travels and life in the palace, and ended by saying it would be useless, and inconvenient, to change her number, as Michael's people would discover it anyway; she will handle getting him to accept she is staying married to her husband whom she dearly loves, and convince him to stop calling her. A sensation of jabs in her chest during her entire discourse made her feel like she was being traitorous to Michael, with her own husband, and she saddened doubly.

Edward sensed it and said dejectedly, "It appears this isn't going to be easy, for either of us. You made me suffer through giving you the details of my infidelity so that you can stop wondering and move on. But you're not allowing me the same concession, so I guess *I'll* always be wondering, and have a harder time moving on." He stood up, his broad shoulders suddenly slumping as his face furrowed with sorrow, "I need to go for a walk, alone. See you later."

The remorse for Edward she had been suppressing surfaced, she wanted to go and find him, tell him that he and he alone was the keeper of her heart; but visions of Michael, his loving face, and the brief yet plenteous devotionally amorous, multifarious life they shared, kept hauntingly disturbing her, holding her back.

She called her parents and children on Skype and spoke with them for nearly an hour, reluctantly having to end the conversation as the family had to go on a prearranged nature hike in one of the beautiful mountainous areas in the north end of Tobago near Starwood Bay, with more family and friends who were vacationing nearby. With warnings to be careful but to have fun, she hung up and called The Children's Home in Trinidad. She spoke to them for half an hour and followed that with two short business calls, one to the family's main offices, another to their recycling plant. Beginning to feel somewhat caught up with her regular life, she walked onto the beach, scanned it and the sea for Edward and not seeing him, took to the water for a swim.

Drying her hair, she barely heard the shrill of the bedside phone through the whine of the blow-dryer. Dashing to it she felt an old thrill at hearing his voice, "Would you like to drive out to Bathsheba? I have a Minimoke. We could stop somewhere and have dinner on the way back."

They took in the rugged eastern side of the island with as much delight as the contrasting tranquility of the western side on which they stayed. The vibrant waves of the Atlantic Ocean crashing against rocks and sand, then calmly, peacefully receding, only to come immediately dramatically back to crash again, seemed to symbolize the tides of their life, with its fluctuating turmoils and serenities.

Walking the beach, both became lost in myriads of thoughts, accumulations of emotions descending upon them; but they were unable to speak, the words simply hung in the air between them.

Almost at the end of the beach Edward stopped abruptly and faced her, "I think you should know I'm having a really difficult time trying to ignore what you told me you did with...him, everything you did with me. All the...special things, that I thought would always be just ours. It's eating my guts."

He turned away and looked toward the ocean, "I know I'm accountable for...driving you away...by what I did. But it hurts that you don't seem in any way to feel accountable for...driving me away...to do what I did...by me feeling neglected and uncared for by you. I'm not saying that it gave me an excuse. I know it was terribly wrong, and I'll regret it forever, to have hurt you, hurt us. I just want you to know I'm disappointed that you can't see your part in...why it happened. Not that I blame you in any way, I just feel it would help for you to be able to forgive me. It's going to be more difficult for us to get back to what we had if there is no forgiveness, Elizabeth, maybe impossible."

He looked back at her, the sadness and grief in his aquamarine eyes immeasurable as they misted over. Embarrassed at showing his teary weakness, he turned and walked back down the beach, his head and shoulders drooping, his gait listless and unsure. She stared after him, assimilating his recriminatory words and emotions, cogitating them, dissecting them, and finally, feeling them. An epiphany struck her like a bolt from the blue, shock waves putting wings to her feet as she ran after him. For the first time, the victim understood the possibility of her own culpability in the crime committed against her.

Breathless, she grabbed his arm and spun him around. Seeing her stunned face he misconstrued it to be his undoing because of what he just said, dropped to his knees and clung to her waist, his tears flowing like a river. Moaning pitiably between words and sobs, he begged, "Forgive me. I know I was wrong. It's all my fault. I shouldn't have said what I did. You're blameless. You've got to forgive me, Elizabeth! Or I'll die!"

His agonized condition pained her insides. Each word felt like a blow to her solar plexus and she clung to his head, pressing it against her body. Making soothing noises as if to calm a frantic child, she was eventually able to articulate her words, "Shush, shush. It's alright, my love. It'll be alright. It seems I was wrong too…became too caught up in things…took on too much…didn't have enough energy left for you…for us. I'm sorry. *You* have to forgive *me* too."

His voice rose in protest, "No! It's my fault, I should've helped you more, you were doing good things. I was too wrapped up in growing the businesses-"

She argued, "But you were doing good things too-"

They disputed back and forth about who was right, who was wrong, their voices getting louder with each contention; until Elizabeth became aware that a Barbadian family who had been picnicking higher up on the beach were curiously gathering closer to them. She thought she recognized the father to be a gentleman they had done some business with in the past, and not wanting to embarrass Edward, she said quickly, "Edward, we're drawing a crowd, get up."

"No!" he wailed, "I don't care! Not until you forgive me! If you don't forgive me, I'll stay here and die!"

She hated seeing him emasculated like this, her Alpha giant indomitable life's-partner husband, being reduced to this tragic, pathetic, wretched weakling. She hated them both for all that had happened to cause this. She knew forgiveness was necessary to destroy the pain and odious emotions that threatened to ruin their chance at reunifying, but knew also, it would be long in coming. Repressing this knowledge and her true feelings, as many a woman had done before, she turned his head forcing him to look up at her, "I forgive you. On one condition. That we never discuss either of our infidelities ever again. That's the only way I can forgive you, and you forgive me. We have to forget everything that happened, and start anew."

On the drive back to Sandy Lane Hotel, having come to an agreement on Bathsheba beach to forgive and forget to be able to start their new life together, they developed an unusual shyness, and talked only of mundane things.

At her open door Edward gave her a quick tender kiss, "I'll love you for all eternity," and turned to leave.

Elizabeth was surprised, and hurt, by his uncertainty and lack of self-confidence. This man, her husband, who idolized her, who she idolized, who had tasted and made love to every centimeter of her body, and she his, was afraid to touch her! Glimpsing the yearning in his eyes, she realized the intention behind his inaction was to show her his deepest love and respect, leaving it up to her to prove she still really loved him, and wanted him; so she took the initiative and said softly, "Edward. Don't leave me, ever again."

He took her in his arms and they clung to each other, both their bodies trembling, with fear, reverence, love, and desire.

Seeking each other's mouths in the softly lit room, they kissed with the intensity of new lovers, yet with an old hunger for what once was. Both tongues plunging deep, exploring the dark wet recesses of places once long ago familiar but now in need of rediscovery, their centers of consciousness became awash with salacious memories of the past. Edward no longer felt lost, he was home again at last. Elizabeth still felt lost, but knew she had to make a start to try to find her way home.

She led him to the bed but a self-consciousness came upon her as she sat. He knelt before her and lifted her blouse over her head exposing her bare breasts, her soft pink nipples puckering and hardening before his famished eyes. Ignoring their enticement, he took her face in his hands and kissed her tenderly and lengthily, wanting her to know he was not just about having sex, but about making love to the whole of her, mind, body, soul.

This only served to bring on a hesitancy for her as a poignant vision of Michael appeared, kissing her in a similar fashion when they made love on the rug in his office at lunchtime, the day she left, for the last time. Just a few days ago. *Oh my Godde, they are so much alike! Michael, go away! This is my husband, to whom I am bound for life. My bond with you must be severed. Please go away. Leave! Now!*

She forced her eyes open, grabbed Edward's face and stared into his adoring eyes, allowing herself to deliberately absorb him. *Here is Edward. My Edward. My husband. My lover. My partner. My children's father. We are forever bound together. Our history has been rich, with joy, and with sorrow. It's time to bury the sorrow, and give the joy a rebirth. He loves me, and always will. I love him, and always will.*

She reached down to lift off Edward's T-shirt, and he held her hands stopping her, "No, leave it on."

Guiltiness resurfaced, "But my love, I want to feel all of you completely against me. I love you. I don't care about how thin you got, it's only temporary anyway-"

He took on a sheepishness, "It's not that-"

She grabbed the bottom of the shirt and swiftly raised it up intending to caress his breasts and kiss his nipples, but backed off in shock, "Jesus! What's this? What happened? You look like you've been beaten!"

A large part of his chest was covered with many small bruises, but he smiled, "I *was* beaten. Deservedly. By this woman that I adore, who I'll let beat me anytime as long as she allows me to make wild passionate love to her afterwards-"

"*I* did that! That first night when you denigrated Mic-? Oh my love I'm so sorry. I didn't mean to hurt you...I just lost it. You know I would never intentionally do something like this, I'm so sorry. Forgive me?"

Edward threw her backwards on the bed and lay on top of her, his loving look changing lasciviously as he whispered huskily, "Yes. Like I said, you will now have to make up for it by making wild passionate love with me."

Wrapping her arms around him she kissed him with a vengeance, pulling his puffed out bottom lip into her mouth and sucking on it, then she did his top lip letting it go only as he began to do the same to hers. Biting gently, teasing her lips, he pulled her tongue out with his own, then let it travel deeper into her mouth toward the well of her throat as he began to caress her breasts. Leaving her mouth he traveled to her ears with wet soft kisses, whispering, "You are mine and mine alone. I am yours and yours alone. I'll love you forever, till death-"

Without thinking, lost in the stimulation of her erotic senses and forgetting who she was with, whispering she added, "and even beyond."

Edward chuckled softly and whispered, "Yes. I like that…till death and even beyond."

Hearing Edward saying Michael's words felt like someone slapped her on both cheeks to awaken her from a faint.

She opened her eyes to see Edward's gaunt but still familiarly handsome face moving towards a breast, and she sat up quickly, "Edward, I…I'm not ready. It's too soon for me, for us. I'm sorry. I need more time."

Edward looked into her bewildered eyes, a sadness entering his own suddenly bewildering eyes, and without a word, he stood, pulled down his T-shirt, and walked out the door.

Elizabeth fell back on the bed overcome with consternation. Here she was with her husband who she adores, who adores her, and even though he had hurt her so badly as to almost destroy her feelings of self-worth, she had healed from it, and encouraged by his remorse, grief, and loving promises of an even better life than before, wanted to renew their life together. She had desired him just now, wanted to make love with him as they had countless wonderful times before, but trepidatious hesitation had crept into her, and as much as she despised the unwelcome interloper, she could not evict it.

She became filled with a sense of betrayal of Michael, as if she were committing adultery, with her husband Edward.

Edward strode onto the beach, violently kicking the sand. Had it been physically possible he would have inflicted those kicks upon himself, and then, if only he could get to, *The fucking prince, I'll kick him to hell and kingdom come.* He acknowledged that, *The royal bastard's spirit,* haunted Elizabeth and prevented her from fully giving herself back to him. Recollecting the love he had minutes ago seen in her eyes while feeling the heat of desire coming from her body for him, Edward, he decided that that acknowledgement was not acceptance. He ran back inside, not to her room but to his, to prepare her seduction, in his space, on his ground, where, *The Fucking prince,* would not be allowed to intrude.

He called the front desk requesting certain items be sent to his suite immediately, with the promise of a big tip. He then fiddled with the control for radio stations until he found one that played music for romance, after which he paced and planned until his requirements arrived.

Alone again, Elizabeth developed self-deprecation along with self-pity. She was in the unfortunate societally impossible position of loving and wanting two spouses equally, a condition only men had dominion over in ancient times when patriarchal bullies forced the demise of the Goddess religions, and still today in a few oppressive and archaically ignorant societies.

Seeing as she was already legally bound to Edward and had a family with him, she knew she must eradicate Michael from her life. She rationalized if Edward and she were to have a future together, she must consciously banish Michael from her head, and their bed; for indeed, she had seven years ago made her bed with Edward, and now they must forever lie in it together, alone.

Ethics and principles overruling emotions and sentiment, she reconditioned her mind. She went to the bathroom, urinated, left her panties off, and slipped into an ivory lace and silk long peignoir set Ruth had purchased for her, and opened her door. Edward was standing there barefoot, about to knock.

Not speaking, both hearts racing, they absorbed each other slowly. Elizabeth saw the fire of desire in his eyes and immediately herself became inflamed. Edward saw his beautiful virgin bride of seven years who was coming to get him, already prepared.

CHAPTER
44

Edward lifted her up in his arms, "Let's promise each other we'll never be separated again. Please, my love?"

Elizabeth riveted her amber eyes on his aquamarine eyes, "What's going to happen when we have to travel separately to faraway places for business?"

A compliant smile deepened the dimples on his cheeks as he nodded, "Okay. No more than ten days apart. Agreed?"

"Well, I guess that's doable. Alright, agreed."

"If one of us has to be away longer than that, the other will join him or her. Agreed?"

"Agreed. Now, are you going to negotiate anything else standing in the hallway or are you taking me somewhere?"

He turned his back to his door which he had jammed ajar with a shoe and pushed it open. Kicking the shoe out of the way and the door shut, he swung around for her to take in the romantic ambiance he had created for her, for their first reuniting night of love. Her eyes widened as she emitted a gasp, "It's absolutely beautiful, Edward."

The room was lit with scores of flickering votive candles. Dispersed around the suite were two dozen crystal bowls with frangipani flowers floating in them, their sweet perfume permeating the air. Feeling suddenly heady, she was grateful he still held her in his arms because she would have surely swooned. She rapidly banished another comparison between her two loves as the memory of what Michael had done for her on their first night of love came rushing back. Intuitively sensing her distraction, Edward brought her back to focus on him with a deep passionate kiss. He dropped onto the bed with her, expeditiously disrobing her while whispering declarations of eternal love. Leaving her mouth he bathed the rest of her face in soft moist kisses, traveled down to her neck and ended in her ear, all the while whispering sensual and loving allurements. Licking and nipping his way down to her breasts, he nibbled on a nipple and she produced a small cry, whereupon he opened his mouth wide and gently suckled her breast, his exploring fingers finding her wet welcoming portal to what will be his final destination. Assiduously, he massaged her walls with two fingers going in and out, preparing her, hoping she would release some of her sweet juices as soon as he could get there to drink.

Reveling in the mellifluousness and deliciousness of his ministrations, she released all thought from her mind of Michael, her first love, to let her body again be free to be captivated by Edward, her first lover. Stimulated to the point of needing full penetration, she suddenly felt selfish, doing all of the taking and none of the giving, her guilt intensifying as she recollected how long it had been that Edward was denied of her loving. She sat up, resolutely pushed him down to lie on the bed, and swiftly pulled off his pants. His engorged penis flapped back to slap against his abdomen and the size amazed her. Uncontrollable thoughts invaded the space she had made in her head, *My Godde, he is the same size as Michael!* Then, though unable to see perfectly in the peach colored dim light, she remembered, because of all his years in the tropical sun, almost every weekend in a swimsuit, Edward's was slightly tanned in color. Somehow, this little detail made a huge difference. She was able to banish Michael again, and concentrate on Edward.

Crawling onto him, she laid her breasts on his phallus and moving her upper body stroked it up and down between them. Edward groaned with delight. Slowly, she crept up to his face, plastering his chest and neck with sucking kisses on the way, whispering the sweet nothings she knew he needed to hear. Arriving at his mouth, she kissed him hard and long with a desperate passion, as if their lives depended on their uniting fluids for their very survival.

In need of a deep breath, Edward held her face and gently eased himself from under her, thinking to go down to feast on the delectable parts of her he had missed and wanted so badly these past eight terrible months. Not surprisingly with lovers of seven years of abounding sexual experiences together, the same thought came to Elizabeth, and she went up on her hands and knees so that he could take full advantage of what he wanted, what she needed. His lips kissed and sucked her external lips, then his moist tongue explored her internally, covering every nook and cranny in the vestibule of her pink flesh as she moaned in ecstasy. Feeling a clitoral climax coming on, and wanting to give him the same pleasure he was giving her, she pleaded softly, "Wait. I want to taste you too. Stop-"

He murmured, "No," and sucking a finger quickly, he inserted it into her other orifice as his tongue and lips returned to his original spot. Moving adroitly in both openings, he expertly brought her to an excruciatingly pleasurable orgasm.

Collapsing on the bed, she called to him to lie next to her so that she could catch her breath before she could return his epicurean pleasures. Knowing his wife better than she knew herself, he ignored her, rolled her over, and kissing her mouth deeply, entered her vagina deeply simultaneously.

Moving harmoniously together, he brought her to a second climax as she felt his semen fill her to overflowing. They rapturously screamed each other's names in ecstasy.

He shifted his body and fearing he was going to leave her, she grabbed his buttocks and pressed him to her. He had no intention of getting off her and kissing her mouth, whispered, "Don't worry, I won't leave you. I can't. I'm home at last. Are you home with me, my love?"

A familiar euphoria flooding her, Elizabeth sighed, "Yes. I'm home, with you, my love."

They did not depart his room the next day and night, only infrequently leaving the bed for the bathroom, and to grab a drink of water or orange juice and mixed nuts from the mini-bar. They needed no nourishment other than what their love could provide. Waking up together the following day, they immediately made love again. Resting in each other's arms afterwards, Edward asked if she needed some fresh air and perhaps a swim.

Elizabeth kissed his chest and pressed against him, "Let's just go home, Edward. Let's go home to our children."

Coming out of Trinidad Customs at Piarco International Airport, Elizabeth spotted the twins immediately, despite the usual large crowd. They were the only two white children jumping up and down and screaming wildly, "Mummy!" "Mummy!"

Running up to her, arms outstretched, they threw themselves at her, toppling her onto the laughing and prepared Edward who had dropped their luggage to the floor ready to catch her. She enveloped them in her arms, fighting back tears and laughing happily, until the children began to cry. She looked up at her parents who had stood back out of the way to give the reuniting family their space, to see they too were crying.

Zarna and Zethan began to bawl inconsolably, "Mummy! Mummy! Don't leave us again! Ever! Please! Promise!"

They would not stop their tearful pleadings though she kept kissing and hugging them with comforting words, "There, there. It's alright. Mummy's here now. Everything's alright. I'm home with you again. I love you more than anything."

Eventually, with her heart breaking to see the frightened state her once happy children had gotten into, she was forced to do the only thing that would assuage their fears, calm them down, and shut them up. Acquiescing to their pleadings, she made a promise to never leave them again. A promise that even the gaping strangers around them knew a beautiful woman like her, with the universality she exuded, could not possibly keep.

Michael threw his pen down on his desk and stood up, "I can't do it, Pa. Can't think. Can't concentrate. Sorry. I'm no use to you like this. I must get away from here for a while. From everything that reminds me of her." His head and shoulders fell as he emitted a miserable sigh. Eyes suddenly filling with virulence his voice became sardonic, "I wish *he,* was dead."

Concealing his shock at his honorable son's remark the King responded imperturbably, "That can easily be arranged, but neither of us could live with it."

Michael looked back at his father with woebegotten eyes, "I spoke to Susan, she and Aunt Anne are going to take over my duties, as best they could. I've indefinitely postponed events that require only my presence and no substitute. The family'll help you in every way possible. Uncle Patrick says you can rely on him, but please be careful. I'll send out a press release saying I'll be in Africa for a while and can't be reached. I'll say I'm studying the effects of the mosquito and malaria situation. With what happened to Mama I think it'll be believed. Forgive me Pa but I'm useless like this. I just can't perform to a proper standard. My mind isn't here. I hope you understand."

His Majesty looked upon his sorrowful son with loving compassion, "Of course son. Take whatever time you need. Where will you go?"

Michael shrugged, "Don't know. Anywhere away from here. Where I can't see her, sense her, smell her."

"You'll take Jenkins? Or Brian?"

"No. I want to be alone. Don't worry, I'll wear a disguise. I'll be careful. I'll have my phone with the micro weapon. I'll rent a car. Or

take trains. Roam around Europe awhile. You'll be alright, won't you?
You've recovered so well-"

The king promptly gave one of his famous benevolent smiles, "I'm
in the best shape ever. Mark is too. Our only concern is your happiness. Just focus on yourself, son. Go heal your hurt, and then you can
retrieve happiness again."

Haunted by the memory of Elizabeth, and what was no longer
to be, the grief-stricken Michael restlessly roamed all over Europe.
He carried only a backpack containing two casual changes of clothes
and in his wallet, his special false identification, pseudonym credit
card, and a thousand Euros. His mind as desultory as his wandering body, the heaviest luggage he carried was the unbearable burden of profound sorrow that filled his heart and weighed down
his soul.

With no family or servants around to force food on him, he hardly
ate, or slept, but imbibed heavily in whatever local wine was available
from the region he was in, hoping to numb his mind and body against
his loss. This proved to be futile, the pain was too great, the wounds
too raw to be salved.

Gradually he sank deeper and deeper into the dark cold hell of that
nefarious place in the psyche called, 'Depression.'

Uncaring for neither vanity nor hygiene, he let his beard, moustache and hair grow till they almost matched each other in straggly
unkempt length. His facial expressions became limited to sullenness
and despondency. As time passed, with what little one could see of
it, his handsome face became gaunt and colorless with sunken lifeless
eyes. His once perfect muscularly salubrious physique became loose
and scrawny as his body weight decreased, and his mental despair
increased. Visions of him dragging Edward off Elizabeth's naked body
frequented his mind and tore at his gut. He would temporarily destroy
them with her angelic face smilingly beckoning him to her. Wanting to

kill the pain of being denied his only desire, his days were spent drinking himself into a stupor. Dragging back to a hotel room each night he would lie awake in bed for endless hours staring into the darkness, until the yearning for Elizabeth overpowered him. He would then scream her name repeatedly till his voice became hoarse, then break down into uncontrollable sobs.

The nights he went out to listlessly wander the streets and bars, people would at first stare at the disgusting looking stranger, then quickly dismiss the solitary red-eyed scruffy young man as just another misanthropic drunk or drugged university student bumming around Europe; or, yet another lazy good-for-nothing roving vagabond. He stopped calling home to check on everyone after the first day as the King assured him that, "Everyone and everything is doing splendidly." Unfortunately, this only served to give him the freedom to be left alone to wallow in more self-pity, and bottomless grief.

His Majesty sat back contemplatively in his chair after hearing Jenkins' latest report on Michael's whereabouts and his deteriorating condition. Michael had turned off his phone and the G.P.S. was no longer functioning but he still wore the engraved Breguet watch, the peace-offering gift from his father following their terrible argument over the King taking a 'mistress' after the Queen had been dead for two years. Previous to giving him the Breguet, Jenkins had secretly had installed, at the King's instructions, the most advanced micro-tracking device. Becoming more worried about his sinking heir, the King decided to send Brian and Eric to furtively follow Michael to keep a closer watch over him.

Wearily, he looked at Jenkins, "What the hell happened to my son, that self-assured, intelligent boy that I raised to be a strong, super-confident, intrepid man?"

Jenkins said melancholily, "He fell in love, Sir."

Priscilla came to mind and the King irritatingly swept a hand away from his body as though brushing away a painful memory, "He's been in love before."

"Not really, Sir. Not like this. Elizabeth was his first true love, and it seems, will be his last."

His heart going out to his forsaken son, the King said exasperatingly, "God damn this thing called 'love'!"

Jenkins smiled sadly with understanding, "You don't truly mean that Sir. Without love nothing else really means anything."

Every morning, as soon as Edward and the children left for work and school, a sobbing Elizabeth would listen to Michael's messages he had left on her phone the day before, record them on a disc, then delete them from her phone.

She had started keeping the ringer silenced with only the vibration on, and retrained herself to always look at the caller identification before answering. It was tortuous enough to hear his pleas, she could not compound the pain they were both suffering by speaking with him. After five days he stopped speaking and simply played songs, all bemoaning love and heartbreak. Another two days later, he became silent.

The day Edward and she were leaving Barbados, while Edward was settling the bill at the front desk, anxious to know from an impartial source how Michael was doing, she had phoned Jenkins.

It distressed and frightened her to hear his condensed factual account of Michael's deterioration. She had to end the conversation when she heard Edward returning and promised she would call the next day. When she did so, three times, Jenkins didn't answer, neither did he return her messages. She hoped it was because Michael's melancholia started lifting, and perhaps he was even back home. Two days later, Jenkins left a message simply stating that he was joining Brian and Eric, who had been clandestinely following Michael to keep an eye on him.

The first week after she returned to Trinidad, Elizabeth's life was totally absorbed by settling the twins in their new classes at school, ballet, football, and music. The hours in-between were spent running to work for an hour at The Children's Home, then to her office at Richardson Enterprises, then to her office at Du Beauchamp & Company, then a quick check at their Recycling Plant, and then, after late lunch appointments, back to Edward's office at Du Beauchamp & Company for a daily "*emergency meeting*" that Edward always required.

These 'emergencies' turned out to be his impatience and inability to wait until night to again enjoy his wife's company, and her body. He would tell his internally amused but externally discreet secretary they were not to be disturbed as they had, "*important business,*" to discuss. Locking his office door, he would take Elizabeth in his arms, kiss her carefully so as not to smudge her makeup, and then, fully clothed except for pants, they would make love on the couch where just hours before sat some of the most important and influential people of Trinidad, who had actually come to discuss bona fide '*important business.*'

Wanting to spend more time on repairing their marriage, and bringing stability back into their children's lives, they started refusing some social invitations, which were always plenteous in Trinidad to people of their class. They judiciously accepted only those pertaining to special occasions and anniversaries of family and friends, and events that were important to their businesses, which were more than enough to cover many ordinary people's lifetimes.

Eight days after she returned, Michael broke his two days of silence. Not with words but snippets of songs with references to death, and Elizabeth was revisited by lugubriousness. The first snippet was a sentence from their favorite Tina Turner song 'Simply The Best' from which he played the only sad line in the entire song, "*don't break us apart, baby I would rather be dead.*" Then came snippets bemoaning "*impending doom*" and "*my darkest hour*" from a song by Killers, one of her favorite groups. Next were morose words from Terry Jacks' 'Seasons In The Sun,' *"goodbye my friend it's hard to die."*

A line from John Denver's 'Annie's Song,' *"let me drown in your laughter, let me die in your arms,"* bringing back memories of when he first played it, contradictorily to woo her after they met, was even more upsetting; but the piece that brought her into a state of sheer panic was the last one by Harry Nilsson singing, *"I can't live if living is without you, I can't live, can't live anymore,"* because she could hear Michael's sobbing voice singing along with Nilsson.

She pressed Michael's number immediately. It rang endlessly, not stopping for his usual voice message. She kept trying his number on speed dial for half an hour when the ringing eventually stopped, and for a second, so did her heart.

Thank Godde! "Hello Michael." There was no response, but she knew he had picked up, she could hear him breathing heavily, like stifled sobs. "Michael, speak to me." Silence. She pleaded, "Darling, please speak to me." More silence. "Please darling, I know you're there." No response. "Michael, for Godde's sake, speak to me! Please darling, please," she begged impassionately, her voice cracking as the tears began to drip down the back of her throat and the front of her eyes.

The silence combining with her pounding heart deafened her until she heard a click, and Nilsson sang again, *"I can't live, can't live anymore,"* and the phone went dead.

CHAPTER
45

*E*lizabeth became frantic. She kept pressing 'redial' but knew in her terrified soul as the meaning in Michael's messages sank in, he was not going to answer again. He had given up. Never in her wildest nightmares would she have believed it possible that her indomitable, happily playful, 'knight in shining armor' prince, who so skillfully, valiantly and completely, rescued her from her depths of despair, could actually sink even lower than hers into his own despairing, disastrous, depths.

She called Jenkins, who answered immediately, and didn't give him a chance to greet her, "Where's Michael!?"

Jenkins' voice was missing its usual calm, "At the appartamento in Venice, we followed him here yesterday."

Memories of their romantic stay in Venice flashed tauntingly at her, "No! Not Venice!"

Jenkins's voice became seeped in desperation, "Elizabeth, he looks terrible! He must've lost twenty pounds or more."

Elizabeth felt her heart jabbing at her ribs, "No! He has no weight to lose! Oh Godde, Jenkins, he's given up!"

Jenkins took on an irritated tone, "Of course he's given up on you, that's why he's in this condition!"

"No, no, not just on me! I mean totally given up. He's played me a bunch of songs about wanting to die!"

"Well I guess it's not surprising, he's grieving for you. But he'll pull through. I know Michael, he's strong and extremely intelligent, we just have to give him time-"

Fear dominated her voice, "No Jenkins, this is different! He won't even speak to me anymore! He only played these pieces of songs about dying! Listen!"

She played back Michael's last communication for Jenkins. He listened attentively and was grateful they were not on Skype so that she could not see he had to sit down. He was so shaken by this death-seeking stranger that Michael had become, someone he could not relate to at all, but faked a calm voice, "He does seem to be a little more distressed than we originally thought-"

"And he's ended up in Venice! I know why! Jenkins, you have to get him a woman! Immediately!"

Jenkins was appalled, "What? What're you saying?"

"He needs a woman's body...to feel alive again!"

He felt her desperation, but his reality prevailed, "Elizabeth that's crazy, the only woman he wants is you."

She persisted unhesitatingly, "Well that's not possible so you have to find him someone who looks like me...not some hooker either... make sure she's on the pill...uses condoms...she doesn't know who he is...have a doctor check her before...and after...you know-"

Jenkins interrupted her desperate ramblings, "That's ludicrous! Michael's not going to want *any* woman. Besides, do you know how difficult it'll be to find someone like you?"

"You've enough men there, you *must* do it! I know Michael...how passionate he is. He needs to...to be held. Comforted. It's our only hope! Please do it! Now!"

Midmorning of the following day she received a call from Jenkins in response to four voice-mails she had left, "We'd found a pretty woman with your hair color but he rejected her. Practically threw her out after she tried to…seduce him."

"Oh no! Wait. What size was she?"

"Well, she was petite, but with a good figure."

"The problem's the size. She needs to…fit…against…him. She shouldn't try to seduce him immediately…just talk…touch a little… then caress him, see how it goes from there. He needs the female touch. Find somebody more suitable. Quickly!"

Elizabeth could not believe the irony. She, who just days ago possessively wanted Michael for herself alone, was preposterously the choreographer in having him get sex and comfort from a stranger! She turned her thoughts back to the importance of the task, knowing that once again, the responsibility was on her, to save Michael.

Jenkins called the next day to say they had found a beautiful woman close in size and shape to Elizabeth's physique, but Michael rejected her also.

Michael had then phoned Jenkins and Brian, cussed them out in the worst way and told them to stop their foolishness, if they really want to help him, they need to bring Elizabeth back, if they can't, then just leave him "*to hell alone.*"

Jenkins begged Elizabeth to come back for a quick trip, just to explain to Michael in person in more detail why she had to leave him and return to Edward and her family. He felt this was necessary, because of the sudden shocking manner in which she left, for him to be able to have closure and get on with his life. Elizabeth told him such a trip was impossible.

Not only would it create an enormous upset to her still healing family, but she felt it would be even more devastating for Michael to see her again and for her to leave him again. She made no mention of the same effect it would have on her.

Less than an hour later she played back voice-mails that were left in rapid succession from the King, Elena, Susan, Anne, Megan, Mark, Brian, Eric, and Jenkins again, all pleading for her to return to speak to Michael as Jenkins had proposed. Several remarked that if only they could get him to return home and keep him busy, they would have a better chance of lifting him out of his melancholia. Each person left assurances they had tried everything possible they could collectively and singularly think of to lure him out of his deep grief, with no success, and she was their last resort. She kept calling Michael at intervals throughout the day. His phone simply rang, his voicemail now inaccessible. Not knowing what to say, she didn't respond to any of the royal's voicemails.

That night she was awakened from a restless sleep by Edward taking her in his arms, "What's the matter, my love, why're you crying in your sleep?"

She felt her wet face, "Oh...I didn't know I was."

Edward turned on his bedside lamp and looked at her, "Tell me what's upsetting you sweetheart. Remember, we promised each other complete honesty from now on. So, what's wrong?"

She had every intention of keeping the promise of undeviating honesty they made to each other during one of their reconciling discussions, but didn't feel it pertained to Michael, seeing they had also agreed to not bring up references to their infidelities ever again, "I'm sorry, I can't."

"What? Why?"

"Because it has to do with a problem with Michael, and I don't want to hurt you by discussing it."

Edward sat up, "Elizabeth, if something's upsetting you this much, it concerns me too. You must tell me."

She went to her desk, unplugged her phone from its charger, turned it on and played some of Michael's desperate messages and death declaring songs, to an increasingly reluctantly sympathetic Edward. *You poor bastard I know what you're suffering, I've been there. But she's mine, not yours. Find your own woman, leave mine alone.*

Seeing her tears forming Edward took Elizabeth in his arms, "My love, he'll be alright. He's a grown man, with a lot of responsibilities to distract him from...his grief. His family needs to rally round him, give him support, and companionship-"

Irritation building, she wriggled out of his arms, "They're doing everything they can. He wants to be alone. Jenkins said he's lost piles of weight, rejected any kind of companionship, including attractive women. They're at a loss at what else to do. Listen." Playing their voicemails, tears spilled from her eyes with each anguished imploration.

Hearing the pained pleas from all the royals greatly disturbed Edward, and seeing Elizabeth's reaction to them exacerbated his agitation to the point that he became filled with anger, at himself, at Elizabeth, at Michael, at the entire royal family. He shook as he stood up, "Look, Elizabeth, he's not a child! For crissakes, he's three years older than me, has probably had the experiences of four lifetimes because of who he is. He'll be fine in no time. I think it's very wrong of his family to pressure you like this, begging you to go up there to "*save him,*" knowing what it will do to your own family-"

His seething anger infecting her, she interjected raising her voice, "They're desperate! I know how they feel! *You* know how they feel! How *he* feels!" She broke down sobbing into her hands. He pulled her into his arms but she pushed him off, "Don't touch me! This is *your* fault! *Our* fault! It's because of *us* this has happened. *We,* are responsible, and *I,* have to do something about it! I've tried phoning him but he won't answer! I don't want to go, but I don't know what else to do!"

Edward felt enormous fear take hold. It stimulated his take-charge propensity, he determined he was not going to risk losing her again. He must show his love in the way she needed it under these circumstances. Picking up the phone, he called their travel agent and left instructions on her voicemail for her to book Elizabeth, and him, on the first flight tomorrow.

Elizabeth grabbed the phone from him. Searing him with a defiant look, she spoke into it, "Cancel that, Angela. Edward's not going. I'll be going alone."

Edward turned away as she hung up the phone but she reached for him, "Your presence would only make matters worse, my love. I have to fix this alone. You've no reason to be afraid. I love you. I'm here now, aren't I? I'll be back in just a few days." She led him back to their bed.

As in the way of a smart wife, she made love to him as if he was all that mattered. As in the way of a desperate husband, he made love to her because she was all that mattered.

They were both deep in divergent but fear-ridden thoughts as Edward drove Elizabeth to Piarco International Airport, when Jenkins called, "Elizabeth, you don't have to come. We're taking Michael home. His Majesty had a heart attack."

"Oh Godde! How bad is it? How is he? How is Michael?"

"Michael looks like death warmed up. Fortunately, His Majesty's heart attack was mild, with care he'll recover, but at least providence provided us with a reason to get Michael to agree to come home, where we can keep him distracted till…he gets over you."

"Yes, thank Godde. His Majesty's illness has certainly made him an unwitting hero in saving Michael. Please tell His Majesty he's in my thoughts and prayers, as is Michael. By the way, shouldn't he be starting physical therapy?"

"Oh, you remembered, about that."

She swallowed, "About everything. You will keep our agreement, not let Michael know…that I was coming?"

"Of course. Thank you, Elizabeth. Goodbye."

Edward was the exemplification of the perfect husband, partner, and father. He went to extremes to ensure the return to happiness and normality within his family, and its perpetuality, pandering especially to Elizabeth's needs and comforts.

Even though they had a competent and reliable cleaning lady cum laundress for six days a week, and a couple to assist with parties, he insisted Elizabeth employ another live-in maid to assist Tilda. This would lighten Elizabeth's domestic responsibilities and allow her more time and energy to pursue activities that most interested her, giving her the fulfillment he knew she needed. He was not chancing her ever getting over-tired again. Seeing she would have to overseer and share the servant's quarters with her, Tilda was given the task of finding a suitable woman for the job, and was able to recruit her beloved first-cousin from St. Vincent.

The family took a long weekend and Edward flew them all to that island, including the immensely excited Tilda who had not seen her birth-land and Vincentian family in several years.

Elizabeth and the children took to Evangeline immediately. Though not as pretty as Tilda, and more heavyset, she had the same sweet kind disposition, and everyone knew she would fit perfectly into the family mold. It was on this trip that Elizabeth and Edward learnt from Evangeline's mother, Jean, of the terrible secret Tilda had been keeping since she was twelve. She had been repeatedly raped and her life threatened if she told, by her mother's common-law husband, who was also her mother's uncle, until she became pregnant at fourteen. Whereupon her unknowing mother threw her out of the house for "*disgracin' de family wid some good-for-nothin' boy.*"

Jean took her in, and only after the baby was born, "*lookin' all retarded like,*" did Jean manage to coerce out of Tilda who the father was to the deformed baby. It was then that she had to assure the guilt-ridden Tilda that she was not at fault for the baby's condition, but it was because, not only was he Tilda's great-uncle, but the baby's father was also her own.

This shocking revelation served to endear the courageous Tilda, and her innocent child, spawned out of rape and incest, even more to Elizabeth and Edward.

That night in their hotel room, after making the gentlest love to each other, they discussed the fact that Tilda's story was not such a rarity, Elizabeth and Jane having come across similar cases at The Children's home. Elizabeth expressed and exhibited sorrow at the

ongoing plight of still too many females the world over being subjected to such atrocities and abuse, and who often have nowhere and
no one to turn to.

Touched, Edward resolved to assist her in raising the rest of the
funds needed to finish the extension and pool at The Children's Home,
declaring, "If we have to, we'll take it out of the profits set aside for
our Du Beauchamp Company expansion."

Elizabeth kissed him softly, "You're so wonderful to even think that
way, but the Company needs to expand if it's to survive and thrive
in today's unstable economy. Besides, it won't be necessary to use
Company funds. As soon as I get the children and household settled
with Evangeline, I'm calling Gloria Goldman in New York to ask her
to carefully examine and negotiate all the offers I received for my
speech, and narrow them down to the most important and profitable
five or six. I'm sure I can raise the required amount."

She could not see the alteration in Edward's color in the dim light
of their romantic candles and the hotel's mosquito coils, as it changed
from golden bronze to pale ivory. But she heard the angst in his voice,
"My love, that's not a good idea…too dangerous. After what little
you told me happened in Europe, I really believe you need to…post-
pone…doing your speeches for a while, at least until the world climate improves toward eliminating violent religious fanaticism."

It was on the tip of her tongue to say "*you sound just like Michael*" but
defended her position instead, "That'll never happen if people are left
to be ruled by ignorant, archaic beliefs. There's more danger in that
than in anything else, Edward. The continuation of backward thinking only feeds the continuation of similar actions, and we'll never be
able to get beyond discrimination, oppression, and the persistence of
global fragmentation. Making world peace unachievable. The more
enlightened of us have to keep trying to proselytize, enlighten others, or all will be lost. Remember the profoundness of what Trinidad
and Tobago's founding father Dr. Eric Williams said, "*Education is
Emancipation*." If humans don't learn the truths behind their indoctrinations, people will never know real freedom. They'll continue to

be imprisoned in beliefs that some celestial being, not humans, are responsible for our condition. The cycle of greed and violent stupidity will persist until everything is destroyed. You know that Edward, that's why you were so supportive before. Furthermore, if I can make good money doing my speeches, what better use for it than to make what life they have more comfortable for our most disadvantaged humans."

Edward gave her an admiring smile, "You are so beautiful, in every way. I'm not trying to change the subject, sweetheart, but it's late and we can discuss this further when we get home. But right now, you angel-devil, you have turned me on and heated me up again." He reached for her hand and wrapped her fingers around his fully engorged penis.

She giggled, "You're incorrigible. Our discussion will definitely continue at home, until I get my way. But, for now, I'm going to have my way with you, and put my mouth to the subject at hand."

She engulfed his phallus like no one else could, performing her distinctive version of fellatio, till he reluctantly begged her to stop when he felt his orgasm approaching.

Apart from not wanting her to be left out of feeling the immense pleasure he was enjoying, he had a need to taste her as well, and whispered throatily, "Come over my face."

She readily obeyed and knelt over him.

His tongue and lips masterfully exciting the lips of her labium, he plunged his tongue deep into that mysterious inner sanctum passage of her vagina, through which his seed had passed six years ago and planted in her womb. Through which nine months later, his matured seeds in her fertilized ovum passed back out in the form of their precious twins.

An epiphany hit him. *I'll stop her, keep her safe, the best way I know. The way it's been from time immemorial.* He took hold of her hips, pushed her down his body till he could look in her eyes and whispered, "I hope you haven't gone back on the pill?"

She knew his intention immediately, "No, I've been so busy since my return I keep forgetting to get it. I don't think I'm ovulating now anyway-"

He rolled her off him and lay on her, "We'll see about that." He placed his hands under her bottom, lifted her up to meet him and rammed his penis into her vagina with a vengeance, and did not stop his forceful pumping motions until she reached her orgasm and his seed emptied till dry. Propping up his upper body on his elbows, he stayed in her, which he knew she liked, that drenched feeling from their combined fluids that signified the complete unification of their two bodies.

Though tonight, his purpose went deep. And he wanted to safeguard it stayed entombed in her womb.

The year Elizabeth flew back from New York to Trinidad with the Grangers for the Christmas holidays, she was introduced to Edward's younger sister Vanessa at a fete, who immediately liked her and invited Elizabeth to her birthday party at her parent's home the following evening. Now nineteen and being out of the Trinidad young people's social scene since boarding school in Europe at fourteen, Elizabeth was thrilled to make a new Trinidadian friend who was not a cousin.

Edward, also back for the holidays from Yale University, was speaking to his father on the far side of the pool in their spacious back garden, when she walked into the party. Despite the already congregated huge crowd, their eyes met immediately.

The sparks they both felt connected the large space between them instantaneously, Cupid's arrows simultaneously piercing them both; a clear-cut case of 'love at first sight.'

The love-struck twenty-year-old Edward handed his cocktail glass to his father, "Hold this please, Dad. I have to go meet my future wife."

Elizabeth recognized there was something extra special about the tall handsome lad with the dazzling aquamarine eyes who came over to introduce himself, and never left her side for the entire evening, holding her deliciously, dangerously, close, when they danced. It never occurred to her that in many ways he was very much in stature and manner like the European Prince who had first stolen her heart a year ago, at a ball at Don Frederico Del Rico's palace in Spain.

Dreams and fantasies had abounded then. It was months before thoughts of the prince would take a sabbatical from her conscious mind, which was encouraged by the relentless wooing of the maturely debonair and handsome Don Frederico. Still young and impressionable at eighteen, she had succumbed to his charms but not his seductions, agreeing to accept his impressive engagement ring with the idea they would marry after she obtained her degree. The persuasive Don was anxious to have an heir, and his older ex-wife, who he had recently divorced after six years of marriage, appeared to be barren.

Originally with intentions of becoming fluent in Spanish and other languages so that she could join the diplomatic corps after university, for four months Elizabeth traveled frequently to Spain. She stayed in her own assigned suite at Don Frederico's palace under the chaperoning eyes of alternately her mother Gabrielle, Ruth, her childhood best friend Judith, or an old aunt of the Don's.

Although they liked the charming and gracious Don, neither her parents or Ruth approved of the match, finding him shiftily urbane, and at forty, too old, for their still maturing virginal precious Elizabeth, who was overflowing with dreams and ambitions. They were concerned he would eventually try to dominatingly stifle the intelligent and headstrong young woman, and failing, with a divorce already in his past, may think nothing of another in the future, and their child would be devastated, especially if there were children involved.

However, having faith in the commonsense of the girl they so lovingly and carefully raised, they cautiously gave her their opinions and advice, but acted with understanding in the hope her infatuation would soon come to an end.

Their hopes eventually bore fruit after Elizabeth and the Don argued one night, in his bed. With the natural sexuality and curiosity of an eighteen-year-old girl, together with his amorous cajoling, she had clandestinely been visiting him every night after the household had gone to sleep.

The Don was at first enchanted by her insistence she remain a virgin until their wedding night, and therefore respected her wishes that they indulge simply in kissing and gentle minimal touching, in the dark. This particular night, after months of excruciating frustration, satisfying himself completely only after she would leave with masturbations, the sexually experienced Don attempted to mount her saying he could not keep his promise any longer, she must give herself to him tonight.

She had to aggressively push him off while threatening to scream "*rape*" if he tried to force her.

With a menacing voice he gave her an ultimatum, "Either submit now or I'm going to resume a sexual relationship with my former mistress, until you do."

Elizabeth and Ruth were on the plane back to New York the next day, her finger devoid of the ostentatious engagement ring.

After that misadventure, she saw the jet-setter Don only occasionally at parties of mutual friends, and would cling to whatever platonic boyfriend was nearby to escape his flirtatious attempts at persuading her to return to him.

A year later she returned home for her first Trinidadian Christmas in several years, met and fell in love with Edward, and after four months accepted his marriage proposal.

Two years later, at twenty-one and twenty-two, with their Bachelor's Degrees completed, they were married in the same Catholic Church in which his parents were married, witnessed by four hundred family, friends, and parent's business associates. Edward's uncle was the officiating priest at a Papally blessed High Mass.

Despite the enormous crowd, their wedding reception still had the ambiance of an intimate affair as it was held at Elizabeth's parent's luxurious Ellerslie Park home, the pool in the back garden covered with a Plexi-glas dance floor and lavishly decorated white tasseled tent.

In true Trinidadian fashion, the newlyweds danced to a popular band, and a Disc Jockey, with their guests, into the wee hours of the morning till exhausted.

They consummated their marriage, and their love, at the upside-down Trinidad Hilton that first night together, the next day flying out to London for a three-week European honeymoon.

CHAPTER
46

*F*atally thrown back into royal double-duty, Michael had little time to dwell on the loss of his beloved. That is not to say he was not still obsessed with Elizabeth. He persisted in trying to reach her whenever he had a rare spare moment.

He would phone while running along palace hallways from one area to the next, while being chauffeured to and from events, whenever he happened to be alone at a hurried meal at his desk, and even when sitting on his 'other throne.'

Elizabeth never answered but later listened to and recorded every message. Some were imploring, some reminiscing, some chastising, some forgiving, but all were loving, and Elizabeth imprisoned her tears through every one.

Twice Edward caught her listening to Michael's messages, but though it pained him greatly, he acted with graceful insouciance, simply remarking that Michael needed to find someone else and allow everyone to get on with enjoying their lives. Elizabeth, feeling her own pain as well as that of both her great loves, would shut off her phone saying she could tell he was getting there, and felt sure he would soon desist from calling. She didn't believe her words, neither did Edward.

Edward still felt he was walking an astronomical tightrope in his marriage, the feeling aggravated by a new fatigue exhibited by Elizabeth, despite all his efforts to make her hectic life easier. He feared she was succumbing to melancholia.

Not actually feeling ill but aware something unusual was affecting her, she went to see an old school chum from when she attended St. Joseph's Convent School before going to boarding school in Europe. Their friendship was renewed when Sabrina Ramkisoon returned from America as an obstetrician-gynecologist, became Elizabeth's doctor, and delivered her twins.

After examining her, Sabrina's brown complexion took on a special glow she could not conceal at moments like this, "You're not to worry. Everything's great, you're in perfect health."

Taking in Elizabeth's suddenly bewildered look and misting eyes, Sabrina knew she must put the feelings of her patient, and friend, before her own unprofessional feelings which had surfaced. Gently, she took Elizabeth's hand, swallowed, and said softly, "Elizabeth, you know you don't *have* to go through with this. I know you didn't intend to have any more. If you don't want to-"

Elizabeth brightened and said decisively, "I want to. I *need* to."

Sabrina smiled excitedly, "Great. Now, from the approximate dates you've given me of your last period, and from when you ran out of the pill, had sex with the Prince, and then Edward, I can safely say this is definitely Edward's child. Go home with a clear conscience, and make your husband happy."

While driving home to give Edward and the twins the exciting news, Michael called. His telepathy touched her, she had been thinking about him too much recently, and missing him. Something compelled her to answer this time. She pulled into a quiet alley in the bustling overcrowded capital city of Port of Spain. The joy in his voice at hearing hers brought on extreme sadness for her. She knew she must now tell him with finality, to never call again. Without responding to his loving enquiries as to how she was, she said bluntly, "You cannot ever call me again. You *must* let me go, Michael."

He matched her bluntness, "I can't, Elizabeth."

She ignored the lump that was developing in her throat, "You *have* to darl…um…Michael."

He caught her catching herself from calling him 'darling,' "Oh? Was it that easy for *you* to let me go?" She didn't answer. "Elizabeth, *have* you let me go?"

Emotionally fatigued, she decided, no more lies, even though this truth will be paradoxically painful yet comforting for him, she sighed, "No."

That one word was the catalyst for Michael's decision, "I'm coming for you. And the children."

She spoke with forced determination, "Michael, no! I have to stay here! My life is here. I'm…I'm…preg…it's too late for us, Michael. It's too late!"

He spoke with resolution, "That is not your philosophy, nor mine. It's never too late-"

"*This* time it is, Michael! This time it is! Oh Godde Michael, stop torturing us both. There's nothing you can do now, but let me go. I've moved on. I have Edward and my children. You must find somebody else to call your own. It just can't be me anymore!" Clicking off the phone, she let it fall in her lap, rested her head on the steering wheel, and set her tears free.

Three days later she was in her home-office responding to e-mails from her agent Gloria Goldman in New York, when Tilda knocked on the door, "Madame, a guard's here deliverin' a huge box but won't let me sign. Says you have to do it personally."

It still amused her that Tilda addressed her in the old-fashioned manner of 'Madame.' She suspected it was because Tilda didn't like the formality and length of 'Mrs. Du Beauchamp,' but felt it disrespectful to call her by her first name; although Tilda insisted it was because she considered it, "De proper way. Mih aunt worked for rich white people all her life and said so."

After she signed and the strange delivery-man left, thinking the box contained something for the baby the elated Edward wanted to surprise her with, she and Tilda set about opening it. To her amazement, it was filled with her clothes that she had to leave behind in the palace when she ran away from Michael, with the exception of her royal blue gown, and she knew why. It was the gown she wore on the night she and Michael first gave themselves completely to each other. The romantic fool kept it as a memento.

In the middle layer of the clothes lay several jewelry boxes and on opening them, she was shocked to see he had not only sent her own sapphire and diamond pieces given to her by Edward for their seventh wedding anniversary, but also those of Michael's great-grandmother that matched them.

She was even more shocked to see all the gold, ruby, diamond and pearl pieces of his mother's that he had her wear with the red gown to The Ambassadors Ball, the next day telling her about his secreted illegitimate teenage daughter in Greece. Amongst the jewelry boxes lay a small parcel that was gift wrapped in gold paper with a white silk bow and a card attached. She told Tilda the box was sent by The Grangers, and waited until Tilda left the room carrying some clothes to attempt to fit them in Elizabeth's closet, to open the gift. Opening the card, her hands shook as she read Michael's handwriting.

'Happy Birthday, my Darling Elizabeth

I wish you today, and always, Life's Splendid Seven Gifts: Love, Peace, Wisdom, Joy, Health, Wealth, and the Time, to enjoy it all. Most of all I wish you were here with me, today and every day, till death and even beyond.

With all my love always, I give you my heart, M.A.S.

P.S. Please promise me you will pass your 'old faithful' watch on to Zarna, and always wear the new 'forever loyal' watch I had made for you. It will keep you safely on time, always. Please don't try returning anything. I'll just keep sending it back to you. Everything is really yours, meant for no one else but you. As is my heart. M.A.S.'

Having vowed to her unborn babe not to upset it by the shedding of any more tears for Michael, she stifled the urge to cry. *You're never going to let me go, are you, Michael? Ah well. Neither can I ever let you go.*

But you mustn't know it. No one will. You'll stay secretly locked in my heart. Alongside Edward.

Inside the gift-wrapped box there were four items, the watch he referred to, two compact discs, one with the love songs he had played for her in the past, the other The Pan Am North Stars classical steel-band music they had danced to, and a red velvet ring box with a note attached.

She read it immediately on seeing inside the box, the ruby diamonds and pearls ring that matched the other pieces.

'My darling Elizabeth, this was my mother's favorite ring. I intended to give it to you the night of the Ambassadors Ball, but didn't after I saw how you reacted to my idea of announcing our engagement, which I now regret. Please wear my mother's ring, especially when you wear the set, she would have wanted you to have it. I know in my heart, from wherever she is, she loves you, almost as much as I do. Yours forever, M.A.S.'

Taking off her engagement and wedding rings that Edward had brought to Barbados and slipped back onto her finger the morning after they reconciled, she tried on the Queen's ring. It was a perfect fit, as though it was made for her. She immediately put it back in its box.

She examined the watch. It was exquisite, and surprisingly, not ostentatious. Though slightly larger than her Baum and Merceir, it had a classic simplicity about it. The face was surrounded with tiny diamonds, there were similar diamonds at each digit, and the band and casing design was sturdily crafted in equal parts of weaved platinum and gold. It was obviously meant to suit virtually any occasion. What struck her as odd was there was no manufacturer's stamp on it or on its case, no literature, and no warranty. She wondered about the meaning behind his wording, "*It will keep you* 'safely' *on time.*"

Edward awakened her on her birthday with an outstanding erection, and an equally outstanding diamond eternity ring, which he placed on her ring-finger on her right hand.

That night she showed it off to over two hundred family and friends at a surprise birthday party he threw for her at his brother's nightclub.

He was elated to see Elizabeth's beautiful face lit up in a dazzling smile for most of the evening. While dancing, his eyes closed as he relished the feel of her body against his, he didn't see two escaped tears that fell on his shirt as they swayed in rhythm to Elvis's, 'It's Now Or Never.'

Edward's plot to stop Elizabeth from doing her speeches simply by getting her impregnated was foiled by Gloria Goldman.

The day before Elizabeth told Gloria in confidence that she was pregnant, Gloria had successfully negotiated speeches in four different European countries, which would be lucrative for both herself and Elizabeth. When she phoned Elizabeth to give her the good news, Elizabeth gave hers. Though Elizabeth articulated much uncertainty about traveling that far and leaving her family for long trips again so soon, and now the new complication of her pregnancy, Gloria would not be discouraged.

A career woman to her core, having never allowed herself to, *"get caught up in the business of motherhood,"* Gloria was not going to let her plans of *"making a tidy little nest egg"* be thwarted by the mere pregnancy of someone else.

Within three hours she phoned Elizabeth again with offers to do five speeches, "All in your neighborhood, honey. Two in the Caribbean, three in South America. You'll be away just a couple days at a time. Less money, but we'll make it up back in Europe after the babe is born. I'm sending you an e-mail with the particulars right away. But *phone* me with your decision. In the affirmative, of course."

Two hours later, while having a late breakfast on the veranda with a view of the sea before making her rounds of the companies and other appointments, Elizabeth was surprised to hear Edward's car speeding up their steep driveway in the middle of the morning, followed by what sounded like a heavy truck.

Entering the veranda, he gave her a quick peck on her nose. She looked at his obviously worried face, "What's going on?"

He was curt, "That's what I'm hoping you'll tell me."

She stiffened, "What do you mean?"

Pulling out his phone he showed her a text message he received an hour ago: '*Edward you must protect Elizabeth. I'm doing what I can but it's difficult for me to do it properly from here. If she continues doing her speeches at the present time she'll be in extreme danger. Please take action immediately. Michael.*'

Elizabeth was first astonished, then annoyed. *How the hell did Michael know. How dare he text Edward! Interfering in my life!* She began explicating Gloria's latest proposals, but then showed him Gloria's e-mail to finish the explanation.

She touched his tense face, "My love, I've not made any decision, I was going to discuss it with you tonight. I'm really mad at Michael for texting you. I don't know how he found out, you know I haven't been speaking to him. He must've had someone hack into my computer. I'll have our expert see what can be done to stop that. But he's just being melodramatic about my needing protection-"

Edward interrupted agitatedly, "Sweetheart, stop! I was just sent the transcript from your speech and Q'n'A in Europe, and, a copy of a threat to your *life*! I don't want to upset you in your condition but," he raised his voice in controlled anger, "why the hell didn't you tell me all that went on?"

"It wasn't important-"

He was shaking inside but hid it well, "Not important! Your *life* was threatened, woman! If you don't care about that, I do! And think of your children! The twins, and now the one you're carrying. You want them raised without a mother? And have you considered you might be putting *them* in danger too?"

"Stop it Edward! Now *you* are being melodramatic. Nothing's going to happen to me or the children. In any case I haven't made a decision yet, but I was leaning towards postponing the speeches until after the baby's born. I'm concerned about the twins' emotional state, they still cling to me when they're home from school, and when they're at ballet and soccer they keep looking to make sure I'm still there, and aren't paying attention. I feel it's too soon for me to leave them. Okay, that's it. I'm going to e-mail Gloria and tell her we have to postpone everything for a year. I hope that makes you happy." She looked at him squarely, "But understand this, I *will* resume my speeches as soon as my family's life is stabilized and nothing you or Mi...*anybody*, can do, will stop me!"

She left the house immediately, undesirous of dealing with any further expostulation and not wanting to be around him, or anyone. Cancelling her appointments for the rest of the day, she drove to Maracas Bay. There, she sat in the churning surf, fully clothed except for shoes, in an attempt to cool down; and contemplated on choices, constraints, and the lot of mothers everywhere, whose lives were so seldom under their own control.

Returning home to her quiet exclusive neighborhood near the top of Goodwood Park after lunchtime, she found her garden to be a noisy beehive of activity with workmen of every description buzzing all over the place in a variety of undertakings.

There was a ditch digger, a carpenter, and a mason, building a guard hut beside the electronic gate, two more masons adding another two rows of concrete blocks to the already tall wall that surrounded the entire property, and four gardeners planting more thorny bougainvillea bushes along the inside of the wall.

At the side of the garages were more construction workers building an outside bathroom for security guards, so they would not have to use Tilda's and Evangeline's. Beyond that more workers had started on the foundation and steel supports for what would be a new baby's nursery adjoining the master bedroom upstairs, which would create a covered porch for the servant's quarters below. A wrought-iron manufacturer was measuring the windows for reinforcing the burglarproofing that was already in existence. Edward, their building contractor, and a man from the Housing Authority, were in the garage poring over house plans on top of a makeshift carpenter's table.

With just polite hellos to the contractor and the Housing man she swept past Edward, who shortly after followed her into their bathroom where she was stripping off her wet clothes.

She swung around and accosted him, "What the hell are you doing? Wasting money turning our home into a bloody fortress! I said I was postponing my speeches! You don't trust me?"

He acted insouciant, "That has nothing to do with it. Based on what I only just found out happened in Europe, I'm taking precautionary measures in case some religious fanatics decide to…try something. I've hired another driver for the office and I'm giving you Carl fulltime to chauffeur you and the children. He always carries a gun and a Taser, and I'm having Tasers and mace brought down from Miami by special courier for you to have on you from now on. I'll keep some in my car. I got permission from the Superintendent of Police, he's Carl's cousin. I've hired round the clock armed security for the house-"

She felt a loss of power, "No! Edward, no! We're not going to lose our privacy! Nor am I going to lose my independence to drive because you're over-reacting to Michael's drama."

He fought the same feeling as hers, "Your…the…bloody prince, has nothing to do with this! *I* am about protecting you, and our family, from whatever idiots might be out there-"

She calmed herself, "You're panicking unnecessarily. People don't even know where I am. I still have no website for my speeches, and I never use the Du Beauchamp name anyway-"

Edward threw his hands up in exasperation, "Great! Now I have to worry about protecting your parents as well!"

Flicking her wrist at him she turned away, "Calm down Edward, my parents are perfectly capable of protecting themselves. Have some faith in humanity, will you," removing her wet underwear she stepped into the shower, "now leave me alone. I'm itchy. I have to wash off sand and salt from Maracas Bay."

She turned the shower on and he stepped in with her fully clothed, "What're you doing! You'll ruin your shoes, and pants!"

He pulled her into his arms, "I don't care. I hate it when we fight like this. Please, just humor me for a while and agree to all the new steps I've taken to protect you…us? Let's just try it, at least until after the baby's born. Alright? Give me one less thing to worry about?"

Seeing deep furrows take over his handsome but still gaunt face, flashing back to all the stresses he had to endure during their separation, she felt an extreme compassion come upon her, combined with overwhelming love and appreciation, "Alright."

Kissing him, she helped him out of his clothes. Before the water had time to remove the saltiness from her body, eating with delicious enjoyment, he did it for her.

That night after everyone was asleep, she snuck into her office and called Michael. She knew he would be deep in sleep because of the time difference and she would get his voice-mail. She left him a scathing chastisement for his audacity in texting Edward and interfering in her life. She concluded by saying though she still loved him and always will, he needed to respect that she felt the same way about the man she was already married to, who was the father of her children, and if he really cared about her he must cease meddling in their lives.

After that, she didn't hear from Michael again. Edward's elation was noticeable, Elizabeth's disappointment was concealed.

By the end of three months the Du Beauchamp and Richardson families had adjusted quite well to all the new security and modifications to their normal routines. They still spent most weekends either at Monos island with Edward's family or in Tobago with Elizabeth's, sans visible security guards.

Through their chauffeur Carl's connections with the police Edward obtained a seldom permitted license for a gun, and was able to purchase a revolver with a safety lock, which he kept always within reach. Elizabeth kept her taser and mace continually accessible in her handbag and was extremely vigilant about keeping them locked and away from children.

She was grateful for her time with Michael and dealing with matters of constant security and protection. It made this new lifestyle more acceptable and less disconcerting.

Though people at their echelon in Trinidad were always careful about security and lived with caution, including alarm systems for homes, vehicles, businesses, and security guards occasionally, all of their lives, the continuous presence of guards, weaponry, and extra surveillance and scrutiny of every stranger regardless of color or gender, was not something Elizabeth and Edward had ever thought would become a normal component of their everyday lives.

CHAPTER
47

Michael and his father were discussing Michael's love-life, or the lack thereof. He told the King about Elizabeth's last blistering message, the added pain it brought, and along with it his renewed hopelessness for them to ever reunite.

The king gave his still too thin heir a sympathetically encouraging smile, "Well son, you should look on this as a sign to get on with your own life. You've been lost and lonely for too long. It's unhealthy. Believe me, I know." Unsuccessful in hiding his underlying worry, he added slowly, "Listen, I understand Princess Teresa still pines for you, has turned down several exceptional proposals. You know, Michael, it is possible to learn to love someone, especially someone who loves you so much. Though she's only twenty-two, she'll mature with the position she'll attain, which she was groomed for. And, she's very pretty, you'd make beautiful babies together, be sure of an heir with her. I'm not pressuring you. Take your time, just think about it." His Majesty left him to ponder on his suggestion, saying that he'll be back in an hour after his meeting with a trade delegation from France.

Michael rose from his desk and walked over to look out the window, concerned about his father's health, a union with Princess Teresa the furthest thing from his mind.

In the distance he could see two swans on the banks of a pond frolicking in a mating dance, white flashes of frenzied wings, feathers flying wildly in the air, the cob trying to mount the pen. His eyes wandered over to an oak tree nearby and took in two squirrels scrambling around its trunk as though in a game of tag, the more enthusiastic male attempting to catch the coquettish female. He was overcome with envy, *What is wrong with you animals, don't you know spring is long gone? So what if it's hot, it's almost autumn, you dopes.*

When his father returned he was still gazing out the window, his eyes with a pained faraway look. He sighed resignedly, "Alright Pa, make the arrangements."

His father could not believe his ears, became unsure of exactly what his son meant, "Pardon? Arrangements?"

"For a marriage with Teresa."

"Really? Are you sure? Have you thought it out carefully-"

Not daring to look into his concerned father's eyes of wisdom, Michael interrupted, "I'm sure. I guess it's time to get started on those babies everybody wants."

Elizabeth spent the day at home helping Tilda, Evangeline, and Lucy and Kenneth, the couple who assisted with parties, to organize and cook a five course sit-down dinner party she and Edward were throwing that evening for the new American Ambassador and his wife. The guest list included two other diplomats and their spouses, and three government ministers and their spouses.

The Chippendale dining table with its fourteen chairs, inherited from Elizabeth's Richardson grandparents, was beautifully set by Elizabeth and Tilda with Rosenthal china, Baccarat and Waterford crystal goblets, and a conglomeration of rare antique sterling silver cutlery inherited from the Du Beauchamp family, given to Elizabeth and Edward as part of their wedding present from Edward's grandmother.

Two silver six-armed candelabras were also wedding presents from family members; as was three Lalique crystal rose-bowls Elizabeth filled with red hybrid anthurium lilies and leaves, freshly cut from under the Julie mango tree in the back garden. The rest of the mansion was decorated by her florist cousin with roses and flowering orchid plants.

Sitting at the top of each place setting, in shell-shaped silver and gold place-card holders they had purchased in Monaco on their honeymoon, was a card with the name and title of the guest to be seated there.

With the reliable, and armed, chauffeur Carl collecting the twins at school and dropping them off at her parent's home in Ellerslie Park for a Friday night sleep-over, Elizabeth had time to indulge in a much needed relaxing bubble bath at four o'clock, the guests not arriving till seven.

Sitting naked at her dressing table, she had just finished applying her makeup when Tilda knocked, calling out that Elizabeth's cousin from Europe had dropped in for a visit and was waiting in the drawing room.

Puzzled, Elizabeth called Tilda into the room as she grabbed a silk leopard-print caftan, "Which cousin?"

Tilda smiled shyly, "Don't know, Madame. He didn't give de guard his name, said he wanted to surprise you. De guard let him in cause he speaks somethin' like you, came in a fancy car, and he really handsome too. Like a movie star."

Elizabeth's face lit up, "It's Jamie! My favorite cousin, and I didn't get to see him when I was in Europe…he was traveling. How exciting. We'll have to squeeze him in at the dinner table somehow." She raced down the stairs, leaving Tilda to tidy the bathroom, in case any of the guests tonight would want a tour of the beautifully appointed impressive mansion, which often happened at parties.

Entering the drawing room, there was no sign of Jamie, and seeing the sliding doors to the outside terraces still closed, she assumed, drawn to the lavish setting that could be seen through the Grecian columns, he had wandered into the dining room to check it out. Her assumption was correct, he was bending over some family photographs in silver frames that sat next to a silver tea and coffee set on a Tudor styled mahogany sideboard.

Hearing the swish of her silk caftan, he straightened up as she called out excitedly, "Ja...Michael!"

They stared at each other for a second. Elizabeth swayed in shock. Michael stepped toward her, she stepped toward him, and automatically melted into his arms. He began to hold her tight, but not wanting him to feel her bump she stepped back, at the same time that he was realizing it was inappropriate for her to feel his which had uncontrollably risen.

Finding her voice, she whispered, "Why did you come?"

Wishing he could come right out and say he was there for a last-ditch effort to convince her to come back to him, but now knowing of that impossibility after everything he had learnt and seen of her world, he instead stared into her misting eyes, "I felt I had to tell you this in person, before it hits the media. I'm getting married. To Princess Teresa."

She felt her heart and stomach constrict but managed a smile, "Congratulations. I'm so glad you've fallen in love again, Michael. I've been so worried about you-"

His voice cooled, "I'm not marrying because I'm in love, Elizabeth. I'm marrying to start a family so that I can get on with the life destiny has carved out for me."

Taking in his skinnier but still handsome face along with his words, she felt illogically both sad and happy, "You're not in love with her?"

His demeanor stiffened, "It may be beyond *your* comprehension, but I'm in love with only one woman, and will be for all eternity. But since you don't want me, I have to use somebody else to have a family with."

Blood gushed through her heart, "Oh Godde, Michael! It's not that I don't want you, I do want you! But I want my family too. And since

I can't have both, I have to choose the one that destiny had already carved out for me!"

His coolness heated to an obstinacy, "You and I were a family Elizabeth. Your children would've become mine, they're part of you, and we would've had more together."

She pleaded, "Michael, don't do this? Please? It's not achieving anything, it only serves to bring back the pain we've both suffered. Leaving you was the hardest thing I've ever had to do in my life. But I've recovered from it." She hoped she sounded convincing enough to conceal her lie, and continued quickly, "You have an amazing life ahead of you darl...Michael. You are destined to accomplish great things for humanity. You must take every advantage of a marriage with Teresa to cement the unity in Europe your family has given up so much for, worked so hard to achieve."

Glancing at the opulent table and around the elegant room, bitterness entered his voice, "I see why I didn't have enough to offer you. You're already queen of your own palace here."

Her heart aching for him she reached for his hand, "You know this has nothing to do with why I had to leave."

He squeezed her hand till it hurt, and looked over at the photographs, "Your children are beautiful. Ours would've been too. Well," his face took on an unmistakable contempt, "I'd better leave before... *he*, comes home," he let go of her hand, "Goodbye, Elizabeth." Turning around quickly, he walked out the Costa Rican hand carved mahogany front door, and got into the car were Brian and Eric waited.

Speeding past Tilda who was coming down the stairs to offer refreshments, Elizabeth almost tripped on her caftan.

Seeing the tears streaming from her eyes Tilda followed her to her bedroom, "Oh Gord, Madame, wha' happen? Somebody dead?"

Sobbing embarrassedly, she mumbled, "No, nothing like that, my...cousin...had to leave. And, I miss him."

Compassion flowed from Tilda, "Don' mind. You'll see him again soon. And look how you spoilin' all your nice makeup wid all dis cryin,' and it not good for de baby. Don' cry. I goin' get you a cool drink." Tilda felt an old fear revisit her. *Madame cryin' so hard, just like when I catch her so many times when she and Sir stopped sleepin' in de same room for all dose months and months, den she got so thin, started travelin' so much alone. But den dey come back from Barbados so happy, just like before Sir moved into de guest quarters. Now wid de baby comin' everytin' was perfect again. Until dis handsome strange 'cousin' come here upsettin' everytin'.*

Unable to get her tears to stop, Elizabeth did what she always resorted to when emotionally upset, speed-walking. She donned her exercise clothes, ran down the stairs, and on grabbing her car keys, bumped into Tilda.

Tilda showed her revisited fear, "Where you goin'? You still cryin', and you have guests comin' in two hours. Carl gone for de day, you can't drive yourself-"

Elizabeth mumbled, "I'll be back in time," and raced off in her car. Tilda rested the glass of cold orange juice she was bringing for Elizabeth on the granite counter, picked up the kitchen phone, and called Edward.

After maneuvering through traffic and tears as she drove past The Queen's Park Savannah lined with flowering tropical trees, and across from it the culturally diverse, magnificent, some neglected and dilapidated, mansions, which represented important aspects of the island's ethnic history, Elizabeth parked her customized Cadillac Sedan at the bottom of Lady Chancellor Hill. She didn't speed-walk but ran up the three miles long steep and winding hill.

Arriving almost at the top exhausted, she brushed away some tears to better see a group of people standing at the summit who were taking in the awe-inspiring panoramic view.

On the hills to the left was a montage of rich greens and multi-colored wild tropical trees, palms, and flowering bushes, and in the distance, The Trinidad Hilton Hotel built into a steep hillside of the Belmont neighborhood. In the far distance could be seen mangroves in the marshy swampland of the mouth of the Caroni River, where massive flocks of Scarlet Ibis come to nestle at sunset, thrilling locals and tourists alike. Looking down the center past more trees, rooftops of houses peeking through, lay the expansive lawned tree-lined Savannah at the bottom of Lady Chancellor Hill. Just past it shone the colorful cluttered capital city of Port Of Spain. Beyond that in the farthest distance flowed the serene azure Caribbean Sea, fishing boats, luxury liners, and cargo ships, cruising in and out of the bustling harbor. To the right, the more restful green forested hills and valleys completed the magnificent scenery.

Seeing the group consisted of four robust black men, terror gripped Elizabeth. She regretted her foolhardiness at coming up the hill alone, and, leaving her weaponry locked in the glove compartment of her car.

Granted, she had not heard of any attacks on women in this isolated area for quite some time, but then, she had been away for two months and since her return had been so busy with resettling her life, her family, and her marriage, she had been unable to get together with her girlfriends to get caught up on the latest gossip. Nor had she had the time to discuss with her mother what was the newest 'mauvais langue.'

Just as she was turning around to make a run for it, hoping to meet and be rescued by some other exercisers who may be coming up the hill, one of the men called her name.

She turned and wiped her eyes as the man walked towards her, "Elizabeth, it's me, Jimmy. Jimmy Brown. Oh gorsh, yuh cryin'? Wha' happen? Somebody dead?"

Recognizing one of Edward's tennis partners, she went into a crying fit of relief mixed with her sorrow, and began to contradictorily chuckle at the same time, *What is it with West Indians, the only time one cries is if "somebody dead"?*

Jimmy wrapped his arms around her. She dropped her head on his shoulder in order to hide her embarrassment, the other men gathering around. In typical Trini fashion, they began to make jokes in the hope of lightening what looked like a serious situation. One said, "But Jimmy, what you do to de girl to make her cry so?" Another teased, "Jim, one look at yuh ugly face and yuh make even de most beautiful woman cry."

Jimmy did not take kindly to the raillery, "Allyuh shut up. This is mih friend, mih tennis buddy Edward's wife. Yuh can't see she badly upset. Elizabeth, wha' happen, doux-doux? I hope is not Edward have yuh upset, he'll have to answer to me."

Unable to speak through her sobs she lifted her head and shook it, when Jimmy said, "Talk of the devil, the man himself."

Edward jumped out of his Jaguar, ran to the group, and Jimmy released her to him. He picked her up in his arms and winked at Jimmy, "Thanks Jimmy. Elizabeth's pregnant and a little emotional these days. You know how it is."

Jimmy smiled in commiseration, "Oh yes. Mih wife was the same way for weeks with the last baby. Take care of her, buddy. Call mih when yuh can get in a game, awright?"

"Definitely. Thanks again."

Edward drove into one of the side streets off Lady Chancellor Hill, and parked in the empty driveway of one of the new mansions under construction that belonged to a friend.

Seeing how distraught Elizabeth still was, he knew he had to calm her down before going home to get ready to face their guests in an hour. He reached over to take her in his arms but she resisted and he sighed frustratedly, "It was *him*, wasn't it? Your so-called 'cousin'?"

She nodded and pulled some tissues out of a box.

He hid his rising resentment, "Why did he come?"

"He came to tell me he's getting married."

His risen resentment became evident, "Huh, that's not the reason. He could've done that over the phone."

"He felt he should tell me in person."

Edward hit the steering wheel with his palms, "No! He came hoping to get you to change your mind! To go back with him. If you weren't pregnant would you have gone back with him? I need to know, Elizabeth."

Wiping her teary eyes, an act she silently promised her fetus would be necessary for the last time, she looked in her husband's troubled aquamarine eyes, and repressing multifarious emotions, said clearly, "No. Now let's go home. Our guests will soon be there."

Elizabeth pulled herself together remarkably well, physically and emotionally. She had no choice.

There was a lot more to this dinner than merely honoring the new American ambassador. The other invited guests, especially the government ministers, were expressly selected for some political manipulation in the hope they would get the government to reconsider part-funding the extension for The Children's Home, now that Elizabeth was postponing her speeches.

She donned a sexy low-cut but flowing black gown that did not reveal her prenatal condition, and with it she put on a charming and happy demeanor, *I do this for the children. My own pain is irrelevant compared to theirs.*

By all accounts the evening was a huge success.

The delicious gourmet meal and excessive partaking of excellent wines and liquors unleashed an outpouring of compliments, with promises from everyone to assist in raising funds for The Children's Home. On leaving after midnight with effusive gratitudes and platitudes, the spirituous guests left with Elizabeth's e-mail address, gushing with assurances they would be in touch by the end of next week.

Within four days thank-you notes arrived from everyone, several via e-mail. The American ambassador and his wife sent a basket of imported fruits and their personal cheque for five hundred dollars for The Children's Home, with information about charity foundations in America she should apply to for help.

With sobriety now prevailing, the government ministers had their assistants e-mail Elizabeth with regrets that, once more, there were, "No funds in this year's budget for The Children's Home," and she, "should try again next year."

Oh sure. Where've I heard that before. Though disillusioned, she still sent off information packages to the American foundations, but recollecting what happened with the International Foundation in Europe, and given the tenuous world economy, held out little hope for positive responses.

She e-mailed Gloria in NewYork and told her to firm up dates for a year from now, for her to resume her speeches.

Two days later her bank manager called, "Elizabeth, you need to come down to sign some papers so I can release the million Euros that came in for The Children's Home."

She almost dropped the phone, "A million Euros! Where's it from? The Foundation said they couldn't give us any more-"

The manager, her father's longtime black best friend and golfing partner whom she grew up calling 'Uncle' out of respect, interjected, "It's not from them, Princess. Sorry, I've been sworn to secrecy about this, it came in yesterday, I checked it out personally. It's all legitimate, the money's here for you to finish The Children's Home, Princess, so come in and get it."

She immediately called her father, hoping his golfing buddy had divulged some classified information, as men have been known to do on the golf course just as frequently as on a lover's bed.

Her father was uninformed of the situation and said when it came to confidential matters, his friend was highly principled and trust-worthy, but he would still be attentive to what he might let slip on the golf course tomorrow. The next evening her father called to say he was unsuccessful in breaking his friend, neither in his confidences or in his game, but she was obviously blessed by the person who his friend said referred to himself, strangely, not as her 'guardian' angel, but as her "*archangel.*"

She told Edward the Foundation in Europe came through after all, then went into her home-office, locked the door, and called Michael,

"Why did you do it? I can't accept it. I can send this back, unlike all the jewelry you gave me, which by the way, I've put in my secret safety deposit box at my bank in safe-keeping for your daughter."

Michael sounded melancholy, "Please don't do that, the jewelry is yours, to be worn only by you. And the money is irrevocable, its appropriation is specifically for The Children's Home, you have to accept it. I'm begging you, Elizabeth, please don't do any more of your speeches until I can keep you safe. You promised me once before-"

Hearing the strange sadness in his voice, she did not want to refuse to promise and start a quarrel, so she interrupted, "How is your arm? Are you still in therapy?"

He chuckled amusedly, "Trying to change the subject? It's fine, I no longer need therapy. Are you going to keep the promise you made when it got damaged? You know if you really care for me like you say you do, you will."

"Oh? Blackmail? It's beneath you, Mr. Prince. I'm no longer making promises I can't keep. But know this, I do care for you. I love you beyond reason, which is to my personal detriment. However, I'm extremely grateful for everything you've done, for me, and the children. I'll never be able to reciprocate, tangibly, you know that. But, you're often in my thoughts and prayers, more than you'll ever know, more than I should legally have you there. I wish you only eternal happiness. I will not call you again. Goodbye Michael, my Archangel."

The next day, there was a long, happy-sounding voicemail from Michael. He told her how wonderful it was to hear her angelic voice again, and to know she still loves him. He had wondered what she was thinking when she backed away from him when he embraced her in her home. It had hurt to think she was repulsed by what often happens to him when he's around her. He still knew in the depths of his being they were meant to be together, and he didn't know if he could hold out for another lifetime for that to happen, and wondered if she herself could. He then assured her that his upcoming marriage was simply one of convenience to ensure the monarchy would have a male heir as soon as possible, that she, Elizabeth, was his only love; though he would have to give his wife his body, his heart and soul belonged only, and always, to Elizabeth.

Three months later, Michael was married to Princess Teresa. It was not the typical royal wedding with the usual pomp and ceremony. It was understated by the standards one had come to expect of this royal family. There were three hundred invitees comprising family, closest friends, heads of foreign royalty and heads of state of European countries only.

The official excuse given for the "*smaller intimate wedding*" was that Prince Michael was still healing from wounds sustained in the assassination attempts on him, but he would be in perfect health for his big coronation next year, to which all persons who may have been excluded would be invited.

The media was quick to speculate that it was such a "*quiet affair*" because Princess Teresa was already pregnant, and she was the one not in good health. This was quickly dispelled when the bride's pictures were splashed everywhere displaying the tinniest waist, which she had secretly cinched in with a corset. No mention was made of the false smile pasted on Prince Michael's face, the bride's true elation taking all the glory.

Elizabeth meanwhile, was blooming. In her fifth month and feeling healthier than when she was growing the twins, she was able to reorganize the construction for The Children's Home and hire an assistant for her co-founder, Jane Thompson. At Edward's insistence she hired and trained her own assistant, which allowed her to reduce the frequency of her visits to check on the smooth running of their various businesses, giving her extra time to indulge her family, and indulge in a healthcare and exercise routine. Taking a sabbatical from the University Of The West Indies, she postponed getting her Master's degree from the Arthur Lok Jack Graduate School of Business for another year.

A month earlier, before she got "*too big and uncomfortable,*" Edward had taken her and the children for their last sailing "*fling*" through The Grenadine Islands on their fifty-two-foot yacht. Because the crossing from Trinidad could be rough, even treacherous, Edward decided he would take only his two teenaged but strong and capable nephews to help him sail to St. Vincent. Two days after they left, Elizabeth, accompanied by one of their pilot friends, flew herself and the children in their plane to St. Vincent where Edward and the boys were safely waiting, to sail them through the heavenly Grenadine Islands.

They had a marvelous time, sailing languorously from island to island during the day, swimming in the most pristine of warm waters, catching fish and lobsters, then cooking them at their moorings in safe harbors at night. After the children had gone to sleep, Elizabeth and Edward would swim in the nude and make love in the tropical waters under the starlit sky.

Only once, during a sail to Mustique, did Edward catch Elizabeth with that faraway look that frightened him so often in Trinidad. Noticing that though she was not actually crying, tears were misting in her eyes, he had his older nephew take over control of the steering wheel. Grabbing his guitar, he sat down beside her and sang a soulful version of John Denver's 'My Sweet Lady,' singing more emphatically when he got to the finishing line, "*I swear to you our time has just begun.*"

Elizabeth was enjoying a lie-in. She had gone back into bed after the twins left for a playdate at their cousin's. The numerous Christmas parties and pre-Carnival fêting was beginning to get tiresome. She had also organized and hosted their own Company's large Christmas party at home last week, and this took a toll on her already depleted energy.

Earlier, Edward had awakened with his usual erection. Knowing he had arranged for Carl to drive the twins, instead of the cold shower that had recently become his substitute for pleasure on such occasions when the pregnant Elizabeth was asleep, he rolled over and embraced her, hoping she would give him his desired response, which she did.

After they had languished in a slow, sensuous session of lovemaking, Edward showered and left for the office. He promised not to stay out late at the Christmas Eve parties which were held throughout the day by many companies around the city, where courtesy dictated he should put in an appearance. Elizabeth told him he should also pop in to at least two of their friend's parties that evening as she was not up to it. Apart from the busyness of the holiday season and the tiredness that had recently overtaken her, from the time she first learnt of her pregnancy she stopped drinking alcohol, and was no longer amused by the silly behavior exhibited by those who still drank to excess, as so often happened at the many parties.

Edward reluctantly agreed that he should go as their friends might feel insulted if neither of them showed up, though he was not in a partying mood, especially as she would not be with him. He had cut back drastically on imbibing alcohol since awakening to it being the primary cause of his near-disastrous 'indiscretion,' now curtailing his drinks to no more than two or three at a fete, or two red wines or Scotches at a dinner or cocktail party. Aiding him with this resolution was the tragedy of losing two of their friends as a result of drunk driving.

The first death was caused by a drunk driver speeding up the Churchill Roosevelt Highway last New Year's morning after an Old Year's Night fete, and crashing into the car in which their friend was sitting unbuckled in the backseat. She was flung through the car door which opened on impact, landed on her head, and died instantly.

The second friend's death occurred when a boatload of drunks coming back to the mainland at night from Gasparee, Down The Islands, hit their friend's boat at top speed from behind. He was thrown into the water. Both speed boats went out of control and ran over their friend twice.

Two of the drunks were also thrown out of their boat, and unable to swim with incapacitated equilibrium in their highly intoxicated condition, subsequently drowned.

As horrendous as these tragedies were, Edward now felt the tragedy he had caused to his precious love Elizabeth, his marriage, his family, his life, made them pale in comparison.

CHAPTER
48

"*M*adame, a strange guard is here wid a big wooden toy box of Christmas presents for de children, but says he's instructed not to leave until you saw it."

Michael, what have you done now?

The man gave Elizabeth a thick envelope which, on seeing Michael's handwriting, *For the Children of Elizabeth Angelique Richardson*, she quickly pocketed. After he left, Elizabeth, Tilda and Evangeline, opened the box, carved on the outside with representations of numerous toys, in the family room to check its contents. It was filled to the brim with a treasure trove of the most exquisite handcrafted polished wood toys of every description, from various European countries. Each was tied in a brown velvet bag and wrapped in bubble wrap.

Elizabeth admitted to the housekeepers she was just as awed at their beauty and craftsmanship as they were, she herself having never seen any toys quite like these before. While admiring them she pondered on the love, thoughtfulness, and generosity Michael demonstrated by this gift of future heirlooms not just to her twins but to her, her family. Recognizing the effect it will have on Edward she thought she should hide them until after Christmas, when hopefully, given extra time, he would be in a more secure frame of mind to accept them calmly.

Edward, however, putting his priorities in perspective, decided against continuing partying at offices downtown, to spend the rest of this exciting day with his family. He phoned Carl and told him he would pick up the twins at his older sister's house himself, and instructed Carl to collect their already assembled Santa Claus bicycles at his younger sister's house, and hide them in the storage at home.

Elizabeth and the housekeepers were deliberating as to where would be a good hiding place for the box of toys, when they heard Edward and the children coming through the kitchen door from the garage, their chatter and laughter filled with the joy and excitement of Christmas Eve.

Not seeing anyone in the kitchen, the cheerful group robotically meandered into the family room where most of the children's toys and games were kept in a corner of the large room. The adult's toys of built-in liquor bar with six barstools, billiard table, dart board, musical instruments, television and music and all its accompanying systems for entertainment, took up most of the space left by comfortable but tasteful furniture. These included a hand-carved mahogany entertainment center, an overstuffed u-shaped sectional couch, two reclining chairs, an oversized coffee table, one adult and two children's rocking chairs, and two end tables with lamps. An entire wall was covered with a carved mahogany bookcase filled with great literature, and the odd asinine novel.

The three startled women stood up and Elizabeth, hiding her astonishment, enthused, "What a nice surprise! You all decided to come home early."

Zarna and Zethan bolted toward the toys sticking out of the box and elatedly began to pull them out, unwrapping them two and three at a time. "Did Santa come early?" Zethan enquired, the amber eyes inherited from his mother widening in wonder.

"Don't be silly," Zarna corrected, her inherited aquamarine eyes from her father glistening delightedly, "these must be presents from somebody else."

Elizabeth sat back down shaking slightly, shrugged at Edward, then smiled at her children, "That's right Zarna, a cousin in Europe sent them for both of you. Do you like them?"

Picking up a doll that wiggled at all its joints, Zarna said fervently in her still babyish voice, "I *love* them!" and clasped the doll to her chest while grabbing a rabbit by its ears, its head bobbing.

"Me too!" Zethan chimed in as he vigorously shook a snake in one hand and a fish in the other, each one's body sinuously jiggling as though alive.

Edward looked at Elizabeth with a raised eyebrow, "Sweetheart, may I see you in the drawing room, please."

Walking into the drawing room behind him, before he had time to say anything, she spoke apologetically, "I'm sorry, but you came in just as the girls and I were trying to decide where to hide them. They came a short while ago. We have to let the children have them, now that they've seen them-"

Edward interjected clasping an imaginary doll to his chest, imitating Zarna, "And *love* them! They'll hate me forever if I took them away. And, I must say, they're really unique, I've never seen toys like those. I assume they're handmade in Europe too. Nothing cheap there, that's for sure." He became serious, "So, what did *he* send *you*?"

"Nothing, Christmas is for children, remember?"

She noticed relief flash across his face as he joked, "He probably wanted to put a blow-up-doll in there for me, not the regular kind, but one that would blow *me* up."

She smiled coquettishly, "I'm happy to see you handling this so well. I *was* expecting you to blow up."

Edward kissed and squeezed her gently, "It's Christmas. I'm not going to let anything spoil it for anyone. And I'm the luckiest man alive, *I* have the best gift right here in my arms."

She kissed him passionately, with relief, love, and joy, "And I have the best gift right here in my arms too."

He returned her passionate kiss and lifted her up in his arms, "The kids are going to be busy with those toys for a while. Shall we go upstairs and enjoy each other's gifts?"

"Definitely. Merry Christmas, my love."

Sitting on her toilet after she and Edward had exchanged their gifts of each other, Elizabeth remembered Michael's envelope still in the pocket of her dressing gown that had fallen on the floor when Edward undressed her. She tiptoed into the bedroom, retrieved it, and sat back down on her toilet to open it. Inside she found a silk pouch containing a simple gold chain, from which a three-inches-tall three-dimensional but flat-backed gold angel, with amber eyes, hung by small rings attached to the back of the tops of each opened wing. These allowed the angel to slide freely on the chain, giving the impression it was flying. A classic Christmas card accompanied it, and in his hand he wrote, *For my forever Angel, all my love always, Michael, your forever 'Archangel,'* and he drew a smiley-face next to his usual two intertwined hearts.

Finding her gone when he awakened from a nap, Edward called out, "My love, where're you? Don't leave me. Come back to bed." She re-pocketed the envelope and naked still, curled up against him. He clung to her and whispered, "I'll love you forever. Never leave me or I'll die." Responding to him with a sensuous kiss, they became aroused again, and fervently made love again.

Lying in the sleeping Edward's arms afterwards, reflecting on their exceptional qualities and all the wondrous times she had shared with Edward and Michael, Elizabeth counted her blessings. *In this one life, how fortunate I have been to love, and be loved, by two of the most extraordinary men that ever graced this planet.*

Christmas Day brought joyful reality to the twin's fantasies, they got everything they wanted and more, but most of all, they had their loving parents acting normal again with each other. Elizabeth and Edward had an agreement between them that whatever monies they would spend on each other's gifts, they would give to The Children's Home. Both broke the agreement but not with extravagant gifts as in the past. She gave him an onyx and gold-plated desk-set he had admired at a jewelry shop in Long Circular Mall, he gave her a pair of two-carat diamond stud earrings to replace ones she lost "*somewhere in Europe.*"

The traditional Trinidadian Christmas Lunch was celebrated at Elizabeth's parent's home with the extended families of both Richardson's and Du Beauchamp's in-laws, and ended as usual with more family and friends dropping round in the evening to party, be serenaded by Parang minstrels, dance, sing, and make merry.

Being less in a party mood than a family mood Elizabeth and Edward decided they would not stay in Trinidad for the many Old and New Year's parties. The day after Christmas, Boxing Day, which Trinidad celebrated like all countries of the British Commonwealth, their family attended another large merry party at Edward's parent's home. The following day they flew up to Miami with Edward's older sister, her husband, and their two youngest children who were one and two years older than the twins.

The families cheerfully accepted the insistent invitation to "*bunk-in*" at the spacious home of Elizabeth's childhood best friend Judith, her husband, and three children, even though they could have afforded staying at a nice hotel. Trinidadians being inherently sociable and hospitable enjoyed the camaraderie of 'camping' together, especially with people they had not seen in awhile, when there was a lot of catching-up, gossip, laughter, sometimes tears, in which to indulge. Being able to 'visit' only on Skype the past two years, the two best friends were thrilled to spend some physical quality time together.

Having given their baby furniture to Edward's youngest sister when she became pregnant with her first baby, Elizabeth and Edward needed to purchase infant furniture for the recently finished nursery, and spent the next two days shopping. After organizing the coordination of the shipping of their various purchases to a container that would be going down to Trinidad with parts for one of their factories, Edward rented the largest S.U.V. available, and drove the excited gang up to Disney World.

Because Elizabeth was starting her sixth month of gestation she was unable to go on most rides with the children. Judith and Careen happily stayed with her, while the three beleaguered fathers had to endure the torturous rides and screams of frightened delight from their masochistic offspring, but did so with fortitudinous enthusiasm. The mothers spent their waiting-time indulging in the latest gossip and philosophizing about it, while silently praying for the safety of their families. In-between the enjoyably horrific rides and a multitude of gastronomic indulgences, the three families took in a number of parades and shows for four exhilarating days, before the Trinidadians headed back home to their normal interesting lives.

George Davis was beginning to show some frustration, "Look, Michael, we've gone through the band ten times and haven't found them. I tell you, they're not here. I'm sorry for not being knowledgeable about their whereabouts, but, as you now know, we've been gone for a year and only flew in from Australia yesterday. If I didn't love my Carnival so much, and you hadn't shown up with your problem, I'd be asleep in bed with my wife."

Michael pouted saying sarcastically, "Which reminds me, thanks for not inviting me to your wedding-"

George laughed but was adamant, "I *did* invite you. It's not my fault that the palace must've tossed the invitation."

"That's only because I get thousands of invitations from strangers. If you'd remembered to put my personal code on the envelope, I would've gotten it, and would've been here. And by the way, *you* never even responded to *my* wedding invitation."

George laughed again, "I was buried in the outback in Australia, brotherman. Just as well, based on the reason for you being here, it doesn't sound like you have much of a marriage."

Michael's demeanor saddened, contrasting sharply with the band's three thousand joyful Carnival revelers that danced and sang exuberantly around him, and George felt bad. He put an arm around Michael's shoulders, "Come. The band's going to rest in a square round the corner. My aunt lives up this street. She and her maid have been cooking for three days. We're going to eat lunch there with a bunch of band members. It's tradition. Maybe somebody there will know what happened to Elizabeth and Edward."

Walking into Aunt Millie's Woodbrook house, even with all the windows wide open, their nostrils were deliciously assailed by the spicy pungent smells of exotic Creole food. Dropping the feathered headpieces and tasseled wristbands of their costumes on a chair at the door, to be retrieved on their way out when going back to rejoin the band, George introduced Michael simply as an old friend from Harvard.

Aunt Millie immediately took hold of, "De handsome white Yankee," led him to a long buffet table festooned with food in abundance, piled his plate high with several foreign looking substances with rich aromas, and sat him at the dining table.

George sat next to him with a similar plateful of food, and began to explain to Michael what were the strange looking victuals in which he was about to bravely plunge. "The dark green thing sitting on top white rice is Callaloo, a thick soup made with okra, coconut, spices, a local leaf tasting something like spinach, and crabs. The yellow corn thing on banana leaf is Pastelle, filled with mincemeat, chicken, pork, olives, raisins and spices. The brown rice with chicken and salt-beef is Pelau. The fried bananas are actually Plantains. The brown peas with pigtails and onions is Pigeon Peas. The tomato-cucumber-onion salad you could recognize, and, oh, the bowls Aunt Millie just put beside our plates have Souse. It's basically cooked 'trotters'-pig's feet, and pork chops, with cucumbers, pickled in salt, lime, onions, garlic, pepper, etcetera." George grinned at his white 'brother,' "You feeling adventurous?"

Recalling their multifarious escapades during their University days, Michael grinned complicitly at his black 'brother,' "Always," and the two men dove into the tasty colorful food with vigor.

Halfway through the hearty meal, a beautiful voluptuous multiracial masquerader in a wisp of a costume approached Michael, "You the Yankee lookin' for Du Beauchamps?"

Stumbling to his feet Michael stuttered, "Ye…yes," as the woman's practically bare large breasts almost poked his eyes.

She eyed him flirtatiously, "They not playin' mas' this Carnival. Elizabeth's pregnant and in Tobago at her parent's beach house. And Edward's on a long business trip in China."

Michael almost threw his chair over as he staggered backwards, "Pre...pregnant? How pregnant?"

The woman threw her head back with a jamette guffaw, then looked him over as she sucked her teeth in a loud, long steups, "Oh. So you is one of those men who think a woman can be 'a little' or 'a lot' pregnant. Pregnant is pregnant, yuh hear. Anyway, the way I heard it, she was away for a long time and when she was comin' back, Edward met her in Barbados for a little honeymoon and she got pregnant."

Michael tugged at the heavily beaded collar of George's costume, "Let's go."

Baffled, George stood up, "Go? Go where, Michael?"

Michael muttered in his ear, "Tobago. I have to see her. Help me find a taxi to get to the airport."

George laughed, "Taxi? This is Carnival! You not going to find any taxi to the airport, brother."

Michael pulled George out to the front gallery, "It could be my child she's carrying, George. I have to find out. I have to get to Tobago."

George was stuporous, "Jesus! What you telling me brother? That really possible? You two had unprotected sex?"

Michael feigned sheepishness, "Well, she was on the pill, but you know nothing's foolproof, and...I never used a condom. And, we had...a lot of...sex."

George's handsome brown face paled to beige under the red and gold stripes of his masquerade make-up, "Jesus Christ, Michael! This is a helluva situation! You're my brother and everything, but Edward is too. These people are among my closest friends, we're like family. Edward is tutulbay, bazodee, stupid, over Elizabeth. And she over him. I'm still having trouble believing what you told me she said he did, even drunk. No wonder she was so shocked and felt her marriage was over. Now, mind you, I can see her falling for you. Actually, you remind me a lot of Edward. And I can't blame you for falling for her, every man would, she sweet too bad. And is one sexy lady, from the little Edward's said, she definitely has supap. But she and Edward only had eyes for each other. Christ! This could be a helluva mess! Look Michael, your own wife's already pregnant, why you don't just forget Elizabeth and leave well alone?"

Casting aside his question as to what the hell is 'supap,' because of the sexual connotation, Michael was certain Elizabeth had it, his expression became forlorn as he looked at his longtime university friend, "I love her, George. I'll never love like this again. You know me, all the fun times we had dating piles of gorgeous women, nothing like this ever happened to me. I...I didn't come to break up her marriage, I just had this yearning to see her one last time. Now I understand why. I have to find out if this child is mine, George. Put yourself in my place, brother. Wouldn't you feel the same way?"

Taking in Michael's downhearted demeanor, plus his reasoning, George had to admit, as man, he would feel exactly the way Michael did; but he had to tell him of the impossible logistics of being able to get a taxi without prior arrangements, to take him all the way from Port Of Spain to Piarco Airport on a Carnival Monday.

Aunt Millie came bustling out to them, "What you boys doin' here, yuh not finish eatin'-"

George spoke up apologetically, "Sorry, Auntie, my friend had an emergency come up and needs to get to Piarco. But my car's all the way in the Savannah, and you know how impossible it'll be to get a taxi to go Piarco today-"

Millie didn't hesitate, "Take my car. And get him some of yuh cousin Jerry's clothes, they'll fit him. He goin' get too much picong goin' back to America in that skimpy costume."

Michael squatted behind bushes at the edge of the beach under coconut palms, observing her carefully. Fortunately she was alone, her parents had driven off in a jeep with the twins after which the maids went into their quarters to rest.

Facing the gently lapping waves of the Caribbean Sea, she was under a large umbrella, stretched out on a chaise, wearing a brief orange bikini, reading a book. A small C.D. player rested against her huge glistening belly. He gathered she was introducing the baby to classical Steelband music at the earliest age. He recognized the piece she played softly, it was the one they danced to at Jamestown's dinner party. An ache developed in his belly as he watched hers, rounded and ripening with her navel protruding slightly, fittingly causing a resemblance to a lactating mother's enlarged breast. His heart swelled as he took in her elongated body, still illogically so slim despite the huge bulge where her flat abdomen once existed, her naturally voluptuous breasts even larger now. *Are you carrying my child, Elizabeth? My son? Tell me the truth!*

The ring of her phone which lay beside a glass of tangerine juice on the table next to her shattered the serenity. Not really wanting to speak, she took her time picking it up, saw the crown on the caller identification and answered immediately, "Mental telepathy. I was just thinking of you. How're you?"

"Not as well as you, it would appear."

Stunned, she sat up, "Wha...what do you mean?"

"Why didn't you tell me you were pregnant, Elizabeth?"

"Because it doesn't concern you."

"Then there was no reason to hide it, was there?"

Her voice turned strangely remorseful, "I...I didn't want to hurt you...for you to know that I...had sex with Edward, so soon after leaving you...um...seeing...him. But Michael, he's my husband, we have a rich history together, and two children. We...we love each other. I had to...forgive him." She shifted her tone perkily, "How did you find out? You'd be shocked to see me, big swollen belly looking like, as Trinis would say, I 'swallowed a watermelon seed and it grew.'"

"I think you look incredibly more beautiful than ever."

"What! You saw me! How? Wait! Where're you?"

"Behind bushes with red puffy flowers to your right."

Elizabeth dropped her book and stood up to look at the Ixora bushes. Michael raised a hand, waved, and she ran over. He stood up and embraced her but she said quickly, "We should sit behind the bushes, somebody might come along and see us." He cleared leaves off a spot next to the trunk of a coconut palm to expose soft white sand, helped her to sit, and sat beside her.

Thinking of the baby, she slowed her racing heart, "What're you doing here?"

His heart now racing, he kissed the inside of her palm, "I felt strangely compelled to see you. Now I know why-"

She spoke, he thought, a little too quickly, defensively, "He's *not* yours, Michael. My gynecologist worked out the dates. He's definitely Edward's."

"Oh, so it's a boy. You had an ultrasound?"

"No. I don't need to, I just know."

"Oh? The famous mother's intuition?"

"I guess. How is your new bride?"

He looked away from her, picked up a stick and doodled in the sand, "I suppose you heard the rumors are true, she's pregnant. I made sure she could produce an heir before we got married, which as you know is the only reason I married her. But I want to talk about you. How're you feeling? You look amazing."

"I feel amazing, I haven't been sick once during this pregnancy. With the twins, I had nausea up to five months. Is Teresa keeping well?"

He uttered a miserable sigh, "She looks fine but complains constantly. I haven't seen her be sick but she says she's been, a lot. And, says it's too painful to...have sex. I thought that kind of thing only happens in the last months."

Elizabeth felt her heart constrict as the love that filled her for Michael turned to hate for the selfish frigid woman he married, "Michael, if she's healthy, that kind of thing shouldn't happen at all. A normal woman is often able to have gentle sex up to delivery."

Turning to look at her his expression was one of innocent surprise, "Really? Did you…with the twins?"

She turned away shyly, "Yes. It's perfectly natural. Unless something's wrong, of course."

He threw the stick away and dropped his head, "Nothing's wrong. I find her cold, unfeeling, no passion. About anything."

The constriction in her heart spread as she thought of the terrible frustration he had to endure. He of all people, her strongly passionate, loving, sexually creative, playful prince, who argued with her the first day they met that he was going to marry only for love, was now stuck in an arranged marriage to a woman he did not love, who would not even give him the pleasures and comforts of the human touch.

Feeling a jab in the small of her back, she stretched out to support herself on her elbows, "Michael, I have to lie down, sitting like this is uncomfortable in my advanced condition."

He stripped off the borrowed polo shirt, rolled it up and placed it under her head, "Rest your head on this."

Relieved to see he regained the weight he lost when grieving with the loss of her, she lay her head down on the improvised pillow, her amber eyes shining with love and joy to be physically close to him again.

His silvery-blue eyes sparkling with love and desire, he lay on his side next to her and, as he had done every morning when they had awakened together, kissed her forearm scars from the wounds she had sustained during the second assassination attempt on him, "I love you Elizabeth. I miss you so terribly. Do you miss me?"

She would not look at him but could not lie anymore, "Terribly. Especially these last three weeks that Edward's been gone, you've been on my mind, far too much."

His voice rose with utter disgust, "He's been gone three weeks! With you so pregnant? *I* would never leave you for that long, Elizabeth."

She felt she had to defend Edward even though she resented him leaving on such a long, but apparently necessary, business trip, at this time. They had promised each other to never again be separated for more than ten days when they reconciled in Barbados. *Ah well, another promise broken*, "It couldn't be helped. We're expanding our recycling plant and the manufacturer in China misunderstood our requirements on the equipment they're making for us, Edward had to go and sort it out. Nobody thought it would take this long."

Michael scrutinized her face, "Are you absolutely positive he's not mine, Elizabeth? I have this gut feeling, no, it's more a peculiar spiritual feeling, that he belongs to me, to us."

She looked at him steadily, "Absolutely, positively, definitely, he is Edward's, Michael. So please don't think that way. Besides, you already have your own-"

"Can I at least touch him? Touch your belly? Please? I don't think Teresa will allow me to touch hers. Please?"

Seeing the agonized plea in his eyes, she felt pangs of pain and remorse mingle with her undying love, "Alright."

He opened his hands and spread them out gently on her abdomen. At that moment, the fetus moved, her abdomen shifted pointedly upwards towards his hands as though the baby was trying to break out.

Elizabeth cried out, "Oh!" and Michael sprang back.

His face gleaming, he said excitedly, "Did you see how he responded to me? He knows it's me!"

She laughed nervously, "Don't be silly. He's just shifting his position. He does that from time to time."

Bending over he kissed her softly on her lips, "He should've been ours." He kissed her harder with the fiery passion he felt only for her. Her ethical mind told her to resist but her hungry deprived body told her differently as the familiar desire for him reclaimed her, and she returned his kiss with equal passion.

CHAPTER
49

A flock of seagulls flying overhead yakked noisily, startling Elizabeth out of her succumber. Reluctantly, she turned her head away, "Michael, no. We shouldn't."

He sighed dolefully, then whispered lovingly in her ear, "You're all I dream about, being with you, in every way. My fantasies of you are the only sex I have now."

Assimilating his words, an overwhelming compassion joined her passion, she recognized his suffering was never-ending. Lacking not even a shred of guilt she said clearly, "Take me."

He sat up and violently hit the sand next to him with his fist, "No! I'm not going to have you give me some kind of 'pity-fuck' Elizabeth! I'm sorry, I shouldn't have told you. Forget everything I said. I…I'd better go."

He moved to stand but she grabbed an arm pulling him back down, "No, don't leave like this," tears filled her eyes, "I feel this is the last time we'll see each other, please don't leave angry. I wasn't proposing any 'pity-fuck,' I want you. I always will. I love you. I pity us both."

Taking her in his arms, he stroked her hair and caressed her naked back, "Shh, don't cry, it'll upset the baby. I didn't mean to upset you.

You know I'll love you forever, I want nothing but happiness for you, I just wish I was the one sharing your life to ensure it."

She kissed the bullet scars on his arm, "You'll always be a part of my life, my darling, no matter we're apart."

Sitting up, he took her face in his hands and kissed her deeply, sucked on her lips and tongue ravenously, then allowed her to suck on his. His hands roamed under her bikini top and caressed her prenatal breasts causing her hardening nipples to pop out. Gently, he suckled each one as she moaned with longing.

He whispered, "God, how I miss all the sweet noises you make when we made love. Will you let me make love to you my darling, one last time?" She didn't answer. She didn't need to. Her wriggling body against his, her soft hands reaching down to release his hardness from the borrowed trousers, told him all he needed to know. He knelt beside her, struggled out of the trousers, pulled off her bikini bottom and kissing her gently on her mouth again, whispered, "I've dreamed about tasting you like this," and went down to savor the pregnant lips of her core.

Her head whipping about in ecstasy as he feasted on her creamy juices, he became slightly concerned she may hurt herself but he could not stop, so delighted with this new flavor her gestation elixir was giving him, and the gratification he was giving her. Lapping up the last of her cream as she writhed in a final spasm of orgasm, he felt a strange satisfaction as if this was all he needed, took her in his arms and just held her tight against him, whispering loving gratitude.

She sensed what he was thinking but knew him too well. She reached down, encircled his distended penis and placed it at her readied opening, but he backed away.

She commanded lovingly, "You must love me completely."

Initially desperate to put his stamp on her baby and feel his phallus brand him in her womb, he currently thought to put her comfort before his own, "I'm nervous I'll hurt you...and him."

She chuckled as she tenderly touched his face, "You can't. I want you. I know you want me. Come in to me. Love me my darling, let me love you."

He kissed her and slowly, gently, entered her place of ultimate plea-sure. Moving harmoniously together on the soft Tobago sand, coconut palm fronds swaying rhythmically above in the cool Caribbean breezes under the warm tropical sun, for the last time, Elizabeth and Michael, filled with love and life, took each other into paradise.

At seven-thirty in the morning, Edward and the twins having already left the house for work and school, Elizabeth's phone vibrated next to her thigh, startling her out of a doze. Slightly annoyed, she wondered, *Who's calling so early, knowing that I'm only just back home with a newborn?* Then she thought it was probably her concerned mother who was supposed to have moved in to a guest suite for a few weeks to assist with the baby, but had contracted influenza.

She looked warily at the caller identification, but overflowed with love on seeing the crown, "Hello Michael."

"Hello Elizabeth, is this a bad time?"

"No, actually, I'm sitting in my rocker nursing the baby. I had a son. Four days ago. We came home yesterday."

"I know. I didn't think I should call before, I thought you needed to rest," he said softly. She no longer wondered how Michael always knew of important events in her life, and never thought to question him. She simply accepted that was how it would always be, and no more did it irritate her but in actuality comforted her with a strong sense of security.

He continued lovingly with concern, "How're you? Was it diffi-cult? Was it terribly painful?"

Remorse entered her loving feelings, "I'm fine. No, it wasn't ter-ribly difficult. He's a big boy, weighed nine pounds six ounces so it wasn't easy to push him out. The twins were only a little over six pounds each. But it was pretty quick, he was definitely in a hurry to be born."

"Can you reach your computer, go on Skype?"

"I can, but Michael...I'm...breastfeeding the baby."

"Darl...um...Elizabeth, I *have* seen your breasts before."

She blushed and knew he was blushing too. She also knew she could not deny him this request, she had denied him far too much already, "Alright, but I should warn you, I look absolutely dreadful. I haven't had much sleep, he's a greedy little fellow, and honestly, I can't remember if I even brushed my hair this morning. And...I'm a bit heavier than when...you last saw me."

Stretching over to her computer on the desk across from her, she turned it on. As a result of her last beseeching request of him for them to try harder to forget each other, they had not spoken since Tobago, two months ago. Although, unable to completely sever their bond, they did exchange musical voicemails several times a week.

Michael lit up her screen, his face disturbingly serious, but as handsome as ever. She immediately noticed he still wore his hair the way she had told him she liked it, longer than he did before they met. He was sitting at his desk in a navy-blue business suit. Under it he wore the blue and white striped hand tailored shirt with white collar and cuffs, the sapphire and diamonds cufflinks, and the baby blue silk tie; presents she had bought him at Bergdorf Goodman's when they were in New York for her speech. Behind him on a credenza, she could see the Venetian-glass cherub vase they designed together and had made when they were in Murano, Italy.

Her heart raced up, she took a deep breath to slow it down, the baby appearing to feel the change in her for he squirmed and stretched, but then greedily resumed sucking. Michael's mouth fell open and his eyes widened in awe, but he remained silent.

Elizabeth gave him a weak smile and said slowly, "Well?"

His face softened and his voice filled with wonder, "This is the most beautiful thing I've ever seen."

She smiled shyly but became choked up, and she now, was unable to speak. He rapidly absorbed the sheer beauty of the madonnaesque scene before him. A strange spirituality enveloping him, he genuinely felt he was in the presence of God.

He too became speechless but his thoughts were limitless. *My beautiful perfect Elizabeth. Your lush hair disheveled, wrapping around your shoulders and infant son like a protective veil. Your moistened eyes encircled with fatigue and darkness, yet emanating the brightest glow I've ever seen come from them. Your voluptuous breasts, massively swollen with milk for the nutrition of this precious babe. The extra weight you've put on giving you an added sexuality that I can't explain. Even in this circumstance, you excite me so! God, I wish I was there. I want to touch you, to touch the baby. I want to hold you both.* Finding his voice, Michael said earnestly, "You've never looked more beautiful. He's so beautiful...who does he look like?"

Elizabeth gave a soft little laugh, "Well it's too early to tell really. Everyone says he looks like me, except for his hands and feet, they're big...like Edward's. Anyway, he's going to keep changing every day, so we'll see."

Michael swallowed the saliva that had rushed into his mouth, *I have big hands and feet too,* "Will you send me pictures regularly, of you and him?"

Elizabeth gulped a gasp and looked down at the baby. She made a pretense of having to shift his body in order to rearrange his blanket around him, giving herself time to compose the words she felt necessary but would be the least hurtful, "Why put us both through that, Michael? Teresa is going to give you your own beautiful baby in a few months' time-"

He interrupted dejectedly, "It's not the same, Elizabeth. She's not you. This picture before me now is the one I always had in my head, and heart. Had you stayed with me a few more days this would've been my reality. He would've been mine...ours."

She wet her lips and forced a smile, "Michael, there's no point in bringing that up now. You have so much to look forward to. You'll have your own son to enjoy-"

He said sadly, "It's a girl. We found out yesterday-"

She interrupted with exaggerated enthusiasm, "Perfect! You love girls! They love you! And you've lots of time to make more babies. Out of the six you wanted, you're bound to have some boys. So even if you can't get the government to change that ridiculous tradition, the monarchy will still continue. Your family will remain securely in place-"

Stopping her, his expression turned sullen, "I only wanted six with *you*. Actually, four is what we agreed on, remember? I doubt Teresa can even handle this one, much worse six! She's not you, Elizabeth. She doesn't have your strengths-"

"But you do, Michael. And you'll get her good nannies. It'll all work out in time darl…Michael. You'll see."

She saw his expression become dubious then sad. He didn't respond to her forced attempts at confident assurances. She felt that familiar ache in her heart, the ache not just for him but also for her. *Fight, you fool! Fight this feeling! Your own heart's been broken twice. And you've obviously done irreparable damage to his.* She struggled to find the right words to uplift him, but the baby having sucked in too much air and in need of belching, sputtered. "I have to burp him, Michael."

Michael perked up and smiled broadly, "Go ahead," he said quickly, showing great interest.

She became amused, not just by his remark as though he was granting permission, but by the way his demeanor rapidly rebounded from one of sadness to happiness. It was gratifying that he could get so excited just to see a simple natural act of a baby being burped. It did not occur to her that it also greatly pleased him to see her breast fully exposed and enlarged with milk as she removed the baby, held him to sit on her knee, and proceeded to pat his back. Michael's eyes widened when he saw how much larger and brown in color her usually pink nipples had become, nobody had told him about this strange phenomenon. He wanted so much to be there. To lavish her with soft kisses, to taste her sweet milk, to suckle her beautiful breast alongside the baby, the baby that should have been theirs.

Looking up from the baby, seeing Michael's staring eyes and his elated smile, she realized she had forgotten to cover her breast. She quickly left off patting the baby and pulled her nightgown over it, "Sorry," she murmured.

He looked and sounded hurt, "*I'm* sorry. Sorry you felt you had to cover yourself from me. After all we've been through. All that we meant, still mean, to each other."

She could not control herself any longer. Her hormonal condition not helping, her eyes filled with the tears that so long ago had gathered in her soul.

Seeing what was happening to her, he fought his first impulse to reach out and hold her through the screen, and then the second impulse to kick himself for being so thoughtless, "Darling, please don't get upset. I didn't mean to upset you. Please don't cry. Unless you really have to, that is, if you need to, to release some emotions, but please, not because of me and my stupidity?"

Holding back the gush she was damming, she wiped away the teardrops that escaped, picked up the happily burped but still hungry baby, and quickly placed him at her now leaking other breast. Michael noticed the trickle of milk that had oozed out of her nipple before the baby latched on to it and smiled, primarily at himself, that he could be so enthralled by all that mother nature and his Elizabeth had exposed to him this day.

Settling the baby, she also settled her emotions, "I'm fine. Don't blame yourself for my silly state. It's just post-partum hormonal stuff, it'll soon go away. You've so much to learn. Have you been doing birthing classes with Teresa?"

He shook his head pitiably, "She doesn't want me there, finds it all too embarrassing."

Her remorse returned. "Really? But surely you'll be able to see the birth of this child? You missed out on your first, and you really should experience how awesome the whole process is."

"You know I always wanted to when you and I…anyway, she won't allow me in the room, given strict orders that I'm not to be there. Her doctors have agreed as they don't want to upset her. She won't even allow the birth to be videotaped, says it's too degrading for anyone to record her in that condition. The only concession she gave me was to allow Megan and Aunt Claire to be with her. She wouldn't even let

Aunt Anne and Susan be there, despite our pleadings. Said some nonsense about it'd be like having you there."

Guilt joined her remorse, "Oh no! I'm so sorry Michael. I know
how much you were looking forward to the whole experience. But
can't you do something?You're not powerless after all, you're not just
the father, you're heir to the throne-"

"Look Elizabeth, it's not important any more. If you don't mind,
I'd rather change the subject."

"Oh, alright," she agreed ruefully.

The ex-lovers looked at each other in awkward silence awhile, the
only sound the soft sucking noises of the feeding infant; but gradually
the silence became comfortable, loving, bonding, familial.

The baby stopped sucking, stretched his legs, balled his hands into
tight fists, gave a soft grunt, his pink cherubic face turned bright red,
he squeezed his eyes shut tightly, pouted his rosebud lips, and Elizabeth
got her first whiff of his bowel movement.

Seeing the radical change in the baby from absolute contentment
to looking like he was in serious pain, Michael was startled, "My God!
What's happening? Is he alright?"

Elizabeth laughed, lifted the baby up, sat him on her knee, and
began to pat his back again. This time she deliberately ignored her
exposed breast, deciding to give Michael what little pleasure she still
safely could, "He's fine. He just filled his diaper, that's all."

Relieved, Michael joined in her laughter, "He looked like he was
about to convulse into an epileptic fit."

Her motherliness took on a wifeliness, "That's how they look
sometimes, when they're about to, release.You'll be enjoying all these
new fun things soon enough."

His expression rapidly saddened again, "I hope so."

The ache in her heart returned and she dropped her eyes, just in
time to see the baby's liquid excrement seeping out of his cloth diaper
onto her nightgown. "Michael, I'm sorry, I have to go. He, we, both
need to change."

He displayed an understanding smile, "Oh, I see. Do you mind if we visit like this every couple of days, or at least once a week?" When she didn't answer immediately he continued, "Every couple of weeks? Once a month? I…I just want to have this experience with you…I don't know if I'll have it…otherwise. What would be convenient for you?"

Enjoying this time with him, she also wanted more, and to give him more, "I can't say right now. Just try next week around this time, but not on weekends. If I don't pick up, it'll probably be because…I'm not alone."

Observing a look of abject loneliness creep into his openly expressive blue-gray-silver eyes, her compassion and heartache increased, and she knew what she must do, "Michael, will it be confidential if I send you some things to Jamestown's? Will it get to you and only you?"

"Of course, Susan and John will make sure of it. If you send it by certified mail and put the code I gave you at the left top of the envelope, no one will open it but me. Do you have their address?"

She deliberately hesitated, "I don't think so, voicemail it to me later. Goodbye darl…Michael, I must go now." She quickly shut him off, she could not risk making a mistake. He must never discover that Susan and she secretly corresponded and spoke on the phone regularly. He must not know how much she needed to keep a close connection to him, to get intimate unpublished news of him. She could not chance him finding out she had not let go of him, that she could not let go. Susan had been only too willing to become her informant. Having grown to respect admire and love Elizabeth, she felt this was a way of surreptitiously keeping her in the royal family fold without hurting anyone. She appreciated how much courage and strength it took for Elizabeth to leave Michael as she knew Elizabeth still greatly loved him, always will, and must be suffering terribly in silence.

Having changed the baby and put him to sleep, Elizabeth had a quick shower, slipped on underwear, a cotton dress with an elasticized top, and a pair of sandals. She took a box out of her desk drawer and dropped it in her handbag.

Pumping enough breast milk to fill a baby's bottle, she called Tilda and Evangeline to come upstairs and showed them where she had placed it in the mini-refrigerator in the new kitchenette adjoining the nursery.

She gave the two women an unnecessary amount of detailed instructions, and telling them she was running out for a short while, warned that nobody besides them should even come near the baby, "on pain of death."

Grabbing her phone and bag she ran downstairs to her car.

CHAPTER
50

Carl, polishing the chrome and brass hubcaps of her already spotless Cadillac, seeing Elizabeth dressed and carrying her handbag, stood up and said, "Good mornin' Madame. How yuh feelin'?" and reached to open the passenger door to the backseat.

Smiling at him, she said quickly, "Good morning, Carl. I'm well thank you, and you?" Not waiting to hear his answer, she hopped into the driver's seat and continued, "I'm driving myself today. Don't worry, I have my weapon. I'm just going down the road, I'll be back shortly. Stay in the house, protect my family, the guards are all here, I trust?"

Carl looked horrified, stuttered "Ye…yes," then reminded her she only just had a baby, should not be driving, and that was what he was there for. She assured him she was perfectly fine and was not going far, and drove off leaving the worried man still shouting his protests.

Relief filled her on seeing there was a short line at the post office. She was nervous about leaving the baby, even though she knew he would be safe and well nurtured in the loving and capable hands of Tilda and Evangeline. Taking the small box out of her handbag, she looked at the copy of the digital video disc, its title written in her own neat hand: '*Delivery And Birth of The Baby Boy of Elizabeth Angelique Richardson.*'

The next six months saw a return to contented normality within the Du Beauchamp household. Back in her regular exercise routine and nursing the big baby often, Elizabeth soon lost her "*baby fat*" and regained her perfect figure. Everyone was ecstatic with the cherubic baby, even the initially jealous twins, who, with loving attention and encouragement from their parents, grandparents and nannies, became entranced by the interesting, constantly changing, live 'plaything.'

With enormous pressure from both their parents to, "at least have *this* baby baptized Catholic," Elizabeth and Edward again had to defend their belief that no child is born with sin and needs to be cleansed. Like the twins, they were not going to have him brainwashed by any religion while still a vulnerable child. It would be up to their adult children to choose what they wanted to believe, after they had been educated and seen a good bit of the world, learnt its history and cultures.

To appease their families, they did what they had done when the twins were a few months old: they had a family and friends Sunday brunch at home for, according to what was printed on the invitation, a '*Blessing and Naming Ceremony.*'

They invited members of the Catholic clergy who were friends of their parents, other religious leaders and friends of theirs from Catholic, Protestant, Hindu, Buddhist, Jewish and Moslem faiths, and all their other spiritual and secular friends. After jointly announcing the baby's name was Thane, Elizabeth and Edward asked everyone to give him their blessings for a long and happy life. Scores of well-wishing short and long speeches later, and after innumerable champagne toasts, everyone happily, ecumenically and unitedly, partook of a Creole and European feast. The Goddess statue, impressively housed under a clear crystal dome on a marble pedestal placed in a prominent corner of the living room, 'watched-over' the many curious, some censorious, but politely non-enquiring, guests.

Edward continued to do everything in his power to ensure the repairing of his once broken marriage, letting Elizabeth have her way in most matters, even showing support for her renewed investigations into resuming her speeches when Thane would be a year old and she would stop nursing him. He suspected Michael still kept in touch with her although she assured him he didn't, and he observed there was no longer any evidence of it.

Afraid of the answer, he never asked if she still loved Michael. He however could not hide his hatred of Michael whenever anyone innocently remarked about his activities that had been reported in the media, and Elizabeth developed an imperturbableness on such occasions that impressed even her, which did help to calm Edward down somewhat. Getting back to a healthy exercise and diet routine, he regained fifteen pounds, lost the gaunt pining look, and again became the 'handsome hunk' Elizabeth had married. He remained focused on keeping his family happy, well provided for, and safe.

One of the things Elizabeth kept hidden from him was the extreme danger she and Michael had faced together. She knew she could never tell him she was the mysterious heroine acclaimed in the media, who had saved Michael's life when she, wounded, had to take over driving his car after assassins shot him while she was sitting next to him, shots still being fired at them, his bodyguard Tommy getting murdered hanging out the car behind.

Neither could she ever tell Michael the whole truth about Edward's infidelity. She would not be a participant in providing ammunition to the intense hatred that existed between the two men who had never even met, that she so loved, illogically equally. She still fought with the demons of distrust and blame of Edward, but kept that battle within.

Sometimes feeling cursed with her excellent memory she knew she could never forget his infidelity. Visions of him with the other woman tortured her more than just after their every disagreement, but she somehow managed to find the strength to disallow them following her and Edward into their bed. It was no consolation to know Edward was also haunted by similar visions of her with Michael. It hurt deeply to know Michael must also be suffering through analogous visions of her with Edward, *Whoever said "Time heals all wounds" should also have warned scars remain, and though they don't fester, they still pester!*

As he requested, every month she sent Michael a few photographs of her and the baby, some of which included the adoring, and adorable, twins. On receiving them he was thrilled, and would immediately call her, often asking for videos of the baby's, and the twin's, progress. Not wanting to keep him living with hope, she always lied saying she was so busy she kept forgetting to make some, but hid copies in her secret safety deposit box at her bank of the multitudes she actually did make. She kept their conversations short and impersonal, always using the "extremely busy" excuse, the pain of losing him unyielding.

Concerned about his father's unstable health, Michael kept a grueling schedule, permanently taking on more control of His Majesty's reign, on top of his own royal duties and supervising the administration of the royal family's investments. Fully healed and back up to his healthy weight, he still secretly yearned for Elizabeth, hiding it well in front of everyone by the attentions he lavished on his pregnant, demanding, spoiled young wife, whenever he would take what little time he could stand to be around her. He continued to be a spokesperson and advocate for the nonpolluting, *"Greening and Saving,"* of planet Earth, traveling to address conferences and symposiums on the ecology, climate change and man's influence on all of it, at the invitation of governments and organizations worldwide.

Knowing what an asset Elizabeth would be to him in this and in every regard, combined with her passion that his wife lacked not just in their bed but in too many matters of huge significance, he missed Elizabeth almost unbearably.

Two invitations of great importance coincidentally arrived at the Du Beauchamp's mansion on the same day, one by special courier. Elizabeth and Edward happened to be at a parent-teacher's meeting at the twin's school, and after entering the house, while going through the mail together, Tilda brought them the imperial looking envelope that had arrived by courier. It was an invitation to Michael's coronation.

The invitation that came by regular mail was to Elizabeth's favorite cousin Jamie's wedding. Both invitations were addressed to Mr. and Mrs., both events were in November, both to be held in the same country. Elizabeth showed her excitement about Jamie's wedding but acted nonchalant about Michael's coronation, although that thrilled her more than the other.

During dinner with the children, Edward brought up that subject, "You know I'm going to Germany to check out a printing press for our new Caribbean magazine. What do you think about us taking the family to Europe for a couple weeks in November? The twins will probably get to experience snow for the first time, they'll miss some school but they're young and smart, they'll catch up. Besides, the education they'll receive from the trip will more than make up for it. We'll take Tilda so you'll be free to visit with your family, she'll babysit while you're at the different wedding festivities. Unfortunately, my appointment in Germany is at that time. Afterwards, I'll meet you all in France at my relatives' farm for the last week. It'll be nice for them to meet the kids and vice versa, especially seeing that you never got in touch with them when you were in Europe...sorry, shouldn't have brought it up. Er...you'll have to decide what you want to do about... the other invitation. I'm definitely not going."

Zarna and Zethan began to chatter excitedly about the prospect of their first European trip and seeing snow. Elizabeth said softly in-between their glee, "I will not be going either. But the rest of the trip sounds wonderful." *I'm calling Gloria.*

In bed that night after assertive love-making Edward held her tight against him, "I know you really want to go. To his coronation."

She responded softly, "I already told you I'm not going."
Edward surprised himself as much as he surprised her, "Maybe you should go. It's a historic once in a lifetime affair. And a huge honor to be invited, I'm shocked he invited me."

"He knows I would not consider it without you."

"Huh. I doubt that's it. He probably wants to show off to me what you sacrificed. Sorry, I shouldn't have said that. Especially now he's a new father and looks really happy with his pretty wife. Look, if you want to go, I'll support you in your decision. Thinking about it, it's a really big deal, the social event of the century. God alone knows how long monarchies are going to continue, his might even be the last coronation on the planet. Maybe you should reconsider, you might regret not going to something this big."

She kissed his chest and said firmly, "I'm *not* going."

The ornately gilded coach could barely be seen behind the twenty perfectly matched white horses, their proud riders astride, splendiferously decked out in red, gold, and black uniforms, white ostrich plumes atop their gold helmets fluttering in the wintry wind.

"Look Mummy! Here they come!" Zarna shrieked with excitement. Zethan jumped up and down like a Jack in the Box.

The coach drew nearer, the horses hooves thundering and vibrating on the street, as did Elizabeth's heart in her chest. "Wave your flags, sweethearts," she shouted above the din of the crowd, all excited to see their new King, "wave like mad, it'll make him happy."

The coach slowed down in front of them to make the turn into the palace gates. She could not tear her eyes away from the handsome crowned head next to the open window, where white gloved hands could be seen waving magisterially. An intense spiritual feeling came upon her, she had to say an affirmative prayer. Closing her eyes for an instant she prayed that as he starts the official journey to fulfill his preordained destiny, that he would be safe, happy, and satisfied with what he has, *Vaya con Dios, mi querido.* Putting his feelings before hers, with a jab in the pit of her stomach, she wished his wife would find passion, and he would find pleasure in her, and at last fall in love with the beautiful new young Queen, now radiantly, proudly, smiling beside him. *Where I was to be.*

The rising roar of jubilant cheers around her brought her back to earthly surroundings. She immediately became aware of his eyes on her, looked at the window of the coach, and caught his gaze. His mouth twisted as if to speak, but he just stared, sadness invading his fixed smile as their eyes locked. The coach began to pick up speed and he turned his head to look back at her. Then he looked at the eight-month-old baby in her arms, his eyes widening in recognition.

Suddenly, all she could see was the back of the coach through springing tears and a muddled mass of jet-black horses and riders in royal blue and gold. Her thoughts drifted back to the first time he held and kissed her in the back of a royal car, and how beautiful and perfect it was.

Tears trickled down her face. Zethan, still jumping up and down beside her, caught sight of them, frowned, and asked with concern, "Mummy, why're you crying?"

Tilda and Zarna quickly turned their attentions to her, Tilda pondering on the strong resemblance the new King had to Madame's handsome cousin who had come for a short visit over a year ago, and made Madame cry then too.

Patting her tears away with the clean burp-cloth she carried for Thane, Elizabeth smiled and said softly, "Darling, they are tears of happiness. I always cry when I'm deeply touched by something beautiful. Now, come along, we must hurry and get away from here…I mean… away from these crowds, it's…too noisy for Thane."

The others were totally perplexed at her last remark as the happy laughing baby seemed to be having the best time of all.

King Alexander, at his insistence, had moved to smaller apartments before Michael's wedding, relinquishing the palace's premier residence so that the future King, Queen, and offspring, would have the largest home; and, at Michael's insistence, at last had Elena move in with him.

Walking quickly to their new apartments, Michael, in front of Teresa, was preoccupied, ignoring her. At the end of the long corridor his valet, Roger, waited to assist him disrobe. Standing next to Roger was a nanny, the five-month-old baby, Princess Sara, in her arms. Michael stood still for a moment and looked at his daughter. Teresa rushed past him, her celadon silk-satin gown brushing against the inattentive King. His heart always filled with delight when he saw the baby, but today his heart strings pulled him in a different direction. He turned on his heels and walked hurriedly away to his office.

Opening the door, he flung his ceremonial red velvet robe trimmed with lynx fur onto a chair. His crown and scepter having already been taken by the museum curator when he arrived at the palace, to be put back in their cases under protective glass, he whipped off his imperial sash, medals, and the rest of his coronation regalia and tossed them onto an overstuffed armchair.

A somber expression consuming his face, he pressed a number on his phone and spoke brusquely, "Jenkins, come to my office."

In less than three minutes Jenkins was at the door, "Something wrong, Michael?"

He responded tersely, "Close the door."

Jenkins closed it quickly. Turning to face Michael, he sensed he was restraining some anger, but could see an ironic tenderness in his eyes.

Michael spoke abruptly, "She came."

Jenkins showed his befuddlement, "She? Who?"

"Elizabeth. She was at the coronation."

Jenkins looked stupefied, "But she sent the R.S.V.P. back in the negative," *which I know hurt you to the core,* "and those two seats you made us save in the cathedral anyway remained empty during the ceremony, I kept checking."

Michael raised his voice, "She wasn't *in* the cathedral, she was right *here,* in the crowd just outside the palace gates!"

"No!" Jenkins sounded surprised, but knowing Elizabeth, he was not.

Michael continued with excitement entering his voice, "I saw them. She had the three children with her, and the nanny. Elizabeth was holding the baby in her arms. He's really big. He's beautiful, like his mother-"

Jenkins interrupted with relief, "That's good, they say it's good luck when a boy looks like his mother."

Michael said slowly, deliberately, "He looked at me, he doesn't have her eyes, nor Edward's," he paused, looked hard at Jenkins, and questioned testily, "what did she name him, Jenkins?"

Jenkins shifted his feet, visibly exasperated, "I told you months ago, she named him Thane, in honor of her deceased paternal grandmother. She was Scottish like the ancient name. It meant 'lord,' apparently." Jenkins had purposely avoided telling him he read somewhere it meant 'King' to ancient Vikings.

Michael spoke acerbically, "I don't mean *that* name. And by the way, you forget, *I* have Scottish blood in me-"

Jenkins' frustration became evident, "Oh come now, Michael, it's miniscule compared to hers-"

Michael interrupted coolly, "What are his other names?"

Jenkins feigned ignorance, "Other names?"

Michael's own frustration bordered on anger as he raised his voice again, "Yes! *Other* names. She would've given him *other* names! You never told me those!"

Barely controlling a stutter, Jenkins shifted his feet again, "Sh...she never mentioned those, to anyone, not even Edward."

Michael arched a fractious eyebrow, "But *you* know!"

Jenkins dropped into a chair with a desperate sigh. His composure evaporated as his head fell forward in defeat. He looked like an exhausted general who had just lost his last, hard fought, battle.

Resignedly, he said softly, slowly, "Alexander, Stephen."

Michael's jaw hardened at the same time his eyes softened. He slapped a hand down on his desk, "I knew it! I felt it in my very soul! Find her, Jenkins! Bring them all here! Now!"

JUST THE BEGINNING

THOUGH YOUR STEPS MAY FALTER
PERSEVERE WITH THE CLIMB
YOU WILL ACHIEVE THE SUMMIT
AT THE APPROPRIATE TIME

Patricia D'Arcy Laughlin

Made in the USA
Lexington, KY
23 July 2013